THE VIRGIN MOTHER

*Thanks for you
Support & Encouragement
Dy Noel*

THE VIRGIN MOTHER

DY NOEL

TATE PUBLISHING
AND ENTERPRISES, LLC

The Virgin Mother
Copyright © 2016 by Dy Noel. All rights reserved.

No part of this publication may be reproduced, stored in a retrieval system or transmitted in any way by any means, electronic, mechanical, photocopy, recording or otherwise without the prior permission of the author except as provided by USA copyright law.

This novel is a work of fiction. Names, descriptions, entities, and incidents included in the story are products of the author's imagination. Any resemblance to actual persons, events, and entities is entirely coincidental.

The opinions expressed by the author are not necessarily those of Tate Publishing, LLC.

Published by Tate Publishing & Enterprises, LLC
127 E. Trade Center Terrace | Mustang, Oklahoma 73064 USA
1.888.361.9473 | www.tatepublishing.com

Tate Publishing is committed to excellence in the publishing industry. The company reflects the philosophy established by the founders, based on Psalm 68:11,
"The Lord gave the word and great was the company of those who published it."

Book design copyright © 2016 by Tate Publishing, LLC. All rights reserved.
Cover design by Norlan Balazo
Interior design by Richell Balansag

Published in the United States of America

ISBN: 978-1-68301-990-9
Fiction / Christian / Romance
16.05.20

1

Norwalk

She awoke to the thrumming of an alarm slowly getting louder. Diana hated the alarm clock, any alarm clock. At least with her alarm clock, there was a double alarm set. Other alarms woke you with a blaring horn that left you clinging by your fingernails to the ceiling. Diana's alarm started quietly and slowly crescendoed. It rarely ever went to the horn level; she was usually aware of it by the second crescendo. However, it may take her three or four beeps to get out of bed to hit snooze. Her habit of hitting snooze was why she needed a double alarm.

She had to be to work by six a.m. *I got to get up*, Diana said to herself.

Her name was often associated with the roman goddess of the moon. Her father always scoffed at such a comment. He would retort that her name means "given by God." Either way, she was a night owl by nature, and for some reason, the Lord seemed fit to give her early morning jobs. She flung the covers off her and rolled to the edge of the bed. Because of the height of her bed, all she had to do was roll out feet first. There was no need to get up off the floor—just roll to a stand.

This morning she was puzzled. Not for the four thirty wake-up call but because of the dream she had last night. This wasn't just any dream; this was one sent by God. How did she know? Dreams that were sent from God didn't disappear with the morning rush. They just had an "I'm talking to you" call to your spirit. Those who never had those dreams before just didn't understand it. Several times she had tried to explain it to church friends and family. She finally gave up trying. This dream—this dream she didn't understand. Maybe God would tell her what it meant later.

It was normal for God to give her dreams. He often gave her dreams and visions, ever since she was a very young girl. It wasn't till she was in her late twenties that He started audibly speaking to her. Now the Lord did both, depending on the situation.

As Diana brushed her teeth, she pondered why. Why did she let the guy grab her? Why was she running? What was she running from? The one thing she knew for sure, the guy did not mean her harm. He was saving her from something.

Diana searched her mind...did she know the guy? No, no, she didn't. She couldn't see his eyes though. The eyes tell a lot. This guy grabbed her from behind, which would normally get most guys into serious pain. It wouldn't be from her fists—no, she never could punch anybody. Her elbows and feet, however, those were another story. Even her fingernails left scars on her brother, no matter how short her mother cut them. This guy, a guy that looked like a cowboy, said to her, "I won't hurt you." He had saved her, pulling her from danger. Danger from what? The thought made Diana's heart race.

"Knock it off, girl!" Diana irritably told herself.

She turned and quickly grabbed her phone and her drink off the dresser. She walked upstairs and grabbed her work bag and purse then, as quietly as possible, walked out the door.

On the way to work, Diana still heard the echo of the cowboy's voice, "I won't hurt you." It was a deep voice, smooth and calming. A voice that often put goose bumps down her arms and made the hair on the back of her neck stand up. Even though at the time she was grabbed she was not calm, his words and his voice calmed her. She relaxed against him, a reaction far from her norm. She actually felt...safe there near him. She'd wished the Lord had given her more information. She had asked the Lord to tell her more, but there was no response.

Everything was put in the back of her mind as she clocked in for work. She was a custodian at the Honeywell's apartment building in Des Moines. Not what most people would expect from a Bachelor of Arts degree university graduate. It wasn't what she wanted to be doing at this time either. She was a teacher, and she loved it. She had originally started working there for the pay raise so that she could get her endorsement in Spanish. Her intentions were to get the classes she needed and then take the last semester in Spain. That was her plan...God, however, had other plans. Eight years later, she was still cleaning lounges and scrubbing bathrooms. She had tried to get a secretarial position, one that wasn't as hard on her body. A college graduate with five years of teaching experience should count for something, right? Apparently not. She couldn't get into a different position, and she couldn't leave; she needed the insurance.

As she bent down to pick up the candy wrapper that someone graciously threw in the corner of the stair landing, her knees popped. She was often told by those she met that she didn't look her age. Her body, however, told her she was older than she was—an effect of the big C. C meaning cancer and its treatment. She was three years out from the last chemo Treatment, but her strength was coming back very slowly.

She wasn't afraid of death, not really; it just wasn't her time. Too many promises the Lord gave her that had not come about yet. She stood looking out the window and shook her head. She can hear her brother's voice in the back of her mind: *God could put everything together in the snap of His finger.* She'd just sigh and tell him, "Not everything."

Diana loved her brother, Dewayne, very much. She was the baby and only girl. With that being said, her brother and her were close; they rarely fought. Her brother was always there when her dad wasn't able to be, at least up until Dewayne married Abbie. Things just grew farther and farther apart since then. She kept telling herself that that was the way it had to be: "Husbands, cleave to your wives" (Matt. 19:5). Sometimes it helped; most of the time, she just felt like an oddity. She guessed for today's standards, she was an oddity.

Diana and Abbie never really got along. Diana was more of a tomboy; Abbie was a city girl or Southern belle, as she often referred to them. They are beautiful, bubbly women that were great hostesses. However, when it came down to doing actual physical work, they couldn't or wouldn't do anything. They considered all that stuff not their problem and left things in a disaster. That was just the surface of the conflict between Diana and Abbie. Some problems Diana didn't understand herself. She tried not to think about all that junk; she had done everything she could do. She really didn't like conflict, but with her and Abbie, there's always conflict. She would always try to give Abbie a wide girth just to avoid the fight to come.

Now as for her nieces (Liza, eighteen; Kim, sixteen, Angie, the youngest, thirteen) and nephew (Jared, fifteen), she would do everything she possibly could for them.

Clive

Two weeks later, Diana still didn't know the dream's meaning, nor had it faded from her mind. She could hear some of the church people saying it was just a fanciful dream of a single, lonely female.

Diana had to smile at that thought. She has had some of those dreams before. Like Kevin Sorbo as Hercules, coming in and fighting for her. He would hold her in his strong muscular arms, at the end scolding her for being at the wrong place at the right time. When she was a teenager, it was John Schneider as Bo Duke. He would come racing in with the General Lee, rescuing her from Boss Hogg or some other fiend, kissing her as the sun set. Yeah, she had those dreams. She is human, although some would debate it. Oh, how she hated waking up from those dreams; she was a sucker for blue eyes. She thanked God who had blessed her with a wonderful imagination. She would just continue those dreams in her mind for days later. She would change the situations and events to make the dreams more romantic or exciting. In her twenties, she knew when those dreams came; it was her time of the month the following week. Those were just estrogen-filled fantasies of a young female. She hadn't had those dreams for three years now.

God's dreams are different though; they don't fade. You can't change them when you don't like what was going on. They spoke to your soul, to your very being. The problem—God didn't always tell you their meanings right away.

Diana was wondering if it was a warning or just a heads-up. Then there was the man; a connection between her and her "rescuer" was building in her mind. She also knew that she could easily make a mountain over a molehill, extremely easy. She had to control her emotions. "Reality, Diana, get some reality in there," she said out loud.

She could hear the voices in her mind, *Why would anybody want you? You're too old. You're too fat. You're no fun.*

"Oh, shut up," Diana simply stated. She looked at the mirror and wondered what would happen if people could hear the voices in her head. *Yeah, they'd put me in a padded cell and throw the key away,* she figured.

She wasn't crazy. Those were just the voices from her past. A past that everybody thought was shielded. She was a pastor's kid, *charmed* as it were. At least that's what most people thought. Her parents hardly ever fought, and both her brother and she were well loved. The Lord had always supplied the family with their needs. However, even a pastor's kids are affected by the evil of the world.

She was around five years old when she awoke from a nap in an upstairs bedroom of her grandparents' house. A large rough hand was touching her in a ways it should have never done. God had warned her father that she was in danger. Her father came into the house yelling for her; not that she heard it. Her ears weren't working right at that time; but her uncle's did. He stopped touching her and slowly left the room. She didn't tell her parents, not until she was sixteen, of what had happened. She saw the hurt in her dad's eyes; he had failed her. He didn't of course; she had no doubt that he saved her from it going far worse. Her mother just cried. They had seen the change, but they didn't know why. She was no longer the happy, bubbly little girl whom everyone enjoyed. She was shy, withdrawn, untrusting. Oh…she was still pure, at least physically, but she was no longer naïve; that was stolen from her. She no longer trusted people, especially men. Only her father and her brother were allowed close to her. Looking back, she often hid behind her bother whenever she felt insecure, or she held near her parents. She wouldn't let herself get caught in a situation where she felt that helpless again. Usually, the Lord warned her of "danger," and when He warned, she didn't need a second warning. She would up and move to where she had an escape as fast as she could and not be obvious about it.

As she prepared the equipment for her job, she got to thinking about things. The advantage of her job was that she had nine hours to talk with God. Not many distractions to divert her attention, multitasking as it were. It was also a disadvantage because there was nothing to divert her attention from working herself up into a frenzy. The last time she did that, the Lord had to talk to her sternly to get her settled down. Normally, the Lord talked to her in a calm, still voice. She almost always responded quickly to Him in that way. Luckily, there were only a few times that God had to get strong with her. Right now, she would take anything from Him; her mind goes too many places given free range.

One of the places it went: she was going with the kids to Adventure Land soon. Was that where something was going to happen? With her nieces and nephew there, she would never leave them in harm's way. Where would they be if it did happen? She didn't like the way her mind was going now. She quickly grabbed the cart and headed up to the third floor.

2

Altoona

She met up with the kids Saturday morning. Today was the day that they were going to Adventure Land. Diana was worried that this was when the Cowboy (that was what she named her rescuer) would show and the situation would be in play. She prayed to God that it wasn't; she did not want the kids hurt. Although Liza and Jared could cause any would-be attacker to have second thoughts.

Liza, the oldest, is not only very tall; but her six-foot-one body had the attitude to go behind it. She was a spitfire and fought like a wildcat when it came to protecting her brother or sisters. Well…at least protecting them from outsiders anyway. Kim, the next girl, she is what Diana was when she was a kid. In truth, under it all, Diana still was; Kim was a peacemaker. Kim is a brain in English and very intuitive. Alas, she ran a little shy on the common sense area. Jared, the only boy, was six-feet-two and clever as all get-out. He is very strong for what most thought was a beanpole. It was Kim and Angie she was most worried about. Angie, being the youngest, was as of yet just a free spirit. She spent most of the time lost in her own world, seemingly oblivious of what was going on around her.

"Lord, not today, please," Diana prayed softly under her breath.

Kim noticed that Diana was somewhat occupied. She put her hand on Diana's shoulder and asked her, "Is everything okay?"

Diana looked in the rearview mirror to see Kim's eyes and said, "Yeah. I was just thinking of something I saw earlier…it's nothing."

"You sure?" Kim insisted.

With Kim's question, all the kids, except Angie who had already put in her earbuds to listen to her own style of music, were looking at Diana.

"No…it's kewl. So what are we going to hit first?" Diana asked. She was relieved when the kids chimed in with different suggestions. She didn't want to explain herself, nor did she want to ruin the day.

It was decided…they were going to hit the roller coaster first. The kids made her promise she would ride with them on it; although Diana was not going to enjoy it. Next was over to the Scrambler, then it was up to a whim as to what ride was next. Diana was relieved that nowhere in the park looked like the setting in her dream.

The day went great; they all had fun, and Diana was able to let her hair down. As they were heading to the car, Angie was complaining that she was hungry, and Jared and Liza were poking fun at the couple that stood ahead of them at the Zipper. Apparently, the lady wanted to ride and her date was trying to weasel his way out of it. Diana chuckled; she had not seen that commotion. She forced herself to ride the roller coaster, but she did an absolute "Not gonna happen" with the Zipper. She really didn't like heights, and the thought of willingly getting into an enclosed box to spin around at fifty feet in the air was not her idea of fun. She instead went and got a cold sweet tea and sat down on the bench and watched the kids ride.

Kim was holding her hand on the way to the car, telling her all about what she could see from the top of the Ferris wheel—another ride Diana didn't take. Diana pressed the button to unlock the car, and the kids were starting to run ahead of her to get in. Just as she was getting in to her car, she felt a presence that was exciting and in an odd way comforting to her; there was also a sense of something heavy and dark that sent a chill up her back, but she wasn't able to figure it out at the time. *Is he here?* she thought.

She tried to look around to see him. *Why would he be watching me? That makes no sense. You're just freaking yourself out, girl. It's nothing… you're just tired.* Diana had finally convinced herself of that. She hooked her seat belt, started her car, and took the kids home.

Urbandale

Ben was late picking up his kids. He promised to take them to Adventure Land earlier that week. The boss, however, wouldn't let him do the paperwork the next morning.

"Do it while it's fresh in your mind. We don't want any mistakes on the report," his boss said.

Of course Ben's kids understood; they quickly headed out the door and climbed into the SUV. Bless their hearts; Benjamen James Jr., or BJ, was fourteen; Kaira was twelve; and the twins, Brock and Kora, were four. He loved them dearly. He hated missing time with them; but that's the problem with working with the Homeland Security nowadays. Most of the time he wasn't home till late and out the door early in the morning. He was good at his job; his boss said he had a nose for it. Ben's intuition was above normal; many in the office believed he was psychic. He got a sense of satisfaction when he saw the bad guys get what was coming to them. His wife, Katherine, knew this.

She had always encouraged him with his job. Even when it meant he had to miss anniversaries or birthdays. He knew she spent hours sending prayers for a safe return and for the Lord's protection. Ben felt that she talked with the Lord so much…she wanted to go "home." A stab of anger ran through his heart. He and the Lord were still not on speaking terms; it wasn't fair. How can he tell the kids about the love of God when God took their mom from them?

Kora reached over and took his hand. "Will you ride on the Scrambler with me, Dad?"

"Definitely, pumpkin," he replied, smiling down at his excited little girl. She ran and jumped at BJ, asking him for a piggyback ride, which BJ willingly gave to her. He was glad the kids were close…they had to be.

"Dad, you really need to update your wardrobe," Kaira stated.

"I like my clothes…what's wrong with them?" Ben asked.

"You look like you just came in from a roundup, seriously," Kaira scoffed.

Ben wore his normal blue jeans, plaid shirt, and his favorite cowboy boots. He did come from the ranchland of Nebraska, but it had been years since he had been to a roundup; he missed those times. "Well," he said as he pulled on his shirt and examined it closely. "You can take the boy from the ranch, but you can't take the ranch from the boy." Ben smirked at his fashion-forward girl.

BJ spoke up and said, "At least he's not wearing his cowboy hat and huge belt buckle."

"Nah, I'd hate to spend the whole time hanging on to my hat instead of enjoying the rides," Ben added.

As the family started for the entrance, Ben looked over at some kids laughing loudly as they were walking through the parking lot. There was a lady in the lead. He'd say late twenties, early thirties, except the taller girl behind her was in her teens herself. She was plain-faced, no makeup or jewelry. Not skinny—farmer's stock was what his father use to call them: a lady who can work. She was tall, somewhere around five-foot-eight, but not as tall as the four kids following her. She was well endowed, but not like those playboy bunnies that his partner seemed to like; no, she was modest. Looking at her, he'd have to say she was a beautiful woman. There was something about her, something that was familiar. He just couldn't put his finger on it. Glancing at the kids, he noted that they looked similar enough to know that they were family but looked different enough that to Ben's eyes, they had to be from different fathers. Two looked similar to their mom; the one with her dark hair and nearly white skin looked nothing like her. The youngest one had the dark hair of the oldest girl but with olive-colored skin.

Figures. Another single mother with a different father for each kid, Ben thought.

Something pierced his soul. It seemed to say to him, *You're wrong.* He wanted to look back and take another look, but they were at the ticket office, and his kids were asking him questions. He shook his head to clear his thoughts. He said "sorry" seemingly to nobody and gave his card to the lady behind the window. *I shouldn't be so judgmental,* he thought.

In the same parking lot, a man stood in the shadows. As he watched Diana and the kids walk across the parking lot, he smiled. Slowly he walked to the car parked near the exit. He watched Diana drive to the exit on the far side. He was making a mental note of everything she did, what she wore, where she went. He noted that she did not drink any alcohol, nor did she smoke; she would move away whenever someone lit up around her. One time, at the apartment building, Diana had to walk through a group of tenants that were standing outside the back door smoking. She only made it five steps away before she started coughing. He'd hoped that she wasn't weak; the Sheikh would be upset at that. Maybe she had a cold then. He decided he would only put good things in his report to the Sheikh. He was very specific in his instructions on what to look for. He started his engine and headed for home to send in his report.

Continue to observe her. Note when and where she is alone. Look for routines…times that would be good for us to intercept her.

—The Sheikh.

3

Clive

Amid had lived in the Honeywell's apartment building for a year. Diana was the third female he had told the Sheikh about. If he was wrong with her, the Sheikh would probably kill him; she wasn't even on the radar at first. He was surprised to hear the comments of the other custodians when they were outside during their break. She wasn't married, she wasn't dating anybody; he heard one custodian say that she thought Diana was "asexual, a self-proclaimed nun." The group mumbled something; a couple of them shook their heads in disagreement. "She's not normal, that's for **** sure" was the final comment Amid heard.

It was then that he started looking closer at Diana. She was larger than what the Sheikh wanted; that could easily be remedied once she was with the Sheikh. He had to make sure she was what they said she was. He asked the other residents in the building, he checked the police records and tried to check her medical records; "Stupid HIPAA law." He found her on Facebook and tried to get her to add him as a friend several times. Since she didn't know any of the names that he used, she wouldn't let him in. She was different then the other girls; they were more than willing to talk to his made-up lures. Not Diana; she was cautious. It came down to him following her when she left work.

The Sheikh arranged for Amid to rent a car from the local Hertz dealership. It made it a lot easier to follow Diana. He was sure that she was single and seemed to be free. She spent a lot of time with her brother's kids. She also did a lot of work with the kids at her church. She was actually leading a very simple life. The only excitement to her life, at least in his mind, was when Diana was off work and driving around. He noticed that Diana loved to roll the windows down, open the sunroof of her Chevy, turn up her music, and drive rapidly around traffic on the highways of Des Moines.

She almost always pushed the speed limit, and she would weave in and out of traffic, swerving around semitrailers and slow-moving vehicles. He could see the pleasure it gave her on her face. He had to admit that it reminded him of riding his horse through the scrub in the early morning dew. For him, it was a sense of freedom; he figured it was the same for her.

With a vehicle to track her, he quickly learned that she had a routine. From work, Diana would head to one of three places. She would either go to Wal-Mart, Sonic, or church then she would go home in the Norwalk area. Then there were days that she would leave town; he couldn't follow her then. He didn't know if she was meeting up with a boyfriend or maybe just visiting family in other towns.

Now he needed to look for a time that she was alone. He knew it had to be at a place with little chance of someone hearing her and easy for the team to get her into the vehicle. He ran his fingers through his hair as he thought about her schedule. This wasn't going to be easy.

Downtown Des Moines

Ben came in to work, poured himself a cup of coffee, and started walking toward his desk; he was headed off at the pass. His partner, Richard "Dick" Richmond, called to him from the director's office.

Dick was the typical gumshoe stereotype and polar opposite of Ben. Dick was a stocky man, only five-feet-seven inches tall. He had never married, didn't have any children, at least none that he claimed, and he had no filter whatsoever on his mouth.

Ben often thought that the director put him with Dick to get him to quit. It was either that or he wanted Dick to quit. Somehow, Ben and Dick were able to make the partnership work. Ben walked into the director's office and said, "What's up, sir?"

Director Charles Zenon was old-school and originally came from San Francisco. Charles started out as a beat cop working, clawing his way up in the ranks. He reached detective status back in the '90s. From there he moved into the Department of Homeland Security; he'd been the director of the DHS office in Des Moines for six years now. He knew the agents hated him, but he didn't care. He wasn't here to be their friend; he was here to get the bad guys off the streets.

He had a situation developing, one that worried him a lot. Since no actual crime had been done, at least none reported, he needed things to go quietly and carefully. He knew that Ben had the charisma and charm to slide through the hardest of barriers. Plus, Charles felt that Ben's training with special ops in the Gulf War may come in handy. Then there was the fact that among the many languages Ben was fluent in, he spoke Arabic and Farsi.

Dick, well, Dick had advantages too. It was mostly because of his contacts with the lowlives in the city. For some strange reason, those people liked Dick; probably because it took one to know one. Intelligence, or intel, was the life force of staying ahead of the bad guys, and Dick had his hands in it.

Dick smiled up at Ben and said, "Looks like we finally have some action in this no-man's-land."

Charles was not happy with that comment. He liked it when it was quiet. Quiet means no major, big bad guys for them to deal with. The DMPD could handle the minor infractions. Charles knew Dick hated this place; it was too boring for him. Ben looked back and forth from Zenon to Dick. "So, is somebody gonna fill me in?"

Charles stood up from his chair, moved to the blinds, and closed them. "HQ sent over some intel they just received from the FBI. It appears we have a terrorist sleeper group working here in the city."

Dick rubbed his hands together like he was warming them up. "Finally!" Ben just stretched is six-foot-four body out in his chair, crossing his ankles. He steepled his fingers up against his chin and listened attentively.

Zenon continued, turning on the TV to show a picture of a young Arabic man. "This is Amid Aliah, twenty-three years old. He's lived in the States for three years. He now resides at Honeywell apartments and attends the university as an engineering student. He is a suspect in two disappearances: one in San Francisco with a twenty-two-year-old woman and one in New York with a fourteen–year-old girl. As of yet, nothing is sticking."

Ben looked down at his fingernails. "So what you're saying is he's a serial that's planning another disappearance?" Ben's voice was dark and as smooth as a rich, full-bodied Colombian coffee.

"Possibly," Charles continued. "But HQ doesn't feel he's working on his own. They feel he is working with this guy." He clicked to another picture. This one was of an old man in a turban, obviously from the Middle East, and apparently wealthy. Charles turned to his men, "This is Alawi Mohamed Akeem, a.k.a. the Sheikh. He was with Saddam's elite forces when they attacked Kuwait."

Dick, in his snide cantor, stated, "This one obviously got away."

Charles, giving Dick the evil eye, then continued. "He has a compound near the Syria-Israeli border. The FBI intercepted some conversations between Amid and Alawi's camp. It was something about looking for a woman. We are not sure what they are looking for or why. What we do know is Amid has apparently zoned in on one. He has been instructed to find an opening. HQ is sure something is going to happen soon."

Ben had a sinking feeling in the pit of his stomach, one that made him want to lose his breakfast, except he hadn't eaten any breakfast. "Do we know who Amid is watching?" Ben asked.

Charles pointed the remote at the TV. "They think it is this woman. Her name is Diana Henderson, forty-five years old, single, no kids, and lives with her parents."

Dick smirked and, with a chiding tone, said, "What, they don't have enough housekeepers in the Middle East? Why in the **** would they want her?"

Ben's heart was in his throat; he'd seen this woman. *So those kids weren't hers,* he thought. *Told you,* reprimanded the voice in his head. Ben pulled his mind back, focused in, sat up, and gleaned as much info as he could.

"We don't know why they are targeting her," Charles said, answering Dick's question; then he turned to Ben. "Ben, I need you to keep an eye on her. Don't be seen and don't show your hand unless it is absolutely necessary."

Dick clapped his hands. "Yeah, some good, old surveillance time. Just like the old days, huh, Tiger?"

"Not so fast, Dick,' Charles injected. "I need you to get with your contacts. Find out what's up with this Amid. Anything and everything you can possibly get. Follow every trail. Ben will be doing solo time, at least for now."

Ben was grateful for that decision. He didn't need a 24/7 dive into societal debauchery.

Dick was not happy; he cursed in disgust. He had hoped he would have a chance to break those high-and-mighty principles of Ben's. He'd given Ben a break for the last couple of years. He knew that he was having trouble dealing with his wife's death. *Long enough,* he thought. *This time…I'm gonna break them.* He had bets already going with some of the other agents in the office.

They walked out of Zenon's office. Ben walked slowly to his desk, sat in his chair, and grabbed the phone. "Gonna call Becca?" Dick asked. Ben nodded. "Tell her she owes me a date."

Ben cringed at the thought of his baby sister on a date with Dick. "Not while I'm alive," he said under his breath. Dick was out the door and Ben was listening to the phone ring. He would need to give Becca a heads-up, just in case he needed her to come and watch the kids.

4

Norwalk

Ben had been on stakeout for four weeks. Zenon arranged for a rookie agent to come in and watch the house over the nights. With that arrangement, Ben was able to go home at night to be with the kids. Diana was, for the most part, very routine and hardly ever alone. If she wasn't with her parents, she was with one or more of her nieces or her nephew. When they weren't around, she was with people from her church. The only time she was alone was while she was in her car or while she was at work. While waiting for Diana to start her workday, Ben tried to put himself in Amid's shoes. *If I was looking for a time to nab her, when would that be? The logistics of trying to take her in her car was huge, especially the way she drove. No, it would have to be while she was at work.* "It'll go down while she's at work," Ben said out loud.

Diana came out of her house and jumped into her car. Ben instantly looked at the clock: a quarter till six. "Here we go!" he exclaimed with a smile on his face. He knew she was running late. That meant California stops, speeding, and passing any car in front of her. He was surprised with the way she drove her car. Even more that she hadn't been picked up for speeding. When he checked her record, it was clean. He felt rather exhilarated following her and the way she drove. *A little bit of excitement to get the blood moving*, he thought. This morning didn't disappoint him.

Ben chided her as he pulled to the curb and turned the car off. "You're lucky this time, ma'am, there wasn't much traffic on the road." He knew she couldn't hear him of course. He often had a one-sided conversation with her, commenting on things she did or didn't do. He was to meet up with the rookie agent that had been relieving him during the night. Ben had to report to the office this morning. The rookie and he had worked it out where Ben would come back at two a.m. so that the rookie could catch a few hours of shut-eye then relieve him at eight a.m. so Ben could get to the office. The rookie met up with him at the Honeywell apartments

Ben made it to the office by a quarter after eight. He quickly grabbed a cup of coffee and headed for the director's office. Dick was already in there and telling Zenon what he had spent the last four weeks doing. Zenon indicated that he had some info that would prep them for what was coming in. Ben tapped on the window and opened the office door.

"It's about time!" Dick sneered. Ben gave him a polished smile as he sat down by the desk, stretched his legs out in front of him, and crossed his ankles as he sipped his coffee.

"So, what did you find out from your snitches and habitual eavesdroppers?" Ben jeered.

"Well, to start out with, Amid has been visiting with some heavies over in the industrial area the past two weeks. According to my intel, this group of Arabs came in by bus from Chicago. They're mean, hot tempered, and not friendly at all," Dick said matter-of-factly.

Ben looked over at Zenon. "A couple of street guys came asking for a little handout. They were in the hospital for a couple of days," Charles filled in.

Ben whistled. "Fun guys all the way I see."

Dick continued, "Some of the guys have said that they have seen a lot of activity in one of the warehouses. They have vehicles and crates of stuff coming in at all hours of the night. They're getting set up for something."

Ben rolled his eyes. *Thanks for the obvious statement pard*, he thought.

"Ben, what did you come up with?" Zenon asked.

"Well, for starters, Ms. Henderson is fairly routine. She works a six-to-three shift, Monday through Friday. From work either she goes and buys a drink then heads home where her parents are, or she goes to her church to meet up with a group there. The weekend shifts a lot, except—"

"Sundays," Dick interrupted. "Where she spends the day at church. Right?"

Ben acknowledged, "Actually…yes." He had to admit; he rather enjoyed listening to the sermons he heard from his car while keeping an eye on her. He had stopped going to church after Katherine passed. He felt that the people always pitied him. It made him feel uncomfortable. "Seriously, Ben, I think she could outdo your high-and-mighty principles," Dick jeered.

Ben smiled at that. Diana and he have a lot in common—or at least did have. There was a stab of pain that shot through his heart at that. He knew he was wrong with how he was acting toward God. *I really should go back to church*, Ben thought. It would be a small church; he never did like the big congregational churches; that was Katherine's choice. To him, it was a little impersonal. Smaller churches had a closer human connection. At least that's the way he felt.

His thought process was interrupted by Dick's cell phone playing "Bad Bad Leroy Brown." Dick answered, "Shoot…uh-huh…okay, thanks for the heads-up." Dick looked up from the phone. "The warehouse is cleared out. Nobody…nothing is in there."

Before they could deduce what the call meant, Zenon's phone rang. "Director Zenon," he answered. "Got it. Stay put till we get there." Charles hung up the phone and looked straight at Ben. "Something is going on at the apartment building. There are people lurking outside, and there's been several calls to the security office by the tenants," he said flatly.

Ben and Dick were out the door in a flash; Charles was right on their heels. As the men headed out of the office, Charles called out to all in the room, "Agents, gear up! Everybody to the Honeywell apartments. I'll fill you in on the way." Agents flew from their chairs and ran out the door.

Ben couldn't get the car to go fast enough. His head was spinning, his heart nearly pounding out of his chest. He was glad that Zenon filled everybody in and organized the whole thing before they all arrived. Everyone knew where to go as soon as they got there.

Ben finally got his mind under control and concentrated on the task at hand. He heard that the DMPD were on scene and waiting for their arrival. They would help wherever they were needed. Ben and his crew took the east side of the building. Dick and his crew took the front, and he also volunteered to clear the building. Charles and his crew were in the back, and another crew was on the west side. As they pulled up, they heard the fire alarm sounding. People were just starting to exit the building. Ben quickly radioed Amid and Diana's descriptions. "Hold these two if you see them," he stressed. Ben couldn't help but fear the worst. He had come up to the retaining wall twenty feet from the east-side exit. He watched the stair windows intently to see if anybody was coming out. He saw movement on the third floor's door.

Clive

Diana had just finished cleaning the public bathrooms on the east side of the third floor hallway. She had been uneasy all day; something was on the wind, but she didn't know what it was. She was just leaving when the loud speaker announced, "All tenants, evacuate the building."

The fire alarm sounded, and lights started flashing. *Great*, Diana thought. *This will put me behind schedule. What a time for a stupid drill.* She started pushing her cart to an out-of-the-way space when she saw Amid coming toward her. "We'd best get out of the building and report," Diana jested.

Amid brought a knife out from his coat pocket. "Not us. We have another task to do."

Diana cocked her head and looked at Amid. "What are you talking about?"

Amid replied, "We are going to meet up with some friends. Then we will be taking a trip." Diana's mind raced quickly, grasping any possibility. She decided to go for a block-and-run strategy. Probably not the best plan, but it was all she could come up with. Just then, her phone rang. Amid pointed to the phone and signaled her to give it to him.

"You won't need this anymore," Amid scolded. He took her phone, threw it on the floor, and stomped on it, smashing everything.

Diana snapped. She shoved the cart with its unsecured broom and mop-handle towards him, then turned for the stairwell. *Lord, help me please!* she prayed. She moved as quickly as she could, just stepping on the front of the stair so she could run down them. She was more afraid of Amid catching her than she was of falling down and breaking her neck. She heard Amid yelling heated words that sounded like cursing to her; though she didn't understand what he said. She was flying down the stairs, finally reaching the exit door. She hit the bar and ran through. Her eyes immediately closed from the pain of the bright sunlight hitting her. Her momentum carried her about fifteen feet from the door. She stopped to get her bearings, blinking feverishly trying to see where to go. She heard Amid hit the window on the second floor landing. She turned and saw the people who went out the front of the building to her right. She figured if she got caught up in them, Amid could catch her; he would be too close for her to get away from him and his knife. She felt a strong urge to run straight, head for the parking lot and her car. *Yes, I can get away in the car*, she thought. She started to run again. Within four steps, she was passing the retaining wall. *There's hope...I'll be okay*, she thought. Suddenly, someone grabbed her, pinning her arms to her side and pulling her back toward the building. The force of the sudden stop had temporarily stunned her.

Ben had seen Diana running down the stairs followed by Amid. His heart jumped, his mind raced. He wanted to run over there to help her, but then they wouldn't get the guy that was stalking her. *Lord, give her strength*, he prayed absentmindedly. He was watching intently and was grateful when he saw Diana bolt out the side door. It was very obvious that she was blinded by the sunlight, but she was almost to him. His heart stopped when he saw her pause.

"Come this way, babe, come to me," Ben said quietly. When he saw that she had decided to head straight toward the parking lot, he quickly prepared to grab her. *It would be like wrestling a steer in a rodeo*, he thought. However, unlike the steers, she could use her elbows, fists, feet, and knees. He knew he would have to secure her tightly. Just as she passed the retaining wall, he reached out and grabbed her across the chest, pinning her arms to her side. He could feel her heartbeat pulsing frantically, her body shaking from the adrenaline coursing through her veins. He heard her gasp for breath. Because of the sudden stop, her feet came out from under her so he easily, pulled her toward the wall. She was stunned, but only temporarily. He could feel her muscles start to tense; she started to fight against him in order to free herself. He needed to calm her down quickly before she hurt herself. "I won't hurt you," he quietly said into her ear. He heard her breath hitch; she stopped pulling against him. With no tension pulling away from him, Ben ended up pulling her tight against his chest. He felt a surge of energy shoot through him from the tip of his toes to the top of his head. He felt a connection to her, like when two powerful magnets with the opposite polarity near each other. *Knock it off, you idiot*, he scolded himself.

Ben heard Dick say, "Going in," over the earpiece. He listened as Dick's crew cleared each room on each floor. *But where was Amid?* Ben wondered.

Ben and Diana heard the side door open; Diana tensed up. With ease and fluidity, Ben slid out from behind her and guided her up against the wall. "Stay still," he quietly instructed. He moved toward the edge of the wall to watch and see where Amid was headed.

Amid came out looking frustrated and scared. He was looking around to see Diana. Not seeing her, he headed toward the back. *Maybe she's hiding back there*, he thought.

Ben saw Amid heading for the back of the building; there were some hiding places back there. Ben gave a heads-up to Zenon, telling him that he had Ms. Henderson and the suspect was heading toward him.

Dick's voice came over the headset. "Third and fourth floor cleared."

Diana could only hear one side of the conversation. This wasn't helping her nerves at all. She started looking around, wondering why she hadn't recognized this place from her dream. As she was looking toward the street, she saw a tan SUV with black-tinted windows pulling up and parking near the corner across from the apartment. She felt a dark heavy presence come over her; it was one that set off alarms in her soul. She gently touched the cowboy's arm. "Please tell me that tan SUV is one of yours," she said hopefully even though she knew it wasn't.

Ben turned and looked at the direction Diana was staring. "Unfortunately…no," Ben replied coldly. "Dick, how are we coming?" he said in a hurried tone. "There's a suspicious vehicle on the southeast corner, tan SUV," he continued. Ben started directing Diana toward a space that was between the wall and a nearby bush. He looked at her and nodded.

Diana understood; she was to stay hidden. She was bristly, like every ounce of her was on alert, clear down to her toes.

"Building cleared," Dick reported.

"Suspect is coming down the sidewalk toward the SUV," came over Ben's earpiece from one of the agents. Ben moved toward the edge of the bush. He watched Amid as he neared the SUV; the side door opened. He could see there was some discussion going on, and then he saw Amid crawl into the vehicle.

Ben touched his earpiece and announced, "They're about to head out." Just as the SUV was pulling out away from the curb; there was an explosion. It rocked the apartment and everything around it. Diana felt the shock wave pass through her. It was strong enough that it pushed her against the bush. She couldn't help it; she let out a little scream. Ben was knocked to the ground. He heard Ms. Henderson scream and looked back at her to make sure she wasn't injured. He quickly turned to see were the SUV was. He heard the tires squeal and turn down the main road. He touched his earpiece, "Zenon, we need an APB out on a tan SUV license plate BVR 23."

"On it!" Charles replied.

Ben looked to see where the explosion was. He could see smoke coming from the back of the apartment.

"The bomb went off in a dumpster. The fire department is already attending to it," came over the earpiece.

I bet they are kicking themselves for pulling the fire alarm now, Ben thought. He turned to attend to Diana. He helped Diana get up off the ground. "Are you okay?" he calmly asked her.

Diana nodded. "Just a few scrapes and pokes, nothing major." Diana brushed the leaves and dirt off her pants. "Who are you?" she asked.

"Agent Tigere with Homeland Security, ma'am," Ben stated.

Diana's eyebrow arched up and her head tilted. "Tigere? You don't look or talk like you're French." In truth, he didn't look French, Italian, or Spanish. He looked like he was the proverbial all-American boy. He was about six-feet-four and well built. He had brown hair and lightly tanned skin; he looked and acted like the men you would see rounding up cattle or throwing bales of hay around her grandparents' farm. His eyes were the color of sapphire blue, like what you see in the deep mineral pools of Yellowstone. He was probably just as dangerous.

"No ma'am, my great-grandfather was originally from Spain, thus the last name. I'm from the Midwest," he declared with a slight grin.

"You obviously were expecting this. Can you tell me what in the world is going on?" Diana asked.

"I need to meet up with my director. Come with me," Ben commanded.

Diana didn't like being left out in the dark, especially when it concerns her. She grabbed his arm. "Why me?"

Ben could see the bewilderment and apprehension in her eyes. Eyes that were dark gray, like the dark storm clouds that move across the plains.

"I don't know yet, ma'am, but I'm gonna find out," Ben assured. Diana stayed behind Agent Tigere as they walked to the front of the building. Diana saw the police taking notes and attending to those who were hurt from the shock wave. She was glad nobody was seriously hurt. Nobody except for Mr. Rogers; you could hit him with a cotton ball and he would say that you broke his arm. Diana was walking three feet behind Ben as they neared a group of men, one of them intently looking at an i-Pad.

"So did the tiger get his prey, or has he lost his touch?" Dick asked as he looked up from the i-Pad. Not seeing Ms. Henderson, he smiled and stated, "Hmm...I'd say the tiger has lost his touch." Just then Diana came around the side of Ben. Dick, caught off guard, commented, "Pictures don't do you justice, lady."

Ben wanted to punch him in the face. "This is Agent Richman, Ms. Henderson, my partner. Agent Richman, this is Ms. Henderson."

Dick just nodded at Diana. "Zenon wants us to meet up in the office," he stated.

Ben turned to Diana, "You will need to join us as well, Ms. Henderson."

"I need to get my stuff and let my boss know that I am required to leave," Diana inserted. "Also…it's Diana." The men gave her a quick nod of acceptance. Ben escorted Diana to her break room to pick up her stuff while Dick called her boss. When Diana grabbed her bag, she chuckled. Ben turned to look at her. "I was heading for my car when you grabbed me. My keys are in this bag. I wouldn't have gotten far, would I?" she stated as she knocked herself in the head.

Ben just shook his head. He understood that for her inexperience, she did try her best. "We need to get going, Diana," Ben said. She turned to follow him out the door.

"Do I follow you or what?" Diana asked.

"You will ride with me. Leave your car here. I'll bring you back afterward," Ben replied. She was apprehensive about leaving her car there, even more so about being alone with him in his car. Ben didn't give her the option; he took her arm and guided her to his car.

Downtown Des Moines

Back in the DHS office, Ben, Dick, and Diana where sitting around a desk. Dick, trying to play the proverbial bad cop, implied that she was in cahoots with Amid and did this as a terrorist stunt. Diana, after the second time of repeating herself, refused to acknowledge Dick's questions. Ben had to admit she had strength. Dick started cursing, which got an instant disapproving glare from Diana. It was one that went through Dick like a dagger, deep down to his soul. He actually apologized for it. Ben's mouth dropped open. Never, ever, in his three years of being with Dick, had he ever heard him apologize for his mouth. When people showed contempt for it, he would do it even more.

Diana turned to Agent Tigere "I've already told you before. I have no idea what Amid was doing, what he wanted, or why I was involved."

Ben smoothly but coldly replied, "I am sure you are not in with Amid," glancing over to Dick. "However, you are his target. Now all we have to do is figure out why. Until then, we will have DMPD assign an officer to you to keep you protected." Diana didn't like the idea of having a stranger watching her, but she didn't talk against it either. Ben stood and held a hand out to Diana. "I'll escort you out to meet your assigned officer."

Diana took his hand and stood up. "What about my car?"

"He can take you to get your car," Ben said as he guided her to the door.

Walking outside the DHS building, Diana saw people moving in and out. It was business as usual for them. As they came to the bottom of the stairs, Diana could see there was a police car waiting for her. It wasn't till the officer came out of the car that she saw who it was. "Ali!" she exclaimed. She ran over and gave the officer a hug.

"Your car awaits you, Milady," Ali said as he gave her a bow.

"Obviously, I don't need to introduce you two," Ben said indignantly.

Diana turned to Agent Tigere. "I'm sorry. Agent Tigere, Ali. Ali, this is Agent Tigere."

Ben shook the officer's hand. "You're a little light for being Arabic,' Ben conjured.

Ali smiled, "No, my real name is Alejandro Luis Garcia Lopez. My friends call me Ali. I attend Milady's church. When I heard about what went down this morning, I volunteered to be her protector. I can be around and nobody would know the better."

Ben raised an eyebrow. "Milady?" he questioned, looking down at Diana. Diana blushed a little. "It's my nickname. A long story. Maybe sometime I'll fill you in."

All of a sudden, they heard a vehicle racing down the street by them. It was a cargo van, heading straight toward them. The side door opened and two men dressed in black, faces covered with ski masks, hung out; another was hanging out from the front passenger window. They had SKS automatic rifles in their hands, and they started shooting. Ben and Ali threw Diana to the ground and both covered her. Diana heard the riffles going off; some women screamed, and men ran up the steps. As the van neared, the back doors swung open; a large bundle wrapped in a tarp and held closed with bungee cords was thrown out. It rolled within five feet from where the three were huddled. Ben, using Ali's patrol car as a shield, crawled to the front of the car and fired back at the van. He fired three shots, one hitting the arm of one of the men. The fellow assailants fired back at Ben, hitting the front of the patrol car and taking out a headlight. They shut the doors and were speeding away when the DMPD came in pursuit, zooming by like a line of NASCAR racers at the Indy 500. Diana could feel the wind draft caused by the cars roaring by. Ben went over to check on Diana and Ali. They had just stood up and were looking around.

As Ben neared them, he heard Officer Lopez exclaim, "Dear Lord Jesus!" Diana and Ali were staring at the package that was thrown out of the van. Diana couldn't believe what she was seeing. The main strap that tied the package closed had come off when it hit the ground. The wind bursts from the patrol cars going by had cause part of the tarp to come open. She could see two hands, a foot, and a leg, but they were in an unnatural position. It was a body in the package—a dismembered body. One that was wearing a shirt like she had seen Amid wearing earlier.

Ben followed the gaze of Officer Lopez and Diana. "Officer, take Ms. Henderson back into the office," he said over his shoulder. He went over to the body in the tarp. He heard Officer Lopez trying to get Diana to move; Diana was frozen, like a bronzed statue you would see in a park.

"Diana…please, come on," Ali pleaded.

"God help me!" Ben exclaimed as he looked up at Diana. He walked over to stand directly in front of her. He could feel her stare burning straight through his stomach. She wasn't seeing him; she was seeing the horrendous image that had seared itself into her mind. Ben gently took her chin and raised her head so he could see her eyes. Eyes that were no longer the dark gray but the slate blue—the color you would see on the seas in a storm, churning up waves of water. Her eyes were beckoning for a rhyme or reason of what they had seen, looking into his for answers. She was lost, struggling to maintain control, looking for a lifeline; those waves now filled her eyes near to overflowing, pleading for help.

It wasn't that Diana didn't want to leave. She wanted to erase from her memory the last fifteen minutes. Even losing the last twenty-four hours wouldn't have bothered her. She couldn't do what Ali was asking; her body wouldn't respond. Something, gratefully, blocked her vision. She felt a hand lift her head; it was Agent Tigere. She was gazing into his eyes, looking for any reasoning. His eyes were no longer the cold, dark sapphire blue. They were warm, even caring, and more of a dark cobalt blue like the crater lakes high in the mountains. She saw no answer in them. There was no help with understanding the hideous thing in front of her. It was his voice, however, that penetrated her mind.

"Diana, go with Officer Lopez," Ben said in a low, calming tone. Diana felt Ali's hand on her arm. Tears were starting to roll down her cheeks. She turned and allowed Ali to guide her back into the office.

Charles instructed Officer Lopez to bring Diana into his office. As Ali guided her to the couch, Charles introduced himself, "I'm Director Zenon. Would you like a cup of coffee, Ms. Henderson?" Diana shook her head. *No...she looks more like a tea drinker, more delicate*, he thought. "How about a hot cup of chamomile tea?" he continued.

Diana looked up. "Yes…please."

Charles motioned for her to stay put as he went to fix a cup. He was glad he had started some hot water at the same time he started a new pot of coffee. It was going to be a late night. He added sugar and cream to the tea; he wanted to add some rum, but being at the office, there was none to be had. *It would have settled her nerves*, he thought.

"She loves it that way," Officer Lopez stated as Charles passed by him. He gave the officer a quick nod of acknowledgement and went into the room. He stayed with her for a few minutes but then left to deal with activities going on outside. It was almost ten at night before the forensic team and the coroner were done with the site. The gunmen were aiming above the people's heads; it was only a distraction. The only shots that were of any consequence were the few fired directly at Ben. Unfortunately, those shots took out Officer Lopez's radiator and headlight. Now, with things done outside, Ben turned his attention to what had to be done inside, with Diana.

He headed back into the office. As he came in, he saw that Officer Lopez was still standing outside Zenon's office, guarding Diana. Ben smiled. "Hope your wife isn't going to kill you."

"Nah, I already sent her a text. She knew it was necessary," Ali replied.

"Where in the world did she get the name Milady?" Ben queried as he motioned toward the office where Diana was.

Ali smiled. "She'll have to tell you the story. I assure you once you get to know her, it fits her."

Ben's expression changed. "How is she doing?"

"It's hard enough for me to wrap around it, much less her. Thank you so much for getting her to move. I was afraid I was going to have to carry her. I don't think I would have made it. My legs were rubber bands. I know I would have dropped her," Ali stated. He got very somber and quietly stated, "She cried herself to sleep."

Ben entered Zenon's office; he saw her on the couch, legs pulled up to her chest—a luxury that she was unaware of. Nobody sat on Zenon's couch but Zenon himself. He could smell the chamomile aroma lingering through the office. *Zenon is going all out here*, Ben thought. He'd have to admit that she needed it. He also understood why she had fallen asleep. Her mind, unable to comprehend what it had seen, needed to reboot. Ben lightly touched the back of his hand to her cheek. He felt the ridges of salt left behind from her tears. She slowly opened her eyes. He softly said, "How are you holding?"

"That was Amid, wasn't it?" she asked.

"Yes," he replied.

Diana continued, "I recognized the shirt. W-why did they do that to him?" she softly asked.

She had to have a reason, so Ben gave her only what she needed. "I'd seen this before, not so nicely packaged but the same outcome. It is both a warning and a punishment. A warning for those who would be protecting you, a punishment for Amid, for failing his assignment."

"You saw this before?" Diana said in disbelief.

"Yes, in the Gulf War. It was common for the Republican Guard to use some type of execution to cause others to obey," Ben said as he looked at a knothole in Zenon's desk. "The Arabic culture can be very harsh."

"So now what's going to happen?" Diana asked.

"Well, now we know what type of people we are working with. However, you can't stay at your home. I've arranged to take you to a safe house." Ben stated.

"What about Mom and Dad? Are they in danger?" she anxiously asked.

"We don't believe so. However, Officer Lopez said that he and his family will be glad to take them in for a few weeks. Apparently, he has a large acreage out south. He feels he can keep them safe there," Ben said flatly. Before Diana could argue, Ben concluded, "It has to be this way. There's no other choice."

Diana felt defeated. *Lord, what are you doing? Would you tell me what is going on?* she prayed.

As Ben brought Diana out of the office, Diana saw Ali waiting. He moved over to her and gave her a hug. "I'll take care of the pastor and your mom…I promise." Diana just smiled. Ali could see that this whole thing was breaking her. "Hang in there, sis. We'll find out the reason later."

Diana nodded and walked with the guys out to Ben's car. "Sorry about your car, Officer Lopez. Hope your captain doesn't blow a gasket," Ben teased.

"Nah, don't worry about it. It was due for a tune-up anyway," Ali jested. "By the way, after what we just went through, you best just call me Ali," he added.

"Mine is Ben," he replied. Ben took one of the company's vehicles and drove them over to get Diana's car. After a thorough look-see to make sure there was no bombs on it, Ali drove the car to Diana's house, even with Diana's major protest.

5

Norwalk

At the Henderson's, Ben explained to them what had happened and what needed to happen. He also told Diana's parents that she was going to have to go to a safe house. Pastor Henderson did not like the whole idea. It took Ben and Ali's assurance that it was for Diana's safety. Of course, it wasn't just her parents that Ben had to deal with; thanks to the news reporters. Dewayne, Abbie, and the kids were all there. It was Liza and Jared that gave Ben a drilling. Kim and Angie sat near Diana; he could tell that she and the kids were very close. Ben was very patient with Diana's niece and nephew; they reminded him of his own kids. Finally, with all the discussion done and over with, the Henderson's packed their suitcases, loaded the cars, and gave hugs all around. Kim stayed with Diana till they had to leave. It was Diana that assured her that she would be okay. Only after that did Kim let her go and headed over to her parents' car. Diana climbed into the DHS's car and waited for Ben. It was a dark-green Enclave, an SUV that she had been eyeballing for a few years. It just wasn't in her budget to buy, not even a used one. Once they were out of sight of the family, Diana let herself go and began to cry. Ben had to give it to her; she put up a strong front. He had no doubt that she would do whatever she could to protect her family.
He tried to break the silence. "Hopefully, all this will be over soon and you can get back to your family."

She simply repeated, "Hopefully." It was hard for her to leave her family, even harder for her to go for an unknown amount of time without being able to see the kids. She worried that whoever these guys were, they may use the kids to get to her. She prayed that God would put a shield of protection around her family. Then she sat quietly as Ben drove north on Highway 28.

"You did very well tonight. I know it's hard to leave your family," Ben added.

"I'm more worried about these guys using them, or worse, hurting them," Diana added.

"You are very close to your nieces and nephew," Ben continued. He was just throwing things out to get her talking. Diana just nodded yes.

She saw that they turned east on I-80 then north again on I-35. "So, how far are we going?" she asked.

"A little ways out of the city. I have a friend who helps us out when we need a place. He's a little eccentric, but I think you'll get a laugh or two from him," Ben replied.

"Not that I doubt you, but I'm having a hard time finding anything funny about all this," she snipped.

"You're exhausted, you saw stuff nobody should ever see, and you've had to leave your family. It's been a very hard day all the way around. A good rest will help," Ben encouraged.

She only looked at him. It would take too much energy to disagree, energy she didn't have. He was right, she was very tired; she closed her eyes to listen for some answers from the Lord, and apparently, fell asleep.

It was quiet for a long time. Ben glanced over at Diana; she had fallen asleep. He also was hoping for the Lord's protection not only for his family but also for Diana and himself.

His friend Scott was his college friend and fellow soldier. He knew he would need his help, just as he knew that this wasn't going to be over any time soon. He felt Diana's pain, her confusion, and her loss of security. It was a little discomforting for him as well. He hadn't really been around another female, other than his girls and his family, since Katherine. Now here he was, driving with a woman to a safe house for an unknown amount of time. A woman, that ever since he saw her in the parking lot, he felt drawn towards. A warm feeling started radiating from the pit of his stomach. It warmed him clear through to his heart. He shook his head as if to shake the feeling off and concentrated on the road ahead of him.

6

McCleary Land

Diana, startled by the engine's idle, realized she had dozed off. "I'm sorry," she said as she adjusted herself in the seat.

"Don't worry about it. As I said earlier, it's been a long day," he replied.

Diana, looking around and not seeing anything familiar, asked, "Where are we?"

"It's just a pit stop for the night. We won't be able to get to the safe house in the dark. We'll have to sleep here. My friend is coming to guide us the rest of the way in the morning," Ben stated. Diana looked and saw a Quonset building. Ben put the car in park, got out, opened the sliding door then he returned to drive the car in. There were several other vehicles inside. She saw tractors, four-wheelers, and a couple of pickups all in various stages of disrepair. It reminded her of her grandpa's shop out on the farm. Not that her grandpa had four-wheelers; they used horses or pickups, but the rest was quite normal for her.

She looked at Ben with a startling realization. "Is there a bathroom? Or do I need to find an outhouse?"

Ben laughed; it was a full-hearted, gratifying, smooth laugh. "There's a bathroom in the back, right-hand side corner. I wouldn't think you would be the type who knew what an outhouse was," he chided.

"There are a lot of things you don't know about me. Don't judge a book by its cover," she reprimanded as she headed for the bathroom. On the way back, she saw that there was a kitchenette and a small fridge in the back. Once she was done and before she headed back to the car, she stopped at the fridge and grabbed a bottle of water. Getting back to the car again, Diana asked, "So we get to nap in the car…huh?"

Ben looked up. "Well… it's either in the car or in the back of one of the pickup trucks," he replied, giving her a Cheshire cat grin.

Diana understood the jest and blushed. "I think I'll save that option for another time, another place. A man whose nickname is Tiger shouldn't be trusted," she quickly replied. Although he was amused at Diana's blush and quick reply, it bothered him that she didn't trust him.

"Oh, tigers are very trustworthy. You're either prey or competition," he chided.

"Oh? No third option, huh?" she smarted back.

Ben had a big smile on his face and an eyebrow arched up, but he kept his eyes closed.

Diana continued, "Hmm...so I'm food or competition." He simply nodded. "Now that that's clear, I might have to go build a cage to sleep in. I'm not allowed to run away, and I pretty sure I don't want to be eaten." She grinned.

"Nah, you're safe for now. I'm too tired to do either tonight," Ben jested.

Diana gave him a smile, got into the car, and reached back, grabbing her pillow.

Ben opened his eyes and watched her. He didn't understand why in the world she had to have her pillow. Her parents told him that she never goes without her own pillow. As she was settling in and getting comfortable to sleep, he saw why. She was a person who cuddled things, so she held a pillow as she slept. He smirked a little; Katherine didn't really like to cuddle. She held to her side and he stayed on his. Of course they got together at least a few times, but then again, they weren't trying to sleep then.

Diana spoke out, "Just a warning: I've been known to snore a little." She didn't bother to open her eyes. She didn't want to see his expression.

"That's okay. As tired as I am, I may snore a lot," Ben injected. They both quieted down and fell asleep.

Diana woke with a start. Her eyes as big as silver dollars; she wasn't able to breathe. She felt Ben's hand on her arm. "Shh...just hold still." The sliding door of the Quonset had just been opened. Someone was walking near the car. Diana felt like her heart was trying to beat out of her chest. As the footsteps passed, Ben slowly reached for the car door and quietly released the handle so he could gently open it. Whoever was walking, walked toward the back of the building. Ben slid out of the car and softly shut the car door. Diana tried to stay still, looking as if she was still asleep. It was hard for her to do; she was scared to death. For a while, she couldn't hear anything. Then she was sure she heard someone at the fridge. She slowly rose up to see what was going on. Nobody was around, so she slowly and quietly opened the car door, slid out, and then gently closed the door. She went and hid behind one of the tractors.

Ben went up the side of the Quonset. He had his gun out and held it near his shoulder. As he approached the guy who was standing in front of the fridge with the door open, he crept up behind him and pointed the gun in the middle of his back. "Freeze!" Ben commanded.

"Jeez...Ben, give me a heart attack," the man said.

It was Scott, Ben's best friend. They were roomies in college, back when Ben was looking to major in Linguistics and Scott was majoring in Zoology. They had hit it off right away. It was Scott who convinced Ben to go into the military for the benefit of travel and funding for school. Scott was six-foot-two with dark-auburn hair and vibrant green eyes. His grandfather lived in Scotland, and he spent a lot of time with him, so he had a tendency to throw out a heavy Scottish brogue. In truth, he was raised down South, in Georgia. He normally spoke with a slight Southern drawl. He was attractive and muscular and had the typical Southern charm that comes from being raised by a horde of women. Like Ben, Scott was in the special ops and had fought in the Gulf War. Ben put his gun back into its holster. "Tell me about it. You should know better than to sneak up on a sleeping person."

"I didn't sneak up. I've been here for the last two hours, keeping a watch on things. It's about time y'all woke up," Scott chided. As the two men walked back toward the car, they saw that the passenger door was slightly ajar. "She's a fast learner," Scott stated and winked at Ben.

"Yeah, just enough to get herself in trouble though," Ben said annoyed. "Come on out, Diana. It's safe!" Ben yelled.

Diana slowly came out from behind the tractor and walked toward the car. Scott smiled. "Smart choice of a hidin' place."

"Thank you, sir," Diana agreed.

"Diana, this is my best friend, Scott McCleary. Scott, this is our pigeon," Ben replied. Diana gave him a look of disgust. Ben simply smiled at her.

"A pleasure, ma'am," Scott said with small bow.

"Thank you, sir." Diana smiled.

"Don't give her a big head. She's bad enough as it is," Ben injected. Diana gave him a raspberry and walked to the car to get her stuff to clean up with.

"You won't wanna do that yet, ma'am. Y'all just get all dirty again in a few minutes," Scott asserted.

Diana turned and looked at the men who were just starting to look over the four-wheelers. "I'm at least going to brush my hair and brush my teeth. I'll clean the rest when we get there," Diana stated as a matter of fact. Both men just shrugged their shoulders and continued to prep the vehicles. Moments later, Scott loaded a trailer that he had attached to his four-wheeler with the luggage. Ben was waiting for Diana; she would ride with him. Diana looked at the situation and prayed that God kept them on the road or trail or whatever they were going to be driving on. Scott came over and grabbed her stuff and put it into the trailer. She put the helmet on and hopped on behind Ben. "You'd better hang on tight. It's going to be a bumpy ride," Ben joked.

"That's what I'm worried about," Diana said nervously. Scott locked the Quonset doors, and then they took off. They went through trees, mud, streams, and fields. Diana was enjoying herself immensely; she even let out a "Wooh–hoo!" a few times. Right up until they started climbing through the sand hills. Diana could feel the four-wheeler lose traction in the sand. On top of that, there were blowout and sharp drop-offs; just holding on to the handgrips wasn't enough for her. She had no choice; she grabbed on to Ben. Her thought was that if she went, he went. Her prayers were constantly going up to God that he kept them from rolling.

Ben had always enjoyed the ride to the cabin. He noticed that Diana was afraid of the edges. The closer he got to them, the tighter she held on to him. He just couldn't resist; he would purposely ride the ridge. They had been riding for forty-five minutes before they crested a hill and stopped for a minute. Diana saw a log cabin down in the valley. There was a lake about fifteen feet behind it and a thick standing of trees all the way around. She figured that this cabin would be hard to find if you didn't know what to look for.

Ben heard Diana say, "It's beautiful." *You're unusual for a city girl*, Ben thought. They drove on down into the valley. When the group came to the cabin, they parked the four-wheelers in a nearby shed.

Scott dismounted and, while brushing the dust off himself, said, "Did we all survive?"

Ben piped up, "I think Diana's fingers are imprinted permanently into my chest."

"If I was going, you were going," Diana stated.

"You like me that much, huh?" he teased.

"Well…the way I see it, you being bigger than me, you would go to the bottom first, and I'd have a softer landing," she quipped back as she was brushing the dust off herself.

Ben and Scott looked at each other and smiled. "Don't go there bro," Scott finally declared. Diana, seeing their look, turned beet red and quickly turned in hopes that the men didn't see it. Of course they did; she heard them chuckling. She was grateful that they didn't take it any further. She grabbed her pillow and toiletry bag and headed to the front door of the log cabin. Ben went and grabbed the suitcase and his travel bag then followed her.

As Scott unlocked the door, he gestured upward. "You can have the loft, ma'am," he said.

"Um, is there a bathroom up there?" Diana timidly asked.

"Yes, ma'am, well, a half bath anyway. There's a sink and toilet. The full bath is down here on the right. There's a kitchen on the left," Scott added.

"That will work…thank you." Diana nodded.

Scott looked at Ben with a questioning expression on his face. "She must go a lot during the night," Ben surmised.

Diana was getting things placed in her mind when she heard something coming from the kitchen. She was greeted by a beautiful golden retriever. As Diana held her hand out for the dog to smell it, she looked over to Scott. "That's Pete," Scott announced.

With Pete's approval, seen by his wagging tail and nudging head, Diana reached down and scratched his ear. She continued to check the place out. She noted that there were no other bedrooms or beds on the main level. "Where are you two sleeping?" she wondered.

"The couch pulls out to a bed," Scott motioned to one of the two couches.

"One will keep watch during the night while the other sleeps," Ben added.

"Do you think they will find us clear out here?" she said worriedly. Both men shrugged their shoulders. Not getting a real answer, Diana turned and climbed the stairs to the loft. It was ruggedly beautiful. It had the typical slanted ceiling, but it was high enough to not have to bend over to get into the double bed. There was only a railing separating the loft from the lower level. The pinewood slats were stained in a warm golden-honey color and ran throughout the area. There was a door at the center of the far wall that went out to a balcony. Diana walked out onto the balcony and gasped; it was so surreal. It looked out toward the east; part of the lake could be seen between the cover of trees. It was tranquil and beautiful; she thought she could just stay out there and forget everything from the yesterday. The bathroom was very small, but it would do for what Diana needed. She grabbed a change of clothes, her bathroom stuff, and a towel then headed for the shower downstairs. The other two took their showers after the hot water tank had a chance to recoup. After everyone was clean and everything was put away, the group got together over an early dinner. Scott made his "famous" chili. He had placed all the fixings out on the table—everything anybody would want with their chili. There was Fritos, cheese, sour cream, jalapeños, onions, hot sauce—you name it, it was there. Ben and Scott went to town, chowing down on several bowls.

Diana, not wanting to be rude, said she wasn't very hungry—which wasn't a lie; she was still worried about the family's safety. She went to the kitchen and made a peanut butter sandwich and grabbed a bottle of water. She came back and sat down at the table and asked, "How long do you figure we'll have to hide out?"

"I really don't know," Ben said solemnly.

"We're stocked with all the stuff we need for a month. If it goes longer than that, we could go hunting," Scott replied excitedly. He and Ben used to go hunting quite often. Lately, they have both been too busy.

Ben saw Diana's demeanor drop. "We can't rush this stuff. If we come back too soon, you will be in a lot of danger. Better safe than sorry," Ben concluded. Diana nodded in agreement, but she was already missing the family.

7

McCleary Land

It had been five weeks since the group started hiding out in the cabin. As of yet, neither of the men would let Diana out of their sights. She was going stir-crazy, and she knew it. Her phone was destroyed, so she had no music. She wasn't allowed to bring her laptop; Ben told her it wasn't secure, and she couldn't go for walks outside. The one comforting thing Diana had was Pete. Since the first day she arrived, Pete rarely left her side. Scott often accused her of stealing his dog. This morning, Diana woke to a conversation that Ben and Dick were having over his laptop. She wanted to see what the men were talking about, so she patted Pete and got out of bed. She came halfway down the stairs and sat down. She was in a lightweight sleep shirt with Scooby on the front and a pair of shorts; she didn't think it would cause any problems.

Dick was filling Ben in on what the FBI and DHS had come up with so far. Dick reminded Ben that they had found the tan SUV the first night. It was abandoned in the parking lot of a warehouse in the industrial area. Everything was wiped clean of all fingerprints; what clues they did find were pointing to a local gang. The gang that was incriminated was hopping mad and looking for blood. They didn't like getting blamed for stuff they had nothing to do with. At least that was what the ears on the street said. Dick started telling them about the van that had screamed by them in front of the DHS office when he started stumbling over his words. Ben looked up from his notes after there were several pauses and bumblings. He could tell that Dick was adjusting something on his screen. Ben asked, "Are you okay?"

"Huh? Oh yeah," Dick said distractedly.

Ben looked at the screen and happened to glimpse the reflection of Diana on the stairs, listening. Her long legs uncovered and her long light-brown hair wild around her face. The sun was just coming through the window of the loft door. The morning light revealed a silhouette through her shirt. Ben's eyebrow arched up; he shook his head but had to admit she was pleasing to look at. "Concentrate, Dick!" Ben reprimanded.

Diana was straining to hear what was being said; she had to start lip-reading to understand Dick; she couldn't see Ben's face to read him. She wasn't sure what Dick was looking at that was making him so distracted.

"Hmm, oh...yeah. The van was just found in the Raccoon River. Apparently, one of the speedboats forgot to pull their anchor in all the way before they started off. It caught it," Dick chuckled. "The boys are okay. They'll be working off their bill to fix the boat to their parents for a while though. Of course, all prints and clues were destroyed by the mud and water," he concluded. He was still adjusting things on his computer screen and let his appreciation slip out. "Wow."

"That's enough Dick," Ben said annoyed. "I'll check back later. Bye." Then Ben closed the link. He finished writing something down on the tablet in front of him. "You really shouldn't tease Dick, Diana," Ben said over his shoulder.

"Seriously. If seeing my knees caused him that much problems, he needs more help than I thought," Diana disputed.

"I can't argue that he has problems, but you don't have to add to them. He was drooling all over his laptop," Ben stated. He, himself, had to focus on writing the data down so he didn't stare.

She couldn't believe she was the one causing his problem. "I'll go get cleaned up and dressed to cover my legs," Diana said exasperatedly.

Ben watched her go back up the stairs. *She's obviously unaware of what the sun is showing*, he thought.

Scott came in from the kitchen. "Oatmeal is ready!" he announced.

"Be down in a minute!" Diana replied from the bathroom in the loft.

Scott had noticed that it was the one meal that she ate. She didn't seem to be eating much of anything else, and it worried him. Pete came down from the loft. "Well, good morning, traitor," Scott said.

"You shouldn't be so hard on him, Scott. I just have a way with animals," Diana scolded.

As they were finishing breakfast, Scott got a call on the landline. "McCleary. Yes, why? Huh-huh...okay, I'll go check it out. Thank you for the heads-up." Scott hung up the phone.

Ben and Diana were just watching him, looking for an explanation. "Yes?" Ben asked.

Scott looked straight at him. "We've got problems." Diana's stomach turned over. "That was the police department. They were calling me to tell me someone broke into my Quonset off of the highway. I'm to go down and meet up with them to tell them what was taken."

"It could be just a coincidence," Ben said. He didn't believe that for a second, but he noticed that Diana turned ashen white and was trying to break the tension.

"Ben, you're gonna need to come with me to check your car," Scott stated. Diana looked hopeful; she didn't even care if that meant facing the blowouts again. She would be able to get outside.

"Don't even think about it," Ben said, looking directly at Diana. "You are staying out of sight. Even if it means handcuffing you to the headboard," he continued. Diana looked totally dejected. She knew better than to argue; she didn't want to give him a reason to tie her up. He'd probably do it. She threw herself to the back of her chair.

"It's for your own good," Scott said.

"Yeah, I know," she quipped. Ben and Scott got their four-wheelers out and ready to go. Ben didn't want to leave Diana. He didn't believe the terrorist found them yet; he just didn't trust Diana. She seemed to draw trouble to herself.

"She'll be fine," Scott assured. "She's not gonna find much to get into trouble with over here. She's also got a good mind, and she knows how to use it," he continued.

"Her using it is what's worrying me," Ben added.

Diana stood at the door of the cabin and watched the men ride away. *At least I'll be able to check things out now,* she thought. Once she knew that the men wouldn't see her, she went and grabbed the spare shed key and went to check it out. She found the usual mechanical stuff, some emergency supplies, odd and ends of stuff. She also found some fishing gear; she smiled at that. She would still be in hiding, nobody is around, and she would get to enjoy some good ole fishing time. She found a shovel and quickly dug up some worms behind the shed. Even Pete helped her dig some up. Diana looked around and found a wide-brimmed hat to block the sun from frying her face then went out on the dock and totally enjoyed herself.

Scott and Ben got down to the Quonset in less than thirty minutes. Scott greeted the officer waiting for them. "Hey, Kevin...this is my friend, Ben. He has some stuff in here too," Scott pointed out. The men turned and went to check out the damage. The sliding door was obviously pried open. Ben headed for the car as Scott and Officer Kevin looked at the other things around the building. Ben noticed scratches around the locks of the car door. He put a pair of gloves on and did what he could not to disturb the scene. The glove box was emptied onto the seat. The emergency kit was pulled out from under the passenger seat. The trash can was missing from the back and in the hatch, the spare tire was slashed, and the carpet was ripped up and pulled out. They were looking for anything to trace Diana. Ben checked under the car to see if a tracker or something more dangerous was put underneath. He found nothing there; however, he noticed the gas tank had a small hole in it. He was just about to check the engine when Scott and Officer Kevin came around.

"Other than some bottles of water and a package of bologna, nothing else is missing. It looks like nothing was damaged," Scott stated.

"I can't say the same for my car," Ben said irritably.

Officer Kevin looked at the car. "Wow, looks like they were looking for something really hard," the officer replied.

"Yeah, my boss isn't going to be happy," Ben added. The officer took his book out to write down what the damages were. Ben didn't tell him about the gas tank or about the trash can missing. Scott just watched and listened. As Officer Kevin finished his notes, he told the men that the report would be done tonight and the insurance company would be able to view the report in the morning. Scott thanked the officer and walked him to his car. Ben got on the phone and called Zenon.

Scott walked back toward Ben's car. "So what did they really get?" he asked.

"From what I can see, they took the trash can, probably to see if there's any proof of Diana's presence, and they put a hole in the gas tank. I hadn't looked at the engine yet. I'll let the forensic crew take care of it. They'll be here in an hour," Ben concluded.

"I'd say that it was definitely the same people. It couldn't be more obvious. If they tracked your car to here, it won't be long before they will start looking for her in the nearby houses," Scott deduced.

"Yeah, I know…but it will take them a while to get to us." Ben, not wanting to give anything away, stayed vague. He wasn't sure if the place was bugged or not. "We'd better get the door fixed. By the time that's done, the team should be here," Ben said nonchalantly. He really wanted to get back to the cabin to keep Diana safe. With this break-in, he knew it was only a matter of time. Scott went back to the cabinets and started pulling out tools and equipment to fix the door. The two men worked together in silence. Just as they put in the last screw, the forensic team showed up. Ben took them to the car, showed them what he saw, and pointed out that the gas tank was punctured. The forensic team started working immediately. Scott gave them the padlock to lock the door with when they were done. The lead of the forensic team told them she would take care of the rest and to go ahead and head back.

They didn't have to tell Ben twice; he was ready to go. Scott, however, was busy flirting with the lead. "Scott! We need to get going!" Ben insisted.

At the Cabin

The water was wonderful; Diana had already caught two good-sized bass and an awesome perch. She was sitting at the edge of the dock with her feet dangling in the water. Pete was sitting right beside her. The fish weren't biting at this time, so Diana closed her eyes and just lay back on the dock, petting the grateful Pete.

Ben and Scott again took less than thirty minutes to return to the cabin. When they took the four-wheelers to the shed, Scott immediately tensed up. The shed was unlocked. He looked over to Ben; Ben took his gun out. They cautiously entered the shed and thoroughly checked everything out. Then they moved to the cabin. They each took a side of the door. Scott didn't have a gun, but he didn't need one; he could be deadly with his hands and feet. Ben slowly turned the doorknob and carefully opened the door. They quietly went through the entire cabin; there was no sign of trouble, but there was no sign of either Diana or Pete. Ben was frantically searching his mind, running through every scenario possible. It was Scott that came up with a possibility. "Hey, I just recalled. I didn't see my fishing rod in the shed or my mom's sun hat."

Ben rolled his eyes. They both headed toward the lake. Sure enough, as they neared the lake, they heard Diana singing. "She has a beautiful voice," Scott pointed out. Ben was too livid to give her any praise. They saw that she was lying on the dock, fishing pole in the holder, legs in the water, and Pete right beside her. "Now that's not a typical thing to see from a city girl," Scott again pointed out. As they were watching, Diana got a bite. She sat up and took hold of the fishing pole. A quick tug, and the fish was hooked. She reeled it in and pulled it out of the water. It was another good-sized bass. She stood up and pulled the leader from the water, hooked the bass on before pulling the hook from the bass's mouth, and then she put the lead back into the water. She was still standing up when Scott came up with a great idea. "Let's give her a little lesson." Scott had a devilish look in his eyes, and Ben knew he was going to try to scare her.

"I'm not sure that would be a wise thing to do," Ben guessed.

"Nah, what's she going to do? Scream, scratch, cry? Whoa! I'm really scared," he teased. Ben stayed hidden so he could watch, unsure of what was going to happen. He also didn't want to give Scott away. Scott had called Pete over to him using a dog whistle. He gave him the command to stay but leashed him to a tree anyway. Diana hadn't noticed Pete not being by her; she was busy with putting on another worm. She threw her line back out into the water. Scott came up quietly behind Diana; he could hear she was still humming. Slowly he came around and grabbed her by her neck and her arm, pulling the arm behind her. "Come with me…quietly." He spoke with an English accent so she would not recognize who it was. She froze and allowed him to pull her back a few steps. Unfortunately, what Scott couldn't see because he was behind her Ben saw very clearly. At first, Diana's eyes showed terror, but then Ben saw the steel, cold glare shine through. Before he could react to diffuse the situation, Diana thrust her elbow into Scott's abdomen. Scott recoiled and grunted from the pain. Then Diana kicked her heel backward into Scott's knee. The shock of her reaction caused Scott to start to lose his balance. Diana took advantage of it and heaved back pushing her attacker back toward the water; Scott fell in.

8

McCleary Land

Diana took off, stopping only for a second at the end of the dock to slip her shoes back on; the wide-brimmed hat fell off behind her. As she ran down the path she heard her attacker fall into the water, which gave her precious time to find something to fight with. She was too busy thinking of what to use that she ran directly into Ben, who was standing ready to catch her. "Easy…Diana, easy. You've taken care of him very well," he smoothly and calmly said.

Diana, realizing it was Ben who caught her, stopped and looked at him with a questioning face. Ben gently led her back to the lake.

"Ack, woman!" Scott said, climbing out of the water. "Ther be ah weld kawt in dat un," Scott replied in a strong Scottish brogue, looking at Ben.

Ben had to laugh. "You, who has a degree in zoology, don't know that a cat, when it feels threatened, attacks."

"Well, you'd know all about cats, wouldn't you," Scott sneered as he rubbed his stomach.

"You just have to know how to pet them," Ben stated as he reached up and caressed Diana's head. Diana's body instantly moved toward Ben's touch. She immediately froze and blushed at her body's reaction. She was mad at herself for endorsing the caress, but what riled her even more was when she looked up at Ben, she knew that he noticed it. He had a smug smile on his face because of it. It was more than she could take; she instantly elbowed him in the side, and when he loosened his grip on her arm, she took off running.

Ben saw that in the instant that he touched her head, Diana's eyes turned to an emerald green with just a small ring of gold next to the pupil. It pulled something in him somewhere down deep in his being. Unfortunately, it only lasted a fleeting second, and then they were a dark, steel-gray again. He felt Diana's muscles tense and quickly moved to avoid her retaliation. She only got in a glancing blow with her elbow. For that reason, and the fact that he has a longer stride, it only took Ben a few steps to catch her again. This time he grabbed her by the arm and swung her around. Regrettably, she lost her footing and started to slide down the embankment on the side of the path. Ben tried to stabilize her but wound up slipping and falling with her. When they came to a stop, he was on top of her.

"Would you get off me," Diana blazed infuriately.

Ben could see she was furious but couldn't help himself; he had to rib her more. "Actually I'm quite comfortable here," Ben replied, smiling.

"So...is the tiger looking for that third option? Or...maybe he just likes playing with his food?" Diana quipped. Ben gave her a broad, malevolent grin. Diana tried to squirm out from underneath him. She could feel the sticks and twigs under her jabbing and poking into her back; she didn't care. When she found that she couldn't wiggle out, she started trying to hit him. He just grabbed her hands and held them above her head, which brought him down toward her face.

"You won't win this one, Milady," Ben teased. He held her there till he saw that she was running out of steam. Now that she was calming down, Ben started to release her; then he heard a motorboat out on the water. Scott, who had gone to untie Pete, heard it too. He signaled Ben to stay down as he headed for the dock. He didn't have time to figure out why Ben was on the ground or where Diana was. Ben looked down at Diana, his eyes the deep-sapphire-blue again, and Diana could see the seriousness in him. "Hold still and don't make a sound," he whispered.

Scott met the motorboat on the dock; there were two patrolmen in the boat. The patrolmen asked, "Have you seen a young lady walking around out here?"

"No, not that I've seen. Why?" Scott asked.

"You live near here, sir?" they continued.

"Yes, sir, I've been in the area for several years. Is this lady a runaway?" Scott inquired and followed the line of sight of the two officers.

The men looked toward some movement they caught out of the corner of their eyes. "Whoever's over there come out now!" they commanded.

Ben came down close to Diana's ear. "Stay here and lie still. They can't see you, you're too low." Ben kissed her on her cheek. "Oh man, you guys ruined everything!" Ben jested with big gestures and stood up. "I've been set up to scare him for several minutes now," he continued, giving them a big smile.

"Where are you from, sir?" one of the patrolmen asked.

"This is my cousin, James. He's up here visiting me for a few weeks," Scott injected.

"So, you two have been fishing?" the officers inquired, looking at the fishing pole.

"Yes sir…do you want to see the fish?" Ben asked.

Scott went and pulled up Diana's leader to show the fish.

"You guys had good luck today," the officers acknowledged.

"Yes, sir, it's supper tonight," Scott stated.

While Ben and Scott were over talking to the men in the boat, Pete found Diana and was standing near her. Diana felt that same dark presence she'd felt just before Amid tried to take her; she just couldn't connect the dots yet. She commanded Pete, "Protect." Pete immediately turned and took a guard pose, growling at the men in the boat. The officers looked again over to where Ben had been hiding. They saw a dog near the area and noticed that it was taking an aggressive stance.

"Well, we need to continue looking for the young lady. If you see anything, be sure to let us know," one of the officers gave him a card with phone numbers on it. "You guys have a good night," they concluded.

Ben and Scott could see the men didn't want to take on the dog. Scott was glad he had taken the time to release him. The officers scanned the rest of the area; not seeing anything else moving, they backed the boat out and turned it around. Scott and Ben waited on the dock till they were out of view. They slowly walked toward the cabin, Ben easily reaching down to pick up the hat that fell off of Diana. Once under the cover of the trees, Ben went over to where Diana was hiding. Scott came over and praised his dog for being such a good boy. Pete was elated with the attention. Ben knelt down beside Diana. "We need to get back to the cabin." Diana agreed and allowed Ben to help her up.

She saw that Scott had the fish she caught and thanked him. "I always hated cleaning these things. That's why I don't fish," Scott said in disgust.

"I can clean them…if someone would kill them," Diana said sheepishly. Ben and Scott looked at her. "I can't kill animals, even fish," she added.

Ben just shook his head. *Typical city girl*, he thought.

Scott replied, "You can't kill anything, but you have no problem taking my kidney out…huh?"

"You scared the crap out of me. I reacted out of instinct," Diana contradicted.

"A cornered animal, I told ya," Ben added.

Scott looked between Diana and Ben. "Definitely a feline: purring one minute turning and attacking the next. I guess it takes one to understand one," he taunted.

Ben just rolled his eyes. As they turned to walk back to the cabin, Ben saw Diana's back. "Holy cow…girl! Do you do anything halfway?" he said angrily. Scott looked to see what Ben was ticked off about. Diana's shirt was shredded in the back. They could see her white skin and the runs of blood going down her back. Diana turned and looked at him. "How bad did your back get cut up?" Ben growled.

"So I've got a few scratches. I'll live…I assure you," Diana insisted. Ben went to look at Diana's back.

"Now's not the time to look, Ben, we need to get inside," Scott prompted. Ben ushered Diana inside; Scott went to dispatch the night's supper.

Ben took Diana directly to the loft. "Take off your shirt," he commanded. Diana just stared at him in disbelief that he would ask such a thing. "Lord help me!" he steamed. "Just turn around and lie on your stomach on the bed," Ben directed. Diana did as she was told. Ben pulled his knife from his pocket and slit the back of what was left of Diana's shirt clear to the collar. Then he undid her bra and tucked the hooks under and off to the side. "Just a few scratches…my Aunt Fanny! Stay here. I need to get some stuff," Ben said as he went down the stairs. He was so mad he could spit tacks.

Scott saw him come down. "How bad?"

"She's not going to be happy. I've got to pull a lot of thorns out and some of the cuts go deep. I don't think she needs stitches, but I may need to superglue some closed," Ben explained.

"Wonderful, so I guess that means I clean the fish." Scott grimaced.

"I'm sorry, just gut them for me. I'll take care of the rest later," Diana yelled down.

The men looked up toward the loft. "You're not supposed to be moving," Ben yelled back.

"Whatever!" she snipped back. Once Ben was downstairs, she went ahead and took her bra off and put it under her pillow. She thought she would die when he unhooked it in the first place. She readjusted herself and lay there as she was told to do.

"I'm gonna need your help. Hopefully, just to hold the light for me," Ben told Scott quietly. Ben went back up to the loft followed by Scott with a spotlight.

Diana held still as much as she could, but she would twitch as Ben pulled the thorns out. Scott couldn't help but notice Diana had a nice figure; at least what he could see of it. She wasn't a skeleton covered with skin. No, she had some meat on her; even so, she was nice to look at. Her skin was not quite white; there was a definite pink tone in it. It just verified that all those red highlights in her long light-brown hair were natural. Ben, trying to get Diana focusing on something other than what he was doing, asked, "Why didn't you attack me like you did Scott?"

"You mean besides that fact that you had my arms pinned to my sides and I couldn't get the right angle to kick your knee?" Diana replied.

"Well...yeah...but then you seemed to just give up," Ben chuckled.

"I don't think you would believe me if I told ya," she retorted.

"Try me," Ben countered.

Diana, only being able to see Scott, looked up at him.

Scott winked at her. "He's probably heard it before," he added.

"I knew that someday it would happen," she curtly answered.

Ben stopped and looked at Scott then back to Diana. "What do you mean?" he questioned and then went back to pulling a stubborn thorn that sank deep into her back.

Diana winced. "I had a dream earlier, like a month or so ago, that it was going to happen. I knew I was running from something. I just didn't know what. I was caught by a man that said he wouldn't hurt me. I couldn't see his face, but I saw his clothes, so I called him Cowboy." With that comment, Ben grinned. Scott looked over at Ben and chuckled.

"If it hadn't been for that dream, you would have gotten the same reaction Scott did, probably even more so. I don't know why I didn't recognize the area, but it didn't click until that day," Diana stated. Ben believe what Diana was saying. Scott, on the other hand, had heard of a lot of things that God has done, but this was new to him. What amazed him more was how much at ease she was with it.

He watched Diana's face, looking to see if she knew how unusual she was. He noticed her eyes were a medium blue it was almost...calming. "Wumen! Ho' manie coolurs do yur ayes chanje?" he asked in a Scottish brogue.

Diana smiled and chuckled, "I have hazel eyes. Both my brother and I do. Mine will go from green to blue to gray and any variation in between. It depends on what color I'm wearing and what my mood is."

With that, both men laughed. "We've seen the mood thing already."

Diana gave them a raspberry, then continued. "My brother's goes the opposite way in colors. His will go from green to brown to gray, though most of the time they are brown," she ended. Then she grimaced as Ben used the superglue to seal up the two deep cuts.

"Hold on, I'm almost done," Ben said calmly. He simply washed the rest of her back to clean off the blood. Diana didn't yell, cry, or scream the whole time. The only thing Ben heard from her was a gasp of air and a jerk when he went to put the ointment on. "Sorry, I'm trying to be careful," he said.

"No, you didn't hurt me, it's just…cold!" Diana assured him with an emphasis as he dabbed on more.

As he finished, he told her that she wouldn't be doing anything but lying on her stomach for the rest of the night. "You move around too much and you'll break open those gashes," he explained to her. "Why didn't you tell me I was hurting you?"

"I didn't feel it until I got up off the ground. I figured they were just little scratches, nothing more," she replied.

Ben figured that being unsure of the two officers *or whatever they were* made her not register pain. "What do you want to eat?" he continued.

"I'm not really hungry right now. I just want a glass of milk," was Diana's response. Neither Scott nor Ben liked her response. Ben had noticed that she weighed noticeably less than the first time he caught her. Scott had already mentioned to him that she wasn't eating much. At first they figured it was just all the stress of the things going on. Now they were thinking she was becoming anorexic. Diana looked up at Scott. "If you could, would you put the fish in a bowl of buttermilk and put them in the fridge? I'll cook them up tomorrow. They're better that way anyway."

"I don't know if I have any buttermilk," Scott said scratching his head.

"Just take some milk and add a couple of teaspoon of apple cider vinegar to it. I know you have that. It'll work that way too," Diana stated. Scott agreed and went downstairs to cook up something for Ben and himself. Ben looked over at Pete, who was lying on the floor, waiting for him to get off the bed. "I'm not sure it would be a good idea to let Pete up here. You don't want an infection," Ben said.

"He doesn't usually lie on me, just beside me," she informed him.

"Still, I think it would be best if he stayed with Scott tonight," Ben insisted. "Is there anything you need before I go downstairs?" he asked.

"In the medicine cabinet, I have two pill cases. I need the blue one," she said.

Ben went and got the pill case, noticing the various pills that she was taking, most of them being supplements. He also brought in some Tylenol. *She would need these too*, he figured. He put the pill case and the Tylenol on the nightstand. Diana gave him a smile. "If you need anything else, I'm just downstairs," he added.

Ben asked Scott to call Pete down from the loft. When he came, Scott gave him the command. "Stay." Pete did, but he kept looking up to the loft.

Ben took a glass of milk up to Diana along with a plate of cheese and crackers. "Just in case you do get hungry," he said trying to encourage her to eat. Diana just smiled.

He came back downstairs, and knowing that Diana would try to hear what they were talking about, the guys went and sat outside on the porch as they ate. Scott was the first to voice his mind. "Do you think they were actual patrolmen?" he started.

"Nope," Ben said flatly.

"So they have found us," Scott added.

"I don't think so. They didn't see Diana, but they will be watching to see if she's here," Ben offered.

"Do you think it's her ability with dreams that they're after?" Scott wondered.

"I doubt it. I have a feeling it's a lot more sinister than that," Ben concluded.

They sat contemplating for a while. Then Scott asked, "Do you remember way back when you had a dream about that lady?"

"Yeah...sort of. I was what eighteen...twenty years old?" Ben stated.

"I remembered you told me she had green eyes," Scott added.

"Yeah...her name was Ariana something. She wore a hijab and lived in the Middle East," Ben said irritably.

"Oh, you didn't tell me that," Scott continued.

"I don't remember it all. It was probably just a dream from studying the Middle East," Ben insisted.

Scott dropped it and changed the topic. "So what's plan B?" Scott asked.

"Well, for now, we stay here. With her back cut up like it is, she'd get an infection if we go on the lam. As it is, we are going to have to find some Benadryl or something. Her back was already starting to break out from the toxins in the thorns," Ben said disgustedly. He was madder at himself for teasing her and making her squirm underneath him. He knew she was already embarrassed, but he enjoyed being close to her. *All right...so I admit it*, he said to himself.

"I'm worried about her not eating," Scott added.

"I know. She's already lost ten to fifteen pounds," Ben continued.

"If we do have to leave and eat off the land, she won't last," Scott injected.

"I need to think on this. There's something we are not seeing," Ben ended. The men went back inside. Ben went to check on Diana, who was already asleep. He glanced over to the nightstand. She not only drank all the milk but ate most of the cheese and crackers. *So you were hungry…huh, babe,* he thought. Diana's shoes were still on, so he went and took them off, placed a light blanket over her legs, and then went to take the glass and plate to the kitchen. He heard her talking, but it wasn't in English. Was she speaking Hebrew?

"I have been calling you. Will you hear me now? Come to me and hear my words and you will be blessed. Come to me once more," Diana said in Hebrew.

Ben froze for a second, then he checked once more to see if Diana was actually sleeping; she was out cold. He was shaking from his head to his toes; there was no way he could deny what he heard. There was nothing in the records saying she knew any other language. *No she didn't know what she was saying,* Ben was sure of it. That meant there was only one possibility; it had to come from God. He knew that he wasn't close to the Lord anymore, but to go to this extreme—wow. Ben took the glass and plate to the kitchen and started washing them.

Scott came in. "You okay, bro?"

"Yeah, just had a weird encounter," Ben stated.

"What, with Diana?" Scott asked.

"No…well, not directly anyway. She's asleep." Ben looked at his hands and started to clean his fingernail. "I just had a direct message from the Lord."

Scott stood by the counter and waited for Ben to continue; when he didn't, he pushed, "And?"

"I'm going to have to do some major reconnecting. I'll take the first watch. I need some alone time," Ben said over his shoulder.

Scott pulled the bed out from the couch, turned down the sheets, and then went to the bathroom to change clothes. *Lord have your way,* he prayed.

Ben and the Lord had a good long talk. It was just coming to an end when Scott came out to relieve him; Ben was flying high. He felt energized and refreshed after being with the Lord. He couldn't believe he let things get so far off whack. He wasn't ready to sleep yet; he just lay there staring at the ceiling. Then he glanced to the loft area; with that, his mind went to the situation with Diana not eating. He was thinking about the meds that she was taking. *Lord…what's going on with her?* he asked.

Look at the records, Ben heard from the Lord.

Ben jumped up and grabbed his laptop. He had a lot of hoops to go through in order to find what he needed, but eventually, he got there. He was scrolling through her medical records. Like Katherine, Diana went through cancer. Unlike Katherine, hers was in her colon. He continued to read through all the information. Then he saw what the problem was:

> Patient has problems with hard-to-digest foods and spices. These cause her bowels to give her problems with work and life activities. Patient deals with problem by avoiding these "trigger" foods.

So that is what it is. She has a dietary restriction that she didn't bother to tell us about. Ben was fuming. *Lord help me with this woman. She's gonna drive me crazy*, he prayed. With the problem shown, Ben was able to catch a few hours of sleep.

9

McCleary Land

He awoke to Diana stirring up in the loft. She must have had to use the bathroom because he heard the bathroom door close and then a few minutes later open. He was listening to her mumble something about her shirt, and then he heard her say something about her back. He lay still so not to give Diana a clue that he was awake. He lay there watching her with semi closed eyes. He saw her grab her shower bag that was near the railing then climb down the stairs.

Diana was trying to be as quiet as she possibly could. She knew the guys were going on little sleep. Her shirt was ruined, parts of her back hurt, the rest itched like crazy. She decided she was going to take a shower; it would make most of her feel better, and maybe…just maybe help her back. As she rounded the corner to head to the shower, she heard Ben. "Why didn't you say something, Diana?"

Diana turned slowly and walked to the hide-a-bed. "What are you talking about?" she asked.

"Take a seat," Ben directed. Diana sat down on the edge of the bed. It was disconcerting for her to sit on a bed with a guy in it and her shirt barely on, but she felt it must be necessary. "Why didn't you say that you couldn't eat the stuff we've been eating?" Ben asked again.

So much for the HIPPA law, Diana thought. "It's hard to explain to those who don't understand what I had to have done. Besides, I have been eating. I eat the oatmeal, I eat a lot of the trail mix that Scott has made up, and if I'm still hungry, I eat a peanut butter sandwich," Diana debated.

"Diana, you're losing a lot of weight. You wouldn't survive if we had to leave here to stay out in the woods," Ben argued.

"So…I'm losing weight. It is probably helping me out more than not. I'm not starving to death," she continued.

"Girl, I'm trying to keep you safe. You're not making it easy," Ben said furiously.

"You have been keeping me safe. I know my body. I know what I have to do to make it easier for you to do what you need to do. This is what I have to do," Diana directed.

Scott walked in at that time. "I expected you two to be sleeping, not arguing," he said jokingly.

Ben looked over to Scott. "I found out the reason for the lack of eating. She's not able to eat the beans and spices we've been eating. Her intestines have been compromised."

"Well, why the devil didn't you say so?" Scott asked irritably.

Diana threw her hands down on the bed in exasperation. "I'm not starving. I'm doing just fine. Now if you two are done, or even if you're not, I'm going to go take a shower," she declared.

"Wait a minute, Diana," Ben stated. "Scott, turn on the light." Scott turned on the light. Ben, who only had pajama pants on, started to scoot over to the edge of the bed where Diana was sitting. Diana, temporarily blinded by the light being turned on, was trying to get her eyes adjusted. It was then that she saw that Ben had no shirt on. His arms were muscular but not to the point of where they hung out like one of those cartoon apes. He had a tattoo on his right arm, but she couldn't see it well. She saw that it had an eagle and a gun in it. His chest was very well defined with washboard abs and a thin line of hair down the middle. Diana had to admit she liked what she saw.

Scott, seeing that Ben had no shirt on, started to rile him. "Man, put a shirt on! You'll scare the poor girl to death."

Ben just turned and looked at him. "Look at her, she's in total shock," Scott continued.

Ben looked over at Diana; she gave him no indication that she was bothered by him not wearing a shirt. To him, she seemed to be enjoying it. Ben looked back at Scott. Scott was busy looking for a T-shirt that would fit Ben. "You should be ashamed for contributing to the delinquency of the innocent."

With Scott's statement, Diana burst out laughing—a full, unrestrained, beautiful laugh. Both men turned to look at Diana to see what caused this joyful outburst. "Scott...God bless you, but you've got a weird way of thinking. Seriously, do you think I've never seen a man's chest? I'm not a sixteen-year-old that just came from a convent in Siberia. I'm a forty-five-year-old woman that works as a custodian in an apartment building. That's comparable to working in a coed dorm to help you understand. If you'd just let your mind go on that information for a minute, whatever you're thinking...it's been there. Now before Mr. Tigere gets too big of a head, I was actually studying his scars. The one on the shoulder, I'm assuming a shoulder surgery. The one on the right side, however, is puzzling me. At first I thought maybe a gunshot wound, but it's long so it's not consistent with a bullet. Then I thought it was a knife wound, but it's too jagged. It would have had to be some weird knife. So...I'm at a loss."

Both men were amazed that Diana talked as long as she had. It's the most they've heard from her at one time since the beginning. Scott still dumbfounded. "There ain't no way you're forty-five."

Diana just rolled her eyes and continued, "Truth be told, Mr. McCleary, I'm the one that would be causing a problem. I'm sitting on a bed with a shirt, which in my opinion is not covering much, and with two men in the room. If it was any other situation, I'd be in real danger. Men of a different ilk would take my present dress and position as an invitation. I know for a fact that Ben is stronger than me. He has proven that twice already. Now that you know how I respond, Mr. McCleary, you'd probably be able to restrain me as well. Maybe not quite as easily, but still you'd probably win the war."

Ben sat with an impressed smile on his face. "The shoulder was a torn rotor cuff. The right side was from being gored while working in a rodeo."

"So *cowboy* was a good way to describe you," Diana acknowledged. Then looking back at Scott with a sober face, she added, "As far as the delinquency of an innocent, don't worry...innocence was taken away a long time ago." Ben didn't like that comment and glared at Diana. She simply shrugged her shoulders.

"Turn your back to me, girl, let me see how it's healing," Ben directed. She did as he asked. Ben flipped the shredded pieces of the back of the shirt over her shoulders in order to see her back. Diana wrapped her arms around her chest to keep the shirt on and herself covered. Ben gently stroked his hands over her back. He was trying to feel if there were any other thorns left that he may have missed. His hands were warm and soft. As they glided gently across her back, a shiver ran through Diana. "Easy...Milady," Ben chuckled.

"Where in the world did you get the nickname Milady, ma'am?" Scott asked.

"It came from when I was waitressing in my twenties. The kids would come in regaling everyone with their latest conquest or midnight soirees. I didn't like hearing it, or their continuous swearing, so when they started in, I would walk out onto the floor where they couldn't say it. The guys bestowed the name Milady on me as a slam. I took it as a compliment and kept it," Diana stated.

As Ben was checking her back, he could feel her muscles relax and loosen up with his touch. *She's a sensual person. Touch means a lot to her. It's probably why she didn't let people get close to her. It makes her too vulnerable*, he thought. "Is your back itching?" Ben asked.

"Let me put it this way. I'm about to let Pete go to town digging on my back," she sneered.

"Go take your shower. Afterward, I'll put some Benadryl on for you. Then we will sit down and work out a meal plan," Ben said snickering.

Diana rolled her eyes and shook her head. She got up and went to take a shower, which felt wonderful. She didn't want to get out. It wasn't till the hot water started running out that she decided to leave it and got dressed. When she left the bathroom, she could hear Ben talking with Dick. Since she had no restraint on the "girls" and had on a very loose shirt, she figured it would be best to stay in the kitchen. She didn't want to be accused of "teasing" Dick again. Scott saw Diana standing in there and signaled Ben. "Hey, pard, hold on a sec. I need to do something."

Ben closed the laptop down enough that Dick couldn't see anything. Then he signaled for Diana to come out and sit on the couch. Diana gratefully obliged, keeping her arms crossed across her chest. Once she was behind the screen, Ben opened the top. "What was it you needed to do?" Dick asked.

"Don't worry about it, continue telling us what you found out," Ben pressed.

"Well, the latest is these would-be kidnappers are searching for a lady they're calling Ariana Ava. The problem is, nobody knows who she is," Dick informed them.

Scott's eyebrow shot up and Ben turned an ashen color. Diana was looking between both of them. She stayed quiet while they were still linked with Agent Richman. Ben, after getting himself composed, asked "So they are still in the area?" Dick nodded, confirming the statement.

Scott piped up and asked, "Is there anything on a missing lady in the reports?"

"Yes, there was. They found her. Unfortunately, she didn't make it. They are still looking for her murderers. Why? Do you think it's the same people?" Dick asked. He started looking through papers he had on his desk.

"Maybe…but it could be a coincidence," Scott replied.

"Okay, thanks for the information, Dick. I'll check back with you later," Ben completed.

"Hey...Ben! Where is Ms. Henderson at? I don't see her there," Dick persisted.

"I'm here, Agent Richman, I'm just listening," Diana chimed in.

Ben figured Dick just wanted to gawk at her again, but he went ahead and asked, "Why did you need to know?"

"Listen to this. That lady they were looking for, listen to her description. She was five-foot-seven, Caucasian, light-brown hair, blue eyes, early to mid-thirties. It sounds a lot like Ms. Henderson," Dick added. Now Diana turned ashen. Scott and Ben wished that Dick had said that when she wasn't in the room. It just couldn't be a coincidence; they must be up in the area now. Ben signed off with Dick then closed the laptop.

"Okay, it looks like we need to start looking for a plan B," Scott flatly stated.

"Yeah, I'd say in a day or two. Let's get the meal plan done first then we'll plan out the next step," Ben arranged.

"So...you two, who is Ariana Ava?" Diana injected.

"We don't know her personally. It was a person I saw a long time ago," Ben said calmly. Scott just shrugged his shoulders. Then the guys pushed to change the topic. "Let's get some paper and a pen and get the lists done." An hour later, Scott, with the lists in hand, left Ben and Diana alone. Ben wanted to get some Benadryl on Diana's back. He could tell that she as very uncomfortable. "Are you ready to get some help for your back?" Ben asked.

"*Please*...it's driving me crazy. Of course the shirt sticking to it isn't helping either," Diana replied

"Head on up. I'll go get the Benadryl," Ben stated. Diana headed up to the loft. She was trying to figure out how she was going to uncover her back without uncovering the rest of her. Ben came up with the Benadryl. Seeing her looking through her shirts, he pulled out his knife and turned it around in his hand.

"No, now...wait a minute. I can't afford to lose any more shirts," Diana stated holding her hand up to stop him. She thought for a second. "Okay...I've got it. Hang on, I'll be right back." She headed to the loft's bathroom. A couple of minutes later; Diana came out of the bathroom. She sheepishly entered into Ben's view, having a bath towel held in front of her, leaving her back totally exposed. She looked at Ben with apologetic eyes.

"Come on over here. I'll hold it closed so you can lie down on your stomach," Ben said. He knew that she was totally out of her comfort zone and extremely embarrassed. He did his best to stay disinterested, but had to admit it was very hard to do. *God, give me strength*, he prayed. Diana allowed Ben to hold the towel closed so she could get on the bed. Once she was set, he opened the towel so he could get to her back. It was a good thing that she did come out with just a towel. It uncovered her shoulders, where he found more thorns. With no one to hold the spotlight, Ben had a little more trouble getting these thorns out. It also didn't help that the thorns were already infected. "These are going to hurt a little…I'm sorry," Ben said apologetically.

"Do what you have to do. It'll only get worse if they don't come out," Diana responded. It took Ben with a needle and tweezers to get these thorns out. Once he had those out, he started putting on the Benadryl. Diana gasped deeply when Ben dropped some of the ointment on. "I think you're doing that on purpose," she quipped.

"Umm…maybe just a little," he laughed.

"You turkey," she fired back. "So, since I'm just lying here holding a towel, just how long do you have to spend in the gym every day?" Diana asked, trying to get her mind on something else other than being exposed.

"About an hour every day after work. It helps me de-stress before heading home to the kids," he answered.

"You have kids?" she asked as she turned her head to the side.

"Yep…four of them," he said.

"So you're married," she said flatly, but she really didn't want to hear the answer. Her heart was starting to ache.

"I was…her name was Katherine," Ben stated. Diana didn't like that she couldn't see his face. She couldn't tell what he was thinking or feeling. He was too good at hiding it in his voice. It was hard enough to read him while watching him. Sadly, with only a towel on, she would compromise herself to turn to look at him.

"How old are your kids," Diana asked.

"The oldest is fourteen, the next is twelve, the younger two are four," Ben flatly replied.

"Younger two?" she questioned.

"Yep…I have a set of twins," he answered. Diana always wanted to have children; she always wanted a set or two of twins. Genetically, she had a high chance of having twins. There are sets of twins on both sides of her parents' families. "Since we're asking personal questions, what about your comment earlier?" Ben injected.

"Take it at face value. I'm sure you know what I meant," Diana softly stated.

"How old were you?" he asked.

"When I was five years old," Diana cautiously replied.

"A family member or a stranger?" Ben pushed.

"An uncle," she briskly answered.

Ben had seen and worked with many a kid that went through abuse. He just never thought about a pastor's kid going through it. He didn't see anything in her records that said anything about it. He wanted to find out more, but he could feel the tension build in her back; he knew enough, so he let the topic go. He changed to a neutral topic instead.

"You don't happen to speak Hebrew do you?" Ben asked.

"Nope…well, I guess I know one or two words. *Shalom* and the names used to describe God. Why?" she asked.

"Just curious. I went to college for a degree in language. I just wanted to know if you spoke more than one," he continued.

"I speak Spanish, but I wouldn't say I'm fluent in it though. That's the only other one, other than English of course. So you studied language, how many languages do you speak?" she asked.

"Umm…let me see, Spanish, French, Italian, Latin, Arabic, Hebrew, Greek, Farsi, some German, and a little Japanese. So that makes what, ten? Oh and English…of a type," he concluded.

"Are you telling me you have all that and you didn't get a degree?" Diana quipped.

"No…I have a degree. I just don't work in the area of my degree," he replied.

"I understand that. It's the same for me," she acknowledged. Conversation just dropped off after that. Ben was forcing himself to focus on just getting the Benadryl rubbed in. He started working up on her shoulders where he found the thorns he had missed. Diana's muscles were relaxing again. His hands could feel her breathing slowing down. He could see she was enjoying what he was doing…so was he—that was what was making him struggle.

Diana got lost with the "work" Ben was doing. At that time she didn't think it was weird; it just felt good to her. But then she promptly became aware that his hands were starting to shake; they slowed down as they moved across her back. She had a suspicion of what might be going through his head. A lump started to develop in her throat; her mind jumped in that she was letting a stranger touch her.

Just then, his fingers dropped down onto her side and went across a ticklish area. She couldn't help it. She flinched and started to giggle. "Okay…I guess I found a ticklish spot," Ben injected.

"If you tell anybody, I'm gonna have to hurt you," Diana scolded.

Ben laughed. "That might be interesting to see. Let me grab the towel, then you can get up." While Ben was holding the towel together, Diana got up off the bed. Once she was standing and could hold the towel herself, he let go. A strand of Diana's hair was sticking to her lip. Ben reached over and moved it behind her ear. He let his fingers trail down her neck, across her shoulder, and down her arm. She watched his fingers go down her arm then glanced up at him. Ben saw her eyes were the emerald green he saw yesterday; he was sure he saw a glint of impishness flash in them. He was drawn to her in a way he had never felt before. He wanted to kiss her so badly every ounce of him was screaming it.

Diana read him like a book; she knew exactly what he wanted to do. "It looks like the tiger is hungry," she taunted. She stood there looking deep into his eyes—eyes that turned the dangerous sapphire blue.

Ben was able to restrain himself, forcing himself to take long slow breaths, but it was taking all of his strength. *Just turn and go downstairs, you idiot. You've never let a woman play you before. Don't start now,* he scolded himself, but he just stood there looking at her.

Diana continued, "Careful, Tiger, this prey isn't incapacitated yet. Although, I'd have to admit, my hands are a little busy at the moment." It was more than Ben could take; his arms started to reach for her. Diana backed up a few steps. "I think I'd better go and get a shirt on before I have to call Scott to bring a chain back with him—one strong enough to hold a tiger."

Ben's mind went south with that comment; he couldn't help it. His sapphire eyes flashed, and he beamed a mischievous smile. He was still watching Diana walk away. Once she shut the door of the bathroom, Ben said to himself out loud, "Yeah, and I'm gonna go take a shower. A very, very cold shower."

Diana stood by the closed bathroom door. She had to tell herself to breathe. *Control yourself, girl…he's forbidden fruit,* she told herself. "Lord, isn't this situation hard enough? Why do I make it play out this way?" she prayed out loud. It took her fifteen minutes before she was breathing normally with her heart rate down to acceptable beats, until she had herself under control. When she came out, she went and remade the bed, straightened the room up; then she went downstairs.

10

McCleary Land

It took Scott four hours to get back to the cabin. Once he was there, Ben and Diana went to help unload the supplies. Ben didn't want Diana outside, so he told her to put things away; he would help bring it in. In truth, neither of the guys wanted to risk her being seen. Once all that was done, Scott went and put the four-wheeler and trailer away. When he walked back into the cabin, he called Diana over and gave her a brown paper package. "Since one of your shirts was ruined, I got you a replacement," Scott said. Diana opened the package; it was a halter top. It had a tie at the neck, four rows of tiered material in a variegated blue to purple color, and then it tied again at the waist. She looked up at Scott. "Well, it covers everything but the back. So you won't have your shirt sticking to you," Scott said as he shrugged his shoulders.

Diana quipped back. "If I didn't know better, I'd say it was a conspiracy." Ben and Scott just stood there grinning. They weren't going to make a comment and step into a trap. Diana left to go put the shirt on. She wouldn't promise anything, but she agreed to try it on. Her T-shirt was sticking to her back and causing it to itch again. She didn't think it would be a good idea to push Ben, or herself, so soon. She wasn't all that sure where Scott stood in the scheme of things either. She had a fairly good idea that he was a player type. Someone that, though she did like Scott, she normally kept at arm's length. In the bathroom, Diana tied the top strings around her neck. The shirt was actually long enough; a major surprise to her. As she tied the waist, she actually smiled at her reflection. The halter was a size smaller than she would normally buy. In truth, she would never buy a halter to start with, but she did look good with it today. "See, not eating much hasn't hurt me at all," she said out loud. She decided she could live with it and walked out of the bathroom. She knew that she would be teased mercilessly, but she would just have to deal with it.

The guys were waiting in the kitchen to see if she would wear it or not. Scott was afraid that he may have bought a size too big for her. It was his best guess that she was a medium, but he bought her a large to give extra room for her endowments. They heard the bathroom door open and saw Diana come out. They both smiled with approval. "Well, at least there will be no need for the towel again," Ben jeered.

Scott's eyebrow shot up, and he glared at Ben. "Obviously, I missed something, something that I definitely want to know about." Ben just gave him a broad, boastful smile. Diana turned and got busy doing something in the fridge. Scott continued, "Come on, man. You know it's not good to let my mind wander. Fill me in."

"It's nothing, nothing happened. We just needed to get stuff on her back, and she didn't want to lose another shirt. So she used a bath towel to cover up with," Ben flatly stated.

"And you enjoyed every bit of it too, didn't ya?" Scott reprimanded. But in truth, he would have loved to have been there himself. He was actually thinking that maybe after this was all said and done, he would ask Diana out for a drink or something. Diana was busy working on the fish for supper. She had to keep as much pride as she could, even if it was only her and the Lord that knew her feelings. She was getting worried that Ben might be getting to know her enough to be able to read her; it was very disconcerting to her. She liked being able to hide her thoughts. It kept her out of trouble. She grabbed the fish bowl out of the fridge, got another bowl and filled it with cold water and added salt to it. She found a good fillet knife, some old newspapers, and a shopping bag. She quietly slipped out the door while the guys weren't looking. She hoped the guys were too busy discussing things to notice her slipping out. As she walked off the porch, she grabbed one of Scott's baseball hats to help shield her face from the sun. She put the hat on and pulled her ponytail through the hole. The solar heat felt wonderful on her exposed back. She started humming as she slit the sides of the fish with the knife, then working the knife in, going down to the rib ledge, and working the meat off and around them. She was grateful that her brother took the time to teach her how to fillet a fish. It had proven useful many times.

Diana was outside working on the fish for about thirty minutes before she heard, "You know very well you're not supposed to be out here," Ben scolded.

She knew she would hear a scolding eventually, so she was not surprised. "You don't want fish scales all over the counters in there, do ya? They're a pain to clean up, and I'm not in open view. Plus I'm almost done," she countered.

"Maybe...but you've been out here long enough to burn your back," Ben added.

"The solar heat actually feels really good on my back. It's not burning hot yet, it's probably just red. I might actually get a tan. Besides, I just need to finish this last fish. It's half done," she ended.

Ben came and stood on the other side of the table. He watched her easily skin the last fillet and put it in with the others in a saltwater bowl. "Take your fish and get your derriere inside. I'll clean up the rest," he demanded. She just glared at him. He met her glare with his own "evil eye." She shook her head then turned and took the fish back inside. Ben grabbed the bones and took them out to the far side of the trees. *I might as well give something a free meal. The way it's going, it might wind up being a meal for us later*, Ben thought. Diana cooked the fish with a little garlic, mayo, paprika, salt and pepper, and lemon. She also fried up some french fries for a side. Scott told her that she could cook fish for him anytime. Ben said he would only allow it if he could go fishing with her. "You enjoy your meal more when you are the one that actually catches it," he stated.

"Sure, as long as you don't mind getting out fished by a female," Diana jested.

"Tigers are excellent fishers. There's no way you could out fish me," Ben jabbed back.

"All right you two, cut it out. Since Diana cooked, one of us needs to do the dishes. Which one of us will it be?" Scott asked.

"Flip a coin, or rock-paper-scissors?" Ben asked.

Diana interrupted, "Since it's a beautiful night, may I be allowed to go sit on the front porch?" She really hated having to ask permission to do things; she had to bite her pride.

The guys looked at each other then Ben shrugged. "Take Pete out with you. If he starts barking, you get your butt inside," Scott declared.

"Thank you, kind sir," Diana gestured with a low bow. Scott rolled his eyes.

"Come on, Pete," she said as she patted her thigh. Pete quickly responded gladly. They went and sat on the stairs of the front porch. Diana started petting Pete; he lay down and stretched out for a tummy rub, which she gladly did. She sat looking at the stars, breathing in the cool clean air, and thoroughly enjoying the peacefulness. *Fall will be coming in soon. With all these trees, it has to be utterly breathtaking*, she thought.

Scott soon came out and joined her. He sat on the railing, his back leaning up against the house. For a while, he sat quietly then looked down at Pete, who in his mind thought he found a new mistress.

"I still can't believe you're forty-five," Scott mused.

Diana just gave him a smile. "Ben lost the coin toss, I take it."

Scott nodded in agreement. "Can I ask you a question?" he continued.

"Sure," Diana said.

"How come you haven't been married and had a couple of kids yet?" he queried.

"Let's just say I'm very particular." She looked over at him. She saw he was questioning that statement. "Before any questionable mind-set develops, I'm not homosexual, asexual, or anything other than what God set from the beginning," Diana stated. Scott just gave her a look. "Yeah, I've heard it all before" Diana shrugged. "I about gave some of my cousins a heart attack when I started dating guys. They thought for sure I was going to join a convent," she continued. She giggled and said, "It definitely would not work. I like 'sugar' too much." Diana turned her head as if she heard something then she smiled. Since the dream, she has always been able to feel a warm, peaceful, kindred spirit when her "rescuer" was watching. It just took her a while to figure it out.

Coming from the South, Scott knew what kind of "sugar" she meant. He was surprised that she used that term much less she would admit to liking it. "Where did you learn to use that term?" he chuckled.

"I have friends from down South. I picked up their lingos and accents," she replied.

"You don't act like any pastor's daughter I've seen," Scott said, shaking his head "So what happened to the other guys? The shoe didn't fit?" Scott continued.

"Umm…no, I can definitely say it didn't fit. I guess I'm not the easiest female to deal with. I'm a little too independent and stubborn. A few of them are still my friends though. They're kind of like brothers now. They're married with kids of their own, and in truth, seeing their marriages, I thank God for unanswered prayers." She smiled.

"Again…you don't act like a pastor's daughter," Scott reiterated.

"And what do pastor's daughters act like, Mr. McCleary?" Diana turned and flashed an impish grin.

"Well…umm, I mean…,' Scott stumbled around.

Then Diana added, "Do you want to put your two cents in, Mr. Tigere? Or are you content to just observe?"

Ben stepped out of the shadows of the doorway where he had been listening. *You aren't that hard to handle. You just have to know what keys are needed to control you*, Ben thought.

"Dang, Ben, how did she know you were there? I didn't even know you were standing there?" Scott said amazed.

Diana turned and smiled at Ben, waiting for a reply. "I believe I'll watch Scott dangle for a while." Ben smiled. Scott growled at Ben then looked back at Diana. He knew he stepped into a trap that there was no way he could possibly get out of on his own.

"Should I help you out, sir?" Diana smiled at Scott. "There are two views. One is a chaste, innocent, gullible girl who can't exist in the 'real' world. The other is a rebellious, loose, lascivious girl who plays the angel at church and acts the devil every other time," Diana concluded.

"Well yeah…I guess that pretty much sums it up," Scott ashamedly agreed. "I kind of had you originally in the first category, but you don't fit there. However, you don't fit in the second one either," he quickly inserted.

"Yeah…don't worry, Scott, I'm not offended. It's a fact. Most of the PKs I grew up around didn't stay with God. A lot of the girls went the latter of the two, partly because they never understood where they were in the scheme of God's plan. The guys pretty much turned their back on everything their fathers' stood on. I blame the congregation mainly. They have always required the pastors' kids to walk a standard that isn't possible for them or their kids to walk themselves, much less PKs who are still finding their way in God. The rest of the blame is on the parents. They taught how to look the part but never the whys and reasonings behind it. You have to have a direct relationship with God, or you'll never make it," Diana concluded. She looked up and saw the expressions on the guys' faces. Scott was processing what she said; Ben just stood there leaning against the doorpost. "Sorry, it's a sore spot for me. Someday I'm gonna have to write a book or something on it," Diana said, looking back at the trees.

"My turn to ask a question. What happened to Katherine?" Diana asked. Scott looked over to Ben then looked out at the stars. He had no clue if Ben would give her an answer or not.

Ben studied Diana for a while. She wouldn't look at him. He figured she was embarrassed by her question. *You should be*, he thought. Then he started piecing together the few times that she got ardent about a topic of discussion. She was still trying to place him in his walk with the Lord. That's the key for her on whether she can trust him or not. "You and Katherine had a lot in common Diana, you both had cancer. You made it through. She didn't," Ben said flatly.

"I'm sorry," Diana said remorsefully. "It must be hard for you and your kids. Forgive me." she could feel his pain.

"She wanted to go home. Apparently…you didn't," Ben replied.

"It wasn't my time yet. Too many promises haven't come about," Diana finished. They sat there quietly for a little while, just admiring God's creation. They were enjoying the quiet breeze blowing across the trees, the clear skies showing the stars so brightly they look like a sequined studded cloak; the sounds of the night tranquilly singing in their ears.

It was Ben who broke the silence. "I've got plan B worked out."

Scott and Diana looked at Ben for the rest of the information. "We'll stay on Scott's land, but we'll head farther north. We'll work out of a debris hut. It's naturally camouflaged and will keep us warm and dry. However, it means that we are going to be in tight quarters for a while," Ben informed them.

"Scott…do you have any chains to bring along? We might need to use them to contain a big cat," Diana teased. Scott looked at Diana with a questioning face. She was looking directly at Ben. Scott could see the mischievous look on her face. Ben, however, had the look of total frustration.

"You are definitely a rare breed, girl," Scott said, shaking his head.

"I'm an oddity. At least that's what I've been told,' she added smiling. Then Diana gasped and quickly turned to face the trees. Pete alerted at the same time. She could feel a cold dark presence; she was frantically looking for something along the tree line. It was Pete who pointed toward the direction of danger. Diana glanced back at Scott and Ben. Her pupils were dilated to the point of her eyes being nearly black; only a small ring of gray remained. She turned and looked directly into Ben's eyes. Ben did a slight nod of his head and gave her a wink. Diana didn't hesitate; she shot up and went inside.

Ben looked over at Scott. "We've got visitors coming." Scott told Pete to heel, for which Pete immediately obeyed. Ben stepped forward to stand by the top of the stairs. Scott moved and sat down on in the middle of the stairs followed by Pete. Pete started to growl, then he went to full warning barks. It was then the guys heard, "Hello, in the cabin…FBI, can we come up?"

Ben replied. "Come up slowly!"

Two men came out of the tree line and walked toward the stairs of the cabin. "Can you contain your dog please?" they asked.

Scott stood up and walked Pete to the door of the cabin. He signaled Pete to go inside; just before closing the door, he commanded Pete, "Protect." With the dog contained, the two FBI agents walked all the way up to the cabin steps. "Sorry to interrupt your evening, gentlemen. We are looking for two suspects involved with the death of a lady ten miles to the south of here," they stated.

"You two must not have much of a home life. It's really late," Ben stated.

"Do you mind showing us your badges?" Scott asked.

The FBI agents each showed their badge. "Are you guys the only ones here?" they asked.

Ben spoke up, "So are you guys under Agent Klein or Sherman?"

The two FBI agents looked at each other. "We are under agent Sherman. How do you know him?" they asked.

"I've helped him out of a couple of jams a few years ago. Why don't you give him a call? Tell him the tiger is hiding," Ben articulated. The agents really didn't want to involve their boss. Finally, one of the agents pulled a cell phone out of his pocket and turned to talk on it. The other stood near the stairs and watched his partner on the phone.

"You two are beyond believable," Scott whispered to Ben.

Ben looked perplexed at Scott. "What are you talking about, bro?"

"You and her. How did she know they were coming? There was no sound. How did you know what she was thinking? On top of that, how did she know you wanted her to go into the cabin?" Scott said in awe.

The FBI agent that was on the phone said his salutations to his boss and closed the phone. He turned around, looked at his partner, then looked at Ben and Scott. "They're in the clear, Kal. They're on our side."

Scott took the opportunity to ask, "Were there any other unusual people around tonight?"

"There were a couple of guys camping out about two miles to the south. They say they were fishing for walleye. It all seemed to be okay," one of the FBI agent replied.

"Thanks for the help, Agents." Ben shook hands with both of them. The agents walked back to the trees and went out of sight. Ben and Scott waited until they were sure it was safe, then they walked back into the cabin. They looked for Diana; when they didn't see her, Scott told Pete to find his mistress. Pete headed for the loft then stood by the door. Once Ben opened the door, Pete went out and sniffed around till he came up to a tarp in the corner next to the house. In the dark, it looked like one of those gas grills.

"Good boy, Pete," Ben patted him and sent him down to Scott. Ben moved his hand down the back of the "grill." "Come on out. It's safe."

The tarp started rising upward. Then it opened up to reveal Diana as the tarp fell to the ground behind her. "I don't think that will be the truth till we find out why in the world these people are trying to find me," Diana said with a shaky voice. Ben heard the tremble in her voice and saw the fear in her eyes. He just pulled her near him and held her. Not only was her voice shaky, but her whole body was shaking. He, unfortunately, felt the same way. The difference between her reaction and his—he had been trained to face danger. She hasn't been. He just held her, stroking her back, forgetting about the rash and cuts on it. "I don't think it would be a good idea to be running around with just a towel on again," Diana stated.

Ben pushed her back to look at her face. He realized what he was unconsciously doing. "Sorry, I forgot about your back," he said.

"Actually, the sun did it some good. Only those two areas that were cut bothers me," Diana stated coolly. "You've had to take care of me the last couple of times. Maybe I should have Scott treat my back tonight?" she suggested. Ben's eyes, though she couldn't see the color, went narrow and cold. She broke down and started to chuckle. "Do I see the face of disapproval?"

He didn't want Scott to treat her back; in truth, he didn't want any other guy touching her. *Knock it off. You're not a teenager…you're being stupid*, he said to himself. He looked at her face and realized he was getting played. He reached over and brushed against her tickle spot. Diana flinched and giggled. "You know what they say: laughter is the best cure. Shall I give you a large dose of medicine? I'm sure I can find more than one of those," Ben said wickedly.

"Oh…no…you…don't!" Diana said as she started darting around. She had just dodged his hand as he went to catch her; she reached up and poked him in his side. She hit one of his "buttons" right away.

"Hey now, you're gonna start something you'll regret," Ben warned. He grabbed her left hand but had a little trouble getting the right. Diana just kept swinging around to elude him, laughing as she snuck jabs in. She found a couple more "buttons" that made Ben jerk. He finally brought her left hand across her chest, bringing her back up against him. With that, he easily caught her right hand and brought it down to her left, so he was holding her in an embrace from behind. *She does like to play, doesn't she*, he thought.

Diana loves to laugh; it was the best medicine for her in any situation. However, right now, being held in Ben's embrace, she felt a wave of security and belongingness enveloping her. She could smell his cologne, feel his heart beat through her back, feel his breath blowing past the side of her face. *This is dangerous, girl*, she said to herself. "Does the tiger think he has caught his prey?" she teased.

"It does seem that you are fairly trapped to me," he jested back.

Scott, who had walked up the stairs, saw Ben holding Diana. He turned and quietly backed down the stairs. *Figures. Lord, when is it my turn?* he sneered. "Pete," he called. "Go get your mistress," he commanded.

All of a sudden, Pete came running up the stairs and started jumping against Ben. Diana started laughing. Ben was frustrated but nonetheless reached down to calm Pete down. They heard Scott calling out, saying, "Ben, you've got a text from Dick."

"Be right there," Ben said disappointed.

"The tiger isn't having much luck keeping his prey today," Diana teased.

Ben had a mischievous look on his face. "You don't know much about tigers, do ya? Unfortunately, we've got a situation that needs to be resolved."

"Hmm…yes. Saved by the phone. I guess the tiger is gonna have to go hunting again on another day. The prey may be hard to find next time around," Diana, still teasing, stated.

"I think the tiger knows very well how to find what he wants. Once he's singled out one, he'll track it down," Ben jested back, then he leaned down. "You can't get away from a tiger that's on the hunt for you," he whispered in her ear, kissed her neck, then let her loose. A shiver shot up Diana's back and down her arms, causing goose bumps to show. Ben noticed and gave her a broad grin.

She turned and shoved him into the room. "Go answer your text," she commanded.

Ben came down the stairs and walked over to the kitchen. Scott was sitting on the counter, eating some ice cream. "You're a pig," Scott derided. Ben looked at him, waiting for him to finish his thought, even though he knew what he was thinking. "It's just not fair, you already had one," Scott said frustrated.

"What do you mean? I have no claim to this one," Ben fired back.

"Oh? Don't deny there is chemistry between you two—one that has been there longer than just the last four or five weeks," Scott added.

"You think so, huh?" Ben chided.

"Are you kidding me? You two were carrying on a conversation tonight and not a word was said—it's insane. I've never seen it before, not even with you and Katherine," Scott scoffed. Ben looked at Scott, his indignation starting to rise. "Now, I'm not saying you and Katherine didn't love each other. You were devoted to each other. However, she was in her world, you were in yours. I don't know, maybe it was because she was ten years younger than you or something. Diana—now Diana can sense when you're near. She reads you almost as well as I do, and she only met you five weeks ago," Scott continued.

"We'll see. I'm not sure I'm ready for marriage again," Ben said flatly.

"Well, from what I saw, if you're not ready to consider marriage, you're heading down the wrong road bro," Scott scolded. Ben studied Scott. Scott didn't want to look up at him.

"I figured you sent Pete up. A little bothered under the collar, were ya?" Ben jabbed.

"I just figured you two needed some space," Scott scoffed.

Ben just shook his head. "You're making a big deal out of nothing," he said over his shoulder. *I'm not even looking for anybody else...what is his problem?* he thought. He went over and grabbed his phone. He scrolled through to the window that had text messages. Dick left a short message: "Check e-mail ASAP." Ben went to the table and started his computer up. He tried to open his e-mail but it wouldn't download. "Scott, do you have satellite here?" he asked.

"Yep, why...what's up?" Scott asked as he watched Diana come downstairs and sit down on the couch.

"I can't get my e-mail,' Ben stated.

"You can get it from your phone, can't ya?" Scott asked.

"It's not protected. If I take it to the phone anybody with a brain can open it," Ben scoffed.

"I wouldn't say anybody. I have a brain, and I can't do that," Diana said under her breath.

Unfortunately, the guys still heard it. "Well, the only thing safe I can say is...ah...well, there's nothing safe to say," Ben mocked. Diana stuck her tongue out at him. It was her normal nonverbal sign that she didn't like what was done or said. "I'll have to take a rain check on that offer. I'll collect it later," Ben stated.

Diana looked confused for a second. Then she remembered back when she was in high school; one of the kids told her that if you stuck your tongue out at a guy, you wanted to be french kissed. She looked over at Ben and realized what he meant. Her heart skipped a beat and her face went beet red. Ben beamed a broad smile.

"Don't make promises you can't keep," Diana shot back.

Scott just had to laugh at the both of them. "Diana, stop distracting Ben from his work." Diana looked down. She couldn't believe she let herself get caught in such a schoolgirl trap. *And that was a pathetic comeback*, she scolded herself.

"God help me!" Ben said frustrated. "Apparently, the net is down. I can't view my e-mails," Ben said as he stood up.

"So…do we use a phone or wait till morning to check it?" Scott asked.

"We can't risk a breach. I'll check it first thing in the morning," Ben concluded.

"Okay, so in the morning, I'll go look in that area we were talking about before supper and find a good campsite. Then I'll be back to help get things prepped," Scott added. Diana had a sickening feeling in her stomach. *These people are getting too close…things could go bad soon*, she thought. *Lord, help us and keep us safe*, she prayed. Ben and Scott looked over to Diana, her eyes dark and empty. She had vanished into her thoughts and far away from the conversation going on in the cabin. Her face was vacant and dull.

Scott stood looking at her; he understood why guys tended to take her under their wing like a sister. There was a spirit in her that called out of them a desire to want to shield her. She was very independent and definitely not helpless, but still there was a type of vulnerability in some ways.

Ben tenderly called out to her; "Diana…you need to go up and try to get some sleep. You'll need all the energy you can get tomorrow."

"I'll take the first watch, Ben," Scott injected. "That way I can get some sleep before heading north."

Ben nodded in agreement. Looking over to Diana, he asked, "Do you need some Benadryl on your back tonight?"

Diana wanted to say no. Most of her back was good; however, those two stupid cuts… "I suppose I better. At least I don't have to change. You should be able to treat it this way," she added.

"Aww…now that's just not fair," Scott quipped. Diana smiled but kept her face looking down at her fingernails. She knew she was blushing.

Ben rolled his eyes. "I'll go get the stuff, just stay on the couch. We'll take care of it there."

After Ben treated Diana's back, she headed up to the loft. She had a hard time finding sleep. She lay there on her stomach, holding a pillow, thinking about all the possible things that could go wrong. *I wish I had my phone; I need my music playing.* The verse, "Therefore do not worry about tomorrow, for tomorrow will worry about its own things. Sufficient for the day *is* its own trouble" came into her head. But Diana was worried. It wasn't till God came down and she felt His spirit holding her that she was finally able to fall asleep.

Ben was having the same problem as Diana. He was running through every scenario and how to counter things going wrong. He basically slept light; he heard every time Diana turned; his eyes opened at every noise. The men after Diana were close; he just knew it. *Lord, help me to protect her. Guide me and lead me in the way I must go*, he prayed. An hour before he went to relieve Scott, he went to check the laptop again. This time he was able to load his e-mails. When he opened the one that Dick sent him, it only had a picture of a scenic view. It was an old dam in the picture, and the dam had a few cracks in it. Ben just shook his head. "Dick, what are you doing?" he wondered. Ben went out to switch with Scott.

"Was she able to go to sleep?" Scott asked.

"Yeah, about an hour ago, she finally went out," Ben replied.

"She's scared, not that I blame her. I'm on edge myself," Scott commented.

"I know, and she has the most to lose," Ben agreed. "Go get some sleep. We need to get out of here…soon."

11

McCleary Land

There was something more to Dick's e-mail; there's something that he missed. He needed to look at the picture again to see if there were hidden messages or something he hadn't seen. He waited till the sun was up before he went back inside. Scott was getting ready to head out and look for a good campsite. Diana was still sleeping; the guys had decided to let her sleep. Scott left to check out the northern acreage, and Ben went back to the computer to look at Dick's e-mail again. He sat staring at it for what seemed to be hours; he just couldn't get what it was he was missing.

"Pretty picture," Diana said.

In an instant, Ben had reached back and pulled his gun out and aimed it at her. Diana gasped, dropped her stuff, and jumped back. She stood there in shock, looking down the barrel of a Magnum. It took Ben a second to realize what he did. "God help me! Don't do that, girl," Ben snapped. He looked over to Diana; she was just getting ahold of herself. The look on her face made him feel very guilty.

"I'm sorry, I didn't mean to surprise you. You usually hear me coming down," Diana stated shakily.

"No, it wasn't your fault. I wasn't paying attention," Ben countered.

"Was that the important e-mail Dick sent?" she asked.

"Yeah, but I don't see what is so important about it," he wondered.

"What dam is that?" she inquired.

"Umm…I don't know. Why?" Ben wondered

"It has a leak in it. Look, see here, it's a darker color running down. That dam is going to break soon," she pointed out.

"That's it! There's been a leak in the office. He's warning us about a leak," Ben said immediately. "I can't believe I didn't see that."

"You're tired, you would have gotten it," Diana encouraged. She started walking to the kitchen.

"Where are you heading?" Ben asked.

"I'm just gonna have a shower, then I was hoping to sit out on the deck upstairs," she stated.

"Shower…yes. Deck…forget about it. Girl, they know you're here now. I'm not going put a Christmas bow on you and hand you over to them. You go outside by yourself, you'd be walking right to them," Ben scoffed.

Diana looked down. "You think they are waiting just outside the door?"

Ben didn't want to scare her so much, but for Pete's sake, she needs to be realistic. "Diana," he said to make her look at him. "Diana!"

She looked up at him, her eyes a light gray. "I don't like being trapped in a cage. Even as lovely as this place is," she quipped.

"I understand, but it has to be done. We'll be out of here soon, then you'll have all the space you need," Ben stated. He kind of figured she would make a joke with that comment…but she didn't.

"Yeah…I guess. I'll go take my shower. I'll be back in a little bit," she informed him. She walked back to the bathroom, and he heard her shut the door. Last night has really brought her down. *Maybe she's just tired herself*, he thought. Diana closed the door, and she couldn't help it; she started to cry. She sat there on the floor, next to the door, holding herself, and bawled for a good five minutes.

This is for my glory. I will not leave you…even when all are taken away, she heard from her Lord.

Lord…as you wish, give me strength. Keep the guys and my family safe. I couldn't bear it if any were hurt. I am your servant, she replied. Diana got up and took her shower. She pulled her hair back then headed out into the kitchen. She knew that things were going to go bad in Ben's and Scott's eyes. It had too because she knew, eventually, she would be taken. She had to trust the Lord that He would keep them and her safe. She decided she wouldn't tell the guys. They wouldn't understand it; plus, if the Lord wanted them to know, he would tell them.

Ben watched her come into the room. He was sure he heard her crying in the bathroom but didn't feel he should intervene. *Sometimes… crying it out is a good thing*, he said to himself. She seemed to be in better spirits. He thanked the Lord for helping her out.

Scott came back a little after noon. "I've got a spot picked out, but it's not going to be easy getting there," he pointed out. "That's to our advantage," he continued.

Ben nodded in acceptance. He figured if it was going to be a hard hike to get there, they would need all the daylight possible; Diana would need it. "We'll head out first thing in the morning," Ben stated. The three spent the rest of the day packing food, clothes, and supplies for the next two weeks. There was a debate about whether or not Diana would have a backpack or not.

"I can carry something! I was raised working, and I'll continue working till *I* have to be carried around," Diana insisted. Ben still didn't agree with it, but Diana was so stubborn; she won the debate.

"I'll take the first watch, Ben," Scott said, laughing at the conversation. "You two, go get some sleep," he stated as he walked out the door. Diana headed up to the loft. Most of her stuff was packed away; only her pillow was out. Ben came up a minute later. "How's your back?" he asked.

"It's good. I won't have a problem using a T-shirt tomorrow," she declared.

"I want you to wrap this around at least two times to cover those cuts," Ben said as he handed her a roll of Ace wrap. "It'll protect them from the backpack rubbing on them."

Diana took the Ace wrap. "Thank you," she said. Then she gently grabbed Ben's arm. "Ben, just in case, thank you for everything you've done."

Ben turned and looked her dead in the eyes. "What are you planning on doing?" he asked starkly.

"I'm not planning on doing anything. It's just a feeling, sort of," Diana answered.

Ben, still looking in Diana's eyes, knew there was something she wasn't telling him. "Diana?" he firmly questioned.

"I'm just saying. You've had to leave your family, you've been stuck with me for what…five weeks. You and Scott are going without sleep, and we've got murderers at the front door. That's a lot of crap you two have had to deal with. I just wanted to say thank you for all you and Scott have had to do," Diana stated.

"I do miss my family, but so do you. It's not your fault that we are out here. That lies totally on the murderers. Now if you have any intention of doing something stupid, I'll turn you over my knee and spank your butt," Ben declared. He got a slight smile and a flash of impishness in those eyes of hers, but it was gone quickly. "Now…do I have your word you won't do something stupid?" he ensued.

"No, I'm not going to do anything stupid. Well, try not to anyway." Diana smiled.

"Good, I'd hate to have to handcuff you to me. It's really an uncomfortable way to try to sleep. Now...go get some sleep," Ben said over his shoulder then went downstairs. Diana lay down on the bed. Pete gladly joined her, lying on the opposite side.

Ben went and lay on his bed, his mind focusing on what Diana had said. *She knows something is coming up, but she's not telling us what*, he thought. *Well, crap...I guess I need to learn ESP to read that woman's thoughts*, he chided.

It was somewhere around one a.m.; Scott, not seeing or hearing anything around, went to get the trailer hitched up. Ben would be coming out in an hour to spell him. They were planning on leaving around six that morning. He went into the shed and started pulling the trailer around. As he was hitching it up; he heard something lock. He immediately turned the lights off. He slipped around to the shed door and tried to open it; it was locked shut. He moved around to the side door. It had been barricaded. *God, help us*, he prayed. He went to get the hatchet. He had to get to the cabin ASAP.

Diana sat up; the dark presence had sent a chill over her. She heard a thump then Pete yipped. She reached over to pat him and felt something sticking out of his side. It was a dart, Pete had been tranquilized. She heard another thump and she felt something hit her arm. She reached over and pulled it out. "Be...n," she started to say but fell back on the bed. Ben heard Pete yip and immediately grabbed his gun from under his pillow. He slid out of bed and was working his way to the loft when he heard a thump. Then he heard Diana start to call for him, he also heard her fall into the bed. Then there was silence. He was almost to the stair when he tripped on something and started to fall. There was a loud bang and a flash of light. Then there was blackness.

12

At the Cabin

Ben woke to somebody slapping his face. He desperately worked to clear his mind. "Ben, come on, bro, you've got to come to," Scott said as he worked to revive his friend.

"Diana?" Ben asked as he opened his eyes. He was still seeing stars.

"She's gone. They used a tranquilizer on her and Pete. You, bro, have been shot," Scott said flatly.

"What? I was shot? No…I tripped on something on the floor, but I don't remember being shot," Ben said in disbelief.

"That was probably a blessing. They only gave you a flesh wound. If you hadn't have fallen, they would have hit your heart," Scott said matter-of-factly.

"How did they get past you?" Ben asked Scott.

"I stupidly went out to the shed to get the vehicles set up to go. They locked me in. It took me a half hour to get out. By then they were gone as well as Diana," Scott said angrily.

"If you had been on the porch, they would have killed you as well. I'm sure they thought they killed me, but I tripped and hit my head on the coffee table," Ben said as he found the dried blood that came from his head.

"I heard a helicopter just a little before I got out. They must have been waiting for an opening. We have to go after her man," Scott declared.

"Yes, we do, but we have to go to town and get things arranged. And…we have to tell Diana's family we failed," Ben said regretfully. Scott's face told everything: he felt and looked miserable.

"Let's go! I'll drive. You'll have to ride with me, bro. You still have a concussion," Scott demanded. Ben didn't put up much of an argument. He was still very dizzy, and his head was killing him. They took only what they needed and put it into the trailer. They left the rest packed in the backpacks in the corner of the cabin. Scott drove like a bat out of hell back to the Quonset. In the Quonset, they took the Ford pickup near the sliding door. "It's in the best shape mechanically. It just looks like a piece of crap," Scott told Ben as they threw the stuff in the back. Again, they were off and heading for the office in Des Moines. Ben dreaded the thought of facing the Henderson's. He failed, and Diana was paying for it.

She's alive…I am with her, Ben heard from the Lord. *Lord, keep her safe, let her know I'm coming for her*, he prayed.

Once at the DHS building, Ben and Scott headed to Zenon's office. The agents were surprised to see the men, especially Ben in his current condition. Dick glanced up, saw Ben, and headed to meet them.

"Hey, man, are you okay?" Dick asked.

"I'll be fine," Ben said as he knocked on Zenon's door.

"Enter," Charles replied.

Charles looked up to see who was knocking. Once he saw Ben, he told Dick to close the door and shut the shades. "I think introductions are in order," he replied, motioning toward Scott.

"Sir, this is Scott McCleary. He's a fellow Special Ops soldier and a very good friend. It was his place that helped us hide out for so long," Ben stated. "Scott, this is my boss…Director Zenon," he ended.

"Good to meet you, sir," Scott said as he shook the director's hand. "Wish it was in better circumstances," he added.

"Fill us in Ben," Charles said as he sat back down in his chair. Ben explained what had happened and that he failed to keep Diana safe. "Sir we need to leave ASAP. They may be on a plane heading out of the States already," Ben said with urgency.

"First, Scott, take Ben to the hospital. Get him patched up. Second, Dick, talk to your people. Find out if they're still in the States or not. I'll do some calling and deal with the paperwork. Hopefully, we'll have the clearance for you two by tonight. With the way you're looking, Ben, you'd best clean up after the hospital. I'll go talk to the Henderson's," the Charles concluded.

"The parents are only part of the problem. Watch out for her nephew and nieces. They are very close," Ben added.

"Understood, now get out of here before you drip blood on my Oriental rug," Charles stated.

Scott took Ben to the hospital. There they did a CAT scan on his head; once they were sure there was no hematoma, they cleaned the area and used superglue to close the gash. Then they turned to the gunshot wound. The doctor said that the bullet went straight through. However, he would need to stitch the flesh together.

Ben was antsy. "Just get it done, Doc," he replied. With the doctor's order to keep an eye on him for twenty-four hours, Scott took Ben to his house. The kids were luckily still at school and the day care. Ben didn't want them to see him looking like this. "I'll go get cleaned up before the kids come home. You can use the upstairs shower," Ben said to Scott.

"No problem, bro. I'll just hit the fridge first," Scott said as he headed to the kitchen. Ben just rolled his eyes and headed to his room. He made sure he plugged the cell phone in then pulled a change of close out and put them on the bed; then he walked into the bathroom. The doctor said no shower 'til the stitches were pulled out, but he could at least wash the blood out of his hair and do a sponge bath. He wanted to clean up quickly—originally to be ready for when the kids come home, but also he hoped that he would get clearance to leave tonight. He couldn't help but worry about what Diana might be going through right now. Once Ben was cleaned up, he went and found Scott still in the kitchen. Scott was busy devouring a fried chicken leg. "Scott…head in before the kids see ya. You're liable to scare the twins looking like a hobo," Ben teased.

"Nah, they'd just run over and tackle me to the ground like always," Scott said between bites. Now with the chicken leg gone, Scott turned to head toward the bathroom.

"I Want a New Drug" started playing; it was Ben's phone ringing. "This is Ben…yes, sir…got it. I'll wait for your call. How did it go with the Henderson's?…I figured they would…thank you, sir. Good day," Ben ended the call.

Scott had stopped moving once the phone rang and waited for the information. He stood watching Ben's facial expression and listened to his tone. "And?" he asked.

Ben didn't like the info, but really, it was what he expected. "We can't leave tonight. Some hang-up in the White House. Zenon is going to have to pull some strings and call in a few favors to get the okay. It's gonna take some time. Dick's people say that there's no sign of the kidnappers. He's figuring they are already on their way to the Middle East. Diana's parents were very understanding and overall took the news well. Her niece and nephew didn't take it well at all. Liza and Jared were furious," Ben concluded.

Scott felt sick. "Do you think she'll be able to hold out?"

"I hope so…I pray so. She's a strong woman, but that's not necessarily a good thing over there," Ben agonized. He felt just as sick as Scott looked. *If Diana doesn't play by their rules, they could beat her to death or even behead her. God, help us…help Diana*, Ben prayed. As it turned out, Ben and Scott had four days to spend with the kids and Becca. It wasn't that Ben didn't want to be with his kids, but he was worried sick about Diana. The guys agreed not to talk about the case in front of the kids, and they only mentioned what was necessary to Becca. They did what they could to put on a good face.

13

Day 1 of Diana's Kidnapping

Diana tried desperately to avoid the black void that was pulling her down. All sound was becoming distant. Then there was no sound at all. She remembered hearing what sounded like a gunshot just before succumbing to the poison shot into her. To her, this was what the bottomless pit would be like. All that was missing was the gnashing of teeth, but that would mean that there would be feeling. Where she was at now, there was no sense of anything. Slowly, very slowly, Diana saw a small point of light. She focused on that light, wishing it…almost willing it to grow. And it did grow. It warmed her, bringing her out of this horrid void she was stuck in. As she fought her way back, she started to hear voices. There were people talking, but it wasn't words she recognized. Her sensation of touch started to come back also. She was lying on a couch, but it seemed to her like she was in the air. As she tried to open her eyes, she instinctively called for Ben; she regretted it. Her head was spinning so fast that it made her nauseous. She closed them again. Swallowing was near impossible because her throat was so sore. It made her call near to being inaudible. Eventually, she did finally open her eyes. As she slowly sat up, she checked out her surroundings. Now that she was waking up, she realized that she was in an airplane. She could see that she was in some type of Muslim robe. *What happened to my clothes? Who…changed my clothes?* she fretted. She tried to sit up; it was then that she found out her hands were tied. There were two Muslim women sitting opposite from her. Diana was looking around, trying to see Ben or Scott. She asked the women across from her if they saw two other men like her on the plane; they looked at each other and started talking. They were speaking a different language. *Arabic maybe?* Diana wondered. She saw a man in a turban sitting near the cockpit; he turned and looked at her. He motioned with his hand, pulling it across his neck like someone cutting a throat open. Diana just glared at him; he in turn just laughed. One woman got up and went to a small room in the back of the cabin. She came back with a bottle of water. She opened it and tried to give it to Diana. Diana wanted something to drink. Her tongue was stuck to the roof of her mouth and her throat was very raw and sore. She just didn't trust what they were giving her. She didn't want to go back to the black void again. The woman was insistent, and seeing that Diana was not taking the water, she took a drink then tried to give the bottle of water to her again. This time, Diana took it. "Thank you," Diana said. She figured that if it was drugged, the women wouldn't be willing to drink it herself. The water tasted wonderful. Diana's entire body tingled with the liquid. She tried to drink it slowly. She may not get another, and she didn't want to worry about using the bathroom. Especially with her hands tied and in the getup she was wearing. She turned to try to look out the window, but the shade was pulled down. She was in the process of lifting it up when the man by the cockpit started yelling. He hurriedly stomped over and closed the shade back down, pushing Diana out of the way. Then he began to yell at her. She had no clue what he was saying; she pretty much shut him off after the first two syllables. The man, seeing that she wasn't paying attention, turned and slapped her across the face. Diana's eyes went steel gray, and she just glared at him. The two women across the aisle started in. They and the man were in a heated discussion. All Diana could figure out was that they didn't approve of him hitting her. Diana didn't approve of it either. She searched her soul, praying that what the man said was being cruel. *Lord, I'm trusting you to protect my family and friends. Please tell me, did they kill Ben?* she prayed. The Lord came down and met her in that plane. However, all that He did was hold her and assure her that He was in control. Diana accepted that and hoped for the best. She sat quietly, singing a song in her head. About an hour or so passed when Diana felt like the plane was going down; her eardrums were popping in and out. That was exactly what the plane was doing. One of the women came over and attached her seatbelt then went and sat down and attached her own. Diana felt the tires bounce off the tarmac three times; then the plane came to a slow crawl as they turned. Diana couldn't see much, but she saw the plane had stopped in the middle of a lane. The door was opened by one of the men in the cockpit. With her hands tied, Diana couldn't release her seatbelt. Again, one of the women came over and took care of it. The woman signaled her to stay seated. The man that sat near the cockpit came over and grabbed her by the arm and pulled her up. He told one of the women something, for which the woman came over and hooked a scarf over Diana's face. Then the man jerked her toward the door. She had a hard time seeing where she was going; the sun was blinding her. The man didn't care; he pulled her down the stairs, yelling at her something she didn't know. There was a limo waiting a little ways from the plane. The two women had already climbed in. The man shoved Diana in and then shut the door. He walked around and climbed in on the front passenger's side.

The limo's windows were tinted, making it so that no one could see inside the vehicle. Diana, however, could see out. She was looking for anything to tell her where she was. Finally, as the limo exited the small airport, she saw a sign written in three languages. One was English; she was in Qatana, wherever that was. The limo drove through the small town then turned toward the north. Diana had no idea where or what she was going to do next. She knew at this time she would have to just wait it out. It was only about twenty minutes before they were entering another town. This one was much bigger. The sign as they entered the town said Damascus. She was in Syria! *This is so not good*, Diana thought. She watched the vehicle weave in and out of traffic. They stopped at an older building. There was a medical symbol in the front. Then one of the women checked Diana's scarf. She wanted to make sure she wasn't seen. Then she put her finger up to her lips, telling Diana to be quiet. The two women exited out the curbside door. The man came around opened the door and pulled Diana out on the roadside door. She was led into the building and through different hallways winding up, being pushed into a room in the corner. She was not going to like what was going to go on in here, and she knew it.

Luckily, the man stayed outside the door; only the two women were in there with her. They came over untied her hands and started removing all the extra coverings Diana was put in. She was down to just a tan linen robe that they left on her. They signaled her to sit down on the examination table. She didn't want to, but since there were only two chairs and the women were taking those, there wasn't going to be much choice. Ten minutes later, a doctor-looking man came in followed by a nurse. He nodded to the women then to Diana. The nurse came over and put a blood pressure cuff on her, took her blood pressure, then went and wrote it down on a clipboard. The doctor came up and listened to her heart. Then in broken English, he said, "Deep…breath." Diana obliged him. He checked her reflexes in her knees, elbows, and ankles. Then he signaled for her to lie down on the table. Diana shook her head a little. He put his hand on her shoulder and was gently pushing her to lie down. She went ahead and lay back. He felt around on her abdomen, pushing down on her. Then came the time that Diana was worried about; she saw the nurse bring over a low light. "Bring up legs now," the doctor said.

Oh…no…you…don't! Diana thought; she refused to comply.

The doctor, nurse, and the two women were talking over in one corner; Diana took her chance. She jumped off the table, opened the door, and ran out before the group knew what was going on. She ran past the man from the plane that had been shoving her around. He obviously was not expecting her to run. He was yelling something at her. Diana just turned around the corner. She was trying to remember how she was led in so she could get out. The man was chasing her, but she had too much of a lead. Another man came out of a room, attempted to grab her; she dodged his grasp. She turned again down another hallway, thinking it was the one that led out. She saw a door at the end of the hallway; unfortunately, a guard appeared and grabbed her just in front of the door.

He had an evil smile of conquest on his face, but he made a fatal error. Diana and the guard were standing face-to-face. Diana brought up her knee quick and hard. The guard fell to the side, grabbing himself; he lay on the ground in a fetal position. Diana normally wouldn't have done that except in a life-and-death situation. To her, this was life or death. She jumped over the guard and went through the door.

Diana stood for a second in shock. It was a type of waiting room. She had no choice; she had to try to get through it. She started off again. The men were closing in behind her, yelling all the time. Diana could see the outside doorway. She was almost there, just a few more steps. Suddenly, a large man dressed mostly in white grabbed her from behind. He was holding tight to her arm; another joined him, grabbing the other arm. She was fighting like a wild woman. She may have to go back, but she wasn't going quietly or willingly. The man from the plane came and stood in front of her. Diana expected at the least a slap across the face, at most…a major beating. He did neither. Instead, he quickly covered her face with a white cloth. Diana figured it was probably filled with chloroform or something the like. She tried not to breathe it in. She was trying to get the cloth off her face, but the man held it tight. Her body, in need of oxygen, took over. She inhaled the sweet sickening stuff. She fought it as much as she could, but her body went limp. The large man in white easily threw her over his shoulder and took her back to the exam room. He and the other man tied her wrists to the table. Then they brought her knees up, tied a rope around her thighs and shins, and then tied her ankles to the table.

The chloroform did not take her to the black void. Diana could feel and hear what was going on around her but was unable to stop anything. She was still fighting the ropes, trying to get freed from what she knew was coming. The doctor came in to finish his examination. She felt the extreme burning and pressure. The burning made Diana's mind start to reconnect to the rest of her body. She pulled, twisted, and yanked on the ropes holding her. She could feel the ropes start to cut into her wrists and ankles. The pain of the ropes brought her more and more conscious. The doctor was measuring her, for whatever reason. Diana heard the nurse speaking, and the doctor stopped what he was doing. He said something to the nurse then he spoke to Diana. "You stop fighting, you bleeding." Diana wasn't going to stop fighting. It wasn't in her nature to give up. The more the ropes cut into her, the more she could pull out of the ropes, and the more she was able to think. She felt someone holding her arm still, something cold was put on her arm, then there was something stinging her. They gave her a shot of something; Diana could feel the drug pulling her into the black void again. She fought for all she was worth to stay awake, but the drug won the battle. She slipped back to the void.

Diana started coming out; she was dressed as a Muslim woman again. Her wrists and ankles were untied and bandaged. The women who came in with her were waiting to take her out. The doctor came back in. "You have scars, what from?" Diana wasn't going to tell him; she just looked at him with a cold stare. "You tell me, yes?" the doctor asked again. Diana tried to say no, but her voice was gone. She shook her head...no.

The doctor turned to the two women; he told them she was a good prospect. She was pure, but he didn't understand the scars on her abdomen. He then told them to take her to the compound; he would come out in a week to check on her.

Diana was aware of the conversation going on, but of course she had no clue what they were saying. They attached the scarf over her face again before they left the room. The women had to help Diana walk out to the limo. Diana was walking like a drunken person. As they were climbing into the car, four Syrian soldiers came and stopped the limo from leaving. They pulled Diana out of the vehicle. The two women were arguing...struggling with the soldiers. Diana didn't understand a word of what these people were saying. All she knew was she was not able to stand there while they argued things out. Her head was splitting open, she couldn't focus her eyes, and her mouth was drier than Death Valley. She started to lean back against the limo. A soldier yanked her back up. She was about to fall down in a heap on the ground when one of the women grabbed her arm to steady her. The soldiers took Diana and the one woman to a jail. *I've been arrested,* Diana thought. *What was I arrested for?* The soldiers told her nothing; they said nothing to the other woman either. Diana thought that maybe she was told over at the limo, but Diana didn't know for sure. Once they were locked into a cell and alone, Diana turned to the woman that came with her. "Since we're going to be in the same room for a while, what is your name?" The woman shook her head, not understanding what Diana was asking. Diana tried again. "I'm Diana," she said as she pointed to herself. "You are?" Diana pointed toward the woman.

The woman said, "Aisha." She was pointing to herself. She turned and pointed to Diana and said, "Ariana Ava."

Diana shook her head. "No, I'm Diana."

Aisha reinforced that Diana's name was Ariana Ava. The name sounded familiar, but Diana couldn't place it at the time. Aisha insisted that Diana take the only cot in the room. She went to the corner and put her cloak that covered her head down on the ground. Diana was going to let Aisha take the cot; she wasn't going to sleep anyway. She was very uneasy, uncomfortable, and hurting from the cuts in her wrists and ankles. She was also hurting from the examination. There was an ache not only physically but emotionally. Memories that she had buried a long time ago came rushing forward to the front of her mind once more. Emotions were overwhelming her; Diana began to cry. She turned to God for help. *Lord…I need you*, she prayed. She sat there holding her knees up to her chest, head down lying on the side of her knees, and her eyes closed. She was rocking back and forth like a child. Diana felt warmth come into the room. It filled her from the inside out, and she could feel God's love and His arms holding her. Then there was a light in the room, driving all the shadows away. Diana just basked in the glow. As she looked at the light, a form came into focus. An angel stood beside her.

"Be at peace and rest. The Lord has heard your cry and has sent me. I will be here with you…standing guard. You will be safe," the angel said. He came over and touched Diana on the top of her head. Diana instantly felt the headache melt away; her eyes were able to focus once more. She could swallow without pain. She thanked the angel and praised God for answering her cry. She laid down and fell asleep.

All the while this was going on, Aisha saw something totally different. She did see the light fill the room, the form coming from the light, and it spoke to her as well. However, what Aisha saw was a warrior in white instead of an angel. The warrior in white told Aisha, "Let no harm come to this woman. Tell your husband any harm that comes to her will be recompensed on the whole compound." The warrior disappeared, and Aisha was afraid. She looked over toward Ariana; she had gone to sleep. Aisha didn't know how she was going to tell her husband, but she was going to have to try.

14

In Damascus's Jail

Diana and Aisha were woken up at sunrise by a soldier banging on the bars. The soldier gave the women two cups of water and a couple of bowls of what looked like cream of wheat. Aisha was the one who took it from the soldier and brought it over to the table. She put a cup and a bowl in front of Diana, and then she sat down on the floor with hers. Diana had no clue of what the bowl was, and she knew she couldn't drink the water. So she left them on the table and walked to the window to look out. The sun was just rising over the small tan houses on the east side; it created a kaleidoscope of fuchsias, oranges, and purples. *It's gorgeous. Thank you, Lord*, Diana thought.

Aisha saw that Ariana was not eating anything. She picked up the bowl and walked over to her as she was standing by the window, looking out like a caged bird. She tried to get Ariana to eat, but she struggled to get her to understand. Ariana just kept smiling and shaking her head no. She was worried the warrior in white would think that she was in harm's way. She didn't know what to do.

It was day two of the women's confinement, and Diana still didn't know why she was there. Aisha was determined to get her to eat, but there was no way to explain why she couldn't. The soldiers did bring a coffee for the lunch and supper meal; even so, Diana couldn't risk it—not that she would choose coffee. She didn't like American coffee even with all the sugar and milk and stuff. Being a history buff, she knew Middle Eastern coffee was much stronger. Diana was beyond thirsty and knew she won't last long without water. She wished she would have been conscious enough to have grabbed her bottle of water out of the limo. *Would have, could have, should have…won't do you any good now*, Diana told herself.

Around two p.m., according to the sun's shadow, a soldier and another man came to their cell. The soldier took Aisha out; the man that came with the soldier came in. "Do you know why you are here?" he asked in broken English.

Diana shook her head. "No, no I don't. What have I done?"

"You here for the disregard and public embarrassment of the guard at the clinic," he said. "Do you know what such crime is punished by?" he continued. Diana again shook her head no. "If he would have been permanently harmed, you would be killed. Since he was not…punishment is only a beating," he said.

Diana thought, *Oh great…I just got my back healed.*

"You…will not be beat today," he stated. "The guard has signed an agreement with your guardian."

Guardian…I don't have a guardian here, not a physical one anyway, she thought.

"You go home tomorrow to your guardian," he finished.

"Who is my guardian?" Diana asked.

The man didn't respond to that question. He just got up and walked to the cell door, yelled something, and the guard showed up to open the door. Aisha wasn't with him. Diana was alone in the cell, but she was okay with that. It gave her time to freely talk with the Lord. She quietly hummed the song, "I Love You Lord." She felt His presence immediately and basked in it, gaining strength from His spirit. Her communion with the Lord was cut short by the sound of an explosion. Diana went to the window and looked to see what was going on. She saw a white smoke cloud rising from the area she thought was around the clinic. People were running around yelling something, some people were looking to hide, some people were running toward the epicenter of the explosion. Diana knew the Middle East is an unstable place. Any little thing could cause someone to get upset; then fighting would break out. *Ben was right…it is a harsh culture*, she thought. With that thought, her mind went to Ben. She trusted the Lord to keep the ones she loved safe, but did that include Ben? She couldn't deny that she had feelings for him. She loved to jest and tease with him, though it gets frustrating when she can't control her own body. Did the Lord take him home? What about his kids? Surely the Lord wouldn't do that to them so soon after losing their mom. Diana's heart started racing, a lump formed in her throat, and she started feeling sick.

"I have control," the Lord spoke to her in His calm, still voice.

"Lord, did you take him home?" Diana asked. The only reply she received was the Lord's arms holding her. She trusted the Lord, but the thought of Ben being killed lurked in the back of her mind. Aisha was allowed back into the cell; she immediately grabbed Diana and pulled her to the door. The guard let them out and led them to the door of the building. Aisha opened the door and pulled Diana outside. Once outside, Diana saw the limo waiting by the curb. Aisha hurried her into the vehicle, and they hurried out of the city. Not that Diana wanted to stay in the cell, but she worried that they were breaking the law somewhere. The man said that she wasn't to leave till tomorrow. The last thing she wanted was to have the soldiers breaking down the door to take her to a hanging. As she looked around, she saw her bottle of water in the mini fridge. She quickly grabbed it up and chugged it. At first, her body tingled with the infusion of water, but not long after, her stomach started knotting. She wondered if maybe they poisoned the bottle of water.

15

In Israel

Ben, Scott, and Dick finally got the go-ahead to leave for Israel. Dick was to stay at the embassy in Tel Aviv to be the go-between for Ben and Scott to Zenon. Ben and Scott were to go to the air carrier USS *Wilson*, from there they would be airlifted to any area near where they need to be. The guys landed in Tel Aviv at eight a.m. It had been four days since Diana was taken. Ben knew she was alive, but what might be happening to her was worrying him. Scott was feeling the same way. Both men were spending large amounts of time praying for her protection. Dick went to check in at the embassy. Ben and Scott wanted to do some legwork before heading to the *Wilson*. The intel they last received was a private jet left from Des Moines heading to Syria. Israeli radar picked them up as they passed through; they said it landed at Qatana. The guys knew that private jets often landed in Qatana for passengers going to Damascus. So they rented a car and headed to Damascus. They had clearance to go through the checkpoints when they left Des Moines; that didn't mean that it still worked now. Praise to God, they did. Scott still had some friends he had helped out some years back. He and Ben were going to call in a favor. As they came into the city, they noticed the people were on edge more than normal. Scott figured it might be better if he went and talk to his friend alone. Looking at the faces of the people watching them, Ben agreed. "While you're catching up on old times, I'm gonna go check with the local police. Maybe they will be willing to share," Ben told Scott.

    Scott nodded. They arranged to meet back in the lobby of one of the hotels. Ben let Scott off at the marketplace; he then drove to the local outpost. He prayed he would be able to get some information about Diana there. Two hours later, Ben came in and sat at the high bar waiting for Scott. He had a lot to tell and a lot to worry about. Scott came in about fifteen minutes after Ben arrived. He found Ben sitting at the high bar and headed over to the open chair.

Ben didn't like the look on Scott's face. *This isn't going to be good*, he thought. "What ya got?" he asked as Scott sat down.

"Well, Diana was here. She came in as a passenger in a limo and stopped at the local clinic. It just so happened that my friend was taking his son to the clinic for a cut on his leg. He said a white woman came out with only her linen robe on. She was being chased by a couple of orderlies and a security guard. She almost made it out of the building before one of the orderlies caught her. He said that woman fought like a wild dog, even with two of the men holding her. It took some chloroform to subdue her. Apparently, you are the only one that can control that cat. Anyway, he said that he didn't see the woman leave, but he was in the room with his son for about an hour and a half," Scott ended.

Ben had to smile at Scott's comment, but then reality hit him. "Okay, I can fill in the next points. One of the security guards caught Diana before she got out to the lobby. She kneed him." Scott instantly winced. "He had to go to the hospital himself. With his disgrace and humiliation, he pressed charges. Diana was arrested and held for two days. She was found guilty, but a 'guardian' stepped in and made an agreement with the guard. According to one of the guards, her beating will be done at the guardian's compound to the south east of here. She wasn't supposed to leave until today, but something happened that made it necessary for her to leave yesterday afternoon," Ben added.

"Shoot! We just missed her," Scott said frustrated.

"Yeah…something happened. What happened?" Ben wondered.

"I think I can fill that part in. Apparently, they had brought Diana here to have her looked at by a doctor," Scott stated.

Ben was trying to stay calm, but inside he was furious. "That explains why she made such a commotion."

"Yeah…no kidding. Anyway, there was an explosion at the clinic. One of the oxygen tanks exploded. A doctor, a nurse, and two orderlies were injured. The doctor has two broken fingers, the nurse has a broken collarbone, one orderly is in a coma, and the other has a broken femur. Do you want to guess who the people were that were involved with Diana?" Scott furthered.

"God said that He was with her. They must have made Him upset," Ben responded.

"Oh, there was another unexplained injury to a security guard of a private jet. He got his hand smashed by the luggage conveyor belt today," Scott included.

"I have a feeling that wasn't just a freak circumstance," Ben added.

Scott asked, "So what's the next step? Over to the sea?"

"Yeah, I wanna get a look at a map. Then maybe some recon," Ben figured. The guys hopped back into the car and took it back to Tel Aviv then caught a flight over to the *Wilson*. The captain showed them a topographic map of the area where Ben and Scott easily located the Sheikh's compound in the southeast corner of Syria, near the Golan Heights. There were several small towns near his compound; that could cause a problem with the drop.

The captain suggested that they go for a night drop tonight so the guys could get a good look around. It was to be a new moon, and there were no storms reported in the weather forecast. Scott was a little hesitant, but Ben was all for it. For him, the sooner they got Diana out of there, the better. The chopper left at ten p.m. with the guys on board. They had their cantinas, night vision goggles, maps, and the rest of the supplies they might need all packed into small stashes on their uniforms.

The captain was right: conditions for a drop were optimal. Scott and Ben had no problems avoiding the patrols from various military sects. They got within three hundred yards of the Sheikh's compound. They were up on the hills looking down into the buildings. Each was looking for different areas. Scott was looking for where the guards stayed, where the weak points in the walls were, what the guards were armed with. Ben was looking for where the Sheikh stayed, where the civilians might be, and more importantly where Diana was being held at. "We're coming, Diana, hang on. We're coming," Ben said under his breath.

Scott said a prayer asking the Lord to continue keeping her safe. The guys headed back to the pickup point and waited for the chopper to get them. There were too many patrols walking around for them to compare their notes. They had to wait 'til they were back to the ship. The chopper came in quiet and low, just barely touching the rail down for the guys to jump in, and then it was up and gone in a flash. The flight back to the *Wilson* took thirty minutes; it was after midnight when they finally landed on the flight deck. They went to the mess hall to grab some coffee and sat down with their notes and planned the next step.

16

In Syria at the Compound

Diana arrived at the compound late in the afternoon. To her surprise, there was a large stand of trees to the west and south of the area. She could see a mountain ridge on the north. Sadly, everything else was blocked out by the tall wall that surrounded the compound. She could see guards walking around; some carrying automatic rifles, some only had a scimitar sword hooked on their waist. There were children playing in the courtyard—at least they were until Diana step out of the limo. No one looked happy there—definitely not happy she was there, at least in her eyes. Aisha led Diana to a building that looked Persian in design. It had lattice-style windows, decorative mosaics, and gracefully pointed alcoves. Diana followed Aisha into a hallway where at the end of it, two large men stood guarding a door. One was black at about seven feet tall and around 375 pounds or more; he looked like a cross between Magic Johnson and Mr. T. The other was Arabic, not as tall and definitely not as muscular at about six feet tall and around 400 pounds. She wanted to turn and run, but Aisha grabbed her hand and pulled her with her. As they neared the two guards, who were eyeing Diana critically, they turned and opened the door. Diana was led up the stairs and into a room where three other women obviously lived. There were colorful curtains hanging from the walls separating different areas in the room. Sheer curtains hung across the windows. Several colorful pillows and cushions scattered throughout the room. Some of the ladies were dressed in plain beige or tan clothes, in a type of Persian design. These ladies had their hair braided and to the side. The others were dressed in the head covering of a Muslim woman, but their robes were lighter and in muted colors instead of the black. The two guards slowly closed the doors behind Diana and Aisha. *Another gilded cage to keep me in*, Diana thought. Once the doors were closed, the ladies rushed over and hovered around Diana. They were pushing and shoving, trying to check her out. Diana didn't like it at all; she had to fight the urge to scream for space. They pulled the scarf off that covered her head, pulling her hair with it. Diana reached up and held her hair so that it didn't pull out with it. They were pulling and prodding, poking and pinching. Diana's temper was just about to go off when an old woman stood up and shouted something.

The woman was obviously respected by all there. She looked to be somewhere around mid-sixties, and with the lines on her face, Diana figured she had hard life. *This woman must be the first wife of the owner of the compound*, Diana thought. She came over and stood in front of Diana. She would normally be face-to-face with most of the women there, but Diana towered at least a foot over her. She looked over her shoulder, said something to a lady standing near the wall, and turned back to Diana. The lady quickly grabbed a stool and brought it behind Diana. She put her hand on Diana's shoulder and pushed down. Diana understood that she was to sit down on the stool, so she complied. The old woman walked around Diana. She combed through her hair and felt it; she grabbed her chin and checked her face. While holding her chin, she put the other hand on Diana's forehead and pushed her head back, opening Diana's mouth to check her teeth. Next, she moved to Diana's hands and feet.

What next, a strip search? It isn't gonna happen, Diana thought.

The old woman said something to the girl by the wall again. She came over and encouraged Diana to stand up by grabbing her arm and pulling up. Diana stood up; the girl took Diana's coat off her. She went to take the linen robe off Diana, to which Diana shook her head no and crossed her arms around herself. The old woman smiled but then called out to somebody.

The black guard that stood outside the room opened the door and came in. The old woman said something to him; he looked over to Diana and started walking toward her. Diana had an instant rush of fear run through her. She looked dead in the eyes of the large man walking toward her. It was hard for her to believe, but she didn't see darkness in them. She saw a kindness, one that she hadn't seen from the men over here. Even still, she wasn't going to let him touch her. The guard came and stood in front of her; he didn't hold her down, didn't make any threatening moves toward her in any way. Diana just stood there looking at him, watching to see what he would do. He signaled for her to give him the linen robe. To which she shook her head no. He pointed to the robe and then to his hand; again Diana shook her head no and held tighter to herself. He glanced over to the old woman, who signaled him to continue. Diana steeled herself and prepared to fight if necessary; though she knew that the guard would win without much problem.

He looked down on Diana and reached out to grab her; Diana dodged him and ran over to the opposite side of the table, putting as much space between her and the man. She saw a knife sticking out of some meat and grabbed it. The girls in the room screamed and scattered to the far side of the room. The old woman just stood where she was. She then called out again, and two more guards came in, raising their swords to take Diana on. Diana backed up and ran to the corner of the room, holding the knife out. She shook her head no and readied herself to defend herself.

The black guard turned and watched what Diana was doing. He said something to the two guards who had just come in; they put their swords away and moved to stand by the door.

Diana didn't want to hurt anybody; she just wanted to be left alone. She was tired of people taking privileges with her that they should never have. She saw the black guard watching her, his eyes still not mean or cold. She thought she saw empathy toward her in them. The old woman told the black guard something. He put his hand up in a halting move; then he walked over to her. On the way, he grabbed a piece of cloth off the pile of pillows.

When he got close enough, he held out the cloth in one hand and pointed to the knife then held out his other hand. Diana wasn't sure what he wanted. She looked at his face trying to understand. He quickly dropped the cloth, drawing Diana's eyes to the cloth; then he grabbed the wrist of the hand that held the knife. Diana felt a sharp pain shoot through her arm from the pressure put on her wrist from his grasp. She instantly dropped the knife. He held on to her wrist and watched her face as he bent down and picked up the knife. Tears were filling her eyes; she willed herself to stop and not cry. The bandage around her wrist started to turn red as her wrist was starting to bleed again. He put the knife in his belt, picked up the cloth, gave it to her. Then he pointed to her linen robe. This time, Diana agreed to give him the linen robe but pointed to him and signaled that she wanted him to turn around.

He grinned but then turned around so that his back was to her. He was big enough to block anybody from seeing her. She slipped out of the robe, and then wrapped the cloth around her like a wrap. It was big enough to go around two times. When she was done, she said, "Okay." The guard turned around and Diana gave him the robe.

He nodded and then walked back to the old lady. One of the girls—Diana figured she was a servant—came over and took it from him. He nodded to the two guards blocking the door, signaling them to leave. He also walked back to his position outside the door. Diana had no idea what he was going to do with that carving knife in his belt, but she wished she still had it.

The old woman signaled to Aisha, who quickly came over to Ariana and slowly took her hand. She pulled her out of the corner, saying something in a smooth voice, then led her to a room in the back. When Diana walked into the room, she saw there was a huge clover-shaped tub in a terra-cotta color. It was built into the floor and filled with water. There were small white flowers floating in it. *At home I would have called this a pool*, Diana thought. Diana smiled; she wanted to clean up, but she turned and looked behind her. All the women were standing in the door, watching her.

Aisha followed Ariana's line of sight and apparently understood why she was apprehensive. She called to someone. A servant appeared in the room; she had some cloths in her arms. The servant and another girl started to reached up and hang the cloth over the doorway. Diana bowed to Aisha and smiled. Aisha pulled Diana's wrist up and began to unwrap the wound. She did the same for the other wrist and her ankles. Diana unwrapped the cloth around her and climbed into the tub. It was warm and felt downright wonderful, melting away the knots that tied up her back. She closed her eyes and just lay back in the water, sinking down so that the water came up to her neck. She smiled as she stretched her legs out was glad that she didn't even come close to touching the other side of the wall. About fifteen minutes later, Diana felt a presence that wasn't Aisha. She opened her eyes to see the old lady sitting nearby. The old woman looked at Diana and pointed to her. Diana, not understanding, just cocked her head to the side. The old woman reached over and traced the scars in Diana's shoulders. With the language barrier, there was no way that Diana could explain anything. She just shrugged her shoulders. She went ahead and lathered up and cleaned herself. She looked for some shampoo to do her hair but found none. She saw the old woman signaling and said something to a servant. The servant climbed into the tub with Diana, which sent Diana to the opposite side of the tub. The servant slowly approached Diana, grabbed her arm, and pulled her toward the middle of the tub. Diana moved hesitantly, not knowing what was going to happen. The servant wanted Ariana to turn around. When she did, the servant started to scrub her back.

As much as Diana didn't want anybody touching her, she did need to make sure her back stayed clean. The last thing she needed was an infection in those two cuts. The servant moved from washing her back to washing Diana's hair for her. Diana had to admit…it felt good to have someone "play" with her hair; it was immensely relaxing for her. When the servant was done, she climbed out. Diana saw a different one coming over with a towel for her to use. Diana submitted to the obvious hint that time was up and climbed out of the tub. She knew the old woman was checking her out the whole time; it made her very uncomfortable. *At least it wasn't the entire compound watching. The woman isn't seeing anything she hasn't seen before*, Diana thought. Once Diana was dried off, the servants brought in clean robes. These were dark blue in color and thinner than her previous robes. Diana thought the style of clothes belonged more with the Persian culture, not the Islamic culture. *At least the clothes covered my stomach*, Diana thought. The servants helped Diana to get dressed. They combed her hair and fixed it then started adding jewelry. They went to put earrings in; then they realized that she didn't have pierced ears. They looked over to the old woman.

The old woman signaled for one of them to go for something. The others started to prepare Diana for the piercing. Diana shook her head no and covered her ears with her hands. The old woman again called for something. A few minutes later, the black guard that stood outside the door was standing in the doorway of the room. He came in and waited for his orders. Once he received it, he came toward Diana again. Diana looked straight at him and said, "No. I don't want earrings! I don't need pierced ears!" She forgot that he didn't understand a word she was saying. She was still covering her ears with her hands, shaking her head no. She was near to crying; this was just too much. He looked at her, slowly grabbed her wrists, and started to pull her hands away from her ears. Diana didn't let him pull her hands down at first; he said something in a low calm tone and pulled harder. She couldn't fight his strength; her hands moved away from her ears. He crossed her arms across her chest and turned her around to hold her tight. He was saying something calmly and softly to her. Diana was crying now; she was still shaking her head no, so much so that he couldn't control her head. The black guard called over his shoulder, and a minute later, the other Arabic guard came in. He joined them and put his hands on each side of Diana's head, holding her head still. The old woman came over, grabbed Diana's earlobe, and quickly shoved the post of the earring through. Diana sucked in air; tears were streaming down her face as her ear shot pain through her head. The old woman put a salve on both sides of the earlobe. Again, Diana tried to fight them as they turned her head to reach the other ear. There was no way she could fight against these two men. Her earlobe was grabbed, and a post shoved through it; salve was put on both sides. Once the old woman was done, the Arabic guard holding her head let go and walked out the door. The black guard loosened his grip but waited till Diana stopped sobbing before he stood her back up. He again said something calmly and quietly to her. Although Diana had no clue of what he said, she knew that he didn't want to hurt her. She looked into his brown eyes, saw no danger, no darkness; he was just doing what he was told to do. There was no way that she could tell him that she didn't blame him; she was just furious at what the old woman did. Now it was a mute point. It was done, and there was nothing she could do now. Once the Lord got her out of there, she would take the stupid things out and let her ears heal.

The old lady brought Ariana back into the big room. All the girls were excited at what she looked like. Aisha brought a plate of food over to her, wanting her to eat, guiding her to a cushion on the floor. Diana refused; she didn't care if they did call the black guard in. She wasn't going to eat that stuff. He would have to shove it down her throat, and even then, she would throw it up. She moved over to the corner, sat down, and held her knees. The salve must have had some deadening in it; her earlobes were totally numb now. She saw Aisha coming over again with a cup. She also had some other stuff in her hands. She gave the cup to Diana, who took it and put it down on the floor beside her, knowing full well that it didn't make Aisha happy. But at this time, she didn't care.

Aisha carefully grabbed Ariana's arm. She pulled the bracelets off so that she could get to her wrist. They were bleeding, even more so now because of her fighting with the earrings. She carefully rubbed salve around her wrists. She heard Ariana suck in air and tried to apologize but knew Ariana didn't understand. She pulled out the clean linens and started to wrap them around her wrists; as she finished, she tied it. Aisha had to put the bracelets back on; it was Bibi's command. She didn't understand why Ariana didn't want jewelry on; they were gifts from the Sheikh. Then she pointed to Ariana's ankles to check them. She was glad when Ariana offered them to her quickly; they were raw and near bleeding as well. As Aisha finished with the ankles, she saw that Ariana was exhausted. She headed over to Bibi to find out where she was going to sleep.

Diana appreciated what Aisha did. If the salve was the same stuff that the old woman put on her ears, her wrists and ankles will stop hurting her soon. She watched Aisha move over to the old woman, watched as they were discussing; she was just hoping it wasn't more stuff to torture her with. She saw Aisha walking back toward her; it was making her nervous.

Aisha took Ariana by her hand, motioning her to follow her. She saw that Ariana was reluctant to come. Aisha understood that; she had a lot of stuff done to her these last three days. She guided Ariana over to a bed near Bibi's bed. Ariana looked at her, seemed to understand what she meant; smiled and laid down on the bed. Aisha let the netting fall down around the bed and gave Ariana a bow.

Diana was grateful to Aisha; she was very tired. She gave her a nod of thanks when Aisha bowed to her. She tried to lie on her side, but the stupid earrings kept jabbing into her neck. She put her arm up to make a hole to put her ear in it. She no more than closed her eyes, and she was out.

It was late when Diana opened her eyes; all the other ladies were asleep in various beds around the room. She saw that her bed was near the old woman's, but she definitely didn't want to wake her. She needed to go to the bathroom and had no clue of where she needed to go. She quietly got up and started to walk around. She went down the hallway just passing the tub room. She looked in and checked in the other rooms. Finally, in the last room on the left, she saw what she needed. It looked more like what you would see in an outhouse, with a low bench with three cutouts on the top with toilet lids attached. It was the odor what was the clincher; this was what the ladies were using. She was grateful that she was able to hold everything long enough to get there. She took a big breath and then held it and went in to finish her business. She found a bowl of water and some towels on a counter. Diana took one of the towels, got it wet, cleaned herself off, then put the used towel by the stool. She walked back out into the hallway only to run into the black guard again. She looked up, afraid of what was going to happen. He just patted her head and smiled then led her back to her bed. As he walked her back, Diana saw that the old woman was sitting on the side of her bed frowning. The guard said something to her, helped Diana back into her bed, then returned to his post.

Do the guards sleep out there, or do they get time to go to their own rooms to sleep? Diana wondered as she laid back down. She turned and watched the old woman lie down, her frown still in place; then she turned over, putting her back to her. Diana put her arm up to give space for her ear and fell back to sleep.

17

In Syria at the Compound

The morning started early. Diana awoke to the scurrying of the servants bringing in breakfast. The old woman and the other ladies were already up and moving around as well. Diana got up, made the bed, and walked to the window. The morning was another beautiful sunrise. She heard a horn of some type play and saw the men all heading to a tower in the center of the courtyard. The women also were standing in a line facing east. Aisha signaled her to come by her. Diana just shook her head no. The old woman frowned at her then turned and said something to Aisha. Aisha bowed and stood at the ready. There was a man's voice coming across a loud speaker, singing something. Diana recognized then what was going on. It was the Muslim tradition to pray toward Mecca. This was one of those times. She knew full well that she would not be allowed to walk outside the room, so Diana went over to the room that had a tub in it, walked over to the window, and did some of her own prayer time. She thanked the Lord for the sunrise and the night's sleep. She prayed the Lord give her strength for the day's trials. She started singing the song, "I Love You Lord" in her head then she started to hum it, which moved to quietly singing it. She felt the Lord's spirit come down to meet her. She communed with the Lord there in the bathroom, gaining strength and peace from her Lord. She sat quietly in His presence, waiting to hear from Him.

I have told you, and I say it again—I am with you. You will come home safe once more. This is for my glory, the Lord said in His still, calm voice.

Yes, my Lord, I'm sorry for doubting. Thank you for your confirmation. Show me what I am to do, she prayed. Again, the Lord, understanding her heart, came and held her in His arms. She quietly sang, "I Will Serve Thee." Diana happened to glance over by the door; she saw a young girl standing in the doorway. She looked to be somewhere around fourteen maybe fifteen years old. She was watching her, listening to her. The girl didn't seem to be scared, so Diana signaled her to come over. The girl slowly came over to her and sat down on the floor beside her. Diana asked, "What is your name?" The girl didn't answer. Diana tried again, pointing her finger at herself, "I'm Diana. You are?" She pointed her finger at the girl.

The girl shook her head no. She pointed her finger at Diana and said, "Ariana." Then she pointed her finger at herself and said, "Mahala."

Diana pointed at the girl and said, "Mahala?"

The girl nodded and said, "Mahala." The old woman came to the doorway and ordered something toward Mahala. The girl immediately jumped up and left the room. Then the old woman signaled the servants to come in. They headed toward Diana and started to change her clothes. They put her in a simple beige robe. They didn't put a cover on her head or a cloak on her. Diana had a bad feeling about it. Something was going on, and she knew she was not going to like the outcome. She figured the black guard was going to be coming in to do something to her.

It wasn't the black guard that met them when the old woman led her to the door; it was a totally different guard. He grabbed her by the arm and pulled her out of the room like she was a rebellious dog. Diana jerked her arm free from his grasp. He went to grab her again, but Diana pulled away from him. She signaled for him to lead the way. When he started walking down the hall, he turned around to make sure she was following behind him; she was. The guard led her across the courtyard. As they were walking through the area, Diana looked around at the different architecture. She saw a building that looked newer but was built in the style of an old Hindu pagoda. Another building was built in the traditional Jewish design. Of course there was the Islamic tower in the middle of the courtyard. She didn't get why there were so many different architectural styles just in this one compound. It didn't make sense to her. The guard stopped just outside a large building with double doors. This building was what Diana expected to see in the compound; it was built and decorated in the typical Moorish style, including the elaborate mosaic paintings and domes. Diana could hear a large crowd on the other side of the doors. The alarms in her head were going crazy. She hesitated to move forward. The guard, seeing her hesitation, grabbed her arm and pulled her with him as the double doors opened. He walked her in and pulled her through the crowd of men waiting to see the exhibition.

Diana heard the venom in the voices of the men surrounding her, the dark cold presence near to suffocating. It was encouraging the envy, hatred, and revulsion that was so obvious, even without her understanding the words the crowd was saying. She saw the building had an open courtyard itself. The crowd of men stood around the open courtyard, except for on the west side. On the west side of the courtyard, there was an awning and a platform with one large ornate, Moorish wood chair in the middle of it. In the center of the courtyard there was a stone table about three feet long and stood three feet off of the ground. The guard brought her to the middle of the court yard just feet from the table. He kept ahold of Diana's arm to make sure she stayed put. She figured he was waiting for someone to take the chair.

Diana stood there praying God would give her wisdom and strength for what was to come. The Lord had told her several times that He was with her and in control. She saw a man come in from the west side of the building. Was he the one that ordered her to be kidnapped? Was she finally going to find out what was going on? Probably not. She wouldn't know what he was saying to start with. As the man sat down on the chair in the middle of the platform, Diana got a good look at him. He wore a black-and-white patterned scarf on his head, a black sash tied like a head band around that, an untrimmed beard, and a malicious smile on his face. His eyes were dark brown—almost black, cold, dark, and wicked. She could feel the evil in him crossing the courtyard and overflowing everything. He wasn't tall, maybe five-foot-seven in height, and kind of stocky in build. The man that took the chair signaled to someone behind them. Diana looked back to see what or who he was signaling to. She saw a man make his way through the crowd. As he neared, Diana recognized him as the security guard at the clinic. She remembered what the man that came to visit her in the jail cell said. He said that she was to be beat for what she did. He also said that it wouldn't be on that day; apparently, it was to be today. *God, give me strength*, Diana prayed. The security guard came and stood beside them, looking at Diana with vengeance in his eyes and a foul smile on his face.

The leader, who had sat down in the chair, told a guard on his right side something. The guard turned, took a few steps behind the platform, and then returned with an armful of long poles made of cane. He came toward them with the bundle, lying them on the ground just on the south side of the table. With another nod of the head from the leader, two more guards came toward her; they each had a rope in their hand. Diana's heart was racing; in herself, she was -already fighting a war. Her flesh wanted to run, her mind was countering, saying she would never get through the crowd, and her heart was crying out to God. So many voices spinning around in her she thought she would pass out. In the middle of this storm, Diana heard God's voice loud and clear: "Trust Me."

Diana stilled the other voices and calmed her heart. She allowed the one guard to bind her wrists. She only winced because they were still very sore. Then the other guard bound her ankles. Then they lifted her up and put her on the table, turning her over so she lay on her stomach. They each took and end and pulled on the rope, tightening them to keep Diana stretched out on the table. Diana had seen a caning before, some years back; it was on the news about a man who had been caned. She thought that it was only an Asian custom, but clearly she was wrong. She kept saying in her mind, *I trust you, Lord...I trust you, Lord...I trust you, Lord*, more to steel herself than anything. She saw the security guard pick out a cane, move over and center himself to her body, and raise the cane to strike her. She lowered her head down so that if he tried to hit her head, her arms would take the brunt of it. She heard the rush of the wind around the cane as he used all his strength to bring it down to hit her. She braced for the impact. Just as she was sure it was going to hit, the cane broke apart. The broken piece fell to the side of her and onto the ground. The other half of the cane was still in the security guard's hands. His face flushed red with anger and embarrassment. The crowd of men laughed at him, which just added to his anger.

The security guard went and picked up another cane, checking it over carefully to make sure there were no cracks. He again centered himself to strike her back again. He raised his arms and brought the cane down hard, only to have it do the same thing just inches from hitting the woman's back. Rage was flashing in his eyes, driving him into madness. The crowd wasn't laughing quite as loud this time. They were watching him as he went and picked up another caning stick, checking it for soundness. He again tried to hit her, not caring where or how well; but again, the cane broke.

Mahdi sat there watching the entire affair, trying to figure out what was going on. The security guard started shouting at Mahdi of how he is being cheated. Mahdi came down from the chair and stood in the courtyard. He told the guards holding the ropes to let her up. They released her ropes and allowed her to untie her wrists and ankles. The security guard was still yelling about being cheated out of justice and retribution. Then he started yelling that she was a sorcerer.

Diana had no idea what the men were saying or doing; she just wanted to get the ropes off herself. She no more than untied her ankles when the security guard grabbed her and held a knife up to her throat, yelling something in her ear. Diana looked around to see if there was any way she could get to safety. There was a ladder in the corner that led to a rooftop, but that was all she could see. She felt the knife pushing into her neck; she was going to have to do something soon. *Lord, now what?* she asked. Suddenly, she felt the knife move away from her neck, and she didn't wait to find out why; she reached down, grabbed the gun from the security guard's belt, ran to the ladder, and climbed up onto the roof and backed herself into the corner, steadying herself to be able to shoot the gun if she needed to.

18

In Syria at the Compound

Taggee awoke to Aisha running into the room. She told him that they were going to kill Ariana. He walked outside to see what she was talking about. He saw a man trying to cane Ariana; he saw a warrior dressed in white standing near her, sword at the ready. He looked at the faces of the crowd and noticed that they did not see the warrior. Looking back at Ariana, each time the security guard went to hit her, the warrior would cut the cane in half. Taggee saw that Mahdi let Ariana up; he saw her untying the ropes, so he turned to go back into his room to get some much-needed sleep. He heard the crowd starting to call her a sorcerer and glanced once more over his shoulder before going inside. He saw the security guard holding a knife to Ariana's throat. Taggee didn't hesitate; he pushed the crowd apart to move toward them. It didn't take much before the crowd parted for him—the advantage of being seven foot tall. He reached the middle of the courtyard in a few steps. He was glad that the guard didn't see him come up behind him. He reached down and grabbed the hand that held the knife, pulling it away from Ariana's neck. Taggee knew full well with Ariana's latest history and what her tendency was when she is terrified, she would bolt. He saw her grab the gun from the guard's belt, turn, and run to the highest spot she could get to in order to get away. He was glad to see that she used her brain and took a spot that couldn't be seen from the ground or for the men to get a shot at her from the wall. Even still, her reaction was not going to lead to a good outcome. Mahdi was taking notice, which was never good.

The men were all shouting, yelling for her to be shot before she killed someone. Taggee looked at Mahdi. "Let me get her, she will not shoot me." Mahdi nodded and told the men to be still by holding his hand up. Taggee moved toward the building that Ariana was hiding on.

He knew she would shoot the person dumb enough to use the ladder, so he called up from the ground, "Ariana, come on, tigress…I will not let them hurt you." He knew she would not know what he was saying, but hoped that she recognized his voice. He also knew he had to keep his voice calm and smooth. "Ariana, come on down," he called again.

Diana waited for the attack to start; she knew they would not let her go. Surprisingly, it wasn't a fight she heard now from the men. She heard the crowd of men quiet down; she heard someone calling for Ariana. Knowing that they would not use her own name, she learned to recognize the name Ariana. The voice was calm and soothing; then it clicked. It was the black guard that was calling to her.

She slowly inched her way over to see what he was doing. She looked over the edge of the roof and saw him standing on the ground, looking at her. His head was only a foot or two below the roofline; if she had chosen a lower roof, he would have been able to reach her without much problem. She glimpsed over the crowd; saw the anger in some, fear in others. With the man that was in charge, she saw something else, something that she chose to block out for the time being. The black guard said something to her that brought her back to focusing on him. He was signaling her to come down, to come to him. She was out in the open now; she saw the guards on the wall had aimed their guns on her. She would never make it back to the corner without being shot. She watched the black guard's eyes closely, looking for any sign of deceit. She heard the Lord telling her to go to him, so she slowly crawled over to the ladder. The black guard followed her over and steadied the ladder for her. He again said something, which at least to her, sounded like an encouragement. As she backed down and reached his shoulders' height, he reached over and grabbed the gun from her waist. Diana froze for a second, a fleeting thought passed through her mind to go back up, but the black guard had a hold of her arm now. He wasn't hurting her, but he was making sure she didn't run. As she reached the ground, the crowd started running in toward them. She immediately started to pull on the black guard's grasp, but he held her tight. It was the crowd that he was addressing now.

"Stop!" he shouted, putting his hand up to reinforce it. "Do you want to tell the Sheikh that you killed his prize before he has a chance to see her? I don't think you will get much mercy from him when he finds out, do you?" Taggee stated. He could feel the urgency in Ariana to escape the mob's wrath. He was commanded to keep her safe, and that he will do until his dying breath. He noticed she stopped pulling when the crowd stopped coming. She was a tigress, full of her strength and power, but wary of dangers. He also knew that Mahdi saw it too. He would have to be extra vigilant watching her now. Mahdi would want to tame this cat.

Diana saw that the black guard was calming the crowd down. She stayed close to him as he started walking her back to the building where the women stayed. She watched every movement in the crowd; she could feel the heavy presence nipping at them. It would only be a matter of time before the Lord was going to have to deliver her—deliver her or take her home.

Taggee took Ariana back to the harem. At least for now she will be safe. Mahdi will bide his time till after the Sheikh decides. However, he noticed that Ariana was losing strength; she was also looking very pale. He heard Aisha telling Bibi that she could not get Ariana to eat or drink; she could not get her to understand. Taggee hoped that the Sheikh would come home with an interpreter or another answer tomorrow.

When Diana entered the big room, the ladies all just stared at her. She could see fear in their eyes, even with the old woman. *Too bad she didn't have that yesterday. I wouldn't have these stupid things dangling from my ears and pulling my hair*, Diana thought. She heard the old woman yell something at the black guard. He shook his head no and replied something.

Ben, I could really use your language skills right now. You wouldn't what to pass them along, would ya? she thought with a sly smile. Then that nagging thought that he might be gone from this earth ran through her head. She heard the black guard call to some of the servants, who shyly came from the corner and quietly moved Diana's bed from near the old woman's to by the window on the opposite side of the room. It was not far from Aisha's and Mahala's beds. In truth, that didn't bother Diana one bit. The black guard led her over to her new spot and let go of her arm. She looked at him and mouthed, "Thank you." He gave her a quick nod then headed out the door.

It was late afternoon; most of the ladies gave Diana a wide girth, only Aisha and Mahala came anywhere near her. At first they were timid around her as well, but when Diana signaled that she wanted to braid Mahala's hair, Mahala smiled and gladly came over to her and allowed her to fix her hair. Diana started to french braid her long dark-brown hair. She used to play with her nieces' hair all the time. Diana's heart started hurting; she missed the family. She knew her parents would be worried sick about her. Liza, Kim, Jared, and maybe even Angie were probably mad at Ben for her disappearance. Dewayne and Abbie might even be missing her by now. She wondered what was going on at home now; was the church family standing by hers? She knew Ali and his family would support them; she wasn't so sure about some of the others. *God, be with them. Help them to understand your plan. Help me to understand your plan*, she prayed.

Aisha brought over some food and a cup of coffee for Diana to eat for lunch. Diana was without food long enough that it wasn't bothering her not to eat. However, she was getting very dry; it was causing her problems otherwise. She was in a lot of pain when she went to the bathroom. Even so, for her to drink the water was out of the question. She was thinking really hard about the coffee. It was boiled; any bad stuff would have been killed with the heat. Diana took a sip and choked. She just couldn't bring herself to swallowing that tar and acid. She would have to gulp it down, and with it being hot, that wasn't possible.

Aisha was glad to see Ariana try to drink the coffee. She was worried that she would die of thirst. She saw Ariana take a sip then she started to cough. She saw Ariana shudder and sputter with the coffee. Aisha didn't know what to do; she went back over to Bibi to get her advice. Bibi just shrugged her shoulders and said, "When she gets thirsty enough, she will drink." Aisha wasn't sure about that. Ariana was very strong-willed; only Taggee seemed to be able to get her to do anything, and that was with a lot of encouragement. She made her mind up that she would talk to the Sheikh about it when he comes home tomorrow. Bibi won't be happy about it, but something must be done.

Diana sat quietly as the group did their evening prayers. She just sat looking out the window, rubbing her wrists and ankles; she was missing home terribly. She lay back and closed her eyes, thinking of the fun times she had before all this. She soon fell asleep. She woke up late in the night; the ladies were all asleep. She didn't need to use the bathroom, she didn't hear anything, so why was she was awake? She looked out the window, admiring the mountains. She unexpectedly felt a familiar pull in her spirit. She knew the feeling well: Ben was near. The question was, was he near in spirit or physically? Tears started running down her cheeks; she had to work hard not to sob out loud. Inside, her heart was breaking.

19

In Syria at the Compound

The sun came up over the mountains and hit Diana in the eyes, waking her from a restless sleep. The ladies were scurrying about in an unusual speed today. Some of the servants brought in the food for breakfast, others were cleaning the rooms, making the beds, and helping the old woman, Aisha, and Mahala get dressed. The morning call for prayer was being made. Diana sat on her bed and did her own devotions while looking out the window. She softly hummed the song, "Be Still and Know That I Am God." She felt the Lord's arms come and hold her, giving her needed strength. She didn't feel well today; the lack of water was more than likely the reason why. She knew that she was starting to run fevers. Infection was growing in her, and soon everybody would know. With the ladies' prayers done, Diana got up and headed to the bathroom. Of course with little going in, none was going out. Aisha met Diana in the hallway and led her to the room with the tub; she took the wraps off her wrists and ankles and shook her head. Aisha signaled to Diana to get in. Diana didn't hesitate; she climbed right in.

    Diana's wrists and ankles were still hurting bad; yesterday's event didn't help it at all. They were bright red and sore, but she didn't see any red lines coming from them. She tried to scrub them well, gritting her teeth the whole time, blocking out the pain shooting through her. There was only one servant in the room; she was the one that usually helped Aisha. The servant reluctantly came and scrubbed Diana's back and washed her hair. Diana smiled and gave the girl a nod. The girl gave her a quick smile but quickly got out of the water as if lightning was going to strike her. Mahala's servant girl brought a towel in for Diana and walked with her back to her area. Aisha and Mahala had already picked out what they were going to put her in. She was surprised that there was a pair of pants for her to put on. They matched the scarf she was to wear on her head. They both were in a deep purple; the linen robe and the coat was in an off-white.

Aisha gave Ariana the pants to put on; she seemed happy to have them. She herself preferred to have her legs free, but at least she got Ariana to do half smile. As she put the linen robe on, Mahala wanted to do her hair; Ariana sat down and let her go free. She smiled the whole time Mahala worked on her hair. She even closed her eyes and seemed to relax. Aisha had to work on Ariana's wrists and ankles. The ropes they used on her yesterday made them swollen and red again. She put salve on them and then wrapped them with clean wraps. Then she moved to change out Ariana's earrings. She wanted to put large hoops with small rubies hanging in the middle of them on. Aisha had trouble removing the first set of earrings. Ariana's ears were starting to heal over the posts. She turned them slowly to loosen the crust from the post. Ariana opened her eyes and bit her bottom lip. Finally, the post came through the earlobe. Aisha went and grabbed the salve again, and once the new earrings were put in, she put salve on the front and back. She had to do the same thing on the other side.

Once Mahala was done doing Ariana's hair, she put the purple hijab on. She added a delicately woven head chain over the top of it. It was three strands of gold, knotted in the back, and in the middle of the front there was attached to it a small gold diamond that had a teardrop ruby hanging in the center of it. It hung down on Ariana's forehead and tied in well with the earrings that Aisha picked out. Then Mahala attached an opaque white veil with gold trim in the hem to the hijab. She didn't pull it over her face yet. It would be needed later. The last piece that Aisha added to Ariana's outfit was a necklace. She noticed that Ariana didn't like jewelry, so she looked for something simple. She found a necklace that had a thin gold chain and only three emeralds on it in the middle. She felt it brought out the green that was showing in Ariana's eyes. When they were done making her up, Diana was led over to the old woman. Diana thought that it was to get the old woman's approval for what they did to her. The old woman came up to Diana and checked her over thoroughly.

Bibi looked at Ariana's arms and didn't like that she didn't have any bracelets on. Aisha argued that Ariana's wrists were really bad from the ropes yesterday. Bibi just scowled at her. Aisha backed down and went to get some bracelets. She tried to get the bigger ones that wouldn't ride on Ariana's wrists. She grabbed a couple of sapphires, a diamond, and a jade, a couple of pearled ones, a ruby, and an emerald bracelet and brought them to Bibi.

Bibi took the emerald and the pearl bracelet and put them on Ariana's right wrist. She grabbed the ruby bracelet but then told Aisha to get the gold herringbone to go with it. Aisha winced at the thought of the gold bracelet. It was to be tight on the wrist; it would cause Ariana's wrist to hurt. She gave Bibi a bow and went to go get it. It only took her a few minutes to put the other bracelets back and find the gold one that Bibi had asked for. She approached Bibi and gave it to her. Bibi put the gold bracelet on first, wrapping it around three times so that it molded to Ariana's arm. Then she put the ruby bracelet on the bottom to cover the wraps that she had to have on. Once that was done, she stood back and looked at the whole picture. She saw that Ariana was very pale and her face was thin. She told Aisha to line her eyes and put a plum shadow on her eyelids. It would detract from the pale skin tone. She noticed there were no rings on her, but figured that she would go without them. Aisha agreed and went to work gathering the supplies.

Mahala took Ariana back to her bed to finish what Bibi wanted. She could see that Ariana did not like the bracelets riding on her wrists, watching as Ariana was working to loosen the gold bracelet, but said nothing. She knew that Ariana had no clue why she was being clothed so finely. She looked around and saw that nobody was watching her. She adjusted the hijab and the ruby in the earrings. Then very quietly, she whispered into Ariana's ear, "The Sheikh comes home today."

Aisha heard Mahala speak English to Ariana. It was strictly forbidden for any of the compound to speak anything other than the old language; she called Mahala down immediately. If she was heard by Bibi or any of the men, Mahala would be whipped. Mahala recoiled from being caught speaking anything other than Farsi or what Bibi called the old language; she sank back behind Ariana. Looking at Aisha, Mahala realized that it was a warning and not to do it again.

Diana was surprised to hear English spoken here. When Aisha called Mahala down, she gave no indication that she heard anything; she did not want Mahala to be in trouble. She thought the man yesterday was the Sheikh, but Mahala said he is coming home today. So who was the other guy? There were just too many questions and not enough answers. She would have to continue to wait until things were revealed. The one thing Diana knew, some of the people knew English but were not allowed to speak it. She wondered if the black guard knew English as well, but why were they not allowed to speak it? It would help solve a lot of questions if they would talk to her. Diana did her best to hold still when Aisha started to line her eyes. She knew better than to fight it; at least it wasn't foreign to her. She often used eyeliner when she dressed up for Halloween. Though to Diana, the girls were putting the black on very thick. The liner felt different than the stuff she normally used. It was heavier and oilier than hers. Aisha signed that she wanted Diana to close her eyes, so Diana did. It allowed Aisha to put eye shadow on as well.

20

On the USS *Wilson*

Scott and Ben started the morning by checking in with Dick. Dick told them that they had a suspect to who was leaking the intel to the terrorist. As of yet, he had not been arrested. Also apparently, the Sheikh was looking for an interpreter. The word on the wind is that he has a new business adventure that they can't communicate with.

"About how many soldiers does the Sheikh have under him?" Ben asked.

"According to the latest intel, there are about forty to fifty men. The obstacle is his second in command…Mahdi. He's the backbone behind the Sheikh. He's ruthless, brutal, cruel, and methodical," Dick concluded.

"How many women do they have in the compound?" Scott asked.

"As far as we know, the Sheikh has four wives, each has a female servant. However, there are two main bodyguards—at least one is always on duty. Other guards may help out, but supposedly only these two men are allowed in."

"Three guesses as to why only these two and the first two don't count," Ben stated.

"The rest of the guards are either single or live outside the compound. So what's the next step?" Dick inquired.

"I'm gonna get into the compound today," Ben informed Dick.

"How ya gonna to accomplish that, Tiger?" Dick probed.

"Well, you said he needs an interpreter, so I'm gonna make myself overly available," Ben stated.

"I'm not sure it would be a good idea going in there with no help," Dick protested.

"What am I, chopped liver?" Scott quibbled.

Dick really didn't like the fact that Scott took over his place as Ben's partner. What made it worse was that Scott was just as high moraled as Ben. The two together made it impossible for him. "Oh…I forgot about you, Mr. McCleary," Dick replied.

"Scott is going to be the contact person between you and me," Ben stated flatly.

"Oh…and just how is he supposed to contact you while you're in the compound?" Dick asked.

"Ancient Chinese secret." Ben stated smiling.

"Fine…keep your **** secrets. Just don't choke on them," Dick said annoyed.

Ben smiled. "We've got to get going, pard. We'll keep you in the loop as much as possible." The men signed off and went to the conference room to go over their plan. "He really doesn't like me, does he?" Scott detected.

"Don't take it to heart bro. He's surround by morality, it makes him uncomfortable. He has bets out that he'll get me defiled this year. You're threatening that plan," Ben added.

Scott just rolled his eyes. "Haven't you been with him the last three years? He hasn't learned yet?"

"Obviously not," Ben replied.

"So how are we going to get you in the compound as an interpreter?" Scott asked.

The captain walked into the room with some papers in his hands. He informed the guys that the Sheikh and one of his wives has been staying in Damascus this past week. It's been said that he's interviewing for an interpreter. The guys looked at each other and smiled. "Thank you, Lord," Ben said, looking up to heaven.

"Now, how are we going to stay in touch?" Scott asked.

"Remember how to do your calls, don't you?" Ben asked.

"Of course…oh, okay…I gotcha. Now what about if you get into trouble?" Scott continued.

"We'll just have to wing it. Time's running out for her, I can feel it," Ben said somberly.

"Trust the Lord, bro. He said He's with her. He's got it all planned out," Scott encouraged.

"I just wish I knew the who, the what, and more importantly the why from Him," Ben pondered.

"You and me both, Ben. I guess He will tell us in His own time, just hang on," Scott deliberated. The guys got their equipment set up and packed. Ben was dropped off just before sunup outside of Qatana.

Scott was dropped off in the mountains to the northeast of the compound. The guys would have to walk to their destination from the drop points. Scott hightailed it to a cave he saw when they were scoping the compound out last night. He made it there just before eight a.m. He checked the cave to make sure nobody or nothing else was already using it, hid his tracks, and camouflaged the cave so that it looked like it wasn't there. Then he began setting up camp. Ben made it to Damascus just before noon. He walked down the main street, interacting with the locals, making sure they knew he spoke both English and Farsi. He stopped and chatted with people in one of the hotel lobby, a historical building, and then went to the street markets. He seemed to be getting nowhere. *Lord...I need your help here*, he prayed. Ben walked over to the end of the street and sat down on a bench next to spice cart. He adjusted his sunglasses and watched as the people were visiting and buying different things. He chanced to look over to the table where the person was selling rugs. An Englishman was trying to buy a specific rug, but the vendor was presenting him with a different one. Ben walked to the Englishman. "Do you want some help?" he asked.

"Oh yes, please. I want that small purple-and-green rug over in the corner, but this gentleman keeps trying to give me this black-and-red one," the Englishman stated.

Ben easily told the vendor what the Englishman wanted. The vendor explained to Ben that the rug the Englishman wanted had already been bought. Ben turned to the Englishman and explained the dilemma that the vendor was having. "Well bloody Nora! It would have been the bees' knees in my tea room. Ah well," the Englishman stated. The Englishman thanked Ben for his help then tipped his hat to the vendor and walked away. Ben also thanked the vendor and walked back to the bench. He sat there a few minutes and then walked over to the vendor selling teas. He asked if she sold chamomile tea; she told him no. He waited another thirty minutes before he figured he had spent enough time here and started walking away. As he was heading out of the street market area, two men came up beside him. One of them tapped him on the shoulder. Ben turned around to address the man.

"Do you understand what I am saying?" the man asked talking in Farsi.

Ben replied in Farsi, "Yes, I speak your language."

Then the man said, "You need to come with us. We would like to offer you a job."

Ben looked at the men and said, "Excuse me?"

"Our boss is having a problem communicating with a new business endeavor. He would like to offer you a job as an interpreter for him," the man stated.

"Well, I'd like to see what the terms are first," Ben added. All the time he was thanking the Lord for opening the door.

"Please come with us," the man said. Ben followed the men to a limo in the street over from the market. One of the men opened the door and signaled to Ben to get in. Ben climbed into the limo only to be face-to-face with the Sheikh. Off to the side of him was a woman. "So you are the man whom the tea woman said spoke our language."

"Yes sir, I'm James…James Johnson. I speak several languages. I'm working on a thesis about languages and cultures," Ben said.

"Are you a professor or something?" the Sheikh asked.

Ben shook his head no. "I'm working on my master's degree, sir."

"Aren't you a little old for being in school?" the Sheikh said skeptically.

"Yeah…some thought so. I had to put my master's degree on hold. I got married and money became tight. Just recently, money became more available, so I started working on my master's again," Ben replied.

The Sheikh seemed to accept Ben's response. "I am going to offer you a chance to get up close with our culture and language," the Sheikh gleamed. The limo doors locked, and the car started to pull away from the curb. Ben acted startled and tried the doors. The glass that separated the driver's seat and the back area dropped down. The man that showed Ben to the limo sat, holding a gun at Ben.

"You best just settle down. I'd hate to have to clean up the leather when we get home," he threatened.

Ben sat back in the seat. He put on a dejected face for the men; inside he was doing backflips. *Thank you… Thank you.… Thank you, Lord*, he prayed. It took about an hour before the limo Ben was taken in pulled into the compound. Ben looked around everywhere to see if he could get a glimpse of Diana. The limo pulled to a stop in front of a large double door, doomed building. The men opened the limo door; the Sheikh stepped out, adjusted his sunglasses, and walked toward the double doors. Then the woman stepped out and headed across the compound. The two guys stood waiting for Ben to get out of the limo. Ben came out slowly looking around. The two guys lost patience and pulled him the rest of the way out and pushed him toward the doors. They flanked him and took him into the large building. He saw that there was an open-aired courtyard in the center of the building. The Sheikh went through and into his room. The two men took Ben into a small room off to the right. They locked the door and left Ben alone in the room.

Luckily, the men didn't do a search of Ben's pockets. He reached in and pulled a small microphone out; it looked like a tooth cap. Ben quickly put it in over his molar and bit down to secure it. The microphone had a 120-hour battery, so he had five days to get Diana and himself out. He hoped he'd make it out in three. There weren't any windows in the room and just a bed along the wall. There was no way he could do a mic check with Scott 'til he gets outside.

He sat in the room for another hour before a guard came in. "You… come out here. Don't make any sudden moves, or you will be shot where you stand," the guard told him. Ben walked out slowly from the room. There was a crowd of men grouped around the courtyard. The Sheikh was sitting on a platform in an old, ornate Moorish chair. There was an awning over him to give him shade. There was a man standing to his right; Ben figured he was the Sheikh's right-hand man, Mahdi.

Ben pulled his sunglasses slowly out of his pocket and put them on as the guard led him to the left of the Sheikh's stand, the Sheikh addressed the crowd of mostly men. "Here is the answer to our problem. Mr. James is going to be our interpreter."

Ben sheepishly raised his hand. "Ah, sir, you have not told me who I will be interpreting for or what I will be paid for my services."

Mahdi glared at Ben. The Sheikh simply said, "You will meet your student soon. As far as what you will be paid, you will be given a place to sleep, food, and water. If you do not agree to these terms, you will be given to the ISIS group for them to do as they wish. Do you agree to these terms?"

"Hmm…I don't think I have much of a choice, sir. So, yes, I'll agree to your terms," Ben replied.

"Good…now that we have that business done, tell Taggee to bring Ariana to me," the Sheikh said to one of the guards by the door. The guard gave a quick bow and headed out the door. Ben stood almost in shock. Ariana was the name of the woman in his dream way back when. *Maybe it is a common name in this area*, he thought.

Ariana was ushered to the door of the ladies' building. Aisha attached her veil and smiled at her. Diana noticed that Aisha, Mahala, and the old woman all had a black scarf and black robe on. They didn't cover their face though. As Diana walked out the door, she met the black guard. He brought his hands out from behind his back; there was a cord in his hands. Diana looked up at his eyes. He said something and then moved toward her. She stood there watching what he was going to do.

He was still talking to her, keeping his voice calm and smooth. When he reached her, he reached down and took one of her arms. He tied the cord around her wrist. Then took the other wrist and tied them together.

Well, I guess this is what I get for running yesterday, Diana thought. The black guard didn't yank or pull on the cord; he simply put his hand on her back and guided her across the courtyard. He kept a hold of the cord, but it mostly just hung loose. Aisha and the other woman walked in front of her. As they neared the double doors, they opened, and the women walked in. Diana could hear the crowd of men on the other side; she hesitated. The black guard simply patted her shoulder and led her in. The crowd parted for the black guard, and Diana followed him. He stopped just behind the other women. One of the guards came and took the cord from the black guard. He pulled on it and jerked Diana out into the courtyard. The sun was starting to set, but it was high enough that it was hitting Diana in the eyes. She couldn't see much, but she was feeling a lot. She felt the cold dark presence all around her. She was also feeling Ben; he was near.

Ben looked at the woman that the big guard brought in. He felt that magnetic connection stir through him, Diana was near, but he couldn't see her. The woman was in a dark-purple hijab and an off-white tunic. She was decked out with pearls and rubies. She had an emerald necklace that was just slightly showing through the white veil that covered her face. Her eyes where heavily lined and shaded with purple eye shadow, but she kept them closed. Her face looked drawn, and her skin pale. Ben just about blew the whole operation when he heard the woman say in Spanish, "¿Son físicamente o sólo en espíritu?"

Ariana is Diana! Ben realized. He replied to her in Spanish, "Abre los ojos y ver."

"No puedo, el sol está en mis ojos," Diana stated in Spanish.

With that, the Sheikh slammed his hands down on the arm of the chair. "What is she speaking? Is she not American?" he fumed.

"She is speaking Spanish, sir. There are many Americans that speak Spanish only. However, I will find out if she speaks English in a minute. What she was saying was that she cannot see, the sun is hitting her in the eyes and making them hurt," Ben informed the Sheikh. The Sheikh motioned for her to move forward. The guard jerked on the cord and pulled her into the shadow of the awning. Ben saw Diana wince at the pressure of the cord. He was also surprised that the guard that brought her was obviously upset at the harsh jerk on her "leash."

Once the sun was out of Diana's eyes, she opened them; she nearly fainted. "Dicen que lo mataron," she told Ben.

Ben saw that her eyes were green—not the emerald green he saw in the cabin, but a type of jade green brought on by the purple in the hijab. He recognized the eyes he currently saw were the same eyes he saw in his dream way back when. A lump formed in his throat. Ben glanced over toward the Sheikh. He saw that the Sheikh was getting mad. "Do you speak English, ma'am?" he asked Diana.

Diana heard the anger in the Sheikh's words, even without understanding what he was saying. She also realized that Ben was not letting the people know that he knew her, she stayed very formal. "Yes, I speak English, sir," she replied.

The Sheikh sat back in his chair. "Good, she is from the land of the eagle," he said satisfied. "Mr. James, ask her to tell me about the scars on her stomach," he commanded.

Ben didn't know she had scars on her stomach. *Duh...she had cancer, idiot*, he chided himself. "The Sheikh wants to know about some scars on your stomach? Ben asked.

Diana stood straight, her eyes changed to the steel gray. "Ask him why he needs to know that for?"

Ben interpreted what she said for the Sheikh. He was not happy with her reply but knew that she was very private. "These American men have let their women have too much freedom. They need to learn respect again," the Sheikh replied and nodded to Mahdi. Mahdi came down and stood in front of Diana, raised his hand, and backhanded her across the face. Diana's face flew to the side; it stung, but the slap only steeled her mind into not sharing any info.

Ben had a hard time holding himself still. They would kill both of them if he blew his cover. He happened to look over at the big guard. He could see in the guard's eyes that he was just as upset about her being slapped. He felt that in some ways this guard was going to be an ally to his endeavor. He looked back over to Diana, who had regained her composure. He also saw that all the guard did was set her resolve. The Sheikh told Ben to re-ask the question. Ben again asked, "He wants you to tell him about your scars, ma'am."

"It is my business, not his. It is my body, not his," Diana replied.

Although Ben didn't want to interpret her reply, he reluctantly did. Diana would not have spoken in Spanish if she was sure no one else spoke English. The Sheikh nodded to Mahdi. Mahdi smiled, turned, and slapped Diana again; she fell to the ground.

Ben wasn't going to be able to stand by much longer; luckily, he didn't have to. One of the ladies dressed in black came running forward. She bowed before the Sheikh. "Milord, the warrior in white warned us not to hurt this woman. Please, stop Mahdi or we will be cursed," she implored. Ben wondered who this warrior in white was. "Where was he now?"

The Sheikh held up his hand for her to stop. "Bibi said she had strength. We just need to teach her respect," he replied. The woman backed up and returned to the other ladies. She was sad, and Ben could see she was worried for Diana. Diana stood up and glared at the Sheikh and the man that was hitting her.

Ben had to do something before Mahdi broke her jaw. "Ma'am, it might be best to tell him. It does not do any good to be beaten for something so trivial," he said to her.

Diana was furious as she looked over to Ben. She could see that it was tormenting him to see her being hit. He was to protect her, and she was putting it at risk. She weighed the pros and cons. It hurt no one to tell where the scars came from; she only had to swallow her pride. "Tell him it is the result of having the disease of cancer and the treatment thereof," she finally replied.

Ben told the Sheikh what Diana said. "Why so many cuts?" the Sheikh asked.

Ben interpreted his question. Diana's ire was growing. "One was the main cut to take the cancer out. Another was needed to bypass my lower intestine 'til I was done with the chemotherapy. Some of the others were so they could drain the fluids or hook in pain medication. Anything else you want to ask that you don't need to know?" she sputtered.

Ben knew that that reply would get another slap, but he interpreted what she said. Sure enough, Mahdi, this time with a closed-hand, struck Diana again. Ben could see he was thoroughly enjoying what he was doing. It was the big guard who stepped forward to Diana's aid. He bowed to the Sheikh. "Milord, she will be no good to Allah beaten to death," he stated.

"He has been the only one to control this woman, milord. He just doesn't want to lose his power over her," Mahdi declared. "Give her to me, milord, and I will make her pliable." Diana just stood there watching the conversation between the black guard, the Sheikh, and the man who was hitting her. She didn't have a clue of what was going on. She could only stand and watch and try to get the stars out of her head.

"No…not yet, Mahdi. If she proves to be unworthy, then you may have her," the Sheikh replied. Then he turned to Taggee. "You have been able to control her, huh? Then get her to drink something before she collapses. Aisha, bring some wine," he commanded.

Aisha bowed, turned, and went to the table near the awning. She poured some wine in a glass and gave it to Taggee. Taggee turned and tried to get Ariana to drink it. She only shook her head no. "Come, tigress, you need to drink something. It will be good for you," he told her.

Diana didn't know what was in the cup that the black guard was giving her; she could only shake her head no. She couldn't risk it. The Sheikh watched the whole event. Finally, he said, "Taggee, give the cup to Mr. James. See if he can get her to drink it."

Taggee turned to James. "You get her to understand, this is her last day if she does not drink. Soon her kidneys will shut down, and she will die," he informed Ben. That was why he needed to get to her today. It must be close to three days if they are worried about her kidneys shutting down. Ben took his sunglasses off; then took the cup and walked over to Diana, followed closely by Taggee. He stood in front of Diana; he was close enough to see that she was beyond dehydrated—she was sick. He held the cup up for her, but Diana just looked at it.

Ben took a big drink. "It is just wine, Milady, it will help your system. Take it."

Diana slowly reached up and took it, hesitantly put it under her veil, and took a sip. It was bitter and burned her throat. She coughed several times.

Ben turned to Taggee but said it loud enough for all to hear him, "I don't think she has ever drank wine before."

"Make her drink it all," the Sheikh commanded. "It will loosen her tongue as well." Ben didn't bother to tell her why the Sheikh wanted her to drink it all. He wanted her to drink it all because with almost three days of no liquid, she had to have an infection growing. "Drink it all, Milady, you need it in you."

Diana didn't want to drink any more, but she saw the worry in Ben's eyes; she couldn't tell him no. She finished the cup, slowly so she didn't start coughing again. Taggee saw that the cup was gone and held his hand out for it. Diana handed it to him; he went and refilled it and gave it back to her. She slowly drank the new cup. She could feel her body tingle with the infusion of liquid. She also was starting to feel dizzy. She drank half of the cup but gave the rest back to the black guard. He smiled and told her, "Well done, tigress, well done."

Ben stood by and watched the black guard interact with Diana. He could see that he cared for her. His attention was commanded by the Sheikh. However, he was allowed to stand near her. "Now, Mr. James, ask her if she has had children," the Sheikh commanded.

THE VIRGIN MOTHER

"Milady, the Sheikh would like to know if you have had any children," Ben stated matter-of-factly. Diana was feeling light-headed. She didn't like the feeling at all, and she weaved where she was standing. Ben tried to steady her, which brought a response of guards rushing in to pull him away from her. Ben held up his hands in surrender; the guards shoved him away from her and took him back to the other side of the platform. Taggee came and steadied Ariana. He wasn't blind; he knew that there was a connection between these two. He just didn't know what it was yet; he held his tongue. Ben repeated the question once Taggee had steadied Diana. "Milady, they want to know if you have had children. Are you still a virgin?"

Diana turned and glared at Ben. "The answer is no, I have not had a baby. I can't have children. They know full well I am a virgin. Their doctor has already checked that," she emphasized. Ben felt rage burn in his stomach' he knew she was hurt with their "physical," and he felt her pain. He was able to control is rage and calmly interpret what Diana said to the Sheikh.

To Ben's surprise, the Sheikh jumped up and clapped his hands. "See, Allah has made this woman to be his chosen one. You will tell her everything I say, Mr. James," the Sheikh commanded. Ben simply nodded. "You, Ariana, have been chosen to carry the son of Allah, Mohamed reincarnated, the new Messiah. He will bring the three great religions together and rule the world. He will be of the chosen race, born of a mother from the land of the eagle, a virgin prepared by Allah. Her son will bring the holy war, the jihad, to reorder the world," the Sheikh declared. His men cheered and clapped. Ben was in utter disbelief of the Sheikh's insanity. It was Diana that put everything to a halt. She threw her head back and laughed a hard, despising laugh. The Sheikh's face went red with rage.

"You are totally insane, sir. The Jews will never accept a Messiah from another race, even if you are cousins. Their Messiah comes from the house of David. The Christian's know the Messiah has already come, and I don't believe Islam will accept an American as the 'virgin' mother," she declared. Mahdi came and punched her in the face, knocking her unconscious. He went to kick her as well, but Taggee stepped in and intervened.

Taggee glared at Mahdi; Mahdi weighed whether or not he wanted to take Taggee on. He smiled an evil smile and backed down then turned and returned to the right side of the Sheikh. The Sheikh looked at Ben. "You will tell me exactly what Ariana said. Leave nothing out. I want to know word for word."

Ben told the Sheikh exactly what Diana said. Seeing how Mahdi didn't wait for an interpretation, he knew that Mahdi and probably a few others, knew English. Confirming the reason why Diana spoke in Spanish, she knew they would be listening to what she said. *Thank you for using your brain, girl,* he thought.

Diana started to come around; Taggee squatted down next to her. "Taggee, take Ariana back to her quarters. Aisha, check on her bruises," the Sheikh stated.

Taggee leaned down and scooped Diana up into his arms. "Come on, tigress, let's get you home," he said. He left the courtyard followed by Aisha.

Before he walked out the doors, the Sheikh called out, "When you get done with her, come back here. I have a new charge for you to keep an eye on." He was looking over at Ben as he finished. Taggee simply nodded in comprehension.

Taggee carried Ariana all the way to her bed. He carefully checked her jaw, hoping it wasn't broken. Even though it wasn't, he could see the bruising showing up already. Aisha came in. "I'll take care of the rest, Taggee. Go ahead and head back to the Sheikh before Mahdi kills the interpreter as well." She was not happy with the Sheikh letting Mahdi strike Ariana. The warrior in white will surely curse the compound now.

The Sheikh addressed Ben now. "You called Ariana Milady, why? Do you know this woman?" he implied.

"Milady is an old English term we use to honor women in authority. However, I know what family this woman comes from. It is obvious to me in her eyes," Ben coolly replied.

"You mean because they change colors?" the Sheikh pried.

"Yes and no, hazel eyes are not uncommon in America, many have them. It's something else I see in them that confirms it to me," Ben declared. "She is a child of the King," he stated.

"America doesn't have a king. Do you mean the president?" the Sheikh asked.

"No, her father is not in this realm. He is the Maker of all here—everything. I see Him in her eyes. He will not look kindly to her being hurt." He had hoped to put a little fear into the men here; it would give her a little protection. He didn't realize the fire that was already burning here about her. An older woman approached the Sheikh; she didn't bow, didn't stop at the bottom of the steps. She boldly approached him. "See, my husband, she needs to be killed or given to the factions. She is a danger to us here. The women are scared of her, only Aisha and

Mahala go around her. She will teach rebellion to them," the older woman affirmed.

"Calla, what is your opinion with this? You were with her in the plane and at the clinic," the Sheikh asked. Bibi didn't like that her husband asking for Calla's opinion. She was his first; he should listen to her.

"I know that your security guard on the plane got his hands smashed by a luggage conveyor the day after he struck Ariana for trying to look out the plane's window. The ones that gave her the physical at the clinic were injured a couple of days later by an oxygen tank exploding, which wouldn't mean much except only those four were injured. The security guard at the clinic, the one you gave the horse to and said he could cane her here at the compound, was bucked off that same horse and drug through a cane field, cutting his back up. There are a lot of events that seem to revolve around those hurting Ariana," Calla replied with a bow.

"Mr. James, do you believe in curses like my wives do?" the Sheikh asked.

"I don't know whether I believe in curses or not, but I do not believe in coincidences," Ben replied.

"I will think about it, Bibi. Till then, she stays in the harem," the Sheikh replied. "You on the other hand, Mr. James, you are going to stay in a cell near Taggee. You make any unwarranted attempts on Ariana and he'll rip you apart. Is that understood? You are to teach Ariana the pure language and interpret for us until she understands," he ended.

Taggee, who came in while Calla was talking, bowed to the Sheikh and eyed Ben. Ben had no doubt that if Taggee thought he was a threat to Diana, he would do what the Sheikh said. "Take him to a room above yours, Taggee," Mahdi stated.

Taggee signaled to Ben, and Ben followed him out of the courtyard. Outside the building, Ben had the chance to find where Taggee stood with the Sheikh's plan.

"You called Ariana *bermadeh*. I didn't know that there were tigers in this area?" he commented.

"I was not raised here. Where I am from, there are tigers. Ariana, unlike the other girls Amid sent here, didn't bawl or cower like a mouse. She is strong and powerful but weary like a cat. When she first came here, the girls tried to get her to take a bath. She didn't understand what they were wanting and fought them. I was asked to take her robe from her. She went and grabbed a knife and backed into a corner to defend herself. I looked into her eyes and saw that she didn't want to hurt anybody, she was just scared. It was then that I saw that if you come against her with force, she will attack. If you come to her calmly, she will yield, just like a cat," Taggee expounded.

"You are the only one who can control her then?" Ben asked.

"Until you…yes," he replied.

"She only listened to me because she understood me," Ben replied to blow off suspicion. "If she is like a cat, maybe you should give her warm milk to get her to drink," he added. He knew full well that Diana would drink milk. It would be a way of getting liquid into her. He looked at Taggee; he noticed was in deep thought. *Lord, help him to understand*, he prayed. Taggee took Ben to his house, led him upstairs, and showed him the room that he would be staying in. "You will stay here. Oh, by the way, if you do try to do anything against Ariana, I will personally see to it you do not see another day," Taggee stated flatly. He locked the door once Ben was inside.

Ben's room wasn't much bigger than the room in the Sheikh's house, but here there was a window. He would hear Scott now. "Did you hear everything that happened bro?" Ben said. He heard an owl call from the northwest. "Then you know that we can't leave tonight. She's sick. They may not know it yet, but I can see it in her eyes. She'll need at least two days of liquid. I hope Taggee took the hint. I highly doubt she's eating yet either. The Lord will have to open that door. Don't get yourself caught. That's an order," Ben said out loud. A coyote howled; Ben smiled and lay down on the bed.

That evening, Aisha brought a cup of warm milk over to Ariana along with some meat and bread. Ariana looked at the cup, smelt it, and smiled. She sipped at the milk until it was gone, but she did not eat any of the meat or bread. *At least she is drinking something now*, Aisha thought. There was a lone coyote calling outside the wall. *They usually don't come this close*, she thought.

21

In Syria at the Compound

Ben awoke to the rapping on the door; he sat up as the door opened. Taggee opened the door for one of the Sheikh's wives. She entered the room, her face covered with her hijab. Taggee came in and stood by the door. "I need your help, Mr. James," she requested.

"I will try my best, ma'am. What is it I can do for you?" Ben replied.

"I am Aisha, I have been with Ariana since America. She will not eat. Bibi, the Sheikh's first wife, keeps saying she will eat when she's hungry enough, but she's getting sick. She will die soon if I don't do something. I need you to explain to her that she must eat," she implored.

"When my wife had cancer, she had a lot of broths and crackers. Her stomach couldn't handle spices and strange foods. Maybe you should try those," he said simply. It was the first time he talked about Katherine and didn't feel sad or angry; it was surprising and refreshing.

"Your wife had cancer? I would think it would be hard to leave her alone and come over here," Aisha stated.

"My wife died from cancer. Ariana is a strong woman to have come through it like she seems to have," he advised.

"Yes, she is strong. That is not a good thing for us. I mean women, here. She was lucky Mahdi didn't try to break her jaw last night. Anyway, you will come and explain to her that she must eat?" Aisha asked.

Ben looked over to Taggee. "I'm not sure Taggee will allow me to be near Ariana, especially where she's at right now."

"Arrangements can be made for a meeting in a different place. You are to be teaching her the pure language, if you recall," Taggee injected.

"I will do what I can, ma'am," Ben stated. Aisha bowed, turned, and headed for the door. Taggee opened it for her, and as she walked through, he turned and stated, "I would suggest you get cleaned up. We wouldn't want to ruin her appetite before it even starts." Then he closed and locked the door.

Ben looked at his shirt, smelled it, and turned green. "Yeah, I guess I do smell like something dragged around by Pete." He found a basin filled with water and towels off to the side. He was busy washing up when Taggee came back in. In his arm were a tunic, pants, and a scarf for him to put on.

"Why did Ariana talk to you in the language of Spanish?" Taggee asked.

"I'm not sure. Maybe she thought I was Hispanic. I was dirty enough to look like one. From the gist I'm getting, she has had no one to talk to for several days. She was probably grasping at straws," he surmised.

Taggee sat looking at him. He saw the scar on his shoulder and side. He also saw a new injury up on his chest. *He must be a soldier for somebody*, he noted. Taggee also recognized the same spirit in him that he saw in Ariana. A little more polished maybe. He was a cool calm one where Ariana was the fervent, passionate one. *Yes…they are two sides of the same soul*, Taggee thought. Then he frowned; he was the servant of the Sheikh; he must do as he is told. He must keep Ariana pure for her to be given to Allah.

Ben saw that he was being "scanned." He wondered what was going through Taggee's mind. What was he thinking? "You look like you just ate a persimmon. Did I miss a spot or something?" Ben asked.

Taggee just looked at him. *Cooler, slyer than Ariana, but the same soul*, he thought. "We must be going," he said to avoid Ben's question. He stood and opened the door; Ben walked through it and down the stairs. As they left Taggee's house, Ben slipped on his sunglasses. Taggee led Ben over to a table that had been set up outside the harem. There was an awning put up over it to shade the users. Taggee waved his hand for Ben to take a chair.

Aisha came over to Ariana with milk and some cheese. Ariana drank the milk quickly and did pick up a piece of cheese. She was looking at it carefully; she took a taste of the piece she picked up then finished the rest of it. However, she didn't take another. Aisha checked on her wrists and ankles and saw that they were not healing as fast as she thought they should. She went ahead and put the salve on and rewrapped them. Mahala and Aisha had picked out a green hijab and a lighter-green tunic. The veil was a pale-peach color with white pearls sewn on it. This time, Bibi didn't require bracelets, but she was to wear earrings and a necklace. Mahala picked out a simple pearl necklace, so Aisha picked out plain gold hoop earrings. With the inspection done with, Aisha took Ariana out to the table.

Diana liked the color of the scarf and coat but wished she didn't have to wear all the jewelry. She was glad that they started bringing her milk. It was richer than she was used to. She figured it was more than likely goat's milk, but at least she was drinking liquid. She tried the cheese, but she just wasn't that hungry. She followed Aisha out of the building; her heart jumped to see Ben sitting at a table. She worked to gain control; she didn't want Ben beheaded in front of her, nor did she want Ben to read her. She also saw the black guard standing nearby, watching her intently. *Keep everything formal, girl*, she told herself.

Aisha signaled for her to sit down. Diana sat carefully, working to not look at Ben's eyes. She may not be able to read him, but he could read her. "Mr. James," she stated.

Ben was glad she was keeping things cool. *Well done, babe*, he thought. He saw that the green scarf made Diana's eyes a sky blue. He also saw that though there was more life in her eyes, she was still quite sick. He was gonna have to work fast. "Milady, I have been instructed to teach you their language. Apparently, my well-being is dependent on it," he informed her.

"You definitely have a task before you sir. My name is—" Diana was saying, but Ben interrupted her.

"I've been told your name is Ariana. Would you like me to use that instead of Milady, or would you prefer to be called what our chaperon calls you?" he stated.

"What does my large friend call me?" Diana asked.

"He calls you a *bermadeh*. It means 'tigress,'" Ben said.

Diana's eyebrow arched up, her face stern. "I had a couple of good friends, one of them was called tiger. They told me that they killed him. I don't know what happened to my other friend."

She wouldn't look at him; she didn't want him to read her, but he heard her meanings between words. "I'm sorry they did that. Since they didn't say anything about your other friend, I would say he is alive."

Diana looked up and glanced at Ben. Her eyes flashed. "For now, I suppose it would be best to call me Ariana. Since you are to teach me their language, you can start by telling me their names. What is the name of my defender standing there?" she asked.

"Our chaperon's name is Taggee. He is the main guard of the Sheikh's harem," Ben informed her.

"Harem? I've been staying in the harem? If he thinks I'm gonna marry him, he's got another thing coming," she flatly stated.

Ben saw her eyes flash gray. The old Diana was still there; they haven't even begun to break her yet. "I'm not sure that is his plan from what I understood from yesterday afternoon. Now, back to lessons," Ben continued. "The Sheikh has four wives. You already know Aisha, and I believe you know Mahala, the newest one. The older woman is his first wife, Bibi. The other is Calla."

"That fourteen-year-old child is the Sheikh's wife! That is insane," Diana fumed.

"Milady, this is a different culture. Learn it quickly. Your life may depend on it," Ben said carefully.

Diana looked over to Taggee. She saw that he was getting agitated. "Your name is Taggee." She saw that he didn't understand her, so she looked over to Ben.

Ben turned and interpreted what Diana said. Taggee in turn bowed to Diana and smiled. "Okay…now, the next area, the food," Ben insisted with an impish gleam in his eyes.

Diana looked at him like a deer in the headlights. *Busted*, she thought. She went to try to explain herself, but Ben interrupted her by going on about the different types of foods typical of the area. He told her how they were made and what was in them. It was good that Ben did interrupt her; she could have blown his cover trying to explain herself. "I'm not sure my insides would handle any of this stuff," she stated shyly.

"I would suggest maybe some broth from lamb or a vegetable broth. Especially if you have problems with foods," Ben informed her. "The one thing that is important is that you tell people what you need… or know."

Diana looked at him; she wished he would take those stupid sunglasses off so she could see his eyes, and yet maybe it's best she didn't. She knew exactly what he was hinting at. Why did she not tell him about what she was sensing? "Some things can't be explained or should come from the official source," she slung back at him.

Ben simply gave her a nod of understanding. While they were talking, Aisha's servant girl came and left a tray of meats, bread, and cheeses, bowed, and left. Mahala's servant girl brought over a couple of cups and some coffee, bowed, and left. Diana looked at the food and coffee and shuddered. Ben could see that she turned a little green around the gills. He turned to Taggee. "Can Ariana have some chamomile tea and some milk?"

Taggee signaled to the girls standing nearby. He told them to bring some tea and milk to Ariana. They bowed and scurried off to get what they needed. Soon they came back with a small steaming pot and glass of milk. They placed it in front of Ariana and backed away.

Diana looked at the steaming pot. It was ornate with its white ceramic base with blue filigree. The steam was wafting up in delicate strings from the pour spout. She caught a whiff of the steam and smelled chamomile; she glanced up at Ben. He smiled at her behind his coffee cup. She reached up and poured a little in her cup, brought it up to her nose and smelled it, then slowly took a sip. She reached over and added a little milk from the glass given to her and then took another sip of her tea. She smiled and gave Ben and Taggee a nod. Taggee smiled at her, and Ben gave her a nod back.

Ben was pleased at Diana's response. He couldn't help but feel admiration and appreciation for everything she has gone through. He would love to be in a different setting and situation. He knew there were barbs going through her head that she's holding back. She was doing her best to stay neutral, but she couldn't hide the glimmers that shoot through her eyes. He had to give it to her; she tried her very level best. The best she could do to hide it was to look down so no one could see her eyes.

Taggee called a halt to the lessons for the time being. It was coming up to suppertime; he could see that Ariana was getting tired, and the Sheikh wanted everybody to eat together tonight. Aisha came and took Ariana inside. Taggee took Ben back over to his room. "We will be eating with the Sheikh tonight. Get yourself prepared," he told Ben.

Diana was allowed to lie down for a while. She was glad to have tea to drink, but it wasn't sitting as well as she hoped on her stomach. She closed her eyes for just a minute, but fell asleep. She awoke to Aisha shaking her, calling Ariana. She opened her eyes, noticing it was dark outside now. It was cold, and she shivered as it spread across her. She had a hard time getting herself motivated. Aisha and her servant quickly got her changed and ready to go to dinner. Diana finally got herself focused and mentally prepared for the evening's escapades. They quickly walked out the door, meeting up with Taggee to escort them to the Sheikh's abode. Diana struggled to focus her eyes on where she was going. *Come on, girl, wake up,* she told herself.

They entered the building and were led to a side room. The doors opened up to a huge room, lavishly decorated with red curtains with gold tassels and purple cushions. There were three large crystal chandeliers hanging from the ceiling, gold candlesticks lining the tables, and china plates that looked like they came directly from China themselves. Each place setting had a gold goblet, a crystal wine glass, and gold engraved silverware. Diana just stood there in awe. Taggee saw that Ariana was amazed at the richly decorated room. He reached down, putting his hand in the middle of her back, and guided her to her seat near the Sheikh. He thought that she looked paler then before but threw it out thinking it was the pink hijab that made her look that way. He waved to Ariana to sit down on the cushion; she did so without rebuttal. Then he turned and stood behind Ariana by the wall.

Mr. James was sat next to her so that he could interpret what was being said not only by the Sheikh but by Ariana. Several other people were sitting around the table. The Sheikh's four wives were seated one chair down and across from them. Mahdi took the first cushion on the opposite side of Diana. There were several people that Ben didn't recognize seated at the table. Ben glanced over to Diana, and didn't like what he saw. Diana's eyes were red and swollen. *She has fever eyes*, he thought. She was very pale, almost white as a sheet. He had hoped that the fluids going into her would improve her health. It may have been too much too fast. The Sheikh came in and sat down at the head of the table. Once he sat down, the servants brought the food they were to eat. The first course was a *gundi*, a chicken-based soup with chickpea dumplings. Diana slowly ate the broth of the soup; she couldn't bring herself to eat the balls floating in it. The broth felt good going down her throat; but felt like a lead ball in her stomach. The next course was *fesenjān*. This was a duck casserole with a pomegranate puree and ground walnut sauce served over rice. Diana just couldn't bring herself to eat it. The presentation was beautiful; she just couldn't eat. The third course was *biryani*. This dish was ground mutton, cooked a special way and served with a special type of bread. Diana just sat there. She desperately wanted to go back to bed; she just didn't feel well. Ben was not the only one to notice she was not eating; he looked over to Aisha and Mahala and saw the concern on their faces. Bibi and Calla seemed to be more upset that Diana was dishonoring the Sheikh by not eating.

"Ariana, you do not eat...why?" the Sheikh asked.

Diana, understanding her name, had looked up toward the Sheikh but then looked over to Ben to tell her what he had said. "He asks why you are not eating," Ben interpreted.

"I'm not feeling very well tonight. I felt it best to not to push my stomach," she replied.

Ben told the Sheikh what she said. "Perhaps something cooler would be better?" the Sheikh suggested. His servants came out with the fourth course: an ice cream made of saffron and rose water was brought out. Diana tried to eat it but only managed a couple of bites.

Ben leaned over and whispered in Diana's ear, "Try some wine…it may settle your stomach." He watched her reach over and pick up the goblet and took a sip of the wine. She was able to drink and not cough this time when she took a sip, but she still winced at its sour taste. She had been told that drinking wine was an acquired taste—one she had not acquired yet, nor was she more than likely to. It was put in the category of coffee. Others may drink it; she would rather not. She managed to take one more sip before putting it down on the table. She heard the people chatting back and forth, all seemingly enjoying the feast. All at once, things started spinning around, then everything went black.

Diana seemed to just crumble. She fell into Ben's lap, unconscious and boiling hot. Ben had just taken a bit of cheese and had it stuck in his throat when she fell over. He was not able to call out or say anything for a few seconds. Taggee came running over; he felt her head and looked over to the Sheikh. "She has a high fever. I will take her back to the room."

Bibi looked over to her husband. "She is contaminated. She will spread it to all the girls. You cannot take her there. Have her stay with Taggee. If she contaminates them, it is no major loss," she suggested.

The Sheikh agreed to have Ariana taken to a room in Taggee's house. He signaled to one of the guards and told him to go get the doctor. It was Calla that spoke this time. "The doctor is in the hospital himself. They had to remove two of his fingers. They had became infected after the explosion."

The Sheikh was uncertain of what to do next. He was conferring with Mahdi when Ben spoke up. "I can try to help her. I took care of my wife when she was very ill," he stated.

"It looks like I have no other choice. Aisha, you will stay with Ariana. You are not to ever leave Mr. James and Ariana alone. Understood?" the Sheikh commanded.

Aisha gave the Sheikh a bow. Taggee picked Ariana off Ben's lap and carried her to his house. Ben followed them. *Lord, guide me in what to do. Please don't take her away as well*, he prayed.

"You'd better be praying, bro. I need all the help I can get. She needs it," he said softly.

An owl hooted several times; Aisha and Taggee looked up. "That is not a good sign. It's the sound of a bad omen," Taggee said. He took Ariana to the room across the hall from where he had taken Mr. James. He gently laid her down on the bed.

"I will need some water and towels. We need to bring her fever down. Aisha, if you would, I need you to remove the hijab and veil. It will be best if the earrings were out too," Ben asked.

Aisha turned and looked at Taggee; he gave her a nod. "I will get some water and towels," Taggee said. Aisha went and removed Ariana's veil and hijab. She folded it up nicely and laid them on the table near the window. Then she went and took out her earrings and laid them on top of the folded clothing.

Ben moved over next to Diana. "I need you to stay here, please. I don't want to be accused of taking privileges. I need to check her out to find where the problem may be," he stated flatly. Aisha stayed near Ariana. He started with her wrists and ankles. He asked Aisha, "Did these get changed this morning?"

"Yes, I changed them myself," she replied.

"Did you see any red lines or puss pockets on them?" he continued.

"They are red and swollen, but there were no lines," she informed him. She watched as Mr. James checked her eyes, felt her neck, leaned down and listened to her heart, and then he started feeling her stomach. As he moved around her stomach, she flinched and groaned when he pushed in the area of her kidneys. "Shh…Milady, it appears you have a kidney infection. This it's not going to be a fun ride for you. But you're strong, you can fight this," he said. He wasn't sure she heard him or not, but it was worth a try. Taggee came back with a basin full of water and some towels. Ben dipped a towel into the water, wrung it out, then laid it on Ariana's forehead. "We gave her too much liquid at one time. Her kidneys were too close to shutting down to handle it. We'll just have to see if they will start up again," he told them.

It was a long night; Ben stayed near Diana, constantly switching the towels to cool her down. Taggee had left to get more water; Aisha had fallen asleep in the corner of the room. Ben took a risk. He leaned down and whispered in her ear; "Milady…you have to fight. You can't leave now, I won't let you go. Listen to my voice. Fight your way back to it." He stopped when he heard Taggee coming up the hall and backed away from Diana.

Taggee put the basin next to the bed. "I can take a turn. You need to get some sleep," he told Ben.

Ben just shook his head. "No…I'll stay here and keep her cool. However, you might need to give Aisha a place to sleep," he stated, nodding his head toward the corner where Aisha had fallen asleep in.

"Aisha tried to get her to drink. She was very worried about Ariana. She likes her a lot," Taggee told Ben.

"I'm sure she did. Ariana seems to be a very strong-willed woman. She will only do what she wants to. It's not Aisha's fault. It is good that she has a friend here," Ben stated. He knew very good and well how strong-willed Diana is. He also knew why Diana didn't eat or drink here. It really wasn't Aisha's fault; the blame went solely on the Sheikh and his insane plan.

Taggee went to get some more blankets, made a bed down on the floor for Aisha, and brought her over to it. Then he went and got a chair and sat it in the corner where Aisha was and sat down on it.

He watched Mr. James work to keep Ariana cool; taking the towel, wiping her face and neck, then each of her arms. He remembered when he was living with his mom; one of his cousins ran a high fever. His mom stripped her down to just a cloth that covered her middle. She was constantly wetting down her head, neck, arms, and legs. He figured that Mr. James really wanted to do the same thing to Ariana. However, where they are now, he would be killed for it. Around three in the morning, Diana started to shiver. She had sweat running down her head and neck but was shivering from the fever. Diana desperately tried to find warmth. She curled up in a ball and said, "Cold." Ben jumped when Diana started to talk. He looked at her eyes and realized she had no clue she was saying; she wasn't really there. "I know. Keep fighting your way back, Milady, don't give up," he whispered to her.

22

In Syria at the Compound

Diana remembered the feast, remembered trying to drink some wine, then everything went black. Later, she knew she was being carried and then laid down somewhere. She could feel somebody's warm hands checking her throat. When the person checked her eyes, she thought she saw Ben looking at her. He then started to feel her abdomen. She soon found herself out of her body, standing behind Ben, watching everything. She saw herself flinch and heard herself groan when he pushed down on her lower abdomen, but she really didn't feel it. She heard something behind her and turned to see what it was. She was standing in a walkway that led through a beautiful garden. The path looked like it was made of paver blocks, but the blocks were clear like glass. They were illuminating a golden light and wound around a huge garden. The plants in the garden were gorgeously full and lush. She saw every color and shade of green that she had ever known. The plants looked similar to ones she'd worked with at home or seen in magazines, but the blooms and their colors were different. All the blooms were either full and at their prime or new buds starting out. She didn't see any dead or wilted heads on any of the bushes. The aromas she smelled made Diana feel tranquil and calm. There were white columns similar to the marble columns seen in the Grecian temples, but they were freestanding. Each column was covered with what looked to be climbing roses, but there were no thorns, and the blooms didn't look like a normal rose bloom. The path wound around, making several turns until widening out to a terrace. There was a bench swing next to a waterfall. The water cascaded eight feet into a catch pool at the bottom. It wasn't one of those splattering falls that, if you sat or stood near, you would be soaked. The clear, refreshing water came down in a shimmering sheet, unbroken by rocks or protruding obstacles, just plunging into the pool ringed by lilies and water plants.

Diana loved to swing on swings. She sat down on the swing and savored the sound of the waterfall, the smell of the garden, and the colors all around her. She felt the urge to wait there until she met someone; she didn't mind waiting. She stayed there, swinging back and forth, closing her eyes, and soaking everything in. Soon she saw who she was waiting for. Jesus came and sat by her. She smiled widely and gave him a big hug. "This place is wonderful. It's so beautiful and peaceful. Thank you, my Lord."

"You are welcome, Diana, I'm glad you like it," He said to her.

Diana heard someone saying, "You can't leave; I won't let you."

She looked over to Jesus. "Is this what the angel meant when he said that I would make it home safely?" There was sadness in her heart. She knew there wasn't supposed to be, but she felt it just the same.

Jesus, of course, knew her heart and thoughts. "You don't want to stay here with me?"

"Yes and no. I've wanted to be with you so many times, but there are so many that will not understand. The kids for one. You gave me promises that I've told them about, saying that they will come true. If I leave now without those promises coming about, what will that do to them? My parents, if I leave, who will help them? Dewayne and Abbie won't help them, and it's too much for the kids to take on. I need to be there for them. Most of all, I just feel I haven't even begun the work you wanted me to do. Am I wrong?" Jesus just smiled at her. She could feel the overwhelming love flowing from him. It was like waves coming onto the shore. She was so torn, wanting to be in both places and feeling like she would have to choose.

Jesus pulled her close to him and held her tight. "No Diana, you do not have to choose. I brought you here so you wouldn't have to be alone. You're body is very sick, but I'll take care of it shortly."

"Was this what the Garden of Eden was like before the fall?" Diana asked.

Jesus nodded. "This is just a small portion of what is prepared for the children." He smiled. Jesus continued to stay with her, giving her comfort and understanding. They sat there on the swing for what seemed to be hours, talking.

Ben kept wiping Diana's head and arms up until dawn. Taggee had dozed off in the chair; Aisha was out several hours earlier. Ben went and sat down on the floor across from Diana. "She isn't going to make it, bro; we don't have the support she needs," he said quietly. He just put his head back for a minute; but he fell asleep.

They all woke up with a start when they heard a woman gasp. They all looked toward the direction of the sound. Mahala was standing in the doorway, holding a tray of coffee. She was staring at something; they followed her gaze. Standing near Diana was the warrior in white, but he wasn't alone; Jesus had come to visit as well. Taggee initially went to draw his sword but, seeing the warrior in white again, quickly put it away and knelt down. Mahala and Aisha were just in total awe. Ben bowed his head. "My Lord."

"Be at peace. I am not here to harm you," the Lord stated.

Aisha was near to crying. "I tried to warn him, I did. I tried everything I could to help Ariana."

"You did as I asked. The turmoil coming is not on you or Mahala," the Lord told her. "Taggee, you are fighting inside yourself. To stop the struggle, a decision must be made," the Lord informed him. Then the Lord turned to Ben. "No, my child, it is not her time. She is to return." With that, the Lord walked over to Diana and touched her abdomen. Then…they disappeared. Ben looked down at Diana; she was no longer shivering. He touched her forehead; she was no longer running a fever. She was in a restful sleep.

Thank you, my Lord, for giving her more time, he praised.

"You weren't making it up," Mahala said to Aisha once she could speak. Aisha shook her head no. She seemed to have a peace show in her face. She was carrying a heavy burden thinking the warrior in white would blame her for the attitude of the compound. Taggee was deep in thought. He robotically took the coffee from Mahala, brought it to the table, then started to serve the coffee to all in the room. Ben gratefully accepted the cup; he needed something to wake him up. The thing that stuck in his head was what the Lord said about the turmoil coming. He hoped Scott heard all that, but he couldn't ask 'til later.

"Mahala…will you stay here with Ariana? That way Aisha can go and get cleaned up," Taggee stated. Mahala nodded yes. "Mr. James, you need to get some rest and cleaned up as well. I will stay here with Ariana. She is getting some much-needed sleep," Taggee told Ben. Ben went to argue but knew he had better get a few hours of sleep, especially if they are going to get out of here soon. He walked across the hall to his room and closed the door. Once the door was closed, he asked, "Were you able to hear any of that bro?" Ben heard a falcon shriek. It meant he didn't hear it. "Well…we just had a couple of heavenly visitors. The Lord healed Diana. She's going to be fine. However, He said that there's something coming. We'll have to get out of here soon. Make sure Dick has everything in the ready." An owl hooted. "I'll give you more detail the next time I see ya," Ben ended. He lay down on the bed and went to sleep. He didn't wake up for six hours. It was somewhere around three in the afternoon when he started moving again. He noticed that Taggee had brought a clean change of clothes. He got up, washed up, then tried the door; it was unlocked. He opened the door and walked to Diana's room. Mahala was still in the room with Ariana, but Taggee was gone.

"How is she doing?" he asked her.

"She is still sleeping," Mahala said.

"Where did Taggee go?" Ben questioned.

"He went to check on Aisha. He will be right back," she answered.

Ben stayed by the door. He didn't want Mahala or himself to be in trouble. He didn't have to wait long before he heard Taggee coming up the hallway. "Thank you for the change of clothes," Ben said to him.

"The doors were unlocked. You didn't make a break for it, why?" Taggee asked him.

"I need to see this through," he said, nodding toward Diana. "Besides, I didn't figure I'd get past all the guards."

Taggee gave him a nod of acceptance. "Mahala, Bibi wants you to go to her. I will stay here till Aisha comes back." Mahala gave a look of loathing but gave a bow and headed out the door. She wanted to ask Ariana or Mr. James about what she saw and heard. It would have to wait till later, but she was going to make sure she asked.

"May I go in now?" Ben asked. Taggee waved his hand to signal to go in. Ben came in and knelt down beside Diana. He felt her forehead; there still was no fever. Not that he expected there to be one. The Lord doesn't do things halfway. Diana started to stir, turning her head toward his touch. She opened her eyes, blinking to get them into focus. "Hello, kitten," Ben said.

Diana enjoyed her time with the Lord. He was the one who told her it was time for her to return. He walked with her back down the path. He gave her a hug, to which she gladly hugged him back. "I will always be with you. You just have to stop and listen for me," Jesus told her. "Diana, you will need to leave there soon. You are here for a living witness to some who would never have heard otherwise. Be prepared to help them out," He continued.

Diana heard Ben talking to somebody. She had to struggle a little to get her eyes to open; she must have been really sick. She was glad to see Ben there. "Still having to take care of me, huh?" she said. She saw him grimace at that comment.

"Yeah…well those of us that speak the same language have to stick together," he replied and smiled when he saw her worry about what she said. If Taggee understood her, he would have to deal with it later.

"How do you feel Milady?" he asked.

"I really need to use the bathroom if you want me to be totally truthful," she replied. Ben had to laugh at that; it was a good sign. He interpreted what Diana said to Taggee.

Taggee laughed and smiled a broad smile. "The bathroom is downstairs. I will take her down," he stated. Ben wasn't going to argue with him. Although he was sure Diana was down at least thirty pounds, she would be hard for him to carry down the steep stairs. Taggee, on the other hand, probably wouldn't even know she was there except for getting her five-foot-eight length down the twenty-four-inch width of the stairs.

Taggee carried her down the stairs, set her in the room, turned, and walked out the door. She was glad that he let her have some privacy. She was worried that it might burn really bad. Her bladder must have been close to bursting, but she thanked the Lord that it didn't burn at all. She walked out of the room and met up with Taggee. He walked her back up the stairs to the room. She was a little wobbly; Taggee had to steady her a couple of times, but for the most part, she made it on her own.

23

In Syria at the Compound

Since Ariana was better, the Sheikh decided that his wives, Ariana, and Mr. James would join him for supper. It took him getting strong with Bibi to get her to agree. Things were just now starting to go as he planned. The doctor that was to perform the "miracle" may have lost two fingers, but he could still work a hypodermic syringe. The Sheikh gloated with the power he was going to gain; then his thoughts were interrupted by Mahdi.

"Milord, we have a problem. Some of your wives have been heard not only speaking in English but praying to a false god," Mahdi informed the Sheikh.

"Which of my wives needs to be made an example of?" the Sheikh fumed. Mahdi called for them to be brought in.

Taggee went to collect Ariana, Mr. James, and Aisha from his house. When he got there, Aisha wasn't there; it was Calla. She had Ariana decked out and dressed, her hijab and veil on already. He had a strong sense of devastation looming around him. "We have been summoned to the Sheikh's home," he said. Ben and Diana could see he was in distress.

Diana's heart was racing; she had to force herself to breathe. *Lord... guide me and give me wisdom*, she prayed.

Ben had alarms going off in his head. It started when Aisha didn't come back when she should have. The fact that Calla, a woman that didn't seem to want anything to do with Diana, came instead was a flag. Mahala, who has wanted to be nearby, also was not coming around—another flag. Now with Taggee's face, the alarms were going off like a foghorn now in his head.

Calla didn't seem to be surprised by Taggee's announcement, at least not in Diana's opinion. She was up and out the door in a flash. Taggee held out his hand to Ariana. He helped her up and then down the stairs.

She was still a little pale, but there was a fire in her eyes. They had made sure that she was drinking liquid and even got her to eat some bread and cheese. Once they were down the stairs, he looped her hand over his arm and escorted her across the courtyard.

Ben followed Taggee and Diana. She wasn't taking the long fast strides that she normally would. So he knew that she was still a little weak. However, her eyes were clear; there was a fire and sometimes even mischievousness in them. The old Diana was on the way back. Now came this impromptu meeting; it didn't feel right. Things could really hit the fan, and he needed to be ready. *Lord…give me wisdom and strength*, he prayed. They entered into the Sheikh's house. The men were all gathered around the open courtyard. Bibi and Calla stood on the right side of the crowd. The Sheikh was sitting in his chair; Mahdi was to his right on the platform. Taggee brought Ariana to the front of the crowd; he signaled Mr. James to go to the left side of the platform in front of the stair.

The Sheikh, once he saw everybody was present, stood up. "I have called you together as a witness to treachery and sacrilege." He motioned for something to be brought in. Diana's heart fell; it was Aisha. Her face was uncovered, and you could easily see that she had been beaten. The bruises on her cheeks and lip were extremely obvious.

The Sheikh looked at Mr. James. "You tell Ariana what I say. She needs to know the retaliation of treachery."

Ben looked over to Diana. "Ariana, the Sheikh wants you to know that what you are to see is caused from treachery and sacrilege." Ben may have had his sunglasses on, but she could tell in his voice that this wasn't good. She was searching for what she should do.

The Sheikh continued speaking. "This woman…was found praying to another god, this false messiah called Jesus." He then looked over to Mr. James and motioned him to tell Ariana. Ben reluctantly told her what was said. In truth, Diana wasn't there when the Lord made himself known; she really didn't have anything to do with it. The Sheikh finished out, "She refuses to deny him. She is now cut off from her family, from everybody here. She will be thrown out to the wolves and factions." He signaled to Mr. James to tell Ariana.

When Ben told Diana what was said, she started to cry. Taggee on the other hand was fuming. Ben could see the anger and betrayal in his eyes. The guards then brought in Mahala. Her hair was braided and her head uncovered. She was wearing just a tan robe. Diana saw that her hands were already tied. "This woman has broken the law. She spoke in an unholy language." The Sheikh motioned to Mr. James. Ben repeated what the Sheikh said for Diana. He saw Diana's eyes flash steel gray. *This isn't going to be good. I'm too far away to control her, and she won't stand by and do nothing*, he thought. He debated whether he would be able to control her anyway. She's far too strong-willed and stubborn. Two guards brought Mahala out to the middle of the courtyard. One guard kicked her in the back of the knee to make her drop down. The other stepped on the rope that tied her hands making her bow. They brought a leather whip out with two tails about three feet long.

Mahala was already crying. Diana heard Aisha saying something to Mahala, crying the whole time herself. She looked over to Ben, trying to get him to tell her what she was saying, but he wouldn't tell her. Ben was steeling himself to endure what he was about to see. He hated seeing anybody tortured, but a woman was even worse. The guard hit Mahala once; she cried out. Diana could not stand by any longer. Before Taggee knew what happened, Diana took off across the courtyard, heading toward Mahala. "No!" she screamed.

She heard Ben yell, "Diana…no!" She wasn't going to stop. Once she reached Mahala, she used her own body to cover hers. Aisha was yelling something to her, but of course she had no clue of what. The guard was unsure of what to do. He had heard of what happened to anybody that harmed Ariana. He wanted no part of being cursed. He looked up to the Sheikh for guidance.

The Sheikh was busy glaring at Mr. James. "How do you know her by that name?" he fumed.

Ben calmly said, "She told me her name." He was putting two and two together. Aisha was beaten to get information about who spoke to Diana in English. It was probably an out to get them to stop hitting her. He figured she was the one praying to God. The fact that she would not deny him was worthy of praise.

"Then you can tell her to move away or be whipped as well," the Sheikh steamed.

"Ariana, the Sheikh says that you must move away or be whipped as well," Ben stated calmly.

Diana looked at Ben. She couldn't see his eyes, but he could see hers; he would know that she wasn't backing down. "I will not let a child be whipped for helping me understand what in the world was going on. You can tell him that for me," she firmly stated.

Ben looked at the Sheikh and translated what Diana said to him. He tried to take the heat off her words, but there was no doubt of her intention. Ben glanced over to see what Taggee was doing. He was standing there like a statue. However, Ben could see in his eyes that he was fighting in himself as to what he should do. Ben remembered the message given to him: "You have a choice to make." *Lord, help him*, Ben prayed.

"So be it," the Sheikh stated. He saw that his guard didn't want to hit the chosen one, so he signaled Mahdi to take over. Mahdi had an evil smile on his face and a gleam in his eye as he took the whip from the guard. He circled around the two women, teasing them.

Diana kept Mahala covered even with Mahala trying to get her to move away. "I will not let you take this. You were only trying to help me. He is in the wrong," she told Mahala. Mahdi came down with the whip, hitting Diana across the middle of the back. Diana felt a slight sting, but because she was wearing the scarf and a coat, it didn't do any damage.

Mahdi didn't like that it had no effect on Ariana. He brought the whip down again, harder. The hijab ripped. He smiled at that. It wouldn't be long before Ariana would start actually feeling the whip. Then he would hear her cry out. Another stroke was taken; it was starting to rip the cloak.

Ben called out. "Ariana, you are going to start feeling him. You need to move back."

"No…I won't…I won't leave her!" she yelled back. Mahdi brought the whip down again. This time, a part of the tail made it to her skin. Diana gritted her teeth; she was not going to give Mahdi the satisfaction he wanted.

"Ariana, move back. I will be okay. You don't have to do this. I don't want you to do this," Mahala cried to her in English.

"I will not leave you," Diana repeated to Mahala. Mahdi took another swipe. The tails cut into Diana's back, the sting just reinforcing Diana resolve.

Mahdi smiled at the sight of seeing the red marks on Ariana's back. *You will be broken…I will be the one who breaks you*, he thought. He laughed a nefarious, wicked laugh as he circled around the women again. Before Mahdi could take another hit, a guard called from the wall. Everybody looked up to see what he was yelling. The guard was pointing to the sky; it was turning almost black, and the wind was picking up. Ben yelled out, "A sandstorm is coming!" Then a gust came through the building, throwing the double doors wide open. The men scattered; trying to get back to their homes. The two holding Aisha left her standing there. Once they were gone, she came over to the other two girls.

Ben ran over to Diana, Aisha, and Mahala. "We have to get out of here…now!" he yelled to be heard. He looked up to see Taggee standing near him. *Which way did you decide to go?* Ben wondered. Diana looked up at Taggee; she watched him intently.

"Mr. James, you must go while the storm is here. They will not be able to follow you 'til it passes. I will take care of Aisha and Mahala. You take Ariana. She belongs with you," Taggee told Ben.

Ben nodded. "Diana, we have to leave. Taggee will take care of Mahala and Aisha. We need to move."

Diana looked at Ben then at the girls. "I'm sorry you had this happen to you. I didn't want you two to be hurt," she told them. Aisha was pushing her toward Ben.

"You go with Mr. James…Taggee will take us to safety. The storm will hide your tracks. You must go…go!" Mahala fervently said.

Diana looked at Ben; she was worried about the girls. "Trust the Lord, Milady. He knows best," Ben said.

She nodded and grabbed his arm. "Put your head down and cover your mouth with your scarf. Don't breathe the sand in," Ben told her. She put her head down and held on to Ben. He put his arm around her and guided her out of the compound. Even if the guards were still out in the open, they would not be able to see them through the sand. He could hardly see where he was going. He trusted the Lord to guide them.

It was really hard to walk against the wind and sand. To Diana, it felt that they had walked halfway across Syria by now. Her legs were screaming in pain. *Man…I really need to start working out*, she thought.

Ben could tell she was getting tired. He was basically pushing her forward to gain ground. "We need to find some kind of shelter…at least 'til the storm passes," he said.

"Have we gone far enough away from the compound?" Diana asked.

"I'm not sure…we'll find out later," he replied. Ben thought he saw a shadow to the left of them. A rectangle-shaped shadow, possibly a house or a stable. He guided Diana toward what he saw. Praise the Lord he wasn't seeing things. There was an abandoned house in that direction. The house looked like it had been abandoned for at least a year. There wasn't any furniture, no dishes, not even a bed. It was just mud walls and wood shutters. Ben pushed Diana in, locked the door shut, walked over to the window, and locked the shutters shut. The sand slowly started to settle. Diana could see clearer now. The wind was still deafening, blowing around the small house. Diana took the scarf off then started brushing the sand out of her clothes, face, and any other groove or place the sand hid. She had a hard time getting the sand out of her hair. Some of the problem was because her hair was knotted from the wind, some because her back was hurting her.

Ben looked over. "Here, let me help you."

Diana laughed. "Do you have a brush hidden somewhere I don't know about?"

"Not that I know of, but I can reach places you obviously can't," Ben said, seeing her grimace. He came over to her and started to untangle her hair, using his fingers as a comb. Her hair was long and soft. There was a slight curl to it that gave it a lot of bounce when it wasn't weighed down with sand and dirt. Fifteen minutes later, he had her hair untangled, but he kept combing through it. "You shouldn't have ran over to Mahala, you know that, don't you?" he asked.

Diana opened her eyes; she had been lost with Ben combing her hair. "I couldn't stand by and watch her get whipped because she was trying to help me," she softly said.

"Mahdi wants to break you...you know. He gets a kick out of it," Ben stated flatly.

"I noticed. I also saw what he did to Aisha. A fourteen-year-old shouldn't have to face that," she insisted.

"That fourteen-year-old is a woman in this land. Most are mothers by now," he informed her.

She just shook her head. "It's not right, I don't care what they say."

"Mary, Jesus's mother, was more than likely about fourteen years old. Are you trying to tell the Father that He was wrong?" he pointed out. She shook her head again but stayed quiet.

Ben put his hands on her shoulders. "It's a different culture, Diana. I know it feels wrong, but to the women who have grown up in this culture, it's normal."

Ben felt her shoulders drop; her spirit seemed to fall with it. "My Lord told me that I had to come here to be a living witness to some that would have never heard. If I'm not helping, then why did He send me here?"

"You have helped. Didn't you hear why Aisha was beaten? She accepted the Lord as her savior. I believe Taggee did also. They would have never heard otherwise," Ben pointed out.

"Yeah...I guess you're right. Speaking of which, what happened to Scott? Was he the one that was shot?" Diana asked worriedly.

Ben snickered. "I was the one that was shot. Scott got locked in the shed, but he's okay and probably listening to us now if the storm isn't blocking it out."

"You were shot? How bad? Where—" Diana said hastily, but Ben stopped her.

"Shh…it was just a flesh wound, thanks to the Lord. I'll show you the new scar sometime," he said, putting his finger up to her lips. "Now, what about your back, we need to look at it. I know the whip went through at least a couple of times," Ben stated.

"Well, that is going to be a difficult task. One, I have a robe on. Two, I have no other clothes to put on. I also don't see a towel to wrap around either," she cited. Ben got a gleam in his eye. Diana saw it. "Don't even think about it. Besides, you don't have a knife, and I don't have a change of clothing."

"Okay…how about this. I'll give you my scarf for the top, you use the hijab for the bottom," Ben suggested.

"Use the what?" she asked.

"Your scarf…it's called a hijab. Use that to wrap around your waist. I really need to see how bad your back is," Ben insisted.

"I think you have other intentions, but since I can't see it. I suppose I'll have to do what you ask," Diana retorted and walked out of the room.

"Sorry bro, you'll have to miss out again. I have no clue how far we actually got. She is still weak, but her spirits are good. As you can hear, she's fencing words again," Ben said while Diana was out of the room. He went ahead and described the house and what he could see of it before going in. He figured Scott would have to track them to find them. Hopefully, they will be picked up in the morning. Diana came back in with her scarf wrapped around her waist and Ben's scarf tied around her neck. It fell just below the waist, so she was totally covered with the exception of her back. "You know, someday—oh, never mind. It would just get twisted around in the wrong way," Diana said with a little blush in her cheeks.

Ben's eyebrow arched up. "Do I sense an off-colored comment floating through that pretty little head of yours?"

"What's in my head stays in my head. What meanings you want to assign to my actions are up to your off-colored mind," Diana fired back with a mischievous smile.

"Get over here, you imp, let's see the damage," he said, taking her hand. He pulled her down with her back facing him. He wanted to check her back before the last of the sunlight was gone. He could make out the marks left by the whip. Only one actually cut her skin; the others left raised red lines and bruises. "Well, it's not as bad as when you were playing in the woods," he quipped.

"Well, if someone wasn't playing cat and mouse; I wouldn't have had those to start with," she fired back at him.

"Well, you should know tigers are just big cats. They like to play with things," he said smiling.

"Huh-huh. I'll have to get some safer toys for the tiger to play with next time," she said, standing up to go get dressed again. Diana's knee became partially uncovered as she pushed off the ground.

"I don't think that would be a safer alternative toy for a tiger," Ben gloated.

Diana arched an eyebrow up. "You of all people should know what I can do with that. Or maybe I should get a reference from the security guard at the clinic for you," she stated.

Ben got very somber with that comment. "I am sorry you had to go through that. I should have been more prepared."

She looked down at him. "Ben…I knew it was coming. The Lord told me earlier that afternoon. I just wasn't willing to be inspected by any man, doctor or not."

"He told you that afternoon and you said nothing to us?" Ben stated with fire behind it. He stood up and glared at her.

"If I did, what would you have done?" she asked. She could feel the heat in his words.

"Stopped it of course," Ben said.

"It came from God. Would you have stopped what God wanted? You know very good and well you can't do that. Besides, if He wanted you to know, I figured He would have told you Himself," she flatly stated.

"If the Lord tells you something else, you'd better share. If I find out you're hiding anything else from us, I'll turn you over my knee and spank your butt," he insisted.

Diana got an impish grin on her face. She knew very well that he wouldn't get far trying to do that. "Oh, really, that might be interesting to see," she quipped. Then she left the room to change.

"Bring those scarves back when you're done with them," he called after her, only to get hit in the face with one of them that she threw at him. "Where's the other one?" he teased. It came flying in, this time hitting him in the shoulder. He arched back to glance into the room that she went into but couldn't see anything. It was too dark back there. He wondered how in the world she saw enough to throw them. "Have you ever thought about baseball?" he jested.

"Nah, running is not my thing. I prefer swimming," she answered back.

"Are you able to see your way back or do I need to come help you?" he said hopefully.

"You know, Taggee wasn't far off by calling me a tigress. I see quite well in the dark, even to the point of hitting what I'm aiming at," she replied.

"You know, they said he was the only one that could control you in the compound. Why was that?" he asked.

She came walking back in and studied him. "Does that bother you some?"

He looked over to her. "It's my nature to be curious."

She smiled at him. "I studied his eyes. He didn't want to hurt me. He was just doing what he was told. He was never mean, harmful, or malicious toward me. I imagine he called me tigress because anybody who came after me with force got force thrown back at them. Which reminds me—" She reached up and tried to take the earrings out of her ears. They didn't want to come though. "These stupid pieces of junk, I don't want them," she stated as she was working on them.

"Come here…let me see," Ben motioned.

"I'm not totally helpless. It took three of them to get them in. I should be able to get them out," she said frustrated.

"It took three people to get earrings in your ears?" Ben asked.

"Yeah, Bibi insisted I had to have the dumb things. When she couldn't do it, she called Taggee in; but it took both of his hands to hold me down. So he called the other guard in to hold my head. If I wanted my ears mutilated, I would have had it done already. Of course the entire time I had no clue of what was going on or what was being said. It wasn't till Mahala talked to me in English that I knew some of them could understand me. The thing is, all she did was she told me that the Sheikh was coming home. That's all she ever said in English. Just those five words, and she was supposed to be whipped for that. Really?" she ended.

Ben stood up and walked over to Diana, reached up, and worked on the other earring. "I'm sorry," he added.

Diana just sighed. "No…I'm sorry. I'm just tired, dirty, and frustrated. It's never a good combo for me. I open my mouth without thinking."

Ben got the one earring out, moved over, and worked on the other till it was out then pulled her to him and just held her. "So…if I get you tired, dirty, and frustrated, I'll be able to know what's flying around in that head of yours?" he asked.

Diana pinched him in the stomach. He did a quick jerk back and then rubbed where she pinched him. "Come on, we'd better get some shuteye. Hopefully, Scott will meet us tomorrow morning," he stated.

"Umm, two questions. One, how does Scott know we need him to get us? Two, how will he find us?" she asked.

Ben gave her a smile. "A little curious, are we? Let's just say it's an ancient Chinese secret." Diana just stuck her tongue out at him. "That makes two I need to collect on," he pointed out.

Diana just lay down on her scarf and said, "Promises…promises."

"You might want to move a little closer. It gets cold out in the desert," Ben said with a smile.

"I've been told I'm a regular furnace. I'll be fine," she informed him.

"Suit yourself. Good night…Milady," he ended.

"Good night," she whispered back.

Ben awoke to the feel of Diana up against him. She was nudging up against his side trying to find a comfortable spot. She wasn't awake of course; she had no clue of what she was doing. Ben smiled down at her and thought, *You need your pillow, don't ya?* He brushed her hair back off her face and traced his fingers down the side of her face. "Come on," he said as he turned on his side, reached over and slowly grabbed her arm, and put his other arm behind her. In one easy flowing motion, he turned over to his back, pulling Diana with him. Her head rested on his chest, her arm across his middle, his other arm wedged against her back to hold her there. He had to agree, she was a natural bed warmer. He kissed her head. "I always keep my promises, tigress, always."

"Hmm?" Diana asked.

"Shh…sleep, babe," Ben whispered. Diana nuzzled into Ben's chest but adjusted her angle so she was lying more on Ben, freeing his other arm. He reached up pulled her hair off her shoulder then let his arm rest on her waist. He heard her breathe deeply and slowly let it out and then she settled down to a normal rhythm. He felt her heartbeat through his side. He was concentrating on her heart rhythm as he dozed off.

Diana was totally comfortable and in a restful sleep. She woke up only because she had to go to the bathroom. There was no roar of the wind outside now. She suddenly realized she was lying on Ben. *Well…I can't say I mind this, but I hope he doesn't mind*, she thought. She carefully slid out from Ben's embrace, quietly went to the back of one of the back rooms, and relieved her bladder. *Now…do I go back to where I was comfortable or back to my space?* she wondered. As she walked back to where Ben was lying, she paused. "Come on back over here. I'm missing my little furnace," Ben stated.

Diana didn't quibble. She lay back down against Ben, adjusted herself, and pulled her hair back away from her face. She closed her eyes and fell back asleep.

24

In Syria

It was somewhere in the morning; the sun was just starting to rise. Diana had to go to the bathroom again. She noticed that she had put her leg over Ben's leg, his one arm covering hers across his chest, the other down her back; his hand draped over her waist. She sighed deeply and felt him gently caress her arm. As much as she didn't want to wake him or even move for that matter, she had no choice. She slowly pulled her arm out from under his then carefully turned so that his other arm softly fell to the ground; then she backed out and away from him. Her heart was beating so fast, she was surprised he didn't feel it and wake up. She quietly went back to the corner of the room she had gone before.

Ben was abruptly awakened by someone kicking his foot. "Hey, you, American. Where's the woman?" the person asked in Farsi. When the man thought Ben wasn't replying fast enough, he kicked his leg. "You! Where's the other one?" he repeated.

Ben slowly opened his eyes. He saw five masked soldiers surrounding him with assault rifles pointed down on him. "What other one? What are you talking about? I got lost in the sandstorm…this was the first place I found," he replied.

Diana heard men talking and knew it was either a group from the Sheikh or one of the factions she heard about in the news. What was she going to do now? she wondered. Just then, a hand came across her mouth and an arm across her chest, pinning her arms down to her sides. "Shh…keep quiet," she heard whispered in her ear. She turned her head to see Scott, all camoed out. She didn't see a gun, so she wasn't sure what he was going to do. The room she had chosen to use as a makeshift bathroom was through a door and was to the left of the room Ben and she had been sleeping in.

He took her over near the wall adjoining the main room and backed her toward the outside corner; he signaled for her to stay quiet and still. Then she heard him make a yipping sound like you would hear a fox make back home. Ben heard the sound and knew he had backup but made no indication he recognized the sound.

The lead soldier nodded to one of the others to go check it out. The one turned, holding his gun up and ready to shoot, and went through the doorway. He checked right then turned left and disappeared in the left room. They heard a thud and crack; then there was silence. The lead soldier signaled for two more guards to go check it out, leaving just two to cover Ben. The first guard entered the room; there was a crack and another thud. The second guard backing him up brought his gun up and fired two rounds, but then there was a whack and another thud. The lead soldier was mad. "You, get up...now!" he yelled.

Ben stood up. He was actually a head taller than his captors. He kept his hands up in the air where they were seen. The lead soldier signaled for the last of his troop to go check the room out. The guard didn't want to go and argued with the leader. "We have this one, let's just take him back. We should get half the price," he stated.

"No, we go back after we find the woman. The price is for her, not him," the leader fumed. He then made a stronger signal for him to go check out that room. The last of the soldiers slowly walked over to the doorway. He cautiously scanned the doorway and then slowly walked through it. He was making over grandiose movements with his gun, waving it everywhere. He pointed it into the room on the left; a hand came out of nowhere and took the gun away from him then pulled the soldier into the room. The leader freaked out, shooting a barrage of bullets into the wall and doorway.

Ben reacted, bringing a hand down hard on the leader's elbow, dislocating it, and grabbing his gun away from him. Then Ben slammed his arm into the leader's neck. Finally, Ben put him into a headlock, turning his head, and breaking his neck. The leader fell to the ground. Ben made a meadowlark's call, checking to see if Scott was okay. He heard a nightingale's call in reply. Ben slowly neared the left room and then peered around the corner. Scott was over near Diana, his hand on her back; she had huddled down low in the corner. Scott looked over at Ben with a questioning look on his face; the lifeless bodies of the four soldiers sent in to check the room were scattered around on the ground.

Diana's was far from where the guys were, buried deep into herself. She knew Scott didn't have a choice. They wouldn't have hesitated to kill him or her for that matter. She just couldn't get past the fact that they were dead. Ben came over and hunched down near Diana. "Milady…we had no choice," he said softly.

"I know, I just can't—" she paused and started to cry. Ben wrapped her up in his arms and brought her close. *She's still very tenderhearted. That's actually a good thing for all that she's had to endure*, he thought. "Come on, we need to move. More maybe coming," he told her.

Scott wished she didn't have to see that. Ben's life was at stake—not only Ben's, but hers as well as his. Death is never an easy thing to anybody who cares for people. Soldiers are trained to put it in perspective, but Diana wasn't a soldier—at least not on the physical realm of things. Ben signaled for them to stay put; he went back into the main room and grabbed the two scarves. He took the water cantina from the leader and then went back to Diana and Scott. Scott was taking the cantinas from the four men in his area. "I don't suppose you know how to shoot, do you, Diana?" Scott asked.

Diana looked him square in the eyes. "Clay pigeons, yes. People, no way."

"You may not have a choice. Take this," Scott said, handing her a rifle then handing her a cantina.

Diana looked at Ben. "I've never shot an automatic. I've only shot 12 and 20 gauges. I have no idea how to work these things. I'm not even sure I could force myself to pull the trigger," she exclaimed.

"Let's hope you don't have to find out," Ben said as he held out his hand for her to hold.

"How long before Dick can get us out?" Ben asked Scott.

"Not till midnight. There was another attack on a temple, and everybody has upped their surveillance. Plus, we have Taliban crawling all over the place. We need to get to the cave soon," Scott informed them.

"Have you been watching the compound the whole time?" Diana asked Scott.

"Yep, saw just about everything, except what was going on in the Sheikh's courtyard."

"Did you see me up on the roof?" Diana wondered. Scott shook his head no.

Ben looked over to Diana. "What in the world were you doing up there?" he asked.

"That security guard from the clinic. I kneed him trying to get away. Apparently, I sent him to the hospital, so he wanted retribution. When he wasn't able to beat it into me, he decided to try to slit my throat. If Taggee wasn't there, he probably would have. Taggee grabbed his knife hand, and I took the only option available to me to get away. I grabbed his gun, climbed up the ladder, and put myself on the roof in a corner to protect myself," she stated point-blank.

"No wonder Taggee called you a tigress," Ben said as he crawled over a boulder. Then he held his hand out to help Diana over.

"You know you really shouldn't go around kneeing guys, right?" Scott said with a painful expression on his face.

Diana knew that all it took was the suggestion of such an act, and most guys would respond accordingly. "If I didn't think it was a point of life or death, I wouldn't have done it," she quipped back.

"So what was the life or death event?" Scott pushed.

"Do you have any sisters, Scott?" Diana asked.

"Nope...just a brother," he replied.

"Then I don't think I could put it in a civilized manner. Perhaps you can ask Ben about it when an opportunity avails itself," she stated.

"Ben knows, but I don't. That doesn't make sense," Scott complained.

"It makes total sense. Ben has sisters and has been married with four children. Even if his sisters didn't state it, I guarantee his wife did. Though technically, only females can truly understand the situation," Diana explained.

Scott looked over to Ben. "Huh?"

"I'll tell you later, I think our tigress is a little bashful in this area," Ben replied. They had been climbing for about an hour. Diana was running out of energy quickly. She struggled to lift her feet up high enough to get over the rocks. Of course it would have been better if she was wearing hiking shoes and a pair of jeans and a T-shirt to work with. Unfortunately, all she had was a robe, scarf, and a pair of sandals.

Ben looked over to Diana; she was getting pale again. He noticed that she did that every time she was near to exhaustion. "How much farther, bro?" he asked.

"Just over the next rise, why? Are you a little out of shape?" Scott jabbed.

"Nope, but Diana is still on the mend. Her body isn't ready for all this," he pointed out.

"Yeah, I see that. She's getting a little peaked, isn't she?" Scott replied.

"Yep, and she won't drink from the cantina. The water will have to be boiled before she'll drink anything," Ben added.

"Are you kidding me?" Scott said in disbelief.

Ben shook his head. "Nope, no kidding. She almost killed herself in the compound. That's why her kidneys were shutting down."

"The whole time she was there, the entire what...eight days, she didn't drink?" Scott questioned.

"Pretty much bro. Aisha said that she had a bottle of water from the plane that she grabbed from the limo when she climbed in after the jail. So she had a little, but the three days before I got there, none. She's a stubborn one to say the least," Ben responded.

Diana caught up with the guys who were waiting for her. "I'm sorry, I'm trying to keep up," she stated frustrated.

"It's okay, Milady, you're doing fine. Stop for minute, catch your breath," Ben countered. Diana gladly sat down on the rock and closed her eyes. She was forcing herself to take deep, slow breaths.

"What I wouldn't do for a decent pair of hiking boots and a pair of jeans right now," she stated after she had slowed her breathing.

Ben just smiled at her. "It's a little different than taking a hike at home, isn't it?"

"Yeah, more heat, less appropriate clothing—a huge difference," she confirmed. The group heard some vehicles driving on the road not far from them. Diana jumped up and moved toward Ben.

Scott and Ben took her behind some large boulders. "Stay here and don't move," Ben ordered.

"No problem," she replied.

Scott and Ben did a low belly crawl over the top of the rise of rocks in order to see what was going on. A caravan of ATVs with missile rockets were heading toward the northwest. "They're heading toward the compound," Scott pointed out.

"This doesn't feel good. We've got to get into hiding," Ben stated. They slowly backed away from the edge and worked their way back to Diana. As they approached the rock, they heard a hissing sound. They slowly came around the corner of the boulder and saw Diana frozen against the rock. She wasn't moving, not screaming, just standing still, looking at a snake. Scott picked up a stick with a pronged end and slowly worked his way behind the snake then inched his way up till he could reach out and get it. He used the pronged stick to hold the snake's head down to the ground, and then he pulled out his knife and, with one quick motion, removed the head from the body.

"Eww," Diana said as she turned away.

"Woman, do you seek out trouble, or does it just follow you everywhere?" Scott asked.

"At this point in time, I'm not sure I can answer that question, Mr. McCleary," she stated flatly.

"We've got to get going. Feel ready?" Ben asked Diana as she regained her composure.

"Ready or not, we can't stay here," she replied.

"That's my girl," he smiled. It was another hour's climb till they finally entered Scott's cave. He had bottled water, cans of Spam and beans, even a small cook stove. "All the comforts of home, I see," Diana said in a sarcastic manner.

"Yeah well, that cabin would have been better, but somebody withheld vital information from us," Scott snarled back.

"How did you know? You weren't in the mud house all night, were you?" Diana asked astonished.

"Well…yeah, in a manner of speaking, I was there," he replied.

Diana looked around and saw a receiver along the side of the wall near the entrance. She looked at Ben. "I see the receiver, but where is the mic?"

"She know electronics. I didn't see that in the file," Scott jabbed.

"There you go, judging a book by its cover again. I run these things at the church. I'm the one responsible for the system. Where is the mic?" she asked again. The guys were not saying anything. So she worked to figure it out. "The mic had to be small. It had to be easily concealed or the guards would have found it. It had to be somewhere where it's amplifiable to pick up not only Ben but obviously surrounding conversations. It's in the head somewhere. Ear is too obvious. The mouth possibly?" she asked.

Ben just smiled. "I love to watch that pretty little head work. Good job, babe."

Scott just shook his head. "If she keeps figuring these things out, we're gonna have to kill her to keep our secrets."

"Yeah…I know. How do you suppose we should do it," Ben jested.

"I'm not sure. It would have to be original—something classy, not messy or anything as such. I'll have to think on that one," Scott teased.

"While you guys are planning my demise, I'm going to grab some water," Diana said as she reached down and opened a bottle. It tasted wonderful. She started to chug it.

"Whoa…girl, we don't need a repeat! The Lord healed you once, let's not tempt Him again," Ben said, grabbing the water from Diana.

She sat there almost sulking. "I can't drink the water?" she asked.

"Sip it, don't chug it. You'll get sick if you drink it too fast, especially if you've gone all day without any," Ben informed her.

"Well, that would explain that," she said, looking down.

"Explain what?" Ben asked.

"I don't know if you guys knew this or not, but I was in jail for almost two days. I was drugged at the clinic, so I didn't have the presence of mind to grab my bottle of water from the limo before Aisha and I were escorted to the cell. When I was suddenly released and loaded into the limo, I found my bottle of water. I was so thirsty…I chugged it. A few minutes later, my stomach started knifing me. I thought maybe they poisoned my water," she told them.

"Nope, too much…too fast," Scott stated. They got organized again. Scott gave Diana a can of Spam to eat. He and Ben each opened a can of beans. The sun was just setting when they each finished up. Diana couldn't eat more than a fourth of the can. She gave the rest to Ben, looking over to Scott and telling him that they could fight it out.

"You'd better get some shuteye. You'll need your strength to get to the pickup site," Scott informed her.

"Rock-paper-scissors or flip a rock?" Ben asked.

"You go ahead. She'll need a pillow again. I'm not sure I would behave myself if she used me," Scott jabbed.

"Oh…you'd behave yourself. Remember what she did to the security guard," Ben quipped back.

Scott just shuddered. "I can't believe she would do that. This innocent albeit beautiful thing."

"She had her reason," Ben added smiling over at her.

"You want to explain the need for maiming a guy like that? I'd like to know so I don't do such a thing," Scott demanded.

Ben explained that the doctor was trying to give her a physical examination. Diana was already half asleep when Ben moved over by her. He lay down close, pulled her over, and let her settle in. Her head went on his shoulder, her right hand tucked under her face with her palm splayed out on his chest, her left arm tucked between them. Ben put his right arm around her and held her there. A sigh came from her mouth as she relaxed and fell deep asleep.

Scott just shook his head. "Nope, I would not behave myself. Best I just let a stronger man be the pillow," he stated.

Ben just smiled. He had to admit to himself he loved the way she cuddled. Everything just seemed to be right with the world when she was lying on him. He closed his eyes and then fell asleep.

An hour later, Scott came and carefully woke Ben from his sleep. "Hey, bro, you'd better come look at this," Scott told him.

Ben looked at him; he carefully and slowly slid out from Diana's embrace. She softly moaned as he laid her head down on the blanket. He gently pushed her hair back out of her face. Scott led him over to the cave entrance. "Check this out."

Ben looked out over the horizon; the ground was ebony black against the deep purple night sky. He saw lights twinkling like Christmas lights down amongst the trees and hills. *What in the world is going on down there?* he wondered. They didn't have to wait long to find out. While Ben and Scott watched the light show, the finale started. The twinkling lights all went dark; then there was a bright burst of light and a rocket was shot off from near the ground. It sped quickly into the valley where the Sheikh's compound was. The guys not only saw the rocket hit the tower but felt the explosion clear up in the cave. It rocked the ground like a 5.0 earthquake. The walls shook, dropping loose gravel and sand down on those below.

Diana awoke when a tremor wave moved through the ground. She jumped up and realized that Ben wasn't there. He and Scott were over by the cave's mouth; she walked briskly over to them. She had a little trouble keeping her balance with the ground shaking; the dust coming down from the ceiling above her kept falling into her eyes. Ben turned to see that Diana was awake and moving toward them. He reached out his hand to help guide her over to them. Once she had a hold of his hand, he pulled her to his side. She seemed more than content to stay there.

"Now there is a fireworks show," Scott stated.

The first rocket took out the tower, the second hit toward the back of the compound. It was either near or on the Sheikh's home. Diana saw one of the rockets take out the pagoda building. She tugged on Ben's arm. Ben looked down at her. "What about Aisha, Mahala, and Taggee?" she asked.

"If they are still there, which I doubt, there is nothing we can do now," he stated. He felt Diana's grasp tighten around his arm, her head bent down and rested up against him. He reached over and put his arm around her back. He unconsciously was stroking her back, comforting her.

"Is Taggee the guard that helped you guys out?" Scott asked.

Diana nodded. Scott could see she was crying. Tears were running down her cheeks, sparkling when the lights of the rockets came across the air. "Is he a really big guy, like a Shaq-size guy?" he continued.

"That's about the right description for him," Ben stated.

"I saw him and two women slip out of the camp just before dawn this morning," Scott stated.

"Then they aren't there, thank you, God," Diana gratefully commented.

"Umm…what time is the pickup?" Ben mused.

"It was to be at midnight, but they won't come anywhere near here with this going on," Scott informed them.

"With all this going on, these hills are going to be crawling with whichever faction is doing this. What's the plan?" Ben asked.

"I thought you had the head for strategy," Scott quipped.

"Yeah well, I'm not sure I have all the information yet to get anything planned," Ben said as he looked down at Diana.

Diana was watching the fires burning in the compound, noticed the quiet, and looked up from the attack going on and saw that Ben and Scott were both looking at her. "What…I don't understand," Diana stated, looking between the two of them.

"You're the one that withheld information from us at the cabin. Maybe you would like to tell us the rest of the story?" Ben injected.

Diana looked at Ben then over to Scott; they were both glaring down at her. She had the strange feeling of an interrogation coming on. "I don't know what you're talking about. I don't know anything, I really don't," she insisted as she took a couple of steps back from the two.

Ben and Scott looked at each other. "I think we need to have some retribution of our own." Ben smiled.

"You mean making her pay for making us come all the way here, risking our lives to save a woman who didn't tell us what she knew?" Scott added.

"Ben? I told you everything I know. Granted it wasn't till you were here, but that's because I knew you wo—I mean, if God wanted you to know, He would have told you Himself," Diana quickly stated.

"You hold her legs, I'll take care of her arms. I think we can get a little more out of her, don't you, Scott?" Ben suggested.

"I think we might need to do a thorough investigation. She may have some information stored on her person." Scott grinned.

Diana figured out they were having a wonderful joke with her. She also knew that they were backing her into a corner. She figured if she jagged a little, she would be able to get on the other side of them; they wouldn't be able to corner her then.

Ben saw the change in her face. She knew that they weren't going to hurt her. There was a spark that flashed in her eyes; it signaled that she had a plan. *Let's see how you deduce and solve…Milady*, Ben thought.

She saw that Ben and Scott had to separate to get below a part of the ceiling that was less than six feet tall. She took her chance and bolted between them. She quickly darted past Ben's arm then dodged Scott's reach.

"Quick little fox, isn't she?" Scott said turning to go after her.

"A fox hunt then," Ben smiled

"Hey, Ben, I've got something for ya." Scott pull his backpack over, opened the side, and pulled out a couple of glasses and handed one pair to Ben.

"Night vision?" Ben asked.

"Of course. I thought they may come in handy. This isn't quite what I had in mind, but since we've got them, might as well use them," Scott replied smiling. The guys each headed off to opposite sides of the wall. They checked every little nook and cranny of the cave. Ben and Scott kept in touch with each other by using their animal calls. Scott came down to a jut out of rock and noticed there was a toe sticking out from behind it on the ground. He stood there for a while and observed it; he was just about to walk away when he saw it twitch. Scott let out a yip, which made the foot grow very still. He heard Ben's reply and knew that he would be there soon. Ben came up on Scott, standing near an outcrop of rocks. He put his hand up on Scott's shoulder. Scott nodded toward the ground. Ben saw her toe sticking out from the nook she must have been hiding in. They waited there for a few minutes quietly, not making a sound; the foot started to move, slowly. Then a leg appeared out of the nook. She must have had to pull the robe up so she could get up; her leg was bare clear up near to the top of her thigh. There was a wide dark line on the ankle, a dark line that slanted down on her calf, and a dark line that slanted up on her thigh. Scott looked at Ben with a question on his face. Ben's own face was stone cold as if he could tear somebody apart. Soon a hand came around and tightened on the wall so she could pull herself up, her robe falling back down to her ankle. Then they watched Diana slowly maneuver herself out from behind the nook.

Diana stepped out from the crevice she'd been hiding in and slowly started to walk the rest of the way to the cave mouth. She sighed as she could see the moonlight shining in, filling the rest of the entrance. She looked out at the red glow from the fires that burned in the compound. She froze for a second then seemingly to nobody said, "Haven't you two learned it's not wise to startle me?"

"Your sixth sense is getting a little weak. We could have taken you five minutes ago," Ben jabbed. He reached over, putting his hand on her shoulder, slowly sliding it down to just above her elbow. Then he tightened his grasp. She had leaned her head toward his hand when he touched her; when he tightened his grasp, he had her undivided attention. Then she felt someone else grab her other arm. She quickly spun her head around to look at Scott holding her other arm.

"I believe we have found our fox bro," Ben said to Scott.

"Yes, indeed, so shall we do the water treatment or maybe the feather one?" Scott jested. When Diana tried to pull away from them, they simply lifted her up off the ground so her feet couldn't touch. They made sure they didn't grab her wrists, which were still bandaged. "You'd better put me down. You'll regret it," Diana quibbled.

"Hmm…I think we'll start with the water then maybe go to the feather," Ben added.

They carried her back, far back, into the cave. "Do you have her? I've got to go grab the stuff from the entrance," Scott stated.

"I think I can manage her. Go ahead and get the stuff," Ben said as he steadied Diana in his grasp.

"You know I will get you back for anything you have going through your mind," Diana threatened.

"Promises…promises. You really shouldn't promise things that you can't keep," Ben jeered.

"And you are one to talk," she fired back.

"I always keep my promises," he said with a grin. Diana felt him push her into a nook. "I think it's time I collect," he stated. His hand let go of her arm and wrapped around her back. He pulled her into him. His other hand started to play with her hair.

Diana looked up at Ben. "If I were you, I'd think twice about what is passing through your head. I haven't had a toothbrush or any kind of toothpaste for almost a week."

"Point taken," Ben replied. "But I will cash in on that raincheck and any other tally you add to it. I'm positive you will be adding more."

She poked him in his rib, a tickle spot she found earlier in the cabin; Ben jerked to the side but kept her tight against the wall. "That did it. It is definitely going to be water first. Then…well…then we'll have to see," he gleamed. He quickly checked the ceiling height, looked down at Diana, then lifted her up over his shoulder.

"Mr. Tigere! Put me…down!" Diana yelled.

Ben carried Diana into a large cavern then put her down in front of him, keeping a hold of her upper arms. There was a small but nonetheless warm fire glowing in the corner. Diana could see a pool of water toward the center of the cavern. She could see the pool because there was a shaft of moonlight coming through a small hole in the ceiling of the cavern. It let the light in from outside. Tonight it was hitting the pool and dispersing reflection ripples of light all over the walls of the cavern. She could hear the babble of running water from somewhere but wasn't able to locate where it was at. She looked up at Ben; Scott just strolled up beside him. "This is where you've been hiding out?" she asked.

"Aye...lassie," Scott replied in his Scottish brogue. Scott went to put the scarves and the empty cans in a corner. "I supposed you called in your note, didn't ya?"

"Nope...I still have to call them in yet. She's racking up a lot of tallies," Ben stated. He glanced over at the woman that was doing everything she could not to look at him. "I may just have to start marking it on an IOU app. I don't think she's learned her lesson yet. Habits are hard to break. Of course, she may never break this one."

Diana glared at Ben. *So...this is a competition between you two*, she thought. "You know, if this is going to be a competition, I'll have to have data to compare to. So...Scott, when he starts collecting on those, you and I will have to go for a walk?" she smoothly stated, beaming a large smile.

Scott smiled. "I think I could show you some interesting things—rock formations, beautiful sunsets, you name it."

Ben's eyes narrowed, his right hand tightened into a fist. Diana knew she got him riled up, but it didn't last long enough for her. She would have to work a little harder. "You can ask Mr. McCleary, Agent Tigere. It's the female that decides who wins in that kind of competition."

Ben got control over himself; she was playing him. She wasn't going to let her pride go by the wayside of men's ego. Scott wouldn't be able to handle her; he knew that. He figured Diana knew it as well. The only one who didn't know it was Scott. "Do you think you can handle a wildcat at night when you couldn't handle her during the day?"

"Hmm...I don't know. Cats are more active at night. It might be fun to do research in that area," Scott jeered.

"I think we'd better chain this cat up for the night. She's a little too frisky. Unless you think we need to tame her down a wee bit now," Ben teased.

Scott wanted a chance with Diana. He looked between the two of them. Nope...Ben had a claim; he just wasn't admitting it to himself. He saw that Diana was having fun riling him up, and Scott had to admit he was proud of her. She did a good job. The fact that she could play Ben so well was interesting. Ben didn't let women play him; he read them too well. "I'll take her feet, you get those arms of hers, and we'll get to taming this wildcat." Scott smiled. He kind of felt sorry for Diana. If it was just himself or Ben alone, she may be able to hold her own. The two of them together...she had no hope.

Ben quickly grabbed on to Diana's left forearm then tried to get Diana's other arm. He knew what he had to do from wrestling with her in the cabin. Even so, he struggled to get her first arm around her chest in order to restrict her movement. He finally managed; then he grabbed her other arm. Once Ben had her arms, Scott came from behind and went to get her legs. He had to be careful. She was already twisting and turning, kicking and swinging her feet. He got kicked in the shin, whacked in the shoulder, then heeled in the back before he got a hold of both legs. "She's a little tricky, isn't she," Scott commented.

"Put me down! What are you two up to? Let me go!" Diana demanded.

Ben and Scott had their arms full. Even with her arms and legs controlled, she was squirming and twisting in the middle, giving the guys an uneven chaotic walk toward the pool. Diana glanced over and saw where the guys were taking her. Her eyes grew huge; she started fighting even more so. A few times she thought she was going to get her legs free; unfortunately, she didn't have enough time to finish the job. In a last-ditch effort, she grabbed ahold of Ben's shirt. *If I go in… you go in*, she thought. The guys got her to the edge of the pool, counted to three, then swung her in. Ben didn't realize that Diana had a hold of his shirt. When she went in, he was pulled in as well. The momentum of the guys swing may have thrown her deeper than Ben; the point was that Ben got wet anyway. Diana's scream was stopped only because she went under the water. She got her bearings under the water then came up and grabbed a breath. She smiled at the fact that Ben was also pulled in with her. He was standing there, talking with Scott with his back to her—a big mistake. He was standing in water that was up to his waist, so she went underwater and quietly swam up behind him.

Scott was laughing at the edge. "She does know how to get under your skin, doesn't she, bro?"

"You think that's funny, Scotsman? Just think what she would do to you if you went for a 'walk' with her," Ben fired back. Just then, he felt Diana grab him around the neck and shoulder. Diana arched back, throwing his balance off. He fell backward, back into the water. Diana let go of him as he fell and came out from behind him. She was treading water while Ben splashed and sloshed around in the water, laughing her head off the entire time. Ben got his feet under him; Diana wasn't quite tall enough to touch the bottom, but he could. He looked over at Diana, who was laughing at him. He walked up and put his hands under her arms and lifted her up out of the water. He held her there, her hands grabbing his biceps to steady herself. She'd stopped laughing, but the enjoyment of her victory was still shiny in those emerald-green eyes of hers. He turned so that it would be in deeper water and went to dunked her under; she knew what he was going to do, so she tried to hold on to his arms as he was putting her under, but she couldn't. Her hands just slipped off. It didn't matter anyway; he lost his footing and went under again. He quickly stood up. She swam over, arching up just inches in front of him. He caught her up under her arms again and pulled her up to be face-to-face with him. *You're unbelievable*, he thought with a smile on his face. He heard Scott laughing at the edge of the pool at them. Well, mostly at him.

Scott was laughing so hard his eyes were closed, and he was crying. Ben looked at Diana, nodded toward Scott. Diana's eyebrow quickly arched up, and a wicked smile came across her face. Ben gently put her back in the water, careful not to make a sound. They inched up to the edge of the pool; Scott was still laughing hard, so hard, he didn't see them coming. Ben and Diana grabbed his arms at the same time, bringing his laughing to an abrupt stop. He looked back and forth between Ben and Diana. "No…no…no, wait a minute," he said. They pulled on him at the same time; Scott was flung into the pool. He ended up hitting the water in a belly flop, which made them cringe. Scott finally popped up, gasping for air not more than three feet from them.

"That's so not kewl!" Scott sputtered.

Diana and Ben just laughed. Diana started to climb out of the pool and realized that she had lost a sandal in there. "Mr. McCleary, since you're still in the pool, would you be so kind as to retrieve my sandal for me?"

Scott looked around then felt with his feet till he felt the sandal on the bottom of the pool. He bent down and picked it up. "Here…here's your flipping sandal!" he said as he threw it about five feet behind her. Diana stood up to go get her sandal. The robe she was wearing now vacuum sealed to her body since she was out of the water and in the air. Ben and Scott were just enjoying the view; her endowments giving credence to her figure.

Diana tried pulling on the robe to break the vacuum, but it didn't want to release. "Well, God bless it. I hope you two are enjoying yourselves. I guess it I should be thankful that this thing isn't see-through," she fumed as she moved more toward the shadowed area.

Ben was sitting on the edge of the pool; Scott was still standing in the middle of the pool. "Actually, I'm enjoying myself immensely. Obviously, since I've not heard a peep out of Scott, nor has he bothered to get himself out of the water, I'm sure he's quite happy. This is the first time he's had this pleasure from you," Ben jabbed.

"I don't suppose either of you two have a change of clothes for me?" Diana fired.

Ben patted he chest, his waist, then his thighs. "Nope, I'm afraid I don't. Scott, do you have anything?" he asked.

Scott, now climbing out of the pool, smiled. "Actually, I just happened to have a few things here." He walked over behind the small fire and pulled out a bag. He opened the bag and rummaged around in it till he found what he wanted. He walked over to Diana and gave her a bundle of clothes. "Maybe you'd better go over to the fire and warm up," Scott suggested.

Diana chuckled. "Why, so you can get a better view? I think I'd best stay in the shadows for the time being."

"Diana, wait a minute," Ben said somberly as he stood up and walked towards her. His shoes were making a squishing, flatulent sound with every step. Diana giggled, and the closer he got to her, the more she had to work to not break out into a full laugh. He reached into his pocket and pulled out a large pocket knife. Her laughing stopped, and her eyes grew wide again. For an instant, Ben was sure he saw fear of him in her eyes. He slowly reached down and grabbed Diana's robe at the thigh. He plunged the knife in and swiftly sliced outward. He slit the robe clear through the hem. He then walked around and did the same to the other side. The slices caused the vacuum that sealed the robe to her body to release. He put his hand on the side of her face. "You should never be afraid of me. I would never purposely hurt you. Remember that, kitten. Now, I want you to walk over to the fire. I want to see what's up with those marks on your legs," Ben sternly ordered.

Diana just stood there like a deer in the headlights. "How do you kn—?" She just shook her head. Ben lost patience and picked her up and threw her over his shoulder. "Would you put me down? Benjamen—oh, whatever your full name is—put me down!" she balked.

Ben sat her down by the fire. "My full name is Benjamen James Tigere. Now, let me see your legs," he commanded. Diana hesitantly stood so the light of the fire shone on her left leg. She carefully pulled over part of the robe so that her leg was able to be seen all the way to her upper thigh. It was extremely obvious that she was very uncomfortable with the whole situation. Ben carefully checked the lines that went across her calves and thighs. They were red, but he could see that they were healing. "And the reason why you didn't tell us about these?"

"I did tell you. I just didn't think I needed to show you where all the ropes were, unless it was absolutely necessary. You are neither my parents nor my husbands, for goodness' sake," Diana barked as he checked her right leg.

"You got those the same time that you got the burns on your wrists and ankles?" Scott asked.

"Yes. I told you I didn't want that man touching me," Diana snipped.

Scott turned to Ben. "What in the world were they doing to her that they needed to tie her up like that?"

"They were checking to see if she was a virgin," Ben flatly stated.

Scott's eyes went red with anger. Diana was about to break. Her eyes were filling with water; her chin was trembling. *I will not cry...I will not cry...I will...not...* She was trying to keep herself strong. She then felt Ben's arms come around her. He brought her up against him and held her there. She couldn't hold it back anymore; she just broke apart and bawled. Too much to deal with, too much wore her raw.

"I'm sorry, Kitten. I'm sorry you had to go through that. It brought everything to the front again, didn't it?" Ben whispered to her.

She nodded and sobbed. "I'm sorry. I'm being a baby."

"No...you're dealing with skeletons. You can only hide those for so long," Ben countered. "You said God's plan was for you to be here. Maybe some of it was to help you get past those monsters? You know, you don't have to do everything alone. I'm here and only a phone call away when we get back home." Ben made sure his voice stayed calm and low. His mind went back to what Taggee told him. "If you come against her with force, she'll fight with everything in her. If you come calm and slow, she'll be easier to work with." Ben felt Diana take in a deep breath as she tried to get control of herself; he felt her body just totally relax against him. "Those rope burns aren't infected. They are healing. I'm sorry I scared you, forcing you to relive that junk. Forgive me."

"It's the shadows in my mind, Ben, not what you were doing. There's nothing to forgive. I've just got to deal with it," Diana said, looking up at Ben.

"Got ahead and get your clothes changed before Scott over there thinks this is too sappy and goes for a feather," Ben said aloud so Scott could hear him.

"Well, if we do that now, it would be more of a mud pit fight. Although, thinking about it, that might be fun," Scott beamed. Diana flushed bright red clear back to her ears. The guys laughed a deep, hearty laugh.

"We would have to flip a coin as to who would be the one to be hands-on with her. It wouldn't be fair if two of us took her on," Ben stated.

"I suggest you think very hard about that, gentlemen. It did take two of you to get me into the pool, and that wasn't without casualties. It would take both of you to control me, and I guarantee that I will use that to my advantage," Diana pointed out as she wiped her cheeks.

Ben looked over toward Scott. *Yeah…there's a little something in his eyes. She would pit us against each other. Even still…it would be fun to try it someday*, Ben thought. "You know, for now, she may have a point. She'd get us fighting between ourselves while she sat back and watched. I think we may need to concentrate on getting home. Then we'll see about a wrestling match," Ben said.

Diana sighed. *I'm glad they bought my bluff*, she thought. She batted her eyes and said in a Southern drawl, "Ar y'all sugges'ing I'd do a li'l ol' thing like dat?"

"That's pretty good. Where'd you pick up that accent from?" Scott asked, glad she wasn't bawling anymore.

"I have friends in Texas, Alabama, and Kentucky. I picked up their accents after I was with them during the summer," she informed Scott. "Now where may I get changed out of this stupid robe?"

"I don't have a changing room here, Milady. I've never had to use one. So…umm…," Scott said.

"Looks like you'll have to find a corner somewhere, Diana," Ben injected.

"Okay, I know a place I can go. If you gentlemen will excuse me," Diana informed them.

"Are you sure you don't need some help?" Ben asked.

"Nope, don't need any help from you gentlemen in this area, thank you," she emphasized. "I'll be back in a few minutes." She turned and walked back down the path. She was heading to the nook Ben pushed her into earlier. As soon as she was down the path, the men got busy adjusting things for three people in the cavern instead of one. As they were moving things Scott looked over at Ben, "Whether you have staked a claim or not, I'm gonna have to challenge the tiger's territory."

Ben looked up at Scott. "Bro, trust me, you won't get far. Taggee called her a tigress, and he's got her pegged right. That's why Mahdi wants her so bad: she's a challenge."

"Yeah, and I think I may be up for the challenge," Scott stated.

"Good luck, Scott, just remember: I warned you." Ben shrugged. The conversation ceased as soon as Diana appeared in the cavern again. She had a pair of jeans on and the halter top Scott had bought for her while they were staying in the cabin.

"Seriously Scott, you do know that if we have to do any walking tomorrow while the sun is up, I'll be fried within an hour," Diana refuted.

Scott just smiled at her. Ben glanced up and saw what she was spitting about. The halter top was loose on her this time. *We've got to get some meat back on her again*, Ben thought. However, she was right: her back would be fried in less than thirty minutes. "We'll have to think of something when we cross that bridge, kitten," he stated to calm her down. He kept eye contact with her till she gave him a nod.

"I'm sorry Scott. I am grateful, especially for the jeans and hiking boots," Diana sheepishly said as she calmed down. She looked down at her shoes. "I'm obviously tired. I don't control my mouth very well when I'm tired."

"Yeah, well...we all get a clouded mind when we're exhausted. Let's get some shuteye, and then we'll get some food into you before that shirt no longer fits," Scott calmly stated. He waved his hand, signaling her to come and sit down by the fire. She nodded and walked over. *This is what Ben was meaning. She can be falling apart one minute then fiery and quick-tempered the next, laughing a moment later. Funny...I'd never seen that before. We could have a lot of fun making up after fighting*, Scott thought.

Ben was sitting on the ground, his back leaning up against the wall, his legs stretched out in front of him and sipping his coffee. He was watching Diana through the corner of his eye. The glow of the fire caused shadows to dance all around her. *Why am I so upset? She's got a mind of her own and a sharp one at that. Scott's a free agent. He can do whatever he wants. The fact is, Scott would want to fight so he could make up afterward. She's not wired that way. Maybe she'll shoot him down to start with. It would solve the issue...wouldn't it*, Ben thought. "Scott, do you have any gauze and ointment with you?" he asked once he focused his mind back in.

"Yeah sure, I'll dig it out," Scott replied.

Ben pulled his now-dried-off knife from his pocket. "Come over here, kitten. Let's check those wrists for you."

Diana moved over to Ben. "Where did you get that knife? You didn't have it last night." She gave him one of her wrists and watched him cut the bandage off.

"Scott was keeping it for me. I knew they would take any type of weapon from me," Ben informed her.

Diana nodded. Her eyes seemed to go away for a minute or two while watching the fire; then she started asking questions. "Aren't you guys afraid of the factions finding us, you know, from the light of the fire going?" Diana asked.

Scott and Ben looked at her. "They can't see this far into the cave. We're about fifty feet inside the mountain," Scott stated as he handed Ben the gauze and ointment.

"What if they come inside the cave? I mean, water is a treasure in this land, right? Wouldn't they know it's here and want to get some?" she continued.

Ben watched her eyes; now what has her on edge. "Diana, what's going on?" he asked as he finished unwrapping her left wrist. He checked it out carefully; it wasn't infected and looked like it was finally starting to heal. He made sure it was dried off and put the ointment on it and rewrapped it with the gauze, then he moved over to the other wrist. He paused when Diana didn't answer him. "Diana?" She looked over to the opening of the pathway then over to Ben.

Scott walked over to stand beside Ben. "Oh no, you don't, Milady. Ben might be able to read you, but I don't read minds. Say it out aloud, please," Scott injected.

"It's hard to explain, Scott. It's a feeling. A cold, dark, and heavy presence I feel. Something bad is nearby or coming. I just don't know what it is right now," she stated.

"So what, are you a medium or something?" Scott questioned.

Diana rolled her eyes. "I'm not a medium or a witch. I don't believe in ghosts, and I'm not insane. I take it that you don't believe God's spirit tells you things, Mr. McCleary?"

"Umm…I know that he works around me. He influences the lives of those who have accepted Jesus as their Savior. I know that God has used dreams, visions, and angels, but as far as the other, I haven't thought about it much," Scott said.

Ben sat there only half listening to the conversation. *Somebody is near. That's what Diana said. The Lord is confirming it to me. We need to put out the fire and get prepared for visitors*, Ben thought.

Diana continued, "We're to be like Jesus, right? We can't do that by what we are or do. It's only through the Lord's spirit living and working in us that it's possible. If the spirit is living in us and we listen to him, the spirit tells us things."

"Ben, help me out here. Ben? Hello…earth to Ben." Scott elbowed him.

"Huh? I'm sorry. I was thinking we need to put out the fire. We may have visitors," Ben stated.

Scott's mouth dropped open. "So you believe all this spirit stuff?" Diana was watching Ben to see what he was going to answer. Her heart was in her throat; she was praying he would understand what was being said.

"Yeah, Scott, I always have. I just didn't mention it because I knew you didn't," he replied.

Diana blinked and nodded as she acknowledged Ben. She studied him for a minute. She wasn't sure if he said that because he actually believed it or for some other reason. *Don't you dare fall, girl*, she told herself.

Ben was finishing wrapping the right wrist. It was also starting to heal. He noticed she was watching him, reading him. She still didn't trust him, but she definitely felt something toward him—that he was for sure of. *I'll have to somehow show her she can trust me*, Ben thought.

"We'll need to get everything hidden and put the fire out, just in case we have any unwanted visitors," Ben said.

"I've been here almost a week, and nobody has come here." Scott held up his hand to stop the oncoming arguments from both sides. "I'll do what you say; but if I'm right, Diana, you have to go on a date with me," Scott said with a smirk.

"A date? Scott, what do you have going on in that mind of yours?" Diana mused.

"Just a simple date—a movie and dinner, that's all. Do we have a deal?" Scott pushed.

"Why do I feel I need to have a contract with the lawyers reading over every detail?" Diana injected.

Scott held out his hand for Diana to shake it. She looked over at Ben, but he didn't look up; he kept his eyes down, looking at his coffee cup. "Okay, let me clarify what you're saying. I go to dinner and a movie. By the way…there will be no alcohol. If we're wrong about having visitors? Diana restated.

"You don't drink alcohol? I didn't know that…okay, yeah, I'll order you milk instead. It's just dinner and a movie, that's all," Scott confirmed. Diana went and shook Scott's hand.

Scott was sure that they were just being paranoid, but he got a date out of the hassle, so he was content. They all packed up the few things they had and buried it near the wall of the cavern. On the far side of the cavern, there was an outcrop of rocks; it was big enough that they all could hide behind it and not be seen. Ben took the one side, Scott took the other, and they put Diana smack dab in the middle of them. *At least I'll have a shoulder to sleep on*, Diana thought.

25

In Syria

The trio was curled up behind the outcrop of rocks; Diana had given up the fight and fell asleep. She was leaning up against Ben's side, her arms down in her lap; Ben's right arm was around her waist and weaved through one of her arms. Neither Ben nor Scott slept deep; they were basically just resting. It was very early in the morning; Ben knew that because he had heard a rooster crow in the distance. He tensed up at what he was now hearing. It started out faint and distant, a mumbling that was echoing down into the cavern. *There is somebody in or near the cave's mouth*, Ben thought. The mumbling seemed to be getting louder, more distinct. Ben looked over to Scott. Scott was looking at Ben; he signaled that he heard it too.

Diana's eyes swiftly flew open; she gasped. Ben quickly put his hand over her mouth. She looked over to Ben and calmed herself. It wasn't the voices that woke her up; she had the feeling of something crawling up her leg. Now, apparently, was not the time to deal with it though. They sat there quietly, intently listening as the voices drew closer and closer. They started to see light dancing around. The voices were now understandable, the lights were brighter. *They're speaking Farsi*, Ben noticed, which only makes sense. That was the common language of the area. He listened to what they were saying. One of the men was saying that this hunt was ridiculous. She wouldn't even survive a day in the desert. The other man was pointing out that they won't either if they didn't find good water. The third man must have been a servant because he was the one who was loaded with the water cantinas and not offering any advice. They were soon in the big cavern. The men got excited when they saw the pool of water. They ran over and started filling the cantinas. One of the men commented on the smell of smoke in the air there. The two gathering the water blew him off. They told him that this was a common watering spot and some shepherd boys probably stayed the night there.

Diana was trying to sit still; she saw Ben and Scott scowling at her. Something was crawling up her leg, and she could feel it; it was up to the top of her calf now. Diana stared at her legs, knowing that it should be coming up to her knee soon. She was hoping there was enough light to see what it was. When she did see it, it made her want to scream. She saw a gigantic nearly white spider with very long pointed legs crawling over the top of her knee; she squealed.

Ben could feel Diana being antsy; he didn't know what or why she was doing it, but he wished she would stop. He heard a squeal come out of her mouth. He quickly put his hand back over her mouth, scowling at her for being so brainless. He looked at her expression and saw she was watching something in front of her. He followed her line of her sight then saw the cave spider crawling on her knee.

Scott, on the other hand, was letting Ben deal with Diana. He didn't know why she was being such an empty headed female, but right now he needed to keep an eye on the visitors. They had heard Diana's squeal and were frantically looking around for its source. The servant was saying that the cavern was haunted. The other was saying that it was probably a mouse that some cave snake got. The third wasn't convinced and kept shining his light around the cavern, looking for something.

Ben whispered in Diana's ear, "You have to be quiet." He tightened his grip on her arms to hold her still; he also kept his hand over her mouth. She was starting to shake, and Ben had to hold her tight to stop her from freaking out. The men, not finding the cause of the squeal, finished filling their cantinas and started heading back to the mouth of the cave. They were saying that they had to go finish their task so they could get back to their own families. One of the men was hoping that his wife held off having the baby till he made it back. Soon, they were out of the cavern…but the trio still needed to be quiet. They weren't out of the cave yet.

Ben got Scott's attention; he saw Ben signaling him to look down at Diana's stomach. *Why? Why would I need to look there for?* Scott wondered. Then he saw it: a large beautiful cave spider, its long elegant legs crawling on Diana's upper thigh. Scott smiled, reached down, and let the spider climb up onto his hand. It was as big as his hand, but that didn't bother him at all. He stood up and reached over to let the spider crawl off his hand onto the far side of the rock formation. Diana just hung on to Ben, who once the spider was off of her, took his hand off her mouth and let go of her arms. Scott slowly crept over to the path that led to the cave mouth. He worked his way through, quietly and softly, behind the men who came for water. Once they were out of the cave and riding away on their horses. Scott headed back to the cavern. "All clear."

Diana jumped up, started hopping up and down, brushing unseen invisible creepy-crawlies off her, to the point that she was almost crazy with it. Ben watched her until she calmed down.

"Interesting little dance. Is it tribal?" Diana glared at him, stuck her tongue out at him, and continued to brush her arms down. As soon as she realized what she did she slapped her hand over her mouth.

Ben smiled impishly. "Another mark on the IOU app, I see." Diana actually smiled behind her hand, but knew Ben couldn't see it. Ben stood up grinning. "She's obviously not an arachnid lover."

"If it was a praying mantis or a lady bug, I wouldn't have minded it so much. I *hate* spiders and snakes," she retorted.

"If it wasn't for snakes and spiders, the world would be overran with pests," Scott informed her. "Besides, if it was a snake, it would have just crawled up inside your jeans. At least the spider had the decency to stay on the outside," Scott jested.

"They may have their purpose, but not *on* me or where I am at. They keep their space, and I'll do what I can to not kill them," Diana quipped. Scott's comments just made Diana even more crept out. She started to shake out her hair and brush down her legs.

"Now you've messed up all that hair. It's going to be a pain to get all the knots out of it," Ben informed her.

"Oh, shut up. I'll probably be doing this all day, stupid spider," she fumed.

"Looks like you lost your bet bro," Ben stated as he nudged Scott.

"They weren't bad, probably looking for the women that snuck out yesterday," Scott replied.

"Maybe," Ben added. "Still, we did have visitors that were unexpected." Scott just waved his hand behind him as he started to dig stuff out for breakfast. The trio sat down and started eating breakfast. Diana took a bottle of water and ate some of Scott's trail mix. The guys ate some beef jerky while they waited for the coffee to heat. Diana was still very jumpy and Ben just had to take advantage of it. He had a long weed that he picked up as they climbed to the cave yesterday. He came behind her and lightly touched it to her back. She jumped from a seated position to two feet off the ground. Scott just looked at her, seemingly unaware of what her problem was. In truth, Scott knew Ben was brushing the weed against her every time he walked past her. He was biting his cheeks to keep his composure. He watched from the corner of his eye as Ben approached Diana again and touched her back with the reed. Diana jumped again, just not as high.

"Lord, help me!" Diana said as she felt something crawling on her back. She caught a glimpse of Scott out of the corner of her eye. She saw him smile and look toward Ben. She put two and two together; the guys were teasing her again.

Ben waited till she settled down. He knew he was pushing it to tickle her three times. She would catch on soon, but he couldn't resist. He started to walk behind her again, the weed ready to touch her back. As he brushed against her back, Diana's arm came around and wrapped behind his knee and grabbed a hold of his ankle. Ben of course stumbled but was able to remain standing. "You dog!" Diana sputtered as she looked up at Ben. She saw the cobalt blue in his eyes; she also heard Scott laughing.

Ben just reached down and brushed the weed under her chin. "What's the matter, kitten, don't you like this toy? Most cats love it."

Diana pulled Ben's leg up, making him fall backward. She jumped up, ran over, and sat down on his stomach. "Let's test it out then," she stated. "Oh, wait a minute, your back isn't bare. I'll have to use something else." She tossed the weed away and started poking him in his sides; he jerked back and forth.

"Now...you're not thinking well, kitten. You'll get into trouble," he warned as he chuckled. She just kept tickling him, smiling at him the whole time. Ben started to laugh, but then in one effortless movement rolled her under him. The quick change took Diana by surprise. She'd figured she was heavy enough to hold him there; obviously, she was wrong.

"I warned you, now what are you going to do?" Ben said with a Cheshire cat grin on his face.

"I can always try this." Diana smiled and pinched Ben's inner thigh. His leg twitched. It's a common button with her nieces and nephew, so she figured she'd try it on him. Diana's eyebrow arched up, and an ornery smile came across her face. Ben reached down and grabbed her hand. Diana started on the other leg, getting the same reaction. He went to grab the loose hand, but Diana started twisting around. He wasn't as high on her as the last time he had her in the same position. She was able to squirm out from underneath him. As she was pulling herself out, Ben grabbed the other hand.

He pulled her down to her knees in front of him. "I'm in a quandary: let you get a pass or retribution time?"

"I think you might need to take a pass. Mr. McCleary is looking a little green in the gills over there," Diana whispered to him. In truth, she was getting majorly hungry for some "sugar." *Get control of yourself, you idiot*, she thought.

Ben looked over to Scott. "What do you think, bro, shall I give her a pass or tickle her till she pees her pants?" He knew Scott felt that he was hogging all of Diana's time, but she's the one that started it.

"I think I'm about ready to throw both of you two in the coldest part of that pool over there," Scott sneered.

Ben looked at Diana. "That might be fun," he said.

Diana eyebrow arched up. She saw the twinkle in his eyes, but she wasn't willing to walk around in sopping-wet clothes all day. "You'd better think twice with that decision, Tiger. You would have more than just me to contend with," she pointed out.

"As you wish, for now," he said and let her go.

She got up, picked up the offending weed, and broke it into little small pieces. "Don't think I didn't notice your involvement Mr. McCleary. You will get yours, I promise," Diana threatened.

Scott looked over to Ben. "How is she at keeping her promises?"

"She hasn't kept one yet, but there hasn't been an opportunity until recently," Ben stated.

"So, I shouldn't be scared then," Scott replied with a gleam in his eye and a smile on his face. *She actually acknowledged my existence*, Scott thought.

"I'll have to admit, I might need backup. I'll have to make a call when I get home. Once I get her on my side, you'd better be afraid." Diana smiled and started to walk over to the pathway that led to the cave mouth.

Ben gave her a querying eye. "Where are you heading to, kitten?" he asked.

"Someone gave the hint of peeing, and my body decided that it needs to. So if you two gentlemen would excuse me." Diana gave them a bow and headed up the path.

"You're not going to give me a chance with her, are you?" Scott steamed.

Ben looked at him. Diana was right; he was green around the gills. "She started it," Ben quipped.

"Yeah, and you were going to finish it, weren't you? The thing is, if I wasn't here, she'd probably let you finish it," Scott fired back.

Yeah, she had a hungry look in her eye. She probably would have let me... well anyway, Ben thought. Ben just gave Scott a shrug.

Diana was walking back down the pathway toward the cavern. She had just come to the door of the cavern when she thought she heard what sounded to her like a bottle rocket flying near; then there was a small explosion. She jumped out of her skin and ran over to Ben, who was standing near the wall by where Scott was sitting. Ben wrapped his arms around her. "It's okay, kitten. It's a message for Scott."

She looked at him then over to Scott. "That's how we get messages from HQ or in this case, Dick," Scott confirmed.

"Dick is in the area too? Great, can I call my cousin for backup?" Diana asked. "I think between the two of us, we can handle the three of you guys."

"I'd like to meet this cousin of yours, Milady," Scott injected. Diana gave him a quick smile.

"I may be able to arrange that when we get home," she prompted.

"We'd better go see what Dick has for us," Ben stated. The trio walked up the pathway to the mouth of the cave. They had to look around to see where the rocket hit.

It was Diana that found it. "Here it is. I think."

The guys came over to where she was standing. "Yep…that's it," Scott confirmed. He reached down and brushed the dirt back to uncover the shaft of the rocket. He unscrewed the top of the shaft and pulled out some paper. He read it then passed it over to Ben.

Diana watched their faces; they didn't look happy. "What's up?" she asked as she looked into Ben's eyes. She was watching to see what he was thinking.

Ben noticed her studying him; he would have to word it carefully. "The pickup will be this evening," he said.

"Okay, so what's the problem?" she inquired.

"We have to be on the other side of the mountain," Scott added.

"And how far is that?" she asked.

"It's about a ten-mile hike," Scott said flatly.

Diana got very quiet. She was looking at the wall of the cave but not really seeing it. Ben came and stood beside her. "You can do it. You're stronger than you think, Diana."

"I don't have much of a choice, do I? We'd better get going. Umm… what are we going to do about my shirt?" she asked.

"Scott, do you have another shirt she can put over the top of this one?" Ben asked, looking at Scott.

"Yeah, I believe I do. I'll give it to her before we head out," Scott replied. They headed back to the cavern, quickly packed up, picked up, and got ready to leave. Scott gave Diana one of his shirts to cover her back. The shirt—a green plaid, button-down oxford with long sleeves—was too big on her, but she took the tails and tied them at her waist and rolled the sleeves up to stay at her wrists.

Ben came and gave her his scarf. "You'll need it more than I do," he said. He put his hand on the side of her face. "Are you ready?"

"I forgot to ask, probably because I don't want to know. How long do we have to get to this pickup site?" Diana asked.

"We have to be at the site by eight tonight. That gives us twelve hours to get there," Ben informed her.

"I'm guessing that since we have twelve hours to get ten miles, those ten miles aren't going to be easy," she stated.

Ben just grimaced. But Diana wasn't letting him get out of answering her. Finally, he said, "It will be a challenge, but it's not impossible."

Lord, give me strength, Diana prayed.

Ben pulled her to him and gave her a hug, kissed her on the top of the head, then said, "You can do it. I know you can."

Scott came in from the pathway. "So are we set to go?" He looked at Diana. "That shirt looks pretty good on you. You should really think about wearing green more often."

Diana smiled at him. "I prefer more of a hunter green, but thank you for the compliment." She put the scarf on her head and tied it in place with the sash. She wished she had a pair of sunglasses to use, but there was no way she was going to take those away from the guys. Somebody had to see where they were going. Seeing that she was ready, Ben and Scott went and checked and made sure the coast was clear; seeing nobody around, they called for her to come on out. The march had begun.

It actually started out fairly well. The fact that Diana had hiking boots instead of sandals was a big plus. It was about noon when the sun's heat started to bake the area, that she started to slow down. Scott found a spot in the shade of a large boulder to stop for a few minutes to rest and rehydrate. He gave her a bottle of water; as she took it, he told her to drink little sips. She nodded.

They only stopped for about five minutes then started off again. Diana could feel her face burning; she took the tails of the scarf Ben gave her and wrapped it around her face so that only her eyes were seen. It made her face hotter, but at least it wouldn't blister. She saw that the guys' faces were getting burnt as well. They stopped again in a small depression—not much shade, but better than none. Diana thought it must be somewhere around two or three in the afternoon now. She took a small sip of water and looked around. They were still climbing, but she thought she could see the crest of the mountain. "How are we doing on the time?" she asked.

"Not too bad actually. You're doing really good, Milady," Scott stated. Ben just gave her a wink and a smile.

"How much more before we start heading down instead of up?" she asked.

"Oh, about another two hours' worth," Scott said.

"Are you serious? I thought that over there was the crest of the mountain," she quipped.

"Ah…nope, that's just the first of the runs," Scott said flatly.

Diana wanted to scream. She was pushing herself already and they still had a long ways to go. "Come on, kitten…you can make it," Ben encouraged.

They stood up and started off again. They had just crested the first of the "runs" when they heard some distant gunfire. Ben and Scott ran back to Diana and pushed her down to the ground on the backside of the crest. Ben then slowly crawled to the top and looked out over the hill. Scott followed him with a satchel, pulled out a pair of binoculars, and gave it to him; and then he himself looked out over the top, scanning the area thoroughly. At this time, Diana didn't care if they took the next three hours; she needed the rest. She let her head fall back and closed her eyes, willing herself to breathe slowly. She took a small sip of her water; the bottle was half gone already.

"I don't see anything, do you?" Ben asked.

"Nope, nothing. Maybe it was some hunters down in the valley. It can echo quite well around here," Scott replied.

"I've got a bad feeling about it. I suggest we get going again,' Ben stated.

"I agree," Scott said as he nodded to Ben. They looked down at Diana, who was lying back, trying to recoup. "You got more than I thought in you, girl. I figured we'd only be halfway here at this time," Scott encouraged.

"Don't kid yourself, sir. If it wasn't for the fact that it's my only way home, I would have sat back at that first boulder and told you two to go jump in a lake. I really don't do heat," Diana snapped. The guys just snickered.

Ben put his hand on the top of her head. "Come on, kitten, let's get going again." They pulled her up to her feet, and they started out again. The sun was starting to set as they started their final climb to the top of the mountain. Diana looked up at what laid before her and almost bawled. She wasn't seeing any type of path. Some areas were sheer-faced rock. She was not going to make it, and she knew it. She stood there shaking her head.

"Easy, Milady, we're not scaling the rock. There are paths through it, you just do see them down here," Scott said. This time he knew what she was thinking. She didn't have the stamina or the strength to do actual rock climbing. Neither of the guys would ask that of her.

"I'm glad to hear that. I was about to freak out at the thought of me trying to scale those rock faces," she said flatly while still looking at the scene before her.

"How's your water doing?" Ben asked. He'd figured she was about out by now.

"I just took the last of it just a second ago," she informed him. He handed her another bottle. It was their last one, but both he and Scott agreed that she needed it more than they did. They'd get water once they hit the river on the other side.

"Are we set?" Scott asked. Diana slowly stood up and signaled she was ready. Ben had her go between them this time. She wasn't quite sure as to the why, but she'd find out eventually.

It was not easy at all to get over this last part of the climbing. Several times Scott or Ben had to help her up to the top of the boulders they were climbing over. The going was very slow, but eventually they made it to the top of the mountain. It was dark now, but the moon was bright. It lit the ground up quite well. Of course with the sun down, it started to cool down quickly. They stopped for just a moment to rest and catch a drink. Except Diana was the only one who drank anything. "You guys are out of water, aren't you?" she inquired.

"We'll get something at the river below, don't worry,' Scott stated. Diana's bottle was three-fourths full yet. She had slowed down her drinking when they started the hard climb.

"Here, take a swallow. I can't find the place, and the last thing any of us need is someone passing out from dehydration," she demanded. Neither of the guys would take a drink. "Two swallows of water missing isn't going to hurt me none. Come on, take a drink." She forced the bottle into Ben's hand. Ben knew she was going to force it down them if they didn't take a drink, so he took a quick sip. It did help clear some of the grit out of his mouth. Ben handed the bottle over to Scott.

He noticed that Diana was taking off the scarf. "You might want to keep that handy. You may need to wrap it around your shoulders later," he informed her.

Scott wasn't going to drink from the bottle. He went to hand it back to Diana, but Diana crossed her arms across her chest and refused to take it. So he took a quick sip then held it out for Diana to take. This time she took it and put it in the pocket of the pack she carried. "Thank you, Diana. Now listen to me carefully. Going down isn't as easy as you think. We are going to be winding back and forth across the side. The ground is mostly gravel, and you will slide easy if you're not careful. Follow directly behind me, understand?" Scott instructed. Diana nodded her head. She heard Ben fiddling around with something behind her. She turned to see him walk over with a long rope in his hand. He strode over and stood in front of her. He wrapped the rope around her waist, tying it in front of her. Then he passed the rope over to Scott. Diana saw that Ben had already tied the rope to himself. She cocked her head to the side and looked up at him.

"This way if one of us falls, the others can keep them from sliding all the way down. There won't be much left of their skin if they slide down," Ben pointed out.

"To bad we don't have a sled. We'd be down in what, ten minutes." Diana grinned.

Ben smiled. "Yeah, that would be a great idea. I'll have to look at inventing that when we get back to the States."

"All set?" Scott asked.

"Lead on, Captain," Ben replied. Scott started out, Diana followed once she felt the rope tighten, then she looked back to see how far Ben was spacing out.

"Eyes forward kitten, you can't see where you're going looking back here," Ben stated.

She looked toward Scott; she tried to follow directly in his steps, but he was taking longer strides then she was. She started to slip and caught her knee on a rock. She heard Ben whistle and felt both sides of the rope tighten, holding her there till Ben got to her to pull her up. "I'm sorry, I didn't mean to…" she replied.

"It's okay, kitten, just be careful. Use those cat eyes I know you have and watch where you step," Ben said calmly.

"Did she get hurt?" Scott asked as he kept the rope tight.

"Just my knee got scratched. I'll be fine," Diana replied.

"It better not be like the last time you said you just got scratched," Ben warned.

"Well, it will be a lot easier on you if it is. I can reach my knee, so I won't need you to take care of it for me. Even if you did, it will be a lot safer," she replied.

"I wouldn't count on the safer part, but now is not the time to check it. We'll look at it once we get down," he countered with his Cheshire grin in place.

Diana wasn't sure what he meant by that, but it obviously was facetious. "I'm fine, let's get going Scott," she stated.

Scott started out again. Diana noticed he wasn't taking as long of strides as he was before; she was thankful for that. They seemed to have crisscrossed the side of the mountain at least a hundred times and they were still not down yet. Diana wanted to—needed to—stop and catch her breath; but she didn't want to say anything. It was Ben who noticed her staggering a little; he called for a rest stop. Scott turned to walk back toward them, but he lost his footing and slipped. Diana heard the sliding rocks and braced herself with her legs. Ben immediately grabbed the rope in front of her and held it tight. Scott came to a stop about fifteen feet below them. "Are you okay?" Ben yelled.

"Aye, I'm fine," Scott fumed. "You want me to climb back up or do you two want to come down here?" he continued.

"We'll meet you," Ben replied. "Okay, kitten, I'm going to lower you down to Scott. Hang on to his rope, it will take you to him." Diana nodded. Ben helped her up and gave her Scott's rope; then he grabbed on to the rope by Diana's back. "Coming down," Ben yelled.

"Come ahead," Scott replied. Diana slowly started walking forward, taking small sideways steps so that she had a small ledge for her foot. She could feel Ben tugging on the rope, keeping it taut so that if she did slide, he'd keep her from falling. "I'm right here, Milady," she heard Scott say. She saw his hand held out for her to take. She took it and let him guide her to his side. "She's down. Come on bro," Scott yelled up.

"Coming down," Ben stated. Without anybody holding him straight, Ben did a lot of sliding himself. He must have known it would kick up a lot of gravel and dust because he came down just off to the side of where they were standing. The gravel slide he caused rolled past them. Scott held out his arm for Ben to grab to steady himself with. "Thanks, Captain, did you get hurt?" Ben asked.

"I scraped my arm pretty good, but I'll take care of it when we get to the river," Scott replied. "How about you? You were nearly lying down when you came."

"Well, let's just say this shirt is toast," Ben answered.

"Oh? You mean I get to return the favor?" Diana quipped.

"I'm sure you will someday, but not tonight kitten," Ben smiled.

"Well...shall we finish this adventure? I figure we've got about an hour, maybe less, to get to the river," Scott added.

"So what...we have a half hour to get down the rest of the way?" Diana asked.

"Hmm...about twenty minutes," Scott stated.

Diana looked over to Ben. "How's that sled idea coming along?"

Ben smiled. "Sorry, it was pushed out of my head for the time being. I'll get back to you with it later." Scott headed out again followed by Diana then Ben. It took them twenty-five minutes to finally reach the valley floor. All of them were hurting from the scrapes and bruises they received getting down. Diana's legs were rubber bands; her feet were blistered and sore. They walked another fifteen minutes, stopping near an outcrop of trees just feet away from the river. All three of them sat down and leaned back against the same tree, mostly because they were still tied together with the rope.

"I guess we don't need this anymore," Scott stated as he started to untie his side of the rope. Once Scott was loose, Diana tried to untie her knot. She was so tired she had a hard time getting ahold of the rope. Ben reached over and started to untie her. She had given everything she had, but now her muscles refused to go any farther.

"You did good, kitten, more than either of us thought you could do," Ben said calmly.

"He's right, Diana. We hardly had to help you out at all. Thank you," Scott affirmed.

Diana smiled a little smile. It just took too much strength to give any more. "Are we waiting for a boat?" she asked.

"Nope, a chopper is coming to get us," Scott said.

Ben heard Diana say, "My Lord Jesus." He turned and saw her eyes were bigger than dinner plates. "Diana, you're afraid of heights, aren't you?" She nodded yes. She was trying to get herself under control, but in her current state of mind, it was hopeless.

Scott heard the conversation and turned and walked toward them. "Oh, it's great to fly. You feel free and lighter than air." He looked down and saw that she wasn't buying it. He heard the chopper coming up the river. "Ben, it's here! Right on time—8:00 p.m. on the dot."

Ben looked down at Diana; she was shaking like a little child on their first day of kindergarten. He crouched down in front of her, took her chin, and made her look at him. "Diana, I promise it will be all right...trust me."

Diana looked at Ben; she had to read his lips to understand what he was saying. The wash from the blades were loud in her ears. His voice from the dream, *I won't hurt you*, kept ringing in her head. She let him pull her up and walk her to the chopper.

Ben stayed with Diana all the way up to the chopper. He pushed her head down when they neared to load. When they reached the door, he gave Diana's hand to Scott, who had already climbed in. Scott pulled her in; Ben followed immediately.

26

USS Wilson

The crewmen took the packs and bags, then signaled Ben to sit near the cockpit. They were signaling for Diana to sit in the back by a window, but once Ben sat down, she headed straight for him. He signaled to the crew that it was okay and took Diana's hand to guide her around to the seat. She cowered down beside him and held on to his shirt like her life depended on it. The crew slid the door shut and told the pilot to take off. The chopper jerked a little as they lifted off the ground. Diana buried her face into Ben's chest.

Ben was given a pair of headphones so that the crew could talk to him. He asked for a set for Diana, more to block the sound of the motor and blades; he had seen that she was covering her ears with her hands. He also signaled the crew to turn her set off; that way she wouldn't hear what was being said. One of the crewmen tried to give her a pair, but she couldn't hear him; her eyes were closed tight, so she didn't see him either. Ben took the headphones and nudged Diana to sit up. She looked up at him; he reached over and put the headphones on her. She adjusted them to fit her better, but she still stayed right up against him. Ben told the crew that Diana had never flown in a chopper before and that she was terrified of heights; they just smiled at her. Scott was in the back getting his arm taken care of. Once that was done, he moved to the seat on the other side of Diana. "She's not going to look out, is she?" Scott said once the crew gave him a set of headphones.

"Judging from the fact that her knuckles are totally white and I can feel her heart beating like a cheetah that just chased down a gazelle, nope. I don't think she's going to move from where she is," Ben replied.

"Too bad, I think she would enjoy the view if she did," Scott continued.

"In a different situation, I'm sure she would. But with all that she's had to do today, I can't really ask her for more," Ben concluded.

"That's true…she did more than either of us thought she could. God really helped her out," Scott stated. The chopper ride was about an hour long. Diana's body had had enough; it shut down, and she fell asleep. Ben knew when she finally went out; her hands finally relaxed, and he could feel her heartbeat slowing down. He gently laid her head in his lap and pulled her hair out of her face.

Scott looked over and watched him. He had to smile at what he saw. Ben acted much different with Diana than he did with Katherine. Maybe not so much acted; he was always gentle with her, but his approach was different. *Okay, Tiger…you've won. She's all yours if you want her*, he thought.

"Agent Tigere?" the pilot asked.

"Yeah…what's up," Ben replied.

"The captain wants you and McCleary to report to him as soon as you get cleaned up. He also said that Ms. Henderson is to use his room while she is on board," the pilot informed them.

"Thank you. How much farther do we have before the *Wilson*?" Ben asked.

"We'll be landing in five minutes," the pilot stated.

One of the crewmen next to the door tapped Scott on the shoulder then pointed to Diana's leg. Scott looked over and shook his head. "Ben, check out Diana's leg," Scott radioed.

Ben looked down; there was a bloodstain showing through on her jeans just below her knee. "Pilot," Ben radioed.

"Yes, sir," the pilot replied.

"Inform the captain that Ms. Henderson needs medical attention and probably a change of clothes," Ben stated flatly.

"Yes, sir," the pilot responded.

Ben was upset that she was hurt again. She did say she came down on her knee when she slid. She also knew there was nothing anybody could do about it at the time. He asked the crewman to turn on her headphones. He reached down and gently shook Diana's shoulder. She started to stir. "Kitten…we're going to be landing soon. You need to wake up now," he radioed.

Diana opened her eyes. It took her a few seconds to realize that she was hearing people talking through the headphones, another few seconds before she realized that she was still in the chopper. She started to panic and cowered down against Ben.

"Milady, calm down…breathe slowly," she heard Scott say. She looked over to see that Scott was smiling at her; his arm was all bandaged up. She scowled at it. Scott saw what she was looking at. "It's not that bad, just a lot of little cuts in a large area."

She looked up at Ben and mouthed, "I hate this!" Ben just laughed and shook his head, pushed some hair out of her eyes, and framed her face with his hand. She didn't cower back down again, but she didn't let go of his shirt either. She was forcing herself to take deep breaths.

The chopper landed on the pad at nine p.m. Once the blades slowed down enough, the crew slid open the door; then they signaled for the trio to get out. Scott went out first then Ben guided Diana to the door; Scott helped her down then Ben disembarked. The blades of the chopper were still slowing down, so when Scott got Diana out, he took her arm and pushed her head down then started to walk toward the stairs. Ben caught up with them quickly. Once Scott saw him, he let go of Diana. Diana was looking around at the faces of the crew. There were a few women on board; however, most of them were men. She felt extremely uncomfortable and nervous; she reached up and grabbed Ben's arm.

Ben saw that the guys were staring at Diana; he also knew that she was feeling very vulnerable. It didn't surprise him when he felt her grab his arm; he reached down and covered her hand. "It's okay, kitten… you're safe" he said.

"By the look of some of the crew's faces, that's up for a debate. I feel like a piece of meat being paraded in front of wolves that haven't eaten for months," she quipped.

"Scott or I will be with you at all times. They may look, but they are good men, they will be honorable," Ben added.

Scott headed to their quarters to get cleaned up. Ben took Diana to the infirmary to have the medic look at her knee. The medic initially wanted her to take her jeans off. Diana flatly said, "No way." He looked over at Ben as if he could change her mind. "The jeans are ruined anyway. Just slice up the sides so you can get to it," she quipped.

The medic grabbed a pair of scissors and cut up both sides of her jean leg. There was a cut and a place where the corner of the rock jabbed into her knee. "The cut isn't bad. We'll just clean it out good. The puncture, on the other hand, we are going to have to open up to make sure there are no rocks or debris in it," the medic stated.

"Great, more scars to add to my collection," Diana sputtered.

"Don't take it out on him, Diana, he's just doing his job," Ben scolded her.

"I am sorry, sir, it's been crazy for me. I'll try to hold my tongue better," Diana said to the medic, who was readying the tools he needed.

"You do seem to have a problem with controlling that tongue of yours, don't you kitten?" Ben jested.

Diana, not thinking, stuck her tongue out at him again. "Oh goody, another tally on the IOU." He grinned.

Diana, realizing what she had done, rolled her eyes and shook her head. "I'd suggest you space those IOUs out. You're gonna be in a heap of trouble if you try to collect them all at one time," she teased with a wicked smile on her face.

"Maybe, we'll have to see…won't we?" he jabbed back.

The medic, who had heard the conversation, looked at Diana and said, "You may want to lie down while I do this. Do you want your husband to come and hold your hand?"

Diana flushed beet red. "He's not my husband. He's an agent that was assigned to protect me."

The medic looked back over to Ben. "You're protecting her? Then how did this—" The medic didn't get a chance to finish it out.

"It's a long story," Ben stated. The medic saw danger in Ben's face and decided he didn't want to know. "Diana, how are you with needles?" Ben asked.

"Even after three years of treatments and labs, I still *don't* do well with the stupid things," she answered.

Ben walked into the room and stood by the table. He looked down at the medic who was just about to begin. "Unless you want kicked in the face, I'd suggest you numb that." Then he looked at Diana. "And you, ma'am, better lie back. In this case, what you don't see won't hurt you," he commanded.

Diana looked at him, looked into his eyes. She'd hurt him; she didn't mean to. *What did I say that hurt him?* she wondered.

Ben watched her face, saw her reading him; he didn't like that she could read him. He saw her wince when the medic started in with the probe. "Diana, take my hand, squeeze as hard as you like," he told her. She went to take his hand, but he was smart enough to only give her two fingers. Just as she did, the medic moved the probe to a sore spot, and Diana squeezed hard.

"Ma'am, there are some pieces of rock in here. We're going to have to open it up to get them out," the medic said.

"Do what you have to. Just don't start having a party in there," she quipped.

"Diana," Ben said scowling.

"Well…what do you want me to do, turn the air blue with a bunch of words while he digs around in my knee?" she fumed.

"I don't think those words are even in your vocabulary," Ben jabbed back.

"They're not, but I can sure come up with a few," she said as she squeezed Ben's fingers.

"I'm sure you can. It might be kind of interesting to see what you come up with," Ben teased back. He was mostly getting her to concentrate on him; he would take her ire instead of the medic. He thought it was amusing to see her that mad; it didn't happen much.

"I'm almost done, ma'am," the medic stated.

"That's encouraging," Diana sneered.

"I'm gonna have to take drastic measures if you don't stop biting the medic's head off," Ben stated. He had been watching what the medic was doing, but he glanced over to look at Diana. An eyebrow arched up, and an impish look appeared in her eyes.

"And what exactly did you have in mind for drastic measure, sir?" Diana decided to call his bluff.

Ben shook his head then looked back at what the medic was doing. The medic had just finished pulling the last piece of rock out of her knee. He reached over and put it with the rest of them that he had in a dish off to the side on the table. Then he washed up the incision he had to make and put in a few stitches to hold it closed. Finally, he wrapped the whole knee up with gauze. "While you're there, you'd better take a look at her ankles and her feet. She was limping a lot coming off the chopper," Ben stated.

The medic gave him a nod and started to take Diana's hiking boots off. Ben went and started to work on the other side's boot. "How did she get those rope burns?" the medic asked.

"Where else? From rope being tied around my ankles," Diana quipped. Ben looked at her and scowled. Diana just threw her head back onto the pillow and sighed.

"Someone tied her up, and she tried to get away. How do they look?" Ben asked the medic.

"The ankles are healing nicely. Her feet, I'm gonna to have her scrub them good then soak them in Epsom salt tonight and tomorrow. I've got to get some antibiotic to give her to stop any infection from the puncture," the medic continued.

Diana spoke up then. "Ah, wait a minute, sir. I'm allergic to several antibiotics, is it absolutely necessary?"

"I would prefer you had some in your body. What are you allergic to?" the medic asked.

"I can't have penicillin, sulfa, or um…oh, there's one other one—I can't think of it right now," she stated.

"Okay, we'll have to use a topical then. You just listed the only two types of antibiotics I carry in serum form. I'll be right back," he stated and walked out the door.

Diana waited until the medic walked out of the room. Then she looked at Ben. "Ben…I didn't mean to hurt you with what I said…I'm sorry," Diana stated quickly before the medic came in.

Ben looked at her. "Do you only see me as somebody assigned to you?"

Diana made sure she looked directly at him. "At the start…yes, but not now…it's just. I mean…" She was stumbling over her words. She stopped, took a deep breath and closed her eyes for a second. Then looking back at Ben, she reached up and put her hand on the side of his face. "You read me too well not to know something is between us, but—" Diana didn't get the chance to get it out; the medic came back in.

"Here you go, Ms. Henderson. Make sure you keep these dry and put this on the lower cut only. At least till the stitches are pulled out," the medic stated.

"Thank you, sir," Diana said and took the ointment.

Ben helped Diana off the table. "Thank you for your help."

"You might need me to look at your back, sir," the medic pointed out. "It looks like you to fell down the same hill."

Diana chuckled. "We did, sir, when we were trying to get to the pickup site."

"Oh…well, I thought that…well…never mind what I thought," the medic said sheepishly.

Diana looked at Ben and smiled. "Looks like it's your turn, Tiger," she beamed.

"You've wanted my shirt off for some time," he jabbed back

"You're right, payback is a bitch," she stated.

"Diana…when did you pick that up?" Ben was shocked that she used that word.

"Would you rather I used female dog? Nah, that's too many words… one word works much better," she jested back. Ben took off his shirt and let the medic check his back out. Diana wasn't minding the view either, which made Ben smile. She saw the stitches that Ben just acquired from being shot. She frowned and shook her head.

"Ma'am, you don't have to stay here. You can go explore the ship." The medic waved for her to go.

"Nope...she has to stay where I am. I'm assigned to her...remember?" Ben informed him.

"Oh, okay...suit yourself," the medic said as he started to work on Ben's back. Diana saw that he was bringing another needle out, so she moved in front of Ben so she didn't see it.

"You know, we will have to continue that conversation later," Ben said as he held her chin.

"I know. Maybe by then I'll have my head on and I'll be able to talk," Diana said.

"It's not your head I want to hear from," Ben whispered and traced his fingers down the side of her face.

"I know," Diana said and closed her eyes.

The medic slid out from around the table. "I don't see any rocks, I'll just wash it down and clean it up. If you would be so kind, Ms. Henderson, I've only got one tube of that ointment. Would it be possible for you to share it with Agent Tigere?"

"I wouldn't mind sharing it at all," Diana stated with a huge grin on her face.

"Thank you, sir. Oh...just a heads-up, you may see me in here in a few hours. I have the strange feeling she may just kill me with it," Ben stated. He caught the spark that flew through her eyes just a second ago.

"Well, she doesn't seem to be the type to do such a thing," the medic stated as he handed Ben his shirt. He saw her eyebrow raise at the medic's response. *He really has no clue what we are talking about*, Ben thought.

Ben and Diana left the infirmary and headed to the captain's quarters. "The captain wants you to use his room. Scott and I are just across the hall. Go get cleaned up, and I'll be back to get you in a little bit," Ben informed her. He saw she was uneasy and tried to encourage her, but he wasn't sure about all the crew either. He watched as she went into the room. When he heard the door latch, he turned and walked over to his quarters. He was looking forward to getting cleaned up.

Diana entered into the room, turned, shut the door, and locked it. She stood by the door and looked around the room. It was small, but she figured in comparison to what the other rooms looked like on the ship, it was probably huge. There was a desk built into the wall covered with papers. A bunk bed was on the opposite side, made with the typical square corners, and some clothes folded neatly on top of it. She saw that there was an adjoining room; she cautiously walked over and peeked around the corner. It was a small bathroom complete with shower and stool. There were towels hung on the bars on the wall. She smiled; she definitely would feel a lot better showered and clean. She walked back to the bunk and checked out the clothes. There was a pair of khaki pants, a dark-blue button-down shirt with long sleeves, sized XL, and, to her surprise, undergarments. Unfortunately, the one piece of clothing they had for her was a size or two too small for her to use. "Thanks Mom…that's probably why the wolves are circling," she said quietly. She stood there trying to figure out what she should do; the girls had to be contained somehow. *I'll just have to wash out the halter top and dry it out. I'll wear it under the shirt*, she figured.

She took the clothes into the bathroom with her, took off her halter top, and washed it and her jeans out in the sink. She rolled it up into a towel and worked at squeezing the water out of it. Then she finished undressing, climbed into the shower, and cleaned herself up. There was soap and shampoo in the corner nook of the shower wall that she used. She knew from her uncle's stories that showering in a ship was restricted. So she made it as quick as she could; she had to keep her leg outside the curtain so not to get the stitches wet. When she got out, she used the washcloth to wash the one leg, then she dried off, making sure she dried the wraps around her wrist as much as possible. Then she walked out into the other room and put the clothes on that was available to her.

The halter top's material was such that it dried quickly, which Diana was grateful for. She tied it on and put the blue shirt over the top of it. It was way too big for her; she pulled the sides together then tied it at her waist. Then she rolled up the sleeves up to her elbows. She went back into the bathroom and glanced down at the sink; saw a new toothbrush and a tube of toothpaste on the edge. She gratefully used it, glad to have a clean mouth; she figured she took five minutes just at brushing her teeth.

She walked out of the bathroom and was working her hair up into a bun when she heard a knock at the door; she froze for a minute. The person knocked again; she took a deep breath then went to check it out. She walked over to the door and said, "Who is it?"

"Diana, are you ready?" she heard Ben ask. She unlocked the door and opened it. Ben and Scott were waiting in the hallway.

"Just about, come on in," she said opening the door wide. As Ben and Scott walked in, Scott noticed she was wearing the halter top again. "It's growing on you, isn't it," he said pointing to her shirt.

"It's a necessity at this time. What they provided was too restrictive," Diana stated flatly.

"I can imagine," Ben beamed.

"Blame my mom, sir, I had no control over it," she fired back.

"I've got news for you: your momma had no control over it either. Not that I'm complaining," Scott added.

"Yeah, you and about half of the crew," Diana sneered.

Ben had been watching her try to get her hair pulled up. All she had was a rubber band, and she was trying to put it up into a bun. "Are you having some problems?" he asked.

"I really need a brush, and I can't get my arms to work tonight," Diana pointed out. Ben walked over and, using his fingers as a comb, pulled her hair back and quickly braided it. Then he wrapped it around itself, tucked it under the first wrap, and pulled it through.

Scott sat there watching. "Where in the world did you learn to do that, bro?"

"While Katherine was in radiation treatments, she was unable to do her own hair. I did her hair for her," he simply replied. "Okay, Kitten… you're set," he stated, giving her a pat on the back.

"Thank you," she said to him, watching him to see if he was struggling with doing her hair for her. She saw no pain or sorrow in his eyes. *Thank you, Lord*, she praised.

Scott walked to the door. "After you, Milady," he said with a large bow.

"Thank you, kind sir," Diana stated back with a low curtsy then walked through the door. She waited in the hall till the guys came out. "By the way, you two look much better without those whiskers." She smiled.

"Here I had you pegged as one that liked the rugged, bad-boy look," Scott replied.

"There are some guys that need that look. Gratefully, neither of you two do," she replied. They walked together over to the conference room.

The captain was shocked that they brought Ms. Henderson with them. "Do you think it's wise for her to be in on all this?" the captain questioned.

"She's been personally involved in 'all this' already. I don't see a need to block her out now," Ben stated.

The captain pulled up another chair. "As you wish." He thought she needed to be protected from this, but he was old-fashioned. He motioned for Diana to come and sit on the chair he pulled up. Diana moved to the chair she was assigned to. She allowed him to push the chair in for her. "I'm sorry we didn't have an appropriate change of clothes for you, ma'am," the captain apologized.

"It's fine, sir, I've learned to make do with what I get," Diana replied. Ben could tell that even though she was talking calm and smooth, one look in her eyes said that she was on edge. He moved over and sat in the chair next to her; Scott took the chair on her other side. That move seemed to calm her down considerably. The captain, however, wasn't happy that they took those chairs instead of the ones facing the screen, but he held his tongue. The lieutenant and the medical officer came in a few minutes later. They saw that their chairs were occupied, so they took the two open ones at the end of the table. The captain stood up, seeing everybody was there and accounted for, and started the debriefing.

Diana wasn't really paying attention to what the captain was saying; her mind was going on what she was going to say to Ben when the time comes. When she saw the lights were being turned down; her attention was drawn to the screen. The person she saw was Dick.

"Good evening, Captain. Ben…good to see your ugly face again. You don't look any worse for the wear," Dick stated.

"Hey…pard. Good to see you too," Ben replied.

"Is that Ms. Henderson next to you? Man, they didn't feed her, did they? Make sure she gets some food into her ASAP," Dick added.

"I look a lot worse than I feel, Agent Richman, but thank you," Diana stated.

"I didn't mean it that way, Ms. Henderson," Dick backpedaled.

Ben held up his hand. "It's okay, Dick, she didn't take offense to it. I'll make sure she gets some meat back on her."

"Now that we've dispensed with all the pleasantries, may we get on with the important stuff?" the captain snipped. Diana looked down, putting her hands in her lap; she thought the captain was barking at her.

Ben reached over and put his hand on hers. "It's not you, don't worry," Ben whispered. Dick told the group about how the Taliban attacked the Sheikh's compound. Someone had leaked that the Sheikh had a sorcerer and an American there under his protection. They came in and massacred all who survived the bombardment. Diana swallowed hard; she felt Ben's hand squeeze hers. She steadied herself. Then Dick went on about the arrangements of how they were going to get Diana home. The *Wilson* was out to sea for another two months before they were to report to port. Diana didn't like that idea at all; she could tell neither of the guys did either. She was glad that they voiced their opposition to that plan. The last option Dick gave was that they would take a chopper back to Tel Aviv, go through Customs, and take a plane to New York then take another flight from New York to Des Moines.

Diana was barely breathing; her body was a stiff as a board, and she sat quietly frozen. Ben and Scott conferred between each other. "We'll go with the last option," Ben said. He looked over at Diana, leaned over, and whispered, "I'll be with you the whole way. It will be okay, kitten."

"Ben, I don't have a passport or any papers. I didn't come over here legally, remember? How am I going to get through Customs now?" Diana worried.

"Hey, Dick, we've got a problem. Ms. Henderson doesn't have the correct papers to get through Customs. We're gonna need to get them okayed and sent to the embassy ASAP," Ben stated.

"Okay…Ben, I'll get right on that. The papers will be waiting for you when you arrive," Dick acknowledged.

Ben leaned back over to Diana. "See…easily taken care of."

She nodded; she kept telling herself, *It is the best and fastest way to get back home*, but the thought of the flight back in a chopper was brain-numbing.

She felt Ben lean over to her again. "You'd better breathe girl, or you'll pass out, and the wolves will come out of the walls."

She took a big breath and looked over at Ben. "You wouldn't let them take me. I know you."

Yeah, you probably do know me in that area, kitten. You trust me far enough to know that I wouldn't just leave you. It's a start, he thought.

Dick concluded that Ms. Henderson and Mr. McCleary were not to go directly home when they came into Des Moines. They were to come to the office with Ben at the earliest possible time for a debriefing.

"I thought that was what this was?" Diana piped up. Ben and Scott knew she would balk at not being able to see her family. What surprised them was that she voiced it in the conference room.

"It is one of many that you may have to have before you are allowed to return home, Ms. Henderson," the captain stated.

"So when will I be able to see my family?" she quipped. Ben saw her eyes were steel gray, and she was not going to let it go.

Ben spoke up. "She hasn't been able to see her family for two months. They are very close."

"I have a whole ship full of people who have not seen their families in over three months. Your point is what, Agent Tigere?" the captain provoked.

Ben slowly and poignantly stated, "Ms. Henderson is not a sailor, nor is she the enemy, sir. She was taken from her family. She did not choose to take a job that took her away from them. She has not seen her parents for over two months. She's been beaten, drugged, and starved near to death, and I'm sure many other injustices done to her. She does not need to have her own countrymen do the same thing in the name of political sensitivities." Ben's eyes were the dangerous sapphire blue with controlled rage shining behind them. The captain began to back down. Ben felt fingers gently touching his arm; it sent a shot of energy through him. He knew it was Diana's. He looked over at her; he saw her blue eyes looking at him, calming him. He also thought he saw something else, something more than just gratitude. He looked over toward Scott, who was sitting quietly, hands folded together in front of him on the table. Then he looked back over to the captain. "Okay, sir, I believe that we can compromise. Ms. Henderson would at least like to call her parents to let them know that she is alive and not beaten to death somewhere in the middle of the desert. It's the least we can do since she can't go home right away."

"I'll see what I can do," the captain said curtly. "Is there anything else that needs to be discussed?" the captain asked. "Thank you for your information, Agent Richman." The captain nodded.

"No problem. Talk to you later, Tiger," Dick replied.

The captain shut the monitor off. "This meeting is adjourned then, gentlemen," the captain stated. It basically omitted Diana. The sailors stood up and saluted. Ben, Scott, and Diana stood up after the sailors left and headed for the door. "Agent Tigere, do you mind if I have a word or two with you? Alone," the captain asked, scowling at Diana. Diana held tight to Ben's arm. She didn't like the sound of the captain's tone. Ben reached down and took Diana's hand off his arm and led her toward Scott.

"Of course…sir," Ben coldly replied. "Scott, would you be so kind as to take Diana to the mess hall. I'd bet she's dying for some hot tea and get some food into her as well," Ben continued, not taking his eyes off the captain.

"Nawt at awl…Milady," Scott said in his strong Scottish brogue, signaling Diana to walk in front of him. Diana was hesitant to leave Ben.

Ben finally took his eyes off the captain and looked at Diana. "Go with Scott, I will be joining you soon." She saw the look in his eyes; she also knew the look in the captain's eyes. Ben had challenged him in front of his own men; the captain wasn't going to let that go. Obviously, with the look in Ben's eyes, he was up for the challenge.

She felt Scott's arm come around her waist, felt him guiding her toward the door. She turned and reluctantly went with Scott. "He'll be fine…he's a big boy," Scott jeered in the hallway.

"I should have just stayed quiet. I'm so sorry," Diana stated.

"Knock it off, Diana. The captain was out of line. Ben just pointed it out. Obviously, the captain needs a little more fine-tuning that's all," Scott informed her. He led her down to the mess hall.

To Diana, it looked like a gourmet kitchen. "Wow," she exclaimed.

"Yeah, they eat well on these ships. If you need it, they've probably got it." Scott smiled.

"Right now, a chamomile tea is all I want," Diana replied. Scott led her over to the drink station. There were different-flavored coffees, hot chocolates, cappuccinos, and lattes. As Scott was pointing things out, she saw what she was after: a large variety of assorted favors of hot and cold teas. When she went to grab a cup for her tea, she just happened to catch out of the corner of her eye a fridge stocked with milk. "They have chocolate milk!" She smiled. She walked over and grabbed a couple of chocolate milks from the fridge.

Scott just laughed at her. "You're worse than Ben's kids. Come on, let's go sit down." They sat in a booth off to the side of the room. Diana sat with her back to the door. She didn't want to see any wolves coming through. Scott, on the other hand, watched the men and women flow through. Most of them gave them a glance and went about their business; some, however, where letting their eyes do the walking. He noticed whenever someone or a group came in checking her out, she broke out in goose bumps. "You can feel them when they are scanning you, can't you?" Scott asked.

"Most of the time I can, unfortunately. That's what I was trying to explain to you in the cavern. When you open yourself up to the spirit world, it's a whole other dimension of learning. If you open it up to the evil side, you feel heaviness, hatred, envy, and strife in your spirit. If you open yourself up to the Lord's spirit, you feel peace, love, joy, and warmth. You learn to recognize the different spirits in people, to battle the dark, by letting the spirit of the Lord guide you," Diana informed him.

"I don't think I want to know the spirits that are around me," Scott added.

"Whether you know them or not, they are there anyway. I look at it like this: a soldier uses night vision goggles to see in the dark when out on patrol. They use them to keep them from walking into traps and dangers and to see whether the person standing in front of them is an enemy or a friend. God has given us a spiritual goggles to see in this dark world. It's just whether you want to use them or not," Diana explained.

"Yeah…that would be the question," Scott stated.

Scott and Diana sat there in the mess hall quietly for about fifteen minutes. Diana had already gone through her chocolate milk. She walked over to the drink counter and made a chamomile tea. She held the cup like a treasure and breathed in the aroma. "Are we content now?" she heard Ben quip.

"Momentarily satisfied is more like it. What happened?" she asked as she turned to face her champion.

"Only momentarily, huh? I'll have to see what we can do about that," Ben teased. He saw her lips curve up behind her cup of tea, her eyebrow arched up.

"You are avoiding the question, Tiger. What happened?" she repeated. Ben put his hand in the middle of her back and guided her back over to where Scott was. He had her sit down opposite of Scott.

"So was it a knock-down-drag-out or just word fencing?" Scott asked.

"It was more word fencing than anything. He felt I usurped his authority. Unfortunately for him, he made the mistake and called HQ demanding I be taken of this ship and off this case. He didn't like what they had to say," Ben stated.

As they were talking, a group of sailors came through the hall. "That makes the second time," Scott stated, nodding to the group.

"It's more like the third or fourth," Diana countered. Ben looked at Scott then at Diana. She had goose bumps on top of goose bumps.

"I suppose we knew this was coming," Ben said to Scott.

"Yeah…it's been building the last twenty minutes. At least they waited till it was more interesting," Scott jabbed.

Diana looked at Scott then at Ben; she saw the coldness in their eyes. "Oh no, wait a minute guys, you don't need to—" Ben cut her off.

"You're not going to be allowed to take all of our fun away, kitten. Packs always have to see where they stand in the pecking order." Ben smiled.

Diana just shook her head; she could feel them getting closer. She was about to get up and leave when she felt Scott's hand grab onto her arm. "Ya bes kip yursef stil, lassie, dah gents haev a wee bit of tawk'n tu du," Scott teased.

"Hi, y'all," she heard one of the guys from the group say.

"Good evening," Scott replied as Ben turned his chair around to look at the group.

"How may we help you, boys?" Ben asked.

"We just came over to invite the lady here to a dance tonight," the Southern sailor stated. One of the guys behind snickered and was hit by the two sailors beside him.

"That's very kind of you, but I think I'd best get some rest before flying out in a few hours," Diana calmly and coolly replied.

"It just wouldn't be fair if we didn't give you the proper welcome, ma'am. I really wish you would reconsider," the Southern sailor urged.

"The lady has had a very hard day today, boys, give her a break," Scott said. Ben sat there, cleaning out his fingernails. Diana could see by his demeanor and his face he was getting agitated.

"We weren't talking to you, Irishman," a sailor from the back quipped.

Diana chuckled. "I think your geographical education is a little lacking, sir. Mr. McCleary's family comes from Scotland, not Ireland. That would be like saying your young sailor here with the Southern accent came from Montana instead of the South," Diana informed them.

One of the sailors from the side came around and grabbed Diana arm. "Come on, ma'am, let's go have some fun."

"I would suggest you let Ms. Henderson's arm go," Ben smoothly stated.

The sailor snickered. "Look, guys, the big DHS agent has a voice," the sailor jested, still holding on to Diana's arm.

"Would you please let go of my arm, sir. You are only asking for trouble" Diana calmly stated.

Ben saw her countenance change, her eyes a steel gray. She wasn't going to tolerate the sailor's intrusion much longer.

"Aw, don't worry, ma'am. We know how to take good care of you," he stated.

Diana stood up, looking the sailor eye to eye. "Let go of my arm…sir."

Ben and Scott stood up when Diana stood up. They were ready, but they were letting Diana deal with the sailor for as long as she could.

The sailor laughed. "Whoa ho ho, isn't this the same chick that Smith said was called Kitten? Why do they call you Kitten? Is it because you purr when you're petted or because you have a fluffy tail?" He glanced back, checking her backside out.

"Most people call me Ms. Henderson or Diana, my friends call me Milady. Only one person calls me Kitten, and with the trouble he's had to deal with, he could call me 'pain in the neck,' and I'd let him," Diana stated flatly.

"Well, how about you come with us and we'll come up with our own nickname for ya. Right, guys?" the sailor said, turning to the group who all nodded in agreement.

Diana had enough. She swung her foot behind the sailor's leg, kicking the back of his knee, then push him back when he reacted, making him fall. The sailor let go of her arm as he fell. The instant Diana was free, Ben reached over and lifted Diana up and set her down between Scott and himself.

The sailor stood up, rubbing the back of his knee. "What the ****! You little—" Ben did a quick jab with his right, hitting the sailor in the jaw, stopping him from finishing his words. "She did ask you nicely to let her go."

"You're some big-shot agent. Let's see how you do with real men," the Southern sailor stated. Then he looked over at Diana. "We'll have a chat later, sweet cheeks, we need to deal with your bodyguards first. Hey, Stew, would you come out here for a minute?" the sailor yelled.

Out of the kitchen came a sailor. He wasn't extremely tall, only five-feet-ten or so, but he had huge muscles. "What's up, Frank?" he asked as he neared the group.

Diana recognized him. "Chad? Chad Steward, is that you?" she queried.

"Ms. Henderson? What are you doing here? Guys, this is my fifth grade teacher. She's the one that helped me get through school. Wow… small world," Stew stated.

"Yes…yes, it is. So you've been in the navy for how long?" Diana asked. Chad went to answer but was hit by Frank and another sailor in the group of troublemakers.

"How did you get involved in all this, Ms. Henderson?" he asked.

"I was taken by some insane people and brought here. These two gentlemen risked their lives to get me out," she answered.

Chad looked at Ben and Scott then turned to the group. "You guys are on your own. I'm not involved. However, leave Ms. Henderson out of it," he warned.

Scott started to pull on Diana's shirt so Diana moved back behind him. That way she was out of Ben and Scott's way. She had already seen what they could do in the abandoned house. "Scott…Ben, remember these guys are supposed to be on our side. There's no need to kill them," she added.

"Yes, ma'am," Scott tipped his pretend hat.

"You always take the fun out of it, kitten," Ben jeered.

The group of sailors laughed at Ben's pet name for Diana. "Kitten? Does she purr when *you* touch her?"

"Nope…not at all. She's a tiger with sharp teeth when she wants to use them," Ben informed them.

"Let's find out if she bites, guys," the Southern sailor stated. He came up against Scott. The one behind him went up against Ben. Neither of the sailors were a challenge for them. They went down to the floor almost in tandem. "Any other takers?" Ben asked.

"Get 'em guys," another sailor said. The group moved in; a quick kick from Scott took one down to the floor. Ben dodged a punch from one, grabbing the extended arm and swung it around the sailor's back; the sailor hollered. Ben pushed the sailor into one of the oncoming ones. Then he threw a punch into the jaw of the next sailor, felling him to the floor.

Diana noticed that Ben and Scott fought like they were choreographed. This obviously wasn't the first time they fought side by side. Ben was fighting old-school boxing style; Scott had a lot of martial arts in his style, but they worked like a well-oiled machine together. While the guys were busy dealing with the main group, the first sailor Scott took on was coming around. He looked at the fight around him then looked over to Diana. He headed toward Diana.

"So you're a tiger, huh? I'd like to find out how much of a tiger you are," he sneered. Diana had backed into the corner, not because she was afraid. She wanted to use the chair rail and the table to brace herself. She figured her legs were her best defense. "You know, you really need to learn to take a hint," she said.

As the sailor charged her. She brought her legs up, then she kicked out, hitting the sailor in the lower abdomen. The sailor doubled over then backed away, coughing.

Ben saw what Diana did; he grabbed the sailor by the shoulder, pulling him up. "I told you she was a tiger. The last man that did that to her, she sent to the emergency room. Consider yourself lucky."

"You're kidding?" the sailor stated as he was starting to recover.

"Not at all," Ben stated then he did a quick jab with his left. The sailor went out cold. The group that came in to start trouble were lying in various stages of consciousness on the floor when the MPs came rushing in.

"You guys are a little late," Scott sneered.

The captain came striding in behind the MPs. "What the **** happened here!" He turned and glared at Ben. "Do you think you can ******* come in here and just ******* the *** **** ship?"

Diana stood, walked up to the captain, and very calmly and coldly stated, "With all due respect, sir, I'd appreciate you restraining your foul mouth. It is very unprofessional and totally unnecessary. The gentlemen on the floor were insisting I go to a 'dance' with them. I told them no thank you, that I was...and am, very tired. They didn't accept that response. Ben and Scott were helping them understand what I meant when I said no thanks."

"And you have proof of this event, do you?" the captain sneered.

"Diana, show the captain your right arm please," Ben directed. Diana undid the overshirt, dropped it down to her elbows, and turned sideways, allowing the captain to examine her arm. The bruising from the sailor's grasp was already quite evident. The captain wasn't happy, he was trapped; he'd have to discipline the sailors for their supposed actions. "Did you have to do so much damage?" the captain stated.

"Sir, the last man that stood in front of me as a threat, I sent to the hospital myself. The hospital would do no good for the men Ben and Scott last dealt with. I think your men here got off fairly easy," Diana calmly stated.

The captain had no reply to what Diana said. So he turned to Ben and Scott. "Do you always let her do all the speaking?" the captain inquired.

"I've learned a long time ago never to challenge a tigress. You'll come out on the losing end," Scott stated.

The captain turned and glared at Ben. "And you Agent Tigere? Why are you letting this *civilian* do all the talking?"

"She's a strong-willed woman. What do you want me to do, gag her and handcuff her to the table?" Ben glared.

"That might be a good start," the captain stated.

"I'll make sure that your request is known in my next debriefing," Diana fired back.

The captain, seeing that she wasn't going to back down, turned to the MPs. "Take these sailors to the brig. I'll deal with them in the morning. I suggest you three get some sleep and get the **** off my ship," he yelled over his shoulder. The trio watched him march out the door. They looked over to the MPs who were just looking at them.

Diana gave them a smile; "Is he always this way or is it just me?"

"I don't think he's ever met up with the likes of you, ma'am," one of the MPs replied.

Ben and Scott walked over behind Diana. "We're sorry for the mess. She did try to keep us men from a confrontation."

Ben pointed to the sailor at his feet. "By the way, this sailor here might need a little bit more medical attention. She kicked him." The MPs eyes grew large.

Diana looked a little sheepish. "I warned him. I did try to aim higher. Some guys just don't take no until it's painfully obvious."

"She has a tendency to draw trouble to herself. We haven't figured out how to keep her out of it yet," Scott quipped.

"That's true, she does keep us on our toes," Ben added.

Diana slapped Ben's arm. "You know it's true, kitten, you might as well accept it," Ben teased.

The MPs just shook their heads. "You guys better get on out of here. You might have to hold her back the next time the captain comes in." The guys laughed at that comment. Diana just smiled at the group and shook her head. She walked over to the table and grabbed her tea, drank the last of it, and put the cup over in the dish racks.

"Hey, Ms. Henderson, would you like a turkey cheese bagel?" Chad yelled from the kitchen.

"That sounds wonderful, Chad. Will that get you into trouble?" Diana asked.

"Nah…I've got it all made up. Not that I'm complaining, but it looks like your navel is rubbing up against your spine," Chad stated.

"She needs it. Maybe she'll actually eat this time," Ben said, smiling at Chad.

"Well, if she needs more, just let me know. The mess hall is open 24-7," Chad said as he turned to go back to the kitchen.

"Thank you Chad, I really appreciate it," Diana yelled back. Ben reached down and started guiding Diana out the door.

Ben and Scott gave the MPs a salute, to which the MPs returned in kind. Diana just gave them a wide smile and a nod. Then they walked out of the mess hall. They walked up the hallway, up a flight or two of stairs, then down another hallway that led to their quarters. "I have never been more proud of you as I have been today," Ben said as he gently stroked her arm. She just grimaced. "You really don't know what you did today, do you?" Ben asked.

"I slowed you two down climbing over the mountain, acted like a pathetic little twit in the chopper, opened my mouth when I should have kept it shut in the debriefing, caused a fight in the cafeteria, and totally disrespected a captain of our country's navy. I think that's all I've done so far. Oh, and was one of the worst patients a medic should have to deal with," Diana stated.

Ben shook his head. "No…not quite, babe. You survived a hike that most new soldiers would struggle with, you had to face a fear so strong that I've seen it make some freeze up, you stood up for your rights as a civilian, you held your head high and stood your ground not only to a group of testosterone-filled boneheads but to an overbearing, power-hungry captain trying to become a general."

"You know you shouldn't be so hard on yourself," Scott stated.

Diana chuckled. "It's an internal trait. I'm forgiving to others, not so much to myself."

"I'm gonna have to work on that," Ben said with a smile on his face. "Do you think a high dosage of 'sugar' would help sweeten her disposition, Scott?"

"Obviously, I need to be more conscientious. You heard that comment, huh?" Diana questioned.

"Yep. I didn't believe you, but then again, I haven't got all the facts to confirm or deny it yet,' Ben jested. Diana simply looked down at her feet.

She could feel the heat in her face. *I could sure use some "sugar" now*, she thought. The trio started walking down the hall again. They heard hard footsteps coming toward them. Diana had the feeling it was the captain, so she slowed down and started walking behind the guys.

"Diana…why don't you hang here for a few minutes," Ben suggested over his shoulder. She didn't argue this time and stood against the wall. The captain turned the corner saw Ben and Scott then glanced down the hall and spotted Diana.

"I suppose you think you've bested me. You and that little *****," he steamed.

"Ms. Henderson has nothing to do with the quarrel you have with me," Ben stated.

"Who does she think she is challenging me in front of my men," the captain fumed.

"You've had access to the file, didn't you read it?" Ben asked.

"Nope, it's trivial and unimportant," the captain replied.

"Well, let me give you a condensed version then. Ms. Henderson is a pastor's daughter, an elementary teacher, and a three-year cancer survivor," Ben concluded.

"How nice, and what does that have to do with anything?" the captain asked.

"He actually left a lot out, sir," Scott injected.

"Now, if she's had to come through all that, plus all the crap that she went through here in the Middle East, do you think standing up to a man who obviously couldn't care less if she ever sees her family again is much of a jump to her? You've been on this boat too long," Ben calmly stated.

"As soon as you get off my boat, the happier I will be. Dick sent a memo that Ms. Henderson's papers will be at the embassy by 1100 tomorrow. The chopper will be leaving at 0900. I would strongly suggest that none of you are late," the captain sneered.

"Aye, aye sir," Scott replied with a salute.

The captain was throwing knives with his eyes but maintained composure. "Carry on, gentlemen." He marched down the hall. When he walked past Diana, he acted like she was the plague.

Diana walked up to the guys. "I get the strong impression that he really doesn't like me."

"Nah, don't take it to heart. He just doesn't know how to treat a lady. He's too used to sailors," Scott smiled. They started walking down the hallway again. Diana had taken a couple of bites from her bagel sandwich.

"It's good to know that you've decided to start eating again," Ben stated.

"I've been eating since we got to the cave, Ben, or didn't you notice that most of Scott's trail mix was gone," Diana countered.

"Hey...I know something she likes better than chamomile tea bro," Scott injected.

Ben shot an eyebrow up. "Oh...and what would that be?"

"She loves chocolate milk. The woman was literally jumping up and down when she saw it in the fridge," Scott stated.

"I was not, don't exaggerate Mr. McCleary," Diana quipped.

Scott looked at Ben smiling and nodded that she did do what he said.

Diana slapped his arm. "Liar! However, given the option of chocolate milk or something else, I'll take chocolate milk."

"I see. I suppose kittens need their milk, don't they," Ben jeered.

"Yes, we do," Diana stated flatly and walked between them down the hallway. The guys just looked at each other and smiled, then fell in line next to her. Diana got half the bagel sandwich down as they walked; she held the plate up and said, "Anybody want the rest? I'm full."

"I think you can get the rest of that down yet," Ben pushed.

"No, I actually can't. The last two bites were hard for me to get down, I'm really full," she challenged.

"We'll save it for you. Maybe in a half hour you'll be able to eat more," Scott replied. Diana just accepted their answer. She knew better than to argue against both of them. She looked up and realized that they were nearing the quarters they were to stay in for the night. Diana started to slow her steps.

"What's the matter, kitten?" Ben asked.

"Can I ask you guys a favor?" she sheepishly asked.

"Sure, what ya need?" Scott wondered.

"Can I stay with you guys tonight? I'll take the floor, it's just..." She looked down. "I feel awkward in the captain's quarter. The way he's acting, I'll probably get accused of spying or stealing something. I've already spent enough time in a jail, I don't want to spend any more if I don't have to," Diana replied.

Scott and Ben looked at each other. "What do you think, Scott?" Ben asked.

"What, you're in the room too. Why is it my say?" Scott quipped. He knew Ben didn't like her being away from them, especially after the mess hall. If Scott had it figured right, it wouldn't matter where they were; he didn't want to be apart from her. "I've already claimed the top bunk. So it's up to you two to work the rest of it."

"I'll take the floor. I'll be up at least a couple of times anyway," Diana stated.

"We'll figure it out in a few minutes. Go get your stuff and bring it over," Ben replied.

Diana gave Scott a hug then went over to Ben and gave him a hug. "Thank you," she whispered.

Ben cupped her face with his hand. "Go get your stuff, kitten." She handed the leftover bagel to Scott then went into the captain's quarter, grabbed the toiletries, the jeans that she was wearing when she arrived, and the extra pillow and blanket that was lying to the side of the bed.

Scott stood in the hallway smiling at Ben. "What?" Ben asked. "I gave you the option."

"Don't tell me you weren't thinking the same thing. You're uneasy about her being out of sight probably more than she is," Scott jeered.

"We'll get a deeper sleep tonight with her in with us," Ben added.

"Umm…what about the bathroom issue?" Scott asked.

"Well, there's one across the hall. I'll just escort her over there and back," Ben figured.

"Just don't take a long time over there. I don't want to walk in on anything," Scott snipped.

"I don't think that will be a problem, bro. Her mind keeps things on an even keel," Ben said disgustedly. Diana came out of the captain's quarter with an armload of things. Ben grabbed the pillow and blanket. Scott opened the door to their quarter and had her walk in. He put the bagel over by the pullout table. Ben set the bedding down on the edge of the bottom bunk. Diana condensed the toiletries into a small plastic bag she grabbed from the captain's bathroom and put it into the bottom of Ben's locker.

"What are you going to do with those?" Scott asked, pointing to the jeans in her hand.

"I don't want to take whosever's slacks I'm wearing. I'm going to cut the legs off and wear them tomorrow. I'd already washed them in the sink before jumping into the shower earlier," Diana informed him.

Ben had sat down on the bottom bunk. "I suppose you're gonna want me to cut those off?" Ben snipped.

"Nope…I just need to borrow your knife, please." Diana smiled.

Ben reached in and pulled out his knife from his pocket and opened it for her. "Don't cut your finger off," he demanded as he handed her his knife.

Diana went down to her hip on to the floor then crossed her legs. She laid out the jeans, cut the one leg off that the medic cut up, then she matched up the other leg and cut it off at the same length. She was studying the knife, trying to figure out how to close it. "This thing isn't normal," she stated confused.

"Give it here," Ben stated. She stood up and walked it over to him. She turned it so that the handle was going toward Ben. "Someone taught you…smart girl." He took it and clicked something then the blade folded in.

"I'm a daddy's girl." She smiled. "Show me?" she asked, pointing to the knife.

Ben just looked up at her and smiled. "You know what they say about curiosity and cats," he jabbed.

"Yeah, it makes for smart cats," Diana fired back.

"Not quite. You do know those are going to be shorts, right?" Ben inquired.

"Not all that short. It will come above my knee, but just barely. It's longer than what you buy at the store," Diana stated.

"We'll stop at a store and get you another pair as soon as we can," Ben stated.

"Are you afraid her father will see those and not approve?" Scott asked.

"That shouldn't be a problem. I won't be able to see them for who knows how long," Diana sneered. Then she looked up at the guys. "I'm sorry, I need to shut up."

Ben scowled. "That's not why, Diana. Those rope burns make you easily identifiable. I'd prefer to keep things low-keyed."

"In other words, she won't blend in with her legs showing?" Scott knew what Ben was saying, but he saw that Diana didn't get it. Ben nodded. "Well, Milady, khakis or shorts?" Scott asked.

"I didn't think about those stupid things. I suppose I'd better keep the khakis. I'll use your scarf as belt to keep them up," Diana said.

"Well, if you'd get some food in that stomach of yours, you wouldn't have to use a belt," Ben quipped.

"I suppose that was a prompt for me to go finish that bagel?" Diana sneered.

"You should be able to finish it now. Go eat the last few bites," Ben demanded. Diana just rolled her eyes. She walked over and took a bite and started to chew it. She really wasn't hungry, but the guys weren't going to accept that fact. It took her a long time to get the bites chewed and swallowed, but eventually, she was to her last bite. It seemed to be growing in her mouth even though she was swallowing. Finally, she got the last of it down.

"Okay, happy now?" she sneered.

"Yep," the guys said in unison.

"Now, Mr. Tigere, you're supposed to have stuff put on your back. Would you prefer for Scott to do it or me?" Diana asked.

"It isn't going to be me. I'm not a nursemaid," Scott voiced.

"Thank the Lord for that," Ben jested.

Diana grabbed the blanket and laid it out on the floor. "I didn't figure he wanted to. Take your shirt off and lie on the blanket. I can reach it better this way." The guys just looked at her. "When I was younger, I use to give my dad, brother, and an uncle backrubs this way," Diana explained.

Ben just shook his head and took his shirt off and lay down on the blanket. Diana then grabbed the ointment, straddled Ben's back down on her knees, being careful not to put pressure on the stitches, and squeezed some of the ointment on his back. She just laughed as he quibbled about the stuff being cold. "As I said earlier, payback's a bitch."

"Did I hear her right?" Scott looked over the edge of the bunk at them.

"Yeah, that's the second time I've heard her say that. We'll have to figure out the correct punishment for such language," Ben stated. Diana started working the ointment into the cuts on Ben's back. The ointment was petroleum based, so she was taking her time working it in. Diana was purposely giving Ben a backrub. She could feel his muscles were tight; she knew how to relax them. She also noticed the bruises from the night's fight showing already. "That cord of muscles seems really tight. Is it okay I work on them for a while?" she asked. Ben mumbled something and nodded yes; she smiled at his reaction. She looked up at Scott's bunk. "You know, Mr. McCleary, I can work on your back when I'm done here if you want." She felt Ben tense up. "Come on, Tiger, it's only fair. He was risking his life for me as well as you. He lost the bet for the movie date and still was fighting to protect me in the mess hall. It's the least that I can do." Ben's muscles loosened back up. "It's up to you, Scott," she finished.

Scott peeked over the side of the bunk, "Actually at this point in time, I'll take a pass. Maybe once you have a table I can lay on, I'll take you up on it." He didn't figure it would be a good idea to have Diana basically sitting on his butt working on him. It could cause problems—for him.

"It's a deal," Diana stated. She worked on Ben for about twenty minutes. She thought she heard him snoring a few times, but she made sure he was sleeping when she stopped. His breathing was slow and even. "It's about time I found something I can do to give back for what you guys have had to do," she softly stated. She carefully stood up and slowly started putting things back in order. Making sure she didn't make a sound. As she was moving around, she noticed that Scott was watching her. "I'm sorry, did I wake you up?" she asked.

"Nope…I was already awake," Scott answered. "You don't owe us anything, you know that, right?"

"No, you're wrong. I owe you guys my life. I have no doubt I'd be dead by now if it wasn't for you two," she countered. "I do hope I've gained a friend or two in the meantime. That way, I'll have a chance to repay you guys."

"You've gained another brother in my book. I can't speak for Ben, but I have a feeling he's heading for a little more than that," Scott stated, looking up at the ceiling.

"I can never have enough brothers, I'm glad. As for 'the more than that,' it isn't that I'm against it. It's just…complicated," Diana carefully stated. She wasn't sure Ben was still asleep.

"Nah, it's never complicated, it's just whether you accept it or not. The rest works out on its own," Scott countered.

"Yeah…well…I've seen too much evidence to the contrary of that statement. Anyway, since you're awake, would you like to hang out in the captain's quarter long enough for me to use the bathroom?" Diana asked.

Scott just chuckled. "Here I was thinking you might be taking me for a walk."

"I don't actually play around like that. I sorry for the come-on in the cavern. I just needed a weapon, and you were the closest. Forgive me?" Diana embarrassedly stated.

"I figured as such. I will admit, you did a good job of riling him up. It was fun to see. Ladies don't usually get to him that way," Scott said as he got down off the bunk. "Come on, before your bladder explodes." Scott walked her over to the captain's quarters and stood by the door as Diana went in and used the bathroom. Once she was back in the doorway, he started to walk her back to their room. "It's past midnight, Milady. We'd better be getting some sleep." Diana nodded in agreement. When they walked back into the quarters, they saw that Ben had pulled the pillow down from the bunk as well as the blanket. He was lying on his back on the floor, seemingly asleep again. Scott smiled, winked at Diana, then climbed back into his bunk.

Diana took her shoes off as well as her socks; she didn't want to take the time to scrub and soak them tonight. She shut the light off and carefully walked over by where Ben was lying. She lay down beside him on her side, her back toward him, her head on her arm. She listened to Ben breathing; it was slow, deep breaths. She sighed and closed her eyes. She suddenly felt Ben stir, felt his right arm come up under her head, his left arm slowly came across her waist. He pulled her closer to him.

"It's only as complicated as you make it, kitten," he whispered in her ear and kissed her neck. A tremble shot through her; her breath hitched.

Lord…an answer from you would solve this quickly, she prayed. Diana slept soundly for the first time in a long while. She actually didn't have to get up again during the night. The few times she did partially wake up, she felt Ben holding her, heard his even breathing, and fell right back into a deep sleep.

27

USS *Wilson*

She awoke to Ben stroking through her hair. She heard him say, "Time to wake up, kitten…let's get you home." She opened her eyes to see that not only was Ben awake, cleaned up, and dressed, but so was Scott.

"I'm sorry. You guys should have woken me up earlier. Are we going to be late?" she asked.

"Nah, ya still have a little time yet. If it was up to us, we'd have let you sleep the whole flight in. But that would mean we'd have to carry ya, and I don't think the capt'n would smile too kindly on that," Scott teased.

"Go ahead and get cleaned up, then we'll go get some breakfast,' Ben smiled. Diana grabbed her toiletries and the green shirt that Scott had loaned her. She saw Ben was waiting to walk her over. She nodded, turned, and opened the door; Ben was right behind her. Diana headed for the bathroom and shut the door. Ben sat down on the bunk and made himself comfortable. He heard her turn on the shower, the curtain open and close, and the change in the sound of the water when she got into it. He sat there trying to figure out what he was going to do with her. He wasn't sure himself where this was going, but if she didn't talk to him, it wasn't going to go anywhere. It surprised him when he heard the water shut off so soon. Not more than five minutes later, the bathroom door opened. She still had to brush her teeth and take care of her hair, but she was otherwise ready to go. "When did you start taking short showers?" he asked.

"My uncle on my dad's side was in the navy. He told me about the limitations while out to sea. I just figured I'd better abide by them as well," she replied.

"I forgot to ask, how many uncles do you have?" Ben asked, wondering which one abused her. He figured he would eventually find out; but now was just not the time.

"My mom is the oldest of eight, my dad has two other siblings," she said very muffled because she was in the middle of brushing her teeth. She spit out the toothpaste and rinsed and dried her mouth; then she walked out toward Ben, working on combing through her hair with her fingers. "My dad's oldest sister's husband was in the navy. He's the uncle I'm closest too. He's always helped me out when my car broke down or needed work done on it." She smiled.

"Come over here let me help." He pulled the chair out for her to sit on. He knew from the desert that someone "playing" with her hair was relaxing for her. It almost puts her in a trance. He started combing through it with his fingers and watched her close her eyes. "You put me to sleep last night working on my back. Who taught you that?" he asked.

"I used to work on my dad, my brother, and a few other family members' backs when I was younger. I had very strong fingers, and I didn't tire easy. I learned how to slowly work out knots without sending them through the roof. I was a little out of practice though, so I hope I didn't hurt you when I started," she replied.

"Did you miss that you put me to sleep?" he waited a few minutes then threw out the next question. "We didn't get your feet scrubbed and soaked, and you didn't treat your knee as far as I know," Ben softly and calmly stated.

"No, I didn't get my feet soaked, but they are better than yesterday. I treated my knee after I was done working on you. I only had to do the lower cut."

Ben watched and listened. She was starting to talk slowly, softly, her breathing deep, slow, and easy. "Diana…where are *we* going?" Ben asked, combing through the left side of her head.

She sighed but kept her eyes closed. "You heard me talking to Scott, didn't you? I thought you might be listening," she whispered. He stopped combing through her hair and came around in front of her. He crouched down to see her eyes. "Why is it complicated, kitten? Let me into what's going on in that head of yours."

She opened her eyes and looked into those sapphire-blue pools. She wanted to tell him everything. To spill every thought that passed by, but the repercussions of doing so were just overwhelming to her. "My head…it doesn't know where it's going most of the time, Ben, much less with us. The major hold…is…I haven't had confirmation in my spirit yet. I don't…I mean…I can't—"

"Shut the mind down again kitten," Ben smoothly stated, cupping her face with his hand. She leaned into it. "I'm scared…Ben," she whispered. They both heard heavy footsteps coming near the door. Ben stood up just as the captain opened the door.

"What the—?" the captain started to let words fly, but he saw Diana sitting in the chair, arms crossed over her chest, and a glare that stabbed through his eyes into his brain. He coughed into his hand and said, "What are you doing here, Agent Tigere?"

"I came to help Ms. Henderson. Then we we're picking up Mr. McCleary and heading down for breakfast," Ben stated calmly.

"And what exactly were you helping Ms. Henderson with?" the captain had an accusing tone in his voice.

"Agent Tigere very kindly came to help me comb through my hair. You see, I don't have a brush or a comb, so I have to use my fingers, but I can't reach the full length of my hair that way." Diana spoke up. "It is convenient you came in, however, sir. Do I keep the toothbrush and stuff, or do I leave them here?" she asked to disperse the tension.

"They are yours, keep them. I see the shirt you left here. Thank you. Ensign Jenson may wind up raffling it off later today. The pants you still have on," the captain replied.

"Yes, well, I was going to change back into my jeans, but with the fall, I cut open my knee. I had the medic cut the sides of my jeans so he could get to it. I didn't think it appropriate to walk around Tel Aviv in cutoff shorts," Diana calmly stated.

"Well, Ensign Trey isn't going to be happy you took them with you, but I guess it can't be helped," the captain stated.

"As soon as I get home, I'll send these back to Ensign Trey. Please tell him or her that for me," Diana informed the captain.

"I will do so, ma'am," the captain replied.

"Diana, we need to get some food into you before we leave," Ben smoothly stated.

"As you wish," Diana nodded to Ben. She picked up the toothpaste, toothbrush, and the shampoo and soap and walked out the door.

When Ben went to pass the captain, the captain stopped him. "I know very good and well that she stayed with you in your quarters last night, Agent Tigere."

"Yes, she did. With the actions of some of your crew last night, you expected her to trust them?" Ben calmly stated.

"There's a lock on the door. She could have locked it!" the captain hissed.

"Since you simply opened the door without knocking just moments ago, a lock doesn't mean much, does it?" Ben countered. "If you'll excuse me, I need to see that Diana gets some food into her. She's already about thirty pounds less than she should be." Ben backed around the captain's hand that he had placed on Ben's chest to stop him, then walked out the door. Ben saw that Scott was waiting just outside the door of the captain's quarter. He looked at Scott; Scott nodded toward their room. Ben acknowledged and walked over and opened the door. Diana was sitting on a chair, tying her last hiking boot.

"We need to get off this ship before you get court-martialed for mutiny," she jabbed.

Ben chuckled. "Come on kitten, let's get you some milk," Ben jeered. The trio walked down to the mess hall. The place was busy with part of the crew eating while others were dumping trays and heading out for other crew members to come in.

Diana took a deep breath, inhaling the aroma in the air. "That smells good," she whispered. Ben and Scott laughed and pushed her in front of them.

"Go get your breakfast, girl," Scott laughed. Diana looked at the smorgasbord before her. It was going to be another long day, she didn't need to make it any worse; she needed to be careful with her choices. She took a couple of buttermilk biscuits, two sausage patties, three containers of chocolate milk, and a large cup of chamomile tea. She waited at the end of the counter for the guys. They were hung up where the eggs and hash browns were at.

Chad saw her standing there alone and walked over near her. "Is that all you're going to eat?" he stated, studying her tray.

"After almost two weeks of no food, my appetite has shrunk quite a bit," she replied.

"What? Who didn't give you any food, those two guys?" Chad was getting angry.

"No, not them, they're almost force-feeding me because they think I'm not eating enough. I was kidnapped, remember? They wanted me to eat foods that I couldn't eat. So I went without," she easily stated.

"Wha…are you on a restricted diet or something?" Chad pressed.

"Yeah, you can say it that way. I had cancer, I lost part of my colon to it. If I eat spicy foods or foods that are hard to digest, I'll have major problems, so I avoid them," Diana replied. She was hoping that Ben and Scott were about ready. Some of the guys from last night were walking in the door.

"I sorry about the cancer, it's good that they took care of it," Chad said as he followed her line of sight. "Oh, don't worry about them, they won't start anything today. There're too many people in here. Some of the crew heard about last night. The more seasoned crew members were very upset at the commotion they caused. They'd gladly pick up where Agent Tigere and Mr. McCleary ended." He paused for a moment. "I just can't believe, you really sent someone to the hospital? You were never that aggressive in school."

"Yeah, I did, but it was only because it was my last recourse. Just like last night with Frank, he left me no choice," Diana stated as Ben and Scott finally walked over to her.

"Jr. Lt. Steward, good to see you," Scott greeted.

"Good morning, Mr. McCleary. I was trying to get Ms. Henderson to get more to eat. I didn't have any luck with it though," Chad replied.

"Yeah, well compared to what she's been eating, that's a feast. Thanks for trying though." Ben smiled. He looked down at Diana's tray. "I see meat, dairy, and bread. That's at least three of the five food groups."

"I may grab an apple for later, so there is four," Diana shot back.

"What…no donuts or rolls? Where's the sugar at?" Scott questioned.

Diana got an impish look in her eye as an eyebrow arched up. "I'm afraid they don't have the kind of 'sugar' I like available here."

Ben met her eyes. "Remind me to deal with her when we get to New York."

"Yeah, I would say so. Your kitten is a little playful today," Scott laughed. Chad just looked between the three, not following what Diana said.

Diana turned and looked at Chad. "Since I don't think I'll have time to say it later, thanks for all you've done."

"I didn't do anything, Ms.—" Diana cut Chad off.

"I'm not your teacher anymore, you're a man in the navy. It's Diana. By you not doing anything, you did a lot. Thank you." She put her hand on his arm.

"You're welcome, Diana," Chad replied. "Man, that seems weird," Chad said as he shook his head. "Can I call you Milady? I heard Mr. McCleary calling you that," Chad asked.

"You most certainly may. Tell Rick hi for me," Diana said as Ben reached down and started to guide her to a table.

"I will." Chad waved and headed back to the kitchen. Ben saw a table with three chairs together and nodded toward it. Scott saw it and took the lead, Diana followed him, and Ben brought up the rear. They worked around the crowded space and finally sat down.

"This place is crazy," Diana simply stated. Ben and Scott nodded in agreement. They could hardly hear themselves think, much less hear anyone of them talk. They simply sat there eating their food. Diana took one of the biscuits, cut it in half, and put one of the sausage patties in between them. She always liked sausage biscuits, as long as the sausage wasn't spicy; she had it gone in four bites, which brought a smile to Ben's face. Scott was deep into an "everything" omelet.

Diana was opening the second of her chocolate milk cartons; she was looking around the room. Chad was bringing out more pancakes to the buffet; Frank and a few other of the guys from last night's group were stewing in the back of the mess hall, the captain was standing by the door talking to one of his lieutenants. She happened to let her eyes fall on Ben's face. He had been watching her; she met his gaze and blushed. He nodded toward her tray; she knew he wanted her to eat more. She rolled her eyes and took a drink of milk.

She made up the second biscuit and started to eat it. The mess hall was starting to clear out now; the sound wasn't so deafening. Diana finished all of her chocolate milk but only made it through half of the second sausage biscuits. She was sitting there, sipping her chamomile tea, waiting for the guys to finish eating. "Better finish the last few bites, kitten," Ben encouraged.

"If I could, I would. I assure you I will explode if I eat any more," Diana informed him. She stacked her plates then grabbed Scott's and Ben's unneeded used plates, stacking them on top of hers. She stood up to go put them in the kitchen.

"I'll take them," Ben stated.

"Nah, you're still eating. I'm just going to put these in the kitchen on my way to get some more chamomile tea. I'll be right back." Diana smiled. It was easier for her to make her way to drop off the dishes; most of the tables were empty now. She dumped the plates and placed them on the counter. She walked over to the counter where the hot water was, put a tea bag in, and started filling her cup with hot water. An alarm started going off in her spirit; she quickly glanced around her to see what was coming. It was Frank, just steps away from her; she calmed her mind and acted like nothing was wrong as she finished making her tea.

"Hello, sweet cheeks," he sneered.

"Good morning. It's Ensign Frank, right?" Diana asked.

Frank didn't bother to answer the question. "We have some talking to do 'Kitten,' some clarification, you might say," he snipped.

"I don't believe we do, sir. If you'll excuse me, I want to go drink my tea," Diana calmly commented.

Frank grabbed her right wrist and brought her arm around her back. "It won't take long," he assured her.

Ben noticed it took Diana a long time to return. He glanced over and saw Frank holding Diana's arm behind her back. He stood up and started moving toward her.

"You know, sir, you really need to learn that females are not flapjacks to be grabbed up. You also need to learn that *no* means *no*," Diana quipped.

"Yeah, and I suppose you're the female that's gonna teach me," Frank jested.

"If you insist," Diana stated flatly. She brought back her left elbow and sank it into Frank's side; then she kicked her right foot back, hitting him in the knee. When he recoiled, she swung around then forced his head down and kneed him in the chin. Frank finally let go of her wrist and fell backward onto the floor. Ben was just walking up to her. "Ow ow ow, God bless it, crap, that hurts!" she was saying, holding her wrists.

"I can't turn my back on you for a second, can I?" Ben sneered.

"I wasn't doing anything but minding my own business. He's the one causing the trouble," she quipped.

"Let me see it," Ben said, looking down toward her wrist. Diana slowly raised her arm and held out her wrist. She saw that there was blood leaking through the gauze.

"Every time I start getting this stupid thing healing, some ass comes up and make it bleed again," Diana fumed.

"Diana…your mouth," Ben teased.

"What…the Bible uses that word all the time. You can't tell me that the mind-set of our friend here isn't the same as one," Diana fired off.

Ben started to chuckle. He glanced up and saw the medic coming toward them followed closely by the captain. "Speak of the devil," he stated.

"Agent Tigere, you just can't leave it alone, can you?" the captain steamed. Diana was going to answer, but the captain punctuated, "I was addressing Agent Tigere, Ms. Henderson. I would suggest that you keep that big trap of yours shut." His caustic demeanor was beyond believable.

Ben just stood there cool, calm, and collected. "Maybe you would like to get the facts before passing judgment, sir," he stated.

"Oh? And what facts do I need to add to my stack?" the captain replied.

"How about this one: I did not do this. Here's another, Ms. Henderson was only protecting herself. The last one was there are witnesses to the previous two facts," Ben concluded.

"Are you telling me that this civilian woman took out a trained sailor all by herself?" the captain responded.

"If he was trained, sir, I'm a supermodel," Diana quipped. The captain moved toward Diana. Ben stepped between her and the captain. "Ma'am, if you don't keep your mouth shut, I will personally see to it you don't see the land for two more months," he threatened.

"Your threat is unwarranted and unnecessary, Captain," Ben stated.

Scott came up and stood beside Ben. "You know, if you are really wanting to ruin your reputation, go for it. However, there is a way to prove what Agent Tigere and Ms. Henderson are saying, sir," Scott flatly commented.

"Oh, and what way is that, Mr. McCleary?" the captain said, still holding eye contact with Ben.

"Ensign Steward, would you like to bring your video camera over here please," Scott called out. Chad came out with his video camera in his hands. He pressed a few buttons and handed it to Scott. "Thank you, sir," Scott nodded. Scott hit a button on the camera and handed it over to the captain. Diana looked over to Chad; he was downcast and watched the captain intently. Then she looked at Scott; he met her gaze and just winked at her. She couldn't see Ben's face, but judging from his stance and posture, he was ready to fight. She then looked at the captain. He was stone-faced; his temple was pulsing with the rhythm of his blood pressure, his eyes beady and cold. It seemed to take forever for the captain to watch the video. Her wrist was killing her. The blood, which had soaked through the gauze, was starting to run down her hand. She reached over and grabbed some napkins and wiped the run of blood up then grabbed a few more and covered her wrist with them, holding her wrist in her other hand. She heard the captain exhale; she looked over to see what was going to happen next.

"Ensign Steward, could you tell me why you were recording Ms. Henderson?" the captain asked, turning toward Chad.

"Ms. Henderson was the teacher in the one-room schoolroom I and my brother attended. My brother Rick had a crush on her back then. I was taking the video to show him that she was here and how great she looked. It was just a fluke that Frank walked into the scene. I was about to put it down and help her out when Ms. Henderson took him out herself," Chad ended.

"I trust that you will edit some of that video before showing your brother. I'd hate to have it go viral. It would put a bad light on the US Navy," the captain calmly stated.

"Aye…sir," Chad replied.

"Dismissed…Jr. Lt. Steward," the captain curtly stated. He turned and addressed the medic. "Would you go and see to Ms. Henderson's wrist? She is dripping blood all over the floor." The medic started toward Diana, but he stopped short as he neared Ben. It was Diana that gently put her hand on Ben's back and walked around him. She rested her hand on his arm. Ben looked down at her, took her hand, and gave it to the medic. The medic took her hand and led her over to the table to work on her wrist.

The captain now addressed Ben and Scott. "I obviously underestimated Ms. Henderson. I assumed that since you two were with her, she was unable to protect herself. Therefore her statements were covers for things you two were doing. I admit when I'm wrong. So I do apologize for my behavior."

"It is not us you need to apologize to captain," Scott spoke up.

"Yes, I acknowledge that. I will talk to her as soon as the medic is done with her wrist. Agent Tigere, I have the feeling you are holding your tongue for some reason. Do you want my word that you will not be prosecuted for things said or done?" the captain stated.

"That would be fine with me, sir," Ben coldly stated.

"Fine, you have my word. I will not pursue any retaliation against you or your friend for things you say or do," the captain stated.

Ben looked at Scott and nodded toward Diana. Scott turned and walked away from him. Ben then turned to the captain; his eyes the dangerous deep sapphire blue, his jaw set. "There is only one thing I would like to do at this point in time," Ben stated.

"And what would that be?" the captain questioned.

Ben brought up a right cut, slamming his fist into the captain's jaw. The blow caused the captain to fall backward to the ground. Diana heard the commotion and jumped up to go to Ben.

Scott grabbed her by her shoulders and held her tight. "It's all right, Milady, Ben was just finishing his conversation with the captain. Let the medic finish with your wrist," Scott insisted. She looked up at Scott then over to the captain who was on the floor, rubbing his jaw. Ben was standing there rubbing his fist.

She sighed and shook her head. "I don't think I'll ever understand the male bonding rules." She went back to the medic for him to finish up.

Ben held out his hand to the captain. The captain smiled and took it, letting Ben pull him up off the floor. "I guess I deserved that," he stated. "Now I know why the admiral called you a tiger. I'll deal with Ensign Smith. He's a good sailor, he just needs an attitudinal adjustment. Give him a few years under his belt here and you two might actually be friends," the captain said.

Ben looked over toward Diana with her eyes closed as the medic started to stitch the gashes that opened up on her wrist. "I doubt it, sir."

The captain followed Ben's gaze. "She's quite a woman. Is she always a spitfire?"

"Yep…pretty much. Only a few people have learned how to control her, and that's only when she wants to let them," Ben answered.

The captain looked at Ben and then over to Diana. *They are two of a kind…these two. I bet with a little training…she'd probably whip Agent Tigere's butt with a few more moves*, he thought. The captain heard a moan from the sailor lying on the floor behind him. He walked over to the intercom. "Lieutenant Jones please report to the mess hall."

Ben walked over to the table where Diana, Scott, and the medic were at. Ben looked down at Diana, her eyes closed because the medic was stitching the gashes. "How ya holding, kitten?"

"Oh, wonderful, I'm just peachy, can't you tell," Diana snipped.

Scott just laughed. "Milady, I would suggest that you learn to deal with needles. Especially since you seem to always need them jabbing into you."

"Not possible, Scott. After ten years of allergy shots and three years of labs, chemo, and surgeries, there's no hope for me to become adjusted to the stupid things," Diana replied.

"Maybe you'll have better luck getting her to like flying," Ben injected.

Diana opened her eyes and glared at Ben. He winked and smiled at her. She glanced over at Scott. "Good luck with that one too." She accidently let her eyes fall on what the medic was doing. She instantly paled.

Scott looked at her then over to Ben. "You'd better get a trash can. I don't think she's going to hold breakfast down, Ben."

"I'll be fine, just hurry and get done," Diana stated getting her nausea under control.

The medic finished his last stitch. "I'm done with the needle, ma'am. I'll wrap it up with some gauze. It will need to be changed again tonight then twice a day till the stitches are dissolved. One of you two are going to have to take care of that. She won't be able to do it on her own."

"I think we've got it. Thank you," Ben stated. The captain walked over to the table, leaving the Lieutenant Jones to deal with Frank.

"How did we make out?" he asked the medic.

"The previous injury from the rope burn with the added pressure from Ensign Smith's grasp broke her skin wide open. I've cleaned and stitched the wrist closed. Unfortunately, with Ms. Henderson's sensitivity to antibiotics, all I can do is keep it clean," the medic informed the captain.

"Understood…thank you. Now that you have finished here you may want to check on Ensign Smith. Make sure he still has teeth in his mouth, if you would." The captain dismissed the medic and turned to Diana. "I wanted to apologize to you, Ms. Henderson. My behavior and actions were uncalled for and very unprofessional. Forgive me."

Diana sat for a few minutes studying the captain's face. She had the disapproving-teacher glare down. The captain actually started to get antsy. Ben knew she was doing that on purpose, getting a little payback from him. Finally she said, "What's going to happen to Frank?"

"That sailor is going to spend a long time working with Jr. Lt. Steward. I've already instructed the kitchen staff to give Ensign Smith all the nastiest jobs possible. Then we will see where his attitude is at. Jr. Lt. Steward said he guaranteed that he will pay his dues," the captain ended.

"I accept your apology then, and thank you for not throwing Agent Tigere into the brig as well," Diana said.

"Why would I need to do that for, Ms. Henderson?" the captain asked.

"For the event that just happened a moment ago," she stated flatly.

"What event? Did either of you two see what she is talking about?" the captain asked, looking at Ben and Scott.

Diana studied the captain a minute then looked at Scott and Ben. "I'll never understand the male mind-sets," Diana said shaking her head.

"Well, now that you're all put together, Ms. Henderson, you'd best go get your things. The chopper is prepping as we speak. Unfortunately, I was not able to arrange for you to speak with your parents," the captain informed the group and walked out.

Scott and Ben looked down at Diana; she was just sitting there, looking at nothing. "Kitten, come on, let's go get things together," Ben stated smooth and calmly. Diana nodded, took a deep breath, and stood up. Ben grabbed her just under her arm when she wobbled and started to fall. "Diana?"

"I'm all right, I'm sorry. I'm still getting myself settled, that's all," she answered quickly.

Ben steadied her in his arm. She was more than willing to stay there. "Deep breaths, kitten, deep breaths," he whispered. He felt her nod slightly. Then they walked to the quarters they used last night, packed up the few things they had, and headed up to the flight deck. The chopper was just starting the engines. Diana looked out over the water. "I bet this is beautiful at sunrise and sunset," she voiced.

Ben looked at her and rubbed her shoulders. "Are we ready?"

"As ready as I'm going to be," Diana said with a shaky voice. Scott took the lead; Ben stayed with Diana and walked her over. She remembered to keep her head down as she neared. She reached over and grabbed her loose hair to keep it out of her face. Ben handed her to Scott, who was already in the chopper. "Careful with her wrist," he reminded Scott.

"I got her, bro, don't worry," Scott replied as he grabbed Diana's forearm and pulled her in. Ben jumped in as soon as she was stable. Ben headed back to the seat by the cockpit, where he was handed a pair of headphones. Diana followed him, but this time she wasn't cowering up against him. She was covering her ears though; the sound of the motor and blades were nearly breaking her eardrums. Scott picked up a pair of headphones for himself and Diana. He handed them to her as he passed by to sit down on the other side of her. Once she had the headphones on, she straightened up. She was looking around at the crew that was in the chopper. She looked like she was calm, but Ben saw the subtle signs that she was still terrified. Her hands were clinched into a fist at her sides, the knuckles were nearly white, and her eyes wide and stormy sea-gray. Ben made sure that her headphones were on then asked, "How are you holding, Kitten?" Diana turned and looked at him and grimaced. Ben smiled at her. "Remember to keep breathing. I'd hate to have to give mouth-to-mouth in here." She backhanded him in the stomach. She saw the crew was chuckling at them; she shook her head and rolled her eyes, giving them a half smile.

"Hey, Agent Tigere, is she the one that took out Frank this morning?" one of the crew asked. Diana couldn't identify which of the crew asked the question. She looked over at Ben to see what he was going to say.

Ben smiled broadly. "Yeah, I guess he didn't learn his lesson from last night."

The same crew member asked, "Why do you call her 'Kitten'? She sounds more like a wildcat."

"It's more sarcasm than anything, gentlemen. I'm not helpless in most situations," Diana answered.

"She's definitely not helpless, more of a trouble magnet," Scott jeered. Diana slapped him on the leg. "Easy, Milady, you'll break open that wrist again," Scott reminded her.

"Oh…whatever," she fired back. Ben saw that she was started to relax. So he laid his head back and listened to the conversation. The crew did a good job of keeping her from thinking of where they were at. It wasn't till one of them asked if she wanted to look out the window that Ben heard her voice quiver.

Then the pilot came on. "Ms. Henderson, I'm going to need to turn your headphones off for just a minute. I'll turn them back on."

Ben opened his eyes, but he didn't sit up; Diana was watching his reactions. "What's up, Pilot?" Ben asked.

"Sir, there has been a slight change of plans. There were some attacks on Americans in Tel Aviv last night. HQ doesn't want you guys to risk taking Ms. Henderson through town. Agent Richman has her papers and will meet you at the airport," the pilot ended.

"Understood. What about Customs?" Ben asked.

"Agent Richman said he has it taken care of," the pilot replied.

"What's the ETA on the airport pilot?" Ben inquired.

"It's another forty minutes, sir," the pilot answered.

"Roger," Ben responded. Diana had reached over and slowly took Ben's hand. Ben looked over to Diana; he could feel she was shaking. "You'd better turn Ms. Henderson's headphones back on. She's starting to let her imagination rove," Ben told the pilot.

Diana heard the crew talking again in the headphones. "Ben, what's going on?" she demanded. Ben took Diana's hand and was stroking his thumb over the back of it.

"It's just a small change in plans," Ben assured. He heard her gasp; he squeezed her hand. "No hyperventilating, kitten. Breathe." Once he saw her take a couple of deep breaths, he continued. "We won't be able to go shopping for pants until New York. We will meet up with Dick at the airport and go directly to the airplane for the States." Ben looked over to Scott.

"Hey, Milady, where would you like to shop at in New York?" Scott asked, more to divert her attention.

"I've never been to New York. I've not been any farther north than Minneapolis, Minnesota. So I would have no idea," Diana said nervously. The crew took the hint from Scott's question; they all jumped in and started to suggest different places to shop at. Ben noticed that Diana was keeping her hand in his. He intertwined his fingers through hers. The energy he felt from that move was unbelievable. He felt his heart racing in his chest, pounding in his ears; he glanced over at Diana.

Diana felt Ben weave his fingers through hers. Her heart went to her throat; she had a hard time breathing, and she felt her face flush. She looked down till she could control herself then glanced over to Ben. He was watching her. She blinked then smiled at him then looked back out again.

Scott of course was watching both of them. *There you go bro, small simple steps. Let her adjust slowly*, he thought.

"ETA fifteen minutes, everybody," the pilot stated. Ben felt Diana's hand tighten around his; he looked over at her. She was taking short quick breaths again. "Scott, do you have a paper bag in that pack of yours," he asked.

"Nope…why?" Scott queried.

"Diana is going to pass out if she doesn't slow down," Ben smoothly replied. Diana looked up at Ben then Scott. She closed her eyes and forced herself to breathe deep and slow. Ben lifted her hand to his mouth and kissed it. "Good job, kitten, nice and slow," he said. The chopper landed on the side pad of the Tel Aviv airport. Ben, Diana, and Scott hopped off. The crew passed their packs out and waited for them to clear the rotor wash before taking off again. Diana turned and waved as they were flying out. Ben and Scott simply saluted. They walked toward the airport terminal where they saw Dick waiting just on the other side of the fence.

The guards stopped them before passing the fence. Ben and Scott pulled out their papers, Diana held back a little. "Ma'am, ma'am, your papers please," the guard demanded.

"I've got them here, sir," Dick yelled out, walking quickly over to the trio. The guard looked perplexed but took the papers Dick handed to him. Diana was looking for where Ben and Scott went too, but she couldn't see them.

"Easy, Kitten, we're right here," Ben said, walking up behind her.

"She's like a cat on a hot tin roof. You'd better hang on to her so she doesn't run," Scott teased. Diana glared at him. "Now…Milady, you wouldn't want these gentlemen to get the wrong idea of you, would you?" Scott continued.

"You…Ms. Henderson, where do you come from?" the officer asked.

Ben and Scott escorted her over closer to him. "I'm currently from Iowa," she stated.

"And you are here for what reason?" the officer continued

"From what I'm understanding, it's just to switch planes, sir," she answered shakily.

"And you are heading to where?" the officer pressed.

"New York…sir. Why all the questions?" Diana asked as her head cocked to the side.

"All you have to take with you is this pack?" the officer continued.

"That's why I'm heading to New York, sir. To go buy some clothes," Diana was getting testy. She didn't know why all the questions; why was he singling her out? She noticed several other people had came and passed through without as much as a word of hello. She looked up at Ben then over to Scott.

"It's protocol, Milady, it's kewl," Scott answered. Diana questioned that response but didn't say anything.

Dick stepped up. "Is everything okay, sir? Their flight leaves in fifteen minutes, we need to get them on and situated."

The guard studied her photo then looked at her. "I suppose this was an old photo. Okay…I'll let her pass." He handed her the papers and waved her on through and reached behind to take the next person's papers. Ben took her hand and put it on his arm. Dick was pushing through the crowd, making a path. Scott was just slightly behind Diana, carefully scanning the people around them without anybody noticing. They came to the next checkpoint of the airport then went to the boarding tunnel. Dick handed the officer his papers then Ben and Diana handed theirs; Scott was the last to give the officer his as they were waved on through. They got into the plane and seated just before the door was shut. The tickets had them in first class.

Ben whistled when he was seated. "Very nice," he stated. Scott was in the chair behind him. Diana was seated next to Dick. Ben could see she wasn't happy, but she held her tongue and was courteous to Dick. She mostly looked out the window at the people walking in the terminal. The captain came on over the mic system. "We will be taxiing out in five minutes. As of now we are running on schedule and should be taking off in fifteen minutes."

With the door already closed, Scott figured the seat next to Ben was open. He slid out his row and up to the empty seat. "You wanna tell me that Dick didn't plan this?" Scott quipped.

"Yeah, I know. I'm wondering how long she'll tolerate him before she fires off," Ben stated.

"Aye, but she's a smart girl. She'd probably slice and dice him up and he'd never know it," Scott pointed out.

Ben smiled at that comment. It's true her tongue can slice you to the core if she ever put her mind to it. "It's, what, a five-hour flight? I'd wager she'll put a pair of earbuds in and tune him out here in fifteen or twenty minutes. Then she'll probably go to sleep from the boredom," Ben commented.

"I wonder what music she listens to. That's a part we haven't found out about yet," Scott mused.

Ben just shot an eyebrow up. Scott was right; they never found out what music she prefers or a lot of other little things. The plane started moving from the loading zone. It taxied out to the runway where it waited for the go-ahead to take off. Scott made himself comfortable in the seat next to Ben. Ben glanced back at Diana; she was calm, but her eyes were the stormy sea-gray again. *Lord, help her stay calm. Hold her in your arms and keep her safe*, Ben prayed.

"We have been cleared for takeoff. We will be leaving momentarily," the captain informed.

The flight attendant gave the usual instructions of what to do and when, how, and why. They were instructed to fasten their seatbelts for takeoff. Ben looked back just in time to see Dick offering to help Diana with hers. She graciously took the belt from his hand as she told him she's got it. Dick sat back down in his seat and buckled his own seat belt. Diana went back to looking out the window, but Ben noticed her eyes weren't open. They were closed, she was breathing calm and acted like was being held. *Thank you, Lord*, Ben praised. The plane took off, leaving Tel Aviv at ten a.m. That would put them in New York around three or so, Ben figured. "It will be good to get home and see the kids again," he said out loud.

"Yeah, it will. What are you going to do with us tagalongs?" Scott asked.

"I figured since you're not allowed to go home, the least I can do is bring you home with me," Ben stated.

"How do you think the kids are going to take Diana?" Scott questioned. "You know that might be one of the holdups she's talking about. That the kids may not accept her," he pointed out.

"I don't know if she'll let it go that far, bro. I'm not sure I'm ready for it to go that far," Ben flatly stated.

"Yeah, you are, and you know it. You've wanted to kiss that girl since the cabin. That will only last for a short time before you'll want more," Scott scolded.

Ben couldn't argue with him, and he'd just bury himself more if he tried to get around it. He figured it would be best just to stay quiet. What would his kids think of Diana? *Kora and Brock won't be an issue. BJ would probably be fine with it, but Kaira—she's become the woman of the house since Katherine died. She may have a lot of problem with it*, Ben pondered. The plane was only in the air for about fifteen minutes before Diana had put in earbuds and tuned Dick out. She closed her eyes and fell asleep. The flight went as scheduled; no storms or bad weather, no terrorists or bombers, just an easy normal flight. Ben saw that Dick was upset that Diana shut him off. He just shook his head, closed his eyes, and fell asleep as well.

He woke to Scott elbowing him. "What's up, bro?" he prodded.

"Do you want to hear what Diana is listening to?" Scott excitedly asked.

Ben shot an eyebrow up. "How did you find out?"

"I asked the stewardess. She has a computer that reads the stations," Scott stated. He handed Ben a set of earbuds. Ben saw that Scott had music going, so he put the ear buds in his ears. He heard Celtic instrumental music playing.

"You're kidding, aren't you?" Ben jeered.

"Nawt at awl. She likes Celtic music. That's unbelievable," Scott stated with a grin. "Oh, we're about a half hour out, so you might as well wake up. Also…what are we going to do about Diana? She's liable to swing out at Dick if he touches her. He's on her right side," Scott worried.

"Yeah, and she'll get that wrist to bleeding again before she's awake to know what's going on. I'll have to deal with it," Ben concurred. He got up and went to the bathroom. As he came back, he asked the stewardess if she could call Mr. Richman. He needed to talk with the lady next to him. The stewardess looked at Ben for a minute, gave him a Cheshire smile, and agreed. Ben went and sat down in his chair, told Scott what he was doing, and waited for the stewardess to pull her part. "Would Mr. Richman please come to the back of the plane? Mr. Richman, to the back of the plane please," came over the mic system.

Dick looked over to Ben and Scott, who shrugged their shoulders. He got up and headed to the back of the plane. As soon as he was through the curtain that separated first class from coach, Ben moved over. He carefully put his hand on Diana's right forearm. "Kitten, can you hear me?" he asked as he sat down in Dick's seat.

Diana smiled. "I don't have to hear you, I feel you. Did you think I would swing out?"

Ben brought her hand to his mouth and kissed it. "Yeah, actually I was afraid you'd break that wrist open again."

She opened her eyes and smiled at him. "You're probably right. If I hadn't realized it was you, I would have swung out."

"So, you like Celtic music huh?" Ben asked.

"I actually like several different genres. Today was Celtic, tomorrow could be classical or hard rock. It just depends on my mood at the time," she beamed.

"I'd better get back to my seat before Dick comes back. We're almost there, so not too much longer," Ben informed her.

"Thank you," Diana smiled. Ben moved back just as Dick was coming through the curtain. He was angry.

"What's up, pard?" Ben asked.

"They were worried about some backpack as to whether it was one of ours or not. Incompetence of people," Dick fumed.

"It's better than having it lost," Scott injected.

Dick just shook his head. He looked over and noticed Diana was awake, but she still had her earbuds in. "She's an exciting one, hey," he snipped.

Ben and Scott just gave him a half smile and turned to their own business. "He really has no clue, does he?" Scott jeered.

"Nah, but don't be too hard on him. He and Diana started off on the wrong foot. I think he's trying to make it up to her. Clumsily, but nonetheless, he's trying," Ben stated. The pilot came on saying they were in final descent for landing. The seat belt light came on, and everybody fastened their belts. A few minutes later, they were on the ground back in the United States. Soon they would be disembarking.

28

New York

They sat on the tarmac for another twenty minutes before the plane moved to let them disembark. Scott and Diana were the first two off the plane. Dick held back to talk to Ben. "I thought you might like a little break from Ms. Henderson. Did you enjoy your short holiday?" Dick asked.

Ben just smiled. *You have no clue*, he said in his mind. "Oh, she's not bad once you get to know her. You've just hit her at the wrong times."

"Are you kidding me? She's a stuck-up ******* little smart ***." Dick fumed.

Ben just shook his head. "How's it going with finding out where the leak is?" Ben asked as they walked down the tunnel.

"So far we keep hitting dead ends. As of right now, we have nothing," Dick said in disgust. They saw Scott and Diana waiting for them just past the first check station. Diana's eyes were plates again; her head looking everywhere.

"Is everything okay?" Ben asked Scott as they approached.

"Our cat here is totally out of her element," Scott jeered.

"What? Are you saying she's really a country girl?" Ben jabbed as he came up next to Diana. "Here I thought we had a sophisticated, urban woman," he continued.

"I've never seen so many people in my entire life. Even in the church assemblies, we only had ten thousand or so people to move through. How are we going to get through all this?" Diana queried.

"Well, since we have to wait till tomorrow before we can head to Des Moines, it will be easier than you think. We have time to move through all the checks and people. If we were going to switch to another plane, we'd have to make a mad, crazy dash," Ben assured. Dick grabbed his cell phone; apparently, it had started to ring. He must have had it on vibrate because with the noise of the terminal, Diana didn't hear it. She doubted anybody else could hear it either. Ben and Scott waited till Dick was done. "What's up, pard?"

"It looks like you guys are on your own. I'm to report to HQ here to update everybody. Then head home ASAP on the red-eye," Dick grimaced. He pulled an envelope out of his coat pocket. "You're set up at the Hilton, there's money in there. The Director Zenon says don't let Ms. Henderson go wild with it. Your tickets for the flight to Des Moines are in there also," Dick informed Ben. "I'll see you back home, Tiger." He slapped Ben on the arm and walked on through the check station.

"Well, at least I won't have to deal with a migraine on the airplane tomorrow," Diana quipped.

"Yeah, his cologne was quite strong, wasn't it?" Scott remarked.

"Well, let's get out of here and get some clothes. Where would you like to start at, kitten?" Ben asked taking Diana's hand.

"Wal-Mart would be a great start." She smiled. The first thing she was going to buy was a brush, deodorant, and perfume.

"There's a woman after my own heart," Scott chuckled.

"I shop secondhand, Goodwill, and Salvation Army stores usually. So I have the feeling that I'm going to have trouble with sticker shock today," Diana stated.

Ben laughed. "I have no idea where any of those are here. You'll have to settle for a few higher-end stores instead. You don't mind tagging along when Scott and I get some clothes as well, do ya?"

"Not at all. You're stuck dragging behind me. Although, I might ditch ya for a few minutes there," Diana stated, looking down at her shoes.

Ben's eyebrow arched up; Scott actually blushed. "I think we can give you a long leash when necessary," Ben chuckled. He offered her his arm, which Diana gladly took. They started going through the checks and searches before finally reaching the outside of the terminal. Ben flagged down a taxi, and they drove off heading toward the Hilton.

The taxi driver pulled up to the Hilton thirty minutes later. Ben, Scott, and Diana unloaded from the taxi; Diana was just shaking her head as they started walking into the hotel. "Now I know what they mean when they call taxi drivers aliens. That guy is insane."

"A far stretch from driving down I-80, isn't it?" Ben laughed. Diana rolled her eyes but didn't make any other comment, mainly because they were at the counter to check in.

The clerk was on the phone when they walked up. The trio waited patiently for her to get finished with her conversation. "May I help you?" she asked once off the phone.

"We're checking in…Richman," Ben stated.

"Yes, four people in three rooms?" she asked.

"No…we had a change of plans. There are only three, and we'll only need two rooms, adjoining, preferably," Ben informed her.

"Are you still wanting…two queens and a king, or do you just want a king in each?" she asked, typing on the computer.

"Two queens in one room, one king or whatever is available in the other," Ben continued. The clerk stopped typing and eyed Diana. Diana just stood there, smiling back at her. Ben figured that she wanted to slap the clerk and tell her to mind her own business, but that was only a guess.

"We have two rooms, two queens in one, a double in the other, adjoining, and opening up to the swimming pool. Is there anything else?" the clerk asked.

"Sounds perfect, thank you,' Ben replied.

"Rooms 1121 and 1122. The elevator is down the hall and to the left," the clerk stated.

"Thank you, ma'am," Scott injected, and the trio started down the hall. They found the elevator and waited for it to come get them. Once the doors open, Diana froze. It was a glass elevator that they were taking up to the eleventh floor. Scott looked over to Ben and grimaced. "This could be interesting."

"Yeah, I guess so. I didn't count on a glass elevator. I should have known. This is New York. Well, kitten, elevator or would you rather climb up eleven flights of stairs?" Ben asked.

Diana seriously thought about taking the eleven flights of stairs, but she knew the guys wouldn't let her go by herself. "I'd better take the elevator, but don't expect me to be smiling about it," she quipped.

"That's my girl. Come on. Let's get settled so we can go shopping. That should bring a smile on your face," Ben teased.

Diana stepped into the elevator but stayed near the doors. "You really believe I'm one of those women that goes shopping anytime she's upset? Here I thought you knew me better than I knew myself," Diana said sarcastically.

"I do believe you have buried yourself in some deep doo-doo, bro," Scott teased.

"Hmm…ya think? However, I'll let him have a pass—for now." Diana smirked.

"Maybe we should take a better look at the view, Ms. Henderson," Ben said as he was pushing her toward the glass side of the elevator.

"Benjamen James Tigere, you're going to regret it if you don't stop it," Diana yelled.

"There you go again; Promises…promises," Ben jeered. The elevator finally made it to the eleventh floor. Diana was the first out of the elevator; Ben and Scott were laughing as they walked out. The trio walked to their rooms and Ben opened 1121 first. It was large and had a sitting area near the window. There was a double bed in the middle of the wall. "This one must be your room, kitten," he stated.

He walked out and opened room 1122; the room was just as big, but with two queens in the room. There was no room for a sitting area. He walked over and unlocked the door adjoining the two rooms. He knocked for Diana to unlock her side. She unlocked the door and opened it. Scott walked in and claimed his bed immediately. "It's going to be great to have a full bed to stretch out on again, isn't it?" Ben stated.

"I can't believe it's only been a week since I've had an actual bed to sleep in," Scott replied.

"I hear ya. It feels like years," Ben said. He walked over into Diana's room. He saw her looking through the brochure. "Is everything okay, kitten?"

"Oh yeah, the room is great. I might have to lock the fridge so Scott doesn't help himself to the microbar," Diana stated with a smile.

"Let's go get the shopping done so we can relax tonight," Ben stated.

"That would be awesome," Diana agreed. She followed Ben into the guys' room. Scott was already checking out the microbar. Diana looked up at Ben and nodded toward Scott.

"Hey…Scotsman, let's go get some clothes, maybe something to eat, then we can get back here and relax," Ben urged.

"Oh…all right, let's get this over with." Scott grimaced. He closed the door of the fridge. "Maybe we can get some swimming in later. If I remember right, our cat here is a fish in the water."

"I would love to swim, but I have a problem." Diana held up her wrist then her knee. "I can't swim with stitches. I'd probably be in there already if I could."

Ben looked down at her. "We can figure something out if you really want to swim."

Diana's eyes flashed with excitement. She gave him a broad smile. "That would be awesome." The trio headed back down; Diana glued herself to the doors of the elevator. They walked out and hailed a taxi. The first store they hit was Wal-Mart. Diana quickly picked up the things she needed. She ditched the guys in the men's wear department so she could get the undergarments she needed. She also picked up a night shirt and lounge pants. The guys met back up with her as she was looking at jeans. "Why can these places ever have talls? Everything is always too short," she quipped.

"We'll get you some jeans before we're done tonight," Ben stated. "Speaking of which, are we done here?"

"As far as I can go," Diana replied.

"Hey…Milady, did you look for a swimsuit?" Scott asked.

"If they don't have jeans in a tall, they're not going to have a swimsuit long enough either," Diana informed him.

"If you wear a two piece, it wouldn't matter," Scott stated.

"Forget it, gentlemen, I'm not wearing a bikini. So get your mind away from where they are now," Diana scolded.

"She is trying to take my fun away, bro. What are you going to do about it?" Scott whined.

"What am I going to do? Why me?" Ben asked.

"Well, you're the cat whisperer, do some whispering," Scott insisted.

"Yeah…well, I don't think this cat is going to listen to any whispering in that area," Ben replied, looking at Diana. He gave her a wink and started guiding her to the checkout line. The next store was one Diana never heard of, but she found jeans and shirts that fit her. They were way more than she would ever pay for them. Ben and Scott assured her that those prices were normal. They paid for them and walked out of the store. She figured she was done, so the guys went to a store for them to get clothes. They went to a Western store first. While the guys were trying on stuff, Diana's eye caught a beautiful pair of boots. They were dark brown leather, with white pearl insets, a square toe, and fancy stitching up the shaft. She picked it up and looked at the price. *No way.* She quickly put the boot back. She didn't realize Ben was watching her.

"There is a country girl in you, isn't there?" Ben whispered.

"I told you not to judge the book by its cover. My mom's parents owned a farm in northern Nebraska. I spent summers with them while my parents were working at camps and assemblies," she easily replied.

Ben reached up and grabbed the boots. "Ben…no, they're too expensive," she insisted.

"How are you going to stop me?" Ben snipped. He told the sales rep that he needed these boots in a woman's size 10. The sales rep left to pull those from the back. Ben bent down to her ear. "They'd look really good with those black jeans and the white blouse with the lace insets." She looked up into Ben's eyes; she felt herself quiver a little at the thought that shot through her head. Ben's eyebrow arched up. "And what was that thought, kitten?"

"Never mind what I was thinking. That's between me, myself, and I," she jabbed.

"I'd really like to know," he stated.

"I bet you would, but you're not going to," Diana said with a smile. "You can't make me tell ya either," she said then turned to go try on the boots the sales rep brought out.

Ben smiled at her. "You have no clue, babe. There are ways to make you talk."

"Not legal ones," she said in a singsong tone.

"Lord, help me," Ben said out loud.

Scott came out of the dressing room. "Is she getting under your skin again?"

"Not exactly, but close enough," Ben snipped.

"Huh-huh…do I need to start reminding you to breathe?" Scott chuckled.

"Oh, shut up," Ben stated.

"What do we have left to get?" Scott said, changing topics.

"Umm, I think we've got everything, don't we?" Ben mused, grateful for the topic change.

"Oh wait, we don't have swimsuits yet," Scott said, snapping his fingers.

"Fine…we'll go get some swimsuits. But if I see your mouth watering, she's going to be locked up in the room," Ben quipped.

"Spoilsport," Scott sneered. The last shop they went to was a sporting goods store. One of the sales reps came and asked if they needed help.

"Do you mind if I get a woman to help me?" Diana asked.

"Not a problem…Glenda," the rep called out. A girl came out from the back room. She looked like she was all of eighteen years old to Diana.

"How can I help you?" she asked.

"Would you mind walking with me, I'll explain on the way," Diana stated as she motioned for the girl to walk with her. Ben just laughed at her and shook his head.

Scott, on the other hand, was upset. "What, we're not good enough to help her?" he griped.

"She's a cat, remember? Her terms," Ben replied. He looked at the other sales rep. "We can take care of ourselves…thank you." The sales rep seemed upset that he was dismissed.

Diana walked with Glenda, explained in specific words what she was wanting in a swimsuit. Glenda argued a little with her; she thought that Diana would want to show her assets, especially since she had walked in with two "hot bods." After some insistence, Glenda seemed to understand what Diana was looking for. She brought a one-piece, color-block swimsuit. It had a skirt that came about two inches down on her thighs. The back was open, and there was a keyhole slot in the front. Diana thought that it was appropriate, and it was on sale. "This will do just great. Thank you, Glenda."

Diana got dressed and walked out to the checkout stand. The guys were standing there, waiting for her. "Did you find what you needed?" Ben questioned.

"Yep. Definitely not what you two wanted, but I won't have to worry about my conscience tonight. However…if we don't have a way to cover the stitches, it's a mute point," she commented.

"We have that taken care of already, Milady, don't worry," Scott injected. Ben paid for the swimsuits, and they left the store. They hailed a taxi and climbed in when one stopped for them.

"So where do you want to eat?" Scott asked.

"Wherever you guys want, I'm not really hung—" Diana didn't finish her thought. Ben and Scott were scowling down at her. "Never mind, I'll force something down."

"Good. Now, since we won't get an answer out of the lady here Scott, what did you have in mind to eat?" Ben asked.

"I'm in the mood for some Chinese, whatcha say…bro?" Scott smiled as he hit Ben on the shoulder.

"Fine…Chinese it is," Ben replied and instructed the taxi driver to take them to the Royal Seafood Restaurant. It was eight p.m. before the trio got back to the hotel. Ben felt ornery and placed himself by the door, making Diana stand closer to the glass. Diana pushed up tight against Ben. Scott stood at the glass, looking out at the view. Ben actually started laughing at Diana. "Kitten…you're going to get into trouble if you don't settle down." The elevator hit the eleventh floor, and Diana jumped out. They went to the rooms and unloaded their plunder. Diana set about to getting things organized and adjusted.

She was just finishing up when Ben knocked on the door casing. "Are you still up for a swim?" She turned around to see Ben was already in his swim trunks. She glanced quickly but then made herself stay on his face.

"I'll change down there. Give me just a second to grab the stuff."

"You do know that it means you have to face the dreaded elevator again?" Ben teased.

"Well…if you, sir, don't make me move closer to the glass, I'd be fine," Diana fired back.

Scott popped in the doorway. "So are we going or not?"

"Just give me a second," Diana yelled. She turned and grabbed up the swimsuit, robe, and a towel. "Let's go," she stated as she opened the door.

"Aren't you forgetting something, kitten?" Ben asked. Diana turned and looked at him with a question on her face. "Let's say your wrist and your knee?" Ben pointed out.

"Oh crap…I forgot. What are we going to do?" Diana flatly asked.

Ben had a roll of saran wrap behind his back. "Hey, Scott, bring in that medical tape please," he said over his shoulders.

"I almost forgot we had to do some preventative stuff," Scott stated as he came into the room. He also only had his swim trunks on. Diana now had to contend with two well-built males in swim trunks in her presence.

Lord, give me strength, she prayed. *At least they weren't beer-bellied slobs. I think I would puke if they came in with just trunks on and looked that way*, she thought.

Ben was watching her; he noticed that after the first glance, she either focused on their faces or the floor. Her innocence was now quite evident to him. It drew him more towards her. "Hold out your wrist," he directed.

She held her wrist out and watched as he wrapped the Saran wrap around several times. He cut it off then took the tape from Scott and taped the edges down, both top and bottom. "Your knee, my…lady," he stated.

"I can't yet. Take it with you and I'll let you wrap my knee before I jump in," Diana said.

"As you wish," Ben grinned. When they got to the pool, Diana went off to the women's shower room. She changed clothes, being careful to not loosen the tape holding the Saran wrap. She locked her clothes up and walked out to the pool. Scott was already in the water; Ben was waiting at the table with the needed materials. Diana cautiously walked over to Ben, who was teasing Scott and didn't notice her enter the area.

Scott was the first to see her as he was getting out of the pool for another dive. He fell back in, which made Diana chuckle. Ben heard her and turned to address her. "Very good choice, kitten," was all he could get out at the time. She was wearing a black swimsuit with purple insets at the waist. It had a skirt that dropped down two inches on her thighs but did not diminish showing her long lovely legs. The rope burns were now more of a dark pink instead of the dark red. *At least those are healing*, Ben noted. He saw that the back of Diana's swimsuit dropped down to the waist and though the neckline was higher, it had a keyhole opening that showed a little skin. The suit was conservative, giving just enough to encourage the imagination. He forced himself to breathe slowly and keep control. "Come here…let's get you set to get wet." He wrapped her knee several times and taped the edges down. "All set."

Diana stood up, strode to the edge of the pool, and dove in arching upward to surface. Once she broke the water plane, she said. "Thank you, kind sir."

Ben took what she did as a challenge. He stood up and, in two steps, came to the pool's edge then jumped in. Underwater, he looked for her; she had gone to the deep end and was swimming near the bottom. He headed straight for her. She went up and grabbed a breath and went under again. Ben was nearly to her by then. She smiled and took off, away from him; the chase was on. Scott noticed that they were staying near the edges so that he could continue to use the dive board. Diana went and caught a breath then felt somebody grab her ankle. Ben pulled her back down next to him. He saw the joy in her eyes; she was having a blast. He reached over and traced his fingers down her face. She reached up and grabbed his hand; he pulled her to him. She shook her head with an impish smile, used her feet to push off his chest, and swam away. She surfaced for air and glanced around; Ben caught up with her quickly. He wondered what it would be like swimming with her once she was totally healed and healthy. He swam up under her, grabbed her waist, and pulled her down again, keeping her next to him. Diana had felt Ben's hands brush against her hips and then wrap around her waist. She grabbed a quick breath before he pulled her down. She smiled as she turned to look at him; she nodded to have him come up her. Ben and Diana surfaced at the same time. Diana stated, "It looks like you two are getting some attention," nodding toward the balconies. Ben glanced around. Several of the balconies had women in various stages of dress watching them.

Ben gave a bird call to Scott, who had just surfaced from a dive. "It looks like a relaxing swim is up, bro."

Scott looked at him then, after Ben nodded upward, looked around. "Well now, that depends on how you look at it," Scott replied with a gleam in his eyes.

"It's more attention than I would like around," Diana stated as she noticed some men walking out and winking at her. Just moments later, several clusters of people came into the pool area. Diana looked at Ben. "Looks like our game is over. Sorry, Tiger." She swam to the steps and walked out. Ben was rather upset at the intruders. He watched her get out and walk across to the chair where she had thrown her robe. He also noticed a couple of guys walking toward her.

This isn't going to end well, he thought. He swam to the side and hopped out. There were some ladies sitting at the table where he left the tape and saran wrap. They got excited when he neared them. "Excuse me, ladies," he stated as he reached across the table and grabbed the stuff, turned, and walked away. He heard them voice their disappointment when he left. He rolled his eyes, and quickly caught up with Diana by the door. She had grabbed her stuff from the locker, but she didn't take time to change. He reached her just as she was getting irritated by the guys surrounding her. "Excuse me, gentlemen. Diana, are you ready to leave?" he smoothly asked her.

"Definitely!" she replied. "Mr. McCleary," Diana waited until he acknowledged her. "I've hit my limit tonight. I'll see you in the morning." Ben gave him a salute and guided Diana out between the intruders. Ben took her back to her room, locking the door behind them. "Does Scott have the key to get in?" Diana asked.

"Nope...I'll have to wait to let him in before I go to sleep," Ben replied. Diana was going to start working the tape off her wrist. "You might want to wait on that," Ben stated. She stopped, cocked her head to the side, and waited for him to finish. "You're going to need to wash all that chlorine off yourself," Ben continued.

"Oh yeah...I guess I'd better do that. I'll be back out in a little bit," she replied.

"Take your time. I'm going to go wash up as well," Ben stated. Diana headed to her bathroom, Ben headed for his; neither were happy with cutting their swim time fun short. It was more fun than Diana had had in a long time. It didn't take Ben long to wash up. He put his pajama pants on and headed over to the sitting area in Diana's room. Diana was just coming out of the bathroom; she had on a pair of lounge pants and a sleep shirt. Her hair brushed back off her face to air-dry.

"I got the tape off my knee, but I'm having trouble getting it off my wrists. It's pulling too much," she stated.

Ben walked up to her and lifted her arm; he put pressure on the wrist holding the skin still as he started working on the tape. Diana grimaced as he pulled on the tape. "Are you ready?" he asked.

"Just don't open that stupid thing up. I don't want an ER visit tonight," she stated through clenched teeth.

Ben held the stitch area tight then quickly pulled on the tape, stripping it off her arm. Diana sucked in air. "Sorry...kitten," Ben stated. He switched positions for a better hold on her lower tape. "Ready?" He saw Diana grit her teeth and nod. He quickly pulled the tape off her arm. Diana jerked a little; he checked to make sure it was dry. "Hang tight. I'll go get the gauze and rewrap it," he stated as he went to his room, coming back in within a minute.

"I forgot to rewrap my knee. Do you think I need to?" Diana asked.

"For the time being…yeah, you better. Let me take care of your wrist first then we'll catch your knee," Ben stated. Diana held her arm out for Ben to wrap. The wrist was still very red and sore from that morning. "Is it hurting you?" he worried.

"A little…but it's not unbearable," Diana stated.

"Take some Tylenol or aspirin when we get done here," he demanded.

"Yes…sir," she quipped. He finished her wrist and taped the end of the gauze down. He had Diana sit down on the bed and started to raise the pant leg to get to her knee. Diana finished pulling the pant leg up to uncover it. "How's this one feeling?" Ben asked.

"It only hurt when I accidentally brushed it up against the plane seat," she replied.

Ben reached into his pocket and pulled out the ointment. He put it on the lower cut of her knee then proceeded to wrap it with gauze. "It's looking pretty good. Those stitches will be out in a few more days," he replied. As he pulled her pant leg back down, the back of his hand slid down her leg.

Diana's heart rate sped up, and her calf contracted. *Knock it off, girl*, she scolded herself. "My turn," Diana spoke up. Ben's eyebrow arched up. "Your back needs to be treated, sir," she continued. When Ben just sat studying her, she replied, "Doctor's orders."

"Fine…your room or mine, Nurse Henderson?" Ben jabbed.

"You're here, we might as well take care of it here," she stated. "Give me the ointment and lie on the bed," she continued. Ben went and lay on his stomach on her bed. She climbed up and straddled him. She wasn't mean this time; she put the ointment on her own hands and warmed it up first. She started rubbing the ointment on the slices on his back. Ben's arms were up under his chin, his eyes closed as she worked on his back.

"You need to go into the massage business, kitten," Ben stated.

"All cats give massages, have you forgotten?" she teased. She saw Ben smile and could feel him relaxing; it made her feel good that she could help him. She continued until she knew that he dozed off. She carefully climbed off him and went to take some aspirin.

She climbed back on the bed near the pillows and watched him. *Is he the one, my love?* she asked the Lord. *I don't want to get in any farther 'til I know. Please give me an answer*, she continued. She nearly jumped out of her skin when he turned over and laid his head on her thigh. She couldn't help herself; she started slowly stroking her fingers through his hair. *I could easily handle waking up next to you, sir, for the rest of my life*, she thought; but then she frowned. *If it's not the Lords will, it will be a living hell. No…I'll wait for the Lord's confirmation.*

"You're fighting too hard, kitten. What are you afraid of?" Ben opened his eyes and looked at her face. Diana's hand froze for a second; then she went ahead and finished the stroke.

"You have soft hair…I like it," she said. "I knew you wouldn't stay asleep long," she continued, giving him a smile.

"Thank you, and you're avoiding the question," Ben snipped. Sitting up and making Diana look at him by taking her chin. "Diana…what are you afraid of?"

"Afraid…of getting out of the Lord's will, of hurting…," she said softly.

"Hurting what…Kitten? You're afraid of letting me in because of what, hurting me?" he guessed. Diana's heart was hurting; she didn't know the best way to answer him. He wouldn't understand, and she knew it. Ben wasn't going to let her go without answering. She could see he was getting mad.

"I…" Diana hesitated. Then there was a knock at the door. "That's probably Scott," she stated softly.

"God help me," Ben stated agitatedly. He got up and unlocked their door and opened it; Scott walked in, his robe on his arm, and still dripping wet.

"You missed out on the fun, bro. Some of the guys and gals were upset that you took Diana away. A catfight broke out," Scott stated.

"I think I'm going to be sick…eww," Diana quipped from her room.

"This is New York, we're not in the middle of cattle trails here," Scott continued. "You look a little upset bro. what's up?"

Diana quickly injected. "I had just finished treating his back."

"What did you do, put him to sleep again?" Scott jabbed.

"Yep," she replied. "I think I'd better get some sleep. What time do we need to leave?"

"Around ten….Diana. I'll make sure you're up in time to eat," Ben stated.

"Good night…Ben and Scott," she softly stated. She didn't want to face Ben yet. She didn't know how to answer him; she didn't want him to pull away from her. She pulled the covers back and climbed into bed. She angled the pillow so that she had something to hold. She felt the tears rolling down her cheeks as she slowly drifted off to sleep.

Ben was sure he heard her crying. He moved over and laid down on his bed. *I've pushed her too hard. Why is she so afraid? Something has made her put a major wall up. It's more than what she has said so far.* Ben thought about it till he fell asleep. Scott came out of the shower, saw that Ben was out. He went to check on Diana; she was out. Something happened between them tonight. He wasn't sure if it was good or bad yet; he'd have to figure it out tomorrow. He shut off the lights and went to bed himself.

29

New York

Ben woke up around six a.m. He went and started the coffeepot, got shaved and cleaned up, then he got dressed. By the time he was done with all that, Scott was awake.

"I take it she still isn't talking yet," Scott stated.

"Nope…she is scared of something. Something that has made her build a major wall up. I thought she was about to say it last night, but she clammed up again," Ben replied.

"Small steps, Ben…small steps," Scott encouraged. Ben got a cup of coffee and went into the sitting area in Diana's room. While he was out, Scott got busy cleaning himself up and was getting ready. Ben quietly turned the chair to face Diana. She was still sleeping soundly, holding on to the extra pillow. Her long brown hair was wild and partially covering her face; her breath was slow and deep.

Lord, what can I do? Why won't she tell me what she's so afraid of? Ben prayed. He knew, by her reactions when they were together, that she wanted him near. She trusted him enough to know he would protect her. He also knew she was fighting within herself. What part was fighting which, he wasn't totally sure. He sat there quietly sipping his coffee, thinking, rationalizing, trying to figure a way to solve his current problem. The sun didn't start coming up till seven thirty; he'd have to wake her up soon to get ready and get something to eat. He was worried that she would pull back from him after last night.

Scott had just finished getting ready. He went and got a cup of coffee for himself then came in and sat down. Ben turned the chair to its original place. "Are we taking her to the meeting or is one of us staying here?" Ben softly asked.

"I don't see you being allowed to miss the meeting, and I'm not sure she wants to be away from you," Scott quietly replied.

"I'm not sure she'll want me around this morning," Ben stated sadly.

"Somehow I highly doubt it. Did you guys fight or something?" Scott wondered.

"No, we didn't fight. I just pushed her too hard for an answer," Ben said, quietly fuming.

"Well, you know as well as I do if she was truly upset at you, you'd be in major pain now," Scott teased.

"Yeah…I hear ya. If she lets me hang around, I'm gonna have to teach her a few new ways to defend herself," Ben snickered.

"I'll go start another pot of coffee for us. You'd better wake her up," Scott stated and walked to the other room.

Ben nodded, sat his cup down on the table, and walked over to her bed. He carefully sat down on the edge of the bed. "Kitten…it's time to wake up, babe," he said as he brushed her hair away from her face. She didn't really respond. *She's really out this morning*, Ben thought. "Diana…come on, honey, it's time to get up." He brushed the back of his hand down her face. Diana's eyes slowly started to open. "There you are…you were out cold, babe."

Diana felt Ben's warm hand caress her face. *At least his not mad at me*, she thought. "What time is it?" she whispered.

"It's just before eight. It's time to get the day started," Ben informed her. She pushed herself up and turn to a sitting position.

She was trying to get her eyes to focus; she kept rubbing them. "Sorry, my eyes don't want to work this morning," she stated.

"It's probably from the chlorine in the pool last night," Ben stated flatly. "Or it's from you crying."

"You heard…I—" Diana started to say, but then the phone in the other room rang. She heard Scott answer it then Scott came to the door between the rooms.

"Bro, it's for you," he said curtly.

Ben got up and walked to the other room. Diana sat on the bed, straining to hear what was being said. She heard Ben say, "I'll call you back in a minute. I need to change phones." Ben came to the adjoining door. "I need to take this on the cell. I'll be back later." He nodded to Scott and smiled at Diana. "Better get ready, kitten," he said over his shoulder as he walked out the door.

Diana looked at Scott. "Where did the cell phone come from? He didn't have that on the ship, did he?"

"I'm not sure. We'll ask him when he gets back here," Scott replied. "I'll go over to the other room. Go ahead and get ready." He turned and went back to his room and closed the adjoining door.

Diana was working on controlling her anger. "There's a logical explanation. Just keep calm and give them a chance to explain it," she whispered. She grabbed the clothes she was going to wear for the day and went to the bathroom. She washed up, brushed her teeth, and wet down her hair to tame it down. She put on a pair of dark-blue bootleg jeans. The jeans had embellishments on the back pockets, something she usually didn't buy, but the guys insisted she take them. She had to admit they did fit her well; it was just that they brought attention to her backside, something she didn't need. That endowment came from her dad's family; she'd been teased about it ever since she was eight years old. *At least I don't have the hips that usually go with it*, she told herself.

She grabbed the white blouse with the lace insets in the sleeves. It had a square neckline and long sleeves that had pearl buttons on the cuffs. The blouse came down to just below her hips; it had a white beaded string belt that Diana tied loosely. To finish it out, Diana use a white headband to hold her hair out of her face but left the rest loose. She'd put on the boots that Ben insisted she get when it was time to leave. She came out of the bathroom and organized everything into her suitcase that they just bought. She zipped it up and moved it over to the door. She knocked on the adjoining door to let Scott know she was ready.

He opened the door and walked in. "I like it when you leave your hair down. It looks really nice," he stated.

"Thank you. Are we going down for breakfast or are we ordering in?" she asked.

"Do I sense that you are hungry?" Scott smiled.

"Not overly, just very thirsty, but I figured you guys were going to force it down me if I didn't eat," she stated.

"Yes, ma'am, *I* would." Scott smiled. He handed her the menu he was looking at and bowed.

"Oh, whatever." She waved her arm at Scott when he bowed. "Is there any chocolate milk?" she asked as she started looking over the menu. "Do you know what you're getting already?" she asked.

"Yep...I was just waiting to find out what you wanted," he replied.

"What about Ben? Do we need to get him something to eat?" Diana continued.

"Umm, yeah, I suppose we do need to get him something to eat. I'll get him some eggs and bacon—that should hold him till lunch," Scott figured. Once Diana decided what she wanted, Scott went and called it in to room service then came back and sat down in the chair. Diana was already sitting in the other one looking out the window. "So what happened up here last night? There was a definite cold chill between you two, it was very weird," Scott asked.

Diana looked down at her foot, took a deep breath. "He wants to know why I'm afraid to let him into my thinking, my life."

"Isn't he already in your life?" Scott questioned.

"Yes and no. He's in it more than he knows or realizes, but no, there's a large part he hasn't got to yet," she softly stated.

"So…what's the holdup?" Scott asked.

Diana just sat there looking at the floor. Scott saw that she wasn't really seeing the floor; she was deep in her own head. "Diana? It's a simple question."

"I don't have a simple answer," she quipped. She heard the door to the guys' room open then shut. Ben was back.

"In here, bro," Scott yelled. Ben appeared in the adjoining door.

He saw that Diana was all packed and ready. "I like that outfit. It looks really good on you." Ben smiled approvingly.

"Thank you. I've got a question for you," Diana stated carefully. Scott knew what was coming; she was going to hit the fan.

"Shoot, kitten," Ben stated.

"How long have you had that cell phone?" she asked, turning to look at him.

Ben figured she was awake enough to catch that statement. She was going to be furious. "I've had it since the pickup with the chopper."

"And you couldn't let me call my parents on it?" she stated with fire behind it.

"One, on the ship we didn't have the ability to call out. Two, on the plane, it was not allowed. Three, here at the hotel, I was told not to allow it till after the debriefing,' Ben calmly stated. He could see the rage building in her, and he truthfully couldn't blame her. "Diana, I can't use it to call my family either," Ben informed her.

"Mr. McCleary, you knew he had it since the chopper, didn't you?" Diana turn her fire eyes on him.

"Well, umm, yeah I—" Scott started, but didn't get it finished before one of the decorative pillows hit him in the head.

"You lied, you piece of *basuda*," Diana fumed.

"Whoa, I didn't lie. I said I wasn't sure," Scott quickly stated as he dodged another blow from the pillow. Diana flung another pillow at Ben, who quickly dodged it. He glanced over at Scott and nodded toward Diana. Scott winked and grabbed a pillow. He started using his pillow to block Diana's blows. Then he started trying to hit her with his pillow, which she blocked but wasn't able to get any more hits in. She was trying to keep track of where Ben was; he was a few feet from the bed. She threw her pillow at him and then grabbed one of the pillows off the bed.

Ben caught the pillow she flung at him and laid it on the bed. Diana was starting to smile; with the bigger pillow, she was able to get a couple more hits in on Scott. Scott was smiling at her charge. He saw that Ben was in place, so he started charging her. She backed up, blocking his blows; it took all her attention to block Scott. She didn't see that Ben was directly behind her; she back into him. Ben wrapped his arms around her, forcing her to cross her arms; the pillow pinned between her body and her arms. His embrace made it so she couldn't swing, and he made sure he stayed away from her wrists.

"Benjamen James," she yelled. Diana tried to wiggle free; Ben lifted her up so she couldn't use her feet to pry with.

He felt her spine pop all the way up. "Whoa…I just popped your back," he commented.

"Thank you…that felt good," Diana replied. "Now let me go!" She was able to push off one of the chairs with her foot. It pushed both her and Ben onto the bed. Scott came up and grabbed her feet; Ben kept hold of her upper body.

"Now, kitten, are you going to calm down or do we get drastic?" Ben jabbed.

Diana just sat there looking at them, wondering if she could get away. "You wouldn't dare," she challenged; calling their bluff. Except, they weren't bluffing. Ben smiled and nodded to Scott. Scott started tickling her feet; she screamed and tried to pull her legs up, but Scott held them tight. Diana started laughing but was still trying to wiggle free.

After a few minute of struggling, Diana yelled with tears running down her cheeks, "Stop…I need to go!" The guys stopped and let her up. She jumped up and ran to the bathroom; at the same time there was a knock on the door.

"It's probably room service," Scott piped up; he went and opened the door.

The delivery man was looking cautiously into the room. "Your breakfast, sir," he said.

"Thank you, here you go," Scott gave him a ten-dollar tip.

"I thought I heard some screaming in here," the delivery man stated.

"Yeah, I was playing with my sister. She's fine," Scott informed him. The delivery man, not seeing anything bad, nodded and backed out. Scott pulled the cart into the room. Diana was just coming out of the bathroom.

"Did you make it?" Ben asked her with a broad smile on his face.

"Barely, you dogs," she fired back.

"You started it," Scott beamed.

"That's because you lied," she quipped.

"No, I didn't. I just stretched the truth," Scott stated.

Diana started grabbing a pillow again. Ben put his hands on her arms. "Kitten…you can't take on both of us. It's better to stop while you're ahead."

Scott went to their room to go get some more coffee. When he left, Ben turned Diana around so that he could see her face. "I'm sorry. There are reasons why I couldn't let you use the cell phone. None of them were to keep you from your parents or because I didn't trust you," he calmly stated. Diana looked up at him, saw that there was no anger or change in his eyes. She put her hand on his chest. Ben took her hand and kissed the palm; then he slowly leaned down and kissed her. Diana felt the rush when Ben kissed her palm. She saw him leaning down for a kiss, and her heart started racing. When he kissed her lips, she didn't fight it; in fact, she kissed him back.

"Hey, Ben…do you want a cup of coffee?" Scott asked oblivious of what was going on in the other room.

Diana did a quiet chuckle and laid her head on Ben's chest. "Yeah, I'll take a cup a coffee," Ben called back. The two parted and headed for the tray. Scott joined them, carrying two cups of coffee.

"We got you some eggs and bacon, Ben. We didn't know what all you wanted," Scott told him as he handed him his coffee.

"Eggs and bacon will be fine. Thank you," Ben stated. "What did the kitten get for food?"

Diana piped up and stated, "I got cereal, milk, and chamomile tea."

"Someday, we'll have to get her to eat something other than cereal for breakfast," Ben quipped.

"Hey…I had sausage and biscuits yesterday,' Diana stated.

"That's true, bro, she did. However, we do need to get her upgraded to eggs someday," Scott agreed.

Diana just shook her head at the two. "So…what's on the schedule today?"

"Well…I originally was going to let you stay here with Scott while I went to the debriefing, but that's been taken off the list. I need you guys to join me," Ben stated.

"That changed because of the call. Who was it from?" Scott asked.

"Do you remember Allen Thomas?" Ben asked Scott.

"Are you talking about Allen 'the Arrow' Thomas?" Scott stated excitedly.

"Yep." Ben smiled.

"Yeah…how can I forget him? He trained us," Scott said disgustedly.

"He's the head of the FBI here in New York. He needs us to come in as soon as we are done with breakfast," Ben informed them.

Diana had the feeling this wasn't going to be good. It wasn't a danger feeling from God; it was more of her own mind, saying, *Uh-oh*. *Ben's not telling them the whole story. What is he hiding?* she thought.

"Milady? Where did you go?" Scott asked. He saw she was far from the room, deep in her own mind.

Ben knew where she was; she was reading between the lines. *It's going to be hard to keep her calm*, he thought. "Your tea is getting cold kitten…better get to drinking it.

Diana blinked, shook her head, and came back to the conversation. "So…what's going on, Ben?"

Ben winked at her. "There's that curiosity working again. We're really gonna have to put that to work somewhere."

"Good luck on that one bro., you can't even control your own curiosity much less try to channel another cat's," Scott quipped.

Diana smiled. "It's not a total impossibility, just an unlikely challenge."

Ben caught a glint of orneriness flash through her eyes. "Careful kitten, you're not the only one with a large amount of curiosity," he smoothly stated. Diana looked down into her tea; she couldn't keep her mind from going to the kiss Ben gave her just minutes ago. A smile came across her mouth.

"I think a cat's got her tongue," Scott stated. Diana's smile grew exponentially, and her face flushed.

There was no doubt where her mind went. Ben chuckled. *Well, I guess her statement at the cabin was true. She would never make it in a convent*, he thought.

Scott noticed her blush as well. *Obviously, Ben and Diana weren't at odds this morning*, he said to himself.

They finished their breakfast. The guys left to pack their stuff; Diana sat on the bed to put her boots on. As she sat there, her thoughts went to the phone call and why she had to go to the debriefing.

What has happened now? she wondered.

Ben stood at the adjoining door and watched her. Scott came and stood beside him. "She knows something is going on, bro. It's got her on edge."

"Yeah, I know. She's very perceptive. I'm worried about how she'll react once we get to HQ. You know the procedures to get into that place. She's liable to flip out," Ben worried.

"Did you explain that to Allen?" Scott asked.

"Yep, he said that he would see what he could do—whatever that means," Ben quipped.

"We'll find out when we get there. She's smart and strong, she'll get through it," Scott stated. He slapped Ben on the back and went to load the suitcases onto the cart.

Ben walked in and sat down on the bed next to Diana. He put his arm around her back and pulled her to him. "I feel like I'm back climbing that mountain again. Looking at the sheer rock face, not seeing any way through it," Diana stated.

"But there are ways through it, you just don't see them. Scott and I will be there to guide you," Ben assured.

"I bet you're wishing you were assigned to somebody else by now, aren't you?" Diana softly said.

Ben brought her chin up to look at him. "I'm not sorry at all. You do keep things interesting to say the least." Ben grinned.

Diana smiled back at him. "I keep you two on your toes, huh?" Ben nodded, but then he saw her get sober again. "What's going on with the FBI? Why do I need to be there?" she asked.

"Did I tell you I really like your outfit? Those boots just complete the whole look," Ben said, knowing full well Diana would know the topic change.

Diana just looked at him. "You're not going to give me a heads-up, are you?"

"You'll just have to trust me, kitten, it'll be okay," Ben again assured her then cupped her face with his hand. "Hey…we didn't check that wrist of yours, did we? Did you already take care of your knee?" he asked.

"Yeah, I caught my knee earlier. I can't do the wrist, and I forgot to ask Scott to help me," Diana informed him.

"I already said I'm not a nursemaid," Scott stated as he walked in the room. "Better let Ben take care of it. He's the one used to bandaging owies."

"Someday, Scott, you're going to meet up with a pair of eyes that will make you eat all those words," Ben stated.

"Never gonna happen bro," Scott countered. In truth, Diana was the closest one to making him want to. He wished there was another one where she came from. Diana saw a trace of sadness in Scott's eyes. As soon as he saw her looking at him, it was gone.

I know where you are, Scott…I do understand, she said to herself. Ben undid the cuff and rolled the sleeve up so he could get at Diana's wrist. He saw a little blood in part of the gauze, which made it a little hard to pull off her wrists. Diana winced.

"Sorry, babe…it stuck a little," he replied. The wrist was not healing as fast as he thought it should be. She more than likely needed some antibiotics. He rewrapped the wrist with new gauze, taped the end down, pulled her sleeve down, and buttoned it. "All set…Milady," he stated. They grabbed their stuff and headed down to check out.

In the lobby waiting for Ben to check out, Scott and Diana went over to the counter where there were complimentary coffee and drinks out. Diana didn't see any chocolate milk or chamomile tea, but she did see there was hot chocolate, so she was preparing herself a cup.

Scott had just grabbed a cup of coffee; he turned around and saw a short blonde girl blocking his way. She looked to be in her early twenties and dressed like a streetwalker. "Hey…I remember you. You're the one doing the flips off the diving board last night," she said.

"Yep…that was me," Scott stated as he tried to politely get around her. The girl continued to block his way. She looked over at Diana. "You left too early, girl. Some of us were looking forward to playing that game of yours," she stated.

"Diana, this is—I'm sorry I forgot your name," Scott stated. Diana knew full well he didn't forget; he really didn't care to know it. He was just being polite.

"I'm Camie…Camie Whithers, remember?" she filled in.

"Diana, this is Camie. Camie, this is my sister Diana," Scott introduced. He smiled at Diana as he said *sister*.

"I don't see the family resemblance between you two," Camie questioned.

"We have the same father," Diana replied. It wasn't a lie, nor was Scott's statement. They both had the same Heavenly Father. At least that was the way Diana was going to play it.

"Oh…well, that explains it. No wonder you reacted the way you did with Jeff," Camie replied. "You know…for about thirty minutes there, we thought he had passed out from drinking too much. It wasn't till he came around that he told us you hit him."

Diana looked at Scott, saw that he froze for a split second when Camie made that comment, and then continued to drink his coffee. "My brother hit somebody?" Diana questioned Camie.

"Well, now knowing that you are his sister, Jeff was way out of line. He made the comment that he—" Camie was cut off by Scott's statement.

"Well, it looks like it's time for us to go now. Here comes Ben," Scott injected. Diana looked up and saw Ben coming their way. Camie turned to see who they were talking about. "Oh, he was the one that escorted you out of the pool. Is he family too?"

"No…he's Scott's best friend," Diana stated. Ben came up and stood beside Diana; it was extremely obvious that he was getting scanned all the way over there. "Ben this is Camie, Camie this is my brother's best friend, Ben," Diana introduce.

"Ma'am," Ben nodded.

"You know you should have stayed longer last night. Some of us wanted to join in with your game," Camie stated.

"Yeah well…too many players in the pool causes a lot of problems logistically. Besides, Diana was tired, so I agreed to escort her to her room," Ben stated coolly.

"She didn't look tired while we were watching her from above. I think the two of us could have had a blast last night—although three could have been interesting too," Camie said, scanning Ben up and down.

Scott saw Diana's complexion paled with the comment that Camie just stated; it was making Diana's stomach turn. "Well…we really need to be going, Camie. Nice meeting you," Scott said and started to head for the door. He reached over and took Diana's arm. "Come on, sis, we don't want to miss our meeting." Diana was more than willing to follow Scott; she thought she was going to lose breakfast standing there.

Ben came up behind her and put his hand on her back. "We're not in Kansas anymore, Toto," he jested.

"Oh, shut up…I'm still working on keeping breakfast down," Diana quipped.

The taxi driver loaded their suitcases in the trunk as they climbed into the vehicle. Diana took the middle since she had the shortest legs of the trio. Ben and Scott each took a side and folded in. Ben angled Diana closer to him so she could have a little more leg room. "Well, that was an adventure," Scott sneered.

"Yeah…I feel like I need to go take a shower again," Diana snipped.

"So you hit somebody last night?"

Ben looked over at Scott. "That would explain the early arrival and you dripping wet last night."

Scott just looked straight ahead. "I thought the conversation needed to change directions. Jeff just wasn't taking the hint. So…as Diana has stated, some guys need to have it painfully obvious."

"What in the world was he saying?" Ben asked. It was not common for Scott to get riled by words like that. It must have been something extremely bad.

"You don't want to know bro," Scott replied, glancing at Ben then looking down at Diana. Ben acknowledged it. He knew Scott was growing very protective of Diana. She is now his sister. In a way, he was glad that Scott heard it and not him; the kid would have probably had amnesia after he was done with him.

Diana caught the looks between Scott and Ben. She was the reason Scott hit Jeff. He must have been very crude and brash with his words or actions to get Scott to retaliate. She was immensely glad she left as soon as the people showed up. She would be more than glad to stay in her world. She reached over and put her hand on Scott's arm. "Thank you."

"Perceptive little minx. I'll have to be more careful next time," Scott jeered but put his hand over hers and lightly squeezed it.

Ben, who had his arm around her waist, pulled her close and kissed her head. "Yeah, I'm working on figuring out how to keep this cat's ability to draw trouble to herself in check. I haven't come up with anything yet," Ben jabbed.

"Hey...I'm not the one who started all this. I was just minding my own business, doing my job. I can't help it if people are insane," Diana countered.

"Well, one of us could take that precious gift of hers away. That would stop some of it," Scott beamed.

Diana glared at him. "There is only one who will get that gift, and only after certain requirements are made and done."

"Hmm, you know Scott, you may have an idea there: no treasure... no quest," Ben surmised.

Diana jabbed Ben in the side; he recoiled. "Even you, Tiger, are not getting it. Only my husband can have that gift. I promise you that."

What if I was your husband, Ben thought. Then he shook his head as if to clear it out. "There she goes making promises again. Tsk...tsk... tsk," Ben jeered.

Diana knew the guys were teasing her. Truth be told, the thought crossed her mind; all this "stuff" wouldn't be happening to her if she wasn't a virgin. It was the only thing of hers and only hers that she could give to her would-be husband. She had to acknowledge, however, if this 'stuff' hadn't happened, she would have never met Ben or Scott.

She couldn't see her life without these two guys in it now. One of the holdups she had with letting Ben truly know her was that when this was all over, he would say good-bye, and she would never see either of them again. The thought was making her heart hurt.

Ben noticed Diana got quiet; she was fighting in herself again. *I really wish she would talk to me, let me into that world of hers. I could help her with what she was fighting with*, Ben thought. "You're too quiet, kitten. You know we were just teasing you," he stated.

"Hmm…oh yeah, I know. I was just thinking about what if—oh, never mind, I'm just being an idiot," Diana quipped.

"Do they have a mind reader in here Ben? There are days I'd like to strangle those thought out of her head so I would know where she's gone to. It's really frustrating," Scott fumed.

"I hear ya, bro. I'll have to look into getting a mind reader," Ben agreed.

"There are some places you two do not want to go in my mind. You'd lock me in a padded cell, throw away the key, and never ever look back," Diana stated.

The spirit knocked on Ben's heart with her statement. *Read between the lines. Okay, there's one wall. She thinks we will disappear once we get this assignment done and walk out of her life*, Ben deduced. "Diana…Scott and I would never just dump you somewhere and disappear. We aren't going to walk away and leave you," Ben calmly stated.

Scott had help with her meaning as well; it was almost like someone was whispering in his ear what she was actually saying. "You're my sister…remember? The one thing I will always fight for is my family. I will always be there when you call," he assured.

Diana looked at them, closed her eyes, and let go of a big sigh. "Thank you," was all she said, but it was enough. The guys could almost see a huge weight being lifted off of her shoulders.

I can help remove more of those weights if you would talk to me, Ben thought. Then he had Scott's statement from earlier run though his mind: *Small steps, brother, small steps.*

30

New York

The taxi pulled to a stop in front of a three-story building. It looked a little out of place compared to the skyscrapers in the background, but it had ornate columns and a marble stairs leading to the front door. Ben and Scott opened their doors at the same time. Diana took Ben's hand to get out of the taxi. Scott followed the taxi driver to the back to unload the suitcases. Ben and Diana each grabbed theirs, and the trio started walking up the stairs.

Once they were up to the front door, a couple of guards met them and stopped them from going in. Diana saw that Ben and Scott gave them their suitcases. So when the guard signaled for hers, she let him have it. Ben reached down and put his hand in the middle of Diana's back and guided her through the doors. Inside the doors was a metal detector. Ben took his pocket knife, cell phone, and a few coins out of his pocket then walked through. Scott and Diana, who didn't have any form of metal on them, walked through quickly. Then on the other side of the detector, Ben led the group to the opposite side of the wall. There was a single door to the left and a single door to the right. One of the guards came up to them. "Gentlemen, you need to go to the right. Ma'am, you need to go to the left."

"I'll take care of this, Harry," a man stated as he walked toward the trio. "Yes, sir," the guard nodded and went back to his post.

"Ben…Scott, good to see you, boys. Are you glad to be back in the States?" the man asked.

"Yes, sir," Scott enthusiastically replied.

"You would not believe how glad we are to be back in the States again," Ben added. "Sir, this is Ms. Diana Henderson."

"Good morning, ma'am. My name is Allen Thomas, I'm the director here," Allen stated.

"I'm afraid I'm going to have to ask your escorts to part from you for a few minutes," Allen injected. Diana started analyzing the situation and statements. Mr. Thomas was a slender six-foot man. She guessed he was somewhere around sixty years old. He had white hair and a white mustache. She watched his eyes; they were intense, and she honestly believed they could be hard and cold. But at this time, they were a soft and kind—the color of deep chocolate brown.

She heard Ben ask, "Sir, may I have a word with you a moment?"

"Of course Ben," Allen replied. Ben took Allen over to the corner to talk about Diana going through. Allen was explaining that he couldn't bend that rule. She would have to go through the procedures. Ben was still pleading her case when Allen looked over and saw Diana watching them.

"Ben…did you know that Ms. Henderson can lip-read?" he asked.

"No…why?" Ben replied.

"Because she is reading this conversation. She knows that going through this door is going to lead to being tested," Allen injected. Ben turned to see Diana on the verge of running, and in truth, he couldn't blame her. Ben, using a hand sign, signaled Scott to distract Diana.

"Hey, Diana, did you know that Agent Thomas trained us?" Scott asked.

Diana turned to look at Scott, wondering where that came from. "Yeah, I think I did hear you mention that," she answered as she turned to focus on the conversation across the room. She was furious that Ben had turned so that she could not see his mouth. *You'll pay for that, Tiger*, she thought.

She turned to look at Scott, who had been the one to distract her; he was standing there, cleaning his fingernail. "Just because you're my brother, don't think I won't get a payback," she fired.

"What? What did I do?" he replied. "I'm just standing here waiting for Ben."

"Huh-huh and just how did he signal for you to distract me? Don't deny it, I can see it in your eyes," Diana snipped.

"I'm not sure what you're talking about. However, I would recommend that you don't start anything here. We'd be thrown out, arrested, or worse," Scott beamed.

Over in the corner where Ben and Allen were talking, Ben kept trying to get Diana out of the next tests. "Ben, I promise you that I will be near her every step of the way, but I cannot let you go with her. Is she really that volatile that I won't be able to handle her?" Allen asked.

"No, it's not that, sir, it's just—" Ben was cut short by Allen.

"Well, if she's volatile, you'd better get over there and help Scott out. She's looks madder than a wet hen," Allen stated with a smile on his mouth. "It's not often that I've seen Scott unable to charm his way out of female's wrath."

"She's not the normal, run-of-the-mill female that Scott's use to. She actually uses that brain of hers." Ben smiled. "Promise me this: if she starts getting hard to handle, call me before you tranquilize her."

"You have my word, Ben," Allen replied. "Let's get over there and help poor Scott out."

Ben and Allen walked back over to Diana and Scott. Scott was still trying to calm her down. "Do you have your claws out, Kitten?" Ben jested. He put his hands on her shoulders, half expecting her to pull away from him.

Instead she leaned back into him. "You're not out in the clear, Tiger. You'll get yours too," she softly stated.

Ben leaned down and whispered in her ear, "Promises…promises." Diana jabbed him in the side with her elbow, but then she looked up at Ben. He smiled, but then he got very sober. "Diana…you're gonna have to go with Agent Thomas. I promise I will meet up with you as soon as you're done." He felt her tense up. "You have to trust me…kitten." She studied him for a minute then nodded.

"Ms. Henderson, if I may," Allen said, and he offered her his arm. Diana gave him a small smile and took his arm and walked with him to the door on the left. She looked over her shoulder to see the faces of Ben and Scott. They were worried, and it made her nervous.

"Ben and Scott are close to you, aren't they?" Allen asked just to get her talking.

"Yes, they are, they've gone through so much for me. I owe them a lot," Diana stated, looking forward.

"I don't believe they see it that way, but I'm not in the loop. Now, Ms. Henderson, before we go through this door, I need to explain. The people are here to make sure you are not bringing anything in that would blow the place up, infect the staff, or cause problems in anyway. Do you understand me?" Allen stated calmly and softly.

Diana froze. She understood more than he knew. She was in for another "inspection," and she wasn't happy about it. Out of the corner of her eye, she saw movement. She turned to see what the movement was; it was from a couple of guards. She debated on what she should do; she looked up at Mr. Thomas's eyes; they were searching her just as much as she was searching him. Diana saw no danger or malice in his eyes. She caught more movement, and it alerted her to watching the guards. She had the strong urge to run.

Over on the other side of the room, Ben and Scott waited to see if Diana was going to go in. "Bro, if any of the guards start moving toward her and she sees them…we're going to have a problem on our hands," Scott stated.

"I know…I'm hoping Allen hasn't lost his touch. She was already on edge. If he would have just let me go with her, I could have gotten her through it," Ben argued.

They saw Allen talking to her; then they saw Diana freeze. Ben and Scott both straightened, ready to intervene at any second if Diana looked like she was in trouble. Ben saw a couple of guard start moving toward her. *Lord, help us,* he prayed.

Over with Allen and Diana, Allen held up his hand to signal the guards to back away. He calmly but sternly stated, "Ms. Henderson, I will do my best to make this as easy as possible for you, but you do have to go through it. I'll be near you the whole time." Diana heaved a sigh and nodded.

Ben and Scott saw Allen holding the guards off, saw him talking with Diana. His face was stern, but they saw that he was controlled with his movements. Then much to their relief, they saw Diana nod and follow Allen in. With Diana in, the guys turned and went into the door on the right.

Allen held to his word; he was within earshot of her the whole time. The first stop Diana had to do was change out of her clothes for a strip search. They gave her a hospital robe to change into. From there she went to the lab for them to test her blood. Diana made sure they used the spot that her doctor's always used for her checkups. Then she proceeded to watch anything and everything but what they were going to do to that arm.

Allen saw that she was avoiding looking at the needle. "So how long have you known Ben and Scott?" he asked to distract her.

"I've known Ben and Scott for, umm"—Diana giggled—"I don't even know what day it is, much less the date."

Allen shook his head. "You have been through a lot, haven't you? Well, today is Friday, and it is the tenth day of October. I assume you know the year."

"Yes, I know the year, thank you. I've known Ben and Scott for a little more than two months now," she replied. The lab tech finished drawing her blood; she stood and went to the next station.

"This is a cavity search, Ms. Henderson. I'll be standing over there to give you privacy," Allen stated.

Diana grimaced. "If I have to go through this junk again, would you *please* have a female do it?"

"That I can arrange. Let me go talk to the doctors," Allen added. He stood over by the door while they finished with Ms. Henderson. He had to laugh when she made the comment to the female doctor about giving her a picture so she wouldn't have to do any of this for at least three years. When they were done; the nurse led her back to the changing room for her to get dressed. Once she was dressed, she met up with Allen by the door.

"Not as bad as you thought it would be now…was it?" Allen stated.

"That is a matter of opinion, sir," Diana quipped. Allen led Ms. Henderson out to the wide-open vestibule. There were several offices all along the vestibule on all three floors. A high glass-domed ceiling allowed sunlight to flood the area, and with the polished terrazzo floor, it seemed like you were walking outside. Even though Diana was busy looking at the architecture, she felt Ben nearby. He and Scott were standing just ten feet to the side of the door that Allen and Diana walked out of.

Ben walked up behind her. "I didn't hear any screaming, and Allen is still capable of walking, so I assume you were well behaved."

Diana turned around. "It cost you two tallies on that IOU app of yours. And the pie I promised Mr. McCleary has just been thrown out the window," she fumed.

Scott spoke up. "Hey now, that's a little steep, don't you think?"

Allen just stood back and listened to the conversation. Ben looked up and saw Allen almost laughing at them. "I told you she was an unusual female, thank you for taking her through that," Ben stated.

"She is a feisty one, I'll say that," Allen admitted. Diana closed her mouth and blushed; she looked down to try to conceal it. Allen continued, "Now that we have survived. I need you to come with me. There's a reason why I needed you here, Ms. Henderson." As the director led the trio to the far side of the vestibule, a person came walking fast toward Allen.

"Sir, I need Agent Tigere to come with me. There is a situation in one of the rooms," the clerk stated.

Allen looked at Ben. "You had better take Scott along with you as well, Ben."

Diana looked at Mr. Thomas then over to Ben and Scott. She didn't like being left alone in this place, much less with Mr. Thomas. She wasn't feeling danger; she just didn't know the man. Therefore she didn't trust him.

Ben saw that she didn't want him to leave her. "It'll be okay, kitten. Allen will take care of you. Just keep your claws in. He's liable to clip them off if you show them."

Diana looked at Mr. Thomas then back to Ben. She doubted that Mr. Thomas was that dangerous. However, out of respect for those older than her, she stated, "I'll do my best to behave myself," with a smile on her mouth. Ben gave her a wink, and Scott shook his finger at her; then they turned and followed the clerk.

Diana watched them walk out of sight. "They'll be back in a little bit, Ms. Henderson, don't worry. Shall we?" Allen said as he motioned for Diana to come with him.

"You might as well call me Diana. It looks like you'll be stuck with me. Lord help you," Diana sneered.

"I don't mind it one bit, Diana. It beats looking at mug shots and musty files. You can call me Allen," he smiled. He noticed Diana relaxed a little and gave him a smile back. "We'll go into this room here, if you would." He opened the door.

Diana saw that the room was darkened. There was a large window that was letting in light from the room next to it and some type of switchboard on the wall next to the window. She thought she saw another door in the back corner of the room, but the room was too dark for her to see it at this time. She'd have to wait until her eyes adjusted to the dim light. She slowly walked into the room. "Allen, why am I here?" she cautiously asked.

"In just a moment, I'm going to let you see and hear a conversation between one of our agents and a man that came in yesterday from Syria'" Allen stated. "I want you to look and listen then tell me if you recognize him."

Diana looked at him, wondering why she needed to identify him. Ben saw the same people she did. She heard someone entering into the adjoining room. She tensed up, worried about who this person maybe. She just about jumped through the roof. "That's Taggee!" she excitedly stated.

"Taggee?" Allen asked.

"He was one of the guards in the harem they kept me in. He saved my life more than once," Diana stated. She noticed that he was handcuffed and chained to his ankles; she frowned at that. "What has he done to be locked up like that?"

"He's a big guy, and they were afraid that he would cause problems. It's really just a precaution," Allen replied over his shoulder. They watched the conversation for a few moments. Diana couldn't understand what they were saying, which frustrated her immensely, but it seemed to her that the agent kept repeating the same questions.

"Can you tell me what they are saying?" Diana asked.

"The man, Taggee, is asking for asylum here in the States. He says he is a religious refugee," Allen, knowing Farsi and several other languages, interpreted.

"He is, he's a Christian," Diana informed him.

She noticed Taggee's responses seemed to have changed. "What is Taggee saying now?" Allen didn't give her an answer. Diana felt a warm presence that she recognized. She smiled and looked out of the corner of her eye but saw nothing. She then saw Allen flip a switch, which caused a red light to turn on in the room where Taggee and the agent were at. The agent said something, stood up, and walked out the door, pulling it closed behind him.

Less than a minute later, the agent was walking into the room where Diana and Allen were. "He just keeps saying that this woman named Ariana is in danger, he needs to find her," the agent stated. Allen just stood studying Taggee.

Diana spoke up. "He's looking for me. I'm Ariana." The agent just looked at her with disgust then turned back to Allen and started whispering. "Allen, I'm Ariana. That's what they called me in the compound. He doesn't know my real name," Diana insisted. Allen held up his finger for Diana to wait a minute. Diana was getting mad. "Ben, tell them! They won't listen to me."

Allen and the agent turned to her. The agent stated with disdain, "Agent Tigere isn't in here, ma'am. Now if you don't mind, just sit there and be quiet for a minute."

"Allen, she's telling the truth. Taggee is trying to protect Diana," Ben stated coldly. Allen and the agent turned swiftly toward the sound of Ben's voice. They saw him leaning off to the side of the door in the back wall of the room.

Ben's back was against the wall, his arms crossed across his chest, one leg in front of him, the other was bent with his foot up against the wall. Ben's voice was calm but cold. Allen knew Ben like he was his own son; he was irritated. Unfortunately…the agent that was doing the interview didn't know how much trouble he was in.

"That's an interesting trick, ma'am, did you see him behind you?" the agent insinuated.

"No…I did not see him there, nor did you. I don't have to see him to know he's near. Don't ask me to explain, you wouldn't believe me anyway," Diana tried to calmly say, but she was fuming inside.

"By the way, Taggee is asking to see Ariana, not just find Ariana," Ben corrected the agent.

Allen was interested in how Diana knew Ben was there. He himself didn't hear or see him. He may be old, but not that old. "What do you suggest, Ben?" he inquired.

"Let her go in. Have our agent here interpret for them," Ben suggested.

"That man would rip her to shreds in just minutes," the agent stated.

"Taggee wouldn't hurt me. Even when he had the chance to, he protected me," Diana insisted. "Which reminds me, can we take those shackles off him?"

"Sir…this woman is insane!" the agent stated. Ben started walking toward the agent. Diana knew that look; she reached out and put her hand on his arm as he went to pass her. Ben acknowledged her by running his fingers down the side of her face, but kept walking past. The agent started to back up toward the door as Ben neared. Allen stepped forward between Ben and the agent.

"Ben, he's a little green, but he's a good agent. He just doesn't know when to keep his mouth shut," Allen stated over his shoulder…aiming toward the agent standing behind him.

"I can give him a few pointers to help him learn," Ben coldly stated.

"Now, Ben, we wouldn't want Ms. Henderson over there to see me whip you into shape. That would be a little embarrassing, I should think," Allen teased.

"I don't think it would be embarrassing for me at all, however, I will put off my lessons for our new agent until we get to a gym," Ben calmly stated.

Allen debated in himself as to whether he should let Diana go into the room. "Are you sure she would be safe if she went into the room?" Allen asked Ben.

"Almost as safe as if she was with me," Ben stated.

"Ben, why can't you come in and interpret for me. I'm not totally sure he is capable of doing it," Diana argued, pointing to the agent.

"No, kitten. Taggee only knows me as a linguistic student, not an agent. I can't risk being seen as a DHS agent or any other agent right now. I'll be listening in. If he says it wrong, I'll box his ears for him," Ben informed the room.

"Kitten?" the agent smirked.

"Agent Johnson…if you want to keep your nose in its current placement, I suggest you shut your mouth and be quiet," Allen warned. The agent shut his mouth and stood quietly.

"Diana…I'm letting you go in. If at any time you feel threatened or uncomfortable, I want you out of there. Do you understand me?" Allen sternly stated.

"I understand. I know Taggee won't hurt me; I'd be in more danger of hurting this…person. Of course if Mr. Johnson isn't careful, it would be interesting to see if it would be Ben or Taggee boxing his ears," Diana carefully stated.

"Shall we, ma'am?" Agent Johnson asked, motioning to Diana to follow.

"Ben…can you see if you can talk Allen into letting him out of those cuffs?" Diana pleaded as she walked toward the door.

"I'll see what I can do, go on now," Ben encouraged.

As Agent Johnson shut the door, Allen commented, "Now then, how in the world did she know you were there? I didn't even know?"

"She has, shall we say, a sixth sense. She knew I was there before Agent Johnson even walked in," Ben informed him.

"Interesting, and you being so protective of her is because?" Allen pried.

"Let's just say we have a connection. By the way, Scott's just as protective of her, and you know his temper," Ben informed Allen.

"What…are you two going halves on this girl or what?" Allen irritably asked.

"Not at all. To Scott, she's a sister," Ben stated.

"And to you?" Allen insinuated. Ben just shrugged his shoulders. "That remains to be seen."

Diana and Agent Johnson walked into the room. Taggee smiled when he saw Diana. Taggee started talking as Diana sat down. "He says you look much better than the last time he saw you. Are you feeling better?" Agent Johnson interpreted.

"Thank you, yes, I am much better than I was. Mr. James has made it his personal goal to force me to eat." Diana smiled.

As Diana and Agent Johnson continued talking, Allen was probing Ben's mind. "So you are Mr. James to this group. Why?"

"You do know I was the one of them that went in and got her out, didn't you?" Ben questioned.

"I knew two special ops people went in. I knew you and Scott were the ones that brought her over from Israel. I didn't realize you two were the exclusive agents," Allen stated, surprised. Ben nodded to confirm his statement.

"They thought that with my ability to speak the language and Scott's survival abilities, we would be the best choice. Plus Diana isn't known for trusting new people."

"I'm surprised you got her out. She's not trained at all, right?" Allen assumed.

"There's a lot more to her than it seems. A big plus was the Lord was majorly with us," Ben concluded.

Scott came into the room. "What's going on in here? Hey, isn't that the guy who helped you and Diana get out of the compound?" Ben nodded.

"And he's chained up like that...why?" Scott continued.

"Because Agent I-Need-a-Nose-Job is afraid of him," Ben sneered.

Back in the room with Diana and Agent Johnson, Diana asked, "Did Aisha and Mahala come here with you?"

Agent Johnson didn't want to ask him. "Let's stick to what we need to know, ma'am," he stated.

Diana looked him dead in the eye. "Would you please interpret what I asked; I know what I need to know. I don't give a hoot what you think you need to know, Agent Johnson. I don't think you want me to start readjusting bodily parts."

Ben had to hold back a laugh, Scott just whistled, Allen blinked his eyes. "Is she always a spitfire?"

"Only when decorum is not being observed," Scott stated.

"Taggee calls her *bermadeh*...a tigress. She chooses whom she allows to control her." Ben smiled.

"Okay...so we have a tiger and now a tigress," Allen conjectured. Ben's eyebrow arched up; Scott just leaned against the wall and beamed a big smile.

Back with Diana and Agent Johnson, Taggee stated, "Tigress, calm yourself."

"Ms. Henderson, he is saying, 'Tigress, calm down,'" Agent Johnson interpreted.

Diana looked over at Taggee and nodded. She looked back to Agent Johnson. "Please ask him about Aisha and Mahala." Agent Johnson begrudgingly translated what Diana asked. Taggee said what he knew.

"He says that they came with him to the States. They are somewhere in the building," Agent Johnson interpreted.

She looked at Agent Johnson. "You already knew the answer to my question, didn't you?" He didn't reply. Diana wanted to readjust his nose herself. It was Ben that told Allen to signal for her to come out. He saw Diana's eyes go steel-gray. She had hit her limit with Agent Johnson. Allen flipped the switch, and the red light came on. Diana saw the light, drew in a large breath, and slowly let it out. She figured Ben put a stop to the interview; he would think she was getting too upset. Agent Johnson pulled Diana's chair out, he offered her his hand; Diana looked at him, shook her head slightly, and stood up on her own.

Before she let him show her out the door, Diana turned looked at Taggee and said, "I'll see what I can do about getting you out of here." She turned to Agent Johnson and quietly said, "Tell him exactly, word for word, what I said. Remember, I know someone who is listening."

Agent Johnson grimaced and decided that it was best to use her exact words. Taggee smiled at her and nodded. Agent Johnson led her back to the observation room. He opened the door, glad to be rid of her.

Diana walked up to Allen. "Please take those handcuffs off him. He seriously won't hurt anybody if they aren't trying to hurt Aisha, Mahala, or myself. Please, sir." Allen looked down at her. He saw that she was honestly concerned for Taggee. There was something in her eyes that pulled at him as if she was his own daughter.

"Are you sure?" Allen questioned.

"I promise. He means no harm," Diana restated. Allen signaled to Agent Johnson to release Taggee from the handcuffs.

"If he goes berserk, the responsibility will be on your head, Ms. Henderson," Agent Johnson stated.

"I assure you, Mr. Johnson, if you don't threaten the women he has been put in charge of to protect, he will give you no trouble," Diana fumed. Ben came up and put his hands on her shoulders, his thumbs kneading in their area on her back. She worked to tone herself down.

Agent Johnson walked out; she watched from the window to see him enter into the adjoining room. He walked up and lifted Taggee's handcuffs and unlocked them. Then he bent down, maintaining eye contact, and unlocked his ankle cuffs; then he walked out of the room. Taggee rubbed his wrists; he looked over toward the mirror, smiled, and nodded.

Diana turned to Allen. "Thank you, sir. Can you tell me how Aisha and Mahala are?"

It was Ben who answered. "They are fine. They were more worried about Taggee being taken away in shackles. Mahala was getting medical attention when I saw her, but it was minor."

"May I go see them? You don't need to send an interpreter unless you want to. Mahala speaks English," Diana requested.

"Scott...would you mind?" Allen asked. "Scott can interpret for you if Mahala gets stuck", he continued as he looked at Diana.

"Nawt at awl sir," Scott replied in his Scottish brogue. He offered Diana his arm and walked out the back door with her.

"She's an interesting character, very truthful and innocent," Allen remarked. "It seems that you can read her as easily as she senses you, coincidence?"

Ben just stood there looking after her. "How is it that Mr. Taggee knew she was here in this room?" Allen asked.

"Some of it has to do with the connection with our Lord," Ben answered. "To Taggee, she is family. What about you, sir? I think that's the first time I've seen you change your mind with a woman's plea like that. Why did you?" Ben asked.

"She was so sure, so positive that Taggee wouldn't hurt anybody. For a moment, I saw...I saw Elsa in her eyes," Allen stated carefully.

Ben just smiled and acknowledged. "She has that effect on people."

"You love her, don't you?" Allen stated, studying Ben. Ben just stood there leaning up against the wall, studying his shoe. In truth...he didn't have to say anything; Allen knew.

Allen chuckled, which brought Ben's eyes up to look at him. "It would be interesting to train her to work as an agent. Pair her up with you, could you imagine what kind of team that would make? If she's so capable to getting information out of people by looking at them and your prowess at hunting down and detaining, that could be very interesting match."

Ben chuckled with that. "If it wasn't for the fact that she can't hurt anything unless she's mad or scared, it would be an interesting adventure."

"That can be taken care of by training in a specific style of defense. It mostly uses the legs and feet. Apparently, she uses them already anyway," Allen surmised. "Does she know how to shoot?"

Ben chuckled. "You're going to try to recruit her, aren't you? I've not seen her shoot, but she told us that she's shot clay pigeons when she was younger."

"Hmm...interesting," Allen said while stroking his chin.

Ben let out a laugh. "She attracts trouble like bears to a beehive."

"Even better. We wouldn't have to send agents out after them, they'd come to her," Allen jested. "Come on, we'd better go get your little trouble magnet before she attracts some new takers," Allen chuckled.

Ben and Allen walked out of the room. "What are you going to do with Taggee and the girls?" Ben asked.

"I've got a few more hoops to jump through, but they should be released today or tomorrow…why?" Allen stated.

"New York probably isn't the best place to be if you are running from someone. Which reminds me, who was Taggee warning Diana about? He never said," Ben asked.

"He said a man named Mahdi is after her," Allen replied.

Ben froze where he stood; his eyes dilated and turned a very deep sapphire blue. "Ben, what is it? Who is Mahdi?" Allen sternly asked after he saw Ben's reaction.

"Mahdi was the second in command for the Sheikh. He was the one that hit her several times while I was there in the compound. The one that beat up Aisha and was going to whip Mahala except Diana ran over and covered her with her own body. If he's after Diana, she's in mortal danger," Ben said coldly and matter-of-factly.

"Okay, so we need to get her to where she can be hid," Allen stated. He had a list of possible places running through his head.

"It only works for a short time. We had Diana at Scott's cabin. She was safe there almost two months, then they darted her and took her to Syria. There's a leak somewhere. We need to find the leak, then we can hide her until we get Mahdi," Ben discussed.

"New York still has too many people to try to hide her from. You need to head back closer to home. The question is where," Allen injected.

"Aisha, Mahala, and Taggee will be in danger as well. Well, maybe not so much Taggee, but the girls are. We'll go to my house first. Have Taggee and girls meet us there. Dick Richman knows the address. Don't tell anybody else but Dick. Taggee will be an asset in keeping the girls safe. Then we'll go from there," Ben planned out.

"Any ideas as to where the leak is?" Allen asked.

"Nope…I'll give Dick a heads-up and have him reopen it. I don't think it's in the DHS department. Maybe the local police department, or the FBI in the area…I'm not sure," Ben replied. *I should see if Ali could do some checking around in the DMPD*, Ben thought. Ben and Allen walked down to where Diana and the girls were being held. Ben met up with Scott and pulled him aside to tell him what was happening. Allen was called over by one of the clerks.

"Ben, if you have any intention of keeping that cat around, you need to find that trouble magnet and destroy it," Scott stated frustrated.

"I'm working on it…I'm working on it," Ben replied, moving his hands in an up-and-down motion as to hush the tone. They turned to look at their charges.

"The girls have been explaining to Diana how they got out of Syria with the Sheikh's jet. The doctor here says that Aisha has a couple of broken ribs from her beating, but they seem to be healing okay. Mahala only has a few bruises on her back. Apparently, Diana took the brunt of the hits." Scott glared at Ben. "That's what you meant in that house the other day. She had to let you see her back again. I didn't catch all the conversation at that time. The antenna was blown over, and I had to readjust it. I caught something about you being sorry I'm missing out again." Scott held up his hand as to signal stop. "I don't want the details of how you were able to get to her back. How bad did her back get torn up again? I didn't see anything last night, but then again, I wasn't looking at her back."

"There was only one hit that just broke the skin. The others only left welts. They had her in a whole hijab and everything. The layers of clothing protected her," Ben informed him.

"Wait a minute. So Diana was called Ariana and she was dressed as an Islamic woman?" Scott restated.

"Yeah, I already put that together in the compound bro. Yes, she was the woman in my dream way back when. Now, let's keep her alive, shall we?" Ben snipped.

Scott saw Allen come toward them. He had a paper in his hands and didn't look happy. Scott drew Ben's attention to it. "This isn't going to be good."

Ben waited till Allen was near them. "What's wrong now, sir?" he asked.

"These are Diana's labs. Her white count is very high, she has an infection somewhere, and her red blood count is too low, so she's anemic. Did you guys know about all this?" Allen worried.

"It doesn't surprise me, sir. She was dying in the compound. We just about lost her there. The wound on her right wrist doesn't seem to be healing very fast, and we're struggling to get her to eat. She's restricted on what foods she can eat already, but over in Syria, she went almost two weeks with very little or no food, and her appetite is just not coming back," Ben stated.

"Ben, didn't you say she took a lot of supplements at the cabin? She hasn't had those in almost two weeks. Those were probably what her doctor used to boost her system. She may not absorb the nutrients like she should," Scott injected.

"Why didn't the medic give her a shot of antibiotic while he was working on her?" Allen fumed.

"She's allergic to the main antibiotics. He didn't have anything he could give her," Ben stated.

Allen just rolled his eyes. "Okay…fine. Here is the address of my doctor. I'll call him and tell him you're coming and have him look at her ASAP. Get some *** **** antibiotics in her and whatever else she needs."

"Yes, sir. I'll go get her right now and head out," Ben stated over his shoulder. In truth, he was grateful. He was figuring he'd have to get her in once they got back to Des Moines. Her wrist could be twice as bad by then. He walked over to where the ladies where. "Excuse me, ladies, but I need to take Ariana from you for a while. We will see each other later," Ben said in Farsi.

"Does she live with you now, Mr. James?" Mahala asked, still speaking in Farsi.

"No, but we'll talk about it later. I need to take her to get the stitches looked at," he simply stated.

Aisha saw that her right wrist was still bleeding. She knew that meant it was not healing right. "Go take care of her, we will be okay. The man over there said we should be released soon." She pointed to Scott.

"Yes…hopefully today," Ben confirmed.

Diana just sat there watching the conversation between Ben and the girls. She was watching Ben thoroughly; she didn't know what they were saying, but she saw something in his eyes and turned to look at Scott. Something was wrong…again. *Lord, what are you doing now? I was hoping this was done now*, she prayed.

Ben looked over at Diana, knew that she has seen something and was trying to figure out what was coming. "Milady…we need to get going." He reached his hand down to help her up off the floor.

She waited until they were a little ways away from the girls. "What has happened now?" she asked.

"Hang on, kitten…we'll talk in the taxi." Ben gave her a slight hug. He slid his hand down her arm to her hand and intertwined his fingers with hers.

They met up with Scott; Diana was trying to see what was going through his mind. Scott simply smiled and winked at her. "After you, Milady."

Diana tightened her hold on Ben's hand. She didn't want him to let go as she walked past Scott. Ben had no intention of letting go, but it did make him smile that she didn't want him to either. They went through a side door instead of the front door. Their suitcases were in a rack there near the door. They grabbed them and headed out. Scott hailed a taxi; Ben had Diana get in, and he and Scott each flanked her after loading the suitcases in the back. Ben told the taxi driver the address Allen gave them, then sat back.

"Okay…guys. What in the world is wrong? Don't tell me nothing, I can see it in your faces," Diana insisted.

"Well, we got two issues right now. One…you have an infection in your body and you're anemic. We're going to deal with that now," Ben informed her.

"That doesn't surprise me. Well, anemic does, but infection doesn't. Not with how many times this wrist has been ripped open and stuff. I was praying God would heal it. I guess he wants me on meds for a while. Now… what's number two?" she commented.

"We're not done with the mountain yet," Ben stated quietly. Diana looked at him and made him look at her by putting her hand on the side of his face and turning his head. "What is it now?"

"Mahdi wasn't in the compound the other night. More than likely, he was the one who tipped off the factions," Ben quietly stated.

"He's coming after me," Diana stated flatly. Ben nodded and kissed the palm of her hand.

"Didn't you say the guys in the cavern were looking for a female?" Diana asked.

"Yes," Ben replied.

"And, Scott, you told me the guys at that house was after both of us and that there was a reward?" Diana inquired.

"Aye, lassie…wer ya hed'n?" Scott asked in his Scottish brogue, trying to lighten the mood.

"He's been looking for me ever since I left the compound, there's a reward, and how many Islamic people do we have in the States? It's just logistics. Somebody has already told him I'm in New York. They're going to want the money."

Ben leaned over and kissed her head. "There's the problem solver at work."

She blinked and smiled a small smile. "He's probably already in the States," she deduced.

"Yes…he's probably already here," Ben confirmed.

"So what are we going to do?" she asked. "What about Taggee and the girls? Taggee can probably take care of himself, although a bullet would take him out just as easy as anybody else. They're in danger too."

The taxi was slowing down in front of a medical building. "We'll put that on hold for now. Come on, let's get you some help," Ben stated.

Diana looked out. "I've got news for you: if it's anything other than my knee or my wrist, there's going to be something hitting the fan."

Scott got out to help the taxi driver with their suitcases. "You'd better give her some catnip to keep her calm. At least put her on a high for a few minutes," Scott suggested.

"Hmm…I'm up for that suggestion, but it would raise her blood pressure. I don't think she'll want more pills to take," Ben jested.

Diana just gave them a raspberry. "It looks like she's learning, Ben. That IOU app is down to what…one or two. You may be out of luck soon," Scott teased.

"Nah, she's just watching her *p*'s and *q*'s right now. She'll forget and start racking them up again," Ben commented.

Diana just looked at them and started walking to the door. They both saw a spark fly through her emerald-green eyes. "How's the ESP coming, Ben? I would love to know what went through her head just then," Scott replied.

"A little bit of orneriness…that's for sure." Ben smiled. The guys caught up with Diana and walked into the office.

Allen had already called his doctor. The nurse came within five minutes and called her back. Diana asked if it was okay for her to bring her friend back with her. The nurse looked at her suspiciously but said it was okay. Diana pulled Ben with her. "This way they won't get overzealous with an exam," she told him as she grabbed his arm. Ben just shook his head. The first stop was more blood drawn. Diana figured as much but was glad Ben kept her distracted while they were working with the needle. Then they took her to a back room, did all the usual questions, and asked about her allergies to antibiotics. She listed all the medications she had been on and that it had been almost two weeks since she had her meds.

Ben noticed the nurse wasn't happy to be dealing with Diana. *Allen probably threw her schedule off a little*, he thought. The nurse put some gloves on and unwrapped Diana's wrist.

"Yeah, that is a little infected, isn't it," she commented. "Now, if your friend will step out for a minute, we'll have you slip off your jeans so we can get to that knee."

"I can just pull my pant leg up, can't I? I shouldn't need to undress," Diana quipped.

"Diana, it's okay. The doctor probably wants to see where the infection is. I'll step out and you can let me know when you're ready," Ben stated.

If I was married to you, it wouldn't be an issue, shot through Diana's mind. She shook her head and blinked to clear her mind.

Ben's eyebrow arched up. "What was that?"

"Oh, never mind, go stand outside. I'll call you once I'm covered," Diana stated. She knew she was blushing, but there was nothing for it. Ben smiled and left the room followed by the nurse who was muttering something under her breath. Diana took her boots off and shimmied out of her jeans then put her jeans under her and brought up the legs to cover her sides. Then she used the paper "cover" the nurse laid out to cover over her lap. "Okay, Ben…I'm covered," she called out.

Ben slowly walked back in. "So what do you want to eat for supper?" he asked.

"Well, I'm anemic, so what I usually did to prevent that during treatments was I'd eat steak and/or shrimp. I don't know how far I'd get with it though, but it sounds good right now," Diana suggested.

"Yeah, actually it's been a while since I've had anything to chew on. It would be nice to gnaw on something for a while," Ben remarked. He glanced over at Diana, whose face was beet red. "And just what is that reaction from?" he asked. Diana just bit down on her bottom lip. "Ms. Henderson, you are a surprise," Ben jested.

"Oh, shut up…I've just got to get out of my head what just flew in," she stated without looking at Ben. Ben was going to slice with another comment, but the doctor walked in.

The doctor was a little taken back with Ben being in the room. "She doesn't do well with needles. She asked if I would come back with her," Ben flatly stated. He glanced back up at Diana, who had gotten herself under control before the doctor addressed her.

"Okay, miss, let's take a look at that wrist," the doctor said as he carefully picked it up. He turned it this way and that. "How did this happen?"

"It started as a rope burn, but it's been reinjured several times after that," Diana told the doctor.

The doctor asked, "How did you get a rope burn this bad?"

"It's a long story, Doctor. Let's just say it's been reinjured at least three times," Ben injected.

"Who did the stitches?" the doctor inquired.

"The medic on the USS *Wilson*," Diana replied.

"So you've been overseas. That explains some of it. I'm going to need to take these stitches out. We will have to let it heal from the inside out now. The infection will just get worse if the outside skin heals closed before the inside closes. I'll have to give you a shot of antibiotic, and I'll send home with a rinse. I want you to use it twice a day on it." He looked up at Diana to reinforce his directions. Diana nodded.

"Now, let's take a look at that knee. The same medic did these stitches as well, right?" the doctor asked.

"Yes, sir, why would that be a problem?" Diana asked.

"It isn't. It's just that the medic is left-handed. The stitches are angled different than that of a right-handed person," he replied. "The knee looks good. I'm going to go ahead and remove those stitches. It should remain closed now," the doctor stated as a matter of fact.

"What antibiotic are you going to be giving me?" Diana worried.

"Well, since you're allergic to the main ones, I'll have to go with Levaquin. It should help out your kidneys. It looks like they are infected as well. I'm surprised they haven't been hurting you," the doctor commented.

Ben looked up at Diana; he was thinking she was hiding information on him again, and he was about to hit the fan himself. "Nope, they're not hurting at all. I was told that they shut down on me a few days back though," Diana stated quickly. She had seen fire burning in Ben's eyes.

"What, when, how do you know?" the doctor asked.

"She had gone three days without liquid in the desert. Her kidneys started to shut down from it," Ben injected.

"You know this for a fact, sir?" the doctor was actually doubting it.

"Yes, sir. I was there," Ben stated flatly.

"Well then, ma'am, you are a lucky one. It also explains the high toxin levels. I suggest you start pushing the liquid down now to flush your system," the doctor ended.

"I'll make sure of it, sir," Ben enforced, looking at Diana.

Diana, watching what the doctor was doing and not thinking, stuck her tongue out at Ben. Ben whistled softly, which brought Diana's attention to him. With a big smile on his face, he licked his finger and traced a tally in the air. Diana thought for a second and put her hand over her mouth. She started looking around and then looked down. She saw the doctor bring out a scalpel, and she turned sheet white.

Ben walked over to her side. "Are you going to do her knee first?" he asked.

"No, I was going to start on her wrist first. Why?" the doctor inquired.

"If you do the knee first, she can put her pants back on. Then it would be easier for me to distract her while you work on her wrist," Ben pointed out.

The doctor looked up at Diana and saw that she had paled with the sight of the scalpel. "Very well, I'll do the knee first. While she's getting dressed, I'll get the antibiotic ready."

"Diana, lie back a little. Keep your eyes up here," Ben stated.

"Are you thinking you'll be able to read what's going through my brain?" she quipped.

"I don't have to think, I know what shot between those ears of yours. I am surprised. Here I thought such things were alien to your being," he teased.

Diana flinched as the doctor pulled on a stitch that had stuck. "Look over here, Kitten, don't pay attention to the doctor right now," Ben insisted.

"Easier said than done, Tiger, you don't—" Diana started to say, but Ben cut her off.

"You don't want me to take drastic measures. The good doctor might get the wrong idea," Ben jested.

"Okay, Ms. Henderson, I'm done. The skin is healed quite well. Too bad your wrist hadn't healed the same way," the doctor stated.

"It would have if I could get people to stop grabbing hold of it," Diana sneered.

"Well, put your pants back on and we'll start working on the wrist," the doctor said as he walked out the door.

"Give a call once you're ready," Ben stated and headed out the door behind the doctor. Diana jumped down and quickly put her pants back on, but she was having trouble getting her boots pulled on. Without the gauze on the wrist, it was drying out more, causing it to hurt her as she worked to put her boots on.

"Okay, Ben," she called. When Ben opened the door she said. "I can't get my boots back on with this thing unwrapped." Ben came over, bent down, and put one of her boots on. As he was reaching for the other boot, which he accidentally kicked beside the table, he reached up to put his hand on the table to stabilize himself. His hand came down on Diana's upper thigh. He realized it immediately; his breath hitched as he slid his hand down. He heard her breath catch and felt her thigh tremble.

"Sorry, kitten. I was just reaching for your other boot," Ben said with a grin.

"Huh-huh, sure you were, Mr. Tigere," she sarcastically stated.

"You can't prove I didn't do it on accident," he quipped back. Diana just shook her head. Ben went and finished putting on her other boot.

The doctor walked in with the nurse and the equipment he needed to work on Diana's wrist. "Ms. Henderson, would you prefer to lie down?" the nurse asked.

Diana didn't have a chance to answer her. "Yes, she needs to lie down," Ben interrupted. The nurse looked at Ben then at Diana. Diana just nodded yes. So the nurse laid the back of the table down and pulled the extension out for Diana's legs. Diana lay back, and Ben walked up near her shoulder.

"This isn't going to be fun, kitten. Infected skin is more irritated and will hurt easier," Ben whispered in her ear. Diana swallowed hard and prepared for keeping herself still. The nurse and doctor started in on her wrist. The first part of it wasn't a problem, but when it came around to the sides of her wrists, the main areas that broke open when Frank grabbed her, that was another story. As much as she tried to keep her arm still, it kept jerking as the doctor pulled on the stitch to get them unstuck. The nurse was holding her arm down, but it took Ben reaching over and holding it to keep it still.

"I'm sorry. I'm trying to keep it still," she whispered.

Ben, who was just inches from Diana's face, smiled. "I know. Sometimes the body just has a mind of its own," he whispered back and gave her a quick kiss. "You're doing fine."

The doctor finally finished pulling the last stitch. Ben was starting to straighten up when the doctor said, "You'd better stay there sir. This isn't going to feel good at all."

Ben reached back over and held her arm at the elbow. The doctor started rinsing the wrist with the medicated wash. Diana felt like they were using white-hot charcoals to sear her wrist closed. She inhaled deeply and then bit down on her bottom lip. Ben could feel her muscles twitching as they desperately tried to pull away from the cause of the pain. He also noticed she was still holding her breath.

"Breath, kitten, deep, slow breaths," he demanded.

"Almost done, Ms. Henderson, just a little more," the doctor said with encouragement.

"Remind me, the next time someone grabs that wrist to knock every one of their teeth out and then some," Diana sneered.

Ben just laughed. "Maybe I need to get a brace that goes from the thumb to the forearm. That way if they do grab it, it has some protection."

"At this point in time, I'd wear it," Diana sneered.

"Okay, sir, she's done with the rinse. You can let go. Mrs. Whitten is going to finish wrapping it and give her a shot of the antibiotic. It will need to go in the hip, Ms. Henderson. I will also send you home with some pain medication. This wrist is going to be hurting for a while," the doctor concluded.

"Thank you, sir," Ben stated. He didn't figure Diana was in the mood to appreciate his time. The doctor nodded and walked out. The nurse finished wrapping Diana's wrist a moment later. She gave Ben the medicated rinse and some gauze for her wrist.

"Could you step outside for a moment please?" the nurse directed.

"Yes, ma'am," Ben replied and nodded to Diana then walked out the door. Diana was used to getting shots in the hip, so she knew what she had to do. She hopped down off the table and prepped for the shot.

"This is going to burn. I'm just giving you fair warning," the nurse stated.

"Yes, ma'am. This part I'm very familiar with. You will need to cover it, I'll bleed a little," Diana explained.

The nurse at first didn't believe her, but blood started to build as soon as she pulled the needle out. She grabbed a spot cover and walked over to throw the needle away. Diana adjusted herself, grabbed her stuff, and waited to see if the nurse had any other instructions. The nurse gave her some samples of the pain medication the doctor wanted her to have. "You're all done. Have a good day," the nurse said over her shoulder.

Diana headed out the door toward Ben. "Are we ready to go eat?" he asked.

"By the time we get there, probably. Right now, my stomach is all knotted," Diana informed him.

Ben put his arm around her shoulders. "Let's go get your brother. He's probably chewed the arm rests of the chairs by now. He's used to three square meals a day." Diana simply smiled.

Scott was busy talking to a cute redhead when Ben and Diana walked out into the lobby. "As I've said from day one, a Southern charmer," Diana jeered.

Ben gave a quiet bird call. Scott looked up, saw Ben and Diana, then smiled. Diana walked over to where he was. "I'm sorry, ma'am. I need my brother to take me to get something to eat," she smoothly informed the redhead. She looked over at Scott. "Doctor's orders." Scott just shook his head and smiled, told the redhead good-bye, and joined Ben and Diana walking to the door. They asked the receptionist if they could get their suitcases; she unlocked the door for them to reach in and grab them.

In the taxi, Ben told the driver to take them to Outback Steakhouse. "Oh yeah, some meat," Scott stated as he rubbed his hands together.

Diana just smiled and shook her head. She was very hungry for something with substance. She was determined to get as much in as she could; though she was quite sure she would have to have a to-go box.

"Now, Ms. Henderson, you will eat everything on your plate, understood?" Ben insisted.

"I've never eaten there before. How do they cook their meat? If I say medium rare, is it going to be red in the center or just pink?" Diana asked.

"Medium rare, are you sure you would eat it?" Scott asked.

Diana smiled. "I like mine bleeding but warm."

Scott's mouth dropped. Then he smiled and looked up at Ben and said, "Definitely a cat. She has to be, there's no other way to explain it."

Ben chuckled. "If you want it bleeding and warm, you'd better say rare."

Diana sat quietly for a few minutes; she felt Ben's arm come down behind her and wrap around her waist. She let him pull her closer and leaned her head up against his chest. "How's your wrist doing, kitten?" he asked.

"It's sore, and it's going to leave an ugly scar." Diana shrugged. "It is what it is. I'm probably going to have to start wearing my watch on my left wrist. Either that or get a very loose band."

"I didn't realize you are left-handed," Scott injected.

"I sign with my left hand. I can actually can use either for the most part." Diana smiled. Diana noticed Ben's watch and turned it to see what time it was.

"It's four p.m., kitten, why?" Ben stated.

"I was just wondering. What time does the flight leave for Des Moines?" she asked.

"Not until eight; we have plenty of time," Ben replied.

The taxi pulled up to the steak house. "You know, it would have been better if we left our suitcases at the hotel. What are we going to do with them here?" Diana asked.

"This is New York. They're used to travelers coming in with luggage. Most places even have a place to turn your luggage in at so that you can pick it up afterward," Scott informed her. Diana just nodded to acknowledge his statement. Ben got out and held his hand out to help Diana out. The trio went in and ate. Diana had a small four-ounce sirloin and grilled shrimp, Ben had the eight-ounce New York strip, and Scott had the twelve-ounce porterhouse. Diana made it through the shrimp and half the steak before she had to call it quits. She didn't even touch her baked potato. Ben and Scott tried to get her to eat some more, but she just couldn't get another bite in. She sat quietly while Ben and Scott finished their meal.

31

New York

They stayed there at the Outback till six thirty p.m., drinking coffee—or in Diana's case, sweet tea. They headed out, and Ben hailed a taxi; they went to the airport from the steak house. Diana leaned her head against Ben's chest and closed her eyes. Ben had his arm behind her but was holding her left hand in her lap, his thumb caressing the back of Diana's hand; she dozed off.

"You've got her purring," Scott teased.

"I just wish I could take her away and hide her from all this junk. You know, keep her safe, innocent," Ben softly said.

"She has to follow what the Lord has set for her. She knows that. She also knows that the Lord will help her through it," Scott reasoned. "That being said, what is the next step? Where are we going to hold up at?"

Diana started to stir. Ben reached up, cupping her face with his hand. "Shh…kitten. You're okay." He pushed a stray strand of hair away from her eyes. "Taggee and the girls are going to meet up with us at my house. The kids should be with Becca out at the farm. Then we need to decide where to go next."

"She wants you close, you know that, don't ya?" Scott quietly stated.

"You've had the classes—that's typical of an individual who's gone through a traumatic event. They latch on to their rescuer," Ben snipped. Not that he really believed that; he was trying to hedge himself if things didn't work out between them.

"No, bro, it's not that way. You read her so well, but you can see this? Come on, you know better," Scott countered. "You heard her this morning. She held a wall up because she thought we would ditch her. You know, it was kind of weird. When she was talking, it was like someone was whispering in my ear what she was really meaning."

Ben looked over at Scott. "Welcome to the world of the spirit. That was what Diana was trying to explain to you earlier."

The taxi pulled up to the airport. Scott got out of the taxi to get the luggage; Ben kissed Diana on the forehead. "Come on, kitten, time to get you back to home turf."

Diana opened her eyes. "I'm sorry, I didn't mean to doze off."

Ben just smiled at her. "A full stomach has a tendency to do that." Diana just smiled up at him. He opened the door and helped Diana out of the taxi. Diana didn't let go of his hand though. She weaved her fingers through his. He raised her hand up to his mouth and kissed the back of it. "Thank you." He smiled.

They walked in and started going through the check stations. They were almost to the loading ramp when they bumped into Camie again. "Hey…hello again!" Camie boisterously expressed.

Diana saw Scott's face; he was grimacing. "Good evening, Camie," she calmly greeted.

"Are you guys on this flight too? That is so awesome. We can get to know each other better." Camie smiled and walked up close to Diana. "Are you and your guy friend in coach?" she continued.

Diana looked up to Ben then back to Cami; "I'm not sure where we are. I let the guys decide all that stuff."

Camie walked over to Ben and stroked her hand down his arm. "So what do you say, Ben? Are we going to get to know each other better?"

Scott saw Diana's expression. Her eyes were dark gray and cold. She held herself stiff and straight. Scott recognized that she was actually jealous. All of a sudden, Scott felt a hand on his shoulder. He turned to see who it was; there was no one there. What he did see was Jeff walking over toward them. Scott prepared himself for trouble; he turned back toward Ben and Diana. "It looks like we have more visitors coming," Scott stated more to Ben than Diana.

Ben looked over. "Let me guess, Jeff?" Diana felt Ben's arm tense; she glanced around Scott.

Camie, who was still 'mauling' Ben, spoke up. "Yep that's my brother, Jeff."

Jeff walked over, coming up between Diana and Scott. "Good evening," Diana addressed.

"Hello. I'm here to apologize to your brother about my comments last night. I had a little too much to drink," Jeff stated.

Diana watched his eyes. *He's lying. He's here to cause trouble*, she thought.

She glanced up at Ben. Ben looked down at Diana, winked, and proceeded to pull her in front of him and over to his opposite side. Diana was standing between Ben and Camie now. Camie put her hand on Diana's shoulder.

"Hey, Jeff, they are taking this flight as well. Isn't that cool?" Camie informed him.

"I'd like that a lot. Maybe I can get to know names then," Jeff acknowledged. "Like your name, ma'am. I'd really like to know your name."

Diana just looked at him. "My name is Ms. Henderson."

"Why so very formal? Isn't there a shorter name I can call you?" Jeff asked.

"Her name is Diana,' Camie spoke out.

"Diana, that's very pretty. So Diana, if it's okay with your brother here, how about going out on a date with me?" Jeff conceitedly asked.

"I don't think so, sir," Diana instantly shot him down.

"Why not? It would be fun," Jeff insisted.

"One, my brother would mind. Two, my boyfriend would mind. Three, my own conscience would mind," Diana calmly stated.

"Oh, so your brother's best friend is your boyfriend now?" Camie questioned.

"Yep. Things moved quickly," Diana smoothly stated.

"What, this guy here is your boyfriend? You can do better than him!" Jeff sneered.

Ben just stood there listening. He was actually surprised that Diana called him her boyfriend. Jeff reached over to grab Diana's right arm. Diana tried to pull away from his reach, but Camie pushed her into it. Jeff grabbed on to Diana's right wrist. Diana gasped and grimaced in pain. Ben quickly reached down and grabbed onto Jeff's wrist, stopping him from pulling on Diana. "I would suggest you let go of Diana's wrist," Ben warned.

Scott chimed in, "If I were you, I would do what he says. He's very protective of his girl."

Jeff just laughed. "I'm not drunk tonight. He's a little old to be dancing with someone in prime shape."

"Ben, remember what I said I would do to the next person who grabbed my wrist? Would you mind freeing my wrist for me? I can easily deal with this nuisance," Diana sneered.

"As you wish," Ben calmly stated smiling down into her steel-gray eyes. He proceeded to squeeze Jeff's wrist. Jeff started to howl and had to let go of her. Ben then let go of Jeff's wrist. Jeff pulled his wrist back and stood there rubbing it. Ben reached up and put his hand on Diana's shoulder. "I can't let you do what you want, kitten. You have boots on. I don't need every male in a twenty-foot radius going to the hospital with sympathy pains."

"Oh…fine," Diana said in disgust. "You or Scott can deal with it. Go have your fun," Diana asserted. She saw the fear growing in Jeff's eyes; her statement just added to it.

"Whoa…Jeff, let's just let them be. She's a prude anyway," Camie spoke up.

Diana turned toward her. "You've finally figured that out, huh? Why don't you and your brother head back over with the rest of your group?"

Camie started turning the air blue and walked back over to the rest of her group. Jeff, however, did not take the hint; "You ******* *****. Who do you think you are?"

"Would you prefer I stay here, gentlemen, or over there?" Diana said as she shook her head.

"Stay here. This won't take long," Scott beamed.

"You don't know how lucky you are, Jeff. If I let Diana loose on you, you would probably lose your teeth and your ability to reproduce," Ben coldly stated.

Jeff looked at her; he saw an eyebrow arched up, her eyes as cold as an iceberg and a confirming grin on her face. "Her? No way." But he unconsciously covered himself.

Scott was almost laughing; he had to bite his cheeks. *Well played, Milady*, he thought.

Ben put his hand on Jeff's shoulder and squeezed. Jeff started to bend down with the pressure Ben was causing. Diana saw Camie out of the corner of her eye. She was complaining to a security guard over by the counter. "Gentlemen, it looks like we are going to have some official attention soon. You'll have to let Mr. Jeff get back to his group," Diana stated as she nodded toward the counter.

Ben and Scott looked over toward where she nodded. "Too bad," Ben simply stated. He released Jeff's shoulder.

Jeff nervously laughed. "Yeah, it's a good thing the cops are coming. You'd…you'd be in a boatload of pain soon." Diana just sighed and shook her head. Ben looked over to Scott and did a quick nod. Scott smiled broadly.

"I'm sure you think so," Ben said as he started to walk behind him. Then Scott did a quick kick to the back of Jeff's knee and a jab with two of his fingers near Jeff's neck. Jeff fell in a heap on the floor. Ben looked back at Diana, took her arm, and started to guide her to the plane. Scott looked around at the people looking at Jeff lying on the floor. "He must have tripped," he said.

They walked a little ways away. Ben looked over Diana's head and saw Camie standing by Jeff, who was up on his feet now. He leaned down toward Diana. "Shall we make a lasting impression?"

Diana looked up at him then back behind her then back up at Ben. A spark shot through her eyes and she smiled. Ben brought her up to him, and he bent down and kissed her long and hard. Diana still didn't let him collect an IOU, even though Ben wanted to, tried to. Scott saw Ben and Diana kissing. He couldn't believe Diana allowed Ben to make that jump. Then he glanced back and saw the faces of Camie and Jeff. It was priceless. It was then he realized that they were putting on a "show" for the two intruders.

Scott neared where they were "occupied." "Your show achieved its desired effect. If you two are done, we need to get aboard," he teased.

Ben released Diana from his embrace, but Diana stayed near him. She smiled up at him. "Well, we have to make sure the correct message was sent. Didn't we, Tiger?" Diana teased.

"Hey, I'm not going to pass up an opening when it so willingly presents itself," Ben jabbed. They turned to go through the last check station. As they walked up the ramp to load, Ben lifted her arm up to look at her wrist.

"It's not bleeding. I tried not to pull against him," Diana told him. "Please tell me we get to stay in first class again. I don't want to meet up with Camie or Jeff for a long while."

"Yeah, we're in the front. Plus you get to sit with me instead of Dick," Ben gleamed.

"Where did Scott wind up?" she asked.

"He's in front of us," Ben confirmed. Soon they were on their way back to Des Moines. Ben had two bottles of water brought to Diana. He insisted that they be gone by the time they land in Des Moines. Diana argued, but Ben would have none of it. She made him show her where the bathroom was. She'd need it soon, especially after all the tea she drank plus these two bottles.

32

Des Moines

The plane landed at the Des Moines airport at ten thirty that night. The trio had to wait on the tarmac for another thirty minutes. There was a car waiting for them to use in the parking garage; it was a Pontiac sedan. They threw their luggage in, and Ben drove them to his house. It was a two-story cream-colored Victorian-style house, complete with fluted columns and leaded glass decorative windows. Ben unlocked the door and showed them into the living room. They set about getting things organized. Ben went to check the kitchen to see if there was food for them for tomorrow. Scott headed for the bathroom, leaving Diana alone in the living room. She was looking at the pictures and knickknacks arranged on the walls and shelves. She thought she heard someone walking across the floor upstairs. She looked up and listened to the sounds. "Who's down there?" a woman's voice called from the top of the stairs.

Diana didn't say anything. She saw two feet start to slowly descend the stairs. The woman came midway down the stairs. Diana could see she had a bat in her hands; she was on the petite side, long blonde hair, and she was wearing a pair of sweats and a gray T-shirt. The woman saw Diana standing there in the middle of the living room. "Ma'am, you just picked the wrong house to rob," she sneered as she hit the bottom of the stairs.

The woman turned on the light and glared at Diana. It was then that Diana saw the same sapphire-blue eyes; she was Ben's sister. "I'm not here to rob this house. I was brought here by your brother," Diana calmly said.

"I don't believe you. He would never bring a woman here," Ben's sister sneered.

"Becca, she's telling you the truth," Ben calmly declared.

Becca dropped the bat and ran to Ben. "You're home, you're safe, I missed you so much," Becca yelled and jumped into his arms. Her yelling brought a thunderous stampede upstairs. It grew louder as it neared the stairs. Diana watched as several feet came running down. She backed up toward the corner so that she didn't startle the kids. They cornered the newel and ran straight for their dad, all yelling, jumping, and screaming. Diana stood there smiling as she watched Ben hug and address each of his kids. Scott came back through the hallway. It just rejuvenated all the yelling and raucousness. Scott acknowledged each of them but then pushed past, heading to the living room. He saw Diana standing in the shadows. She had a smile on her face, but he could see in her eyes she was fighting back tears.

"Are you okay, Milady?" he asked as he neared her.

"Yeah, I just miss my own family, but I can't go home yet because—" Then it dawned on her. "Scott! I can't stay here, they—" Diana was cut short by Scott putting his hand on her mouth.

Ben stood up and saw that Diana and Scott discussing in the living room. He looked at Diana directly and saw sheer terror in her eyes; she was near to tears. Then he saw Scott stop Diana from talking.

"Diana, we will cross that bridge when we get to it. You need to calm yourself down. Don't let the kids see you scared," Scott reprimanded. Diana nodded and turned toward the window to regain her composure.

"Diana, I'd like you to meet my family," she heard Ben state behind her. She swallowed hard and took in a deep breath. She then turned to see Ben standing next to her. He put his arm around her waist.

"This is BJ…my oldest, Kaira…my oldest girl," Ben introduced. Diana shook BJ and Kaira's hands. "These are my twins, Brock and Kora."

Diana went down on her knees to greet them. "Hello, Brock and Kora. It's good to meet you."

"Why are you crying?" Kora asked.

"I was just watching you guys hugging your daddy. It reminded me of my family," Diana replied.

"Haven't you seen your family?" Brock asked.

"No…I haven't. I haven't seen my family in almost three months," she calmly answered.

"Why…not?" Kora questioned.

"Well, I…umm…" Diana looked up at Ben. He reached down and helped Diana up to her feet.

"She's been out of town for a long time," Ben replied carefully. "Becca, this is Diana. Diana, my baby sister, Becca."

Diana held out her hand toward Becca, who hesitantly took her hand. "Good evening." It was quite obvious to Diana that she was not wanted here—at least not by Becca.

"I'm sorry if I startled you when you came down the stairs," Diana apologized. Becca only nodded. Ben could feel the anger waving off Becca. He also could feel Diana trying to back away from her, but he was blocking her from doing so.

"I thought you and the kids were out at the farm. What happened?" Ben asked.

"Mom and Dad are out on a roundup. The kids didn't want to help out, so I brought them home to catch up with friends," Becca replied.

"Well, munchkins, I know you're all excited and happy I'm home, but it's late, and I've been on the road all day. So, head upstairs, climb into bed, and I'll be up to tuck you in," Ben instructed. The kids all moaned. "Can't we stay up with you for a while?" they asked.

Diana looked up at Ben and smiled but said nothing. "We can have a bowl of ice cream together. Then it's bedtime," Ben stated. The kids all yelled and headed for the kitchen. Becca looked at Ben and Diana, frowned, and turned to help dish up the ice cream. Scott held back to discuss with Ben and Diana.

"Ben, I can't stay here. I'm putting your family at risk," Diana pleaded.

"You're going to stay where I am, Diana. Put that worry out of your mind," Ben commanded softly.

"So how are we going to work this, bro?" Scott questioned.

"I'm still working on it. I could have Diana sleep in my room," Ben suggested.

"That would not be wise in so many levels," Diana quipped.

"It's no different than what it has been, kitten," Ben commented.

"Point taken, except we aren't in the desert or on a ship, we are in your house. Plus, I think your sister would rather shoot me than taint your reputation," Diana pointed out.

"She was extremely cold tonight, bro. she's got a burr in her saddle about something," Scott implied.

"Nah…she's tired and was scared. She'll be fine," Ben commented and walked toward the kitchen.

Diana looked at Scott. "I know that feeling all too well. I'm the intruder here and she wants me out. What am I to do?"

"We'll figure it out tomorrow, Milady, be patient," Scott said and rubbed her upper arm.

"Are you two coming?" they heard Ben call from the kitchen.

"You go on ahead. I don't want any. Thank you though," Diana stated. Scott went on into the kitchen.

As Scott walked into the kitchen, Ben looked up from talking with the kids. "Where's Diana?" he asked.

"She wanted to give us alone time with the family," Scott simply stated. He looked up at Becca, who was beginning to smile.

Ben watched Scott then looked at Becca. Scott was protecting Diana—that he understood. Why was Becca so cold? She's usually very accepting; he'll have to have a talk with her. The kids finished their ice cream, and though they begged for more time, Ben sent them up to bed. Scott was sitting on the back porch looking at the night sky. Becca was doing the dishes. Ben walked over to her. "Why the cold shoulder toward Diana, Becca?"

Becca stopped washing for a second but then continued with the bowl. "I wasn't cold," she replied.

"You were cold enough to freeze most of Des Moines. What's the problem?" Ben insisted.

"Why did you bring her here? You never bring you assignments home. Why this one?" Becca fumed.

"Because she's not just an assignment," Ben stated.

"Honestly, Ben, you leave for almost two months and you come back with a girlfriend. What do you want me to do, jump for joy that you're being an idiot?" Becca replied.

"I assume that you want me to live the rest of my life as a lonely widower. I can never have another?" Ben asked.

"You've only known her for, what, less than two months? What do you know about her?" Becca countered.

"I've learned more about her in the last three months than I would have ever known under any normal circumstance," Ben informed Becca. "I think you would like her if you would give her a chance. You two have a lot in common."

"I do? Or does she have a lot in common with Katherine?" Becca questioned.

"No...I can easily say there is very little in common between Diana and Katherine. Diana isn't Katherine. She won't ban you from the kids or me," Ben softly said.

"Just how do you know that? You've only know the woman for less than two months," Becca sneered. She finished the last dish, walked out, and headed for bed.

"God, help me," Ben said out loud.

"Is there too much estrogen flowing in the house tonight, bro?" Scott asked, walking back into the kitchen.

"I wonder," Ben grimaced.

"So how are we going to do this?" Scott asked.

"You go ahead and take the guest bedroom. I'll have Diana sleep in my room. If nothing else, I'll use the recliner in there," Ben stated. "Once Taggee and the girls get here tomorrow, we'll need to find another place to keep them safe."

"We'll need to go to the DHS office tomorrow as well. Your director will want to know what's going on," Scott informed Ben.

"Yeah, we'll go in after breakfast," Ben agreed.

"Diana… also?" Scott wondered. Ben nodded. The guys walked down the hallway toward the living room. They saw Diana passed out on the couch; Ben smiled. "Well, I don't think you're going to get much argument from her tonight," Scott jeered and slapped Ben on the back.

Ben glared at Scott but then said, "I'll see you in the morning." He walked to the door and made sure it was locked. "You want to hit the light in just a second. My arms are going to be a little full."

"Yeah, I'll catch them." Scott smiled. He watched Ben go over to Diana and carefully lift her arm up and placed it around his neck. Then he slid his arms under her and lifted her up into them, her head on his shoulder, her hair totally covering her face. Ben smiled and walked down the hall toward his bedroom. Scott hit the light off and went to the upstairs guest bedroom.

Ben laid Diana down on the bed and gently brushed the hair from her face. He moved down and took her boots off. He looked down at her wrist. He didn't get it treated tonight, and he didn't want to wake her to take care of it now. *Lord, touch it and heal it quickly*, he prayed. He removed the headband from Diana's hair and laid it on the nightstand; Diana softly moaned. "Hush, babe…sleep," he whispered. He went to his bathroom and changed clothes and washed up a little. He put on a pair of pajama pants and walked back into the bedroom. Diana had curled up into a ball; he knew that she fell asleep feeling insecure. He figured since she was fully clothed, it wouldn't be a problem if she shared his bed. He crawled in beside her, carefully turning her toward him, pulling her in close. She uncurled and nestled into his side. He brought her right arm out and across his chest. He heard her breathe in deep and slow, then it stayed at a normal rhythm. He wondered what he was going to do. She was getting close to letting him into her world, but the situation with Becca put that in jeopardy. Then there was Mahdi; where was he going to hide these women at? Where was he going to put

Diana to keep her safe? In truth, she was safest next to him. That was where she belonged—next to him. He reached over and ran his hand down her face. "You have to let me in someday, kitten," he whispered. She unconsciously moved into his hand. He brought her in closer and closed his eyes. Soon he was fast asleep.

It was around two in the morning; Diana woke herself up when she yelled out "No!" She sat straight up in bed, tears streaming down her cheeks. Ben jumped awake and grabbed his knife he had under his pillow. It took a second for him to realize that she had a nightmare.

He calmed himself down, sat up, and rubbed Diana's back. He could feel her shaking. "Kitten...what is it?" he asked. When she didn't answer, he turned on the light that was on the nightstand. He saw the panic and fear in her eyes. He brought her to him and held her, rocking her slightly in his arms. "Diana, what did you see?"

"Mahdi found me here. He took everybody. He killed Scott and you first then went to each of the rooms, killing everyone. At the end, he brought Kora down, made me watch, I couldn't do anything. I was screaming for someone to come and help, but nobody came. Kora was begging me to help her, but I couldn't reach her. I...couldn't—" Diana broke down and bawled.

Ben lifted her face so he could see her eyes. "Mahdi is not here. You would have felt him. Scott and I will do everything we can to not let him find you or the kids. You believe God is in control, right?" Ben calmly but firmly stated. Diana nodded. "He has told you everything so far, hasn't he?"

"Not everything, but when there was danger, he has always warned me first," Diana said between sobs.

"Okay...so this was just a nightmare. You're in a strange house, you're tired, and the pain medication could be affecting you—so many variables to cause this. We are all here, we are all safe," Ben assured her.

She bit down on her bottom lip. She was still shaking badly. "I'm sorry, it was just so terrifying."

"I bet it was. Since you're awake, do you want to change into something more comfortable to sleep in?" Ben asked. It was more to get her mind focusing on something else. She simply nodded. "Okay...go get your stuff. You can change in my bathroom over there," Ben replied.

Diana glanced around; it was the first time that she realized that she was in Ben's bedroom. "My suitcase is in the living room," she explained.

"Do you want me to go with you to get it?" Ben softly asked, brushing her hair away from her face again. Diana sheepishly nodded. Ben just smiled. "Come on then, let's go." He walked her out to the living room. She walked over to the corner where she had left it. As she bent down to grab it, she saw movement out of the corner of her eye and gasped.

"Easy, Milady. It's just me," Scott whispered.

Diana's body froze; she struggled to get a breath in. Ben walked over and held her in his arms again. He could feel her heart trying to pound out of her chest. "Breathe Kitten, deep, slow breaths. There you go, nice and slow." Ben kept rubbing her back until she was starting to breathe normally. He saw her water bottle on the coffee table and reached over and grabbed it. "Here…take a drink."

Diana's hands were shaking so bad that she could hardly hang onto the bottle. She finally managed a swallow. "Take another," Ben commanded. Diana obeyed and took another drink. She was able to slow her breathing down now. Her hands weren't shaking quite as much.

"I'm sorry, Diana. I didn't mean to scare you so much," Scott softly said. Diana only managed to shake her head no.

"Go to the room kitten, go get changed," Ben softly whispered. "I'll be in…in just a moment." Diana slowly picked up her suitcase and quietly walked back into Ben's room.

"What in the world happened?" Scott asked once she was out of earshot. "I heard her yell, so I came down to check on everything. I've never seen her like that," he worried.

"She had a horrifying nightmare. The ending of it was her watching Mahdi torturing Kora and her not being able to help but having to watch," Ben told Scott.

"Wow…where did all that come from?" Scott wondered.

"She's had to deal with a lot. Kora is about the age that she was when she was abused. Then to have Mahdi after her, I think her mind melted it all together," Ben surmised.

"I often wondered if that wasn't in her background, especially after that comment in the cabin. I just didn't have the heart to ask," Scott softly stated. "I know she just about flipped out when it dawned on her that she may be putting the kids in danger. I wasn't sure she would stay. I think she realized she really didn't have another place to go," Scott added.

"She carries too much on her shoulders. She doesn't have to," Ben whispered.

"Small steps. Although I don't think you'll have too much more to go before she opens up to you," Scott encouraged.

"We'll see…good night," Ben said and walked down the hallway.

"Good night." Scott turned and carefully glanced out the window. *It's safe…get some rest*, he heard in his ear. He nodded seemingly to nobody and walked back upstairs.

Ben walked back into his room. Diana was in the bathroom still. Her suitcase was opened up on the chair. He saw that she had already changed out of her jeans and shirt. They were folded up nicely along the side of her suitcase. He walked over to his side of the bed and lay down on top of the covers. He thought for a minute and reached down and pulled a light blanket out of the nightstand. He figured if she was in her pajamas she might get a little cold. He knew she wouldn't get under the covers. It would be too improper in her mind. He heard the bathroom door open and saw her walk out. She had her black lounge pants on and a sleep shirt. When she looked over at Ben, he saw total weariness in her eyes. The night's episode had drained everything from her. "Come on, kitten, come get some sleep," he softly said. He figured that a baby could probably lead her right now. She had nothing left.

Diana walked over and climbed onto the bed. Ben gave her the blanket, which she draped over her feet. He pulled her up against him, letting her settle in. He put his arm around her back, his other hand holding her hand rubbing it with his thumb. "You're going to be okay. Scott and I aren't going anywhere. Remember, the Lord is with us; his angel protecting us, protecting the entire house. So don't worry. Sleep," Ben softly and smoothly stated. He reached his arm up from behind her and started stroking through her hair. With each stroke of his hand; she loosened up. Soon, she was back asleep again. Ben turned on his side, facing her. She had pulled both of her arms down and in front of her but stayed as close as she could to him. He gently kissed her lips. "Soon, kitten, it'll be over soon. Then you and I are going to have a heart-to-heart." He reached over and pulled her in close, leaving his hand on her waist. His other arm he put under his head. He himself fell asleep again.

33

Ben's House

Diana didn't wake again for the rest of the night. Ben woke up a few times, only to check on Diana, then he went back out. In the morning, when he woke up, he noticed that during the night, Diana had turned over and now had her back to him. Her arm draped over his arm and his hand pulled up and held at her chest. She was still sound asleep, so he gently slid his hand down the middle, flattening it out at her stomach to untwine his arm from hers. His own heart started racing; blood started pulsing in his ears. "You're beautiful kitten. If the Lord wills, you and I will be together," he whispered. He saw her adjust her head into the pillow. He started stroking her hair, using his fingers like a comb; he heard her take a deep breath only to slowly let it out in a sigh. He lay there savoring the moment; then he heard his kids running around upstairs and knew they would be coming down soon. He kissed her neck, pulled his knife out from under his pillow and placed it in the nightstand drawer, carefully slid off the bed, and headed for the bathroom.

After he had showered and dressed, he came out and saw that Diana had curled up into a ball again. He walked over and pulled the blanket up around her shoulders. He wanted her to sleep. It not only helps the body heal physically but mentally as well; both were needed…especially by her. He quietly walked out toward the kitchen and closed the door.

Scott was sitting at the table drinking a cup of coffee. Ben smiled and walked over to the cupboard and pulled out a cup for himself. "Did she sleep the rest of the night?" Scott asked.

Ben was pouring his cup of coffee. "Yeah, she finally settled down. I've never seen her quite so shaken up. She felt so helpless in her dream."

"I guess that's another fear of hers—that she'd be helpless, unable to help those she cares for," Scott injected.

Becca quickly walked through the kitchen and headed toward Ben's room. "The kids have the bathroom tied up. I'm going to use yours," she stated as she strolled through.

"Wait a minute, Becca, you—" Ben tried to stop her. Becca opened the door and froze. She saw Diana sleeping in Ben's bed. She turned and looked at Ben, fire burning in her eyes. Ben slowly walked over and quietly closed the door. He put his hand in the middle of Becca's back and guided her back into the kitchen.

"You two are sleeping together!" she hissed.

"We used the same bed to sleep…yes, but I did not 'sleep' with her," Ben coldly stated.

"She could have slept on the couch. She didn't need to make you share your bed," Becca informed him.

"She didn't make me. In truth…she didn't have much to say about it. She was already asleep on the couch. I carried her in there," Ben calmly stated.

"Are you insane?!" Becca yelled.

"Shh…Becca," Scott scolded.

"I suppose you're okay with him doing this? Giving up on everything he has stood for, throwing it out the window for this woman," Becca emphasized but in a quieter voice.

"What have I given away…Becca?" Ben asked. "If you didn't notice, she is fully clothed. I was clothed—nothing happened." Their conversation was brought to a halt. The kids started filing into the kitchen for breakfast. BJ came in and immediately headed for the fridge. He grabbed the gallon of milk and sat it down on the table; then he went to the cupboard and grabbed a bowl then a box of cinnamon toast crunch. Brock was the next child to appear. He just sat down at the table. Ben saw that he was basically still asleep. "Do you want a bowl of cereal, Brockster?" Ben asked. Brock nodded. Ben moved over, grabbed a bowl from the cupboard, and sat it down in front of his son. BJ was the one that poured the cereal and milk for Brock. Ben went to get a spoon out of the drawer. He brought it over and placed it next to Brock's hand.

Kora came in, heading straight for her dad. She grabbed her dad's leg. "Hold me, Daddy," she said, holding her arms up for him to pick her up. Ben bent down and picked her up, giving her a hug. "Did you want something to eat for breakfast, pumpkin?" he asked.

"Oatmeal." She smiled.

Becca spoke up. "We don't have any made. Are you sure you don't want some cinnamon toast crunch?"

"No…I want oatmeal," Kora insisted.

"I'll get it, Becca. That's what I'm hungry for," Scott injected.

As Scott passed Ben, Ben whispered, "Do extra for Diana. She'll need something in her stomach."

Kora heard her dad say a lady's name. "Where's the pretty lady at, Daddy?"

"She's still sleeping, pumpkin. Her body needs the rest," Ben replied.

"Is she sick daddy?" Brock, now awake, decided to join the conversation.

"Not anymore. She was very sick for a while. She has medicine to help her out now," Ben patiently explained.

Kaira finally came down and entered the kitchen. "Good morning, sunshine," Scott greeted her as he was putting the pan of water on the stove. Kaira just snarled at him.

She walked over to the fridge and pulled out a Boost. "So where's the trespasser at?" she quipped.

"I see you and your aunt have had a nice discussion. Diana is not a trespasser, she wanted to leave last night. I wouldn't let her," Ben sternly stated.

"Don't let her leave, Daddy…I like her," Kora stated.

"You don't even know her," Kaira quipped. Ben gave his daughter a look that made her clam up. Then he turned his attention to Becca.

"What? We just chatted a little before bed," Becca insisted.

"Now listen here, all of you. Ms. Henderson has been through hell and back. She is weak and needing a place to rest. I brought her here because she has no other place to go. I expect all of you to treat her with respect. Am I understood?" Ben ruled.

BJ and Brock nodded. "Yes, Daddy," Kora replied.

Ben sternly looked at Kaira. "Yes, sir," Kaira finally said. Then Ben looked at Becca.

She tried to ignore it but could feel his disapproval. "Oh…whatever," she said.

"Becca…you need to be setting the example. Do I have your understanding?" Ben reemphasized. "Yes…I will be on my best behavior," she sneered.

"I doubt that, but a little improvement would be appreciated," Ben jeered. Becca simply rolled her eyes.

"Hey, Dad, may I go play my Xbox?" BJ asked.

"Sure…go ahead." Ben smiled.

"Can I go with him, Dad?" Brock asked. Ben smiled and waved him on through.

Ben's cell started ringing. He looked to see who was calling. "I'll be out on the deck for a few minutes." He sat Kora down on one of the kitchen chairs. Scott nodded as he put some butter into the boiling water.

Becca was putting the milk away in the fridge. She looked over at Kaira and saw that she was still sulking. "I've got to get some more food here now that your dad and Uncle Scott are home. Do you want to come with me?" she asked.

Kaira looked up. "Sure, it doesn't look like we'll be doing anything fun around here."

Becca looked at Scott. "When my brother gets off the phone, tell him that Kaira and I went grocery shopping."

"No problem," Scott said over his shoulder. He was just adding the oatmeal to the boiling water.

Becca and Kaira walked out of the kitchen, leaving Kora sitting at the table by herself. Kora saw that Uncle Scott was busy and her dad was out on the deck; she carefully walked over to her dad's bedroom and opened the door. She saw the lady sleeping on the bed. She slowly walked up and stood by the bed, watching her. Then Kora climbed up on the bed behind Diana.

Ben came in from the phone call. He saw Scott still working with the oatmeal. "Where did Becca and Kaira run off too?" he asked.

"They decided to go grocery shopping," Scott stated. Ben started walking to the table. He caught a glimpse of light out of the corner of his eye. He looked toward it and saw that his bedroom door was open. He quietly walked to it and glanced in the room. Diana was still sleeping, and directly behind her, softly stroking her hair, was Kora. He walked into the room and moved over behind Diana where Kora was.

"She is very pretty, her hair is very soft," Kora said, smiling up at her daddy.

"Yes, she is, she's very beautiful. Come on, we don't want to wake her," Ben softly said.

"It's okay, Ben. I woke up when she started playing with my hair. I just didn't want to scare her," Diana softly replied. She opened her eyes and rolled over to look at Kora and Ben. "It's a good thing to wake up to. Thank you, Kora," Diana said with a smile. Diana saw that Kora had her daddy's eyes, maybe just a tad bit lighter. She had dark-brown curly hair and a dimple in her left cheek that was quite evident when she smiled. Her skin was a light-tan color. Diana figured that their mom must have had some Native American or Spanish in her background.

Kora gave her a big smile. "Will you let me play with your hair later?"

"I think that can be arranged." Diana grinned.

"All right, pumpkin, Uncle Scott has your oatmeal ready. Go get some." Ben lifted her off the bed and gave her a playful swat on her backside.

Diana watched her walk out of the room then looked over at Ben and smiled. "She's a beautiful little girl, Ben. Don't be upset with her for waking me. I needed to get up anyway."

"How are you feeling?" he asked, sitting down on the side of the bed.

"I'm okay. Did I keep you up all night?" she asked worried.

"Oh no…I went out cold once we got you settled back down." Ben smiled.

"I haven't acted that way with nightmares since I was twelve years old. I don't know why it came back last night," she said, looking up at the ceiling.

"You were extremely tired, stressed, in a strange house, with at least one person that doesn't want you here, and an evil man after you. Do you want me to keep going?" Ben jabbed.

Diana chuckled. "No, I suppose you can stop." She sat up and leaned back against the headboard.

"Did you tell Becca that it was only for a day?"

"Nope, and I don't intend to say anything. This is my house, and last I knew, I was the dad," Ben sneered.

Diana reached over and put her hand on his. "Don't be like that. She's just worried about you and the kids. To her, I'm the one who's kept you away from them for what…two almost three months."

He traced the side of his finger down the side of her face. "Come on, kitten, Scott has some oatmeal for you too. Get dressed, then we'll take care of that wrist, then you can get some food in you." Diana grimaced at the thought of putting that medication on her wrist again. Nonetheless, she got up and grabbed her stuff and went to the bathroom to get ready. Ben walked out into the kitchen where Kora was eating her oatmeal. Scott was looking at the day's paper.

"Is she going to be our new mommy?" Kora asked. Scott dropped the paper down. Ben froze where he stood. "I really like her. Can she be, Daddy, please?" Kora continued.

"I don't know, pumpkin. Things don't always work that way with grown-ups," Ben flatly stated, walking to the fridge and pulling out the milk.

"You like her, don't you?" Kora pressed.

Ben looked over at Scott, who was sitting there near to laughing out loud, seeing Ben squirm at his daughter's questions. Ben poured the milk into a glass and raised it up to his mouth. "Yes, Kora, I like her. I like her a lot." Ben saw Scott raise the paper back up. He also saw that he was snickering behind it. Ben grabbed the dish towel off the counter and flung it at Scott.

"Hey...I was just laughing at the comics," Scott jabbed.

"Huh-huh...keep it up and you'll be laughing on the other side of your head," Ben threatened.

"You haven't been able to do that for over twenty years. You think you can do it now?" Scott quipped. They heard the bedroom door open and saw Diana come out. She had pulled her wet hair back into a simple ponytail. She was wearing black jeans with a white scoop-necked T-shirt tucked in at the waist and a hunter-green sleeveless shrug. She had a black belt with silver medallion and pearl stones studded throughout the belt.

"I like the belt, Ms. Henderson," Kora stated.

"Thank you, Kora. Your daddy and your Uncle Scott insisted I get this one," Diana stated and came and knelt beside Kora. "You and your family can call me Diana."

"Diana...I like that name," Kora said softly.

Diana smiled. "Yeah...my daddy liked that name too."

"You don't like your name?" Kora assumed from Diana's statement.

"Oh...no...it's fine. I just mean my daddy chose my name," Diana replied.

"My mommy chose my name. She said that daddy made up his own names for us later. He always calls me Pumpkin," Kora inserted.

"Yeah, I noticed," Diana said, looking over her shoulder at Ben who was still leaning up against the counter, drinking his milk. Diana winked at him.

"Does Daddy use your name?" Kora wondered.

"Only when he's upset at me. Both he and your Uncle Scott use a nickname for me," Diana replied.

"Uncle Scott? I've never heard him use a nickname for me. Uncle Scott, what name do you use for Diana?" Kora requested.

"I use Milady usually," Scott quickly replied, still reading the paper.

"Milady...why?" Kora pursued. When Scott didn't answer, Kora went to ask her dad. Ben cut the conversation off.

"Diana...we need to treat that wrist. Come on over here," Ben stated. Kora looked at Diana then looked down at her wrist.

Diana stood up and cupped Kora's chin. "Your daddy wants to torment me again."

"What does *torment* mean, Daddy?" Kora replied.

"Diana was just kidding, pumpkin. She has to have medicine put on her wrist. She can't do it one-handed, so I help her with it," Ben informed her.

"Can I help?" Kora asked.

"I'm not sure that would be a good idea, Kora. The last time I looked at my wrist, it didn't look good," Diana hesitated.

"Please," Kora pleaded.

"Go grab a medium bowl. You can help pour the medicine over her wrist," Ben agreed. Diana looked at him.

"It will probably take both my hands to hold your arm still. She's an extra hand," he declared. Diana pulled her sleeve up to her elbow. Kora pulled a bowl out from the lower cabinet and put it up on the counter. Ben measured out the amount of water needed then poured the exact amount of medicine that was supposed to be added. He used a whisk to blend it together. "Your daddy looks like he's cooking pancakes," Diana told Kora.

"Nah…Daddy uses a bigger bowl to make pancakes," Kora replied.

"Oh…so your daddy can cook. I didn't know that," Diana said, surprised.

"There are a lot of things I can do that you don't know about." He turned and grinned at the two girls. "Now…I want you to sit down on the side of the chair," Ben stated, looking at Diana as he brought the bowl over to the table. He sat it down and walked over to grab a cup from the cupboard; he gave it to Kora. He pulled another chair around and sat down in front of Diana so his back was to her. He unwrapped her wrist, carefully pulling at the gauze that was sticking to her wrist. He heard Diana suck in air a couple of times.

"Eww…that looks really sore, Diana," Kora stated as her dad pulled the last of the gauze off. Scott looked over and decided he had something to do in another room. He left, saying, "I need to go check on the boys."

"Okay, pumpkin…I'm gonna hold Diana's arm still. I want you to take that cup and scoop up some of the liquid in the bowl and pour it over her wrist. Make sure you don't get any on you. Can you do that?" Ben instructed Kora.

"Sure, Daddy." Kora carefully dipped the cup into the medicine. Diana knew it was coming; she felt Ben's grip tighten on her arm. Kora started pouring the medicine over her wrist. She instantly went to pull her arm away from it, but Ben held it tight.

"God, help me," Diana whispered and clenched her teeth.

"Am I doing it wrong?" Kora asked her dad.

"Not at all, you're doing great. The medicine stings really bad. That's how it helps heal it," Ben said. Kora started pouring another cup over Diana's wrist; Ben started turning her arm so the medicine hit all the way around. Diana put her head against Ben's back then groaned. "Hang on, kitten…we're almost done," Ben encouraged. He had Kora pour three more cups over the wrist. Diana had tears streaming down her cheeks by the time they were done. "Good job, pumpkin. Now go wash your hands in the sink really quick, then you can come back here," Ben praised his daughter. He pushed the bowl back so he had room to lay Diana's wrist down on the towel. "We'll let it air-dry a little first." He turned around to see Diana's face. He put his hands on the sides of her face, using his thumbs to brush away her tears. He smiled and pulled her toward him and kissed her forehead. "Sorry, babe."

"It has to be done. I just wish it didn't burn like I'm sticking my wrist in a bowl of white-hot charcoals," Diana replied. Kora came back into the kitchen; she looked at Diana.

"Did I hurt you?" Kora said sadly.

"No, it wasn't you. You helped your daddy out a lot, thank you," Diana said and reached over and gave her a one-armed hug.

"You know what?" Kora whispered closed to Diana.

"What?" Diana whispered back.

"I heard Daddy call you Kitten," Kora said as if it was an important secret.

"Yes, yes he did. That's his nickname for me," Diana whispered back, glancing up at Ben.

"Why does he call you Kitten?" Kora asked softly.

"Well…I think that is something you need to ask your daddy. Don't you?" Diana replied.

"Daddy, why did you call Diana a Kitten?" Kora asked, walking over to him, raising her arms up for him to pick her up.

"One of our friends called her a tigress. Since she's smaller than me, I changed it to Kitten," Ben informed her as he picked her up.

"Why did he call you a tigress?" Kora asked again.

"You got your daddy's curiosity, didn't you, Kora. He called me a tigress because when people tried to hurt me, he thought I fought like a tiger. Since I'm a girl, and girl tigers are called tigresses, he calls me a tigress," Diana replied.

"People tried to hurt you?" Kora said amazed. "Is that why Daddy had to leave for so long?"

"Yes…your daddy had to come and get me. I would have died where they took me," Diana said somberly.

"Oh." Kora wiggled out of Ben's arms and came up to Diana and looked at her. She pulled on her arm so that Diana would lean down. Then she wrapped her arms around Diana's neck and gave her a big hug. Diana picked her up and held her in her arm. "I'm glad Daddy got you out before you died," Kora said as Diana put her down in her lap.

"I am too. I'm very glad he brought me here to meet all you guys." Diana smiled.

"Why don't you run downstairs and tell your Uncle Scott we're done working on Diana's wrist?" Ben asked his daughter.

"Okay." Kora slid off Diana's lap and ran downstairs.

"We'd better get this covered up before he comes back up here," Ben said as he sat down facing Diana. "It does look better than it did yesterday. Even if it didn't feel any better," Ben said as he started wrapping the gauze around. As soon as Becca and Kaira come back, we'll need to head over to the office. Zenon wants an update," Ben stated.

"I was wondering when we had to report," Diana chuckled.

Ben was just finishing wrapping Diana's wrist when Scott came back upstairs. "So what's on the schedule?" Scott asked. Diana got up and picked up the bowl that the guys sat out for her to use. She put some oatmeal in it, added brown sugar and some raisins, then added a little milk. She turned and sat back down at the table.

"As soon as Becca and Kaira come back, we have to head into the office. They'll give an ETA on when Taggee and the girls will get here. Then we'll have to find a place to hide everybody," Ben plotted out. He saw Diana go into her own mind; he walked over and started kneading her shoulders with his thumbs. It brought her back to the current conversation.

"I don't think Taggee is a target. Mahdi's preference is women, specifically and apparently…me," Diana commented. They heard the front door open and the girls giggling and walking through the house. It all came to a screeching halt as soon as Becca entered the kitchen. Diana put on a good face. "Good morning, ma'am."

"It's good to see you up and awake," Becca coldly stated.

"Thank you. Is there something I can do to help?" Diana inquired.

"No, thank you. Kaira and I have it under control," Becca replied over her shoulder. "Just sit back and enjoy your neck rub." Ben didn't realize he was still working Diana's shoulders. Even still, she was out of line.

"Becca, I think—" Ben was cut off by Diana turning and putting her hands and his arm.

"I think I'm going to go see what games the boys are playing since the ladies of the house have it all under control," Diana injected. She stood up, placed the bowl and spoon by the sink, and walked toward the door she saw Scott come out of and headed down the stairs.

"Kaira...I need you to go downstairs as well," Ben enforced. Kaira knew better than to argue. She put the cans down and headed downstairs.

Diana didn't like the fact that she was coming between Ben and his sister. There was nothing she could do about it at this time though. She rounded the corner and listened for the sound of kids playing. She followed the sound to where the boys and Kora were. "Did Daddy wrap your wrist back up?" Kora asked.

"Yes, he did. It's all covered now," Diana stated.

BJ paused the game and looked at Diana's wrists. "Your wrists were tied, weren't they?" BJ had his daddy's brown hair color, but his eyes were turquoise. His complexion was fairer than his baby sister's. The shape of his face was quite similar to his dad's though, and he looked like he would be just as tall as his dad.

"Why do you say that?" Diana inquired.

"You have one wrist wrapped and the other has a mark around it," he stated easily.

"Yes...I have rope burns on my wrists. Or at least is started out as rope burns," Diana simply replied.

"So why were you tied up?" Diana heard from the doorway. She looked behind her and saw Kaira walking in. Kaira had dark-brown hair like Kora. Diana didn't know if it was natural or dyed. She figured Kaira had used a straightener on it, so her hair must be curly as well. Her eyes were green, like the color of the spring grass. Her skin was tan like Kora's, but the shape of her face was longer, thinner than Kora's or BJ's.

"I didn't want to be where I was, so I tried to escape. They caught me and tied me down." Diana tried to be careful not to give too much information but still answered their questions. She figured the more they wanted to talk to her, the better it may be.

"Why didn't you just hold still?" Kaira questioned.

"I was trying to free myself from the ropes. I needed to move around to loosen them enough to attempt to pull my hands out," Diana continued.

"Daddy said that you almost died," Brock spoke up. Brock was the mix of his mom and dad, Diana figured. He had his dad's light-brown hair, but his eyes were green like Kaira's with the darker skin tone of his twin sister. Even though he was very young, Diana figured he has his dad's body structure.

"Yes…I was very sick. Your daddy took care of me during that time until the Lord came and touched me," Diana informed them.

"Well, if he healed you, why is your wrist all bandaged?" Kaira sneered.

"This was reinjured while I was on a ship," Diana quipped back.

"What happened?" Brock asked.

"A sailor on the ship wanted to…umm, wanted me to go to a dance with him. I said I didn't want to dance. He didn't accept my answer. He grabbed my wrist and made it tear open. It became infected, and now it has to heal from the inside out," Diana ended.

"Why doesn't God heal it now?" Kora asked.

"Sometimes, God has us go through things that we don't understand, because we don't know His purpose. Sometimes things happen to us just because Adam and Eve fell. We just have to trust that God knows best and believe He is in control," Diana replied.

Diana sat down at the table that was in the room. BJ started playing the game again; Brock sat watching.

Kora watched for a little bit but then turned and asked, "Can I play with your hair again?"

"Sure…if you want to," Diana replied. Kora jumped up and ran over to her and started to comb through her hair with her fingers. Diana reached up and took out the ponytail holder.

Kora was very excited. "I'll be right back."

"Okay…not a problem," Diana acknowledged. A few minutes later, Kora came running back in, carrying a brush and handfuls of hair ties and barrettes. Kora went to town working on Diana's hair. Kaira watched her for a little while but soon joined Kora, showing her how to braid or work with one tie or another. Fifteen minutes later, Ben walked into the room. He smiled at what his girls were doing to Diana's hair. They were actually playing with her.

"I hate to break up the 'makeover' session, but I need Diana to come with Uncle Scott and I. We'll be back later for you girls to continue," Ben smoothly stated.

"Aww…Dad…you're taking all our fun away," Kaira said. Ben just smiled and signaled Diana to come.

"I'd better go girls…sorry," Diana stated as she started taking the ties and barrettes out. Kaira and Kora helped her. Soon her hair was loose and down. She stood up and walked out the door with Ben. They met up with Scott in the kitchen; Diana saw that Becca was busy working on getting everything put away. She also saw that Becca had been crying. "We'll be back as soon as we can," Ben coldly told Becca.

Diana looked up at Ben then over to Scott; she grimaced and quietly walked out with the guys. She knew it was best to stay quiet and out of the discussion that Ben had with his sister. Ben guided her to the car, opened the door for her, and waited for her to climb in. Then he shut the door and climbed into the driver's seat.

34

Downtown Des Moines

God…what can I do? How can I help the situation?" she prayed. Just then the song "Sometimes He Calms the Storm" came over the radio. Diana felt God's arms wrap around her; she understood. There was nothing she could do. She was to be quiet and wait for God to deal with it. The trio didn't say anything the whole time they were in the car. A few times she caught Ben looking at her in the review mirror, but all she saw was sadness in his eyes.

Ben knew that it bothered Diana that she was causing problems between his sister and him. He was also sure that she saw that Becca had been crying when she came upstairs. He didn't want to be that hard on Becca, but she was out of line and had no intention of changing her stand. He glanced back at Diana through the review mirror; she saw him but looked away. He could see the questions, the feeling of guilt running through her head. He would have to talk to her as well, or she'll beat herself up for Becca's problem. Ben turned the corner; the office was just a few blocks away. Diana and Becca's issues will have to wait till later. Ben parked the car across the street from the DHS office building. He got out and opened the door for Diana to get out. She paused a minute, looking at the building. "Are you okay kitten?" Ben asked as he shut the door.

"Hmm? Oh yeah…I was just thinking, remembering, I guess," Diana replied distractedly.

"A lot's happened since that first day we met. I wish it would have been in different circumstances," Ben stated as he started guiding Diana toward the office.

"I wonder if Dick is here today. It's Saturday…you suppose he'll be off today?" Scott hoped.

"Nah...he'll be here. We have Diana with us, remember?" Ben teased. Diana glared at Ben, who just winked at her.

She shook her head. "Scott...if he gets out of hand, do you think you can use those hands of yours and put him down to the floor?"

Scott grinned widely. "I think that can be arranged."

"Now, children, he's not as bad as all that," Ben chuckled. Diana and Scott stopped and stared at him. "Okay...so he is that bad, but he does have a good side too." The trio walked up the stairs together. Ben opened the door for Diana and Scott to go in. Then he guided them to the main office. Diana walked in first. She glanced around at the men working at their desks. Two of the desks were empty; she figured one was probably Ben's desk. Ben took her arm and escorted her to Zenon's office in the back. Scott followed them.

Zenon's office had the blinds closed and the door shut. Ben knocked on the door. "Yes?" Charles called out.

Ben opened the door. "We're just checking in, sir."

"Come on in Ben, bring the others in with you," Charles ordered. Ben opened the door wide and brought Diana in with him. He pointed for Diana to head for the open chair. He watched Scott enter then closed the door. As he predicted, Dick was there and standing near the window. Diana saw that there was another man there when she entered the room—a man that was setting of an alarm in her head; she wasn't feeling the cold, heavy, presence that seemed to be the norm lately, but an alarm was going off nonetheless. Agent Zenon signaled for her to take the empty chair, so she sat down next to the stranger. He looked very familiar, but she couldn't put her finger on it.

"Gentlemen...Ms. Henderson, this is Agent Kal with the FBI. He and his partner have been involved in the project pretty near the start," Charles introduced.

"Yep...I remember him," Scott injected. Ben nodded. Zenon looked at the guys with a question on his face.

"Agent Kal came to the cabin looking for suspects with the kidnapping/murder of the lady earlier," Ben filled in. Charles nodded in understanding then started the session. Ben and Scott filled him in with what happened and what was done while in Syria. Dick explained what he had to do to achieve success at the embassy. Agent Kal went over what the FBI was doing to help Taggee and the girls to get asylum in the States. Charles wanted an explanation of the events on the USS *Wilson* and at the airport in New York.

Diana sat quietly listening and watching Agent Kal. Something wasn't right with him, but she couldn't put her finger on it. Agent Kal asked; "Ms. Henderson, are you staying at Agent Tigere's house?"

"I'm staying in the city, yes," Diana replied coldly. Ben and Scott looked at her, studying her. Scott noticed her posture, her demeanor—she didn't trust Agent Kal. Ben was reading her as well. She was on edge; something was alerting her. It was because of that they were both careful what information was given.

Dick was oblivious. "Isn't Ben taking care of you Ms. Henderson?"

"He has seen that I am taken care of," Diana carefully replied. Dick looked at Ben for clarification. Ben scowled and shook his head no. Dick thought maybe he and Diana were fighting and she was at a hotel now. He would find out later.

Charles asked if there was more to discuss. When nobody added anything, he figured the meeting was over, but nobody seemed to want to leave. Agent Kal's cell phone started to ring. "Excuse me," he said and walked out of the room.

Once he was out of the room and the door was closed, Charles asked, "Okay, Ben, what's going on?" Ben looked at Diana; she grimaced a little.

"There's something not right with Agent Kal. Until I figure it out, I didn't want to give out too much information," Ben explained.

Charles looked at Diana. "You are staying at Ben's house, aren't you?" Diana nodded. "That reminds me. Agent Thomas passed along an order from his doctor. He wants Diana to see her doctor here in three days to check that wrist," he continued. Diana shuddered and grimaced.

Dick chimed in. "Did you really take out that sailor?"

"He gave me no choice. All he would have had to do was let go of my arm and leave me alone," Diana firmly stated.

"There is a reason why Taggee calls her a tigress. Don't corner her, or you will be sorry," Scott laughed.

Charles wasn't humored with the statement. "Where were Ben and Scott? You shouldn't have had to defend yourself in the first place."

"The first time I dealt with our dense sailor, Ben and Scott were dealing with five or so other sailors. The second time…well, I really didn't think I needed an escort to dump my tray the next morning. I figured those sailors were still in the brig. I was obviously wrong," Diana defended. "As it was, Ben and Scott would have wound up in the brig themselves if it wasn't for another sailor's video cam. I would have had no escort at all if that had happened," she ended.

"Like Dick here, the captain had a hard time believing Diana could do the damage she did. It took physical evidence to show him. He thought she was covering for us," Ben calmly stated.

"Would you cover for the guys, Ms. Henderson?" Charles asked suspiciously.

Diana looked directly at Director Zenon. "I haven't found a reason or need to, Director Zenon. However, let me just make this extremely clear. I don't and won't lie," Diana stated indignantly.

"I meant no offense, ma'am," Charles replied.

"She may leave out some information when it suits her, however," Ben threw in.

"Oh, whatever…Ben," Diana quipped.

Agent Kal came back into the room; Diana shut down immediately. "Sorry about that. The three Syrians that came from the compound will be arriving at the airport around ten thirty tonight. Do we have a plan for where they will stay?" Agent Kal asked.

"Agent Richman has that all taken care of, right, Agent?" Charles stated.

"Yes sir. I have it all planned out," Dick replied.

"I would love to know what your office has planned," Agent Kal pushed.

"For reasons of protection and security, we feel it is best to keep as few as possible aware of the exact details. You have my word that they will be taken care of," Ben coldly stated.

"Director Zenon, it was my understanding that your office and the FBI would be working together on this case. This information would help us to protect all that are involved," Agent Kal injected.

"I understand, but at this point in time, I agree with Agent Tigere. We've had trouble earlier in this case that put Ms. Henderson in grave danger. I would just as soon avoid having her go through that again," Charles countered.

"I would greatly appreciate that," Diana injected.

Agent Kal was getting furious, but he knew that he would go no farther with the current group. He would have to have his supervisor lay down the law. "Fine. You will let us know as soon as you can, correct?" he said annoyed.

"Of course, Agent Kal. As soon as it is for sure safe, we will inform the FBI," Charles assured.

Agent Kal left the room and slammed the door. Scott peeked out the blinds and watched him leave the office all together. "Okay, he's clear," Scott stated.

"So what do we have planned, gentlemen?" Charles asked.

"There's an interesting question. The plan at this time is that Dick would pick up Taggee and the girls and bring them to my house. Since they are coming in so late, Diana, Taggee, and the girls will stay overnight. Here's the sticky point. Mahdi is in the States and looking for Diana again. I wouldn't put it past him to go looking for the girls as well, especially if he can't find Diana. So…we need a place for all of us to hide out in. Scott's cabin is out of the question now," Ben stated

Diana piped up, "Ben…your house is out with Becca and your kids there. There is too much danger for them."

Charles nodded in agreement. "A hotel would be too obvious," he added.

"So where does that leave us?" Scott questioned.

"Don't look at me. I've only got a one-room flat over on Broadwell," Dick stated.

"Well, that leaves us only one possibility. You'll have to stay at my family's vacation house to the northeast. It will have the space you need, and for the most part, it's easily protected. The lake will be the only weak spot," Charles settled on.

"Are you sure that will be okay?" Ben asked.

"It's the only option we have. Just don't go trashing the place," Charles insisted.

"They'll behave," Diana inserted. The guys all turned and stared at her. "If I can keep twenty kids in order in a twenty-by-twenty-foot room, Aisha and I can keep two big teenagers under control. Especially if Taggee is there," Diana observed.

"Who's the one that draws trouble to her like a magnet?" Ben quipped. Diana stuck her tongue out at him. He acted like he had a notepad in his hand and pretended like he added a tally. Diana tightened her lips and bit down on them then looked down to the floor.

Scott shook his head. "I guess you're right, bro, old habits are too hard to break." Dick and Charles just looked at the trio. They had no clue what was going on, and it was quite obvious the three of them weren't going to tell them.

"Well, now that that problem is solved—oh…we have your stuff from the cabin. After we processed the cabin, I had them bring it here. It's over in the evidence lockup. Take it with you before you leave. Now, was there anything else that needs to be dealt with?" Charles requested.

"The only thing on the agenda is getting some food into Diana," Ben replied.

"I'm not hungry right now…I'm fine," Diana insisted. Ben and Scott scowled at her. "Oh, whatever…you're going to shove it down me anyway."

"See, Scott, she's learning. It just takes some discipline," Ben jeered. Diana glared at him but kept her mouth under control. Scott put his hand up to his mouth to cover the fact that he was actually laughing at her.

"Okay…go get some lunch. I'll have the house ready for your arrival tomorrow morning. I'll meet you there to give you the keys," Charles concluded.

"Let's go troop," Ben commanded. "I'll see you tonight, Dick."

"Catch ya later, Tiger," Dick replied. The trio left the office and headed for the evidence lockup to gather their stuff. Diana saw her pillow and grabbed it. It took her a while to find her suitcase. Scott grabbed it and his backpack. Ben grabbed his laptop and the other backpack. They signed for their stuff and headed for the car. Ben again opened the door for Diana to climb in. He then opened the trunk and he and Scott threw the luggage in; then they climbed in.

Ben started driving, turning onto the interstate. "Where are we heading to?" Diana asked.

"Home…Becca is supposed to have lunch ready when we get there," Ben flatly stated. He glanced in the review mirror to see Diana. She was looking out the window, but in truth, she was lost inside her head again. "Kitten? Climb out of that hole and talk to me," Ben chided.

"I don't want to cause more problems," Diana softly stated.

"It's not you, at least not directly. As you have said toward yourself, it's in her mind," Ben continued. Diana just bit her bottom lip as if she didn't really believe that totally.

She leaned her head back. She grimaced a little bit. Scott happened to look back at her at that time. "She's hurting again," Scott quietly told Ben.

Ben glanced in the review mirror at Diana. "You didn't take any pain meds this morning, did you?"

Diana looked up at Ben. "Nope, I don't want to take that stuff until I have to. I took it last night while you and your family were eating ice cream. The next thing I know, I'm waking up from a horrific dream, in a strange room, and a strange bed. I don't want a repeat."

"Obviously, her body is innocent in more ways than one," Ben smiled. "We'll get some 'baby' meds when we get home," he teased. Diana gave him a raspberry. Ben and Scott chuckled. Twenty minutes later, Ben pulled up into the driveway of his house. He opened the door for Diana and held his hand out for her to take to climb out. Diana took his hand, her pillow in the other arm. She stood for a moment looking at the house, then shook her head as if to clear it. She turned and followed Ben and Scott who had grabbed the bags and packs out of the trunk. They walked into the house together. Diana followed Ben to his bedroom and left her pillow on the bed. Ben put her suitcase and his pack on the floor in the closet. When he turned around, he saw Diana was looking for something in her toiletry bag. "What are you looking for, kitten?"

"My aspirin. My wrist is really hurting me right now," Diana stated plainly.

Ben walked up to her and held out his hand. "Let me see it." Diana looked at him suspiciously but let him have her wrist. He took it and opened her hand, palm-side up, and started massaging it, working with his thumbs, starting at the lower part of the palm then out toward the fingers.

At first, Diana flinched a little; but as he continued, it hurt her less and less. By the time he finished, she was relaxed, and her wrist didn't hurt as much. "How does that work?" Diana asked. Ben smiled at her but kept working on her hand. He saw her close her eyes and take in a deep breath.

He was just about ready to stop when he hear Kaira at the doorway. "I haven't seen you do that since mom was here," she observed.

Ben stayed calm and made no attempt to hide what he was doing. "Diana was in a lot of pain. I was just helping her with it," Ben injected, still working on her hand. He was starting to ease up with it now.

"Aunt Becca said you two were to come to lunch. It's all ready," Kaira continued.

"Thank you, Kaira, we'll be right there," Diana softly stated.

Ben looked over at her; she was reading him. "What are you searching for?" he softly asked Diana.

"Making sure you weren't feeling hurt from doing this," Diana whispered. "I don't want to cause you more pain," she said, looking down at her hand.

Ben stopped massaging her hand and lifted her chin to make her look at him. "The only pain you cause me is when you shut me out," Ben calmly stated. He saw the words sink deep into her, causing her to turn into herself. Ben traced her face with his fingers; it brought her back out. He pulled her into his arms and started stroking her back.

"I don't mean to push you away. There's so much. I'm afraid you'll not understand," Diana finally stated softly.

Finally…a break. It's a small one…but I'll take it, Ben said to himself.

"Ahem!" Diana and Ben turned to see Becca standing at the doorway. "Your lunch is getting cold. I suggest you two go get something to eat," Becca steamed.

Ben felt Diana recoil at the resentment in Becca's tone. She wanted to leave his embrace because of it, but Ben held her there. "Thank you, Becca…we'll be right there," Ben calmly stated.

Becca turned and stormed off, mumbling something under her breath. Ben just shook his head. Diana put her head down against Ben's chest. Ben reached under and lifted her face toward him. He saw the worry in her eyes. "She'll come around…give her time." Diana just blinked and gave a quick nod of her head. "We'd better go get some grilled cheese and soup before the kids eat it all," Ben teased. Diana smiled at him. They headed out to the kitchen and grabbed their sandwiches and soup. Diana grinned; she thought her family was the only one that ate tomato soup with grilled cheese sandwiches. She grabbed a sandwich then she saw that Ben had grabbed a cup out of the cupboard for his soup. He looked over and asked "Do you want one?"

"Yes, please," she smiled. He handed her a cup and waited for her to fill her cup with soup. She only put a couple of ladles in.

"You can have more than that, you know," he quipped.

"Yeah, but I figure if I get through all this, I'll come and get some more," she stated as she ripped her sandwich in half and dipped part of it into her soup.

"Come on…let's go sit down," he stated over his shoulder. She followed him into the living room. The kids were scattered around. BJ and Kaira each had a recliner, Scott had taken one side of a couch, Kora and Brock were down on the floor, Becca was sitting in a barrel chair; it left a love seat and the other side of Scott's couch to sit in. Diana decided it would be safest and less confrontational for her to take the opposite side of Scott's couch. She'd let Ben have the love seat, but Ben had other things in mind. He reached down and put his hand in the middle of Diana's back. He guided her over to the love seat. She sat down then Ben joined her. Diana looked down at Kora and Brock; she smiled as she watched them carefully eat their sandwiches. In truth, she was avoiding looking over at Becca; she knew she would be fuming.

"Do you like grilled cheese sandwiches?" Kora asked Diana.

"Yes…yes, I do. Especially when I have tomato soup with it," Diana replied.

Brock spoke up. "I don't like tomato soup."

Diana grinned. "You wanna know what?"

Brock looked up and looked at Diana. "What?"

"I didn't like tomato soup when I was little either," Diana stated.

"Did you have to eat it anyway?" Brock asked. Diana shook her head. "No, Mom made my dad and me chicken noodle soup instead. My dad didn't like tomato soup as well."

"We eat what is put before us here," Becca stabbed. Diana saw that Brock was hoping that he could have a different type of soup.

He looked up at her. "You have to do the rules of the house." Diana smiled to take the edge off. She finished her sandwich then drank her soup. She got up and carried it to the kitchen and rinsed the cup out; then she came back into the living room.

Kora had climbed up next to her dad; Diana wasn't going to push her out. Ben saw Diana coming back in. "Hop up and let Diana have her seat back, pumpkin."

"She just wants to be near you, Daddy," Becca chided.

"It's fine, Ben, I'll sit over here by Scott," Diana added.

"Kitten," Ben smoothly said in a warning voice. Diana looked over at him; he held up his hand and signaled for her to come to him.

Diana sighed and walked over to the love seat. "Why don't we do this?" Diana stated. She picked up Kora, turned, and sat down and let Kora sit in her lap.

"Daddy…can we watch a movie?" Kora asked.

Ben looked at his watch. "Isn't it nap time?"

"Aw, Daddy, can't we watch a movie first then we'll go take a nap?" Brock moaned.

"That depends. What movie do you want to watch?" Ben asked.

"I want *Frozen*," Kora piped up.

"No. Not again. We watched it last night," Kaira and BJ groaned.

"How about *Hook*?" Brock asked.

"Aw…do we have to?" Kora quipped.

"Let's get a shorter one," Ben asserted.

"How about *Rapunzel*?" Becca chimed in. The girls agreed, BJ just rolled his eyes, Brock just pouted. Kora jumped down from Diana's lap and ran over to grab the DVD. Kaira put it in and started it up. Kora jumped back up into Diana's lap. Ben saw that Becca was upset at that, but he didn't mind it at all. BJ pulled out his Kindle and started working on something with it. Kaira went back to her chair. Brock started off on the floor but soon he climbed up into his dad's lap. They were only halfway through the movie before Brock went to sleep. Ben turned him to lie across his right arm. He reached over and put his left arm over the top of the love seat, behind Diana's head. He started to play with her hair. Kora was out fifteen minutes later. She was leaning on Diana's left arm, her head against Diana's chest. Brock jerked his leg and accidently hit Diana's wrist. She quickly jerked it up and laid it across Kora's lap.

"You okay?" Ben worried.

"Oh yeah, he didn't hit it hard. I just wanted to give him more room," Diana replied. Ben looked into her eyes; they were a calming blue and totally content. He stroked his hand down her cheek.

Once the movie ended, Ben stood up with Brock in his arms; "BJ, do you want to carry Kora up to her bed for me?"

"I can get her, Ben,' Becca spoke up. She walked over to Diana and paused. Diana just moved her arms so Becca could get a hold of her easier. Becca reached down and lifted her up and followed Ben upstairs.

35

Ben's House

Diana saw that BJ was still looking at the Kindle. "Are you playing a game or reading a book?"

"Reading a book," BJ replied.

"What are you reading?" Diana asked.

"Just a book," he stated. Diana took the hint and let it go at that. Kaira had just looked up then went back to painting her nails. Diana got up and walked to the kitchen. She checked the electric kettle for water then pushed the button to turn it on. Then she started looking for some tea. She found some; it wasn't chamomile tea, but it would work. She looked out the window and saw the deck. She went and grabbed a cup from the cupboard, put the tea bag in it, and poured the now-boiling water in it. She went and grabbed a saucer and a spoon, pulled the tea bag out, and added milk and sugar to it. Then she walked out onto the deck. She saw there was a porch swing over on the side of the deck. She walked over and sat down on it, bringing her legs up so that she was sitting sideways, and sipped her tea.

"Are we content now?" she heard from the side of the house.

"Momentarily so," she quipped back. She glanced over and saw Ben leaning with his shoulder up against the side of the door. He smiled at her and then walked over and sat down on the swing. "What's Scott up to?"

"He went up to the guest room. I'm figuring he's probably catching a few Zs before tonight," Ben replied as he pulled Diana's legs over his lap.

"How is it that you massaging my hand helped my wrist?" she wondered.

"It's based off a holistic medicine. The idea is that by working certain areas of the body—like the hands, feet, or even the neck—you can increase the blood flow, which decreases the swelling in various areas of the body," Ben informed her.

"I'll have to read up on that. It worked very well." Diana smiled. She took another sip of tea then looked over at Ben. He was lost in thought. "Did that bring back memories?"

"No. Not at all," Ben stated then looked at Diana. Her eyebrow was arched up, and an analyzing look was on her face as she took another sip of tea. "You don't believe that, do you?"

Diana smiled. "You went somewhere, so I question it…yes."

"I was thinking that I need to install a swimming pool in the backyard," Ben jabbed.

"Hmm, and what would Becca say about that?" she jeered back. Ben just shrugged. They sat there a few minutes quietly, rocking back and forth. Diana finished her tea and sat it down on the deck.

"Come over here, I've got a few questions." Ben motioned for Diana to switch positions. Diana turned around and put her back up against Ben's side. He wrapped his arm around her waist. "I know you listen to Celtic music, what other styles do you listen to?"

"It would be easier to list what I don't listen to. I don't like screaming, grunge, or most rap because of its vulgarity. It really depends on how I'm feeling what I'm listening to," she informed him.

"Let's say right now, what would you be listening to?" Ben asked.

"Right now, I'd probably have classical or instrumental going. Something soft so we could talk over it," she stated. "If I'm driving in my car, some fast '80s or hard rock. What about you? What do you listen to?"

"I like classical or instrumental in small doses. I listen to the '80s a lot," Ben accounted.

"What's your favorite '80s singer or band?" Diana inquired.

"Hmm, Whitesnake, or Huey Lewis and the News are good. Bryan Adams, Duran Duran are up there too," Ben listed.

"Good groups. I'd have to add Gloria Estafan, Rick Astley, Kenny Logins, and Journey in there for me. Heart is another one," she added.

"Okay…here's another one. Are you a night owl or an early bird?" Ben queried.

"By nature, I'm a night owl. However, the Lord has seen to it that I have had early morning jobs. So I have to be an early bird for them," she replied. "And you?"

"I'm a night owl," Ben added. He looked over and saw her grinning. "And what thought crossed there?"

Diana chuckled, "How interesting it could be if two night owls got together."

"Hmm, two night owls together, yeah that would be interesting, wouldn't it." Ben smiled. He was glad she had no holds and willingly shared her thought. Now if he could just get her to tell him the rest. They went back and forth finding out the simple things that neither knew about the other.

"What's your favorite color?" Diana threw in.

"Hmm, dark greens are okay. But I like blues a lot," he stated. "And you?"

"I like jewel tones: the dark purple, dark green, dark red, and dark blue. If I had to name only one, it would be blue," Diana replied. "How about this one: favorite dessert?"

"I really don't have a favorite. I like sugar," Ben quipped. Diana reached over and pinched his thigh. "Hey now, you'll get into trouble, kitten. I already know your favorite dessert," he teased.

"You know one of them, you don't know the others," Diana jested.

"Oh…there's more?" Ben said excitedly.

"Easy, Tiger, you wouldn't want your sister to have a conniption. Although the one is my very favorite, it is rarely available. I also like dark chocolate and cheesecake," Diana informed him.

"I can arrange it so that the other dessert is always available," Ben teased. He felt her heart rate jump up.

"Are you wanting to put me in a sugar coma? That might be a difficult task, sir," Diana jabbed back.

"That's an idea, it would keep you out of trouble," Ben jeered.

"You and I both know you would be in a heap of pain trying to get me into one," Diana jested. They heard the front doorbell go off. Diana froze for a second; she was searching to see if it was good or bad. She relaxed, she didn't hear any warnings. Ben slid his arm out from around Diana's waist and headed inside. While he was gone, Diana disappeared into the thoughts that were swimming in her head.

Kaira answered the door. There was a policeman standing there. "Is your mom or dad home?"

Kaira yelled. "Daddy!" She heard her dad coming from the kitchen.

"Yeah, squirt, who is it?" Ben asked as he rounded the corner. "Ali… hey, I was about to call you. How can I help you?" he asked as he shook his hand.

"I have a person here that says he belongs to one of the people in the house. Would it be okay to have it checked out?" Ali stated officially.

"Ah…as far as I know all mine are accounted for," Ben stated puzzled.

"You may need to go inside to see if anybody recognizes you," Ali said to someone off to the side. He signaled for the person to step inside.

Ben recognized him immediately. Jared stepped into the hallway; Ali came in behind him. "Oh…yeah, I think that this person may belong to someone here. Go ahead and close the door, and I'll see if I can find that person," Ben said with a grin. He looked down at his daughter to have her go get Diana, but she was all starry eyed at this tall, brown-haired, blue-eyed boy that came in. "Just a minute and be right back," Ben said. He walked out to the deck where Diana was. "Kitten, I think I may have a treat for you. Come with me a second." He smiled.

Diana studied him. *He's too happy for it to be bad*, she thought. She got up and followed Ben back inside. It only took a second for her to hear his voice talking to Kaira. She looked over at Ben who smiled and winked at her; she ran through the kitchen and down the hall. "Budder!" she yelled as she ran over and grabbed hold of him, giving him a hug. He leaned down and hugged her back. "I've missed you guys so much," she said as tears were running down her cheeks.

"It's good to finally get to see you," he said. "You've lost a lot of weight, I could probably pick you up now." He looked over to Ben with a frown.

Scott came down from the guest bedroom. "I am assuming I'm in the presence of one of Milady's family members."

Diana let go of Jared. "Jared and Ali, this is Scott, he's Ben's best friend. He went with Ben to get me out. Scott, this is my nephew, Jared, and my good friend, Ali."

"I'm glad to meet you two. She has been missing her family terribly," Scott said as he shook Jared's and Ali's hands.

"How's Nana and Papa?" Diana asked Jared.

"They're okay. They would be a lot better if they knew where you were and when you could come back home," Jared stated with a little fire in his eyes.

"I see the apple doesn't fall far from the tree." Scott smiled at Ben.

"They took after their aunt quite well," Ben concurred.

"I told her family I could pull this off if I had Jared come with me. I knew your boy was about the same age. Those who didn't know the families wouldn't know if he was one of your boy's friends or not," Ali stated. He looked over at Jared. "I can't stay, that would throw the scam off. I'll be back in a half hour or so to pick you up."

"Thank you Ali," Diana said as she went over to give him a hug. "Jared's right, you're nothing but bones, girl. Are they not feeding you?" Ali questioned.

"You'd better clear this up, Kitten, or your adopted brother and nephew are going to bury me," Ben chided.

"The guys have been almost force-feeding me. I went almost two weeks without food over there, so I just don't feel like eating. It's not their fault," Diana assured.

Ali looked at Ben and Scott. "Yeah, I know, she's stubborn as all get-out. I'll be back later." He slapped Jared on the back and went to open the door. Ben walked over and guided Diana over into the living room so she wouldn't be seen when the door was opened. Scott walked behind Ali and started closing the door. He glanced down the road and saw a black SUV down a block. He thought it was odd, but he didn't want to alarm Diana yet.

Ben saw Scott pause a moment when he shut the door. Scott nodded toward the direction of the SUV. Ben glanced over and saw that Diana was busy catching up with Jared, so he moved over to the den's window and looked out. It looked like it might be FBI surveillance, but he would have to get closer to check it out. "You want to go, or me?" Ben asked Scott.

"She'll know if you disappear. I'll get a closer look. If I'm not back in five, you'd better scoot out of here with her," Scott replied. Diana noticed that Ben and Scott were talking quietly in the den. Something was up, but she didn't want to alert the kids and especially Jared. She kept on as if nothing was off.

"So how long have you been back?" Jared asked.

"I got back to the States on Friday. I had to stay over a night in New York to catch a flight here. I didn't get back to Des Moines until late last night," Diana replied.

"And they couldn't let you call Nana or Papa?" Jared steamed.

Diana put her hand on his arm. "Jared, I'm not out of it yet. They were worried that someone would leak where I am. They're just trying to make sure I don't have another plane ride. Do you understand?"

"You can't be with your family, but he can be with his?" Jared fired while looking up at Ben, who was standing by the post.

Maybe in a couple of years, we can recruit him for the DHS. He's got the look down already, Ben thought

"His family was supposed to be with their grandparents. We have to leave here tomorrow. We are waiting for two more ladies that are in danger as well. They'll be here tonight," Diana said quietly. She didn't know if Ben had told his kids yet or not.

"Hey, Jared, why don't you and your aunt come out to the back deck," Ben suggested. He knew Diana was trying to be careful what she said. But Jared was going to need more information. Out back, they could talk freer. Diana and Jared started walking down the hallway. "Would you like some coffee or milk or something to drink?" Ben asked Jared as he passed him.

"Do you have any root beer?" Jared asked.

"Yep...I do. I'll get you a glass. Diana, do you want some more tea?" Ben stated.

"Yes, please, I'll bring my cup back in and get it," she replied. She led Jared out to the swing and grabbed her tea cup. "I'll be right back," she assured Jared. She came into the kitchen and started working on her tea. Ben was getting a glass of ice for Jared's root beer. "Where did Scott go?" Diana asked Ben.

Ben turned and grabbed a can of pop as if nothing was going on. "He had to do an errand. He'll be right back," Ben easily stated.

She looked at him, searching him. He looked over at her and traced his finger down her face. "Don't worry, he'll be right back. Let's go get your nephew calmed down before he throws you over his shoulder and takes you home."

Diana figured she'd find out the rest later. They headed back out to talk with Jared. "Okay...kiddo. You can talk freely out here. Fire away," Ben stated with a smile.

"Let's start with her wrists," Jared sternly stated.

"Some of that was my doing, Jared. I tried to get away and caused a ruckus, they had to tie me down. But even with that, I was trying to get out of it and caused several rope burns. Then while on the ship to get back home, there was a confrontation, and the right wrist got torn open. Now it's infected, and I have to let it heal from the inside out. Most of the burns are like on my left wrist. They are almost healed," Diana told him.

Jared's next question was, "Why were you taken?"

"An insane man over in the Middle East thought that since I was virgin and could not have children of my own, I was the perfect subject for him to use to bring about a messiah. The child was to be born as an American citizen, with claims of being the reincarnated Mohammad, with ancestry tracing back to the Hebrew and Arabic nations. In his mind, the child would bring about a jihad and unite the three main religions," Diana continued.

"And you losing so much weight?" Jared scowled.

"As you very well know, I can't drink water from just anywhere, nor can I eat certain spices or foods. That's all they had there. I went almost two weeks without food and three days without water," Diana said carefully.

"Three days without water and you would be dead," Jared doubted.

"She did almost die," Ben injected. "Her kidneys shut down. I wasn't allowed to go over right away. I got there on her third day of no water. The Lord had to come down and touch her so that her kidneys would work again."

"But you're not over there now, why are you not eating now?" Jared directed his question directly at Diana.

"I'm just not hungry most of the time. Ben and Scott are constantly after me to eat. I just don't really want to," Diana stated.

"Have her make some homemade bread. She won't leave it alone. She'll gain some weight then," Jared inserted, looking at Ben.

"I'm willing to try that." Ben smiled at Diana. Diana just rolled her eyes. They heard a fox cry just to the side of the house. Ben saw Diana smile and relax a little. *She's starting to learn the calls*, he thought. "If you'll excuse me, I'll be right back," Ben said to the two and walked inside.

"What about the fact that you're not out of it yet?" Jared asked. Diana saw the concern in his eyes.

"The insane man had a second in command named Mahdi. He loves to beat on women until they are broken. I'm his next target. He thinks he can break my spirit," Diana softly stated.

"Is he in the US?" Jared asked. Diana nodded. "Is he in this town?" Jared pushed.

"That, I'm not sure of yet. It is possible, but I hope not," Diana replied.

"Why don't you go back and visit Cousin Rita in Nebraska? If he's here, leave this place," Jared inserted.

"Rita is still in the process of unpacking boxes from the move. Truth be told, he will find me no matter where I go. I don't want to put Rita and her kids in danger. I didn't want to put Ben's kids in danger. They weren't supposed to be here now. That's why they have not allowed me to even call you guys. The danger is very high," Diana stated as a matter of fact.

Diana and Jared continued to talk. Five minutes later, Ben walked back out onto the deck. Diana was still talking to Jared, so he stayed back behind the wall. *Please don't let her feel me. I want to hear what she says*, Ben prayed.

"What about Ben?" Jared asked his aunt.

Diana looked up at him. "What do you mean?"

"You like him," Jared stated point-blank. "I can see it in your eyes."

Diana looked down into her now-empty cup of tea. "Yes, I like him a lot."

"Does he know that?" Jared continued. Diana nodded. "Are you two dating now?" he pushed.

"There really hasn't been time for that, Jared. He was either trying to keep me alive or trying to get me back to you guys. There hasn't been time for dating," Diana quipped.

Jared looked at his aunt. "You're in love with him." Diana looked up at her nephew and gave him a shrug. "So are you going to marry him?"

"Jared, it's not that simple, you know that. He lost his wife to cancer. He may not be ready for another. His children may not accept me. His sister already despises me, and I don't know about the rest of his family. Then there is the call that God told me about way back, when I was your age. It's just not a black-and-white answer," Diana stated.

"Well…what about what God showed you? He definitely fits the description. Maybe he is what God has planned," Jared countered.

"I know, I…ah—well anyway…I just have to wait for God's answer. To go out of his will would make life a living hell for both of us and his kids. I'm not willing to risk that. I can't have a life like my—" Diana stopped her sentence.

"Like my mom and dad," Jared finished.

"And several other couples around, with a few exception," Diana rushed in to calm the hurt she saw in her nephew. "I'm not my brother. I can't live that way." She felt a calm warming presence near. She looked over toward the kitchen door.

"What is it?" Jared asked.

"How long have you been standing there, Tiger?" Diana asked.

Ben came around the corner. "Long enough." Jared looked at his aunt then back at Ben. He wasn't stupid; it was quite obvious to him. But he stayed still; he knew his aunt would work it out in due time.

"Jared, Ali is here to take you back home. Are you ready?" Ben asked.

"Yes sir," Jared nodded.

"Tell Nana and Papa I'm okay, but don't tell them about the rope burns, alright?" Diana insisted. Jared nodded. Diana gave him another hug. "I'll be home soon."

Jared gave her a big hug back. "You'd better be," he chided. He followed Ben to the front door. Jared looked Ben in the eyes. "Tell me you will keep her safe this time."

"With the help of the Lord, this will be all over soon. Then maybe you, BJ, Scott, and I can do some hunting," Ben assured.

Jared smiled. "And my dad as well."

"Really...well then, there's a plan. As soon as we get all this done and over with," Ben stated. Jared turned and walked out.

Ben saw the sun was starting to set. Becca, Kora, and Brock were upstairs playing with their leapfrog. He hollered, "Do you guys want pizza tonight?" There was a resounding yes from all in the house. Ben called out for pizza and then went out to the deck while he waited for it to be delivered.

Diana was standing in the far corner of the deck. Her mind was frantically racing for how she was going to do damage control, or even if she'd be able to. She was sure Ben was going to run for the hills now. *Lord, help me*, she prayed. She heard Ben walking out on the deck. She was bracing herself for the worst. Ben walked out and saw Diana was pulled into herself. He finally got to hear what was going on in her mind. The stuff she was so afraid he wouldn't understand. He walked up to her carefully.

"So, now what?" Diana warily asked. She was steeling herself for rejection. Ben put his hand on her head and caressed down her back. She closed her eyes. *At least he's going to do it nicely*, she thought.

Ben brought his hand up to her face and made her look at him. "You carry too much on those shoulders." She looked up at him; he leaned down and kissed her gently at first, pulling her to him. Her hands resting on his chest, she could feel his heart beating fast. He moved over to her ear. "Come on, kitten, let me in."

She pushed back, looked into those sapphire pools that she wanted to swim in. "As you wish," she whispered. *Lord, help me if I'm wrong*, she prayed. This time when Ben kissed her, she let him in. Things escalated a hundredfold. Ben's kiss became harder, more urgent. She felt his heat and desire for her, and in truth, she wanted more as well. She slid her hands up around his neck, and he pulled her up to him. He moved to kissing and nuzzling her neck. Diana closed her eyes then placed her head down on his shoulder. His hands started to wander across her back.

A thought shot through Diana's mind, one that scared her to death. She had to slow this down. "Ben," she softly called. He moved from her neck and took her mouth again. Diana had to calm herself now as well as Ben. "Ben, we have to stop," she shakily said once he let up on kissing her. She started to push against his chest.

Ben didn't expect the feeling he got when Diana allowed him in. He wanted her to know that he wasn't going anywhere, but it turned into he just plain wanted her. He heard her call his name, but it didn't register until he felt her start to push away from him. He released her from being so close but kept her in the circle of his arms. He looked down at her; a hint of fear was in her eyes.

"Ben, I'm sorry. I…I just need you to slow down," she managed to say.

"I'm sorry, I didn't—" his sentence was cut short by Diana putting her fingers on his mouth.

"I'm not saying no. I just need it to slow down," she restated.

Ben traced his fingers down the side of her face. "As you wish," he whispered. He lifted her up on the top of the railing of the deck. "We need to have a talk. Shall we begin? Let's start with Katherine," Ben stated. Diana looked at him and tried to steel herself. "The Lord and I had a long talk. The topic of Katherine does not hurt me. It hasn't for about a month now," Ben said as a matter of fact. He continued to talk on each of the areas that Diana brought up to Jared, making sure she understood where he stood and making sure she didn't have any other questions.

"There is one area I can't answer. I need more information on it," Ben said, looking into Diana's eyes. "Something about a call and a person God showed you?"

"I'm sorry, Ben, I can't give you that information," Diana quietly stated, looking down at the deck.

Ben's eyebrow arched up; he made her look directly at him. "And why not?" He saw her eyes were a soft, calming blue. It was on the tip of her tongue; he just needed to get her to say it.

"It's not for me to tell you, it has to come from somewhere else," she continued.

Ben stood there studying her, watching her expressions—her… mouth. He reached up and cupped her face with his hands. He pulled her toward him, kissing her again.

Diana saw the hunger in his eyes; she could have stopped him, but in truth, she didn't want to. He was more controlled this time, so she wrapped her arms around his neck. "Don't shut me out, kitten," Ben whispered as he was kissing her. Diana shook her head and kissed him back. The doorbell rang, Ben groaned and looked down; Diana chuckled. "That will be the pizza," he stated. He looked up into those emerald-green eyes. "Shall we?" Diana nodded. He lifted her down off the railing and walked her into the house. He had Diana stay in the kitchen as he paid for the pizza. It didn't take long for the troop to come out of the woodwork to grab a couple of slices. "I got a hamburger pizza for you kitten. Is that okay?" Ben stated.

"That's great, thank you, Ben," Diana replied. She took two pieces and grabbed a bottle of water from the fridge.

Kaira spoke up. "Can I have some of the hamburger pizza?"

"Heavens, yes, I can't eat all that," Diana stated. Ben gave Diana a sullen look. "I'd be sick if I tried to. Even when I was a teenager, I couldn't eat a whole pizza," Diana quipped.

Ben walked over and grabbed another piece of hamburger pizza and put it on a plate and stuck it in the microwave. "I think you can get around three pieces," he proposed. Diana just rolled her eyes at him then walked into the living room.

Scott had grabbed a box from Ben as soon as he shut the door. Diana laughed as she crossed the floor. "I take it you were a little hungry," she teased.

"I don't get delivery pizza out in the cabin; so when I get the chance to get some, I grab it," Scott informed her.

"So where did you go this afternoon?" she easily threw the curveball.

"I don't think I went anywhere this afternoon," Scott replied, grabbing another piece of pepperoni pizza. He glanced up at Diana, who was sitting in the love seat. Her eyebrow arched up and stern glare was in her eyes. *Yeah...she's not buying that one*, he thought.

"So...let's try this again, brother of mine. Where did you go this afternoon?" she restated.

"I just took a little walk," he flatly stated.

"Well, at least that has more truth in it that the first statement. Where did you walk to?" she pushed.

Scott smiled at her. "Why, are you volunteering to go for a walk with me, Milady?"

Diana maintained her composure; she didn't dwell on the undertones that were in that statement. "I would love to take a walk around, but neither you nor Ben will let me," she countered.

Ben walked into the living room. He had caught part of the conversation; he didn't figure Diana would let Scott's disappearance go. It was just temporarily forestalled until Jared left.

"Are you having a little problem with the tigress tonight, bro?" Ben teased.

"She's a little ornery tonight. Didn't you give her any attention yet?" Scott jeered.

"I thought I gave her a little attention. Maybe she needs a workout?" Ben countered. Diana took a bite of pizza. She didn't want to look at the guys; she knew she would turn beet red if she did.

"I simply asked where my brother went this afternoon. A simple truthful answer is all I'm asking for," Diana pushed after she swallowed.

"I think she's wanting to take a stroll with me," Scott hinted.

Diana's rolled her eyes and shook her head. Once she finished chewing her bite, she came back with, "If it meant that you would take me to where you disappeared to this afternoon, sure I'd go on a stroll with you."

"She's getting better at wordplay. You'd have to admit that." Ben smiled and patted Scott on the shoulder. "No...you're not going for a walk tonight. Don't bother suggesting it, kitten."

Becca came into the room next. She had a couple of pieces of the supreme pizza on her plate and a diet cola in her hand. "So how are we going to work the sleeping arrangements tonight, Ben? Maybe Diana could sleep on the floor in my room?"

Diana sat quietly. No matter which way she answered, it would be read wrong. She wanted to stay with Ben, but after what happened just moments ago, that may be a problem. "Actually, Becca, I'm going to have the girls stay with you in your room. I'll let Aisha and Mahala take the girls' beds. Scott is going to move down here, and Taggee will take the guest bed. Diana will sleep in my room," Ben informed his sister.

"Why does Scott have to take the couch?" Becca questioned.

"I'm not going to be sleeping much tonight Becca," Scott informed her. Diana glanced between Ben and Scott. *Something isn't right...but God hasn't warned me. So what's going on?* Diana wondered.

Ben saw Diana watching, listening to the conversation. She was reading between the lines and trying to process what she knew. "Kitten... what's going around in that head of yours?" he asked.

Diana looked up and glanced at the faces now looking at her. She decided she would wait till they were alone to ask Ben. "I wish you had a pool in the backyard," she beamed.

Scott and Ben laughed. They knew she was still piecing things together but didn't want to say anything in front of Becca. Becca just looked at her. "Where did that come from?"

Diana smiled. "We have an unfinished game. I'd just like to finish it someday."

"That would be so awesome to have a pool, Dad. Do you think we could do that someday?" Kaira stated as she walked into the room. She'd had her fill of pizza, but she was still working on the cream soda she had started.

"I don't know, squirt, I'll have to check into it," Ben replied.

"What unfinished game did you start?" BJ asked. He had two more pieces of supreme pizza on a plate and a can of cream soda also.

Diana got an impish look on her face, and a spark flashed in her eyes; "A game of tag. I was winning before we were so rudely interrupted."

"That's not how I saw it. I believe I caught you last," Ben countered.

"Hmm…nope, I'm pretty sure I was winning. What did you see, Scott?" Diana jeered.

Scott looked at Ben then over to Diana; he shook his head. "I think I'm staying out of this one and going to get a cream soda out of the fridge."

"Chicken," Diana jabbed.

"Careful, Milady, I just might have to find a feather again," Scott jabbed back.

"Nah…I don't think you'd win this time. I have back up. It would be two against five this round," Diana warned.

Ben looked at her. "And how do you come up with that, kitten?"

"You two…against BJ, Kaira, Kora, Brock, and myself. I might be able to talk Becca into joining in on our side," Diana easily stated. "What do you think, kids? Do you think we could take your dad and Uncle Scott down?"

Kora and Brock came running in and shouting "yeah!" Diana looked over at BJ and Kaira; they nodded, their eyes bright with excitement.

Diana looked over at Becca. "Would you like to get your brother back for the times he got you?" Diana could see she was trying to talk herself out of it, but she would love to see her brother get some payback. Diana looked up at Ben and gleamed a smile of satisfaction.

Ben arched an eyebrow. "I think we may have a coup on our hands in here Scott. Are you up for a challenge?"

Scott walked back into the room. "She didn't learn her lesson in the hotel yet? Well, I guess we need to do a refresher lesson." He was smiling from ear to ear.

Diana signaled for the kids to come over to her. "Okay, so how are we going to take them down?"

Ben watched as she rallied the kids, even Becca decided to join. *Well done, babe…well done*, he thought. He came around and sat down on the couch. Scott just stood there, leaning up against the doorway. "So have you decided to concede or what?" Ben jested.

Diana looked up and glanced at the guys. Then back down to the conference by her. "Okay…go," she said. Kora and Brock went running toward Scott, each one grabbing an arm. Scott rolled each of them up in his arms and started carrying them around to the chairs. BJ and Kaira headed for their dad, pulling him down to the floor. BJ got on his back as Kaira lay on his legs. With the guys busy wrestling with the kids, Becca and Diana snuck out to the kitchen and got a couple of small glasses of water and put ice cubes in them then slowly headed back to the living room. Diana let Becca take care of Ben; she would get Scott. Diana held back; she knew it would be better for her to wait until Scott was distracted by what was going on with Ben. Becca saw that BJ and Kaira had their dad tied up pretty well.

As BJ and Kaira held their dad's attention, Becca came over and started pouring the very cold water over his head. "Hey! Wait a minute!" Ben hollered.

Scott looked over to see what was going on with Ben. He saw that Becca had poured water on him. He straightened up from bending over the chairs tickling Kora and Brock. When he did, Diana dumped her glass over his head. "Whoa…that's cold," he quipped as he quickly reached over and grabbed Diana around the waist and held her there next to him with the other arm holding her arms across her body.

Ben looked up and saw that Diana had gotten Scott, but Scott had a hold of her. He reached over and grabbed Becca by the legs and pulled her down. "You think you can keep a hold of that one while I deal with this one?" Ben asked Scott.

"I'm not sure, she is an armful, isn't she?" Scott replied as Diana started to squirm around.

"We can help," Kora and Brock said as each of them jumped up and grabbed a hold of her legs.

"Hey…I thought you two were on my side," Diana teased. She'd have to be careful not to hurt the kids.

"Nah…they love their Uncle Scott, don't you, guys?" Scott jeered. The twins smiled and nodded.

Ben straddled Becca, who was lying on her stomach, holding her wrists behind her back to keep her from punching him. "Okay, Kaira, you get her ribs. BJ, you get her feet."

BJ and Kaira smiled and started in. Becca screamed and laughed and wiggled around, trying to get out from under Ben. By the time they were done, she had tears streaming down her face.

Ben looked up at Diana. "Your turn, kitten." Diana knew there would be retaliation, but she wasn't going down without a fight. She started out by trying to pull her arms free from Scott's grip. She got one arm loose and started poking Scott in the ribs. He was jerking around and laughing, so she managed to get the second arm free and quickly started pulling the twins across the floor with her. She knew she wasn't going to get far, but then the twins let her legs go, and she took off down the hallway. Ben caught her just outside the kitchen doorway and picked her up and threw her over his shoulder and brought her back to the living room. "Okay…now, since we don't want to break that wrist of hers open again, I'm going to keep her arms secure. Who wants to tickle her feet?"

"Who's not thinking straight this time…Tiger?" Diana stated quietly. Ben wondered what she was talking about, but then she started tickling him in his sides. It dawned on him that he had left her arms free. She had gotten him several times before he reached up and grabbed the back of her knee. She started kicking and wiggling around with that. He swiftly brought her down off his shoulder and sat down with her on the couch.

"Interesting, I found another one," he gloated. Ben quickly grabbed the forearm on the right arm and pulled it across her chest. Diana started to wiggle out way from him, but before she could get out, he started tickling her side. Diana jerked back across, centering again to Ben. He grabbed the left arm and pulled it across her chest. "So…any takers? No? Scott, would you do the honors then?" Ben threw out.

"It would be my pleasure," Scott replied.

Just then all the kids went and attacked Scott. "Get him!" they shouted.

They managed to hold him down. "I think I'm a little tied up right now bro.; unless you can get your sister to do the honors," Scott chided.

"No sir, we ladies have to stick together," Becca rebutted.

"Looks like we're at a standstill kitten," Ben whispered. Diana gleamed with satisfaction. "Unless…?" Ben stated then slid off the couch, bringing Diana with him, holding her down to the floor while he straddled her. He quickly secured her arms again and held them in the middle of her chest.

"You're still at a standstill," Diana countered. "If you let go of my arms, I'll get out, and you can't do anything without letting go of my arms."

Ben leaned down and whispered, "Have you ever heard of a hickey war? Granted it would be a one-sided battle, but I'm not going to complain."

"That could be interesting to try to explain to people when I get home,' Diana quipped.

Ben gave her a wicked smile. He was mostly giving Scott time to free himself from the kids. "Let's see…where would be a good place to put one?" he teased. "Back below the ear or down here near the collarbone?" He felt Diana's breathing hitch. *Yeah…down there would be an interesting spot*, he thought.

Just then, Diana felt someone grabbing her legs. "Hey now, you're heading for trouble there," she warned. She couldn't see who was grabbing her legs, so she didn't want to fight too much.

"Why do you think I hold both of them down? Safety," Scott jeered. He started tickling her feet. This time it was Diana screaming, laughing, and wiggling around. "What was it she said in the ship the other day? Something about payback" Scott teased.

Diana screamed and laughed and started crying. "Okay…okay, let me up. I've got to go!"

The guys simultaneously got off her, and she jumped up and ran to the bathroom. The kids were just looking at them. "Did you hurt her?" Brock asked.

"Nawt at awl," Scott replied. "She had to use the bathroom."

"What if you hadn't let her up, what would have happened?" Kora asked.

"We'd have a bigger wet spot on the floor than we do now," Ben smoothly stated.

Becca just looked at him. "Surgery?" Ben nodded. "Where?" she continued.

"I'll explain later," Ben calmly replied. He didn't want his kids worrying about any of it. Ten minutes later, Diana slowly walked back into the room. She had her black lounge pants on along with her sleep shirt. "Sorry, kitten, but you did start it," Ben said with a slight chuckle behind it.

"I have time. I'll learn a way to get my payback." She smiled.

"Daddy said you had a surgery. Why?" Kora asked.

Ben went to answer, but Diana put her hand out to stop him. She came around and sat on the couch near him; he was still sitting on the floor. She leaned over next to his ear. "Is it okay to tell them, or would you rather I don't?" Ben turned and looked at her; she was trying to be respectful of his authority. He stroked his fingers down the side of her face. "Keep it simple." Diana blinked and acknowledged what he said.

"I had surgery on my stomach a few years back," Diana stated.

"Do you have any scars?" Brock asked. "Daddy has a scar."

"He has more than one, but yep, I have several. If you connect the dots and lines on my stomach, I'd have a capital letter *G*," she replied.

"Can I see it?" Brock asked.

"Yeah…I'd like to see it," Ben teased.

"Count me in," Scott jabbed.

"No…I don't think that would be a wise thing to do, gentlemen. After a certain age, it's best girls don't go running around showing their tummies," Diana replied. "It can lead to some people acting like wolves." Ben reached up and grabbed that spot behind Diana's knee. Diana jump and slapped him.

"Someday, Milady, I'll see you in a bikini," Scott quipped.

"Not gonna happen bro.," Diana replied.

"Not while I'm around anyway," Ben whispered.

"I'm going to need to do some laundry before tomorrow, if that's okay?" Diana informed them. She saw a glint of something that ran through Ben's head. "That better not be what I think it was shooting across those eyes," she teased. Ben's ears turned red. She actually made him blush, she chuckled at it.

Scott saw it too. "I can't believe that. I think that is a milestone. Never…ever have I seen that before. To think, it only took forty years and emerald eyes to bring it about," he teased.

Ben shot a glance over at Scott. "Careful boy, we wouldn't want to regale the ladies of the times I've observed; now, would we? As for you, kitten, I'm gonna have to give that tongue of yours something else to work on." He looked up at Diana, those impish emerald eyes of hers smiling at him, daring him to try it. Ben looked around and saw the kids and Becca in the room; it would have to wait. He glanced back at Diana; she knew she had a victory at this time. He would bide his time, for now.

Becca sat there quietly during the discussion. Not even hearing what was going on. She wondered what was going on with Diana. *Was she dying, sick, or what?*

"The laundry room is downstairs and on the right. Kaira can show you," Scott injected. "Ben is still trying to deal with the fact that you won."

"Only a temporary victory, but I always win the war," Ben jested.

"Hmm…we shall see," Diana stabbed back. She got up and followed Kaira out of the living room.

36

Ben's House

At nine p.m., Ben sent Brock and Kora up to bed. Becca told Kora she could sleep with her in her bed. Ben went up to tuck them in. In Becca's room, while Kora was settling down, Ben got the cot out and made it up for Kaira to sleep in. "Daddy?" Kora asked.

"Yes…pumpkin," Ben replied.

"Is Diana dying?" Ben looked over at his baby girl. She had read into the conversation and was able to come up with a conclusion. "No, Diana is not dying," he calmly stated. "The surgery was to take what was going to kill her out so she wouldn't die." He saw the relief in Kora's eyes. "Go to sleep now. Becca is going to take you kids to church tomorrow. I'll be gone before you come back. Hopefully, it will only be for a short time."

"Is Diana coming back with you too?" Kora wondered.

"She won't be staying here like now. She'll be able to go home and stay with her own family when I come back," Ben softly said.

"So she won't be here anymore?" Kora worried.

"I have the feeling she'll be around a lot," Ben assured her. Kora nodded and rolled over to go to sleep. Ben kissed her on the side of her head and stroked her head. He went over to check on Brock. He was just finishing brushing his teeth. "All set, Brockster?" Brock nodded and climbed into his bed. Ben pulled the covers up for him.

"Daddy?" Brock asked.

"Yep," Ben figured the kids would have questions.

"I had a lot of fun tonight, can we do it again?" he wondered.

Ben smiled. "It was fun, wasn't it? Listen, Becca is taking you guys to church tomorrow morning. I won't be here when you get back. Hopefully, it will be only for a short time."

Brock nodded in understanding. He rolled over and nestled down into his pillow. "I really like Diana, she's fun," he whispered.

Ben smiled, leaned down, and kissed his son on the side of his head. "Yeah she is."

Becca was sitting at the kitchen table, drinking her pop. Scott and Diana walked in carrying the plates and empty pop cans. Diana saw Becca deep in thought, looked over at Scott, who just shrugged his shoulders, then looked back at Becca. "Are you okay?" she asked.

"That question needs to be aimed more at you I think," Becca sneered.

Scott was going to say something, but Diana put her hand on his arm. "I think it's time for the girls to clear the air. You wouldn't mind keeping the kids occupied, would you?" Diana asked.

Scott looked down at her; he saw that she was determined. He nodded and started walking out of the kitchen. "If I hear a catfight going on, I'll be back to watch," he said over his shoulder.

"Don't get your heart set on that, bro. Neither Becca nor I want to give you that pleasure," Diana jabbed back. Diana went and grabbed a bottle of water from the fridge; then she sat down on the other side of the table. "Now…shall we?" she stated.

"What was your surgery for?" Becca quizzed.

"Cancer, I'm three years out from treatments," Diana simply replied.

"Do you love my brother?" Becca shot back.

"Yes, but before you jump to conclusions, we haven't done anything but kiss," Diana stated neutrally.

"How far do you intend to take it?" Becca asked with a bite.

"I don't know yet, I need to hear a reply from God," Diana calmly stated.

"I won't let you hurt him or the kids. So if you think you're going to ship them off to a boarding school somewhere or take Ben off to Europe and away from his family to start one of your own, you'll never make it," Becca stated with fire in her eyes.

"Becca, I can't have children. If God allows me to join Ben's family, it would be a blessing, not a burden. I know you don't know me, but family is very important to me. I can't believe the Lord would put me with a man that isn't, in some ways, similar. It would be a major cause of trouble for the marriage. That being said, the only thing I play second fiddle to is God. Do you understand what I mean?" Diana carefully stated.

"So you would push his family out of his life?" Becca burned.

"Nope…not at all, but I would have more say in the events of Ben and the kids' life than his parents, siblings, or relatives. There's no halfway in my being. If I'm in, I'm all in. Otherwise, I stay out of it altogether."

"I think that would have to be Ben's say, not yours," Becca shot back.

"That's true, and that's why I'm waiting for the Lord's reply. God knows what I must have and what Ben and the kids need. Only He knows the full picture. We only see a very small part," Diana informed her.

Ben had come down the stairs and saw Scott, BJ, and Kaira setting up to play poker on the floor. Scott looked up at Ben and nodded toward the kitchen. Ben could see he was worried, so it had to do with Diana. Ben turned and walked quietly down the hallway. He could hear the fire in Becca's voice, but he also heard the calm stillness in Diana's. She wasn't being fazed at all with Becca's questions. He heard the whole conversation from the beginning. *Thank you Lord...I needed to know that piece*, Ben praised.

"So...what, you're going to keep Ben dangling on a string?" Becca angrily stated.

"I have no intention of keeping him dangling anywhere. I've tried to keep things neutral. If you haven't noticed, Ben and I have a connection. One that can only be explained by the fact that God has placed it," Diana strongly declared.

"A connection...like what, are you holding something over his head?" Becca replied.

"No...a connection such that Ben can read me without me having to vocalize it, at least for the most part. There is an area he still struggles with, but that's because of me shutting it down...not him. Then there's the fact that I know when he is near, even when I can't see him," Diana explained.

"Ben's always been able to read people. That's not anything new," Becca countered.

"Maybe...but very few have been able to read me. Even Scott can't always read me. You yourself can't read me. If you could, you'd know that hurting Ben, the kids, or you would be the last thing I'd ever want to do," Diana concluded.

"And that you are able to feel him when he's near, so what?" Becca sneered. Diana knew Becca was starting to grasp at straws. She couldn't argue with her reasoning.

"It's an important fact. For example, he's heard this entire discussion," Diana pointed out.

"How so? Are you wired?" Becca questioned.

"Nope, he's standing just around the corner. I figure he's making sure a catfight doesn't break out," Diana informed her.

"He is not, you're putting me on," Becca doubted. Ben, who had been leaning against the wall, straightened and took a step around the corner.

"No, she's not putting you on, sis. I've heard the whole thing," Ben stated as he came up behind Diana. "Now are you done with your venom?"

"Ben, she just needed to get to know me. You men have your ways to bond, sometimes using fists. Females have two ways as well. Some have a tendency to use words. Isn't that right, Becca?" Diana declared. Becca was just sitting there, looking at her brother. She'd thought she was the closest to knowing him. It was apparent that she wasn't; she can't feel his presence. She could, however, see and feel his disapproval of her questions toward Diana. She looked down at her pop can.

"Becca…you were asked a question. Are you not going to give an answer?" Ben sneered.

She looked up at Ben then over to Diana; she saw that Diana wasn't trying to rub her nose in her influence over Ben. She saw kindness coming from her eyes; "As she said, we just were getting to know each other."

Diana smiled. "I think I want some tea." She turned and put her hand on Ben's arm. Ben looked down at her; she winked up at him then grabbed the kettle and walked over to the sink to add water to it then put it on to boil. "Oh…I left my cup out on the deck. I'd better go get it." Diana walked out the door and headed toward the swing. She knew Ben wanted a few words with Becca. She felt it would be better for her to give them space. She went and found her cup, turned, and walked to the rail. She scanned out at the yard and the trees on the outskirts of the yard. She felt Ben's hands come up over her shoulders. "Is she okay?"

"Oh yeah, I think you were too easy on her," Ben replied. "She and the kids went up to bed."

"I've been in her shoes. I just didn't voice it like she did," Diana stated as she turned to look at Ben.

"With your brother and his wife?" Ben asked.

"Yeah…after they were married a year, I saw how she tried to control him. She despised any time he spent with us. It hasn't improved, at least not yet. I'm still praying God will do something," she replied.

"How did you and the kids get so close?" Ben wondered.

"Abbie has a habit of, shall we say, dropping the ball with the kids. They would call to ask if we could help out. Nana, my mom, and I started leaving our phones on for them to call any time they needed us. I would get calls at two a.m. from a bawling girl with nightmares, texts from Budder or Liza asking for advice on things at school, or I'd just take a couple of stressed-out kids for a car ride, letting them voice anything and everything without judging them on it. It built a strong bond between all of us," she recounted.

"Something tells me that there's more to it than just your brother and his wife," Ben probed.

Diana smiled up at him and nodded. "You want every little scrap of information, don't ya?"

"Everything I can pry out of that lovely head of yours," Ben concurred. He caressed his hand through the side of her hair.

Diana grinned and moved towards his caress. "If the pastors are smart, they'd include their children in their ministry. The kids see a lot of the bad sides of people, including the effects of stepping outside of God's will. I can't—I won't—do that. The price is too costly."

"Now we hit that wall of yours…correct?" Ben said, looking down at her.

Diana looked past his shoulder but nodded. *Lord, please…is he the one you have chosen?*

Ben saw that she was crawling back into that hole of hers. "Kitten… come on out of there. Someday I'm gonna have to put a lid on the hole you keep climbing into."

Diana looked down and shook her head. Ben lifted her head back up. "Please, talk to me."

"Only God can tell you what you need to know. It would be just hearsay coming from me. It has to be set in your being. That only comes from Him telling you directly," Diana answered.

"Do you know how special you are?" Ben replied. Diana blinked, wondering where that comment came from. He cupped her face, caressing his thumb over her cheek. Diana smiled at him. He was starting to lean down to kiss her, but the doorbell rang. He just shook his head. He slid his hand down her arm and took her hand. "Shall we…?" Diana grinned and weaved her fingers through his. They walked back into the kitchen. Ben made her stay there until he answered the door. Ben saw that Scott was at the top of the stairs as he neared the door. Ben opened it; he saw it was Dick.

"I thought something happened. What took you so long?" Dick wondered.

"Just being careful, pard. Come on in." Ben opened the door wider. Dick, Mahala, Aisha, and then Taggee walked into the house. Ben shut the door, and Scott came down the stairs, which alerted Taggee. Aisha was the one that told Taggee that he worked with Mr. James. Ben signaled for them to go into the living room. The group sat down.

"Maybe we should clear the air a little here," Ben said in Farsi. "My name is Benjamen Tigere or Ben for short. I work for Homeland

Security. I was assigned to Diana/Ariana to protect her when the Sheikh was after her."

Diana slowly started walking down the hallway when she heard Ben talking. As she neared the living room Scott, who was leaning up against the doorway, looked over and saw her. He winked and smiled at her, but he wanted her to stay behind him. Diana didn't know what was going on, so she obeyed his wish.

"You are not a student then?" Mahala asked.

"Not now. I was a linguistics student twenty years ago," Ben answered.

"Where is Ariana, now?" Taggee pushed. Diana recognized the name; she looked at Scott to get permission to go in. He held his hand out to signal her he wanted her to wait. Scott gave a quiet call to get Ben's attention then did a quick nod toward the hall. Ben understood what Scott signaled; he nodded. Scott gave Diana a nod and let her go in with the group.

"She is here, Taggee," Ben said and looked toward the doorway. Taggee and the girls followed Ben's line of sight and saw Diana coming around Scott.

"Ariana!" Mahala and Aisha said simultaneously. Diana smiled and walked over to them and gave them a hug. "You knew Mr. Ja—I mean Ben before?" Mahala asked.

"Yes…I've known Ben for almost three months now," Diana replied.

"Is he your husband?" Aisha asked. But she had to wait for Mahala to interpret for her.

Diana blushed a little at what Aisha asked. "No, Ben and I are not married," she said as she glanced up at Ben. She quickly looked elsewhere and waited for Mahala to tell Aisha what she said. Diana looked at Mahala while she was talking to Aisha. She saw some characteristics that where similar to Agent Kal. She studied her for a minute or two. Ben and Scott both saw Diana's face change. Ben saw her eyes; they were processing something, something that he knew was important.

Scott didn't know why the change, but it bothered him enough to look over at Ben. He saw Ben was reading her; he would know what was going on soon. He glanced back over at Diana and saw the goose bumps down her arms. *This isn't going to be good*, he thought.

Dick was just staring at Diana; it was putting Taggee on edge. "I don't like the way he stares at her. Are you sure he can be trusted?" Taggee asked Ben. Ben looked at Dick and told Taggee, "Diana would put him to the floor before he knew it. He's just not learned to control his mind yet. However, his is a good man down deep."

Diana felt the scanning that Dick was doing. She looked over at him. "Agent Richman, I don't think you want to start something that would cause you injury. I suggest you control yourself and your eyes."

"Hmm…oh, well I just—" he stumbled. Diana's eyes were steel gray and cold. Dick looked down at his watch. "Well…it's late. I need to go finish some paperwork before I head home. So if you folks will excuse me, I'll be going." He stood up to leave; Ben got up as well to walk him out.

"Man, I just can't get that ******* Scooby shirt out of my head tonight. Did you see her that day, the sun hitting behind her? **** even through the screen I could see her silhouette," Dick explained. But he was burying himself deeper. Diana was reading what the men were saying. She was going to have a discussion with Ben about it later.

Ben let Dick out and stood on the porch. He glanced around nonchalantly; the black SUV was still there. But that wasn't where the warning alarms were coming from. The house was being watched—that was obviously felt. By whom or what was the question.

Diana felt that cold dark presence; she looked up at Scott then started looking for Ben. Taggee was the one that voice the question that Scott had running through his brain. "Tigress…what's wrong?"

Mahala looked over at Diana; she put her hand on Diana's hand; "Taggee wants to know what is wrong?"

Diana looked down at Mahala. "Do you have any brothers, sisters, or family here in the States?"

Mahala blinked, wondering what that had to do with anything; "Yes, I have an older brother here. He works in one of the agencies and one of the reasons why we were able to get out of the office in New York. Why?"

Diana looked over at Taggee and Aisha then asked, "What is his name?"

Mahala still didn't know why the questions, but she replied, "Khaleel. Ariana…what's going on?"

Ben walked back into the house and over to the living room; Diana was on edge. He walked over to Scott. "What's happened?"

"I'm not sure. Both Taggee and I saw her tense up and become edgy. She's asked Mahala whether she has any family here. Apparently, there is a brother working in one of the agencies. His name is Khaleel," Scott recounted.

Diana took Mahala's hand. "Did you see your brother before leaving New York?" Mahala nodded. "Did he give you anything?" Diana continued.

"Yes, he gave me a phone. He said I needed to leave it on all the time. He would call me later," Mahala replied.

Diana closed her eyes for a moment then looked over to Ben. Ben understood why she acted on edge and why the questions. "Mahala, I need you to trust me. I need you to give me that phone," Ben clearly and carefully asked.

Mahala slowly reached into her pocket, pulled it out, and gave it to Ben. "I don't understand," Mahala said shakily.

Ben took his knife out of his pocket and pried the phone apart. Inside the phone was a small tracer. He showed it to the room then proceeded to crush it under his foot. Mahala started crying. "I think we've found our leak. Now, we need to be very careful," Ben stated.

He turned to Taggee and explained what was going on and why he did what he did. Taggee nodded. Aisha was cradling Mahala. "She didn't know, Mr. James, believe me."

Ben nodded then went down on his knee in front of Mahala. "Did your brother say anything that seemed odd or unusual to you before you left New York?" Ben kept his words soft and calm. Mahala was so distraught that her brother would do this that all she could do was shake her head no.

Ben looked up at Diana. "Kitten…come over here please." He got up and walked her into the den. Scott followed her.

"Agent Kal is her brother, that's why the alarm went off this morning," Diana injected. Ben acknowledged what she said.

"I need you to help Mahala remember what she saw and what was said when she talked to her brother last," Ben explained.

"I don't know how to do that," Diana replied.

"You help her focus on the meeting. Keep your voice calm, keep Mahala calm, the rest will be up to the Lord to guide you. It has to be somebody she trusts. You're the only one here that can do it," Ben pushed. Diana nodded. "That's my girl," Ben said as he stroked his finger down her face.

Diana walked back over to Mahala and Aisha then knelt down in front of them. "Mahala, I'm going to try to help you remember, okay?"

Mahala looked at her. "I'm so sorry. I don't want you hurt. I didn't mean to—"

Diana cupped her face, stopping Mahala from completing her sentence. "I understand."

While Diana worked on getting Mahala calmed down, Ben called Taggee over to talk with him. Taggee quietly got up and walked over to Ben and Scott. "What do we do now?" Taggee asked.

"Mahala's brother has pinpointed where Diana and the girls are now. We have to leave tonight to go to the safe house. I will call my director and have him meet you guys there. I need to get my family out of here as well, so I will meet you out there," Ben planned.

"Ben, you know good and well she's not going to leave you," Scott inserted.

"She'll have to this time," Ben coldly stated. "She wants to protect the kids almost as if they were her own family."

Ben heard Diana start to ask Mahala questions to help her remember. "Let's see how much the brother is involved," he sneered.

Diana saw the guys coming back into the room. She looked at Ben's eyes; they were the dangerous sapphire blue, but more than that, they were hard and cold. Like on the first time she saw him. She looked down. *God, help us...we need your guidance.* Diana calmed herself and lightly stroked Mahala's hand. "I want you to close your eyes. Think back to when you last talked with your brother. Okay? Where were you at? Can you see it?"

"Yes...it was in the building there where we saw you and Mr. James at," Mahala replied.

"Was it in the conference room or in the corridor?" Diana guided.

"It was near the bathroom. I had just come out of the door. He came up behind me and pulled me to the side," Mahala answered.

"What did he look like? Did he seem calm or rushed? Was he clean or unkempt?" Diana continued.

"He was clean, but he kept looking over his shoulder. Like he was afraid someone would see him," Mahala replied.

"Do you remember what he said when he first came up to you?" Diana asked.

"He said, 'Welcome to America, land of the supposed free.' He said that I needed to be careful whom I talk to. Not everyone is a friend here," Mahala recounted.

"Did he say anything else or do anything else?" Diana pushed.

"He had a piece of paper in his hand. He kept looking at it," Mahala pondered.

"Was his face happy when he looked at it or sad?" Diana directed.

"Sad...worried...he mumbled something once. I couldn't hear it," Mahala stated.

"When did he give you the phone?" Diana lead.

"He shoved the paper in his jacket pocket. He shook his head and gave me the phone. He told me that I was to use it when I needed him to come get me. That he wished I was not involved in all this," Mahala declared.

"Did he say anything after that?" Diana asked.

"That I was the only family member left. He would protect me, no matter what," Mahala sadly added.

"Did he do anything else?" Diana probed.

"He looked over at a man standing outside the door. When I turned to see what he was looking at, he got upset. Told me to go back to where Aisha was, that he would see me soon," Mahala said as she looked over Diana's shoulder, remembering the look on Khaleel's face.

"Did you see him again after that?" Diana softly asked.

Mahala just shook her head. Diana reached up and rubbed her arm and gave her a hug. "Thank you," Diana whispered in her ear. Diana stood up and walked over to Ben; she looked up at him. He looked down at her and wrapped his arms around her. She needed security, or maybe she saw that he needed strength. Either way, he held her near him.

"We have to leave tonight, kitten," he softly said.

Diana nodded. "I know." He reached up and stroked her hair. They all jumped when there was a knock at the door. Ben pushed Diana away and signaled for Taggee to go near the girls.

Scott grabbed Diana by the arm and pulled her into the living room. Ben walked up to the door and slowly opened it. "Hello Ben, I'm here to give you a helping hand."

Diana recognized the voice the same time Scott did. It was Allen. "You're a long ways from home," Ben jested.

"Yeah, I am. Do you mind if I come in? I'll explain what I've got for you," Allen asked.

Ben opened the door and let him come in. Then he closed and locked the door. "I think we'd better move to the kitchen and shut these lights down out here," Ben suggested.

Allen walked down the hall a little ways. He glanced over and saw Taggee and the girls, then he saw Scott with Diana. "It looks like you may already know some stuff," he assumed. Ben signaled for the group to follow him to the kitchen. Diana told Scott she needed to put her clothes in the dryer so they would be dry before they left tonight. Scott nodded. He signaled for the girls and Taggee to go ahead of him. He walked through and shut the lights off in the front of the house then walked into the kitchen himself.

"You're the black SUV outside," Ben surmised.

"Yeah…we've been watching the house for most the day. I figured you'd finger us quick," Allen replied. Diana came up from downstairs and stood by the downstairs door. She mostly listened.

"So let's compare notes, shall we?" Ben advised. "Mahala, I need you to translate what we are saying for Taggee. Word for word, can you do that?" Mahala nodded. Taggee sat down on a chair so that it would be easier for him to hear everything going on. Allen and Ben went back and forth. Allen had put a task force on finding out where the leak was. He was also the one that suggested that Diana's friend Ali bring a family member over to let them know she was okay. He looked over at Diana when he said that. Diana gave him a smile and mouthed the words *thank you* to him. Ben told Allen that they just now found out about Khaleel, or Agent Kal as they've known him, being the leak. That he had given a cell phone to his sister, Mahala, with a tracer in it.

"I'm surprised you came up with the family tie. It took us a while to connect the dots as it were," Allen praised.

"Diana came up with the family tie." Ben smiled.

Allen looked over at her. "Don't tell me you sensed that too."

"Well yeah, I'd guess you'd call it that. I just used my sense of vision this time. When I saw him at Ben's office this morning, I knew I'd seen his face before, but I couldn't place it. It wasn't until I saw Mahala interacting with Taggee and Aisha tonight that I saw the resemblance," Diana stated.

"Impressive," Allen stated. Ben saw the look in his eye. He knew Allen was seriously thinking of trying to get her to work for them. "Anyway," Allen continued. "Agent Kal's family was killed in a raid about three months ago, just after Mahala was given to the Sheikh." Diana looked over at Mahala; she was crying but continued to interpret for Taggee.

Ben saw the pain in Mahala's eyes. "I'm sorry." Mahala just nodded in acknowledgement. "So you figure that Mahdi is using leverage to get Agent Kal's cooperation?" Ben continued.

"Mr. Ja—I mean, Ben, what is *leverage*," Mahala sheepishly asked. Ben smiled and interpreted the word for them.

"Yes…I don't believe he would willingly do this if it wasn't for the need to protect his sister. I'm sure he already knows what Mahdi is capable of," Allen finished.

"So…we need to get Agent Kal and hold him, if for nothing else for his protection," Ben added. "We also need to get Diana and the girls to the safe house, and I need to get my family up and send them to my parents ASAP," Ben stated.

Allen, Scott, and Taggee all nodded. "Well, with the SUV, I can take the girls and Taggee with me to the safe house," Allen suggested.

"No...I'm staying with Ben. Taggee and the girls can go with you," Diana asserted.

"I told you she'd have a fit," Scott jabbed.

"Diana...I need you to go with Allen. I'll get the kids packed and send them with Becca to the farm," Ben insisted.

Diana just shook her head no. "I'm staying with you."

Taggee chuckled. "The tigress is pretty set on staying with you, sir."

Allen piped up. "Yeah this could be interesting, the tiger and a tigress. Which one is going to win?" Diana didn't know what Taggee said, but she knew what the others were saying. She had no intention of backing down.

Ben stood up and said over his shoulder, "The tiger will win." He walked over to Diana and put his hand in the middle of her back to guide her to his room. "Excuse us for a few minutes."

Allen and Scott chuckled. "He won't hurt her, will he?" Aisha asked.

"No, ma'am, Ben won't hurt her. He's trying to protect her, she's just a little too stubborn to accept it," Allen informed Aisha.

"A tigress's mind is not an easy thing to change. He has a task before him," Taggee stated.

"What I would pay to be a fly on the wall in there," Scott chuckled.

Once Ben had Diana in his bedroom, he shut the door and calmed himself. "Diana I need you to go with Allen. I need to get you out of here. It's not safe."

"I'm not stupid, Ben. I knew that when Mahala said she got a phone from Agent Kal. I want to stay with you," Diana insisted.

Ben walked up to her and sat her down on the bed. He knelt down in front of her. "I'll be coming there as soon as I can get my kids and Becca on their way. I've got to make sure they are safe."

Diana saw the concern in his eyes. She put her hand on his face. "I can help you with that," she softly stated.

Ben reached up, took her hand, and kissed it. "I'd be too worried that you weren't safe. I need you to stay safe. Allen and Taggee will make sure of it," he softly said. He saw a tear roll down Diana's cheek. He reached up and cupped her face with his hand then brushed the tear away with his thumb. "I'll be a half hour behind you, I promise."

Diana looked up at the ceiling then glanced down at Ben. "I'm sorry I put your family in danger. You know this is the last thing I ever wanted to happen."

"I know…but it's not your fault. So if I hear you beating yourself up for it, I'll spank your derriere," Ben commanded. He got a half smile out of her from that. He stood up and pulled her up with him. "You suppose once this is done and over with we might be able to actually have a date?" he teased.

"You'd probably get too bored with me by then," she stated.

Ben tilted her face to look at him. "I'd never get bored with you." He bent down and lightly kissed her lips. Diana reached up and wrapped her arms around his neck and held him there. She was the one that kissed him back hard. Ben wrapped his arms around her, holding her tight against him.

She slowly released him. "You'd better keep your promise Tiger, only a half hour behind."

Ben smiled and kissed her nose. "I always keep my promises. Get your stuff packed." Diana pouted but went ahead and started packing her stuff. Ben walked out into the kitchen.

"So…which one won?" Scott teased.

"Diana will be going with you, Allen. I and Scott will be there as soon as my kids are safely heading to the farm," Ben replied.

"So the tiger has power over the tigress, huh?" Allen jested. "I didn't hear any screaming or things breaking. I'd like to know how you did that."

Scott jumped in, "He probably gave her a large dose of sugar to throw her off balance."

"Not as much as she needs," Ben stated. All of the sudden a wet washcloth came flying through the air, hitting Ben on the back. "Hey now!"

"I see she has good aim," Allen chuckled. Scott let out a laugh, and Taggee sat smiling. Ben just shook his head and threw the washcloth into the kitchen sink.

He walked over to Taggee. "She's going to be on edge when she leaves here. I need you to try to keep her calm and safe. Especially safe, please."

Taggee knew the connection between Mr. James and Ariana; the fact that he was handing her over to him to care for was important. "With my life, I will protect her till this is over with."

"Thank you," Ben said, putting his hand on Taggee's shoulder.

Diana came out of the room. "I've got to get my clothes out of the dryer, then I'm ready."

"I'll give Zenon a call and explain what's up while you finish up then," Ben stated and walked out onto the porch with his phone in his ear.

Diana watched him walk out; Scott saw the fight going on in her. "Hurry up, Milady…your carriage awaits you." She looked over at Scott, gave him a halfhearted grin, and walked downstairs.

"Really tenderhearted I see. Probably the reason why Ben could talk her into going?" Allen observed.

"I have the feeling that if it wasn't for the fact that Ben's kids and his sister are here, she would have won the battle. She's leaving to protect them," Scott conjectured. He looked over to Taggee and the girls. "Keep my sister safe. I'll make sure Ben gets back to her." Taggee nodded.

Diana was coming up the stairs; she heard Scott talking to Taggee. She turned and went into the room to pack the clothes into the suitcase. She was just finishing up when Ben came back in. "You got everything?" he asked.

"Yeah…I think so," she softly replied.

"All your meds?" he continued. Diana nodded. "What about the meds to treat your wrist?" Diana grimaced at that but said, "Nope, I forgot that one."

"Huh-huh, that would have been convenient—everything but the one that you hate the most," Ben jeered.

Diana looked up at him. "I forgot. That's my story, and I'm sticking to it."

Ben laughed and went to the cabinet, pulled the stuff out, put it in her toiletry bag, and walked over to her. "Hang on kitten, not much longer,' he said as he pulled her to him. He felt her relax against him; she breathed in deep then sighed.

Scott came to the door. "Come on, Milady. We've got to get everybody out of here and safe." Diana nodded.

Allen had pulled the SUV up into the driveway. Taggee was helping the girls into the backseat. Ben was loading Diana's stuff into the rear; then he made sure Diana was in with the girls.

"Okay Allen, you're loaded." He handed the address to Allen and closed his door. "I'll be there as soon as I can."

Allen nodded and started the car and pulled away. Ben walked back into his house and started up the stairs.

His first stop, Becca. He walked into the room. "Becca…Becca, wake up sis. You need to get to the farm," Ben said as he shook her shoulder.

"Hmm…what?" Becca replied.

"Becca, I need you and the kids to go back to the farm…now," Ben enforced.

Becca heard the tone in his voice; she quickly became alert. "What… what happened?"

"We've been traced. It's not safe for you guys to be here. I need you to get pack and take the kids back to the farm with you," Ben said as he started to wake Kaira. "Kaira…come on, squirt, wake up. Go get your clothes, pack up quickly." Ben grabbed a bag from the closet and put it on her lap. Becca quickly got out of bed, grabbed her suitcase from under the bed, and opened it up. She went to the closet, grabbed the few things that she had in there, and threw them into the suitcase. Then she headed for the bathroom. Kaira was up and loading her stuff into the duffle bag she used. Ben grabbed several outfits and stuff for Kora and put them in Becca's case.

BJ stood at the doorway of the girls' room. "I've got myself and Brock packed. Uncle Scott is loading it into Aunt Becca's car right now," he confirmed.

"Great job, kiddo…thank you," Ben praised his son. He finished getting Kora's stuff packed. He turned and looked over at Kaira, who was almost packed. "I need you two to listen carefully. I'm sending you out to Grandpa and Grandma's house for your safety. I need you to be alert. If you see anything strange or you feel you are in danger, I want you to call the police. Understood?"

BJ looked at his dad. "Uncle Scott told me. Is Diana going to be okay?"

"I'm praying so. The Lord has protected her this far, I don't see him stopping now." Ben smiled.

"Okay, Dad, I'm all done," Kaira stated. Ben put his hand on her head. "I love you guys, I don't know what I'd do if I lost any of you." Becca came back in from the bathroom, her arms full of the bottles and hair stuff. She threw it into a compartment of her suitcase and then walked over to the drawer and grabbed the rest of her stuff from there and added it to the case. Then she pushed down on it and closed the latch.

"Okay…I'm set," she stated winded.

"Head on down, I'll get Kora," Ben directed. He walked over and picked his little girl up in his arms. She was a sound sleeper, so he wasn't worried she'd wake up. He carried her down to Becca's car and buckled her in. Scott was already down there with Brock, who was fussing a little bit for being woken up. Kaira and BJ crawled in and waved good-bye to their dad.

Becca opened her door to get in. "Are you going to be okay?"

"Once you and the kids are safe, I'll go into hiding," Ben calmly stated.

She was going to say something, but she looked at her brother and just nodded and climbed in. "Don't do anything stupid!" Becca commanded. Ben just waved good-bye at her. Once Becca and the kids were off and on the road, Ben and Scott headed inside. They each had a pack all ready to go. They grabbed it and threw it into the car, did a once-over to make sure there was nothing to burn down the house, then they walked through and locked all the doors and windows and left the house.

Ben was on the road and heading toward Zenon's vacation home. "I wonder how long this one will last?" Ben was basically talking to himself, but he vocalized this thought.

"I'm hoping for at least a couple of days." Scott smiled. "We've had several 'one-night stands' as it were. It would be nice to stick around in one place." Ben nodded and chuckled.

37

Zenon's Vacation House

Allen looked at the girls in his review mirror. Aisha was holding on to Mahala, who was still very upset. Diana was quiet, withdrawn from everything around her. *Ben and Scott said she often pull into herself. That's probably where she is now*, Allen thought.

Taggee also looked back at the girls. He saw that Ariana was gone. "She has folded in on herself," he said to Allen. Allen nodded.

Diana sat looking out the window, looking into the darkness but not really seeing it. She was searching, searching for God's will, searching for the reasoning of Agent Kal's motives, searching on how to deal with Mahala, but most of all, searching for God's assurance that Ben and his family will be safe. She heard Taggee mention something to Allen, but she didn't care to find out what he said. She wanted to stay in her solace for now.

Allen wanted to pull her out but didn't know how to go about it. "Diana, are you okay?" he tried. He looked back at her; she remained looking out the window but nodded. *Ben…how do you pull her out of there?* he wondered.

Taggee looked over at Allen. "Tell her she must trust the Lord."

Allen wasn't used to having God conveyed in that manner, even from Ben. "Diana, Taggee said to tell you that you must trust the Lord," Allen interpreted.

Diana looked over at Taggee, who was watching her, gave him a small smile, and nodded. Mahala looked over at her and put her hand on Diana's shoulder. "I'm so sorry."

Diana looked at Mahala, at the guilt that was swimming in her eyes; she reached over and took her hand and pulled Mahala over to her. She gave her a hug and whispered, "I don't blame you. I'm just worried about the kids. I can't get an image out of my mind."

Allen turned the SUV off the highway and onto a smaller street. He thought he saw a car tailing him. He pulled out his phone and punched a number. "Harry, got a problem. Are you ready? Great...ETA five minutes."

Diana looked at Allen. *We're being followed*, she silently said to herself. Allen looked back and saw her connect the dots. She met his gaze, and he winked at her. She simply gave him a quick nod. "Mahala, I need you to tell Aisha that Allen may be making some unexpected stops and moves. She's not to look around, just keep still and hold on. Do you understand?" Diana instructed. Mahala looked at Diana, nodded, then moved over to speak with Aisha. Taggee heard what Mahala was saying as well. Allen hit the accelerator and sped down the street. Luckily, it was very late at night, and there wasn't much traffic. Diana grabbed on to the handle by her door to steady herself as Allen dodged around the few cars he came up on. Then he made the SUV tailspin left and quickly turned down a crossing street. Diana looked into the driver's side mirror; she caught a glimpse of another car's headlights acting just as erratic as the SUV's. Allen again sped up to pull away from the other car. He gained some leeway from the other car when it got caught up in traffic. Then Allen made the SUV tailspin right and turned onto another crossing street. He accelerated but then quickly turned right again into a parking lot; another quick right, and he headed toward a garage. The door was already half opened and opening wider. Allen didn't hit the brakes until he was inside the garage. The door quickly shut.

"Everybody okay?" he asked, looking around at the passengers.

"That was interesting," Taggee stated. Aisha and Mahala were huddled together, their eyes as big as dinner plates.

Allen turned to look at Diana; he figured her to be a basket case by now. She was sitting there calm as can be.

"I'm fine, Allen. How do we know when we've given them the slip?" Diana asked.

Allen just grinned in amazement. Nonetheless, he said, "I have some friends here that are watching the road. I'm going to go talk to them now. Stay put." Allen repeated his command to Taggee and Aisha in Farsi. Then got out and walked up the stairs to a door on the second floor. They sat there for what seemed like ages, but Diana figured it was probably somewhere around twenty minutes. She heard the second-floor door open and looked to see who it was. Allen came down and walked back over to the SUV. "Our friends are rather determined. They keep circling the area, so we are going to have to change vehicles," he stated.

Diana glanced around the garage. "I don't see any in here big enough for all of us to get into."

"Maybe it's because some things are best kept hidden until necessary," Allen said with a smile. He nodded to the next stall over. Diana looked over there, but all she saw was the large hole in the floor for the men to work on the underside of cars. She looked back at Allen with a cocked head and a questioning look on her face. "Just wait," he grinned.

Diana heard the sound of things being moved around. She glanced over at the next stall and saw the oil catcher and other various tools were being moved out of the way. Then she heard a large motor start up. It was coming from below them. She looked at Allen then at Taggee and the girls, then she turned back and looked at the empty hole in the floor. The hydraulic car lift raised up toward the ceiling; the tire guides were lifted up and moved back. Slowly she saw the hood of a black vehicle being raised up from the hole. She stayed fixated on the vehicle slowly rising from seemingly out of nowhere. When it was all said and done, there was a black limousine waiting for them to drive out of there with. "Okay, I admit it. I'm impressed," Diana voiced.

Allen just chuckled. He told Taggee to get the girls into the limo. "Your ride, ma'am," Allen said as he opened Diana's door. Diana smiled and took his hand to climb out. She went with him to the back of the SUV to grab her luggage and to help carry anything else that needing to go. Taggee quickly came over and took her stuff from her; he put his hand in the middle of her back to have her walk over to the limo. Diana shook her head a little but smiled and allowed him to help her. She climbed in and sat on the seat facing back. After loading and clearing essentials out of the SUV, Allen and Taggee joined them. Allen sat next to Diana, giving Taggee leg room as he took the last seat next to the door.

Diana looked at Allen; "Umm…who's going to drive?"

Allen looked at her. *Inquisitive thing, isn't she? It reminds me of Ben when I was training him some twenty years or so ago.* "The people looking for the SUV will be watching for us, so we have a different driver," Allen informed her. The window separating the front from the back rolled down. Diana looked over her shoulder. "Ms. Henderson, this is Harry. Harry, Ms. Henderson and friends," Allen introduced.

"Pleasure to meet you folks," Harry said, tipping his hat to them.

He was missing a front tooth, and it appeared that he was or had been a smoker, because his teeth were a brownish-gray color. He had a black beard and mustache, both well kept and trimmed. He wore the usual limo driver's outfit. His eyes, like hers, were a hazel color, but there seemed to be laughter behind his. "Likewise sir." Diana grinned.

"Okay, Harry, let's get these ladies under cover, shall we?" Allen said as he slapped Harry on the shoulder.

"Aye, aye…Captain," Harry stated and rolled up the window. Diana watched through the tinted window as the garage door opened up. The limo slowly pulled forward and out into the parking lot. She could feel the weight of the limo as it pulled onto the street. It seemed to fill the entire road. She unconsciously started to rub the area around her wrist.

Allen looked over and studied Diana, saw that she was holding her wrist. "Is it hurting you?"

"Hmm…oh, yeah a little. I don't want to take the pain meds they prescribed to me. I'll grab some aspirin when we get to the house," Diana nonchalantly said. It took Harry another thirty minutes to get to Zenon's vacation house. Diana was a little worried that Ben might get there before them and freak out when they weren't there. As it was, they seemed to have arrived at the same time.

Ben and Scott saw the limo pulling in just behind them. Ben recognized the driver. "They must have had a tail on them. Allen had to switch vehicles." Scott turned and looked at the limo. They watched as Taggee unfolded to get out. Mahala climbed out behind him then Aisha. Taggee led them over to Ben and Scott. They both saw that not only were the girls very tired, they were obviously on the scared side. Allen was the next to unload followed finally by Diana. Allen didn't have to tell her to go to Ben and Scott; she quickly walked over to them.

Diana came up and gave Ben a hug. "I'm glad y'all are safe." Ben held her next to him; Scott gave her a wink.

"Shall we?" Ben signaled to have everybody walk toward the door. He let go of Diana and went to go grab the luggage out of the limo. Scott and Taggee followed.

"Hey, Ben…Scott, good to see you're safe and sound," Allen stated.

"I take it you had some problems," Ben jeered.

"Which problem are you referring to?" Allen asked in a teasing manner.

Ben's eyebrow shot up. "Both."

"Not much as far as Diana goes. She crawled into a hole for the most part. Taggee got her to at least register conversation, but that was all the farther we got her until the Indy started," Allen informed him.

"And what caused the Indy to happen," Scott asked.

"We had a tail. Whoever this person was, he was good. I had to resort to drastic measures to shake him. It's funny. Diana knew what was going on before I said anything. I heard her warn Mahala and told her to tell Aisha. With the speed and all the turns, the two girls were near hysteria, but not Diana. She was all calm, cool, and collected," Allen voiced.

Ben chuckled. "You should see her drive to work in the morning. You probably would have gotten a smile out of her if you would have had music going as well." He watched Taggee walk back over toward the girls.

"She likes a sense of freedom, huh?" Allen jested.

"As long as she has her feet on the ground," Scott injected. The guys laughed, which brought Diana's attention to see what they were laughing about. She couldn't read their conversation, nor could she hear it. She saw Ben turn and look at her, grin, and then turned back around. She shook her head.

"By the way, make sure she gets some pain meds in her. I caught her rubbing her wrist on the way over. She said something about not taking the pain meds prescribed to her. Why won't she?" Allen asked.

"Stubborn little…with everything going on—the medication, Mahdi, putting the kids in danger—her mind melted everything into one horrible nightmare. It really shook her up. So she refuses to take the stuff. I would surmise that her system isn't used to taking anything more than Tylenol or aspirin," Ben informed Allen.

"According to her records, she had a few major surgeries recently. How does that compute with low-dose pain meds?" Allen wondered.

"I haven't found that out yet. Maybe tonight I'll get the chance," Ben replied.

"Considering the late time and the fact that at least two, personally I'd say three, look exhausted. I don't think you'll find out until later bro.," Scott chimed in.

Ben shook his head. "Let's go get our charges tucked in for the night."

Allen, Ben, and Scott walked over to the women. Taggee started guiding Aisha and Mahala to the door. Ben nodded for Diana to head on over; she glared at him but followed Taggee. The rest of them came up behind her. The girls didn't know what to do when they got to the door, so Diana went around and pushed the doorbell.

Director Zenon answered the door. "Come on in, Ms. Henderson," he said as he opened the door wide. He stood there waiting for the entire group to come in. He saw Allen with the group and wondered what was going on.

"Good evening, Charles. Bet you're wondering why I'm here?" Allen stated.

"Good evening, Allen. Yeah, I am curious as to why a New York FBI is clear out here in the midlands," Charles replied.

"Our leak, it appears, is an FBI agent working here in Des Moines. I'm sure you've met him, Agent Kal," Allen informed him. Charles looked at Ben then at Diana then back over to Allen. He had a perplexed look on his face. Allen just smiled. "I see this is the first time you've noticed the skills of our cats over there. It's a little unsettling at first. It took me a while to adjust to it myself," Allen jeered.

"Agent Kal was in the office this morning. I'd noticed that Ms. Henderson was very vague and ambiguous with her answers. While Agent Kal was out of the room, I asked what was going on. Ben said something about not trusting him. I got the strong impression that it was because of Ms. Henderson's actions," Charles replied.

Allen snickered, "Yeah, it's an interesting relationship between those two. They read each other like an open book, often without any words being spoken."

"That's not a good thing. Agents lose focus when they get emotionally involved," Charles warned.

"In most cases, I'd agree with you. These two seem to gather strength from each other. They focus in more when they are together. Could you imagine the possibilities if you partnered them together?" Allen suggested.

"Ms. Henderson is too fragile a person to put her out in the field. It would destroy her," Charles quickly countered.

"She's a lot stronger than you know, Charles. There is steel in that girl. She's fragile in appearance, but there is steel underneath it all," Allen informed him. "Steel that is tempered when she is around Ben."

Charles shook his head. He still saw the woman that was broken at the sight of Amid's demise. In truth, he saw his daughter in her, and as such, wanted to protect her from the monsters of the world. He walked over to the group now sitting on the couches. "If you will follow me, I'll show you the house."

38

Zenon's Vacation House

Diana had been checking the house out as she waited for Director Zenon to finish his discussion with Allen. It wasn't exactly what she expected. She figured it would be this posh, multimillion dollar edifice. It turned out to be a simple ranch-style house. It had an open floor plan. The entryway, dining room, and living room were all open to each other. There were skylights that Diana figured lit up the entire area with sunlight during the day. She would bet that at night with the full moon, it would be bright enough to even cook by it. There was a large fireplace on the one side of the living room. The opposite side of the front door was a wall of windows and patio doors that opened out to a huge covered deck. The kitchen was separated from the living room by a long high bar complete with stools to sit on. There was an island in the kitchen that had a stovetop on it. The fridge was a double door French style with the freezer on the bottom. It had a microwave, double ovens, a dishwasher, and a lot of counter space. Diana noted that everything seemed to be very high-end stuff. It was the type of house she wanted to buy someday.

She was just about to get up and explore on her own when Director Zenon came over to show them around. He took them down the hallway to the right of the front door. There was a bathroom just past the dining room. Then the hall turned left, and there were three bedrooms past that. The first one was a single-bed child's room. The next room had queen bed in it. The one on the very end, the master bedroom with its king-size bed, had a door that opened out onto the deck, and a private bathroom. They all followed Director Zenon out onto the patio. He pointed out that the yard went all the way to the lake some 260 feet away. Diana saw that it was a very well kept yard with rows of bushes lining both sides, marking the property line. In the distance there was a seating area complete with a fire pit. She smiled at that. Charles turned and saw what she was looking at. "I often like to sit out there and just to unwind watching the fire," he quietly stated.

Diana looked at him. "That would be where you'd find me at nights." He smiled and patted her shoulder. He lead them all back into the living room. Diana hung back a little looking at the surroundings. Ben came and put his hands on her shoulders. "Where you at, kitten?"

"Daydreaming, I guess," she replied.

"You can't be daydreaming, it's nighttime," Ben teased.

Diana smiled and turned to look at him. "Let's just go with dreaming then."

"Come on, let's get you inside," Ben said as he slid his hand down her arm and took her hand. She instantly weaved her fingers through his as he walked her back inside.

"Any questions?" Charles asked.

"Is the kitchen stocked, or do we need to have a grocery run?" Scott asked. Diana chuckled. "What…are you planning on going fishing every day for supper, Milady?"

"I wouldn't mind it, but I have a feeling that you gentlemen wouldn't allow it," Diana shot back.

"You're right, it's not allowed," Ben inserted.

"Now, who's taking all the fun away?" Diana jeered as she sat down on the barrel chair next to her and pretended to pout. Charles had never seen the playful side of Diana; he couldn't help but chuckle a little. She looked up at him and smiled.

"No, you don't need to go shopping. The kitchen is fully stocked. There's meat in the freezer. There's also a freezer in the garage you can pull from," Charles explained.

"Thank you, sir, I'm sure it will be great. Thanks for letting us use the house," Ben stated.

"I want a report every day from you, Ben. I don't care if it's somebody that broke a fingernail. I want to know about it. The phone is secure as well as the network. Am I clear?" Charles emphasized.

"Yes sir. I will report around nine a.m. every day," Ben stated.

Charles took his leave and headed out the door. "I need to get going as well. I'll have Harry take me back to the SUV, and then I'll take it to a hotel. I'll keep in touch with you two. If you need me, give me a call," Allen injected.

"Aye, aye, sir," Scott answered.

"Ben, get some meds into her," Allen restated as he looked over and saw that Diana was rubbing her wrist. Diana realized what she was doing as she looked up at him. She put her arm down, shrugged her shoulders, and shook her head.

"I'll take care of it, sir," Ben sneered as he looked down at her. Allen turned and walked out the door.

Ben walked over and looked out and waited till Allen and the Zenon left; then he locked the door. "Hey, Scott, do you want to pull the car into the garage and secure it?" Ben asked.

"You've got it bro," Scott replied and jumped up. Ben tossed him the keys as he passed and headed out the door that led to the garage.

"Okay, Aisha, Mahala, do you two want to share a room or do you want separate rooms?" Ben asked in Farsi.

Aisha spoke up and said. "I think it's best if we share a room. We'll take the second room. Give Ariana the big one on the end."

Diana watched the conversation. Once they stopped talking, she spoke up. "Someone is gonna have to teach me Farsi. I hate not knowing what is going on." Ben just smiled.

"I can help you learn it," Mahala spoke up.

"That would be awesome, thank you," Diana praised.

Ben turned to Taggee. "I'm sure you're exhausted. Why don't you go get some sleep, Scott or I will take the first watch."

"I will, after Aisha and Mahala are down. You need to deal with Ariana and her wrist for now. I will sleep once everybody is settled," Taggee stated.

"As you like. I'm going to need your help with her wrist. Someone has to hold her arm still while the medication is poured on. It bothers Scott too much to see her in pain," Ben asked.

Taggee nodded. "Let me know when you need me."

Again, Diana watched the conversation, but this time she pretty much knew part of it was about her. Both Ben and Taggee looked at her at the end. She saw Taggee get up and start picking up the girls' bags. He said something to them, which caused them to get up and follow him. "We are going to bed now. Have a good night Ariana," Mahala told her.

"You too, I'll see you in the morning," Diana replied. "So how are the arrangements worked out?" Diana asked as she walked toward the kitchen where Ben was.

"The girls are taking the second room. They want you to have the room on the end. We'll leave the single open for whichever one of us men want it. Truthfully, I have the feeling that we will probably just camp out here at night," Ben blankly stated.

"You should have had them take the big bedroom. I'm use to smaller ones anyway," Diana quipped.

"It was their wish. I'm not sure I like the door access directly to you," Ben flatly stated. Scott walked in from the garage. He threw the keys at Ben, who barely looked up to see Scott. Diana didn't know how in the world he caught those keys.

"Everything is secured bro. Who's taking the first watch?" Scott asked.

"One of us. Taggee will go to sleep after the girls are down," Ben said as he started looking through the cupboards.

Diana was leaning on the high bar. "What are you looking for?"

Ben opened a cupboard near the ovens and pulled out a bowl and set it on the counter then looked over at Diana. Diana grimaced. "Go get the stuff kitten. Let's get this over with," Ben softly stated. Diana sighed and slowly walked over to her bag that was on the floor in the dining room. "Since I know you don't like to see this, do you mind telling Taggee I need his help? Then you can go check that door in the master bedroom. Make sure that it is secured or can be secured. Diana will be staying in there," Ben informed Scott.

Scott nodded and headed down the hallway. He hated seeing Diana in pain, especially when there was nothing he could do to stop it. He saw light coming from under the second bedroom's door, so he stopped and knocked on the door. Taggee opened it. "Ben needs your help. It should only take a minute," Scott informed him. Taggee told the girls he would check on them later. Scott headed to look at the door leading to the patio from the master bedroom. He decided he would stay there until they were done with Diana.

"Kitten…do you mind grabbing a towel from the bathroom? I don't know what this stuff will do to marble counters. I'd hate to ruin them," Ben asked.

"Judging what that stuff does to my wrist, it would probably burn a hole right through those counters," Diana quipped. Ben just chuckled and started running the water to heat it up.

Diana passed Taggee on her way to the bathroom. He continued on to where Ben was. Ben looked up and saw him coming. "Her wrist was too infected to close up. It has to heal from the inside out. This medication is to help it stay clean and to heal correctly," Ben informed him.

"Was this all from the ropes?" Taggee asked.

"Unfortunately…no. We had a little problem on our way back to the US. One of the guys grabbed her wrist to restrain her. Diana made him pay for it before I could get to her, but he ripped her wrist open in the mean time," Ben stated.

Taggee just nodded. He knew she would fight if force was used on her. "Do you know where she goes when she folds into herself?"

Ben looked up at him. "Not always." Diana had walked up to the counter with the towel as the guys were talking. Neither was looking at her, but she heard her name at least once.

"So what thing did I do now that warrants a major discussion?" Diana jeered.

Ben looked over at her. "He was saying you crawled back into your hole while you were with Allen. Pouting a little bit that you didn't get your way, were ya?"

"I wouldn't say pouting. I was upset that your family was put into so much danger," Diana countered. "Are they going to call you when they get to the farm?"

"Yeah…Becca will send me a text. It should be coming soon. By the way, it wasn't your fault, quit blaming yourself," Ben scolded. He laid the towel out over the top of the island. He placed the bowl toward one side of the towel. Then he turned to Taggee. "Do you want to hold her, or would you rather I hold her?"

"I will hold her hand and pour, you hold her arm," Taggee replied.

Ben nodded. "She has a strong grip, you may only want to give her a finger or two."

Taggee laughed as he came around the high bar. Diana looked at them. "What did you tell him that made him laugh?" Ben just smiled and shook his head. "You're a brat," she quipped when he wouldn't tell her.

Ben went and grabbed a bar stool for Diana to sit on. "Sit down. I don't want to deal with you jumping around."

"Oh, whatever," Diana sneered, but she sat down and braced herself.

Taggee took her hand, giving her his thumb to wrap her fingers around. That way he could turn her wrist to get a good coating. Ben held on to her forearm, positioning himself between Diana and the bowl. "Whenever, you're ready Taggee," he said.

Diana heard Taggee dip the cup into the bowl. She instantly felt the searing burn of the medicine run through her arm. She sucked in air, and her arm instantly tried to pull away. She immediately tightened her grip on Taggee's thumb. She heard Taggee chuckle and say something to Ben. "You'd better tell me what he said," she demanded through gritted teeth as her wrist was turned and another cup was poured over it.

Ben chuckled. "I had warned him that you had a strong grip. He was just telling me that I was right."

Taggee turned her wrist to the other side to give it a good dowsing. He looked over and saw tears running down her cheeks. "She does not scream with this even though it looks like she should be," he stated.

"No, she doesn't. If she could control it, she wouldn't cry either," Ben informed Taggee.

"That should be the last. I coated it well," Taggee ended.

"It looks good, thank you," Ben replied. Diana felt Ben's hold let up, so she slowly released Taggee's hand then laid her head on Ben's shoulder. Since Diana had released his hand, Taggee walked over to the sink to wash any medication off. Ben moved the bowl off of the towel and allowed Diana to rest her arm on it to air-dry. As Taggee finished drying his hands he walked by and patted Diana on the back. She looked up at him. "I'm sorry, I hope I'm about done with this stuff."

Ben interpreted what Diana said to Taggee. "Tell her there is nothing to be sorry for. She did well," Taggee replied.

Ben interpreted what Taggee said to Diana. Diana gave Taggee a nod.

"I'm going to go check on the girls," Taggee told Ben.

Ben nodded then turned to Diana. She was wiping the tears from her cheeks. "Now, kitten, we need to deal with this guilty complex of yours."

"I think there is another more important topic to deal with. What are we going to do with Agent Kal?" Diana redirected.

Ben moved over to grab the gauze and he pulled the knife from his pocket. "I'm still deciding on that one," he answered.

"I think…no, let me word it this way, I believe he is being forced to do this. To protect his sister," she surmised.

"Maybe, but we don't have evidence to support that assumption. We do have evidence to the contrary," he countered.

Diana just looked at him, waiting for more information. Ben looked up. "We have your reaction at the cabin for one. That should be one flag."

"Agreed, but I didn't have the same warning in Director Zenon's office. If he was bent on evil, the warning would have been the same," Diana injected.

"Then we have the fact that he gave his sister a phone that he knew would lead to you," Ben stated.

"Yes…but Mahala was there too. Why would he want his sister to be in danger as well?" Diana countered.

Ben finished rewrapping Diana's wrist. "Go get some pain meds and get them into ya," Ben enforced. Diana got down from the bar stool, went to her bag, and pulled out a bottle of aspirin. She poured two out into her hand and walked back to the kitchen. Ben had already poured her a glass of milk to take them with. "Sorry, there isn't any chocolate milk for you tonight," he teased.

"So are you done with the torture session?" Scott said as he walked back toward the living room.

"Yep…I'm done. We were just discussing our Agent Kal," Ben stated.

Diana finished drinking her milk. She walked over and rinsed the glass out. Then she looked over to the coffeepot, grabbed the carafe, and started filling it with water. Ben looked at what she was doing and smiled. He came up behind her, putting his hands on her waist, and leaning down to her ear. "You're beautiful…you know that?" Diana just smiled. Ben kissed the back of her neck and walked over to the couch to continue the discussion. Diana finished getting the coffeepot set and started it to running. She then went and sat down by Ben.

"So what have we came up with so far?" Scott asked.

"Well, we have the reaction at the cabin. God obviously warned Diana of danger. Then we have the reaction at the office. God was warning Diana there," Ben recounted.

"But it wasn't the same, Ben. At the cabin, there was an evil presence. In the office, it was more of a caution sign. Something is different," Diana explained.

"So what, a change of heart maybe?" Scott threw out.

"It's possible. If he truly is trying to protect Mahala and he found out that I tried to protect her at the compound, maybe he's changed his mind but is being forced to complete his task," Diana purposed.

"I guess that's possible," Scott injected. Diana heard the coffeepot finishing up. She got up and went to the kitchen.

"I'm not saying it isn't possible, but at this point in time, there is no proof," Ben continued.

"Do either of you take sugar or cream?" Diana asked from the kitchen. Ben and Scott looked at each other. Their minds went to the same place at the same time. Then Scott shook his head as if to clear it.

Ben just chuckled. "I think we'd better stay with black for right now."

Diana heard the laughter in Ben's voice and looked over to see what was going on. Scott's face was beet red, and Ben's ears were almost glowing. She thought for a moment as to what would cause that kind of reaction. As it dawned on her, she felt her own face heat up. She shook it off and walked out into the living room with a cup of coffee for both of them. "If we are done with the trip to the gutter," she scolded.

Ben and Scott looked up at her. "I don't know what you are talking about," Scott threw out.

"Oh...well then, maybe you'd better look in the mirror at the color of your face Mr. McCleary. As for you, Mr. Tigere, that's twice I've made you blush," Diana informed them.

"My face isn't red, kitten," Ben injected.

"No...but your ears were nearly glowing." She grinned.

Taggee came around the corner and sat down on a barrel chair. "I would think she should be in bed," he said to Ben.

"She will be soon," was all Ben said.

"We were discussing the issue with Mahala's brother Khaleel. How much he is doing this on his own will versus being forced to do it," Scott told Taggee.

"What are the opinions?" Taggee asked.

"Diana feels that though he may have started out on his own free will, that he is being forced to do it now. Ben is leaning toward him doing this on his own free will. I'm just not sure yet," Scott filled in.

Diana looked over at Ben while Scott was talking to Taggee. "He's just filling him in on our discussion," Ben informed her.

"I'll have to agree with Scott right now. There is just not enough information to go either way," Taggee stated.

Ben interpreted what Taggee said for Diana. "There is one thing that Mahala said that is odd to me. She said that her brother looked out the door and saw somebody standing there. The part that's odd is that he got mad at her for looking at the man," Diana questioned.

Ben interpreted what Diana said for Taggee. All three of the guys thought for a moment. "I have to agree, this mystery man does tend to lead toward Diana's conclusion bro," Scott added. He then turned to Taggee to tell him what he said.

"It's something to think on," Ben ended. "Kitten...you need to get to bed before I have to carry you in there."

A thought crossed Diana's brain that made her eyes flash. She looked down to contain it, but Ben saw it. He smiled as he sipped his coffee.

"You two are having a conversation over there, aren't you?" Scott scolded.

Diana looked up. "I don't know what you're talking about, brother of mine."

"Huh-huh, then maybe you'd like to explain why you look like you're hiding something and Ben has this huge Cheshire cat grin on his face as if he found something," Scott accused.

"I'm a woman, I'm allowed to hide whatever I want to. As for the tiger finding something, considering where your two minds were just moments ago, I'll leave that to the powers that be," Diana scoffed.

"Ben, get your kitten to bed. She way too playful for me to deal with tonight," Scott teased.

"She'll just be three times worse to handle with a few hours of sleep," Ben countered.

"Maybe you'd better give her something to sweeten her disposition then," Scott suggested. "Do you have any IOUs left?"

"Nope, he doesn't. Too bad, so sad," Diana tossed in as she went to pick up her stuff to take it back to the room.

"I guess you have been a little occupied lately," Scott teased, looking at Ben.

"I always keep my promises. I'll see what I can do to help her attitude," Ben said, getting up to help Diana.

"You'd better start praying for him, Scott. He's gonna need it," Diana teased back.

Ben caught up with her as she rounded the corner. "Somebody is gonna need it, that's for sure," he whispered. Diana figured they both would if they weren't careful. She laid her pillow on the bed and put her toiletry bag in the bathroom. Ben set her suitcase down by the closet and walked over to check the door. He was really uncomfortable about the direct access problem.

Diana came out of the bathroom and looked over at him. "What's wrong, Ben?"

"I really don't like having an outside door where you are sleeping. It's too easy," he stated. Then he kicked himself for saying it. He didn't want to make her worry about it.

"It locks, doesn't it?" she asked. Ben nodded. "Is there a safety bar or something to double secure it?"

"Unfortunately, no. I wonder if Zenon would have a problem with me boarding it up?" Ben voiced.

"I would have a problem with you destroying it. They've got a lot of money into this house. I'd hate to see it ruined," she quipped.

Ben looked over toward the bed. "It's a good thing you got your pillow back. Otherwise, you'd have to go without holding anything tonight," Ben teased.

Diana had taken her clothes into the bathroom to change. She had just finished switching around. She walked out of the bathroom carrying her clothes she wore for the day. "I will always find something to hold. Just some things are better than others," she countered.

Ben was going to add to that comment, but he figured he'd better behave. He walked up to her as she was brushing out her hair. "One of us will be awake all night. If there's a problem, don't hesitate to call out."

"I won't…I promise," Diana assured. She knew Ben didn't want to leave her, much less leave her alone in a room he questioned the security of. She looked up into his eyes, and her heart rate started to increase.

"How about I owing you for a while," Ben suggested as he put his hands around Diana's waist and pulled her closer.

"Hmm…how's your credit score. Is it good enough for a loan?" Diana teased.

"Definitely," Ben said as he leaned down and kissed her. Diana still had the brush in her hand, so she put that hand up behind Ben's neck. Ben probed for entrance, and Diana gave it to him. He could feel her heat, the slight taste of sweetness, but he had to maintain control or he would scare her again.

Diana was just about to start to push away from him when she heard his phone ringing. Ben slowly let up and released her from his embrace. He pulled the phone out of his pocket. "It's Becca." Diana nodded. "Hey, sis. I was just about ready to call you. Is everything okay?" Ben walked over to the door and looked out over the patio.

Diana waited to make sure everything was okay. *Thank you Lord, for helping us*, she prayed.

Scott slowly walked into the room. "Is everything okay?"

"Becca finally called. I don't know whether it's good or bad yet," Diana quietly stated.

"Okay…you keep in touch and call if there's a problem. Yeah, I love you too. Bye," Ben ended the phone call. "She and the kids made it out to the farm safely. She thought she was being followed as she was going through town but the car that she thought was following her, was pulled over by a police car just as she turned on to I-80." Ben smiled.

"Remind me to make Ali a sour cream raisin pie when this is all done with," Diana chimed in.

"You know how to make that one too? You got to make me one Milady. I don't wanna have to drive all the way to Georgia to get one, please," Scott begged.

Diana chuckled. "Yeah, if I'm doing one, I might as well do two."

"Thanks, sis," Scott said as he gave her a hug.

"I've been told she can make bread as well. An official source told me that if she made homemade bread, that she might actually gain some weight," Ben added.

"Hey, I'm game for it. Killing two birds with one stone, you might say." Scott smiled.

"One problem, gentlemen, I can't knead the dough," Diana countered, holding up her wrist.

"I'm sure we can figure something out kitten," Ben injected.

"Fine...I'll see what I can do. Now, y'all get on out a here and let a girl get some sleep," Diana shooed.

"I'm a going, I'm a going," Scott said as he walked out the door.

Ben traced his fingers down Diana's face. Diana could see he was worried. "I'll yell out if I even catch a glimpse of a possible shadow."

"Promise?" Ben insisted.

"I promise," Diana assured. He slowly walked out of the room, closing the door behind him. Diana noticed he did not latch it. She walked over and turned off the lights. She went ahead and cracked the door open then climbed into bed, adjusted her pillow, and held it tight. "It was more comfortable when I had Ben to cuddle up to," she sneered quietly. Then she closed her eyes and slowly went to sleep.

Scott had already started another pot of coffee. He figured neither of them were going to get much sleep tonight. Or at least what was left of the night. He saw Ben walk out into the living room. "You want another cup?" Scott asked.

Ben saw that Taggee had taken one of the couches and gone to sleep in it. "Yeah, I'd better. Not that I'm going to sleep much anyway."

"Withdrawals can be hard to get through. I'm interested in seeing how you handle going through this withdrawal. You're too used to her being near you," Scott teased. "It seemed to me that you were able to sweeten her disposition a little bit."

"Oh, shut up and give me that coffee," Ben sneered.

"Wow...okay, remind me to make sure Diana give you a massage when she wakes up," Scott snipped.

Ben rolled his eyes. "I don't like the fact of someone having direct access to her while she's sleeping. It's the one time she's alone in this house," Ben pointed out.

"I understand that, so what are you going to do?" Scott probed. "Wait till she's asleep and climb in bed with her?" Ben glared at Scott. "Okay...that didn't come out right. But you know what I meant."

"There's no kids here. I could take one of these chairs in and leave the door open. That should keep everything kosher," Ben suggested.

"I would think so. There's room for a chair in there. Activity is freely seen, so neither of your reputations will be tarnished. How will we work night watch?" Scott counseled.

"We'll overlap. I'll just be watching closer to the girls is all," Ben suggested.

"Sounds good. How long before Diana is asleep?" Scott wondered.

"I'll give her about fifteen minutes then go check on her," Ben stated.

"I have a feeling she won't be totally out until you're in there with her," Scott jabbed.

Ben didn't counter; Scott was probably right. She needed him close as much as he wanted to be close to her. He waited until his coffee was done before going in and checking on her.

She was asleep, but it wasn't a deep sleep; she was restless. He came out to the living room to grab a chair. Scott wanted him to take the recliner, but Ben opted for one of the barrel chairs. They were smaller and more maneuverable. He carried it in there and placed it at the foot of the bed. He was totally visible from the hall, but he could easily protect her if someone tried to enter through the door. She was still tossing around a bit. "Shh…kitten. I'm here…sleep," Ben whispered softly. He heard her take a deep breath in and slowly let it out. She seemed to settle down from there. Fifteen minutes later, she was in a deep, restful sleep. Ben lightly rested. He got up a few times and walked through the house. The first couple of times, Scott was awake and watching things. The last few times, it was Taggee that was awake and Scott was asleep. Ben went back and sat back down in the chair in Diana's room.

39

Zenon's Vacation House

Ben was resting in the barrel chair when he heard movement in the living room. He sat up and looked down the hallway. He saw Taggee carefully walking toward the girls' room. Taggee smiled and nodded at Ben; Ben returned the nod. He sat there and watched as Taggee carefully opened the door then slowly, quietly closed it; then he walked back into the living room.

Ben sat back in the chair. He stretched his legs out as much as he could and leaned his head back against the wall. He figured the sun would be coming up soon; then he wondered what they were going to encounter throughout the day. He closed his eyes for a minute.

Diana woke up needing to go to the bathroom. She felt Ben's presence and looked around the room. She saw him at the end of the bed. She rolled over to the opposite side of the bed and carefully climbed out and silently walked to the bathroom. She didn't flush; she figured she would take care of that after everybody was awake. She quietly walked down the hall and out into the living room. She saw that Taggee and Scott were both awake and talking quietly to each other.

Scott looked up and saw Diana standing near the corner of the hallway, "Good morning, sis."

"Good morning…are you two up for the remainder of the time?" Diana asked.

"Yeah…why?" Scott wondered.

"I'm up for the day…I'm going to get Ben to go to sleep for a while. I just wanted to check," she simply stated.

Scott smiled at her. "Good luck on that one."

"Oh, I don't figure he'll stay asleep for long, but a few good hours are better than none," she quipped back. She turned and quietly walked back to her room. She quietly made the bed and arranged the pillows.

Then she walked over to where Ben was. She knew that he could lash out before realizing it was her touching him; she'd have to be careful. She gently touched his hand. "Ben? Come on, go lie on the bed and sleep for a while." She carefully put her whole hand on his. "Ben?" She started to slide her hand up his arm, careful to not make any sudden movement and ready to duck if he lashed out. "Benjamen, come on. Go lie down on the bed and get some sleep," she said a little louder. She felt his muscles start to twitch. "Tiger, your shift is done. Go get some sleep," she said a little louder. Suddenly Ben's other hand quickly reached over and grabbed her hand. She held still but looked up at his face; "Ben…Tiger, come on. Go lie down. It's more comfortable there than here."

Ben, in instinct, reached over and grabbed what was touching him. He quickly registered that it was Diana. He started to stroke his thumb across her hand to calm her and then opened his eyes.

"Your shift is over, Tiger. I'm up for the day. Go lie down on the bed and get some real sleep," Diana softly encouraged.

Ben smiled at her and traced his fingers down her face. "Good morning, kitten. Did you sleep well?"

"I slept very well…thank you. It's your turn. Scott and Taggee are both awake in the living room," she quietly told him. "Come on, get over there," she insisted. Ben allowed her to pull him out of the chair and lead him over to the bed. He sat on the side and took his shoes off; then he lay down on the pillows. "I'll get cleaned up and dressed, then I'll be out of here," she said.

"Don't rush away. I don't mind you hanging around," Ben teased. Diana smiled at him but got up and grabbed her clothes she was going to wear and headed to the bathroom. He heard the shower turn on and the sound of the water change as Diana climbed in. He lay there and listened to the sound of the water; it was calming to him. Soon he fell deep asleep. Diana finished showering and dressed. She quietly opened the door of the bathroom and walked out into the bedroom. She studied Ben, watched him breathe, listened to the rhythm—he was deep asleep. She quickly but quietly put her things away then headed toward the kitchen.

As she passed the living room where Scott and Taggee were sitting, Scott asked, "Any luck getting him into the bed to sleep?"

"Yep…as of a minute ago, he was out cold, but I've learned that doesn't mean much with him. I figured he'll be awake in the next fifteen to twenty minutes," Diana stated. Scott just laughed. She continued to the kitchen and started to going through the cupboards looking to see what she had available; making a mental list of what was where and what she would need. After about an hour of looking and figuring, Diana thought she better write certain things down. She saw the dry-erase board on the side of the refrigerator. She wrote down yeast, coconut, gallon of milk, chamomile tea, and a gallon of chocolate milk with a smiley face by it. She went ahead and pulled out some bacon and eggs from the fridge then turned on the oven and pulled out the pans that she needed to cook breakfast.

Scott and Taggee sat watching Diana move around the kitchen. Taggee noticed that she seemed quite at ease and seemed to know what she was doing. He heard movement in the hallway and figured he'd better go check it out. Scott figured it was one or both of the girls waking up. He heard a door open and then shut. Soon he saw Taggee walking back into the living room. "Are Aisha and Mahala awake?" Scott asked.

"Yes…Mr. Ja—I mean Ben is still out though," Taggee replied.

Scott started to smell the bacon wafting by. "He won't be for long."

By the time the girls were cleaned up and out into the living room, Diana had breakfast near ready. The only thing lacking was how Scott wanted his eggs cooked. She asked Scott to have them come up to the bar and sit down. She placed the plates up on the counter. "How do you take your eggs, Scott?"

"Sunny-side please," Scott replied.

"I also need either you or Mahala to ask Aisha and Taggee if they would like milk, orange juice, or just coffee?" she asked over her shoulder as she went to the cupboard to grab the glasses.

Scott signaled to Mahala to go ahead and translate for Diana. Taggee wanted coffee; Aisha wanted juice. Diana gave them what they had asked for it. She slid Scott's eggs onto his plate.

"Mahala, Scott, what would you like?" Diana continued. She figured Scott wanted coffee, but she just wanted to make sure.

"I think I've had my limit of coffee right now, Milady. I'll take some milk," Scott stated.

"I'll take an orange juice please," Mahala replied. Diana smiled and put them up on the bar. "Ah…Ariana; we don't eat pork", Mahala informed her.

"Oh; I'm sorry. Did you want a different kind of meat?" Diana embarrassedly asked. Mahala interpreted what Diana asked. They all shook their heads no.

Scott looked and saw that Diana wasn't eating. "Milady…where is yours?"

Diana looked over at Scott. "Don't worry…I'll eat in a little bit."

"You'd better…you know very good and well what trouble you'll be in if you don't," Scott warned. Diana smiled over at him as she was looking through recipe books. She wished she was home; she preferred her own recipes for bread and pies. They came out of some very old books.

Ben woke up and looked at his watch. He had been asleep for three hours. He could smell the scent of Diana on her pillow. It was a mix of Pantene, a rich vanilla, with a hint of floral undertones. He could hear talking in the other room so he figured he'd better get up. He had brought his stuff into Diana's room during the night. So he pulled out his clothes and bathroom supplies and headed in to take a shower.

Now that he was clean, he walked out toward the living room. Everybody was up and moving around. "Well…looks like the tiger is done with his nap," Scott jabbed.

Ben looked around and didn't see Diana. He looked over at Scott. "She's out on the patio, bro. Now that you're awake, maybe she'll eat breakfast," Scott informed him.

"She didn't eat with you guys?" Ben snarled.

"Nope…she assured me she would eat later. She hasn't yet," Scott said snidely.

Ben's eyes narrowed. "She will eat now, even if I have to spoon-feed her." Ben immediately headed to the door and out onto the patio. Diana was on the far left side. She was sitting forward on a lounge chair, legs crossed, and flipping through a book, humming a song. She looked up when she heard the door open and close. She had her sunglasses on, so Ben couldn't see her eyes, but she obvious saw his. He saw her recoil and decided he'd better temper his rage. He walked over to her. "Are we up to mischievousness this morning?"

"Not-that-I-know-of," she cautiously replied.

"What was breakfast this morning?" Ben asked.

"The group had some bacon…well Scott had it anyway; eggs, toast, and a drink. I didn't want to wake you up…so I figured that I'll cook mine at the same time I cook yours," Diana informed him.

Ben felt like a heel; she was waiting to eat with him. "Sounds good… let's go eat," he encouraged.

Diana looked at him. "Scott told you I hadn't eaten, and you thought I was going to skip it…didn't ya?"

Ben looked at her, sat down on the edge of the lounge chair, and lifted her sunglasses up, putting them on the top of her head. "I like to see those eyes of yours."

"I am trying to eat more, whether you guys believe it or not. I know full well what will happen if I don't get enough nutrients into me. My parents, and probably you and Scott, will have it IV'd into me. Now, knowing my like of needles, do you honestly think I want to go through that?" Diana scolded.

"Do I start begging for forgiveness now or just call for mercy?" Ben teased. She had put him in his place and did a good job of slicing him. He deserved it, he admitted it. He looked at her, saw that she was debating her options then saw a flash of orneriness in her eyes.

"I'll think about it," she quipped. Ben knew she was playing him; he also knew she'd save it for another time. He looked down at the book she was flipping through; it was a cookbook. He looked up at her. "I was trying to find recipes that were similar to the ones I use at home. I'm not having much luck. The books at home are quite old. By the way, what time is it?" Diana asked.

Ben looked down at his watch; "Ten fifteen....why?"

"You'd better be calling Director Zenon. You're an hour and fifteen minutes late," she demanded.

"Yes, ma'am. You go get our breakfast ready and I'll go call Zenon," Ben stated. He held out his hand for her to join him. She unfolded her legs and stood up, falling against him. Ben held her steady. "Let me guess: your foot fell asleep."

"Apparently, my entire leg fell asleep," Diana said. She struggled to get the blood flow moving again.

Ben sat her back down on the lounger chair and started to rub her leg. "How long have you been out here?" he asked.

"I don't know. I've gone through a few books. Maybe a half hour, I'd guess. I really need to get my watch and put it on my left wrist," Diana replied.

"Which reminds me...we need to treat your wrist again this morning," Ben inserted.

"Well, there goes any appetite I had," Diana quipped. Ben pinched the button behind her knee. Diana jerked and grabbed his hand. "I don't need to take another shower so soon. I'll run out of clean clothes. So, we shall behave...right?"

"I don't know if I can promise that one, kitten. I'll have to think on it," Ben jeered. "Let's see if you can walk now...shall we?" Ben stood up then helped Diana to stand. She slowly put weight down on her dozing leg.

She knocked it a couple of times against the other foot then shook it out. "It's awake now. You'd better get in there and call," Diana insisted. Ben waited until she was walking without a limp, then he guided her back into the house. She headed for the kitchen, and Ben headed for the bedroom to give Zenon a call. Scott, Taggee, and the girls saw the two come in and head for different directions. "What are you doing, Ariana?" Mahala asked.

"I'm getting Ben's and my breakfast. He'll be out in just a few minutes," Diana replied as she started heating up the skillet. She popped some bread in the toaster and laid out a couple of plates.

"What's Ben up to?" Scott inquired.

"Checking in," Diana replied. By the time Ben came back out from talking with Zenon, Diana had everything ready. She'd asked Scott what way Ben liked his eggs. She was just finishing scrambling hers when he walked over to the high bar. She turned off the stove, slid her egg onto her plate, then put the pan in the sink to be washed. "Did you want coffee, juice, or milk, Tiger?" Diana asked.

"Milk please," Ben said as he took a bite of his eggs. Diana went and grabbed two glasses and poured milk into both of them. She came around and sat them down on the counter then sat down on the stool near her plate. Ben cleared his plate and waited to see if Diana would make it around hers. He saw that she had two pieces of bacon, about the equivalent of one egg scrambled, and a piece of toast. She nearly made it. There was only one piece of bacon left. Ben reached over and grabbed it off her plate and ate it. Diana just smiled.

"So what is on the agenda today?" Scott asked.

"I was hoping for some homemade bread and pie," Ben jabbed.

"No yeast for bread here, and I can't find a decent recipe for it. As for the pie…Scott is going to have to wait on his. I was thinking of doing a coconut cream pie though," Diana planned.

"What…no apple or cherry pie?" Ben jested.

Diana saw the flash in Ben's eyes when he said *cherry pie*. "I'm not very good at fruit pies. You'll have to wait 'til Mom can make those. Hers are awesome. I just wish I could call them and get my recipes."

"That could be arranged now kitten," Ben softly said. Diana's head snapped up; there was a gleam in her eye. Ben just nodded to reinforce what he said. "Let's get that wrist taken care of first. Then we'll make a call."

Diana jumped down off the bar stool and gave Ben a big hug. "Thank you…thank you…thank you!"

"She is so much different here than she was over there," Aisha commented.

"She's more open and definitely happier," Mahala added.

"That's because she is where she belongs," Taggee concluded.

Diana heard Taggee and the girls talking; she looked up at Ben for a translation. Ben smiled. "They were just commenting on how different you are here than over there." He rubbed her arm a couple of times. "Taggee, are you wanting to help me again this morning?" Taggee nodded and stood up and moved toward the kitchen.

"I think I'm going to go take a shower," Scott stated and headed toward the hallway. Ben nodded an acknowledgement as he was getting the bowl out. "I need you to go grab a towel from the bathroom, kitten." Diana went to the hallway bathroom; she was just coming out as Scott was heading in. Scott gave her a wink and stepped aside to let her pass. She grinned and patted his arm then headed back toward the kitchen. The girls sat in the living room, watching the movement.

"What are you doing?" Mahala asked as Diana walked back to the kitchen.

"They have to treat my wrist. As much as I try to hold still, I can't control my arm; so somebody has to hold my arm while another person treats it," Diana stated. They sat and watched as Ben and Taggee worked on Ariana's wrist. They saw how much it hurt her to have the medicine put on it. They also watched as Ben comforted her once it was done.

Aisha looked at Mahala then over to Taggee as he walked back toward them. "She belongs to him, doesn't she?"

Taggee nodded. "They are two sides of the same soul."

Ben wrapped Diana's wrist with gauze. "Shall we give your parents a call?" he asked as he finished up.

"We can't yet…they're at church. Dad's probably still preaching," Diana informed him. "We'll have to wait till about one or so to call." Diana sat for a minute, turning back and forth on the bar stool.

Scott walked in from taking his shower, saw that Ben and Diana were talking by the high bar. "So what are we going to do for the day?"

"I really would love to see the town…but I know that will not be allowed," Mahala replied.

Scott just shook his head. "Maybe once this is all done with, then we can take you guys to see the sights, but not right now."

Ben just smiled and watched Diana. He saw she was processing something...then he could almost hear a *ding* as he saw a flash in her eyes; she settled on an idea.

"Could I send a few texts?" Diana asked.

"Unfortunately...no. We'll be using the landline to call, not the cell phone. The landline is secure...the cell phone isn't."

"Oh...yeah, I forgot. I'll just have to wait till one then," Diana said downcast. She hopped off the bar stool and headed for the kitchen. She started to rinse off the plates and glasses to load into the dishwasher.

"I'll do that...you go on," Ben stated as he slid his hand down Diana's arm, stopping at her hand for just a second, then taking the plate from her.

Diana let go of the plate and looked up at Ben. She could feel her heart racing, and her mouth started to water. *Knock it off, girl...* she scolded herself. She quickly got control of herself and walked over to the fridge and grabbed a bottle of water. She figured Ben read her and knew what she was thinking. She didn't look back at him right away; one of them had to keep in control. This morning...it wasn't going to be her.

She walked out to the living room listening to Scott, Taggee and the girls carry on a conversation in Farsi. She looked over and saw a remote control on the coffee table. She picked it up and started looking at the buttons. She found the button that said TV and pushed it.

There was a flap that opened up on the ceiling and a seventy-two-inch flat-screen TV dropped down from the ceiling just above the fireplace. "Kewl," Diana said in awe. The movement brought the previous conversation to an end. Ben, who had just finished loading the dishwasher, walked over to the group.

"I see your curiosity is in full force," Ben teased. Diana just looked up at him and smiled. She got busy figuring what else she could do with the remote. Ben looked up at Scott and grinned. He noted that Taggee and the girls were in awe as well. Diana clicked another button. All the shades on the windows looking out onto the patio started to slowly close. Then she saw that the light in the room was diminishing. There were shades closing on the skylights as well.

Diana giggled. "I love this house." Ben was totally amused at her excitement.

"She's worse than a little kid. Maybe you should take that away from her before she breaks something," Scott teased.

Diana looked up at him and scowled. She held the remote close, up to her heart. "No..." she said like a little kid. She looked over at Mahala and Aisha and winked. They were nervous at first when the TV dropped down, but now they saw that she was playing. Diana looked down at the remote to see what she needed to do to turn the TV on. She clicked on the power button. She heard the TV click on. She waited until she saw the screen lighten up. Then she clicked on the menu button. A pop-up window came up on the screen. The options were HDMI, cable, or satellite. She clicked on satellite and waited to see what came on. What came on was a total shock at least to Diana. She had no clue what channel it was, but what it showed made her want to crawl under a rock. The satellite came on in the middle a very illicit bed scene. All Diana could do was hit the power button and toss the remote toward the chair near Ben. "Okay…here ya go." She brought her legs up into the chair and refused to look at those in the room.

Ben picked up the remote. "I warned you about your curiosity… kitten." There was laughter in his voice. Diana grabbed a nearby pillow and threw it at him. He didn't think she could possibly get any redder. He looked over at Scott, who was hiding his laughter behind his hand. "I guess it's a good thing that there is only one pillow near her," Ben teased.

"I don't know…I had fun with the last pillow fight," Scott jabbed. Diana looked up at him and glared. She then got up and walked out the door onto the patio.

Taggee, Aisha, and Mahala were confused. They saw an image come on the screen then it clicked off. "What happened?" Aisha asked Ben.

"Ariana is innocent, remember? She's not used to that," Ben told Aisha in Farsi. "She is extremely embarrassed."

Taggee stood up and walked to the kitchen. "Well, it is proof that you have not been with her yet," he said quietly.

"No, I have not taken Ariana. I wouldn't do that to her, not without permission," Ben somberly said. He watched Aisha and Mahala get up and walk out onto the patio.

Diana sat down on the other side of the wall. She heard the group talking in Farsi. Usually she would want to know what was being said. She was very glad she didn't know. She heard the door open; at this point in time, Ben was the last person she wanted to deal with. She looked down at the deck. She felt someone move their hand down her arm. She looked up and saw it was Aisha.

Aisha started stroking through her hair, relaxing her. She continued to comb through it until she saw that Ariana was calm. "Someday, when the Lord says, you will be ready for that," she quietly and calmly said. Aisha looked over to Mahala, signaled for her to come and interpret what she said for Ariana. Mahala came over and knelt in front of Ariana and told her what Aisha said. Ariana just gave a quick nod.

Scott moved from the living room and stood in the kitchen near Ben and Taggee. "I didn't expect that reaction. I guess I should have been a better brother," Scott guiltily stated.

"In this case, it is better for the women to deal with Ariana. I have a feeling she would just climb deeper into herself if one of us men neared her," Taggee surmised.

Ben was in his own solitude. Scott looked at him and asked, "Do I need to get someone to read your mind?" Ben blinked and shook his head. "Where did you go, bro?"

"I'll plead the Fifth on that one. I think Taggee is right though. I think we need to give the ladies some space. Do you feel like going shopping, Scott? I saw Diana had a list on the side of the fridge. I'd really like to have some homemade bread," Ben suggested.

"I'd like to try some homemade cooking. Do you think Taggee can handle the fort?" Scott wondered.

"If Scott and I go to pick up some groceries, do you think you can take care of the tigress?" Ben asked Taggee.

"She will be no problem…go get what you need." Taggee smiled.

40

Northeast Des Moines

Ben and Scott copied the list off the fridge, walked out to the garage, and drove down the street. "Where did you go in there, Ben?" Scott asked.
"Trying to put some information together from the morning—the conflicting signals," Ben vocalized.

"You really didn't believe she would sit and watch that, did you?" Scott replied.

"No, but I didn't expect her to pull away from me like she did," Ben worried.

"She pulled away from all of us. Like you said, she was totally embarrassed," Scott injected.

"Yeah, but she was totally withdrawn. I've not had that from her, not even when we first met. She was hesitant then, but just now, she literally shut everything off," Ben continued.

"Not everything. If she had shut everything off, it wouldn't have bothered her to look at you. She kept her eyes down so you couldn't read her. Let the girls calm her down. You'll see that she'll be back," Scott instructed. They drove down to the nearest grocery store, picked up what was on the list and even some stuff that wasn't on the list, then started their way back to the safe house. On their way back, they were pulled over by a police car. "You weren't speeding were you bro?" Scott asked.

"Nope...I'm not sure why they pulled me over," Ben said, waiting for the policeman to near the window.

"Maybe it's Diana's friend Ali," Scott purposed.

Ben wondered; he saw the policeman get out of his car and walk near the driver's side window. Ben rolled it down. "How may I help you, Officer?"

"I'm here to help you, but we must keep up appearances. Do you mind giving me your license and registration?" Ali asked.

Ben and Scott smiled. "You had to work today, huh?"

"Yeah, my shift will be ending here soon. I remember you said you were going to call me yesterday. I never had the chance to talk to you after that. Jared had mentioned that Diana was still in danger. He also told me not to say anything to the pastor or his wife about it. So, how can I help you?" Ali asked.

"Well, I need you to do some looking into things at DMPD. We have a leak...now, we've just traced it to one person in the local FBI office. But we're not sure he's working alone. Before Diana was taken, we had an encounter with the local police that seemed a little...off. I thought maybe you could carefully check into any incongruences that might suggest a worm in the barrel?" Ben replied.

"I can do that. Did your sister get home safely last night?" Ali added.

"I thought that might have been your doing. Thank you, I owe you. Yes, she got out safe." Ben smiled.

"It wasn't me personally, but there is a group of us—at least one in each shift—that have been keeping an eye on things as much as we could. Stacia was on patrol last night. She ran the plates of a car that came from near your house. When she read that it was your sister's car, she kept it in sight. She was far enough back to see that your sister was being tailed by another car, so she thought she'd pull it over for some minor infraction. I think the report said something about not signaling a lane change." Ali smiled.

"I think you've got a sour cream raisin pie coming your way for it. I'd say you'll have to share it with Stacia," Scott added.

"Ain't no way. I'll let Stacia know how much Diana and you guys appreciated her assistance. But the pie is mine," Ali insisted.

"Well, if we want any homemade bread tonight, we need to get going," Ben stated.

"Yeah, Jared made mention that he'd hope you guys would get her to make her dad's bread. He figured it should put at least five pounds back on her," Ali stated as he handed the papers back to Ben. "I'll let you know if I come up with anything. Stay safe and take good care of my sister for me," Ali admonished. Then he turned and went back to his car.

Ben waited till Ali was in his car before signaling and merging back into traffic. He checked back in his review mirror to see Ali merge back in.

Zenon's Vacation House

With a lot of encouragement from the girls, Ariana agreed to come back inside. Once inside, she noticed that only Taggee was there. She looked at him and cocked her head. "Mahala, can you ask Taggee where Ben and Scott went to?"

Mahala asked and Taggee replied. "Taggee said they went to pick up supplies from the store," Mahala translated.

Diana nodded. She saw the TV was still down, thought for a minute, then picked up the remote control. "I'm gonna try this thing again," she stated more to herself than to the group. She clicked it on, waited for the screen to light up, then selected cable from the popup menu. This time the TV came in on the news. Diana hit guide on the remote. She saw that the cable there at the house was similar to what she had a home. "Do you guys mind if I listen to music?" she asked. Mahala translated her question to Aisha and Taggee. All three of them shook their heads no. Diana scrolled down till she found the music channels and selected classical. The station was playing some of Diana's favorite sonatas. She put the remote down on the coffee table and went to grab her water. She looked over at the clock on the oven. She still had another hour before she could call her parents. She turned and asked Mahala. "Do you feel like teaching me some words in Farsi?"

"Definitely," Mahala excitedly replied.

"Great, let's start with some basics," Diana injected. Diana and Mahala went back and forth over how to say things like *good morning* and *good night*. Aisha suggested that Mahala should tell her the names of the objects in the kitchen. So Mahala and Diana headed to the kitchen to go over the various things. The girls were going over some of the silverware when they heard the big garage door open. Diana looked over to Taggee; he signaled for the girls to move to the living room. Then he moved to the hallway that led to the inside garage door.

Ben and Scott locked the car and the garage then started for the door. Ben stopped for a second. "What's wrong bro?" Scott asked, turning toward him.

"We didn't set up a system of letting Taggee know who was coming in. Now if we just walk in, what do you thing is going to happen? I'm pretty sure they hear the garage door," Ben informed Scott.

"Diana should be aware of you, she always has been so far," Scott injected.

"I'm not sure she will be now. I think we'd better knock, we'll get the details down later," Ben suggested.

"The thought of taking on Taggee right now is not a thrilling one. So I guess you're right," Scott agreed. He knocked on the door.

Taggee heard the knock, figured it was Ben and Scott, and went to open the door. "I'm glad you knocked. I was about to take whomever opened the door out," Taggee grinned as he took one of the bags from Scott.

The guys walked into the kitchen and set the bags on the counters. Ben noticed that there was music going, saw it was coming from the TV. "Did one of you three do that?"

"No…the girls got Ariana to come back inside a few minutes ago. She seemed as if she was going to conquer the controller. She turned it to a different place, and it brought up news and a list of different stations. She chose this one," Taggee informed him.

Ben looked out over the room, but he didn't see Diana. "Where did she go?"

"As soon as she heard your voice, she headed to the back room. I think you are going to have to go talk to her. Whether she wants it or not," Aisha insisted.

"Lord, help me," Ben said in aggravation.

"Not in force Ben, calm and gentle, or she will retaliate," Taggee reminded him. Ben nodded. He walked slowly down the hallway. The master bedroom door was closed, but it didn't latch. He carefully pushed the door open. Diana was lying on the bed, holding her pillow.

"Kitten…may I come in?" he asked even though he was already inside the room. She didn't answer. He closed the door, making sure it was latched this time, and walked over to sit down the side of the bed. "Diana," he calmly but sternly said. She still wouldn't acknowledge him. He slid over beside her and started combing her hair. "Diana…talk to me," he said quietly to her ear. He saw her close her eyes, but the goose bumps down her arm told him she was listening to him. "Come on, kitten…am I going to have to take matters into my own hands to make you talk?" he teased.

She opened her eyes and turned her head to look at him. "There you are," he said as he traced his fingers down her face. He saw her eyes soften; they were no longer the steel gray but a soft blue. "I'm sorry you were so embarrassed and I teased you about it," Ben stated. He continued to play with Diana's hair. She still wasn't saying anything, at least not audibly.

Ben tried a different direction. "I met up with our friend Ali on the way home."

"Is everything okay?" Diana softly asked.

Gotcha babe, Ben thought. He knew he could come around in another direction to fix the problem. "Yeah, everything is okay. He remembered that I mentioned I wanted to talk to him when he dropped Jared off. Since there was no chance to talk to him at that time, nor any other time after that, he pulled me over to talk to me."

Diana sat up against the headboard and put her pillow across her lap. She cocked her head to one side. "He pulled you over?"

"Yep…on the way back to the house here. He pulled me over so that we could chat," Ben informed her as he took her hand and started caressing his thumb over the top of it. Diana closed her eyes and leaned her head back against the headboard. "Kitten, don't go back to that hole. You wouldn't want a tiger pouncing on ya now, do you?" Ben jeered.

Diana couldn't help it; her mind went somewhere it shouldn't have. Her eyes flew open, and her face flushed red. "You might want to rephrase that statement Tiger," she said with a little laughter in her voice.

"Nah…I know exactly what I said," Ben teased. He saw her emerald eyes flash for a second. He grabbed her pillow away from her before she could grab it. She jumped up off the bed and stood ready to fight. Ben saw the challenge behind her eyes. He slid off on the bottom of the bed, blocking her way from getting to the hallway door. He slowly started walking toward her. Her eyebrow arched up and she dashed for the patio door; she didn't make it out. Ben grabbed her up and tossed her over on the bed. She went to crawl off on the other side, but Ben grabbed her by her waist and pulled her back. He sat down on top of her, straddling her between his knees, holding her arms off to the side. "Now, Ms. Henderson…we need to have a talk," Ben gleamed.

"What if I don't want to talk?" Diana dared. He bent down and kissed her lips. Diana didn't respond to him at first, but he knew she would—and she did. She was almost breathless by the time he let up on her.

"Are you going to talk to me? Or do I need to loosen that tongue of yours more?" Ben jabbed.

Diana looked up at him. "That all depends on what topic you want to discuss."

"Huh-huh…I guess I need to loosen it up some more," Ben teased as he bent back down and kissed her hard again. He could feel her body start to tremble underneath him. He let up on her. "That should loosen it up enough now," he stated.

Diana knew she was going to be in trouble if she didn't behave herself. She obviously wasn't the strong one today. If he kept going, she would be in over her head.

Ben saw she was trying to regain composure. He waited a minute before continuing. "Are we willing to have a civilized discussion now?" Diana nodded. Ben let go of her arms and let her slide herself up to a sitting position. He swung his leg over and off the side of the bed, freeing the rest of her. He reached over and put his hand on the side of her face and made her look at him. "I don't ever want you to close yourself off to me ever again. I'm I making myself clear?"

"I wasn't expecting…" Diana was still dealing with what she saw. Ben was able to read her now.

"Do you actually think I'm blaming you for that?" Ben scolded.

Diana shook her head. "No, but I couldn't let you see what was thinking. I had to close you out, I needed to get…control."

"My dear Ms. Henderson, the last I saw, you are human. I'd be worried if things didn't connect in that lovely mind of yours," he assured her.

She looked back over at him. "You don't understand…if I—" Diana stopped and shook her head and looked down at the floor.

"If you what, Diana?" Ben insisted. Diana didn't say anything. "Do I have to take drastic measures again?" he threatened.

She looked up but wouldn't look at him. "There are too many souls at risk, I can't lose control."

"As long as we both are trusting in the Lord and listening to His spirit; that will not be a problem Diana. You carry too much on your own shoulders. They are not big enough for all that. Give it to the Lord and let Him carry it. He is more than capable of dealing with everything," Ben stated.

Diana looked over at him, studying him. "You may be right, but I know of several occasions where it didn't work that way. I just don't trust…myself."

"Someday I'm going to find a way to turn that mind of yours off," he sneered.

You've found it. You just don't know it yet. Lord, help me, Diana thought.

There was a knock at the door. "Is it safe to come in?" Scott joked.

"Yes…come on in," Diana quipped.

Scott slowly opened the door. "Oh, good, you're both still alive. I was getting worried there." He saw Ben was leaning up against the headboard and Diana was sitting on the side of the bed. The bed was a total mess. "I see I missed a wrestling match, looks like it would have been a good one to see," Scott jested.

Diana flushed red. Ben glared at Scott. "Was there something you needed?"

"Hmm…oh…yeah, the girls were wondering if they needed to get stuff ready for lunch?" Scott smiled.

"I take it, brother, you're hungry," Diana quipped.

"Hey, what can I say? I enjoy the simple things in life: shelter, food, and water. We've got shelter and water, but I'm lacking food," he stated.

Diana giggled. "Okay, I'll go get something ready for lunch." She got off the bed, went to the bathroom, brushed her hair and pulled it back, then headed out the door toward the kitchen.

"Glad you got her back. How'd ya do it?" Scott quizzed.

"I used a bait and trap," Ben jeered.

"Bait? What bait?" Scott looked at Ben perplexed. Ben simply looked at Scott. "You did not…did you? She should be on a high for the entire day then. It didn't look like she was on a high to me," Scott chuckled.

"She has a high tolerance," Ben stated as he stood up and walked to the bathroom.

Diana walked toward the kitchen. "Are you okay, Ariana?" Mahala asked.

"Yes…I'm okay," Diana replied.

Taggee saw Ben and Scott come around from the corner. "I see you were able to pull her out again. You didn't slap her, did you?"

"No…she wouldn't respond to that. It would have just driven her farther away. I used a different route," Ben stated.

"You know, your route will only work for a short time bro.," Scott said in Farsi so Diana wouldn't understand.

"It will work long enough to keep her safe. After that, I have something else in mind," Ben replied.

Diana looked between the guys. "What are they saying?" she asked Mahala. Mahala looked over at Ben, who shook his head no.

"I think you will need to talk to him for an interpretation," Mahala stated as she pointed to Ben.

Diana was going to say something but saw the gleam in Ben's eyes. She shook her head at the guys and walked into the kitchen.

"See…all I have to do is hint of a little 'sugar,' and she backs down," Ben told the guys, still speaking in Farsi.

Taggee laughed. He reached over and patted Diana on the head as he walked to the living room. Then he said, "You may use that on her now, but she will win out using that same idea on you Ben."

Ben looked over at Diana. "Yeah...you're probably right there Taggee. However, I have a little time to enjoy my victories."

Diana looked at Scott. "Tell me what he said." Scott just shook his head. "I'm not gonna touch that one sis. You'll have to get that from the tiger over there."

"Remember that sour cream raisin pie...," Diana threatened.

"Are you really gonna make me drive all the way to Georgia to get one?" Scott quipped.

"Hey...I can be reasonable. Tell me what he said or forget about that pie,' Diana continued.

"That's blackmail. Ben, she's blackmailing me over here," Scott hollered.

"Some need sugar, some need spanked, some...my dear brother, need food," Diana teased.

"He said that Ben would only be able to use his method on you for a short time," Scott threw out.

"Maybe, maybe not. We'll see," Diana smoothly stated.

Ben looked up at her; the impish little gleam in her eyes was clearly seen. "Tigress...be careful. I'd hate to make lunch wait even longer. Mr. McCleary may pass out from starvation."

Diana's eyebrow arched up; her eyes went a steel gray for a second. She looked over at Scott, who was acting like he was going to die. She shook her head and smiled. Then she turned and went to the fridge, pulled out some lunch meat, cheese, and salad dressing; placing them on the high bar. She went over and pulled a couple of loaves of bread from the bread box. Then reached up and grabbed a bag of Doritos from the cupboard. She brought them over to the high bar. She slid over and grabbed some plates and put them at the end. "Come make your own sandwiches," she announced.

"You're beautiful, you know that?" Scott praised. "Can I get some mustard though?"

Diana chuckled. "I suppose I can manage that." She went back over to the fridge and pulled out not only the mustard but also the ketchup, sat them down near Scott, then pulled the soda out of the fridge as well. She helped Taggee and the girls make their sandwiches then went to get herself a glass of milk. She grabbed the regular milk first, but before she pulled it out, she glanced back in and saw a gallon of chocolate milk she hadn't noticed before. She grabbed it out of the fridge and poured herself a glass.

"I was wondering how long it would take you to see that," Ben said as he came up behind her. "There is some chamomile tea in the cupboard now too." He put his hands on her shoulders and pulled her back to him. She leaned her head back on his chest. "Thank You," she whispered.

"So you do have her purring again," Scott said as he came up to get another sandwich.

"Whatever...Scott. Just because two cats spar doesn't mean that they are fighting. You should know that," Diana teased. "They're just getting to know each other better."

"You two get to know each other any better, you'd better have an agreement between you two," Scott jabbed. He saw Diana flush and Ben glared at him. "I'm just stating the facts." He turned and went back into the living room.

Ben rubbed his hands up and down her arms. "You'd better get yourself a sandwich before your brother eats it all."

"You haven't had any either, so get up there as well," Diana quipped. She poured herself another glass of chocolate milk and then fixed herself a plate. Ben fixed a couple of sandwiches then grabbed a soda off the counter and turned and headed for the living room.

Diana sat down in one of the barrel chairs; Ben took the chair next to her. "Can we watch something or get a different type of music or something?" Scott pleaded.

"Classical and instrumental music helps me calm down. However, since I know that is an acquired taste, you can change it," Diana quipped. She saw that the remote was next to her, so she tossed it over to Scott. Scott scrolled through to the world news and left it there. Diana just rolled her eyes and sat quietly eating her lunch.

Once lunch was done with, Mahala, Aisha, and Diana went to the kitchen to clean up and put things away. "Bosh-ghab," Diana said as she was holding a plate. Mahala and Aisha nodded. Diana put it up in the cupboard and continued to dry all the plates. Every time she grabbed a new plate to dry, she would repeat the word in her mind. With all the plates dried, Diana started on the glasses and asked for the word for *glass*.

Ben and the rest of the guys stayed out in the living room. Ben asked Scott to find a channel that spoke Arabic or Farsi for the group. Diana would be the only one not understanding it. He planned on her talking to her parents as soon as they were done in the kitchen. *That should take a little while*, Ben thought.

The girls joined the group in the living room. Diana was standing behind Scott. She wasn't going to stay in the room; she was planning on going out on the patio. She looked down and noticed Scott trying to work his own neck. She reached down and started working on his shoulders and neck.

Scott felt Diana's hand come down on his shoulders. He froze at first, but as Diana continued to work, he started to relax. She worked on his shoulders for about twenty minutes. Scott looked over at Ben. "You've got to get her to open a parlor." Ben smiled and winked at Diana.

He waited until it looked like Scott was going to fall asleep. "Are you about done, kitten?" Diana looked over at Ben with a question on her face. "It's about time to let your parents hear your voice." Ben grinned. He saw the excitement flash in her eyes. Ben laughed. "Come on then."

Scott turned around. "Thank you sis."

"Not a problem…I told you I would rub your back for ya when you needed it," Diana replied as she moved to follow Ben.

41

Zenon's Vacation House

Ben led her to the bedroom. He plugged the phone cord into the wall and checked it to see if there was a dialtone. "Okay kitten…let's reach out and touch your family," Ben snickered.

Diana just rolled her eyes, but she did pick up the receiver and dialed her house. She sat there listening to the phone ring, "Hello, Henderson's," she heard in the receiver. "Mom…it's me, Diana," she paused for a moment. "Diana! Honey! Diana is on the line!" she heard her mom say.

Ben looked over and saw a tear running down her cheek; she quickly brushed it away. He brushed the back of his hand down the side of her face; she looked up at him and grinned. "I'll check back in later," he whispered. Then he walked out of the room to give her privacy.

He walked back into the living room. "Did she get through?" Scott asked.

"Yeah…she's talking to them right now," Ben stated as he walked over to the fridge to grab another can of soda. He sat with the group watching the news from the Middle East.

A half hour later, he went to check in on Diana. He quietly opened the door and listened to Diana's conversation. "Hey guys…I need to be going. Thanks for the recipes. I know…I hope so…I love you too. Tell the kids hi for me, okay? God Bless…see you soon…bye."

Diana was still holding on to the receiver; she slowly started to lower the receiver, but then she heard an extra click. Her alarm system went berserk, she turned sheet white. She knew Ben had walked in. She turned to him, putting her hand over the receiver. Ben watched her expressions and body posture change. When she looked over at him, he not only saw the alarms going off in her, but his own alarms were going off. He put his finger to his mouth, walked over, and took the receiver from Diana. He didn't expect anybody to be there, but he held it up to his ear to check anyway. He reached over and pushed the tab down to end the call then put the receiver back in its rest. He turned to Diana, who was still sitting on the bed. "It was supposed to be safe…isn't that what Director Zenon said? I would have never called them if it wasn't safe," Diana said in disbelief.

"Kitten…it may not mean it's bad," Ben stated. Diana looked at him in total disbelief. "Okay…okay…we both know it is, but let's get all the facts before we go jumping…agreed?"

"Agreed…are we going to tell the others?" Diana asked.

"We'll tell the guys. Mahala and Aisha doesn't need to know yet," Ben added.

"So, now what do we do?" Diana wondered.

"We continue like normal, maybe just a little more cautious," Ben calmly stated.

"I guess my morning devotionals on the patio are at an end…huh?" Diana sadly stated.

"I'm afraid so babe," Ben replied. Diana was just getting her mind wrapped around the next step when the doorbell rang.

Ben grabbed her hand and pulled her to the living room. He whistled, which alerted Scott. As Ben and Diana rounded the corner of the hallway, he signaled Scott to stay with Diana. Taggee didn't need to be told. He already gathered Aisha and Mahala and was on guard. Ben slowly walked to the door; the doorbell rang again. Ben looked out the side window then opened the door a little. "Ben…we need to talk."

Diana leaned over to Scott. "That's Allen." Scott nodded but remained on alert.

"Come on in," Ben said and opened the door a little wider. Allen stepped around the door and into the entryway. Ben closed and locked the door behind him then motioned him to go on in.

Allen saw that the guys were already on high alert. Glancing over at Diana, he didn't think she was overly surprised. The other two girls were extremely nervous. Ben walked past him, picked up a remote control, and turned off the TV. "Have a seat, sir," Ben offered.

Taggee signaled the girls to go sit down. Scott guided Diana to the nearby couch and signaled her to take a seat. He stayed standing behind the couch. Allen took the nearby recliner, and Ben sat in the chair next to it. As much as Ben didn't want to tell the girls about the latest event, he went ahead and asked Mahala to interpret the conversation for Taggee.

"So what's on the wind, sir?" Ben asked.

"Agent Kal has gone underground for starters," Allen began.

Diana looked over at Mahala. She could see the pain in her eyes. "You don't think he was taken like Amid, do you?" she carefully asked.

"It's a possibility…but I don't think so," Allen replied. "Going through his apartment, we found a journal that he was writing in. It made mention of how at first he didn't think twice about helping the Sheikh to get his hands on you. He had found the cabin that you were hiding in. He made arrangements for two other men to pose as state patrol to separate the guys from you. He had planned to grab you then while they were distracted, but a dog stopped him from getting to you. He also talked about the incident where his partner, Agent Donavan, insisted that they go up and check the cabin out. It was because of the call to Greg that Kal and his partner were pulled out of the area. That's when he came up with the idea of using darts to take out the dog and Diana. Apparently, there was a skirmish between Diana and Scott that made an impression on Agent Kal," Allen said, looking between Diana and Scott.

"Hey, I plead the Fifth," Scott quickly stated. Diana chuckled a little bit.

"I would love to know what happened," Allen insisted.

"I was out fishing while the guys left to deal with a break in at Scott's Quonset. They came back, and Scott thought he would play a trick on me," Diana informed Allen.

Allen gave a fatherly glare at Scott. "I thought I would scare her a little. She knew she wasn't supposed to be outside, and there she was, dangling her legs in the lake, fishing," Scott added.

Ben chimed in, "He did manage to scare her for about thirty seconds. Then she took out his kidney with an elbow and his knee with a backward kick. Then she pushed him into the lake."

"I see…then what did she do next?" Allen inquired.

"I tore off down the dock heading for the cabin until Ben caught me," Diana stated.

"I can see why Agent Kal didn't want to have to wrestle with her. He doesn't have the rodeo background you do, Ben," Allen jeered. "Anyway, the journal entry four days ago says that Mahdi contacted him saying that the American woman had escaped and to be watching for her to return home. He was to intercept her and give her back to him. He also wrote that his sister called him from Damascus, telling him about a woman called Ariana and how she was different from the other two girls. Apparently, you had mentioned that you were to be whipped for disobeying, but Ariana kept you covered and took the hits for you?" Allen looked over at Mahala, who just nodded, then over to Diana.

"I wasn't going to let her be whipped for simply letting me know what was going on. She only said five words in English, that's all," Diana stated.

"And you, Tiger, were able to get her out just after being whipped?" Allen questioned.

"With all the layers on, she was momentarily protected. Only one swipe made it through to break the skin. A sandstorm came up that prevented Mahdi from taking the next hit. I'm pretty sure the next one would have done a lot more damage," Ben stated.

"Half of me really wants to know how you know this, the other half wants to give a fatherly rebuke," Allen sternly stated.

"Sir, Scott was gracious enough to bring an outfit for me to wear to get out of Syria with. One piece of it was a halter top. Not my choice of shirts, but it has come in handy in several occasions," Diana informed Allen. "Plus, the guys let me go swimming that evening in New York. Ben and I had a little bit of a challenge going on. He was constantly lagging behind and therefore he could get a good look at my back," Diana teased.

"That's not entirely true, kitten," Ben refuted.

"She did give you a good run for the money, bro," Scott chimed in.

"Wait a minute. You're telling me that you, Scott Aiden McCleary, gave this woman a halter top to walk in the dessert with?" Allen steamed.

"Well…I—" Scott started out.

"You'd better just take the heat and not bury yourself, my dear brother. I know that look. My dad used it a lot when he wanted to warn my boyfriends," Diana warned.

"And you, Tiger, you are telling me that this woman was out swimming you even though she was anemic and had infection throughout her body?" Allen questioned.

"Well…that might have been a slight exaggeration on my part. I'd say we were about even. Unfortunately, your-well maintained gentlemen here were attracting a lot of attention from the female occupants of the hotel. We had to cut the challenge short, so neither of us knows who would have won," Diana injected.

"We weren't the only ones attracting the attention, Milady" Scott jabbed.

"Yeah…well, all the more reason why I stopped the game and returned to my room," Diana quickly stated.

"Interesting," Allen stroked his chin.

"Kitten, I have a feeling Allen is going to want to offer you a job," Ben laughed.

"Really...hmm, considering the fact that I've been terminated from my previous job; I might look into it," Diana stated.

"Are you serious?" Scott steamed.

Diana nodded. "Mom and Dad just told me about it. I received a letter a week ago informing me of my termination of employment at Honeywell's apartment." Diana glanced over at Ben; he was beyond mad. "Tiger...it's okay. I actually expected it a lot sooner than that. I figured I was fired by the third week out."

"Anyway...back to the problem at hand," Allen refocused. "Agent Kal's attitude toward Ariana/Diana changed after the conversation he had with his sister the next day. The journal states that he told Mahdi that Ariana was not his problem and that he had fulfilled his assignment. Apparently, Mahdi told him either he give him Ariana or he has to give him Mahala," Allen ended.

"Over my dead body," Taggee fumed. Diana wondered what he said, but thought it best to let it go for now.

"That goes for all of us, Taggee. He will get neither of them," Scott injected.

"The point is, though, I can't blame him. Agent Kal will protect his sister. That means he has to give Mahdi...Diana, and now he has gone underground," Allen stated flatly.

"Do we know who he is working with over here?" Ben asked.

"Unfortunately...not yet," Allen informed him.

"Ben...you'd better tell them. The girls are in it already anyway," Diana suggested.

"Tell us what?" Scott queried.

"The landline and net were supposed to be secure, so I let Diana call her parents. When she ended the call and after her parents hung up, there was another click," Ben included.

"Could it have been at her parents' house, maybe two receivers were being used?" Scott threw out.

"I would have been opened to that possibility, except I saw Diana's reaction afterward. It wasn't good, bro," Ben informed him.

"There are days I wished you'd take those special goggles off," Scott fumed.

"Sorry, brother, it's who I am and have been for several years. I can't change that," Diana stated.

"So, now what do we do? Do we have to leave here as well?" Aisha spoke up.

Diana looked over to Scott, since he was the closest. "What is she saying?"

"She's asking if we are going to have to leave here," Scott translated.

"Not yet…we have to come up with another safe house. As of right now, this is still the better option. As Charles said earlier, the weakest spot is the lake itself," Allen stated. Diana looked up at Scott; he shook his head then translated what Allen said. Allen started walking toward the door; Ben and Scott followed him. "I'll fill Charles in…I strongly feel this: don't let these girls out of your sights. I'm hoping for Agent Kal to make a mistake so we can get him before he can get Diana." Scott and Ben nodded.

"Sir, I have a man working on the possibility of an accomplice in the DMPD. If I hear from him, I'll be giving you a call," Ben said as a matter of fact.

"Officer Lopez, right?" Allen asked. Ben nodded. "Charles said something to the fact of him being Diana's brother. How many brothers does she have?"

Scott chuckled and Ben grinned. "She has one biological brother, the others kind of adopted her as their sister," Ben stated.

Scott chimed in. "She has that effect on us. We just kind of take her under our wings. I'll have to ask her someday why she doesn't have as many sisters."

"That may take a task force all by itself," Ben jeered.

"I've got to go. Be alert, be ready, and be strong," Allen said as he unlocked the door and walked out. Ben reached over and locked it again. Scott went and looked out the side window till he saw the car pull out and away.

Ben and Scott walked back to the living room. "Well, kitten, do we get to have homemade bread tonight?" Ben asked.

"I did get my recipe from home, so I don't have a good excuse not to," Diana smiled. She knew it was to break the tension. She had to put on a good face for no other reason but to keep Mahala calm. She went back to her room, grabbed her papers, then headed toward the kitchen. "Mahala, do you and Aisha want to lend me a hand or two?" she asked.

Mahala translated what Ariana asked to Aisha. Aisha patted Mahala on the knee then stood up and signaled to Mahala to follow her. They headed to the kitchen.

"Well, there's at least two of the kitten's sisters," Scott threw in.

Ben nodded. Diana was close to the girls. He figured once the language barrier was down, Aisha and Diana would be very close.

Taggee moved over to the chair nearer to the guys. "So how are we going to change things to increase the protection here?"

"For one thing, the girls are to be escorted by at least one of us at all times," Ben stated.

"Three girls…three of us, that shouldn't be a problem," Scott added. "I don't think Diana or Aisha is going to let Mahala out of their sights anyway. So it should keep two of us around the area at all times," Scott threw in.

"I don't think it is a good idea to have them separated at night," Taggee voiced.

"I agree…we'll do a camp out here in the living room at night. All three girls will sleep out here. We'll stay with the schedule that we had last night. We'll overlap so that two of us will be awake throughout the night," Ben planned. Scott and Taggee agreed. Diana had walked back into the living room while the guys were talking. She wished she knew their plans, but of course they were talking in Farsi. Ben caught a glimpse of Diana out of the corner of his eye. He looked over to see what she needed. "What's up, kitten?"

"Is it okay if we turn the music back on? I'll let you guys choose the station, just don't pick screaming or grunge," Diana asked.

Ben looked over at Scott and raised an eyebrow then looked back as Diana. "Not a problem. We'll get it turned on," he quickly said.

Scott just chuckled. "This could be interesting." Ben gave him an ornery grin and picked up the remote control. Ali had told them that music has a strong influence on Diana's moods. Obviously…Ben was going to find out if it was true or not.

Diana had walked back to the kitchen to put the dough together so it could rise. She had Aisha working on prepping the bread pans. She had Mahala working on the pie crust. She started to add the yeast to the water and sugar when she heard the song "Take On Me." She laughed unrestrained, knowing full well that Ben was playing with her again.

Aisha and Mahala turned and looked at Ariana. Diana looked at the girls. "It's the kind of music I listened to when I was your age, Mahala, a long time ago." She didn't bother trying to explain anything else.

Scott heard Diana laugh in the kitchen when the station started playing. He looked at Ben. "I take it you found out what other kind of music she liked."

"She likes a wide range of styles. This one, as you know, is my style. I'm just seeing what 'mood' it puts her in," Ben replied.

Diana finished getting the dough together and set it in the oven to rise. She then helped Mahala with getting the coconut cream pies done and cooling. Once that was done, the girls started discussing what they were going to do for supper. It was decided that Aisha and Mahala were going to put together a vegetable dish. Diana was to take care of cooking the meat and potatoes. Mahala and Aisha got to work on cleaning and prepping the vegetables. Diana headed to the garage to get the roast out of the freezer. She walked out the door and over to the freezer, shuffling things around to get to the roast. She stopped for a second as she finally got down to the roast. "You're not going to scold me now are you?" she queried calmly.

"The thought crossed my mind," Ben replied. "But I see what you have in your hands, I figured I'd better word it carefully if I intend to enjoy that piece of meat."

"Indeed," Diana quipped.

"Seriously though, you're not to be out of our sight at any time," Ben warned.

Diana couldn't resist. "Now that could be an interesting situation sir. How do you intend to work that with bathroom rights?"

Ben's ears turned red; Diana laughed at him. "That's three times now. Maybe I need to start a tally app," Diana teased as she moved to walk past him.

Ben reached out, stopping Diana from going through the door. "Well played kitten. Even so, other than that; never out of my sight, understood?" Diana looked at him and placed her hand on the side of his face and nodded. She walked through the door and back into the kitchen. Ben followed her in and headed for the living room.

"So what's planned for supper?" Scott asked.

"Roast," Ben replied.

"If she's as good with roasts as she is with fish, I'm gonna marry that girl," Scott teased.

Ben looked at Scott. "Don't think so bro…"

Supper was ready by six that evening. The smell of freshly baked bread and seasoned roast was wafting through the air. Diana and Aisha insisted that they use the dining room for this meal. Ben enjoyed the meal but watched to make sure Diana ate. She did take a small amount of meat and potatoes. He saw she was a little leery of the vegetable dish, but she took a little and picked out what she thought would be safe. He smiled when he saw her grab another slice of bread. He had to admit, the bread was good and was silently thanking Jared for sharing her weakness.

Scott was going in for another big helping of roast and potatoes. Taggee, Aisha, and Mahala were commenting on how they would tweak the roast by adding cumin and baharat; then there was a knock on the door. Everybody froze for a second. Taggee was already close to Mahala and Aisha, but Scott was at the opposite end of the table from Diana. Both Ben and Scott stood up at the same time. Scott moved to stand by Diana; Ben moved to answer the door.

Ben opened the door slowly. "Sir…come on in."

Charles entered the entryway. "Sorry to disrupt your supper, folks."

"With the exception of Scott over there, we were about done anyway," Ben replied.

"Sir…have you had your supper yet? We have plenty here if you'd like," Diana added.

"No, thank y—is that homemade bread?" Charles asked.

Diana chuckled. "Yes sir, just made this afternoon."

"I'll take a slice of that," he eagerly said.

"Help yourself, sir," Scott stated as he placed the plate of sliced bread near the side of the table. Diana reached over and grabbed the butter and her knife and placed it near the bread.

Charles reached down, grabbed a slice of bread and buttered it, then took a bite. "Mmm…a talent lost over here. Did one of the Syrians make this?"

"No sir, Diana made it," Ben replied.

"Aisha helped too. I couldn't knead the dough with my wrist. She took care of that," Diana added.

"Was there some new news, sir?" Scott asked when things seemed to drag along.

"Yes…sorry, I don't get to enjoy such luxuries," he said, swallowing his mouthful. "Ali came and visited with me today."

"What did he come up with?" Ben queried.

"He checked into the possibility of someone working in with Khaleel in the DMPD. He said that the two men you saw up by the cabin were impostors. The names on their uniforms match two officers that were in the hospital for injuries sustained while helping with a factory fire in Cedar Rapids," Charles ended.

"Well, that mystery is solved," Ben stated.

"However, if I may, Ben. Could you follow me for a minute? I need to talk to you privately," Charles said as he put his hand on Ben's shoulder and started walking him to the patio door.

Diana watched as the two men walked out onto the patio. She tried reading the conversation, but Ben and Director Zenon were facing the backyard. Scott put his hands on her shoulders. "It'll be okay, Milady. If it's something important, Ben will tell us."

"Tell you, maybe, I'm not so sure about telling me," she quipped.

Scott felt Diana tense up and started rubbing her neck. "Hang on sis, it can't be too much longer."

Taggee and Aisha quietly asked Mahala what was going on. "One of Ariana's friends found out some information about an incident that happened with her before she came to us. But I think she is more nervous about the conversation going on outside. She really does not like not knowing what is going on," Mahala explained.

"She will always want to know the good and the bad; that way, she will be prepared for either way," Taggee stated.

Ben walked back in with Zenon. He saw that Scott was working on keeping Diana calm. He purposely had Zenon face out to the backyard. He knew she would read it otherwise. He also warned Zenon that Diana would try to deduce what was going on.

Charles walked up to the table and grabbed another slice of bread. "Ma'am…you definitely have a talent." He smiled.

"Thank you, sir," Diana stated as she tried to read him. She couldn't read anything good or bad. *Lord, help me out*, she prayed.

Charles said good-bye to all and walked to the door. Ben followed him. "Allen's right, she's an interesting character. Judging from the look in her eyes, you've got a challenge coming toward you tonight," Charles surmised.

"Very well aware of it, sir." Ben smiled. He unlocked the door and let Zenon out then locked it again. He watched from the side window as he walked down the drive and across the street. Then he walked down the sidewalk out of sight. He turned and joined the group at the dining room table.

Scott sat back down to finish the rest of his plate. Ben sat down and glanced over at Diana. She was quiet but fuming. She looked up at him and, with a cold glare, shot an eyebrow up at him. He had to bite his cheeks to stop from laughing. *That's okay, babe…I know you're furious, but it's for your own good*, he said to himself.

Diana saw that she wasn't going to get any information from Ben at this time; she also saw that everybody except Scott was done eating. She needed to focus in to have a chat with the Lord, to get her emotions under control. She started stacking her plate with the empty plates near her.

She took them over to the kitchen and started to rinse them off. Soon Aisha and Mahala came in with the rest of them. The girls worked together to get things taken care of. The guys moved over to the living room and started moving some of the furniture around to make room for the night. "So what are you going to do?" Scott asked Ben.

"Do with what?" Ben replied as he moved the one couch back.

"You know good and well with what. Are you going to just leave her out on a limb?" Scott snipped.

"It's for her own good," Ben said as he stood up and looked at her working in the kitchen.

"She doesn't know that. As much as you threw a fit for her shutting you off, what do you think she's feeling?" Scott reprimanded.

Ben turned and looked at Scott then at Taggee, who unlike Diana, understood the conversation Ben and Scott was having. "It may be best to have her worry about one specific thing rather than everything," Taggee stated. Ben nodded.

Once the dishes were done and everybody settled down, Diana went and got the pie and started to cut it into slices. She was reaching up to get the small serving plates when she felt his hand stroke down her arm. "I'm sorry," Ben quietly said.

She lowered her arm and turned and looked at him. "Are you going to let me know what in the world is going on?"

"Diana…," Ben said shaking his head. She reached up and grabbed the plates and walked over to the counter, turning her back to him. She started putting the pie on the plates. "Seeing how I'm the one he's after, don't you think I should know what's in the wind?" she countered.

"Don't you think your shoulders have enough to carry?" Ben quipped back.

"You obviously think so, I don't," she shot at him. She put the plates of pie up on the high bar.

"You're short one kitten," Ben teased.

"No, I'm not. I'm don't want any," she stated. She started the teapot and began working on restarting the coffeepot.

Ben grabbed her hands and turned her to face him. He looked into the steel-gray and cold eyes of Diana. "I know you're mad, but I also know you're scared. Let me do my job and protect you," Ben firmly stated. He watched as her eyes turn to a calming blue. "Thank you," he stated as he traced his fingers down the side of her face.

"Hey are those for us?" Diana heard Scott ask from the living room.

"Come and get it," she called out. She looked back at Ben then moved around to the far side of the high bar to hand the plates out. Ben came around and grabbed one for himself and went to sit down. Once everybody had one, Diana went and got herself a cup of chamomile tea then came back and sat down in the living room as well. She sat over with the girls on one of the couches, opposite side from where Ben was sitting.

Scott took another bite of the pie to stop himself from laughing. *Still as stubborn as all get-out aren't you, Milady.*

Ben noted her protest as well; she may be willing to submit control to him, but not without letting him know that she didn't like it.

Taggee laughed. "The tigress is still not willing to let you take all control from her."

"I would say not. That's okay, at least she is contained for now." Ben smiled. Then he looked at Mahala. "She will ask you what was said. I strongly advise you not to tell her. I'd have to take drastic matters to contain her again."

Mahala looked up at Taggee. "He would hurt her?"

"Not at all, quite the opposite, Mahala. My sister doesn't respond to that type of force. Ben has another way of controlling her," Scott filled in. Mahala looked over at Aisha for an explanation. Aisha told her she would explain it later. Aisha saw that Ariana may not be understanding the words, but she saw the look in Ben's eyes. Ariana knew that Ben was blocking anybody from telling her, and she was not happy.

Later that night, while Aisha was working on rinsing the dessert dishes off and handing them to Ben for him to load in the dishwasher she said, "It would be easier for her not to fight you so much,"

"God has created her to be a fighter. I'd be worried if she didn't fight. It would mean she has given up," Ben stated.

"That isn't going to be good for her if Mahdi gets a hold on her," Aisha warned. Ben turned and looked at her. Aisha looked near to being sick. "The first woman Amid sent to us did not pass the examination. The Sheikh was furious at her lie; he gave her to Mahdi, who proceeded to arrange for her to be taken by several of the guards there that evening. I had to attend to her afterward. There was nothing I could do but try to stop the bleeding. The next time I was called in to attend to her, she had been beaten so bad that I prayed she would die to end her pain. She lived, but she was broken. Mahdi only spat at her the next time he saw her. The next day after that, I found out that the Sheikh sold her to an Asian businessman."

"What happened to the second girl?" Ben softly asked.

"She was pure. The Sheikh had the doctor impregnate her. But she was too young and too small. Both the baby and she died when she miscarried. A blessing in truth. The Sheikh had no intention of letting the virgin mother live after the baby was weaned," Aisha said as she looked at Ariana. "That's how bad I was. I was willing to put Ariana through that. I knew it was wrong, but I did nothing."

Ben turned Aisha to look at him. "You did as you were told to do by your husband. You knew no other way. That was the reason why God sent Ariana to you, to show you, Mahala, and Taggee a different and better way. The Lord told Ariana that He was sending her there to help those who could not hear otherwise. He is also going to be the one that deals with Mahdi. We just have to trust Him to guide us in His way."

Aisha looked him dead in the eyes. "And what are you going to do if Mahdi takes her?" Ben looked at Diana. He couldn't wrap his mind around that possibility; he was becoming sick to his stomach. "Ben... what are you going to do?" Aisha asked again.

"I will chase him down, no matter where he goes, no matter how far he goes, until she's back and safe," Ben coldly stated. Then he looked at Aisha. "I will do that no matter which one of you girls are in danger. In the Lord, you and Mahala are my sisters. I will not let him take any of you." Aisha nodded. She had no doubt that Ben, like Taggee, would do everything possible to keep them safe. However, if Ariana was taken, Ben would kill Mahdi. Ben and Aisha walked back into the living room. Ben didn't see Diana and looked at Scott, who was standing over by the corner of the hallway. Scott winked and nodded toward the hallway bathroom. "Where did Taggee go?" Ben asked.

"He said he was going to have a look around outside," Mahala answered.

"Well then, do you ladies want to watch a movie, listen to music, or what?" Ben asked.

"I have always heard people talking about this great Western actor named John Wayne. Do you have any of his movies?" Aisha asked.

Ben and Scott grinned. "I'm sure we can find some of his movies. Let me flip this over to satellite and then we can see if we can pull him up," Ben replied.

"You'd better do that before Milady comes out of the bathroom. I sure don't want a repeat of this morning," Scott jabbed.

"Point taken. If she comes out before I have it changed over, would you mind taking her back to the room and having her bring her stuff up to one of the other rooms?" Ben requested.

"I suppose I can do that. But if I find out that you're doing that to protect my sensibilities, I'm gonna have to knock some sensibilities into your head," Scott stated. In truth, that is exactly why Ben was asking Scott to do that. He, like Diana, was a virgin; and Ben thought it to be inappropriate to expose him to the scene no matter how short it was going to play. He saw Scott's face when the satellite came on this morning. Attention was drawn to Diana because of her reaction, but Scott was just as much in shock at first.

Ben picked up the remote and started switching the things around when they heard the bathroom door open. Ben nodded to Scott, who shot a piercing look at him but then turned to intercept Diana.

"Hey, Milady, since we're over here. Let's get your things moved out of the bedroom," Scott suggested.

Diana looked at him for a second. "All of you girls are going to be camping out in the living room at nights," Scott simply stated. Diana thought for a minute, processing as it were. Then she nodded and headed toward the bedroom. She grabbed her toiletry bag and loaded everything into it from the bathroom. Then she placed it on the bed then loaded her suitcase back up and locked it. As she passed by the patio door, she noticed Taggee out on the patio. He was over in the far corner on his knees and praying.

Scott saw her looking out and walked over to see what she was seeing. "Lord, help us please," Diana prayed out loud.

Scott put his arm around Diana's back and pulled her near. "He is helping us sis, or you wouldn't have heard that extra click."

Diana rested her head on his shoulder. "I wish we were on the backside of the mountain and not still climbing it."

"I know," Scott quietly stated as he rubbed her back. "Come on, let's get you back with the group." Diana sighed and finished getting her stuff together. She moved it in to Aisha and Mahala's room—all except her pillow. That she was taking into the living room. Scott saw that Diana had also gathered Ben's stuff; he grabbed it and put it in the small room next to the bathroom where Taggee and his things were put. As Diana met him in the hallway, she stated, "Maybe you'd better set up that last room like I was there. It would at least give us a heads-up if someone was trying something." Scott grinned at her and guided her into the living room again.

"Well, it's about time, I was about to start the movie without you two," Ben teased.

"You're welcome. I guess Diana and I could have left your things in that bedroom and made you get them yourself," Scott jabbed back.

"Well, in that case, thank you," Ben jested with a large bow. "Shall we then?" He clicked Play on the remote. He saw that Diana had taken one end of the open couch, her legs pulled up with her pillow across them. He sat down on the floor in front of her.

"So what are we watching?" Diana quietly asked Ben.

"The girls wanted to see a John Wayne movie," Ben replied as he leaned his head back against Diana's legs.

"Umm, Mahala isn't going to enjoy much. She'll be exhausted interpreting everything," Diana pointed out. Just then the theme song to *The Quiet Man* started. Diana noticed that the music to the song was the same, but the words were different. The movie had been dubbed in Arabic. "I didn't even know they played such movies in the Middle East," Diana quietly stated.

"They don't. There are enough Arabic immigrants in the States that the companies started putting it in Arabic," Ben whispered back.

"Well, that's an interesting fact to know," Diana commented. Ben and Diana heard the patio door knob start to turn; Ben went to jump up when Diana put her hand on his shoulder. She leaned down and whispered in Ben's ear, "It's just Taggee coming back in."

Ben looked over to see Taggee standing by the door. "We have a movie going if you would like to join us," Ben stated.

"Thank you, I will grab a cup of coffee then I will be in," Taggee replied.

Taggee came back in with his coffee and sat down in the recliner. Scott had taken one of the barrel chairs opposite of the couch that Aisha and Mahala were sitting in. Diana looked over at the clock on the oven. It was only nine p.m. *This day has really drug on*, she thought. She turned and watched the movie. She didn't need to read the subtitles... she knew the movie by heart. It was one of her family's favorite John Wayne movies ranking just below *McClintock!* About halfway through the movie, she started nodding off. She finally gave it up and laid her head down on her arm and closed her eyes.

As the movie ended, Scott glanced around the room. He saw that Diana had fallen asleep. He chuckled and nodded to Ben to look at Diana. "It apparently wasn't exciting to Milady... she went out," he teased.

"It hasn't been an easy day for her bro," Ben jabbed.

"We will need to treat her wrist then we can let her go to sleep for the night," Taggee stated.

"Do we need to do that tonight? Can't we just let her sleep?" Mahala asked.

"No...she needs to get that wrist healed. She will go back to sleep," Aisha corrected.

Ben got up on his knees and turned to face Diana. "Kitten," he said as he traced his fingers down her face; Diana opened her eyes. "Let's get that wrist of yours treated then we'll let you go out for the night," Ben softly said. He saw her grimace at the mention of treating her wrist. He chuckled. "I know…but let's get it over and done with." He stood up and took the pillow and laid it to the side of the couch. Then he took her hands and pulled her up. She stood up directly in front of him; he saw her slowly raise her eyes to look up at him. There were those emerald eyes he'd not seen much all day. "Shall we?" he said, stepping back to give her room to move. He placed his hand in the middle of her back and guided her to the kitchen. Taggee followed them over.

"My turn to go check the outside area," Scott quickly stated. Ben just nodded as he started filling the bowl with water.

"Is there something we can do to help?" Aisha asked.

"If you could, would you grab the extra blankets from the closet next to the bathroom? We will need to put a couple of beds down on the floor," Ben stated. Aisha and Mahala went and started working on getting things set up. Ben started unwrapping Diana's wrist. "You haven't taken any pain medicine for this today, have you?"

"No…I haven't needed to," Diana calmly stated. "Why?"

"If it hasn't been hurting you, I'd say it must be getting better," Ben figured. As he unwrapped the last layer, he inspected it. There was still a small gash around the sides of her wrist, but the top and bottom of her wrist were closed and were a dark pink instead of bright red. He saw no signs of infection or puss pockets around the wound. "It's looking very good, kitten," Ben encouraged.

"Let's hope it shows it by not burning so much," Diana quipped.

Ben gave Diana's hand to Taggee, who patted the backside of her hand. Diana looked at him and gave him a small smile then closed her hand around his thumb. Ben glided his hand down the underside of Diana's forearm. He felt her muscles twitch. "I'll have to check that out another day." Diana slapped him. Ben just laughed then grabbed a hold of her arm. They treated it and started to rewrap it.

Scott came back inside just as Ben was finishing wrapping Diana's wrist. "How's it looking?"

"It's actually healing fairly well. Tomorrow or Tuesday, I'll have to take her to see her doctor," Ben informed him.

"Are you sure it couldn't wait till this was done with? You know Agent Kal knew about her needing to see the doctor in three days. He'll be looking for her," Scott injected.

Diana looked at Ben. "He's got a valid point, Tiger. I may not be able to see my doctor until this is over with."

"No…you'll have to see a doctor. The medication that we've been using is almost out," Ben stated.

"Thank the Lord for that one," Diana quipped.

"Now…now…it could be worse. You could be needing an IV of antibiotics ran into you," Ben suggested.

"Already been there and done that, and no, I would prefer not to revisit it," Diana jabbed.

"Okay then, I can't take you to your doctor, what about mine?" Ben suggested.

"You don't think he'd figure that as a possibility?" Diana wondered.

"No…I don't think he would. Let see what we can do in the morning. Are you going to sleep in what you got on or do you want to change?" Ben asked.

"Normally, I'd sleep in what I have on, but there's flour and stuff on my jeans and shirt. So I'd better change," Diana figured.

Ben walked Diana back to the middle room. Diana knocked on the door, Taggee opened it. He signaled for Diana to come in; after she passed him, he walked out and closed the door. "Go ahead and get done what you need. I'll wait here till the ladies are done," Taggee informed Ben.

Ben nodded and headed back to the living room. The only thing he had planned on changing was taking off his boots. He walked back into the living room and slipped off his boots.

"Do you think she'll go back to sleep tonight?" Scott wondered.

"She's tired enough to, it's just if she lets herself," Ben replied.

"Remember what she told Zenon last night. He had said that most nights they would find him out at the fire ring looking at the fire. She made the comment that that would be where she would go," Scott inserted.

"You figure if we get a fire going, she'll relax?" Ben surmised.

"It will change her mood in one way or another," Scott teased.

"I'd have to shut her mind down to get the other. I'm still working on that puzzle. I'll settle for just keeping her calm right now," Ben sneered.

"Well, I guess putting sappy love songs on would be the wrong choice then," Scott laughed.

Ben walked back to the last bedroom and pulled the pillows off the bed and grabbed the spare blanket from the foot of the bed. He came back in and started making his bed.

Scott watched as Ben made up a bed on the floor. "You're not going to be Diana's pillow tonight, huh?"

"Nope…she has her pillow now. Plus, even though it isn't a problem for us, my sleeping with her may be a problem for Aisha, Mahala, and Taggee. Let's not cause problems before we need to," Ben stated.

"Yeah, I forgot, we have to keep things kosher," Scott quipped. "I sure hope she doesn't have one of those nightmares again. We may have to deal with three hysterical women instead of one."

"She didn't need to take any pain meds today. I think that had a major influence on that night. However, I don't need to be losing five more years of my life if she does have one. I'll see what I can do," Ben informed Scott.

"I'd greatly appreciate that." Scott grinned.

Ben went and turned the gas on in the fireplace and started it up. Then he turned the TV back to cable and started scrolling through the music channels. He first started with Classical; Scott just about died. Then Ben checked out Nightsounds, that was a definite *no*. Finally, he checked out Easy Listening. It was at least tolerable, even still, he turned it down low so it was more of a background noise. "Do you think you can tolerate elevator music for the night?" Ben asked Scott.

"It's better than that classical junk," Scott fumed.

The ladies walked back in followed by Taggee. Diana saw the fireplace going; she looked over at Ben and Scott, who were talking over in the barrel chairs, and smiled. *To bad this wasn't in a different situation*, Diana thought.

"Did I see what I thought I saw cross those eyes of hers?" Scott chuckled.

Ben gleamed. "I believe you did, Scott. I'm sure I saw something there."

"I'm not sure what you two are talking about," Diana stated.

"Huh-huh, I'm sure I can get what's in that head out if I set my mind to doing so," Ben injected.

"No…I'm pretty sure you can't," Diana quipped. "One…I'm not drugged. Two…you're not a mind reader. Finally…what you think you can use would not be allowed with the present company. So I'm pretty sure it's safe to say you can't," Diana stated with a confident grin on her face.

"I do believe she has you confined for the current moment," Scott chuckled.

"Not really…I can throw her over my shoulder and take her back to the bedroom. I'd just have to tell Taggee and the girls that I need to discipline her." Ben smiled.

"Whatever, Tiger," Diana snided as she sat down on the couch. Ben got up and walked around, checking the doors, including the one in the bedroom. When he walked back into the living room, he made it a point to walk near the couch that Diana was sitting on. He rested his hands on the back of the couch directly behind Diana's head.

"By the way, I agree with you. It would be great if this was in a different time and place," he whispered in her ear. He kissed her on her neck and walked back to the barrel chair.

Diana's face flushed beet red, and she bit down on her bottom lip. *Okay...so he is a mind reader. I'll have to be more careful*, she told herself.

Scott watched Ben lean down and talk to Diana. He saw her eyes flash and watched as her face turned beet red. "What did you tell her?" he asked as Ben sat down in the chair.

"Nothing much really. Why?" Ben smiled.

"Because that flash I saw could have started its own fire, and she just about bit through her bottom lip," Scott snipped.

Ben got a conceited look on his face and with a broad smile across his mouth as he said, "Sometimes, she forgets the connection the Lord has given us. It comes in rather handy, especially when she's too tired to fight it."

Aisha and Mahala lay down on their bed and watched the fire for only a few minutes before they were asleep. Ben told Taggee to go ahead and get some sleep; he and Scott would take the first watch. Taggee took the recliner. Scott had shown him earlier how to work it. It was more comfortable than the couch he slept in the night before.

Ben and Scott quietly talked to each other, leaving Diana to silently reflect on the day's events. *I'm sorry Lord. I didn't give you much time this morning or throughout the day, did I? I guess that explains my bad behavior*, Diana prayed. *Thank you for giving me a chance to talk with Mom and Dad. Thank you for giving us a heads-up to the dangers around us. Help me to remember why you're having me here in this place and in this position. Help me to be a witness of your love and glory. Help me to rest in your arms and to do your will with an open heart. Protect my family, Ben's family, and all here. Protect me and hold me in your care, my love.* Diana sat quietly watching the fire and listening for the Lord's instructions and guidance. She felt the Lord's arms come and wrap her up and hold her tight. A peace overflowed her heart and mind and settled in her spirit. She thanked the Lord and basked in His love and mercy. Soon she was asleep.

Ben felt the Lord's presence fill the room; His peace flowed through the house. He looked over at Scott. "Do you feel Him?"

"Yeah…it would be impossible not to. It's like there are angels all around us, shielding us from the evil outside," Scott stated.

"Definitely…Thank you, Lord," Ben praised. He looked over at Diana; she was still sitting up, but she had fallen to sleep. God's peace was so full and close that she was at rest in Him. Ben got up and walked over to Diana. He moved her pillow from her lap, slowly put one arm behind her back, the other he slid under her thighs then gently moved her down so that she could lay down. She woke enough to see what Ben was doing; she turned so she was lying on her side then gave him a smile and closed her eyes. He laid the pillow beside her then he grabbed one of the extra blankets and covered her up.

"Good night, babe. Sleep deep in the Lord's presence," he whispered. He brushed the back of his hand down the side of her face then kissed her forehead. She snuggled down against her pillow. He went to the kitchen and poured two cups of coffee and brought them over to the coffee table between him and Scott. Scott looked at the fire and sipped the coffee. Then he quietly chuckled. "What?" Ben asked.

"Oh…on the way back from moving the stuff out of the bedroom, Diana threw out the idea that we should set up the room as if she was in there and sleeping. That way it would give us an early warning if someone did try something," Scott recounted.

Ben thought for a minute. "That's not a bad idea, bro."

Scott looked back at Ben then back to the fire. A lightbulb turned on in his head. "I could add a few more traps around to slow any would-be assailants."

"I think that would be a good idea. We'll get to working on that once the sun is up." Ben smiled. The guys sat quietly discussing what they could do and making a mental list of supplies they would need to find.

42

Zenon's Vacation House

About three hours later, Ben and Scott had everything set and planned out. As Ben went to the kitchen to refill his coffee cup, he glanced down at Diana as he passed by. She was still in a deep sleep. Before he made it to the counter, he heard her get up and quickly, but quietly, head to the bathroom.

Scott saw her start to fidget just as Ben passed her; then she opened her eyes, glanced around quickly as if to get her bearings, then move toward the bathroom. "She was out deep. It took her a while to register where she was," Scott said as Ben walked back to the chair.

"Yeah…I kind of thought she'd be out the whole night. I guess not." Ben smiled as he sipped his coffee. A few minutes later, Diana walked back into the room.

She went back to the couch and lay back down, adjusting her pillow and blanket. She just lay there looking at the flames dancing around, but she wasn't able to go back to sleep. Scott and Ben watched her lay back down. Ten minutes later, the guys saw she still wasn't going back to sleep.

"What's going on with her bro?" Scott whispered to Ben.

"I'm not sure," Ben replied. He put his coffee cup down on the coffee table then walked back over to the couch. He crouched down in front of Diana. "What's wrong, kitten?"

Diana looked up at him. "I just can't get back to sleep." She simply said as she went back to watching the fire again.

Ben smiled. "So you have a hard time shutting your own mind off…huh?" Diana quickly focused back on Ben; she went to her typical response of nonverbal dislike for comments—she stuck her tongue out at him. "I don't think that would be a good idea babe…you need to sleep. I'll hold off for another time on that suggestion," Ben quietly teased.

Diana, realizing what she did, just rolled her eyes and said, "Whatever."

"I've got another idea. Move down a little," Ben requested. He helped her scoot down some then he lifted her up enough for him to slide in behind her, next to the arm of the couch. He laid her head down on his lap. Once she adjusted herself and arranged the blanket on herself, she settled in. Ben started to comb his fingers through her hair by taking long slow strokes. She smiled and breathed in deep, slowly letting it out. She missed him being close to her. It was her own fault he was distant today; she pushed him away.

She could feel herself relax more and more with each stroke; she slowly closed her eyes. "I'm sorry," she whispered.

Ben watched her eyes, saw them slowly soften, her eyelids getting heavier and heavier. He heard her say she was sorry. He didn't need an explanation; he knew she was saying that to him. "It's okay, kitten, it was an off day." Soon she was asleep again. Ben carefully lifted her head and slid out from underneath her. He laid her head back down on the couch. He waited there to make sure she was still asleep then turned and went back to the barrel chair.

"I see why she doesn't like conflict. She replays it over and over," Scott commented.

Ben just nodded his head and took a drink of his now-cold coffee. He caught movement out of the corner of his eye and looked toward it. Taggee had woken up. "Are you ready for your watch?" Ben asked.

Taggee nodded. Ben looked at Scott. "Go ahead and get a couple hours of rest. I'll go out last."

Scott nodded and headed for the open couch. He had to take the long way around so not to step over Aisha and Mahala, who were asleep on the floor in front of the fireplace. He was out within five minutes of lying down.

"Did the tigress go to sleep okay?" Taggee asked Ben.

"The first time she fell back to sleep real easy. She had trouble just a short while ago," Ben replied.

"What happened?" Taggee asked.

"She woke up to use the bathroom, when she came back, her mind started replaying the day's events," Ben informed Taggee.

"Sometimes that's a good thing to do. To pick up on things that you've missed at the time," Taggee replied.

"True…but not this time. She was regretting the day. It made her stress out about it. It wasn't necessary," Ben carefully said.

Taggee nodded. He looked at the fireplace. "I think I prefer a real fire over this imitation fire."

Ben smiled. "I do too. But those not used to being outside, they don't understand the difference."

"What did your boss talk to you about?" Taggee asked.

"He assigned a patrol car to watch over Ariana's family. He's doing it as a precaution, but she wouldn't see it that way. He didn't want her to know about it. It would make her worry too much. He feels—and so do I—that she already carries too much responsibility on her shoulders," Ben quietly stated.

Taggee looked at the fire. "She would be a wonderful mother. Full of love to give and the heart to care."

They sat there quietly for a few minutes. Then Ben's thought went to what the Sheikh had planned to do with Diana if he had the chance to make his scheme play out. "Were you involved with the other two women Amid sent to the Sheikh?" Ben asked Taggee.

Taggee looked at him. "Aisha told you?" Ben nodded. "I only dealt with the first one for a short time. Once the Sheikh gave her to Mahdi, I never saw her again. The second one was in my care with the wives. She was very frail. I knew that there were going to be problems by her fifth month of carrying the baby. She was small, and the baby was quite big already. The next month, she miscarried, and both died," Taggee sadly said.

"Did you know the Sheikh intended to kill the mother after the baby was weaned?" Ben inquired.

Taggee quickly looked at Ben. "Aisha told you that? No…I did not know. She must have heard that from Bibi. I am glad the Lord took Ariana out of there before any of that could come about."

"Me too," Ben added. The next few hours stayed quiet. Aisha woke up once to use the bathroom but went right back to sleep. Ben was starting to doze off. He got up and walked around, checking doors and things just so he was moving. He had just walked back into the living room when he noticed Diana to start pulling her blanket close around her; she was restless now. At the time he started to register alarms, Diana sat straight up, her eyes as big as plates. "Ben?"

"I'm here, kitten. Stay quiet now," Ben softly stated.

Taggee had jumped out of the recliner without making a sound. Scott was awake and heading toward the patio windows. Ben slowly walked to the patio door, signaling Diana to stay still. It started off deathly still; the atmosphere so heavy you had to force yourself to breath. Then a sound, a faint, hardly audible sound was starting to be heard. It took another minute before Scott and Ben could place it—a helicopter was nearing. Ben signaled Diana to close the patio blinds. She jumped up and grabbed the remote control. She clicked the button and watched the blinds start to close. Then she turned the TV off.

The sound of the helicopter was growing louder. Aisha woke up and glanced around. She shook Mahala to wake her up. Mahala slowly opened her eyes. Ben looked over. "Be still and quiet," he told Aisha and Mahala. Taggee, standing near the side window, kept watch out the front. Diana watched Ben walk to the bathroom, and she heard the shower start running. She looked at Scott, who signaled for her to wait. She then saw Ben head down the hall. He came back out to the living room a minute later. She was trying to figure out what he was doing. She watched him as he moved over to Mahala and Aisha and had them sit on the couch. As he neared her, Diana saw the cold sapphire-blue eyes; it sent a cold chill up her back. "Trust me kitten. I want you to sit here. Stay calm, like there is nothing going on," Ben quietly said. He guided her down onto the other couch; he put his hand over her heart. "Slow your heart rate down. Deep, slow breaths."

The helicopter was very close now. Ben moved back to the patio door. Diana closed her eyes. *Lord, protect us,* Diana prayed. She worked on forcing herself to take deep breaths and then slowly let them out. She let her mind jump to a different place. She faded to the first time she saw Scott's cabin, how beautiful it looked to her. To sitting on the dock, her legs were dangling in the cool water, the sun warm on her skin, Pete lying beside her as she scratched his ear. Then it jumped back to the Lord's garden.

Scott glanced around the room. He looked at Taggee, who nodded that all was clear on his side. He looked at Aisha, who was calming Mahala over on the far couch. He then glanced over at Diana. He heard Ben telling her to slow her heart rate. She was sitting on the couch, her eyes closed; the expression on her face was calm and tranquil. He then glanced over at Ben. He winked then nodded toward Diana. Ben smiled and then turned his attention back to the problem at hand. The helicopter seemed to just keep circling around. Ben wished he had a pair of binoculars so he could see the numbers on the side. He finally turned to Scott, whistled, and signed for the binoculars. Scott nodded and headed over to the small room. A minute later he came back in and handed Ben his binoculars. Ben saw that Diana was back watching the events.

The whistle brought Diana back into focus of the current surroundings. She was maybe not as calm as she was a second ago, but she didn't think her pulse was too high. She saw Scott heading toward her. "Sorry we brought you back, Milady. Remind me to ask you where you went to," Scott whispered and gave her a smile as he went back to his post.

We're going to be running out of hot water pretty soon. I hope they're about done looking, Ben thought. He held the binoculars up and saw the ID. "KLP 108," he said softly.

Diana read what he was saying. She slowly got up, went to the kitchen, grabbed the dry-erase marker, and wrote down *KLP108* on the board. As she headed back to the living room, she grabbed a bottle of water out of the fridge. Her tongue was sticking to the roof of her mouth. She screwed the top back on the bottle and sat back down on the couch.

The helicopter made one more pass of the area then turned and headed back the way it came. The guys stayed at their post until there was no sound of the helicopter. Then Ben and Taggee sat back down in the living room. Scott went and shut off the showers in the bathrooms before sitting down himself.

"Explain to me the reasoning behind the showers being turned on," Diana asked Ben as he sat down on the couch next to her. Ben reached over and pulled Diana up against him. She was more than willing to let him hold her.

"If they were using thermal scanners, they would not be able to tell exactly how many people were in this house. I pretty much figured they would be listening in when they got close enough. The sound of the water would distort that as well," he explained.

"Hey…Milady…where did you go to earlier?" Scott asked.

Diana smiled. "Out on the dock at your place."

Ben chuckled. "Before or after he went for a swim?"

Diana looked up at Ben, a mischievous thought shot through her head, but she simply stated. "While you two were out riding the four-wheelers."

Diana looked at Scott and winked. "I out fished him. He just doesn't want to admit it," Diana told Mahala.

Mahala laughed and told Aisha and Taggee what they were saying. Ben's left hand came over and held on to Diana's right forearm; then he reached down with his right hand and started tickling Diana's side. Diana laughed and wiggled around to move away from his hand. "Are you going to tell them the truth?" he asked.

"I did tell them the truth. I caught four fish while you and Scott caught none." Diana smiled. Ben started tickling her again; she tried to hold his hand away, but he still had a hold of her right forearm. She started sliding off the couch, so he pulled her back up.

"You'd better say all of it kitten…I may not let you go this time," Ben warned.

"What part are you insinuating?" Diana challenged.

Ben arched an eyebrow up. "You know very good and well what part."

Diana grinned. "Oh, you mean when you slipped and fell, or—" Ben started tickling her before she finished her sentence. She rolled, squirmed, and turned. Ben went ahead and let her slide to the floor, still holding on to her forearm to prevent her from damaging her wrist again. He slid down to one his knee beside her. "I'll take drastic measures if I need to. It might put your brother over there into shock if I do. I'd think about telling the rest of the story," Ben warned. Diana looked at him; she was debating the pros and cons.

"I don't know bro. I think she may take on that threat. I'm not even close, and I can read her from here," Scott chuckled. Diana flushed; she unconsciously licked her lips. Then she looked over at Mahala, her eyes were huge. She wasn't understanding what Ben was implying.

Ben looked up at the girls, noted their expression, then over to Taggee. He was studying the situation. "What do you think? Will the tigress yield this time or challenge?" Ben asked him.

Taggee looked at Ben. "I don't think she's ready for a public display yet. So she will yield, at least for the time being."

Ben looked down at Diana. "What did you tell him?" she asked as she started to try to escape his grasp.

Ben simply grabbed her other arm and swung his leg over to straddle her. "Are you going to tell them the whole story?"

Someday, Tiger…this isn't going to work, Diana thought. She looked up at him; she saw he wasn't bluffing. "You know, once my wrist heals, this move of yours isn't going to work," she quipped.

"Oh…I'm not worried. I'll just up it to the next level," Ben easily stated. "Your time is about up kitten. I'm just a simple human, I'm getting very…hungry."

You aren't the only one, shot through her mind. She shook her head to clear it.

The girls thought that she was meaning she wasn't going to tell them the rest of the story. "Why does she not want to tell it?" Mahala asked Aisha.

"I don't think that is what she is fighting, Mahala," Aisha stated.

"It isn't. She fighting the control, not the story," Scott told them. Diana heard the discussion between the girls and Scott. She glanced around the room; the girls were confused. Scott sat there with a smile on his face. Taggee was watching, but was calm. Then she looked back at Ben. "Milady…you won't win this one. Are you willing to pay for the challenge?" Scott chuckled.

"Time's up…kitten," Ben whispered. Then he started to lean down towards her.

"Okay…okay," Diana quickly stated.

"Tell it right," Ben warned.

"I did catch four fish, and the guys didn't catch any," Diana started. She felt Ben tighten his hold on her arms. "They were on the four-wheelers," she ended.

Scott laughed. "I think she has figured out how to twist things so that they're truth, yet not being truthful."

Diana gleamed at Ben. "I told the truth…may I get up now?"

Ben chuckled. "I'll have to be more specific next time." He stood up pulling her up with him.

"I thought she was going to prove me wrong," Taggee stated.

"If she thought it was something more important, she would not have bent," Ben said over his shoulder. He still had not released Diana from his hold.

"Are you going to allow me to know what is being said or do I start closing you out?" Diana quipped. She saw Ben's disapproval of her statement. "If you withhold information from me, I'll withhold information from you," she plainly stated.

"I think she is upping her wordplay, Tiger," Scott said as he headed to the kitchen, biting his cheeks all the way. "She's not going to let you have total control of her yet, brother," Scott said in Farsi.

Ben looked over his shoulder at Scott's comment. "Te diré más adelante," he said, looking at Diana.

Diana accepted that answer; she nodded but looked back at him. "¿Lo prometes?"

Ben released her arms then traced his fingers down the side of her face. "Me prometo."

Scott forgot that she could speak Spanish. He shook his head. *What a mixture.* "Hey…Milady, where are the big pots at?" he called out. He figured he'd do oatmeal this morning.

Diana came around the corner of the bar. "It's over here," She walked over and opened a lower cupboard and pulled a large stew pot out. She handed it to him.

Scott saw something in her look that disturbed him. He grabbed her hand when she gave him the pot. "Are you okay sis?"

Diana was still trying to sort out her emotions when Scott called from the kitchen. Apparently, he was starting to be able to read her as well. "Lord help me, I don't think I can handle two males being able to read me. I must be slipping somewhere," she halfway teased.

"Us males are not all bad. It's okay if you let some of us in," Scott softly said. Diana gave him a smile. "So…are you okay?" Scott re-asked.

"Yeah…just sorting out conflicts in myself," Diana assured. "Since you've got breakfast, I'm going to go jump in the shower. The hot water heater should be caught up by now, and if not, a cold shower might do me some good."

She left and walked down the hall. Ben saw her go towards the second room, saw that Scott was in the kitchen. "Taggee, do you want to keep an eye on her?" Ben asked. Taggee nodded and got up and headed to the hallway. Diana soon walked into the bathroom.

"Ben, why does she fight for control?" Mahala asked.

"She has learned that she can't trust most people. If she really thought she was in danger, I would not have been able to hold her there. She knew I would not hurt her," Ben calmly stated.

"What were you going to do if she had not yielded?" Mahala continued.

Ben looked at Mahala. *Diana was right…she is still a child in so many ways*, he consented. Ben walked over pulled one of the barrel chairs over so that he could sit in front of the girls. "Ariana is pure physically, but not mentally. She was hurt when she was a very little girl. Do you understand what I mean?" Ben carefully stated.

Mahala nodded. "Someone did something forbidden to her."

Ben nodded. "For her to make sure that it never happened again, she shut herself off to others. Only her parents and her brother were close to her."

"Like how she was like in the compound. Aloof and withdrawn," Aisha stated.

"But she wasn't that way toward me or you…Aisha," Mahala countered.

"She was at the start. It wasn't 'til we were in jail that she saw I meant her no harm," Aisha informed Mahala.

"It is a defense for her. If she's closes down, people cannot hurt her. They may kill her, but in essence, that is just sending her home," Ben half teased. "They can't break her if she's closed off to them."

"But she doesn't act that way here?" Mahala responded.

"She trusts us. She knows that Taggee, Scott, and I won't hurt her on purpose. She feels that you and Aisha are her sisters. She will protect you with her life," Ben stated.

"Like what she did for me at the compound," Mahala quietly affirmed.

"Exactly," Ben put his hand on Mahala's head. "Now, as far as today, Ariana trusts me for protection, but she's not willing to give me total control. It makes her insecure, like the little girl she once was. I have to teach her to be secure in not only my protection but my decisions."

"But what made her give in? You said you would not hurt her, so what made her stop fighting?" Mahala pushed.

"Ariana is a full-grown woman. Her body responds to me. If I were to kiss her, she would have to fight not only my control but control over her own body," Ben simply stated.

"So you were threatening to kiss her, something she actually wants?" Mahala questioned.

"Yeah…pretty much." Ben smiled. Mahala looked at Aisha confused.

"She is a strong-willed woman Mahala. She's proud and stubborn. She will hold to what she knows, even if it means going against what her body wants or needs," Aisha stated.

"So what you are saying, even if Mahdi gets a hold of her, she will die before she breaks," Mahala somberly stated.

Ben looked at Aisha then up at Taggee, who had be listening at the corner of the hallway, then back as Mahala. "Yes."

Taggee saw the pain in Ben's eyes. "We won't let that happen," he firmly stated. They heard the bathroom door start to open. Ben quickly moved the chair back over to its spot then walked over to the high bar.

Taggee turned as Ariana walked out of the bathroom. "Do you feel better?"

Diana looked up at him then over to Mahala. "He is asking if you feel better," Mahala quickly translated. Diana saw that Mahala had been crying. She glanced around the room; Aisha was trying to calm Mahala, Ben wouldn't look at her, and Scott was busy in the kitchen. "Yes, much better." Diana nodded to Taggee and walked past to go to Mahala. Mahala told Taggee what Ariana said.

"Mahala…what happened?" Diana said as she sat down beside her put her hand on her shoulder.

"We were just talking…that's all. I'm fine," Mahala stated.

Diana shot a look at Ben, who still wouldn't look at her. He was standing there, cleaning his nails.

Diana pulled Mahala into her arms. Mahala sobbed. "I don't want you to die…I don't want Mahdi to get you."

Diana rubbed Mahala's back. "As much as I don't want it either, it's not in our hands, it's in God's. If it's His will that Mahdi gets me, He will give me the strength to overcome that. If it is His will Mahdi is caught before that, I will praise Him greatly. I didn't want to be taken to Syria, but God said I had to go there. Because of that, I have gained two sisters and a couple of brothers. I would do it again if the Lord said so. Maybe not fight the ropes as much is all," Diana chuckled.

Mahala giggled a little then sat up and looked at Ariana. "You only gained two brothers. What about the third one?"

Diana looked Mahala. "It remains to be seen." Diana looked up at Ben, who was now watching her. She quickly raised an eyebrow and gave him a Cheshire grin.

"Speaking of ropes, we need to deal with your wrist kitten," Ben injected.

"I think it may be best to wait till after breakfast. I don't want the chef to be forced to leave his work," Diana jested.

"As you wish," Ben replied. Diana walked over to the kitchen to see if Scott needed anything. Scott had everything pretty much ready. Diana helped out by grabbing bowls and spoons and placing them on the high bar. Scott brought the oatmeal over and put it on a hot pad. He had already put a variety of toppings out. Diana grabbed the juice, white milk, and chocolate milk and sat it down on the counter. Scott headed over and grabbed several glasses.

"Okay…it's all ready guys," Scott called.

Mahala, Aisha, and Taggee all came to the high bar. While they were busy getting breakfast, Ben took Diana by the hand and pulled her around and to the far hallway. Ben had his arm braced against the wall near Diana's head. "Now, kitten…am I getting the impression that Mahdi is going to get you?" Ben warned.

"No, the Lord hasn't told me anything yet. It is still a possibility though Ben," Diana softly said. "What brought Mahala's tears on?"

"She was worried that I was going to hurt you. I was just explaining my idea of compliance." Ben grinned.

"So how did that result in Mahala crying?" Diana continued.

"Aisha explained that you are stubborn and proud and will slowly kill yourself rather than bend," Ben teased.

"I am usually best at self-preservation," Diana quipped.

"Huh-huh, and not eating or drinking fits into that statement how?" Ben fired back.

Diana looked over his shoulder. Ben took her chin and made her look at him. "How about the last comment you made to Mahala?" Diana grinned, and a spark went off in her eyes. Ben let his hand slide over to the side of her neck. He could feel her pulse racing. He caressed her jaw with his thumb.

"Ben…Diana, you'd better come get something to eat," Scott called out.

"I'm a little hungry for something else," Ben quietly stated.

"Am I understanding you right? You're going to let me skip breakfast?" Diana teased.

"Never kitten...just a slight delay." Ben smiled.

"Ben, Diana?" Scott's voice was getting closer.

Diana went to walk under Ben's arm. Ben quickly reached out and grabbed her by her upper arm and pulled her back to him. "After breakfast and my wrist, you need to get some sleep Tiger," Diana softly said.

Scott came around the corner. "Hey, Tiger...Diana, is everything okay?"

"Yeah, it's fine. Ben thought I implied Mahdi was going to get me. We were just discussing that," Diana stated.

"You'd better go get something to eat, Diana," Scott sternly stated. Diana turned and slowly walked out toward the kitchen.

Ben calmed himself. Diana was right; he was very tired. "Sorry bro., she needed to get something to eat," Scott carefully said.

"Don't worry about it. Make sure she eats. I'm going to go take a shower," Ben calmly stated.

Ben went into the guys' room, grabbed his stuff, then headed into the bathroom. Scott walked back toward the group. As he came up toward the kitchen, he asked, "Did everybody get what they needed?"

Taggee, Mahala, and Aisha nodded. Then Scott asked Diana, "How about you, Milady...did you get what you needed?"

Diana looked behind her toward the hallway then back at Scott. "I'm fine...I'm just dealing with low sugar counts. Suppose I'll make do with what ya got here," she jested.

Scott put his hand on her shoulder. "I'm sorry."

"Oh, don't worry about it. There'll be time after all this is done," she assured him. Once everybody was done, Diana started to clean things up. She made sure there was a little oatmeal left for Ben, though she doubted he would eat any. She was just rinsing the last glass off and putting it in the dishwasher. "Feel better?" she asked.

"Cleaner anyway," Ben replied.

"Did you want something to eat? There's some in the fridge you can warm up if you want," she added.

"Nah...I'm good," he replied. "Let's get that wrist taken care of."

"Then you, Tiger, are going to get some sleep," Diana demanded.

Ben called Taggee up to help him. He saw Scott headed for the shower. Diana followed Ben's line of sight. "You're not mad at him, are you?" she asked as Ben put the bowl down on the counter. "No, ma'am...it's good," Ben stated.

Taggee came and held her hand; Ben held her arm. They both noticed that she didn't react as much as before. "It didn't hurt as much this time, did it kitten?" Ben smiled.

"Not as much…still burned as all get-out. Maybe red coals instead of white ones," Diana quipped.

Ben started wrapping the gauze around her wrist. "We'll have to arrange for you to get to the doctor either today or tomorrow," Ben told her.

"How are we going to do that one?" she asked.

"Still working on that," he quickly stated as he finished tapping the end down. He put his hand up on the side of her face. Diana reached up and took Ben's hand. She pulled him to the living room and made him sit down on the couch. Ben smiled at her.

"You need to sleep. You can't protect me if you're too exhausted to think straight," Diana sternly said.

"Bro. You do need to sleep. Taggee and I will take care of things," Scott assured him.

Ben looked back at Diana. He pulled her down to sit on the couch as well. Then he laid his head down on her lap. "As you wish, I'll stay here," Diana whispered.

Aisha and Mahala watched what Ben did. "He doesn't trust you to keep her safe?" Mahala asked Scott.

"It's more of the fact he will sleep better knowing where she is." Scott smiled. He watched as Diana started combing through Ben's hair. "I'm going to go check the grounds. I'll whistle before coming back in," he told Taggee.

"Well, since I'm being held down, what do you want to do?" Diana asked. Mahala interpreted what Diana asked for Taggee and Aisha. Taggee told her that he was going to keep an eye on things; he'd be walking around a lot. Aisha and Mahala discussed back and forth, finally Mahala asked if they could watch another John Wayne movie. "We can give it a try," Diana said. She had Mahala hand her the remote control that was over between the two barrel chairs. *Lord, don't let this open up with the first scene. I'm definitely not in the emotional state to handle it yet*, she quietly prayed.

She soon found out that Ben wasn't quite asleep yet. "Give it here kitten", he directed. She handed the remote to Ben; he quickly set the TV up to watch the next movie. "Which one do you want?" he asked.

"Ah…I don't know. *El Dorado* or *Rio Grande* I guess," Diana threw out.

Ben clicked on *El Dorado* and gave her back the remote. "If I'm not awake once this movie it over, you are to wake me up." He turned on his back to look at her. "Do I make myself clear?"

"As you wish," Diana said with an ornery grin. Ben turned back over on his side, got comfortable again, and closed his eyes. It dawned on Diana that she didn't think Ben had called Director Zenon. She leaned down. "Hey Tiger, did you give Director Zenon a call already?" Ben nodded. "Sorry…I didn't see you call. I didn't want you to get into trouble." Ben reached up and grabbed her hand and kissed her palm.

Two hours later, the movie was ending. Mahala looked over at Ariana. Ben was still asleep with his head on her lap. "Are you going to wake him up?" she asked.

"I'm gonna have to. He'd be upset if I didn't," Diana softly said.

"Two hours isn't very long…I would think he'd need more. Taggee is here, everything is calm. I'd let him sleep," Mahala replied.

Diana shook her head no. "There has only been a couple of times I've seen him sleep longer. The Lord is going to have to end this soon; for both of our sakes," Diana stated. Diana started working on waking him up. She leaned down. "Ben…you wanted me to wake you up." Ben turned over on his back. Diana cradled his head in her hands. "Benjamen…you wanted woken up," she said a little louder, stroking her thumb across his cheek. He still wasn't really responding to her. His breathing was even, and his body was relaxed. Diana pulled her hair over to the side of her head. She leaned down and lightly kissed him. Ben was already halfway awake. He was just starting to register her voice. Then he felt her lips on his. He reached his hand over and placed it on her head; holding her there, kissing her back.

He let her rise back up; he glanced into her emerald-green eyes. "Thank you."

"I'll have to remember that. It is the safest way to wake you," Diana softly whispered. She looked up at the girls who were watching her and flushed. She couldn't bring herself to look at Taggee. She looked back at Ben.

Ben grinned. "I love it when you get embarrassed at the simplest things."

They heard a whistle from the patio. "Scott has been outside most of the time," Diana informed Ben. Ben gave a call back, stood up, and headed for the patio door. He glanced out then opened the door.

Scott walked in. "I figured you'd be asleep still. Did Milady misbehave or something?"

"I was just following orders, but since I'm free to move, excuse me for a minute," Diana quipped. She got up and headed for the bathroom; her bladder was about to explode. She heard Ben and Scott do a little laugh as she closed the door. Moments later, Diana rejoined the group, coming up and standing by Mahala and Aisha. "What are the guys doing now?" Diana asked Mahala.

"They were talking about how they were going to get you to the doctor," Mahala calmly stated.

Diana just shook her head and said. "Thickheaded..."

"We could always put her in the trunk of the car," Scott teased.

"It would take all three of you guys to accomplish that task," Diana quickly stated as she walked to the kitchen. She was surprised that Scott actually spoke in English and not Farsi.

"I think that was a challenge Tiger...how did you read that?" Scott looked at Diana to see her reaction. He watched her as she calmly poured herself some chocolate milk. Diana knew they were playing with her. She calmly put the milk away, turned, took a drink, and walked up to the corner where the guys were sitting.

"It's not a challenge...it's in point of fact," she firmly said as she turned and walked over to the couch and sat down.

"The tigress is mischievous this morning." Taggee smiled and turned to look at her in the couch. He didn't have to know what she said...he could see it in her eyes.

"I guess so," Scott chuckled. "So are you going to take the challenge Tiger?"

"Not this time. Taggee knows what she can be like when she makes up her mind that she doesn't want something. We'd end up doing more than opening up that wrist of hers," Ben coolly added.

"Taggee had trouble with her too? What happened?" Scott asked Taggee.

Taggee stopped smiling and got somber. "I was instructed to hold her so that Bibi could put earrings on Ariana. She didn't have pierced ears and didn't want pierced ears. I got a hold of her, but she fought so much that I ended up making her wrists bleed. I didn't want to hurt her, not that she knew that. I crossed her arms across her chest so I wasn't holding on to wrists anymore, but it took both hands to keep her body still. I had to call for Ishmael to come hold her head while Bibi shoved the posts through her earlobes." He looked up at Ben. "I didn't mean for her to get hurt. I tried to help her as much as I could."

"She knew you didn't mean her harm. She told me that the first night we left the compound. She was mad at Bibi," Ben assured Taggee.

Diana looked over at the group of guys. Something has changed; they were no longer upbeat. She looked directly at Ben, who was talking calmly to Taggee. Taggee's voice sounded to be in anguish. Diana stood up and walked over to Ben. "What's happened?"

"I had mentioned to Scott that Taggee knew how much you fight when it's something you don't want. He recounted the episode with the earrings. He feels that you blame him for hurting you," Ben told Diana.

Diana went over to Taggee, knelt down in front of him, and put her hands on his. "I never have blamed you for what happened at the compound. That is why I came off the roof when you called. Why I let you tie my wrists again without fighting. I knew you did not want to hurt me. There was just no way I could tell you that at the time," Diana said. Then she looked at Ben to interpret for her.

Ben told Taggee what Diana said. Diana watched Taggee's eyes as Ben was interpreting for her, making sure he understood what she meant. She saw tears forming and running down his face. He looked down at her, said something, then pulled her up to him and hugged her. Diana wrapped her arms around his neck and gave him a hug back. Taggee released her, stood her on her feet, then guided her over to Ben. "Tell her what I said", he stated as he walked out into the living room.

Ben took Diana's hand and pulled her near him. "Taggee wanted me to tell you that you are a definite child of the Lord. You show His love and kindness in what you say and do," Ben interpreted to her.

"I try to be…I pray to be a willing servant," Diana said as a tear ran down her own face. *Thank you, Lord, for using me to be your witness in this situation. Help me to be opened for this next one*, Diana silently prayed. Aisha and Mahala came walking over and grabbed Ariana and hugged her. Diana gave them a big hug too. They pulled her over to the couch and were talking back and forth.

"I didn't mean to start all this," Scott quietly said to Ben.

"Nope…but God did. Taggee was worried that Diana would not forgive him for things done in the compound. He needed to know God's capacity to forgive, and he saw a small part of it in Diana's ability to forgive. Mahala is just starting to understand what the love of God is," Ben informed Scott as he watched Diana interact with the girls.

"I can't believe it took three people to put earrings in that girl's ears. She never fought either of us that way," Scott stated.

Ben looked at Scott. "One…we could explain things to her. She had no clue of what was going on until I got there. Two—and this is the main key—God told her he was bringing us into her life. Have you forgotten her reaction to you when she didn't know who you were?"

"Man, she is every bit as stubborn as you are—maybe even more so," Scott jabbed. "She didn't have earrings in when I came and got you guys. What happened to them?"

"As soon as she had a chance to take them out, she did—well, she tried to anyway. I had to get them out for her. Her body was rejecting them already. I had to work them back through her earlobes," Ben stated.

The doorbell rang. Diana and the girls immediately became quiet. Taggee went to stand by the girls. Ben stood by the hallway wall; Scott went and answered the door.

He looked out the side window then slowly opened the door. "Scott, I brought someone I think you're going to need." Scott opened the door wider to let the two men in. Diana recognized the voice immediately. Allen was paying them another visit. She watched as Scott let Allen and another man in. Ben met them as they neared the hallway and walked into the living room with them.

"Diana, I assume you are doing well?" Allen inquired.

"I'm getting there, sir," Diana stated as she was watching the man Allen brought with him sit down and start rummaging through a bag he brought in with him. Allen saw Diana was cautious and knew it was because of who he brought with him. Allen easily saw that she was not the only one.

He looked over at Ben. "It's becoming a tight family here, isn't it?"

"Yeah, you could say that. You might want to introduce our new friend. Although I'm sure the kitten has already deduced who he is," Ben smoothly stated. Diana shot a look up at Ben for his comment and a questioning glance up at Allen.

Allen laughed. "Yes, Diana, he is a doctor. This is Dr. Jefferson from the SAC base in Omaha. I heard about early this morning from Charles. I knew it would be risky to take Diana out, even if it was to see her doctor. So if you can't go to the doctor, then the doctor must come to you."

"Well, at least you don't have to worry about him getting overzealous here. He doesn't have the equipment to do any of that," Ben chuckled.

Diana started looking for something to throw at him, but she couldn't find anything. Scott broke out laughing. "I told you it would be a smart thing to hide those pillows."

"If you would, ma'am, I need to see your knee as well as your wrists. Could you change into a pair of shorts?" Dr. Jefferson asked. Diana got up and walked to the second room to change her pants.

Ben followed her. "Use the pair you had at the cabin. Nobody has seen those rope burns on your thighs for a while, might as well have the good doctor check those as well."

"If I didn't know better, I would say there is an ulterior motive to that request," Diana quipped. Ben just stayed cool to her barb, but he wasn't going to deny it either.

Diana walked up to him. "Since I don't want Taggee to rip you gentlemen into pieces, you might want to explain to him what is going on." She walked through the door and headed toward the bathroom.

Ben walked out to the living room. "She'll be out in a moment. Dr. Jefferson, I need you to look at the rope burns on her thighs and calves. It's been a while since anybody has seen them. I just want to make sure they are healing correctly."

Allen shot a glare at him. "She had more rope burns than just her ankles and wrists?" Ben nodded. "So she was whipped, starved, and tied up more than normal. Is there anything else you want to tell me? If I was her father, I'd be going to town on you right now. I still may."

Ben heard Mahala interpreting for Aisha and Taggee. "Has anybody told these guys what is going on?"

"I told them that he is here to check her wrist. I didn't know you were going to have him check her legs," Scott piped up.

Ben looked at Taggee and the girls, explained that Diana was coming out with her legs uncovered so that the doctor could see all the rope burns. Just as he finished saying it, Diana walked out into the living room. The doctor signaled for Diana to come to the chair and sit down. Taggee moved over and stood between the area that the doctor was working in and where Allen and Ben were standing. Aisha and Mahala got up and each flanked Taggee but stood to watch what the doctor was doing. Ben nodded to Taggee then guided Allen and Scott to the far end of the dining room.

"I forgot the culture they came from. I am glad to see he is helping you protect her though," Allen quietly said.

Scott was pouting a little. "Spoilsport."

Ben glared at Scott. "So...would you like to fill me in on those rope burns?" Allen sternly requested.

"Sir...I told you that they checked her to see if she was virgin. That's why I tried to get her out of going through a cavity check at NYHQ," Ben fired at Allen.

"You didn't say anything about her being tied up for it," Allen countered.

"Knowing what you know of Diana, what do you suppose she would do?" Ben rebounded.

Allen just shook his head. "From what I saw, she at least didn't get those infected," Allen surmised.

"No. From what she told me, they drugged her to stop her from doing more damage than what she already had," Ben ended.

"So you still think you can handle this tigress, Ben?" Allen smiled.

"Oh…he can handle her. It's the rest of the male population that have to worry about her," Scott jabbed.

Dr. Jefferson came out from behind Taggee and the girls and walked over to Allen. "The rope burns on her thighs and calves are almost totally healed. The lines will eventually fade. The rope burns on her ankles are a little irritated. I would suggest she goes barefoot as much as she can. She said she had some antibiotic ointment left. I have instructed her to use it on her ankles for at least a week. The one wrist is almost healed as well. Eventually, the ring will fade."

"And her right wrist?" Ben asked.

"The top and bottom are good. I'm worried about the sides. I believe she may be using it too much so it's not able to close up like it needs to. It also seems she still may still be dealing with an infection. I have given her another shot of Levaquin. I tried to give her some pain meds, but she says she won't take them," Dr. Jefferson ended.

"Does she still need to do that rinse?" Scott asked. "It really burns her."

"What rinse?" Dr. Jefferson asked. Ben walked to the kitchen, grabbed the bottle of powder, and brought it back to him. "What in the…? Ahem. You have been using this on her wrist?" Dr. Jefferson asked.

"Yes, sir…twice a day," Ben informed him.

"Apparently, the wrist was extremely infected Friday. This medication burns like crazy. I only use it when absolutely necessary. I've seen guys scream their heads off with it. So, no, you do not have to continue with it. The wrist is healed enough that you should be able to use that antibiotic ointment on it then cover it with gauze to keep it clean. I'll send this on to her general doctor. I recommend that she does a follow-up visit in a week, unless infection develops or she starts having problems with it. Then get her in ASAP," Dr. Jefferson ended.

"Thank you, sir," Ben said as he shook the doctor's hand. "Okay…kitten, he's done. Go change," Ben called out. He noted that he didn't have to mention it twice. Diana scooted out from behind Taggee and headed down the hall to the bathroom. Taggee came and stood by the corner of the hallway. The two girls returned to the couch.

Ben got somber. "There is more that you do need to know, sir."

"Oh…what else has your trouble magnet done?" Allen jeered.

"It's not with Diana, thank the Lord. You have a file open on two women that you suspected Amid had kidnapped, correct?" Ben stated.

"Yes, we do. Everything has gone cold though. Why?" Allen asked.

"I know from a trusted source that the fourteen-year-old is deceased. The twenty-two-year-old is probably in China or Asia somewhere," Ben coldly informed Allen.

Allen looked at Ben. "Did Taggee have anything to do with them?"

"Taggee's contact with the twenty-two-year-old was limited to only one day from what I understand. Once the Sheikh found out she wasn't 'pure,' he gave her to Mahdi. Once Mahdi had her broke, they sold her to an Asian businessman," Ben explained. Ben stopped and looked over toward the hallway. He saw Diana standing there, tears rolling down her face. He held his hand out to her. She quickly came to him; he held her tight.

"And the fourteen-year-old, what was Taggee's involvement with her?" Allen asked.

Ben kept Diana against him. "Taggee cared for her after the Sheikh had her artificially inseminated. The girl was too small and the baby too big. She miscarried, and both died."

"If Taggee had little contact with the twenty-two-year-old, how do you know where she was sold to?" Allen questioned.

"The information did not come from Taggee, sir. It is often the custom to have the younger wives be just above a servant," Ben quipped. "One of the Sheikh's wives had to go and clean the twenty-two-year-old up after Mahdi was done with her for the day."

Diana felt Ben's hold tighten around her when he said that. It was almost hard for her to breathe, but she wasn't going to say anything. She knew he was scared, scared for her.

Allen looked over at the two women sitting on the couch. "Does this mean I will be sent back?" Aisha asked cautiously.

"No, ma'am. I thank you…from the families that the girls came from. One will get closure, the other will have a glimmer of hope," Allen replied.

Diana looked at Ben. "Aisha was worried that she was going to be sent back to Syria. Allen was just telling her thanks. He can now give one family closure and the other a little glimmer of hope," he interpreted for her. Diana laid her head back on Ben's chest. Ben looked at Scott; he saw a mix of fear, rage, and disgust run through his eyes.

Allen walked up to Ben. He put his hand on Diana's shoulder; she turned and looked at him. "You have to be strong. Ben says you have a brain and use it quite well, so focus it in on the task at hand—staying hidden. Fear clouds the brain. Don't let this man win by making you afraid. Understand?" Diana nodded. "We will try to get him first, before he can get to you. My word of honor," Allen ended. "Now…I need to talk to Ben and Scott, could you excuse us for a minute?" Allen smoothly and calmly said. Diana looked up at Ben; he released her from his embrace. She hesitantly walked away. Ben smiled; she headed over to Taggee, who put his hand on her shoulder.

Ben, Scott, and Allen turned and walked toward the door. The doctor waited in the dining room. "You don't think we are going to be able to catch him first, do you?" Scott asked Allen.

"No...even here, there are too many greedy people who'd sell their own mothers if it gave them a quick buck or two," Allen replied. "It will take a miracle, but she seems to have a direct connection to that department. We need to be able to trace her position at all times. If, God forbid, he does get to her; we need to track him and get to her before any major damage is done. Any ideas?" Allen asked.

"Well, jewelry is out. She reacts to it," Ben stated.

"Have her swallow a tracer?" Scott suggested.

"Her intestines are too sensitive. I wouldn't want to risk it," Ben countered.

"An article of clothing then," Allen stated.

Ben snapped his fingers. "Give her a wrist brace with a tracer embedded in it."

"Will she wear it?" Allen asked.

"Definitely...especially if there's a risk of somebody tying her wrists up again. She doesn't want that wrist opened up again," Scott stated.

"Okay...I'll get one made up and bring it by in the next couple of hours," Allen agreed.

Allen signaled for Dr. Jefferson to follow him. The doctor walked up to Ben. "I know this is going to be hard, but she needs to get some sleep as well."

"You're gonna have to be the stronger man and be her pillow bro. She'll sleep then," Scott teased.

Allen waved his hand. "I don't want to know. I don't know if I can stay the boss and not the father. Just do your best."

"I'll do what I can to get her to sleep more. And, no...don't try to give her sleeping pills. She won't take them. She wants to keep control of her faculties," Ben said as he saw the doctor pulling a box of pills out of his bag.

"Okay boys...game face on," Allen said as he unlocked the door and slowly opened it. He and the doctor slipped out. Scott closed and locked it while Ben watched from the side window. They walked back to the living room. Everybody's spirit dampened, and tension thick in the atmosphere. Taggee took his hand off Ariana's shoulder; she headed straight for Ben. He immediately wrapped her up in his arms. He stood there holding her, quietly whispering to her, letting her gain strength from him. Scott walked on into the living room, his eyes cold and dangerous. Taggee could see his mind was running on high, planning and scheming. Mahala asked if she needed to make some coffee. Taggee nodded to her. She headed out to the kitchen and got it going. Aisha was worried that Ariana would pull away from her now that she knew her involvement with the other two girls. She was steeling herself.

Ben loosened his embrace around Diana. She looked up at him. "Aisha is going to be worried that you will despise her for the other two girls. You're going to need to assure her," Ben quietly said.

"It wasn't her fault, no more than her being with me was her fault," Diana countered.

"She can't read you, babe. You're going to have to tell her," Ben reinforced. Diana nodded. "Second point, I've been instructed to make you sleep more. Do you have any idea of how that can be accomplished?" Ben jabbed.

"I'm gonna need my traveling pillow. Lord help us. I just don't know how that is going to work with our new brother and sisters," Diana jeered.

"We'd better join the group now, kitten." Diana nodded and turned to walk into the living room followed by Ben.

Diana sat down by Aisha and made sure Mahala was ready to interpret for her. "I'm not upset at you. You were doing what you were told to do by your husband. To disobey would put you in danger and would not help either of the two girls. Do you understand?" Diana carefully stated. She waited for Mahala to tell Aisha was she said. Aisha looked to Mahala to translate what Ariana said. She looked back at Ariana, saw peace and love toward her in her eyes. She reached over and grabbed Ariana and hugged her. Diana held her until she was ready to let go. She gave Aisha a smile as she straightened up. Diana stayed on the couch with the girls.

43

Later that morning

Scott was working outside. Diana figured she would ask him later what he was doing. Taggee had Ben turn on the TV and put on the news for the Middle East. Ben had moved to the high bar after getting himself a bottle of water out of the fridge. Mahala took the opportunity to talk with Ariana; she had questions that needed answered.

"Ariana at the compound, when you were sick, two men appeared in the room. They were dressed in white, and they seemed to glow. Aisha told me that one was the Lord and the other was the warrior in white. Why did the Lord need the warrior with him?" Mahala questioned.

Diana waited for a minute before answering her. *He was to show Aisha and Taggee who I was*, the Lord told her

"The Lord had the angel, the man you are calling the warrior in white, come with Him because Taggee and Aisha had already seen him. He was an introduction to the Lord for them," Diana calmly said.

Mahala asked, "Why did I see them?"

Diana smiled. "To introduce Himself to you. Your walk with the Lord is personal. I or any one of the others can help you, but ultimately, it is your choice to follow and listen. It's your love toward the Lord that determines how far you go with the Him."

Mahala turned to look out the window. Then she looked back at Ariana. "I have heard you mention many times about obeying our husband. I understand for us it is important. But you live here where there is freedom. Why would it be so important to you?" Diana was a little hesitant to answer not because of Mahala but because it would open herself up more to Ben. "You don't have to answer if you don't want to," Mahala responded sadly.

"No…it's not you. It is true here in the States women have freedoms you and Aisha have not had until now, but we are to live more than by the rulings of the land. We are to follow the rulings of the Lord. He has it set up that a husband is to be the head or ruler of the family. As a wife, when and *if* I marry, I agree to put myself under the rules of the man I marry. I am to be his helper and to support him," Diana stated. She almost wanted to see what Ben thought, but she needed to help Mahala. "It goes back to what I just said with your love toward the Lord. The love a husband and wife has for each other determines how long the marriage lasts. Unfortunately, for some people, their love only goes as far as 'What does it do for me?' So some men rule like the Sheikh…a wife is a maid, someone for him to use whenever—just his property," Diana carefully stated.

"It goes the other way too, kitten," Ben threw in. Diana wanted to throw something at him, but there was nothing around her. Mahala asked her to explain what Ben said.

"He is right. In countries that women have freedom. There are some women who are just as bad as the men. These wives are the dictators to their husbands. They use them for money or make them a slave having them do everything while they sit down and do nothing. For some it is just so that they can have a baby. Whatever their reason…it's something other than that they love them," Diana stated.

"I don't understand why you are not married yet," Mahala questioned. "You let Ben rule over you," Mahala stated.

Aisha saw the look on Ariana face. She knew Ariana was getting very uncomfortable. "Mahala! What did you ask her?" she scolded.

Diana looked over at Ben; he was looking at his fingernails. *Lord, help me.* She turned and looked at Mahala, "It is true I let Ben, Scott, and Taggee have control over me more than any other man in my life except my father. Ben a little more so because of the connection that God has put between us, but he does not have *total* control over me. Nor am I bound to do what he or the others ask. If he told me to do something I felt was wrong, I would not obey him." She glanced back at him. He was looking at her, his eyes the dark sapphire blue, but there was a hint of humor in them. Ben knew Diana didn't want to give him more information about her. He also knew that she wouldn't leave Mahala hanging. When he heard her last statement, he looked up at her. She was looking at him, her eyes cool and dark gray, warning him not to challenge her; he was amused with her warning.

"When the time comes that I have *total* control over her, you two will be one of the first ones to know about it." Ben smiled as he talked to Mahala in Farsi.

Mahala giggled but got somber when Ariana turned to her. "Tell me what he said?" Ariana said sternly. Mahala looked over Ariana's shoulder toward Ben, who was shaking his head no. Mahala turned and looked at Aisha.

"You are the one that put yourself between them. You deal with it," she scolded.

Mahala got worried that Ariana was going to be mad at her. "I am afraid I cannot. I'm sorry," Mahala said timidly. Diana nodded her acceptance of Mahala's answer. She got up and walked to the kitchen to get a bottle of water. She watched Ben out of the corner of her eye. He sat there picking imaginary lint from his shirt. She walked to the fridge and grabbed a bottle of water. As she came around the corner of the island, she decided to act. She put the bottle down on the counter, reached over and quickly grabbed the sprayer and turned on the water, hitting Ben in the back. She quickly dropped it down, hitting the water off at the same time; then before he could totally register what was going on, she ran out of the kitchen and down the hallway toward the bathroom—the one room with a door she could lock with no other access.

Ben was expecting Diana to chew him out for not letting Mahala tell her was he said. It surprised him that she walked right past him and went to the fridge. Suddenly, he felt cold water hit his back. He jumped off the bar stool to see what happened. He caught a glimpse of Diana running out of the kitchen. It took him a second to figure out what was going on. He ran and hurdled the first couch, took a few steps and hurdled the second couch, making Mahala and Aisha duck, and landed just a few steps behind Diana as she was nearing the hallway and the bathroom door. He caught her elbow and pulled her back away from the door. He quickly wrapped his arms across her, lifting her up. "You want to play with the water today, kitten? Let's go have some fun with water, shall we?" Ben stated as he pulled her into the bathroom.

"Benjamen James Tigere, let me go! It's your own fault, you egotistical, arrogant, pompous—" Diana fumed.

Ben chuckled as he carried her into the bathroom. He had to use one hand to turn the shower on; Diana squirmed out of his hold and headed for the door. Ben got a hold of her again just inside the hallway. "Now... now, let's cool down that temper, shall we?" Ben teased. He took her back into the bathroom, leaving the door open. He swung her around to put her into the shower, but she had put her legs up to brace against the wall to hold herself out. "You know you're going to get wet, are you going to take it nicely?" Ben warned.

"Of course not," Diana steamed. Ben let her push off the wall, but it was only to take her brace away; the wall was getting wet, and her feet were now wet. He swung her around again to put her in. She went to brace herself again, but her feet slipped on the wet wall. Ben got her into the shower. Diana screamed as the cold water hit her. Ben released her once he got her in. So she reached up and grabbed the showerhead, pulled it down and aimed it at him. Ben reached over and grabbed her wrist. Realizing he had her wrist, he loosened his grip and slid his hand to her forearm. Looking down, he noticed it was her left hand holding the showerhead.

He moved his grip back to her wrist and grabbed the showerhead with the other hand. "You're going to hurt yourself…you'd best stop," he warned. She still tried to aim the showerhead back at him, but then she started to slip. Both of them let go of the showerhead at the same time. Diana grabbed on to his arm to steady herself. Ben pushed her up against the wall to hold her up. One hand was on her upper arm. The other hand didn't make it out far enough to grab the other arm. Diana froze, her heart racing even faster than when she was wrestling with Ben. Emotions and feelings raced through her head and body. Ben slid his hand down so it was now on her stomach to hold her there until she got her feet under her; he could feel her heart was racing. She still had a hold of his arm. He reached over and shut the water off. When she looked at him, he saw a plethora of thoughts and feelings flying through her eyes. "I'm sorry, kitten. I needed to keep you from falling and breaking your neck," Ben chuckled.

"Is she okay?" Ben heard Taggee ask.

"Yeah, she didn't fall," Ben replied.

"Do you want me to take care of her while you get dried off?" Taggee inquired.

"No, it's okay. I'll get her out of here," Ben stated. He heard Taggee move back to the living room. "Diana…look at me," Ben smoothly stated.

Diana blinked and focused in then looked at Ben. "You are going to behave now, right? I don't want an ER trip," Ben calmly but sternly stated.

"I suppose," Diana quipped.

Ben reached over and grabbed the towel from the towel bar, giving it to her to somewhat dry off. The towel was already wet from them fighting. Seeing that she was able to stand and not fall, he moved to the cupboard and grabbed one for himself. "Did I hurt you?" Ben inquired.

"No," Diana curtly stated.

"I am sorry, I didn't mean to do that. I don't regret it, but I really didn't mean to," Ben chuckled. Diana shot a glare at him and went to say something, but she flushed and went to continue drying herself off. Ben saw it but figured he'd embarrassed her enough already; he let it go. Out of the corner of his eye; Ben saw Aisha in the doorway. "Do you want to take her in to change her clothes? I'll get the floor dried up in here," he requested. Aisha nodded. Ben took Diana's arm and started guiding her to the door. She slipped, falling on Ben, who slipped, and both of them fell to the floor. Diana wound up falling on top of Ben. Diana at first was in shock but then burst out laughing. Ben smiled… Aisha was just shaking her head.

"Well, I never do anything halfway, do I?" Diana jabbed.

"Nope…but I'm not complaining." Ben smiled.

"I can tell that." She giggled. "Now how am I going to get out of this?" she smiled. She glanced around; there wasn't enough room for her to go to the side. She'd embarrass herself if she tried to crawl off of him, and she didn't think she could get her feet under her to push up from him. Then she looked down at Ben's eyes; she hesitated. Her breathing sped up; she started to tremble. Diana shook her head as to clear her head. Ben saw the look in her eyes. It was a mixture of hunger, fear, and confusion running through her.

"Hang on a second, kitten," he assured her. He reached his arm across her back and rolled her with him to his side. Now that there was room, he stood up and reached down and picked her up off the floor, guiding her the rest of the way out of the bathroom for Aisha to help. He finished drying the bathroom floor with the towels; then he went to change clothes. Twenty minutes later, he came back out to the living room. Taggee was on the couch with Aisha and Diana. Mahala was sitting in one of the barrel chairs. "Has she settled down a little?" he commented.

Taggee smiled. "Let's just say she's temporarily contained." Scott whistled, so Ben walked over unlocked the door and let him in.

Scott came in through the patio doors. "You took another shower?" Scott queried Ben. Then he saw that Diana had changed clothes and had wet hair as well. "All righty then, what did I miss while working to keep people safe?"

"Ben wouldn't let me translate what he said about Ariana. She got mad and shot him with the sprayer in the kitchen sink and tried to get to the room to lock the door. Ben caught her and threw her into the shower," Mahala informed Scott.

"I just needed to put out the fire," Ben stated.

"I know she loves to swim, but you of all people should know what a cat does when it doesn't want to get wet," Scott sneered.

"Yeah, well, we ended up cleaning the bathroom." Ben smiled.

Scott looked at Diana. "Are you ever going to learn sis?"

Diana glared at Scott. "Oh, I'll learn. I'll learn how to get payback."

Scott looked over to Ben. "You've really got her enraged. Not exactly what the doctor ordered now, was it bro?" he scolded.

"Yeah…well, I'll have to deal with that in a little bit," Ben quietly said. "I suppose I'd better get some stuff out for lunch." Ben headed to the fridge and pulled out the lunch meat and cheese and put it on the counter; then he started to gather all the fixings and stuff. Fifteen minutes later, he called out, "Come and get your lunch."

Aisha and Mahala looked at Ariana. "Come and get a sandwich," Mahala stated.

"You two go ahead. I'll be there in a minute," Diana replied. Taggee stood up, patted Ariana's head, and walked over to the high bar. Ben looked out and saw Diana wasn't coming to get anything to eat. He made her a sandwich and some chamomile tea and took it out to her. He set the plate on the couch by her; he held out the chamomile tea for her to take. She glanced up and saw the cup of tea; she reached up and took it.

"You need to eat kitten. I can't teach you how to fight if you don't keep your strength up," Ben calmly encouraged.

"I know how to protect myself already," Diana quipped.

"Hmm…so you wouldn't be interested in learning how to block somebody from say… pinning your arms to your sides?" Ben smiled. Diana looked at him then looked down to her cup of tea. They sat there quietly, not talking for a while. Diana had her tea half gone but still had not eaten her sandwich. She did lie back against the back of the couch. Ben put his arm up and rested it on the back of the couch; he reached over and started to play with Diana's semi damp hair.

She started to relax with what he was doing, closing her eyes. "I'm sorry for losing my temper. I not getting my alone time with the Lord. He's the one that keeps me on an even keel."

"I understand. It's been stressful, and since you won't let others help take the load off your shoulders, it grates on you," Ben replied. Diana took a deep breath in, her tea now gone; she put the cup down in her lap. Ben continued to stroke her hair. He noticed that her breathing was even, her hand no longer holding the cup. He reached over and took her cup from her lap. He carefully stood up, picking up the plate with the untouched sandwich on it. He walked over to the high bar. Scott was on the kitchen side of the counter. "Scott, could you wrap this for me and put it in the fridge?" Ben calmly asked.

"Yeah…we'll save it for her," Scott agreed.

Ben walked back over to where Diana was. He sat down next to her and pulled her to him, letting her sleep against him. Scott looked out and saw Ben holding Diana while she slept. "I guess he has her purring again. I just wish he'd quit antagonizing her," he said to Taggee.

"I think it is a type of courting between those two. She barbs him just as much, but he is the calm, cool one to her fire and passion," Taggee said.

"Not always. I've seen it where she is the calming one while he storms," Scott countered.

With everybody done with lunch, they all joined Ben out in the living room. "So how far did you get this morning, Scott?" Ben softy asked. Scott told the group about the trip wires he had set up on the sides of the house, the trap he planned to set up at the bottom of the patio stairs, and what he had planned to set up in the bedroom at the end of the hall.

"I was thinking that we may need to teach the girls a few moves for defense. What do you guys feel?" Ben suggested.

"I'm not sure I want Diana to know any more moves. She's hard enough to handle now," Scott teased.

"If I can teach her a better move than what she had in her arsenal right now, it may save us from sympathy pains later bro,' Ben chuckled. Diana stirred at the movement of him laughing. Ben quickly put his hand up to her face, calming her down.

"I would like to know how to protect myself, like Ariana has done," Mahala replied.

Aisha just sat there quietly. Scott watched her. "You don't want to learn it, Aisha?"

"I am not sure I can do that yet. My ribs are still healing. Besides, I'm not sure I can hurt anybody anyway," Aisha countered.

"Ariana doesn't want to hurt anybody. She only uses physical force when she feels threatened," Ben injected.

"I have some questions. The words that Ariana said, what do they mean?" Mahala asked.

"What words?" Scott inquired.

"Ego-sits-ico…er-o-gant…pomp-as?" Mahala queried.

Scott looked over at Ben. "Is she serious…Diana called you those?"

"Something along those lines…yeah." Ben smiled.

"You really had her fired up. I don't think I've seen her that mad before," Scott added.

"So what do they mean?" Mahala asked again.

"Well, egotistical usually means selfish. Arrogant can mean overconfident or overly proud. Pompous means haughty or belittling," Scott informed her.

"So she was calling him a selfish, overconfident, belittling man?" Mahala reworded.

"She was just very mad. She threw whatever word came to her mind at the time," Ben calmly stated.

"I guess it's a good thing she doesn't cuss. I'd hate to think of the words she would have used." Scott smiled.

"At least she doesn't stay mad for long," Aisha stated.

"It's actually unusual for her to get this mad. She's tired, anxious about Mahdi, and worried about everybody's safety. She doesn't want anybody here hurt," Ben included. "She knows I'm not giving her information, and she doesn't like it."

"So...since she's still sleeping and Ben's hands are full, Mahala...do you want to learn a few moves?" Scott asked.

She nodded. "Taggee, would you like to be the attacker?" Scott inquired. He figured it would be safer, not for Mahala, but for himself. Taggee wouldn't feel he was taking privileges. Scott went about showing a few moves to Mahala on how to break free from basic holds. An hour later, Mahala had the moves that Scott showed her down fairly well. Diana started to stir. "Did you have a good nap?" Ben asked.

Diana looked up at him and smiled. She just laid her head back on Ben's shoulder and watched what Mahala was doing. "You left out the basic move that always helps give time to escape," Diana quipped.

"I purposely left that one out. I think there are other moves that work just as well," Scott replied. Diana smiled; she figured she would teach that to the girls out of the sight of guys later.

"Do you feel like eating now?" Ben asked.

"Not really, but you're not going to accept that answer, are you?" Diana sneered.

"Nope," Ben replied as he caressed her arm. Diana shook her head but got up and headed to the bathroom.

"I'll get it in a minute," she stated as she shut the door. Ben got up and went to the kitchen and pulled the sandwich out of the fridge and put it on the high bar. When Diana walked back into the living room, he called her over to the high bar to eat her sandwich.

While she was eating the sandwich, Ben asked, "So what would you like to learn to do?"

"I'm interested in some of the martial arts moves that I've seen Scott use, like what he did to Jeff for example." Diana smiled.

"That has to do with pressure points on the body. I think we can do some work with that," Ben added. The doorbell rang. Scott guided Mahala over to Taggee then headed toward the door. Ben signaled for Diana to sit still and walked to the hallway just outside the kitchen door. Scott looked out the side window, then slowly opened the door. Allen stepped inside.

"How did you come out?" Scott asked.

Diana, hearing Allen's voice, hopped off the bar stool and slowly made her way toward the hallway. "I think we've got a good option here," Allen replied.

Scott and Allen walked to the living room. "Hey, Milady! We've got a new accessory for ya," Scott jested.

Diana looked at the bag in Allen's hand. "It's not jewelry, kitten, don't panic," Ben stated as he came up behind her. He saw her hesitation when Scott said accessory.

"That's a relief. I'd hate to cause another scene," Diana quipped.

"Another scene?" Allen shot a challenging look at Ben and Scott.

"Leave me out of it, I was outside," Scott said, holding his hands up in surrender.

"She was mad at me. I dealt with it, it's in the past," Ben curtly stated. "Let's see what we've got," Ben added, changing the subject. Allen pulled out a wrist brace from the bag. Diana cocked her head to the side and then looked at Allen.

"The doctor said that he thought you were using that wrist too much. So I brought over a brace to keep you from using it," Allen stated.

"Thank you. It's going to be interesting doing the dishes with this one," Diana said as she took the brace and put it on. She was working on securing it when Ben held his hand out for her to give her arm to him. It felt like a spandex material, but it was thicker. It was only about eight or ten inches long and was in a skin tone. Normally it would match Diana's color, but she had spent the last three months either stuck inside or covered head to toe with clothes. The brace tied on the top and then had a flap that covered over the top of the lacing to secure it. She could feel the hard stays that ran up the sides of her wrist. The stay on the outside of her wrist ran the full length of the brace. The stay on the inside of her wrist shaped a *Y* at the thumb.

"How does it feel?" Scott asked.

"It's stiff…but I guess it's suppose to be. It's very different than the braces I used when I had tendinitis in my wrists," Diana determined. She was checking the brace out when she felt the heavy cold presence again. She instantly looked at Ben. Ben felt the hairs on the back of his neck stick straight up.

"Uh-oh...here we go again," Scott stated as he saw the goose bumps on Diana's arms.

Allen looked between Ben and Scott. "What's going on, boys?"

Ben told Taggee to keep the girls close. He was just walking past Diana when something came crashing through the patio windows. Ben pulled Diana down to the floor. Allen and Scott put their backs to the hallway wall at the same time. Taggee grabbed Aisha and Mahala, carrying one in each arm, taking them to the hallway on the other side. Diana lifted her head up to see what was thrown through the window. It was a canister, and it started to smoke out.

"It's teargas!" Allen stated.

"Well, at least we are on the backside of the mountain now," Diana said as she looked at Ben.

"Yeah, but remember how much fun that was," Ben quipped back. "I want you to head over toward Taggee."

"Ah...that may be a problem. I have no shoes on, and there's glass everywhere," Diana pointed out.

"Lord, help me! Crawl back toward Scott then. Stay hidden, is that clear?" Ben commanded. Diana nodded and moved back toward Allen and Scott. Scott reached down and pulled her up then pushed her into the corner on the other side of the garage door.

"Stay down," he told her as he moved back toward the door opening into the kitchen. Ben moved over to the patio door, Scott came to the edge of the high bar, Allen stayed in the hallway not far from Diana. Taggee kept the girls behind him. Ben looked out and saw one person with the launcher thirty feet away from the house. He glanced around and saw two more coming up the side of the hedgerow. He held up three fingers toward Scott and Allen. Just then there was a raucous that sounded like it came from the garage. Allen glanced at Ben.

"One of your trip wires?" Ben asked as he looked at Scott. Scott smiled and nodded. Allen shook his head and moved back in front of Diana. A few minutes later, the garage door slowly opened. Diana tried to make herself as small as she could. Allen flattened against the wall 'til the men came into the hallway. The first man had goggles and a respirator on. When he came in, he was thrown against the wall. Then Allen did a quick chop on the back of the neck; the man dropped to the ground. The second man came in prepared, but Scott had moved back to help Allen. He kicked the gun up so that it shot the ceiling then pulled the gun strap around the man's neck, pulling it tight. He did a couple of quick jabs to the stomach, finishing with a hit to the chest. The man folded. Diana just stayed as still as possible. She saw another man come in while Allen and Scott were busy with the first two. He was taking aim on Allen; Diana whistled to get Scott's attention. The whistle brought the attacker's attention toward Diana. He turned and started heading toward her. She slowly started to stand up. She figured she'd be able to fight back if she had her legs free. As the attacker neared her, she saw a hand come around the attacker's face, grabbing the opposite side and then it jerked quickly. The attacker fell to the ground. Diana looked up and saw Allen standing behind where the attacker was standing. She grimaced. Allen nodded for her to get back to the corner. Ben was dealing with his own challengers. The two men coming up the side of the hedgerow had broken the patio door to enter into the house. Ben was able to disarm one of them and used the gun to knock the second guy out. Then he started dealing with the first one. He overtook the first man after four hits. The guys looked around; there were no other men coming into the house. But it only lasted for a second. Ben glanced out just in time to see four guys aiming their automatics at the house.

"Hit the deck!" he called out as he made a leap for the back side of the far couch. Taggee pushed the girls into the bathroom. Scott ran over and covered Diana, and Allen dropped to the floor near the end of the hallway. Diana heard glass breaking everywhere. Bullets sprayed through the living room and kitchen. Pieces of drywall, wood shards, and stuffing from the chairs and couches filled the air.

"Lord, help us," Diana said out loud. The four gunmen walked into the house, checking for anything to shoot. Allen and Ben nodded at each other. Ben still had a hold of the gun he took away from the first attacker he took out. Ben stood up and open-fired. He took out three men, but the fourth man ducked behind the high bar and was coming through the kitchen to flank Ben. The gunman stepped on some glass on the floor, which alerted the guys to where he was. Allen stood up, looked over to Ben, then started moving toward the kitchen doorway. Ben prepared to take the gunman out if it looked like Allen was in trouble. As the gunman's arms came into view, Allen grabbed the gun and took it away from the gunman then came around the kitchen doorway and fired, taking the fourth gunman out. Ben, Allen, and Scott started checking around the house for more attackers. Scott signaled for Diana to stay in the corner and to stay quiet. As the guys moved through the house, an attacker came through the garage door. He didn't have a regular gun. Diana held her breath; she hoped the goggles made it hard for the attackers to see. She didn't see where the guys were, but she couldn't alert them to the new attacker's presence. The man looked in the kitchen then the living room, then he was turning to the dining room. A piece of drywall that was hanging by the paper fell not more than a foot in front of Diana. The attacker turned toward the noise; he saw Diana, took aim, and fired. She jumped to the side; a dart hit the wall where she was huddled against. She looked at what hit the wall then looked at the attacker. She quickly grabbed the dart out of the wall; the phrase that Allen said at the garage popped into her head: "Some things are best kept hidden until necessary." She kept the dart in her hand for if she would need it later. The attacker reloaded and took aim at her again. This time Taggee, who had been watching the far hallway, came around the corner and saw what was going on. He came up behind the attacker and grabbed the dart gun and broke it, then he quickly knock the guy against the wall, taking out the attacker. Taggee came over and picked Ariana up and carried her over to the guest bathroom. He pointed for her to go in; she nodded and opened the door. Then she locked it, turned and looked at the scared faces of Mahala and Aisha. They stayed in there, Diana and Aisha praying in their own way for God's help. The girls heard two close gunshots. Mahala let out a scream; Diana put her hand over Mahala's mouth to quiet her. They watched the bottom of the door; there were shadows of people walking by. They saw someone trying the doorknob. Diana gave Aisha the dart, looked at Mahala. "Tell her to use it if they come close to her," she whispered.

Mahala interpreted what Ariana said. Aisha shook her head and tried to give it back. Diana insisted that she keep it. She figured with her cracked ribs, she wouldn't be able to put up a fight. Moments later, the door was kicked in.

Agent Kal was standing in the door way. He pointed his gun at Diana. "Let's go, Ariana," he said.

"Khaleel, no let her be! This is wrong, and you know it," Mahala argued.

"I have to, or he will take you. I have to give him Ariana," Khaleel replied. Another man came up behind Khaleel; he aimed the dart gun at Mahala, hitting her in the shoulder. Then he took aim at Diana; she saw that Khaleel was upset that Mahala was darted. He took his eyes off her; she took advantage of it and took a running start and put her shoulder down, driving it into Khaleel's stomach. She ended up knocking both men back. She pointed for Aisha to go to the far side while she was trying to get up herself. She felt Aisha move past her and run down the hallway. She started to move that way too, but the man with the dart gun knocked her over the head with it, rendering her unconscious.

Khaleel pushed Diana off him and to the side so he could get off the man with the dart gun. "Why did you shoot Mahala? We were to get Ariana and that's it!" Khaleel argued.

"I have my orders. I was to bring both girls in," the gunman stated.

"That wasn't the deal," Khaleel stated. While they were arguing, Aisha found a hiding place in the garage. She still had the dart with her, and she held it up to her chest. Khaleel stood up and picked up Ariana, throwing her over his shoulder. The other man picked up Mahala. They headed out to the backyard. Ben, Scott, and Allen were busy dealing with the attackers out on the patio. Ben had been trying to get back to Diana, but every time he got close to getting back in the house, someone would block him. He saw two people coming through the house carrying something. It was Agent Kal and another man; they had Diana and Mahala. Ben started heading for them when a helicopter came in over the lake. They had a couple of automatic rifles aimed at them. Ben went to move toward Diana when Allen grabbed his arm.

"You can't help her if you're dead. We have to come at this in a different angle," Allen stated.

Khaleel walked out onto the patio; he started to feel Ariana move around on his shoulder. He brought her down in front of him and held a knife to her throat. "You're gonna walk now, Ms. Henderson. Don't make me draw blood," Khaleel steamed. Diana was still working on getting her head around. She really wasn't all that awake yet.

She did try to reach up and grab the man's arm, but he pushed the knife closer into her throat. "Diana, don't!" Scott called out.

She cleared her head more. "If you have me why are you taking Mahala, you jerk?" Khaleel didn't give her a response. He was just forcing her to walk toward the helicopter. She saw Ben, Scott, and Allen along the side. "Me encontraste!" Diana looked directly at Ben. She could see fear, intense anger, and extreme danger in his eyes. "Me encontraste!"

Ben nodded. "Yo prometo te encontrare!" The guys watched Khaleel load Diana and Mahala up into the chopper. Just as the chopper was taking off, they heard the sirens of the DMPD coming down the road, screeching their tires as they pulled up to the house.

In seconds, the police walked into the house and started checking the rooms. They made it out the backyard. "Freeze!"

Ali came up behind the group. "These are the good guys. Stand down." Ali walked up to Ben. He didn't have to ask; he saw it in his eyes. *God, help us…help her, Lord*, he prayed.

Allen and Scott started walking back into the house. "Let's see if we have anybody that can give us some information," Allen stated. Ben and Ali fell in behind them. The first thing they did was look for Taggee and Aisha. They found Taggee in the corner by the door. He was starting to come around. He had been darted, but because of his size…the effectiveness was lacking.

Ben knelt down beside him. "Did you see where Aisha went?" Taggee just shook his head. Scott started walking down the hallway and noticed a small footprint left in the powder of the sheetrock heading into the garage.

He stepped out into the garage. "Aisha you can come out now, they've left." Scott saw movement under a tarp in the far corner. He walked up to it as Aisha came out from under it. He saw the tears running down her face. "I've got her, Ben," he yelled. He started to guide her back into what was left of the house. Taggee was standing now. Aisha and Scott walked into the hallway, Aisha seeing Taggee standing, ran to him. "I thought they shot you…I thought you were dead," she said against his arm.

"No, they did not kill me, but they got Ariana and Mahala," Taggee plainly stated.

"Ben, wasn't that the same helicopter we saw this morning?" Scott asked.

"Did anybody catch the ID numbers on the idiotic thing?" Ben fumed. He couldn't believe he failed her again. His head was just spinning with the thought of Diana in the hands of Mahdi, and why did they take Mahala when they had Diana?

Allen looked at Ben; he needed him to focus. "Ben, you promise her you would find her. You need to focus. You're not going to help her by beating yourself up," he chided.

"It was something 108," Scott throw out.

Ali glanced over at the kitchen; it was a total loss. He happened to see the dry-erase board over on the side of the fridge. "Was it KLP 108?" Ali asked.

The guys turned to him. "How did you know that?" Allen asked. Ali pointed to the dry-erase board. The guys came in and looked at it.

"You must have mouthed it when you saw it this morning. That's why Diana got up and went to the kitchen. She read it and wrote it down." Scott smiled.

"I love that girl." Ben smiled. Allen went to call in to find out where they took Diana. The brace should be giving a signal. Ben, Scott, Ali, and Taggee started to look for survivors. They did find a few; the guys were working on squeezing any information out of them they could. There was one specific man that had on a different outfit than the others. Ben and Scott felt that he may be higher up in the ranks therefore would know more information. Unfortunately, he wasn't willing to share. Scott saw that he had some deep cuts in his thigh.

"Why don't we help those cuts out? We have some medication left to put on them." Scott smiled wickedly.

Ben caught what Scott was implying. "Let's see how well he takes burning, shall we?" he stated as he went to the kitchen. He found a pan to use to hold the water and added the last of the powder they had been using on Diana's wrist.

44

At a Warehouse in Des Moines

Diana was allowed to hold Mahala on the way to wherever they were going. It kept her mind off the fact that she was in a chopper again. She actually would rather fight the fear in herself than the effects of the drug they used to dart with. She did thank the Lord for that and for keeping the guys safe. She knew that Taggee was hurt, but she saw him breathing when she was trying to get off Khaleel. She closed her eyes and searched for the Lord. He said He would be there all the time, she just had to calm herself and listen. She felt His presence once she focused in. She heard Him say, "I am here…you will be okay." The helicopter came in for a landing in the industrial area of Des Moines. One of the warehouses had men moving in and out of it, so she figured that was where they were probably heading.

Lord, help me, guide me and keep me focused to overcome this trial, she prayed. The guards came up; one grabbed Mahala and threw her over his shoulder like a sack of potatoes. Another came up and cuffed Diana's hands together then yanked her out of the helicopter. Diana still didn't have shoes on, so she wasn't walking quickly. He hit her across the face, knocking her out, then threw her up over his shoulder. Diana was out long enough that when she finally came to, she found herself in the warehouse near a railing that was at least thirty feet up in the air, with her arms stretched above her head. She glanced around—first to find Mahala then to see how she can escape. She saw that Mahala was stretched out like she was about ten feet from her. She was still out from being darted. Diana managed to turn around to look behind her, making a mental list of what she saw, what was available for her to use, where the exits were. *At least here, the exits are marked*, she thought. She tried her bounds to see if she could pull her hands free. Diana was grateful for the brace Allen gave her. It was keeping the handcuffs from cutting into her wrist. The cold heavy presence came over her, sucking the air out of her lungs. Goose bumps ran down her arms and covered her entire body. She heard someone laughing an evil, wicked laugh.

"Don't even try it. You are mine for now," Diana heard from the far side of the room. Diana's mind started to freeze up.

She heard the echo of Allen's voice: "Fear clouds the mind." Diana stilled herself. *Lord, guide me*, she prayed.

The spirit of the Lord came down and, in Diana's mind, blasted the cold heavy presence away from her. *I am here with you...trust me*, Diana heard the Lord tell her.

She turned herself around to face forward. "So are you that afraid of me that you hide in the shadows?" Diana quipped.

"I'm not at all afraid of you, but once I'm done, you'll be afraid of me," Mahdi sneered.

"Don't count on it," Diana jabbed back.

Mahdi laughed; "Oh…I'm positive of it." He came up and grabbed Diana by the face, "*I will* break you." Diana just glared at him; she almost smiled in defiance. She could see that it bothered him that he had no effect on her. He turned and walked over to Mahala. He checked her neck for a pulse, slapped her face, which she didn't feel, then laughed at her. "We will wait till she is awake. I'll be back," Mahdi said over his shoulder. Diana watched him walk out of the area and through a door.

Zenon's Vacation House

Allen, Scott, and Taggee picked up the gunman that was in a different uniform and tied him to a chair. They suggested that Ali go with the rest of the officers and start sifting through evidence and bodies. Being an officer of the law, Ali was restricted on what he was allowed to participate in. Ben brought over the pan with the medicine in it. "Let's see how much burning this gentleman can take" he sneered. Ben pulled out his knife and sliced the pant leg off the gunman, leaving several cuts from the fighting exposed. He used a cup and scooped up some of the liquid and started pouring it over the gunman's leg. The gunman screamed as if someone put a hot poker on his leg. "Tell me where Mahdi is taking the girls," Ben said. It took ten minutes of "helping" the gunman's wounds before he finally told the guys that they were taken to a warehouse.

Just as they were putting the pan and cup on the counter, Ali walked into the area. "We've got a hit on the helicopter," Ali said as he looked at the gunman tied in the chair.

Allen turned and asked, "What do you have?"

"It's registered to a local business that rents and flies for hire. They have on record that a Middle Eastern man rented the chopper and pilot to fly over the city at five this morning. The pilot said that he was asked to concentrate the fly over to this area. It is also on the books that the same guy rented the helicopter by itself for this afternoon. It has not been returned yet," Ali informed them.

"Okay...he has to be in the city yet. Those types of helicopters don't have the ability to fly far from the area," Ben deduced.

Allen's phone rang. The guys hoped it was the address from the tracer Diana was wearing. "Thomas...got it. We're on the way," Allen replied. "We've got an address. Let's go!"

He didn't have to tell them twice. Both Ben's and Allen's vehicle were beyond hope of use. Ali took Ben and Scott in his car. Officer Stacia took Allen and Taggee in her car. Aisha was driven by another officer to DHS office for protection. They headed for the industrial area. Allen told Ben that he was going to call in some reinforcements. Ben said he was going to call Zenon and fill him in on what happened and where they were heading. "How did he take the news?" Scott asked Ben once he was off the phone.

"He's not happy, but he's more worried about Diana and Mahala. He and some of the guys are meeting us at the warehouse," Ben replied.

Scott saw the expression on Ben's face. He knew what was going through Ben's head; it was going through his as well. "Trust the Lord bro. He hasn't bailed on her so far. I don't figure He will now," Scott encouraged.

"He will give her strength and wisdom," Ali added. Ben just stayed quiet.

Scott laughed. "You've been around Diana too long, Ben. You've learned to crawl into a hole just like her."

Ben turned and glared at Scott, but he had to admit...he wasn't really paying attention until then. *Lord...what are you doing?* he silently prayed.

You'll have to trust me, Ben heard the Lord tell him.

When Ali pulled near the warehouse, he turned off the sirens. The guys looked out to a massive offensive before them. "I guess when Allen says he's going to call in for reinforcements, he wasn't kidding," Scott chuckled. There were DHS agents, DMPD, SWAT, and the National

Guard there. The guys unloaded from the cars and walked into the middle of the mob. The leads of the SWAT and the National Guard were gathered together with Director Zenon by the van that they used as command central. Allen spotted the group and directed the guys that way.

Taggee was uneasy with the mass of people around him. Most of the troop there were not used to seeing a man as tall as him, much less as big. "They do know I'm not their target, right?" Taggee asked Scott as they walked through the crowd.

"Yeah, they're just not used to seeing someone of your stature." Scott smiled.

"So, Charles, how's the outlook?" Allen asked as they neared the table.

Charles looked up from the blueprints to address the guys. "There are fifteen to twenty men in the building. Most of them are on the ground floor. We've seen movement up on the third floor, but we don't know where Diana and Mahala are, and we don't know what defensive they have," Charles ended.

As Charles and Allen were talking, Dick came up behind Ben and put his hand on his shoulder. "Sorry man, but we'll get her back." Ben simply nodded.

"So what we need to do is get a few inside set to pull the girls to safety as soon or before we start the offensive," Allen surmised.

"I think that will be the best hope for Diana and Mahala," Charles confirmed.

"I and Scott will go in," Ben firmly stated.

"Are you sure you can keep yourself focused Ben, no matter what state the girls may be in?" Charles questioned.

"It won't be a problem," Ben said coldly.

"I think it will be advantageous for Taggee to go in with them," Allen stated. Charles looked at him a little puzzled. "If nothing else, he could carry the girls by himself while Ben and Scott clear the way," Allen chuckled. He looked at Taggee and told him what he told Charles. Taggee nodded in agreement.

"Okay, agreed. Let's get this over and done with before we have to carry Diana and Mahala out in a black bag," Charles stated. The thought of his statement just hit him between the eyes. He looked at the group and saw the coldness in their faces. "God, help us," he said as he shook his head and walked to the perimeter.

Inside the warehouse, Mahdi kept track of the growing numbers of troops outside. "Be ready. They won't push too much. We have hostages," he stated to one of his men. He figured as long has he had his two queens, the men wouldn't charge. He walked out of the room and headed out to check on his hold cards. He walked out onto the catwalk, Ariana was there and smiling as he neared. "Are you ready to let us go?" she asked him.

"Oh no…things are just coming together. Soon I'll have the key to your undoing," Mahdi stated.

Diana thought on that statement; then she replied. "You can't get to the key of my undoing."

"We shall see," Mahdi replied as he moved over to Mahala. This time when he slapped her face, there was a response. She was starting to come around.

"Soon ladies…now if you'll excuse me, I need to get the trap set." Mahdi smirked as he walked down the stairs.

Diana thought on what Mahdi said. She figured by the way they were strung up and opened for all to see, they were the bait. Then it hit her: the only ones that would be affected by using her as bait would be Ben or Scott. Mahdi doesn't even know Scott exists, so it's Ben he's after. "Lord help us…control my mind, my love," Diana prayed out loud. Diana heard a moan from Mahala. "I'm here with you. Don't open your eyes right away. You'll get sick," she told Mahala. She wasn't sure she was registering sounds yet, but she had to try to warn her of the darts effects.

Back outside, the guys prepared to head in. They had found an entrance that was only lightly guarded. Scott and Taggee quickly took out the two guards without any problems. Then Ben picked the door lock and quickly entered. Scott still didn't carry a gun, but he did have a knife with him now; Taggee refused any weapon. Ben had his knife and his Magnum with him. They glanced around for any other guards. There wasn't any. Alarms started going off in Ben's head. "This is too easy. Watch out for a trap," Ben whispered to Scott and Taggee. Scott and Taggee headed to the right and started looking for trouble. Ben took the left; he was to look for the girls. As he quietly moved through the building, he heard men talking about the two women upstairs. Ben stayed low and waited to hear the rest of the information. The men said that as soon as Mahdi had his last tool, he would start having fun with the American. Ben watched as the men started walking away on their patrol. He found the stairs leading up to the next floor and quietly walked up them. He looked around the second-floor area and found nothing. A few guards were posted at the windows on the corners, but they were busy watching the troops outside. Ben headed to the third floor. It had a catwalk all the way around with only a railing to stop you from falling all the way down. He stayed near the wall, trying to keep hidden as much as possible. There was an area he couldn't see because the walk took a sharp turn to the right. He slowly worked his way to the corner to glance around it. Once he glanced down the hall, he saw Diana and Mahala stretched up like a side of beef hanging in a cooler. His blood started to boil.

Diana knew Ben was near. He was close enough for her to feel him. As much as she wanted him to come and get her, she knew there was danger for him. "Cuidado! Es una trampa!" she said as loud as she could.

One of the guards in the room came out to check on her. He walked up and stood in front of her. "I can't wait for tonight. Mahdi said he would let some of us guys have a little fun with you. I intend to enjoy myself immensely," the guard said as he ran his fingers down the front of Diana. Diana's face turned stone cold. Her feet weren't tied, so when the guard took privileges; she retaliated. He stumbled backward and desperately tried to breathe.

"You won't be using that anytime soon," she sneered. She had wished she could have hit him harder, but she felt the pull on her wrists and was afraid she'd tear them open if she swung out more. The guard, finally able to breath, came fuming at her. He went to strike her but was called to a halt by Mahdi.

"I told you to check on Ariana, not to touch her. At least not yet," Mahdi steamed. "You seem to like impairing men," he said as he neared Diana. "Until I have my last tool, I think we need to contain those legs of yours," Mahdi said as he grabbed some rope from off the wall. He looked over at the guard. "Do you think you can keep a knife at her neck without getting kicked?" The guard wanted to spit nails.

The guard pulled out his knife and grabbed a handful of Diana's hair, pulling her head back, and held the knife to her neck. "Don't worry, I'll still be able to have fun with you tonight," he whispered in Diana's ear. Mahdi used the rope to secure Diana's legs to the railing. When he stood back up, he smiled and half-slapped her face a couple of times. Then he nodded for the guard to go back to the room. He followed him and shut the door.

Mahala slowly opened her eyes and looked over at Ariana. "Where are we at?" Mahala gravelly whispered.

"We are still in Des Moines, at a warehouse in the industrial district. I know your throat has to be burning like crazy. Try not to talk," Diana said as she looked at Mahala.

Ben, who was watching from the corner, hoped that Scott was nearby. He did a meadowlark call and waited to hear any reply. He saw that Diana had heard it and looked toward the sound. Ben figured that Scott wasn't near the area because he didn't hear a reply. Just as he was figuring out what to do next, he heard a nightingale call. He moved back and waited until he had visual on Scott and Taggee.

Diana looked over at Mahala. "The guys are here. We'll be getting out soon." Mahala smiled and nodded. What happened next was not seen by the guys or Diana. There was a noise coming from the hallway on the other side of Mahala. Diana looked over to see if one of the guys or maybe Allen was coming to get them out of there. It was Khaleel, who neared them.

He came up to Mahala and checked to make sure she was okay. "I've got to get you out of here," he told his sister.

Mahala looked at him. "Ariana too?" Khaleel didn't give her an answer. He started to cut through the ropes that held her hands. Mahala restated, "Khaleel, we're taking Ariana with us too."

Khaleel looked over at Ariana then back to his sister. "I can't get both of you out. I can only take one. I'm taking you, Mahala," he emphasized.

Diana looked at Mahala and whispered. "Go with your brother. I'll be fine, go." Khaleel was just about through the rope when there was a shot fired. Khaleel looked at his sister and then down at his chest. His shirt started to turn red; Mahala screamed as Khaleel fell to the ground. Diana looked around trying to see where the shot came from. It was from the other side of the catwalk. They had a sniper set up there. Mahdi and the other guard came out of the room.

Mahala was crying; the guard bent down and checked for a pulse. "He's gone," he stated.

Mahala screamed then bawled. Mahdi looked at Ariana. "Tsk, tsk, tsk…he wasn't the one I wanted to catch. Oh well, sometimes when you set a trap, you get the insects as well as the rats." He smiled. "I'm willing to wait. I'm sure the rats are nearby now."

"I have no clue. As I've said before, you can't touch what controls me." Diana smiled back.

Mahdi walked up to Ariana. "I will be the one that controls you. It gives me great pleasure to think of the enjoyment I'll have breaking you. It may take me months. Just think: finally to have months and months of enjoyment."

"I honestly don't think you have months and months to live. I hope you're thinking about getting ready to leave this world. You're definitely not going to like the world to come if you don't change," Diana said candidly.

Mahdi laughed and grabbed her face then slid his hand down to her throat and started to squeeze. Diana just glared at him. "If you're referring to that curse of yours, I'm not at all worried about it," he gloated. He walked over to Khaleel's body. "Get it out of here. We don't want to give anything away," he demanded.

The guard called back to the room. Two more guards came out of the room and picked the body up and took it down the stairs. Ben watched from his hiding place. He saw the sniper from across the way. *We'll have to take him out first.* Then there's the unknown amount of guards in the room. *We'll have to neutralize that area.* It dawned on him: the trap was for him. He was the tool Mahdi was going to use to break Diana; he placed his head back against the wall. *How are we going to deal with this problem, Lord?* he prayed in himself.

Ben heard a quiet nightingale call. He did a short meadowlark call and watched to make sure it didn't bring attention. Mahdi looked around, told his guards to get back into the room and smiled at Ariana, then turned and went into the room himself.

Diana heard the calls; she knew the guys were near, but she tried not to give it away. Mahala was lost in grief. Her last surviving family member was now gone. Diana looked over to Mahala. "I'm sorry, but you're not alone. You still have your new family." Mahala looked over to her. "Aisha, me, Ben, Scott, Taggee—we're your brothers and sisters. We'll be by you until the Lord returns," Diana finished. Mahala gave her a half smile. Diana wished she could give her a hug, but it would have to wait.

Ben saw Scott working his way over to him. "What do we have?" Scott asked as he got next to Ben.

"A trap" Ben snipped. Scott looked at him and waited for him to finish.

"Mahdi has the girls hung up like a side of meat as bait. There is a sniper directly across from them. He just took out Mahala's brother. Then there are at least four and probably more in the office on the side ready to jump out at whoever tries to rescue them," Ben stated.

"Well, that sounds like fun. What are we going to do?" Scott wondered.

"We'll have to take out the sniper first. Do you want to take that on?" Ben asked.

"You got it, Ben. I'll take care of him. Then you and Taggee can deal with the office people. I'll take out who I can," Scott added. Ben nodded. Scott worked his way back down to the stairway. He signaled for Taggee to come up and told him what the plan was. Then Scott worked his way around to the other side of the catwalk. Ben watched as Scott ducked behind boxes and crates, working his way to the area he told him the sniper was at. He saw Scott get right up against the wall and glance around where the sniper was hiding. Then he saw Scott head in. Ben prayed that there was only one gunman over there. If there was more, well, Scott would have to deal with it. It was taking Scott longer than Ben thought it should for him to signal. He was starting to get nervous. Then he heard an owl screech. Ben looked out and saw that Scott had the position covered. He also saw Scott signal to Taggee to start out. Taggee started working his way toward Ben.

Once Taggee got to Ben, he asked, "So how are we going to deal with the men in the office?"

"I was originally going to block the door, but this building is apparently not up to code. The door opens in instead of out. So…do you have any ideas?" Ben quipped.

"Is there a way we can take them on one at a time?" Taggee asked.

"I don't know what weapons they have in there. If it was just hand-to-hand combat, that would be a possibility, but if they have automatic weapons?" Ben grimaced.

"We don't have a choice. We're going to have to take that risk," Taggee flatly stated.

"Well, let me do this then. I'll will pull the guards out of the room. You hold back here. I'll go and start getting the girls down. If I can get them out before they know I'm here, that will be great. Otherwise, I'll draw out the group. You and Scott jump in when you can." Ben figured, if it was a trap for him, then they would want him alive—at least for a while.

"I don't like it. They may kill you on sight," Taggee argued.

"They want me to get to Ariana. I heard Mahdi say he was going to use me to break her," Ben answered. "That will mean that he'll want me alive, to make her watch, probably as they torture me. It's the best option we have to get them out of here. I'll take out who I can. But don't let them get too far into things. Deal?" Ben said with a smile. Taggee nodded. Ben started to make his way toward Diana and Mahala. He saw that Scott was watching him, the rifle at the ready.

Diana looked over and saw Ben coming toward her. She closed her eyes. *Thank you, Lord*, she quietly prayed. Once Ben got to her, she whispered, "Ben, it's a trap for you."

Ben smiled, traced his fingers down the side of her face, and whispered, "I know."

"Get Mahala first. She's the liability for him now," Diana stated. Ben nodded and quickly cut Mahala down. Mahala rubbed her wrists and looked at Ariana.

Ben whispered in her ear, "I'll get her. Quietly go around the corner. You'll find Taggee there." Mahala nodded and quickly ran toward the corner. Ben then started to cut Diana's legs free. "Ah…my trap has finally caught the right prey," Mahdi stated, standing in the doorway of the room.

Ben stood up and turned to face him. "I'd figured that Ariana would make you free Mahala first. She was just a, diversion, shall we say. Too bad Khaleel didn't wait. I would have given him his sister as soon as we had you," Mahdi continued. His guards in the room filed out and surrounded Ben and Diana.

"And you want me for what?" Ben coldly stated. "You obviously don't need a translator."

"Oh…no. That's not my need for you. You see, I have this strong desire…a need—to control Ariana. Now, knowing that she was more than willing to kill herself before she would eat or drink in the compound told me that we needed a different tool to control her. Again, Khaleel came in very handy. He told me about the supposed bond between you and Ariana—that you control her. I must say, I am surprised that you haven't bedded her yet. She must be very strong-willed, or you're very weak," Mahdi snickered as he turned to Ben.

"No person controls her. She only listens to God," Ben simply stated.

"Well, we will find out. However, since you have untied her legs and we don't want her using them. We need to move them out of the way." Mahdi walked into the office and then returned with a controller. He moved to an outlet near the office and plugged it in. He hit a button. Diana was raised up by the pulley they had her hooked onto. Ben saw the sheer terror in her eyes, but he made no moves toward her. Then he saw Mahdi hit another button. The pulley moved Diana out away from the catwalk and toward the middle of the open space. She was dangling by her handcuffs over thirty feet in the air. She instantly screamed.

Mahdi grinned from ear to ear. "Isn't that a pleasant sound to hear? I bet she has a beautiful singing voice. Have you heard her sing yet, Mr. James? Or should I call you Agent Tigere?" Ben just stood there; his face was hard, his eyes were cold.

Back outside, Allen and Charles were waiting for the signal saying that the girls were clear. They heard a gunshot earlier, so they had moved everybody into their positions and readied for the go. Then they heard a bloodcurdling scream. Allen instantly felt a cold chill run up his spine. "We can't wait, Charles. We go now," he stated.

Charles nodded in agreement. "Everybody, go! Watch out for Diana, Mahala, and the guys," he warned. Each group had their assignments, and they started moving in. "Charles…I'm going in. Diana won't trust just anybody," Allen stated as he prepped his gun.

"I'll stay here, just in case she runs out," Charles added. He watched as Allen made his way over and into the door Ben used.

On the catwalk, Ben kept eye contact with Mahdi, but he said, "¡Cálmate! Te conseguiré."

"Oh…don't worry so much. I just gave her the perfect front-row seat. Now, Agent Tigere, shall we see how much your pain can affect her?" Mahdi smiled. Ben smiled, looked at the guards circling him, and then gave a nod. The guard directly behind him ran toward him to put him in a chokehold. Ben flipped him over and gave him a right hook into the face. Then two from the side came at him. Ben turned to the side and tripped one; he fell up against the railing and knocked the wind out of himself. The second one got a hold of Ben. Ben threw his elbow into the guard's side, which caused him to let go. Then Ben turned and forced his head up against the wall. The guard fell to the floor. The guard that got the wind knocked out of him came from behind and got a hold of Ben's arms. Another guard from the circle came over and started punching Ben.

Diana closed her eyes. *Lord, help us! Help me get control of my fear.* She knew she had to get to safety. That would free Ben up to concentrate on the guards. She also knew that though the right wrist was protected by the brace, her left wrist was starting to get cut again. She worked to pull herself up on the chain of the cuffs so that she could grab a hold of the hook with her hands. That would relieve the pressure on her wrists. She glanced over and saw Taggee and Mahala to the side. She looked at Taggee and nodded toward where Ben was; then she heard a gunshot. Her heart stopped. She forced herself to look over toward Ben. It wasn't Ben that fell to the floor; it was one of the guards. She tried to look behind her to see who was there, but she couldn't turn her head enough. Mahdi was shocked to see that his sniper took out one of the guards. Then there was another shot. Mahdi saw that the guard that was holding a knife to start working on Agent Tigere fell backward to the floor.

Scott's shot startled the guard that was holding Ben's arms. Ben felt the guard loosen his grip. He quickly flipped the guard to the side and grabbed his head and did a quick jerk. Ben looked up; he had two more guards plus Mahdi. Ben heard the fighting down on the ground floor.

He figured Diana's scream would start something outside. The troops were starting to take the warehouse.

Mahdi was mad; his plans were crumbling around him. He still had the hold card yet. "Get him!" he sneered at the two guards standing near him. They started working their way toward Ben.

Diana looked out across the way. She saw that there were guards coming up the stairs on both sides. She forced herself to glance down and see what was going on below her. She saw that there were guards hiding behind crates about ready to ambush a group of soldiers walking under her. "To the sides, watch out!" she yelled. The soldiers first aimed up at her then the one in the lead signaled to fan out. She saw that the soldiers were getting to the guards before they could move. Diana looked back toward the guards up on third. There was a group nearing were Taggee and Mahala were at. Mahala was watching her. She nodded toward the direction that the guards were coming from.

Mahala tapped Taggee on the shoulder and pointed toward Ariana. Taggee looked out and saw that Ariana was nodding toward something down the catwalk. He then heard the sound of someone coming toward them. Taggee nodded to Ariana and pushed Mahala down low behind the crate. He moved to the corner and waited till the guards came around.

Diana then turned her attention to the guards coming up the stair from the second floor on her left. "I don't know who is behind me, but since you helped Ben out, heads-up. They're coming up the stairs," she called out. She heard a meadowlark song and smiled. "You're welcome, brother." She grinned.

Ben heard Diana guiding people around; he grinned. Now he had to deal with these last two guards, then it will be Mahdi's turn. They each took opposite sides of him—one on the right, one on the left. The one on the right made the first move toward him. He had a knife in his hand. Ben knew he had lost his gun and first knife near the start of the fighting; his pocket knife, however, was still in his pocket. He simply pulled it out, clicked it, and threw it at the guard. It hit its target; the guard fell to the floor. The last guard came up and kicked Ben's hand that had been holding the knife. Ben blocked the guard's leg from coming toward his head and pushed it back. The guard swung around and shifted his weight to bring up the other leg. Ben blocked that as well. Then Ben threw out some jabs to the shoulders and chest of the guard. Diana watched; it was the first time she'd seen Ben use a martial arts style of fighting. She thought that maybe only Scott used that style. She was obviously wrong. She started looking for where Mahdi was. She knew he would be Ben's next target. But he was out of sight. She heard a snap and a groan, which brought her attention back to Ben and the guard. She saw the guard fall to the floor in front of Ben.

Ben looked around for Mahdi, but he didn't see him. A stray bullet came whizzing up, hitting one of the windows in the area. "We've got to get you undercover kitten. Hang on," Ben said to Diana as he moved over to the controller. He hit the button to bring her back toward him. He really wished the pulley would move faster. Another bullet came by and took out the window on the south side. If Diana was still where she had been placed by Mahdi, she would have been hit. Finally, the pulley had her over the catwalk. Ben then hit the button to bring her down.

As she neared the floor of the catwalk, Ben dropped the controller and moved over to her. He guided her down with his hands then reached up to unhook the cuffs from the hook. She grimaced as her arms were being lowered. "I think I dislocated my shoulders," she stated as she tried to bring her arms down.

Ben just smiled. "You never do anything halfway...do ya?" Diana just shook her head.

Ben started picking the lock of the handcuffs to release Diana. "Ben, look out!" he heard Diana yell. He grabbed Diana and was dropping her to the floor. He felt a sharp pain in the back of his head; then everything was black.

Diana was being covered by Ben, but he was out. She saw the blood running down the side of his head. She couldn't do anything. Ben's weight was fully on her and her hands were still handcuffed. She knew he wasn't dead; she felt his breath on her face, but he was severely hurt.

"We have some unfinished business to attend to first Ariana. I wasn't planning on killing him straight out, but I guess plans have changed," Mahdi stated as he rolled Ben off Ariana. He threw the wrecking bar down on the floor and grabbed Ariana by the handcuffs, pulling her up to a standing position.

Scott had aimed the rifle at Mahdi, but Mahdi put Diana in front of him. He couldn't get a clear shot.

Mahdi turned Ariana around as soon as he saw movement across the way. He held a knife to her. "Who do we have here? Another vying for you?" he snipped. "By all means, do come around."

Scott slowly lowered the rifle and walked around the catwalk toward Diana and Mahdi.

"I do believe introduction need to be made. Tell me who he is Ariana," Mahdi demanded.

"This is Mr. McCleary. A friend of Agent Tigere," Diana flatly stated.

"Oh…so he has no tie to you then. Why is he here?" Mahdi snipped.

"He asked me to come and help him," Scott simply stated. He knew why Diana didn't tie him to her. She was trying to protect him.

"Hmm…too bad then. You wouldn't mind throwing that rifle over the railing now, would you?" Mahdi suggested.

Scott pulled it up; he saw Mahdi push the knife closer to Diana's neck. He opened the chamber and dropped the last few bullets out of it, walked over near the railing, and dropped it. Mahdi started walking Diana backward, putting distance between them and Scott. Diana hoped that maybe Taggee was nearby and he would grab the knife and deal with Mahdi; but she continued to be pulled back. Soon they rounded the corner. It was then that Mahdi let Diana up from the knife by her throat. He still had a hold of her and he still had the knife out, but he was forcing her to walk ahead of him. As they walked around the catwalk toward the stairs, Diana prayed God would deliver her. She didn't want to go back to Syria. She was shoved into the stairwell. As she turned to go down the stair, she heard a shot. Mahdi let go of her arm and went back against the wall before the stair. Then there was another shot. She saw Mahdi fall to the floor. She stayed there in the stairwell.

"Diana!" Scott called out. He was afraid that Mahdi may have thrown her down the stairs. Diana heard Scott call and went to the top of the stairwell. She saw him come around the corner. She closed her eyes and took a deep breath. Scott saw her at the top of the stairs and grabbed her up. "Thank you, Lord," he prayed out loud. He wrapped her up in his arms.

Allen, Taggee, and Mahala came up behind Scott. Diana saw that it was Allen carrying the rifle. "You took him out then?" Diana asked over Scott's shoulder.

Scott relaxed his hold on her and turned to let her see. "It's a good thing he still has quick reflexes. He grabbed it as it came down to the second floor."

Diana laid her head on Scott's shoulder. Allen just winked at her, but then he saw her get very somber. "Ben?" Diana asked.

Scott held her tight to his side. "We don't know yet."

"Let's get those cuffs off you," Allen stated as he walked over to her. "Did you get hurt?" he asked as he picked the lock.

"I think my shoulders are dislocated," Diana said calmly.

"We'll send you in the ambulance with Ben and have the doctors check on you, okay?" Allen informed her.

Diana smiled and nodded. "Thank you. That would be greatly appreciated."

"Well, we can't have you walking out with bare feet. I guess we'd better have you carried on down," Scott stated as he looked down and saw that Diana had no shoes on.

Scott looked at Taggee and asked if he was willing to carry Ariana out. Taggee smiled and walked up to her. Diana nodded and let Taggee lift her up. He carried her all the way out. Scott guided Mahala out behind him, and Allen brought up the rear.

As soon as they reached the ground floor, Charles met up with them. "Did everybody make it out?" he asked.

"We need an ambulance to take Diana and Ben to the hospital. Ben is up on third floor with a bad blow to the back of the head," Allen stated.

"And Diana?" Charles asked them.

"She may have two dislocated shoulders," Scott replied. Charles moved to the doorway and signaled for the medics to come in with the stretchers. One stopped in front of Taggee; he laid Ariana on the stretcher and patted her head. The medics secured her in and took her into the ambulance. The other crew carried the backboard up and retrieved Ben.

Diana watched to see Ben, but the ambulance pull away before she could see him being brought out. *Lord…I'm scared*, she prayed.

I am here, she heard the Lord reply.

Thank you for being with me. Thank you for getting me out of there. Is Ben going home now? Or are you going to allow him to stay? Diana asked the Lord.

He is with me for a while…but he will return, the Lord told her. Diana relaxed and lay back. She started singing "I Love You, Lord" in her head.

45

At Mercy Medical Center

The ER doctor checked her out and had x-rays done on her shoulders and arms. Diana made sure they checked her wrists. She came out with a dislocated right shoulder, which they popped back into place and put a sling on, and some glass in her feet and pulled muscles and tendons in her arms and wrists. They pulled the glass out and wrapped her feet in gauze. Then they gave her some slipper socks to walk around in. The left wrist was slightly cut by the handcuffs, but it was above where the rope burn was. They didn't do anything to it. The right wrist, when they took the gauze off, had a slight re-tear on one side of it. They cleaned it up and put the ointment on it and rewrapped the wrist with gauze. She didn't have them put the brace back on it; they just put it in a bag for her then they dismissed her. She headed over to the counter to ask where Ben was. Scott met her at the counter.

"Well, Milady, did you come out without any new scars?" Scott teased.

"They pulled some glass out of my feet, but I don't think it will scar," Diana jabbed back. "Where's Ben?"

"Come on sis, I'll take ya to him." Scott grinned and guided her out into the hallway and up to the fourth floor.

They went down a few rooms and walked into an intensive care room. One of the nurses came over to them. "Are you family?"

"I'm his best friend, but she's his fiancée," Scott replied. Diana's breath caught, and she looked up at him. He heard her gasp when he mentioned her relation to Ben; he looked down at her and simply winked.

"Oh…okay then. You can come in," the nurse said as she moved back to her desk.

"Go ahead sis. I'll be in in a bit. I need to get some coffee," Scott said as he stroked her arms.

"Hey, Scott...thank you," Diana softly stated. Scott turned and tipped his imaginary hat to her and walked down the hallway.

Diana walked into the room and up to the nurse. "What were the results?" Diana asked her.

The nurse looked up from the charts. "He has a concussion. Right now we are just monitoring him. What did he hit his head on?"

"A wrecking bar hit him," Diana said, looking over at him lying on the bed.

"I'm surprised it didn't crack his skull open. He just has a big gash in the back of his head," the nurse said in amazement.

Thank you again, my love. Diana smiled and silently prayed. Diana walked in and went over by the far side of Ben. She reached down and put one hand on his arm. She leaned over and whispered in his ear. "I know where you are at. The Lord told me. When you come back, we'll have to compare notes...deal?" She kissed his temple.

Ben knew he had been hurt; he just didn't know how and how bad. He remembered things going black. He woke up lying on the ground in a forest. He stood up and looked around. It was beautiful and peaceful. He walked down a trail that was in front of him. It wound through huge tall trees then he came to a clearing. There was a fire going and fish cooking over it. He looked around to see if there was anybody around. When he looked back to the fire, the Lord was there sitting on the logs around the fire.

"Come...have a seat," the Lord said. Ben walked over and sat across from the Lord.

"I'm that bad off, huh?" Ben asked somberly.

"Oh...not overly. I made you with a thick head. I just needed to have a chat with you. You seemed a little too rushed to talk long...so I brought you here." The Lord smiled.

Ben heard something behind him. He turned and saw a tiger come out of the woods. Ben instinctively stood up.

"It's okay Benjamen. She doesn't want to hurt you. She's come to be with me; she often comes to me," the Lord replied.

A tigress, Ben thought, which took him to thinking about Diana.

"She's safe," Ben heard the Lord say. "Diana is safe?" Ben reiterated. The Lord nodded as he petted the tigress.

"She a lot like this one here," the Lord mused. "But you already knew that, didn't you."

Ben laughed. "I've noted the similarities. I've always wanted to ask you, how do you control her?"

The Lord looked up with a stern look and said, "I don't. I simply guide her. Take this cat here. I've known her since she was created. She has learned how to trust me through the things she's experienced in her life. Now, I can tell her to go to you." Ben saw the Lord signal the tigress to go to him. The tigress stood up and moved partway toward Ben, but then she stopped. "Now, I guided her toward you, but she has to decide whether to go the rest of the way or not. Hold your hand out to her…don't be afraid," the Lord stated.

Ben held his hand out toward the tigress. He saw her looking at it, smelling it. The tigress turned and looked back at the Lord. "It's okay, he won't hurt you," the Lord told her.

Ben kept his hand out, palm-side down, and waited quietly. The tigress turned and smelled his hand again and then moved toward him. Ben carefully glided his hand down the cat's back. She came up beside him and lay down by his foot. Ben continued to stroke his hand down the cat's back.

"See, I didn't force her to obey. I simply asked her, and for her trusting me, she gets petted." the Lord smiled.

"Will she ever just do as I say?" Ben asked.

"Maybe…eventually the tigress may listen without questioning. She's known me since she was three years old. Even now she questions me, just not as hard. You should have been around when she was in her teens," the Lord laughed. "Oh, she's a stubborn one. She argued with me for months when I told her what I planned for her to do. Then there was one time—she was so mad that she refused to talk to me, just like you did. The difference between her and you was all I had to do with her is hold her for a while. She responds to love, true open-hearted love."

It took Ben a few minutes to figure out which tigress the Lord was talking about. He saw the Lord smile at him. "I've created her to be strong, a warrior with different weapons. Now…we need to talk about you and your work I have for you to do."

Diana felt the Lord's presence near them. Scott came into the room, "I brought you some chocolate milk. They didn't have any chamomile tea downstairs."

"That's great...thank you," Diana said as she moved toward Scott. She took the cartons of milk he brought and shook one of them up and started to drink them.

"Becca and Ben's parents are on their way in," Scott flatly stated.

"I doubt Becca will let me stay here," Diana sighed.

"His parents may. You'll have until they leave before she can demand anything," Scott added.

"I hope so. However, if I don't, I'll go down to the waiting room. You can let me know if there are any changes," Diana replied.

"You don't want to be with your family?" Scott queried.

"You know me better than that, but I have family that needs me more here. You, my brother, and him," Diana said as she nodded toward Ben.

"You've finally accepted it huh?" Scott beamed.

"Accepted what?" Diana smiled and winked at him. She moved back to Ben and held his hand, weaving her fingers through his.

A few hours later, Ben's parents and sister came into the room. "Diana, what are you doing here?" Becca fumed.

"I wanted to make sure Ben will be okay," Diana replied.

"Mark...Sarah, this is Ms. Diana Henderson. Diana, this is Mark and Sarah, Ben's parents," Scott introduced.

"It's a pleasure to meet you," Sarah stated. "You're all we heard about from Kora and Brock."

"Oh...I hope it was good stuff." Diana smiled.

"Mostly stuff about wrestling with their dad and Uncle Scott, and something about your wrists and being tied up," Mark replied. He looked over at her wrists. "It looks like Kora wasn't too far off."

Diana looked down at her wrists and held the one up. "Yeah...well, they're getting better."

"You know Diana, since we're here, you can go ahead and get back with your family," Becca chimed in.

"I will, after Ben wakes up and is okay." Diana smiled. She knew Becca was wanting her out. She let go of Ben's hand and leaned down toward his ear. "Tiger, I'm gonna move back so your family can talk with you." Diana moved back to the far end of the room and signaled for Ben's parents to come and be with him.

Scott moved over to Diana. "You handled that well."

"Thank you...it's going to be a problem with Becca shortly. She's just biding her time," Diana whispered.

"We'll cross that bridge when we get to it," Scott assured her. Diana stayed back and let Mark, Sarah, and Becca each have their time with

Ben. Then Mark and Sarah started to include Diana in their conversation. They went back and forth for the next few hours.

Sarah then put her hand on Mark's thigh. "We need to get you something to eat. Would you like to join us, Diana?"

"No, not right now; I'm not hungry. Thank you anyway," Diana thoughtfully said. She heard Scott shuffling beside her. She glanced over and saw him scowling at her.

"You know how much trouble you will be in if you don't eat?" Scott scolded.

"I'll eat; just not right now," Diana quipped.

"Diana, I'll stay here. You go with Mom and Dad and get something to eat," Becca injected.

"Becca…if she's not hungry, she not hungry. Don't force her to do something," Mark corrected her.

"Actually, in this case sir, Becca is right. Diana has a habit of skipping meals. She will be in a heap of trouble when Ben finds out she did not eat," Scott stated, looking at Diana directly. Diana glared at Scott. "You know I will tell him. Now, are you gonna go with Mark and Sarah by your own free will, or do I have to carry you down?" Scott warned.

Diana shook her head. "It'll have to be in the cafeteria here. I don't have any shoes." Mark and Sarah nodded. Diana moved over to Ben and whispered in his ear. "I'll be back in a little bit, Tiger. My brother is being demanding." She put her hand on his shoulder. Mark, Sarah, and Diana walked out the door to get supper, leaving Scott and Becca with Ben.

As soon as Becca knew her parents were out of earshot she looked over at Scott. "Why did you tell the nurse she was his fiancée?"

"How do you know she's not?" Scott jeered.

"Don't try to fence words with me. He hasn't known her long enough to decide that," Becca steamed.

"Oh…he knows her quite well." Scott smiled. Becca's head jerked up and she glared at Scott. There was no missing what she was thinking. Scott laughed. "There's more to knowing a person than that, girl. You of all people should know he wouldn't do that yet."

"I'm going to get some coffee. I'll be back in a minute," Becca fumed.

Scott watched her walk out then looked over at Ben. "Bro, you'd better come back soon. Diana is compliant for the moment, but Becca is going to push her till she bites."

Becca came back in a few minutes later. Scott and Becca sat quietly for the rest of the time.

Ben's parents, with Diana, came back to the room an hour later. Mark and Sarah headed over to Ben's side. Diana held back by the window. "Well Milady, did you behave and eat something?" Scott teased.

"She did eat, but not much. A bowl of soup and a half sandwich," Mark quipped.

"She did drink three cartons of chocolate milk though," Sarah added.

"Well, at least it was something," Scott jabbed. "Ben, when you get back here, you're gonna have to start force-feeding her."

"Honestly Scott, she's not going to be living with him," Becca sneered. Scott didn't argue, and Diana didn't take the bait.

Mark looked over at Sarah. "Well dear, we'd best be getting home. Becca, are you ready to drive us home?"

"I was thinking of staying here tonight. Did you need me to drive?" Becca questioned.

"Well...it is late, and you know how your father is with night driving. Do you mind terribly?" Sarah inquired.

"No...that's okay. I'll come back up here tomorrow. That way, Diana can go home to her own family," Becca simply stated. Whether or not Ben's parents caught the barb or not was irrelevant to Diana; she caught it. In truth, Diana did need to give her parents a call. She'd do that in a little bit, once things quieted down again. Diana stayed back and watched Mark, Sarah, and Becca tell Ben good-bye.

As Sarah passed by, she acknowledged Scott and Diana giving each a hug. Mark came up to Diana and said, "Someday you're going to have to explain the nickname *kitten* to me. Scott's nickname seems to be more appropriate."

Diana just smiled. "Milady is what most of my friends call me. I'm sure once Ben wakes up and is back to his normal ornery self, he'll fill you in on the other."

Just as Ben's family left, Allen, Charles, Taggee, and the girls came up. Zenon had the agent that was guarding Aisha bring her over to meet up with Malaha, Taggee, and Allen. The nurse frowned at so many people visiting. Seeing how Diana was her patient's fiancée, she let her determine when it was time to cut back.

Allen came up by Scott. "So how did we fare?"

"He has a concussion and has not revived yet. There are no cracks or breaks, nor is there a hematoma," Scott replied. "He does have a possible cracked rib and several bruises."

"How about you, Diana, what did the doctor say?" Allen inquired.

"I had one shoulder dislocated, some glass in my feet, and I have a little damage to my wrists," Diana stated. She saw Scott's face and held

The Virgin Mother

up her hand. "It's a small tear. I didn't need stitches. They only put a new batch of antibiotic on it and rewrapped it. The left side has a ring around the wrist but it's in a higher place. It'll be healed up in a week."

"If you aren't careful…you won't have to wait for Ben to wake up to get spanked. I'll do it myself," Scott warned.

Allen chuckled. "I take it she hadn't mentioned her wrists to you, eh, Scott?"

"Nope…she's withholding information again," Scott sneered.

"The tigress is tired. Aren't you going to take her home for her to get some sleep?" Taggee asked Scott.

Scott shook his head. "I'd have to have Ben to get her pulled away from here right now. I don't think even you would be able to do it tonight."

Diana looked at Scott. "What's up?"

"Taggee thought that I should take you home to get some sleep. I told him it would take an act of God to get you away from here," Scott jeered.

"You're right there, but I'll get some sleep in a little bit." Diana smiled.

"Do you want one of us to stay with you?" Mahala asked.

Diana came over and gave her a hug. "No, that's okay. How are you doing?"

"I'm okay. I think I've cried myself dry now," Mahala slowly stated.

"Where do they have you staying now?" Diana wondered.

Scott was the one that replied. "I have them at Ben's house for now. We'll figure something else out once everybody is healed and awake."

Diana nodded to Scott. "Well troop…we need to go before the nurse starts calling security," Charles stated.

Diana looked at Director Zenon. "I'm so sorry about your house."

"It wasn't your fault. Don't worry about it," Charles replied.

"It was my fault. If I wasn't there, your house would not have been demolished," Diana countered.

"And if you were not staying there, where would you have gone?" Charles corrected.

Diana sat quietly. "No, Ms. Henderson, it wasn't your fault. Don't carry more than you should," Charles scolded. He motioned for the group to started heading out.

"We'll check back on you guys tomorrow," Allen added. The group all turned and filed out of the room. Taggee came over and patted Diana on the head. Diana stood up and gave him a hug. He hugged her back then turned and left the room.

The nurse walked back in after the group left. "Are you going to be staying the night, ma'am?"

"Yeah…both of us are going to be here tonight," Scott jumped in to answer.

"I'll bring in some pillows and blankets then," she replied and headed back out.

Scott came over and started caressing Diana's back. "Are you sure you don't want to go home and be with your family?"

Diana leaned into him and put her head up against his side. "No…I'll call them here in a minute. I want to be here, with Ben," she softly said.

"Do you think he's not going to make it?" Scott worried.

"Nawt at awl", she smiled and winked at Scott. "He's just having a one-on-one with the Lord right now. He'll be back shortly."

Scott chuckled. "You do pick up accents easily. It would be interesting to take you over to Scotland and see what you come back with."

"As long as I don't have anybody trying to kill, maim, or otherwise defile me. Oh…and it's at least six months down the road. I'd be up to it," Diana laughed.

"Why six months, Milady?" Scott wondered.

"It'll take me six months of hibernation to be a reasonable travel companion during the trip," she jeered. Scott laughed. The nurse came in carrying pillows and blankets.

Scott came over and took the load from the nurse. "Allow me, ma'am." Diana noticed that the nurse was being charmed by Scott. She quietly chuckled.

Scott looked over and raised an eyebrow. "And what are you laughing at?"

"Southern charmer all the way aren't ya bro," Diana teased.

"It didn't work much on you now, did it?" Scott jabbed back.

"Oh…well, I'm an oddball, remember?" Diana ridiculed.

"Ya got animor wer ya frum?" Scott asked with a strong Southern back hills drawl. He saw a flash fly through her eyes as she gleamed and raised her eyebrow.

"I know at least one, but I'm not the type to go setting up blind dates. We'll have to see what the Lord does," Diana teased.

"Thank the Lord for that fact," Scott said as he turned to put the bedding down on the couch. "I hate people trying to set me up with one girl or another."

Diana walked over and sat on the chair by Ben. She reached up and grabbed the phone and dialed her parents' house. Scott arranged the bedding and set up the couch for himself. He was going to catch a few hours of sleep. Then he was going to try to get Diana to sleep.

Mercy Medical Center

Scott and Diana had a restless night. Diana, being in the hospital more times than she liked, knew it wasn't going to be a night to get any sleep. The nurses came in and checked on Ben every two hours. Several times the alarms went off for the saline solution or the nutrient bag to be changed out. Eventually, however, they both went out. Scott was the first to wake up to the daylight. He saw that Diana had fallen asleep in the chair hunched over with her head on the side of the bed. He got up, stretched, and then walked over to Diana.

"Milady? Diana, come on. Go lie down for a while. I'm up now," Scott said as he rubbed Diana's back. Then he stood her up when she wasn't responding.

Diana was still basically asleep. Scott simply guided her over to the couch and sat her down in the middle of it. He guided her shoulders back toward the pillow and then lifted her legs up onto the couch. He covered her with the blanket and brushed the back of his hand across her cheek. "I'll be back in a little bit, kitten," he warmly said as he went to use the bathroom. When he came out, Diana was curled into a ball. He walked out to get a cup of coffee. Then came in and sat in the chair.

It was only a short time after that that Allen knocked on the door and walked in. He saw that Diana was asleep then glanced over and saw Scott awake in the chair. "You finally got her to go to sleep, huh?" Allen softly chuckled.

"Yeah, but I doubt it will be for long," Scott quipped.

"He still hasn't woken up?" Allen asked as he nodded toward Ben.

"Nope…I hope he does before Becca comes back up here," Scott simply stated.

"These two aren't getting along?" Allen queried. "That's unusual, they have a lot in common."

"Yeah…both Ben and I have stated the same thing. It isn't on Diana…she's trying to keep out of the fight, but Becca is really pushing it," Scott informed him.

"A little bit of jealousy is what it seems to me," Allen deduced. Scott just nodded. An alarm went off on one of Ben's IV's. Scott grimaced and Allen looked over at Diana. Sure enough, she woke up. Diana opened her eyes and realized she was lying on the couch. Then she saw that Allen was there and it was morning. She sat up.

"Good morning, Diana." Allen smiled.

"Good morning sir." She blinked. She looked over at Scott. "I take it I was totally out. I don't remember moving over here."

"Yeah, the lights were on, but nobody was home," Scott jabbed. Diana shook her head and got up. She folded the blanket and stacked everything in a neat pile.

Then she headed toward the bathroom. "Excuse me, gentlemen. I'll be back in a few minutes."

Allen moved over to the couch and sat down. "So, do we know where these two stand?" he pondered.

Scott shot an eyebrow up. "Are you asking as a father or a boss?"

"Maybe a little of both…so?" Allen pushed. The two guys sat talking.

Diana later came back in. She had used the guest bathroom to get cleaned up. She had taken the sling off and didn't bother to put it back on. On her way back, she picked up a hot tea and glazed donut.

"I can't believe it, she actually chose to eat on her own," Scott jabbed as she entered the room.

"Whatever Scott…I need the energy," Diana sneered.

"Well, since she's back and has something to eat. Do you want to come down and grab a bite with me sir?" Scott asked Allen.

"I've already eaten, but I'd like another cup of coffee," Allen injected. The guys walked out and headed to the cafeteria.

Diana moved back over to the chair. "Good morning Ben," Diana stated as she leaned down and gave him a kiss on the forehead. She held his hand; "How's the talking going? Are you about done? I hope you're not arguing with the Lord. You know he always wins those." Diana sat quiet for a moment then she started humming the song "Behold the Lamb." Before she was through the chorus, she was singing the song.

Ben and the Lord had been discussing things until Ben was at peace. Ben sat there and quietly watched the fire. The tigress had moved back over to lie down by the Lord. As Ben watched the fire, he heard singing floating through the air. It was a female's voice. She sang with no music—acapella. Ben looked up at the Lord.

"Do you not recognize the voice?" the Lord teased.

Ben sat and listened longer. The voice became louder; he recognized the song. It was one that was used a lot in youth groups. As the woman's voice got loud enough, it dawned on him. He was hearing Diana; she was singing. He had forgotten that she could sing. "Is she okay?"

The Lord nodded. "Are you ready to head back?" Ben sadly nodded. "I trust I don't have to take such drastic measures for us to talk again," the Lord scolded.

"No sir…I guarantee it," Ben assured.

The Lord stood up and motioned for Ben to walk with him. The tigress jumped up and started walking beside Ben as they walked slowly down the path. "By the way, I want you to tell her something for me," the Lord stated.

"Of course, sir, but is she not listening to you?" Ben wondered.

The Lord chuckled. "She's had a lot running through her mind lately, some of it caused by you. I've answered her several times, but it gets lost in the storm."

"I'm sorry I tried to take some of the load off her," Ben sheepishly replied.

"In some ways…I know you've tried to help. However, in others, you added to it. Do I need mention the issue with you insisting that she tell the whole story when it only meant that you had to knock your own pride down to let it ride?" the Lord sternly looked at him. Ben wanted to crawl under a rock. The Lord put his hand on his shoulder. "No, I'm not mad. I'm just pointing out that as much as you were trying to help her with one area, you were adding to the other."

"What was it you wanted me to tell her?" Ben asked, still ashamed that he didn't recognize what he was doing to Diana.

"Just a simple word. Tell her I said…yes," the Lord ended.

Diana looked at the clock. She had a sinking feeling in her stomach; Becca would be coming soon. She turned back toward Ben. "Hey, Tiger, I'm just giving you a heads-up. Becca will be coming soon. I know she will demand I go home, and I don't want to fight. I'll have to leave when she demands it. I'll try to get back here as soon as I can, but that won't be easy with her. I just wanted to give you a heads-up. I'll let you know when I actually leave."

Scott and Allen walked back into the room. "Apparently, you were singing…Milady?" Scott asked smiling at Diana.

Diana cocked her head to the side and looked at them. "Yeah, I probably was. Why?"

The guys just chuckled. "I think I was stopped by two nurses and three patients telling me that I needed to get you into the recording studio," Scott informed her.

"Apparently, you have a beautiful voice Diana," Allen added.

Diana blushed. "Thank you. I've always got a song going in my head. When I'm by myself, I often let it out. I didn't figure Ben would quibble too much. If it was bad enough, he might even wake up and tease me." Scott knew it was starting to bother her that Ben wasn't coming around yet. He just walked over and caressed her back. They all looked toward the door when they heard Becca's voice talking to the nurse. Diana dreaded it but knew it was coming. Scott could feel Diana's muscles tense, and he heard her take in a deep breath and let it out slowly.

Becca came around the corner. "Good morning," she beamed.

"Good morning Becca. Did you get your parents home okay last night?" Scott asked.

"Yes, I did. So now that I'm here, why don't we let Diana get home to her family," Becca instantly requested.

"Seriously girl, are you gonna start out that way immediately?" Scott quipped.

Diana put her hand on his arm; he looked into a set of cool, calm blue eyes. "It's okay Scott. I knew she would demand it. I don't want a fight," Diana calmly stated. Allen watched Diana calm down Scott—something that proved to be a challenge for most. Diana stood up and leaned down toward Ben. She put her right hand down by Ben's hand on the bed and her left arm up near his head. "Ben, I have to go now. Becca wants her time with you. I'll try to get back here as soon as I can," she told him. She stroked Ben's hair a couple of times and kissed his forehead. As she started to pull away from him, she froze. Ben had reached his hand out and grabbed Diana by her right wrist. She didn't pull or fight him, but it did twinge a little. He pulled her wrist up to his chest, and held it there. Allen walked out to get the nurse and have her come in. Scott just watched. Becca walked over to the other side of Ben. She reached down and went to take Ben's hand off Diana's wrist, but he wouldn't let it go. When the nurse came in, she made Becca move back. The nurse saw that Diana's wrist was bandaged; she carefully lifted Ben and Diana's hands. She tried to free Diana's wrist, but the more she tried, the tighter Ben held.

Scott saw that they were hurting Diana. "Stop…you're hurting her. Just let him hold her arm."

"Honestly Scott, just pull her wrist free," Becca quipped.

"I don't think so Becca. It will rip that wrist open. That is not going to make your brother happy," Allen calmly stated.

Diana leaned down and started talking in Ben's ear. She didn't whisper this time; she wanted to make sure everyone, especially Becca, knew what she was saying. "It's all right Tiger, I'm here. Ben, listen to me. I need to you wake up. If you want me to stay here, you will have to wake up and tell them that." Diana felt Ben's thumb start to move back and forth across her hand. She pulled back and looked down. She put her left hand on his face, her thumb moving across his cheek. "Ben, babe, you have to wake up now," she restated. She saw that his eyes started to move back and forth.

Ben heard Diana tell him that she had to go. He could hear in her voice that she really didn't want to. He felt her hand near his, so he grabbed it; he wanted her to stay with him. He felt like someone was pulling her away from him and that he had to hold on to her. The more they pulled her away, the tighter he held her. Then he heard her telling him that she was there. She kept repeating that he needed to wake up. He tried to open his eyes, but they weren't responding. "Babe, wake up now," he heard. He opened his eyes for a second. The pain that shot through his head was incredible.

Diana saw him struggling to open his eyes. She saw him grimace with the pain when he managed to open them for a second. "I know it hurts...try again babe," she encouraged. Ben finally managed to open his eyes. Everything was blurry at first, but it slowly came into focus. He looked over to his left, where he felt someone touching him. He saw a nurse, taking his pulse. He glanced over to his right; there was his tigress.

Diana saw him start to register things around him. "There you are, Tiger. Glad to see you back."

He looked down toward his feet. He saw Scott and Allen standing there. "Hey bro, did you enjoy your vacation?" Scott teased. Ben nodded.

"Ben, I'm assuming that you want Diana to stay here, am I correct?" Allen flatly asked. Ben nodded again. "Okay, I promise that I'll make sure she stays. You can let go of her wrist now." Ben lifted her arm up and saw that he had a hold of her right wrist. He brought it up to his mouth and kissed her palm then let go of her wrist.

"It's okay, I'll charge you for it later," Diana teased.

Ben smiled and said in a very raspy hoarse voice, "Promises...promises." He looked back to the left. He saw Becca standing by the wall; she was crying.

Diana followed his line of vision. "Becca, come on over here. Don't make him strain to see you."

"He doesn't want me there, he has you," she steamed. Ben held up his hand and signaled for Becca to come to him. Becca slowly came over.

He cupped her face with his hand and brushed her tears away with his thumb. "Do you think I'm so shallow?" Becca just shook her head no. "Then don't be so shallow yourself," Ben quipped.

Diana had moved back and caught the nurse while Ben was talking to Becca. "Can he have some water?"

"I'll bring a glass in. The doctor will be in this morning to check on him," the nurse stated.

Ben started to look around for Diana. Scott called over his shoulder. "Milady, you're going to get into trouble if you don't get in his eyesight."

"I'm just arranging for a glass of water to be brought in," Diana replied. She came back in and around Scott. Ben pointed to Diana and then, using the same finger, signaled that he wanted her to come to him. He saw the flicker that flew through her emerald eyes and an impish grin on her face. He grinned from ear to ear.

Allen and Scott looked over at Diana. "What in the world did you do?" Allen asked.

Diana looked down to the floor to regain composure then looked up at Allen. "I didn't do anything sir," she stated.

Scott laughed. "They're having one of their inaudible conversations again I'd bet."

Diana looked up at Scott. "I didn't say a thing."

"Don't try to get by me today sis. You're too tired to fight it. I can read you quite well," Scott informed her.

Diana couldn't deny it. Scott had learned to read her—at least partly. She heard Ben clear his throat, and she looked up. She saw him signal for her to come to him; she walked on over to his side.

The nurse came in with a glass of water. "Would you like a sip, Mr. Tigere?" He nodded. The nurse put the straw down for him to take a drink. The first swallow made him wince; the second swallow went down easier. "That should help your throat now," the nurse informed him. "Did you want to sit up a little?" Ben nodded. The nurse raise the bed's head and adjusted the foot of the bed to make Ben more comfortable.

"Thank you, ma'am," Ben replied.

"Nice to hear some voice and less air Tiger," Diana teased.

Ben grabbed Diana's hand and pulled her over to the edge of the bed. "Take a seat, kitten," he commanded.

"I'm not sure that's allowed Ben," Diana said.

Ben just simply pulled her down. He put his arm around her waist and pulled her to him. Diana gave in and just lay down beside him. Ben held her close and said, "Thank you." Diana totally relaxed next to him.

"Well…I can see you're in good hands Ben. I'll check back in before I head back to New York." Allen grinned, slapped Scott the back, and winked at Diana. He put a hand on Becca's shoulder as he walked past her. "You'd really like her if you give her a chance," he whispered. Becca acknowledged his statement. Allen then walked out of the room.

Scott looked back at Becca. "Do you want a coffee girl?" Becca nodded. "Do you want to walk for it, or would you prefer I bring it up for you?"

"I'll go down with you for one; whenever you're ready," Becca quietly stated.

"Let's go then. I need some caffeine," Scott jeered.

They left Diana and Ben alone in the room. Diana tilted her head up to see Ben's face. "How's your head?"

"Wishing it would fall off right now," Ben quipped.

"I'm sorry," Diana replied.

Ben pushed her up so that he could look directly into her eyes. "There is nothing to be sorry for," he emphasized. He saw that she was not accepting his statement. "Diana Nicole Henderson, you are not to take the blame for this. You did not choose this. You did what you could to stop it, understood?"

Diana looked at Ben. "Yes, sir."

Ben pulled her back down to him. "Scott is right, you are too tired."

"I'll be fine. How was your talk with the Lord?" she smiled.

"I'll tell you later. I want to be able to carry on a full discussion," Ben stated. He started to caress her arm.

"You're going to put me asleep," Diana jabbed.

"Good…you need it," Ben jeered.

"What if your parents come in, or anybody else, then what?" Diana softly asked.

Ben could tell she was already going out; he kept caressing her arm. "We'll deal with it when it happens," he softly replied. Diana fell asleep.

Scott knew that Ben was going to put Diana to sleep. He and Becca walked back into the room ten minutes later. He just smiled at Ben. "You have her purring I see."

Ben looked up at Scott. "It didn't take much. She is very tired."

"I told her to go home last night. I was making her go home this morning until you said otherwise," Becca sneered.

"Becca, she wasn't going to leave. She wouldn't have slept at her house any more than she slept here," Ben countered. "Scott, do you want to lay her down on the couch?"

Scott walked over and adjusted the pillows and pulled a blanket out to cover the couch. Then he walked to the bed. He reached under her back and thighs and lifted her up. Diana opened her eyes slightly. "It's okay, kitten, it's just me," Scott assured her. Diana smiled and let him carry her over to the couch. She lay down and went back out.

"We really have to work on getting some weight back on her," Scott griped.

"So, now that she's getting some much-needed sleep, fill me in," Ben queried.

"Where would you like me to start?" Scott smiled.

"How about with Mahdi," Ben flatly stated

"He's dead. Allen took him out when he tried to leave with Diana. The rest of his men are either deceased or in prison," Scott informed him.

"What about the kitten, how bad did she get hurt? I saw a bruise on her cheek, what else?" Ben pressed.

"Only one shoulder was dislocated. She's supposed to be wearing a sling, but you know her. She had glass pulled out of her feet and she re-tore the one wrist. I didn't see it, so I don't know how bad. She says it's only a small rip and she didn't need stitches," Scott listed off.

"I'm going to the bathroom. I'll be back in a little bit," Becca quipped and walked out the door.

Scott slowly turned to Ben. "What else Scott?" Ben demanded.

"For Diana and me to be in here, I told the nurse that she was your fiancée. The nurse told Becca, and I'm not sure if your parents were told or not," Scott awkwardly replied.

Ben laughed. "I can't believe Diana let you say that."

"I'm glad you're not upset," Scott said relieved. "She didn't argue with it, but she didn't confirm it either." For the next few minutes, Ben asked questions and Scott filled him in. Scott kept watching the IV monitors.

Ben noticed it and finally asked, "Why do you keep watching them?"

Scott looked over at Diana; she was still out cold. "If those stupid alarms go off, she'll wake up."

"Well…go catch the nurse. Since I'm awake, I should be able to have this stuff unhooked. That will turn off the alarms," Ben insisted. Scott walked out and went to talk to the nurse.

Becca came back in. Ben waved for her to sit down in the chair next to him. "Where did Scott go?" she wondered.

"I have him chasing down a nurse. I want some of these tubes off me," Ben quipped. "Did you give mom and dad a call?" Becca nodded her head. Becca sat watching Diana for a few minutes. "What's eating ya girl?" Ben finally asked.

"Did you really ask her to marry you?" Becca carefully asked.

"Is that going to be a problem sis?" he posed, taking a drink of his water.

"Don't you think it's too soon?" Becca jabbed.

"Nope...what does Mom and Dad think?" Ben inquired, studying his baby sister.

"They don't know yet," Becca sadly said, looking down to her shoes.

"Good...I'll let them know later." Ben smiled.

"So it is true. Did you already set a date?" Becca pouted.

"Not yet." Ben grinned and put his hand on Becca's head.

Scott came back in the room. "The nurse will be in shortly, it took a little finessing."

"I just bet it did. You got her eating out of your hand already, huh?" Ben grinned.

The nurse walked into the room. "I heard you wanted some of these unhooked from ya. I can take the saline off now since you're drinking. The doctor will be in around eleven a.m. He has to okay the others."

"How long before the next alarm goes off?" Ben wondered.

"About fifteen or twenty more minutes. Why?" the nurse retorted. Ben nodded over toward Diana. "Maybe she should go home for a while," the nurse sneered.

"Not yet, ma'am," Ben glared.

The nurse recoiled. "Sorry sir...not my place."

"That is correct, it's not your place," Ben repeated. The nurse went over and unhooked the saline IV; then she nodded. As she walked past Scott, she grimaced then walked out of the room.

Ben looked over at Scott. "Hey, I didn't tell her to voice her opinion. I just asked her to come and unhook the IVs," Scott countered.

The guys turned their eyes over to Becca. She wouldn't look at either one of them. "Seriously Becca, if you don't knock it off, I'll be the one setting the rules down," Ben warned. Diana could feel the aggression in the air; words were being heard but not registering. She was thinking she needed to wake up, but she really didn't want too. Ben noticed Diana starting to stir; she was feeling the tension in the room. He really wanted her to sleep longer, so he picked up the TV remote and started flipping through channels. He found the music stations and picked out contemporary Christian music. He had the volume down so that people could talk over it, but it would settle the atmosphere. Scott shot an eyebrow up. Ben just shook his head and glanced back over at Diana. She had stopped stirring. *Sleep, babe...we'll deal with the world later,* he thought.

The doctor came in at 10:50 a.m. "Good morning, Mr. Tigere. It's good to see you're awake now," the doctor started.

"Well, as far as I know, everything is working. I'm kind of tied to the bed as it were. I'd like to see if I can function without all the tubes and bags," Ben jested.

The doctor came and checked his eyes, his head, and his reflexes. "Well, all those are working. How about liquids, are you able to keep those down so far?"

"Yes sir. I'd like to get a hold of something with substance, if I may," Ben informed him.

The doctor looked over the chart, wrote something on it, then turned to walk to the back of the room. He saw Diana on the couch. "It looks like Ms. Henderson has had a rough time as well. What did she do to her wrists?"

"How do you know Diana?" Scott asked.

"I'm her physician. So what happened?" the doctor asked.

"It's a long story, sir. You should have had the paperwork already. I'll make sure they send it to you when I get out of here. Any idea as to when that will be, by the way?" Ben commented.

The doctor studied Ben then went back to focusing on his orders. "I'll have the nurse pull the catheter and the rest of the IV's. We'll leave the needle in till we're sure your system is going right. If everything is going well, you will be out by tonight," the doctor replied. He walked on out of the room.

The nurse walked in a minute later. "Mr. McCleary...Ms. Tigere, would you step out for a few minutes?" Scott and Becca walked out of the room.

Ben saw the nurse head for Diana. "No...don't wake her, just pull the curtain."

The nurse nodded and went over and pulled the curtain around. She unhooked the IV's and pulled the catheter. "Do you want to take a shower Mr. Tigere?"

"That would be wonderful." Ben smiled. She pulled a shower cap out of the drawer in the bathroom then she grabbed a Tegaderm bandage to put over the IV lead. She laid out a clean gown for him to put on and a robe to cover his backside. She got Ben set and guided him to the bathroom. He was a little unstable but, for the most part, controlled his walk. "Do you need me to help with the rest?"

"No, thank you. I think I can deal with the rest," Ben replied. She put the shower chair in the shower for Ben to use and told him to pull the cord if he needed help for anything. She walked out and shut the door then walked out into the hall. She told Becca and Scott that Ben was in the shower and that they could go back in if they wanted to.

"Do you want to check out what they have available for lunch down in the cafeteria?" Becca asked Scott.

"Sure...let's go," Scott replied, and they went on down.

Ben loved every bit of the shower. He really wished he could wash his hair but knew that wasn't going to be for a few days yet. He didn't need to use the shower chair, so he just pushed it to the side. He finished up, dried off, and put the gown and robe on. He noticed the bruises covering his sides and back from the fighting. He was amazed that he got out without a fat lip or black eye. He really wanted to shave but didn't have anything to do it with, so he walked back out to the room. He went to the far side of the bed and pulled the curtain back. Diana was still sleeping; he just grabbed a blanket and put it over her. Then went back to the bed and lay back on it. Becca and Scott came back about five minutes later.

"Feel a little better Ben?" Becca asked.

"A ton better. Where did you two run off to?" Ben asked.

"We went to check out the lunch menu of course. Oh, by the way, a milestone moment. Diana grabbed a donut for breakfast this morning without any of us forcing it down her." Scott grinned.

Ben smiled. "That's always a good sign. So what's for lunch?" While Scott and Becca were talking with Ben, Diana woke up. She just lay there for a while watching them talk. She must have been dreaming that they were fighting earlier. She just rolled her eyes at her own stupidity. "Good morning, kitten." Ben smiled.

"Is it still morning? I think I slept the day away." Diana grinned.

"Aw... wal...ya neid tu ge ur res, lassie," Scott teased in his Scottish brogue.

"Hey...you got unhooked. Did I miss the doctor?" Diana realized.

"Yeah...he was in a little bit ago. He said that barring any complications, Ben will be able to go home tonight," Becca chimed in.

"That's great. Thank you, Lord." Diana grinned as she sat up from the couch. She winced a little as she tried to unknot her back.

"You okay?" Ben quizzed.

"Yeah, just sore muscles. The doctor said it was going to take a few days for them to get back to normal. I'm sure you hurt more than I do. How many bruises did you come out with?" Diana retorted.

"Oh…I've got a few nicely colored ones," Ben confirmed.

Diana got up and folded the blankets and put them on the pile along with the pillow. As she was walking out of the room, she stated, "I'll be right back." A few minutes later, Diana came back in and sat down on the couch. The whole group chitchatted back and forth till the nurse came in to find out what Ben wanted for lunch. Diana was glad that she could relax a little around Becca. *Thank you again, Lord*, she praised silently. Scott, Becca, and Diana decided to go down and grab lunch and bring it up to eat with Ben. Scott and Becca headed out; Diana was just walking past Ben's bed.

"Kitten, come here a second," he asked. Diana came over and sat down beside Ben. "The Lord told me I was causing you more stress by the way I was handling you at Zenon's house. I am sorry," Ben stated.

Diana put her hand on the side of his face, leaned in, and kissed him. "There's nothing to be sorry for. I am interested in what else the Lord and you talked about," she softly queried.

"Go get some lunch, then we'll make some plans." Ben smiled. By the time Scott and the girls came back into Ben's room, his lunch was being brought in. Ben looked to see what Diana got; he was pleased with her meal. She had grabbed a turkey and cheese panini and a side of fries. He also noted that she had two cartons of chocolate milk and a glass of sweet tea. Charles, Taggee, Aisha, and Mahala came up to check on Ben shortly after lunch.

"Good afternoon sir," Ben greeted when he saw Zenon come in.

"Good afternoon. It's good to see you conscious and alert. How's the head?" Charles inquired.

"It hurts, but I'll live. Sorry about your house, sir," Ben apologized.

"As I told Ms. Henderson last night, it's nothing to worry about. I knew the risk. I have insurance, and the department is going to kick in some to rebuild it," Charles quipped.

Ben looked over at Diana; he could tell she was still upset about the destruction of the house. "Maybe, once we all get healed up, we can come over and help clean up the mess."

"Maybe…now that this is done with. But you'll have to stay out of the doctor's office for at least a week to prove to me that you're capable of doing something without hurting yourself," Charles stated.

"That almost sounded like a joke, sir. Do I hear a tone of humor there?" Ben jeered.

"How many stakeouts are you willing to work when you come back, Agent Tigere?" Charles warned.

Ben looked over at Diana, who was biting her cheeks to not laugh. "None anytime soon, sir," he shot back.

"If I were you, I'd watch what I'd say then," Charles quipped. He turned to see Diana near to laughing; he winked at her. She nodded to him with a broad smile on her face.

"Now, how are we going to arrange for living quarters for Taggee and the girls?" Charles put out to the room.

"I may be able to help out with the girls," Diana replied. "I need to make a call first. My parents have a guest bedroom with a queen bed."

"Now that this is over, I think I need to go home and touch base with my family," Taggee replied after Mahala interpreted what was said.

"Are you sure you don't want to stay a while here?" Ben asked.

"Thank you…I will be back to visit, but I feel the Lord calling me to a different place," Taggee insisted.

Diana saw the change in the guys' faces. She looked at Ben, cocking her head to the side. "Taggee is going back to his homeland. He feels God is calling him to another place," Ben interpreted for her.

Diana looked over at Taggee, studying him. *I have another work for them. Let them go*, she heard the Lord tell her.

Taggee saw her questioning then accepting what he said. She nodded at him, but he could see the pain in her eyes. "Tell her it is not good-bye. I am sure we will see each other again," Taggee stated, looking back at Ben. "It goes for you as well. For you two are entwined." Ben nodded.

"Taggee says to tell you that this is not good bye. He feels that we will be seeing him at another time," Ben translated for Diana.

Aisha spoke up. "Mahala and I are also going with Taggee. We will help him set up a mission in his home."

"I already know the girls are going with him," Diana quietly stated before Ben could tell her.

"He told you, didn't He?" Ben inquired. Diana nodded. "Come here, kitten." Diana got up and went over to Ben, who slid over and made room for her on the bed. She crawled in. He wrapped his arm around her back and pulled her close. He whispered in her ear, "Don't fight the Lord on this."

She softly replied, "I wouldn't dream of fighting it. It doesn't stop the heartache though." Ben kissed her temple.

Charles looked at Scott. "Does she speak Farsi?" Scott shook his head. "Then who is the *he* Ben is talking about?"

Scott beamed a smile. "The *he* is the Lord. He talks to her, often. He's helped us all through these last few months more times than I can count. Often telling her ahead of time of dangers. Unfortunately, He doesn't give us much of a heads-up. We could have been elsewhere when Mahdi came to your house if He would have."

Charles shook his head. "They are a strange couple. Allen wants me to offer her a job. I just don't think she's got what it takes to be an agent."

"She's really great at organizing things and getting information out of people. You can always put her in as an advisor," Scott suggested. "Least till she can be trained to defend herself. I highly doubt that she will ever be one to take a life. Then again, if they're breathing, they can talk."

"What about you, Scott, feel like a job change? We can always use a good man," Charles probed.

"I don't think Agent Richman would agree with that," Scott quipped.

"Oh well, seeing how he has put in to transfer to San Francisco, I don't think that would be a problem." Charles smiled.

"We're a team sir. If I agree, we work together—Ben, Diana, and I," Scott warned.

"I'll agree to that only if you keep Diana out of the gunfire. My old ticker doesn't need the extra stress on it," he added.

"Agreed," Scott nodded.

"Well, troop, if we are going to get you three on the plane, we need to get going," Charles piped up. "By the way, Agent Tigere, I don't want to see your face in the office for a week. Get rested and healed up."

"Thank you, sir." Ben grinned.

Diana jumped up and quickly moved to Taggee. "You call me any time you need help. I'll see what I can do. Even if it means I have to fly over there to build a house." She looked over to Mahala to tell Taggee what she said.

Taggee listened to Mahala then leaned down and gently gave Ariana a hug. "I will keep in contact with you and the guys." Ben was the one who told Diana what he said. Diana went and hugged each of the girls. She told Mahala to be strong and grow in the Lord.

Charles and the rest walked out of the room. Diana crawled back up next to Ben. She needed to be held for a while. She felt the tears building, and she let them go.

Becca sat quietly and watched the whole event unfolding. It was then that she saw how soft Diana's heart was and why Ben fell for her. She wasn't the devious, conniving woman she thought she was.

Somewhere around 5:00 p.m., the doctor came back in. Diana recognized him immediately. "Good evening, sir."

"Hello, Ms. Henderson. I see you've gotten your rest, what happened to your wrists?" the doctor inquired.

"Well, it started out with rope burns that led to one being opened up when I had to pull it loose from a hold, then just recently, it was hurt a little by me hanging from a hook," Diana smirked.

"I'd ask you what in the world were you doing, but Mr. Tigere said it was a long story. I'm pretty sure all of you would like to go home. So, why don't you hop down and I'll check our hardheaded friend here," the doctor stated.

Diana moved out of the way and headed toward Scott. The doctor checked him out, asked several questions, and studied the chart. "Well, Mr. Tigere, I'm going to let you go home. I want you watched for twenty-four hours. Any sign of pain increasing, blurry vision, blood coming from the cut or from the eyes or ears, I want you back here ASAP. Am I clear?" the doctor admonished.

"Yes, sir," Ben smiled. The doctor signed the dismissal paper and took it out to the nurse. Just as the doctor walked out, Allen walked in.

"So, I see everybody is bright-eyed and bushy-tailed," Allen jested.

"Ben gets to go home now," Becca injected.

"Well then, I arrived just in time to drive everybody home." Allen smiled.

"You going to go home to your family now, or what were your plans Diana?" Becca asked.

Diana noticed there were no barbs, no hostility toward her now from Becca. "I think I'd best be with my family tonight. I figured you'd be around to help out if he needs it," she replied toward Becca.

"I want to chat with your family for a little bit, if you don't mind kitten," Ben injected.

Diana smiled. "I don't mind. Are you gonna come over and meet the rest of my kinfolk, Scott?"

"Do I sense a setup here?" Scott jabbed.

"Nawt at awl. Since your kin are down in Georgia, ya might as well be adopted into mine. My mother makes awesome fruit pies. Between Ben and Becca's parents and mine, you should be well fed," Diana teased.

"Well, since I just made the deal that the three of us will be working together now, I suppose I'd better get to know the families." Scott smiled.

Ben shot up and eyebrow. "What's this about a deal?"

"I convinced Charles to offer Diana a job with DHS. He was already going to try to get Scott in," Allen spoke up.

"There ain't no way I'm going to put her out in the field to be shot at," Ben fumed.

"What kind of brother do you think I am? I don't want her shot, are you insane?" Scott sneered. "She'll be in the office as an advisor, at least until she's trained."

"Charles has no intension of putting her in harm's way Ben. As much as she gains brothers everywhere, she seems to pick up extra fathers as well." Allen grinned over at Diana.

Diana just smiled. "This was all planned out for me, huh?"

"Now…sis, ya know it is all contingent on if you want the job or not. Of course seeing how you don't currently have a job…," Scott started.

"And the pay and benefits are fairly decent," Allen added.

Diana looked over at Ben. "I don't know if the tiger wants competition. Two cats in the same area, ya know?"

Ben looked at his fingernails and started cleaning them. "I was thinking more along the means of that third option kitten. Ya got to admit, we would confuse the daylights out of the offenders." He looked up at Diana.

Diana's eyebrow arched up, an ornery grin shown on her face. Then she turned to Scott. "Let me check it out with the man upstairs. I definitely don't want to be out of his will and working in DHS. I'll let you know." The nurse came in with the papers for Ben to sign. She shooed everybody out to the hall and told Ben to get dressed. Ben came and opened the door once he was ready. "I think we might need to stop at your house and let you change clothes before you come to mine," Diana stated as she pointed out the bloodstains and rips and tears in Ben's clothes.

"I think we all need to clean up a little before heading to your house," Ben added.

"Easy for you to say…I'm not sure my clothes survived the demolition," Diana jabbed.

"Charles had the girls grab your clothes from the room you all were using. They should be at Ben's house already. Yours also, Ben, as well as Scott's," Allen stated.

Diana looked at Becca. "Did you want to come as well? You're more than welcome."

"Not this time. I'm going to run home and pick up some clothes for me and load up the kids and bring them home. The way I see it, Scott's going to go comatose for the next forty-eight hours. So I'll keep tabs on Ben for the next twenty-four." Becca smiled.

"Next time then…I insist." Diana added. The whole group went down to main entrance. Becca jumped into her car and drove out to the farm to get clothes and the kids. Allen drove up to load Ben; Scott carried Diana out to Allen's car; then Allen took the trio to Ben's house to clean up. Ben had Diana use his bathroom once he was done shaving; he went ahead and washed all but the back of his head. Then he carefully combed through it. Diana picked out what clothes she was going to wear. Everything but her perfume and her pillow survived the onslaught. She grabbed it up and headed for the bathroom. Ben listened for the shower being turned on and the sound of the water change before he started to change his clothes.

He had just finished dressing when he heard the shower turn off. "I'm heading to the kitchen. I'll wait out there for you," he yelled through the bathroom door.

"Okay. I'll be out in a minute," Diana replied.

He walked out into the kitchen. "I appreciate you leaving your door open. I was wondering if I was going to have to chaperon you two," Allen jeered.

"Nah, she wants to get home to her family. It's all good," Ben quipped.

Scott joined them a minute or two later. "So are we about ready?" he quizzed.

"Waiting for the kitten. She's just about done," Ben flatly stated.

"I've just got to re-wrap my wrist and I'm ready," Diana stated as she entered the kitchen. She was wearing the black bootleg jeans, the white shirt with square neck and lace insets, her boots, and the white headband to keep her hair out of her eyes. She saw Ben's eyes flash; she smiled. She had pulled her sleeve up to get to her wrist and was trying to work the end of the gauze free to start wrapping her wrist with it.

Ben walked over to her. "Give it here." He reached down and lifted her arm up then lightly slid his hand down the backside of her arm down to her hand. The guys saw her arm twitch, even with her trying to hold it still.

"When did you find that one bro?" Scott snickered.

"While I was treating her wrists the other night." Ben grinned.

"Oh, whatever," Diana quipped as she looked over at Scott. She glanced at Allen but saw that even though he was amused, he was smart enough to stay quiet.

Ben turned her hand around to see the wrist. "You did re-tear it, didn't you?"

"It would have been a lot worse if it wasn't for the brace that Allen gave me," Diana somberly clarified.

"I'm glad it helped. What did you do with it?" Allen asked.

"I put it in with Ben's stuff from the hospital," Diana stated.

Ben noticed she had already put the ointment on it, so he started wrapping the wrist with the gauze. He went to pull the knife out of his pocket then remembered that he lost it during his fight.

"Are you looking for this Tiger?" Scott grinned as he held out Ben's knife.

"I owe you one Scott," Ben stated as he grabbed the knife and cut the gauze.

"Where's the tape at, kitten?" Ben asked as he held her hand. She pulled it out of her back pocket and gave it to him. She saw his eyes flash with the thought that went through them.

She read his thought as clear as day. "Now…now…Tiger, be careful," she teased.

Allen burst out laughing. "I guess she can more than just feel you near, Tiger. She reads you too. Although what I saw from both of you, gentlemen, she must be very good at animal taming."

Ben saw the satisfying gleam in Diana's eyes. He purposely stroked softly down the back side of Diana's arm while holding her hand so she couldn't pull away. "Benjamen James!" she quibbled.

Allen laughed again. "I think we need to get her home to her family, gentlemen…let's go."

They loaded up, and Allen drove them over to Diana's house. "My plane leaves in an hour, so I can't wait for you guys."

"That's okay, Allen, I have a car. It just wasn't available to me. I can take them home," Diana injected. She got out and walked over to Allen's door; she put her hand on his arm that he had on the window ledge. "Thank you," it was all she could say.

Allen reached up and cupped her face. "You are more than welcome Diana. If you ever need anything, don't hesitate to give me a call." She smiled and nodded.

Ben came over and wrapped his arm around her waist. "Until next time sir," he stated.

Allen patted him on the arm and waved to Scott. Ben guided Diana to the other side of the car and they watched him drive off. "Shall we?" Ben suggested as he weaved his fingers through hers.

Diana led the guys to the door and tried the knob. She opened the door and called out; "Mom…Dad…I'm home!"

The guys were there until ten p.m. Mrs. Henderson had made an apple pie earlier that day. Scott and Ben had two helpings. Diana gave Scott what would have been her share since she couldn't eat it. "If I'd known you were going to be here, I would have used nutmeg instead of cinnamon," her mom argued.

Diana went down to her part of the house to grab her keys from the hook. Ben had asked permission to go down after she had left. Mr. Henderson gave it to him. "You've been with her this long and she maintained. I don't figure it will start to be a problem now."

Diana went down and grabbed her keys without turning on the lights. Once she picked them up, she paused. "Can you see where you're going? Or do I need to turn on the lights for you?" she teased.

"I can see you just fine," Ben said as he put his hand on her arm. "But I'd like to see what your house looks like," he whispered. Diana reached over and flipped on the lights. She looked directly into those sapphire pools. There was no missing what he was saying. She was sure he read the same in her. Five minutes later, they heard footsteps coming down the stairs. They came around the corner to see Scott hitting the bottom step.

"What did she do, lose her keys?" he teased.

"Nope…Ben wanted to see the house down here," Diana quickly stated.

"Huh-huh." He gently took her face and turned her head. "You'd better pull your collar up a little bit. I'm not sure your parents are ready to see that a vampire has been sucking on your neck. You've got to be more careful bro. Either that or put them down lower." Diana blushed beet red but adjusted the shirt collar to hide the mark.

"I'll keep that in mind," Ben gleamed. Diana poked his ribs, forgetting the bruises he had. Ben recoiled and winced.

"Oh…I'm sorry…I'm sorry," she said as she put her hand on his chest.

"It's okay…don't worry about it," Ben said as he put his hand on the side of her face and caressed her cheek with his thumb. The trio walked back upstairs. The guys said good-bye to Diana's parents, and she drove them home. Becca was already there with the kids, so Scott hopped out and headed inside. "Are you sure you'll make it home all right?" Ben asked, rubbing Diana's hand with this thumb.

"Oh yeah…I'll be fine. Do you guys have a church you're attending now?" she carefully asked.

"The kids have been going to a church just down the block, but I'm looking for a smaller congregation to join to. I found this church over in the SW that I've heard a lot of good sermons coming out of. I figure I'll check it out this Sunday," Ben jested.

Diana smiled. "Well, that church has a youth night on Wednesday starting at 7:00 p.m., if you would like to bring the kids over. Some of the adults do a Bible study while they wait for the kids to get done."

"What are they studying now?" Ben asked.

"I'm not sure. I'm one of the youth leaders, so I'm with the kids at that time," she smiled.

"I'll ask the kids tomorrow. Do you have any plans on Thursday, say around six or so?" Ben quizzed.

"Well, since I haven't signed any papers to take a job yet, I believe I'm free at that time," Diana teased.

"Great…I'll pick you up at your house. I'd love to sit down and compare notes and talk," Ben planned. "Oh…by the way. The Lord told me to tell you something. It had to do with a question you have been asking him. He told me to tell you *yes*," Ben said, looking down at her hand. He heard her breath hitch; he looked up to see her looking out the side window. "Diana?" he said as he took her chin and turned her head to make her look at him. He could see tears running down her face. But her eyes were not sad; he saw gratefulness in them. "What was your question?"

Diana smiled and put her hand up to the side of his face. "I'll tell you later." A quick glint of orneriness flew through her eyes. He shook his head, slid his hand to her neck, and pulled her to him.

Ten minutes later, Ben walked into his house. Scott was sitting on the couch watching the news. "Did you take my advice or are Mr. and Mrs. Henderson going to have a shock when she gets home?"

"No, I didn't add any more. I didn't mean for that one to happen?" Ben gloated.

"So what…you were just talking all ten, fifteen minutes?" Scott probed.

"Part of it, yes. I just wanted to make sure she got home okay, so I gave her something to keep her awake." Ben smiled as he took his boots off.

"I hope she could see through the windows then," Scott teased.

"Well, she had to wipe them down a little, but she didn't mind it," Ben chuckled.

"Whatever bro. Are you going to bed now then?" Scott asked.

"Nah, a little hyped right now. I'll go grab a can of pop and sit out here for a while," Ben replied.

"Hyped…my aunt Fanny! You're flying higher than a kite. You won't be down for several hours," Scott quipped. Ben only smiled and walked to the kitchen.

46

October 31

Ben and the kids had started attending Diana's church. Even Scott came now and then. Ben talked to Pastor Henderson about starting to work in the church. The Sunday before, Ben had made arrangements to take Diana to dinner on the thirty-first of October. When she asked if it was a casual date, Ben had suggested that he would like to see her in an actual evening gown. Diana had taken Kaira, Liza, and Kim with her to shop for an adequate dress for their date. After much debate and trying on of dresses, the girls came up with one that pleased everybody. Ben picked Diana up at six that evening. It was a cold night, so she had a trench coat on as she came up meet Ben. Her hair was pulled up with small strands of curling locks coming down over her shoulder. Ben was dressed in a black suit and tie. Diana noted that he was still wearing a pair of boots; it was a pair of grey ones instead of brown ones this time. "Shall we?" Ben asked as he held out his arm for her to take. Diana smiled and took his arm and walked out to his car with him. He had noted that she was wearing black three-inch wedge heels and was trying to be careful while walking on them. "Were those Kaira's idea or Liza's?" Ben teased.

"It was from all three. I was content with the two-inch heels, but they wouldn't have it," Diana jabbed. Ben laughed. He took her to the Cityscape Lounge; he had made reservations five days before hand. He walked her in and helped her with her coat. As she slipped out of her coat, he had to force himself to breathe. Diana was wearing a one-shouldered hunter-green sheath dress; it came down to just above her knees, had ruching that went around her waist, and showed her beautiful figure and long legs.

"I can feel that, you know. I'm assuming the girls and I have made a good choice," Diana teased.

Ben leaned down and kissed her neck. "Good enough that I would love to just take you immediately home." Diana blushed. Ben walked her into the room and waited for the hostess. She escorted them to a table over in the corner. The hostess frowned when Ben asked for a glass of sweet tea for Diana and a coffee for him. They finished their main meal, or most of it. He saw that Diana desperately tried to eat everything. Even with the smaller-portion size, she couldn't quite get everything down. Knowing that Diana loved cheesecake, he ordered a piece for them to share.

"You know, while I was with the Lord; a tiger came up to be with him," Ben stated.

"A tiger...wow! There weren't any animals in the garden. It was just me and the Lord sitting on the swing. Not that I'm complaining. It's just interesting," Diana replied.

"She reminded me of you." Ben smiled. Diana arched an eyebrow but waited for him to finish. "The Lord said that He had known her since she was created. I asked him how he controlled her. He frowned at me and said He didn't. He only guided her. She had to decide whether to do as He asked or not," Ben finished as he took a sip of coffee.

Diana smiled. "That's about the truth of it. If the Lord wanted robots, we would still be in the garden. But He wants us to do as He asks because we love Him, not by force."

Ben smiled at her. "Are you ready to head out?"

"I would love to get these shoes off and into something a little less restraining." Diana grinned.

Ben waved the waiter down for the check. With that taken care of, he pushed out to help Diana up. Diana saw how much he had to pay and just about made a comment, but she held her tongue. They walked out to the car and Ben drove her to her house. "Do you mind if I come in?" he asked her.

"You don't have to ask, you are more than welcome here," Diana chided.

Ben walked around and held his hand out to help her out of the car and walked her up to the door. "Diana, hang on."

Diana turned around and looked at him. "Ben, what's wrong?"

"While I was with the Lord, he told me that he wanted me to work as a minister. Specifically with those from different countries," Ben carefully said.

"That's great," Diana encouraged. "So are you going to be working in other countries?"

"The Lord may have me travel to them, but I strongly believe that I'll be working out of the church here or nearby. We have a lot of internationals already around us," Ben replied. He turned around. "Would you be interested in being an important part of that ministry?"

"How…important?" Diana smiled, orneriness flashing in her eyes.

"A very, very important part of it." Ben grinned at her reaction. Ben got down on one knee. "Diana Nicole Henderson, would you marry me and be my partner in the ministry God has called me to?"

Diana nodded. "Definitely!"

Epilogue

Diana lay there thinking of the events of the day. Both Ben and she agreed that it would not be a good idea to have a long engagement. She had wanted a winter wedding ever since she was a teenager; so they had decided on January 31. Diana glanced over at the dress that was disrespectfully dropped on the floor. She slid out of bed and went to the bathroom; when she came out, she slipped on a night shirt and picked the dress up and hung it on a hanger in the closet. She chuckled a little bit to herself. Ben had gotten so somber that evening. He told her he was going to have to break his promise; he would purposely be hurting her, but it should only be this one time. She had just smiled at him and said, "I'm not a sixteen-year-old." He must have told her at least ten times he was sorry.

"Mrs. Tigere, what are you doing?" Ben chided.

"It just seemed to be a shame to leave it all crumpled up on the floor. I was just hanging it up," she replied.

"Come on back here kitten," Ben scolded. Diana climbed back in under the covers and cuddled next to him. "Did I hurt you too bad?" he asked caressing her arm.

"No. If you say you're sorry again, I'm going to have to take drastic measures," Diana sneered.

"You haven't be able to accomplish those promises yet kitten." Ben smiled as he turned her to face him.

"I will. It may take me a while to get them done, but if I say I will do something, it will be done one way or another." She grinned as she warned.

Ben tucked her in next to him and closed his eyes. He continued to caress her back until he was sure she had fallen asleep. He then went out himself, pulling her tight against himself.

Diana went to sleep thinking of how she was going to get retribution from Ben. Then she remembered some of the gag gifts that her family had given her on their "kidnapping" run. Just then it clicked; she knew exactly how to get him back. She fell asleep knowing she'd set her plan in motion in the morning.

Diana woke up early while Ben was still sleeping. She'd have to act quickly if she was going to succeed in her little endeavor. She carefully slid out of bed, grabbed the toy handcuffs that one of her cousins had given them. She carefully climbed back into bed and softly lifted one of Ben's arms above his head. She had put one side of the cuffs on his wrist but didn't tighten it down. She weaved the cuffs through one of the dowels of the headboard, then she lifted his other arm. She noticed he was starting to wake up; so she quickly put the opened side of the cuffs on that wrist. Then she swiftly tightened them up, which made Ben wake up immediately.

"What are you doing?" Ben glared at her.

Diana just simply smiled. "Getting retribution that I promised I would do. I figured out how I was going to get it from you last night. You, sir, are going to be under my control for at least ten minutes."

Ben saw the gleam in her eyes: he was amused. He didn't figure that it was going to be a problem for him. He looked over at the clock by the phone then looked over at Diana. "And what exactly are you planning to do, Mrs. Tigere?"

"Oh...I don't know. I figured I'd wing it." She smiled. "Let me see, I can start up here," she stated as she lightly started to caress the underside of his arms. By the time she got down towards his shoulders, she started to see his muscles start to twitch. She continued to move down his side, hitting a couple of spots that she already knew about, giggling as he jerked because of her. Then she hopped up and straddled his stomach. She noticed his eyes started to dilate. "Now let me see. What was it you said, a one-sided hickey war? I'm up for a try at that."

She spent the next ten minutes learning him, watching his reactions to what she was doing. Ben was okay for the first three minutes, but once her body came into contact with him, it changed. By five minutes, he was asking her to let him touch her. She just smiled at him. "Now you wouldn't want it said that I don't keep my promises now, do you?"

Eight minutes, and he was getting frantic; his body started to tremble and shake as he tried to maintain control. He was pulling on the cuffs. By ten minutes, he was pleading with her to release him. He wanted her to the point of being mad with it. She finally came down and kissed him while she reached up and released the cuffs that he was near to breaking anyway. Diana was laughing as Ben reached up and quickly rolled her under him. She knew how to get to him now. She had no intention of using it to be cruel, but it was something to use as a tease. He slipped her shirt off, and her mind shut down after that; its only thought was her and her husband and the here and now.

Diana caressed through his hair as he lay partially on her. He was out, as least for a few minutes. She smiled at him. She was merciless playing with him, but she was glad she could make him want her that much. It gave her a since of belonging; she belonged to him, and he wanted her. *Thank you, Lord. Help me to be a good wife and mother. Help me to never make him regret marrying me. Build this family around your spirit and your love. Help us to be a good example of what a marriage should be, and help us to continue to walk in your ways*, Diana silently prayed as she held her husband.

"You're not fighting with yourself again, are you kitten?" Ben softly said as he looked up to see her eyes.

"Oh…no, not at all." Diana smiled.

"Here I thought you might be debating whether it was right to nearly kill me or not," Ben teased.

"Why would I want to kill ya? There's no fun it that. I'll just take ya to the edge," she jabbed as she glided her fingers across his back. He just grinned and shook his head.

"You never did tell me, what was that question that you had been asking the Lord about back in October?" Ben stated as he shifted his weight off her so she could move free.

Diana chuckled. "Do you really want to know?"

"Yep…I do," Ben said as he ran his fingers through her hair.

"It was whether you were the one God showed me in a dream back when I was sixteen years old," Diana simply stated. "I only wanted that man because I saw the love in his eyes, love that was directed at me. God told me that the man I saw there was the one He had planned for me to marry. Unfortunately, the Lord didn't tell me his name, nor could I see his face well. Just his eyes were what I saw clearly."

"Interesting…'cause I had seen you in a dream as well." Ben smiled. He pulled her close as he rolled over to his back. They just lay there in each other's embrace, thanking the Lord for the gift He had given to each of them.

"What is Zenon having you do so far?" Ben asked.

"I've be working in the filing room for a good part of it. Apparently, some of your agents aren't good at putting things in alphabetical order," she jabbed.

"What were you doing for the other part?" he wondered.

"So far they had me try out the shooting range, and they are having me do some weight training," Diana replied.

"How did you do with the shooting range?" Ben asked, looking down at her.

"I'm good with the riffles, not so good with the handguns," Diana informed him. Ben just chuckled. He lay there looking at the ceiling; "I wonder what Scott's going to be doing without us around? He'll have one whole week to get himself into trouble."

"Well, I did overhear some of the guys saying that they had 'appointments' with him in the gym, something about a picture or something like that. I hope he doesn't get too banged up," Diana worried.

Ben knew what she was talking about. Scott, Zenon, and himself agreed not to let Diana know about it. He wasn't worried at all about Scott getting too banged up. He was just hoping that the other agents didn't get broken up too much. Scott was downright livid. Ben was glad Dick had already left for San Francisco; he would have been in mortal danger otherwise. At the time Ben saw the picture, he was furious as well. Luckily, the other agents didn't know who the woman was that was wearing the Scooby shirt. The lady's head was turned away. Neither Ben nor Scott were going to tell them either. They just quickly took it off the lounge wall before Diana could see it. It didn't stop the other agents' comments about it, however. Scott had plans on how to deal with it. It would be a one-on-one basis with the understanding that the person wasn't going to mention it any further or he would continue his "practicing" on them. Ben smiled at that. "Do you want to go get some breakfast?" he said as he caressed her back.

"In a little bit. I'm quite content to lie here and watch the sunrise through the window," Diana softly replied.

Ben just beamed a broad smile and lay there, soaking it all in.

CPSIA information can be obtained at www.ICGtesting.com
Printed in the USA
LVOW10s1237290716

497975LV00005B/13/P